The Moon in the Water

Pamela Belle was born and bred in Suffolk, the daughter of a local prep school headmaster. She went to the University of Sussex, and is now teaching in Hertfordshire. *The Moon in the Water* is her first novel.

Pamela Belle

The Moon in the Water

Let me not to the marriage of true minds
Admit impediments . . .
(Shakespeare, 'Sonnets')

Pan Original Pan Books London and Sydney

First published 1983 by Pan Books Ltd,
Cavaye Place, London SW10 9PG
© Pamela Belle 1983
Paperback ISBN 0 330 26919 4
Cased ISBN 0 330 28157 7
Photoset by Parker Typesetting Service, Leicester
Printed & bound by
Collins, Glasgow

To my mother, who took me to Rushbrooke and started it all, and who has known the Herons almost as long as I have.

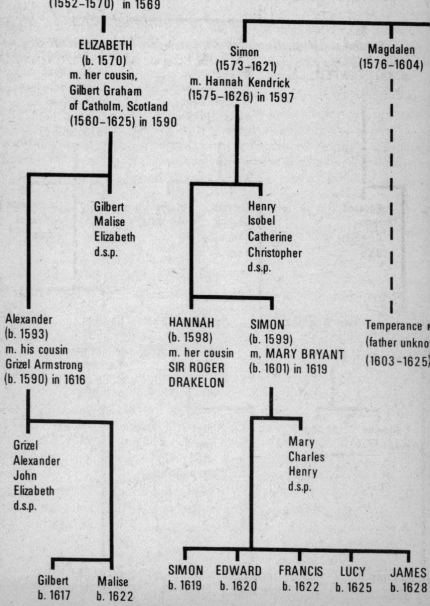

Sir Henry (Hal) Heron (1550–1612), great-grandson of the builder of Goldhay

married

(i) his cousin, Isobel Drakelon
(1552–1570) in 1569

ELIZABETH
(b. 1570)
m. her cousin,
Gilbert Graham
of Catholm, Scotland
(1560–1625) in 1590

Simon
(1573–1621)
m. Hannah Kendrick
(1575–1626) in 1597

Magdalen
(1576–1604)

Gilbert
Malise
Elizabeth
d.s.p.

Henry
Isobel
Catherine
Christopher
d.s.p.

Alexander
(b. 1593)
m. his cousin
Grizel Armstrong
(b. 1590) in 1616

HANNAH
(b. 1598)
m. her cousin
**SIR ROGER
DRAKELON**

SIMON
(b. 1599)
m. **MARY BRYANT**
(b. 1601) in 1619

Temperance
(father unkno
(1603–1625)

Grizel
Alexander
John
Elizabeth
d.s.p.

Mary
Charles
Henry
d.s.p.

Gilbert
b. 1617

Malise
b. 1622

SIMON
b. 1619

EDWARD
b. 1620

FRANCIS
b. 1622

LUCY
b. 1625

JAMES
b. 1628

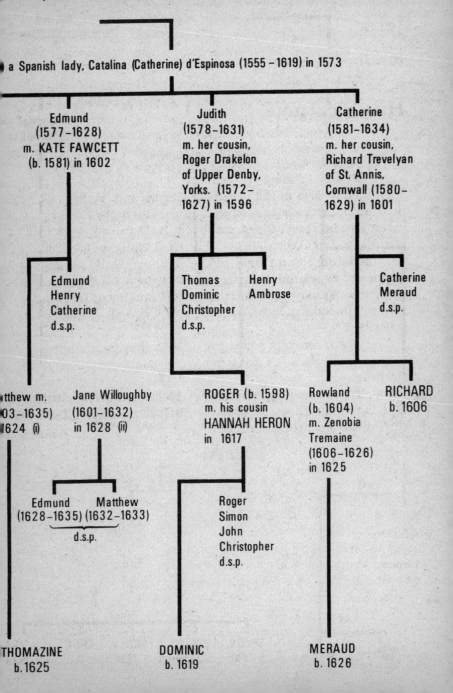

Christopher Heron: trader, privateer and courtier to Queen Elizabeth:

a Spanish lady, Catalina (Catherine) d'Espinosa (1555 – 1619) in 1573

Edmund
(1577–1628)
m. KATE FAWCETT
(b. 1581) in 1602

Judith
(1578–1631)
m. her cousin,
Roger Drakelon
of Upper Denby,
Yorks. (1572–
1627) in 1596

Catherine
(1581–1634)
m. her cousin,
Richard Trevelyan
of St. Annis,
Cornwall (1580–
1629) in 1601

Edmund
Henry
Catherine
d.s.p.

Thomas
Dominic
Christopher
d.s.p.

Henry
Ambrose

Catherine
Meraud
d.s.p.

tthew m.
03–1635)
624 (i)

Jane Willoughby
(1601–1632)
in 1628 (ii)

ROGER (b. 1598)
m. his cousin
HANNAH HERON
in 1617

Rowland
(b. 1604)
m. Zenobia
Tremaine
(1606–1626)
in 1625

RICHARD
b. 1606

Edmund   Matthew
(1628–1635) (1632–1633)
          d.s.p.

Roger
Simon
John
Christopher
d.s.p.

THOMAZINE
b. 1625

DOMINIC
b. 1619

MERAUD
b. 1626

Historical note

The main figures in the story, the Herons and the Sewells, their immediate associates and their various houses, are my invention; however, the world in which they move, both in Suffolk and in Oxford, is not. The Civil War events depicted, including the incident of the Banbury guns, actually happened as related, barring of course the involvement of my fictitious characters, and the Suffolk families of Jermyn, Blagge (including Nan), Hervey and Gage all existed as described.

The poem on page 528 is my own – other unattributed quotations in the story are from ayres, ballads or poems of the time.

Finally, for sceptics, the names Holofernes, Hepzibah and Drakelon all occur in West Suffolk parish registers during the seventeenth century.

Contents

part one:

'Illusion's bubble'

1	Goldhayes	3
2	A bridge of unicorns	54
3	Return of a prodigal	91
4	Discovery	150
5	Rumours of war	197

part two:

'Cold reality'

6	Ashcott	251
7	The red horse	313
8	Pennyfarthing Street	371
9	A killing thing	436
10	The valley of decision	488

part one

'Illusion's bubble'

We were as twinned lambs that did frisk i' the sun,
And bleat the one at the other: what we changed
Was innocence for innocence: we knew not
The doctrine of ill-doing, no, nor dreamed
That any did.

(Shakespeare, *The Winter's Tale*)

chapter one

Goldhayes

I wonder, by my troth, what thou and I
Did, till we loved.
Were we not weaned till then
But sucked on country pleasures, childishly?
(Donne, 'The Good-Morrow')

When I was ten years old, my father died, and my six-year-old half-brother; and in the space of those two days my world was shattered.

It had been a secure, peaceful world, although my up-bringing had been, by conventional standards, a little unusual. My father, twice widowed, was a big, fair, indulgent man, tolerant of childish misdemeanours, and a lover of independence of spirit both in men and in women. He had found it in his first wife, my mother, and lost it abruptly after a year of marriage when she died at my birth. I was, unfortunately, not the boy he had so greatly desired, but he was not a man easily thwarted by such details and encouraged me to run and play and think as freely as if I had been the longed-for son.

He had loved my mother very dearly; she had been his first cousin, and they had been born in the same year and reared together. But he was not, I think, the kind of man to lie forever alone, and by the time I was three years old it was moreover obvious that I was suffering from the lack of a mother – my paternal grandmother, who lived with us, being a somewhat stern and distant figure who concerned herself little with small children beyond catechism or the strap. So my father looked about, and found the young, childless widow of a wealthy Oxford brewer. She was not good-looking, her best feature being her warm and friendly smile, but her kind heart, as well as her Oxford house and chest of plate, were recommendation enough, and he mar-

3

ried her forthwith. Within the year, she presented him at last with a son, a child who with his size and blond hair took as much after his father as I, small, brown and fiercely skinny, resembled my mother.

I did not feel supplanted by my new brother Edmund. I had playmates enough amongst the children who lived in the tumbledown cottages huddled about the walls of Ashcott, my father's ancient and dilapidated manor house in the parish of Adderbury, twenty miles from Oxford, and there were also the steward Will Tawney's growing brood. Nor was my stepmother a threat. Never having had a real mother, nor a nurse beyond babyhood, I welcomed someone kinder than my strict grandmother, someone who could tell stories and comfort childish tears and would not worry about deficiencies in my education – for my grandmother, believing in the virtues of an early start to keep me from mischief, had already begun teaching me to read, and write, to sew and reckon and to pick out hesitant tunes with one finger on her precious virginals. Moreover, with my brother's birth a nurse, a Banbury girl named Alice, was engaged to look after us, and she was young enough to be a friend.

So for a while we were all very happy, until I was seven. In that year, 1632, my stepmother was again with child, and as was her habit remained as active as possible right up to the expected date of the birth. She went as usual to Deddington market, the child due within a fortnight, and on her return the horse slipped coming down the hill to Ashcott, and fell on top of her. I remember too clearly seeing her brought in, screaming with the pains of labour; but it was two days before the baby was born, and so exhausted was she by her travail that not an hour later she died. Nor did the tragedy end there, for somehow the child, a boy named Matthew after his father, had been damaged by his protracted birth and from the beginning it was plain there was something terribly wrong, for he scarcely moved, nor cried, and stared vacantly at the ceiling. It was a relief when Alice found him dead in his cradle at three months old.

I was greatly upset by the death of my stepmother, and at

first missed her sorely; but with the natural resilience of childhood transferred some of my affections to Alice, and ~ne's memory grew dim. My father, I think, took it hard; ~d a kind heart and had been heard to lament that, with ves lost in childbirth, he had no mind to inflict a sin. death upon a third.

So my brother Edmund and I grew in the comfortable, shabby surroundings of Ashcott; the house with its courtyard and gatehouse and the few large, under-furnished rooms and the huddled hovels of the farm workers outside the walls. Our grandmother did her best with us, for she was a good and godly woman, of Yorkshire Puritan stock; but she was often ill, and our father had the most influence. He taught us to ride, to handle dogs and horses and hawks, and treated me as Edmund's equal, encouraging my boldness and directness because, so he said, it made him laugh. So I developed a wilful turn of mind, quick to pride and anger, and Edmund and the village children and the little Tawneys, boys and girls alike, followed me into mischief, for I did not scruple to threaten and upbraid the reluctant and must have struck terror into smaller and fainter hearts.

It was from one of my village playmates, in the spring of 1635 when I was ten years old and Edmund just six, that I caught what was at first pronounced some childish fever; by the time my father and brother had also been infected, it was seen, too late, to be the smallpox. Half the villagers' children died of it, and two of the Tawney girls. I was strong and healthy, and by some miracle I escaped almost unmarked, save for a scar or two along the side of my face. Edmund was weaker, despite his size, and quite quickly died; and despite all that the doctors, and my grandmother who had had the disease as a child, and the elderly relative of my stepmother's who kept the Oxford house for us and who had no little skill with simples, could do, my father within two days followed him to the grave.

And I, Thomazine Heron, aged ten years and four months, was left orphaned heiress of Ashcott, the Oxford house, lands in Yorkshire and in Norfolk which had belonged respectively to my grandmother and my mother, and a thousand pounds' worth of goods and plate.

There was much coming and going that April, whilst I, hung with black like the house, wandered through the high stone rooms, rejected, bereft and bewildered. My grandmother was frequently closeted with imposing strangers, who looked me over rather as my father had been used to inspect a promising heifer, fingered the tapestries and rapped tunes on the silver plate. My bewilderment increased. When, one sunny morning early in May, I was summoned to my grandmother's presence, I went not with my usual gloom but hopefully, grateful at once for some attention after three weeks of loneliness and neglect by everyone but Alice, and eager to discover what was happening. After curtseying, I was directed to sit upon the footstool – my grandmother being strict and old-fashioned demanded a proper deference from children. She looked me over sternly, and then said, 'Your dress is creased, and your apron is disgracefully dirty. Have you been climbing trees again?'

'No, Grandmother,' I said meekly; I had, in fact, been sitting on the battlements which topped the courtyard wall. My grandmother gestured impatiently. 'Well, that does not matter. I wish to tell you, Thomazine, something which concerns you greatly. You realize, of course, that since your father's death you are an orphan and a ward of the King?'

I did not, but nodded.

'It is usual, for one in your position, for your guardianship to be sold by the King's Court of Wards to the highest bidder. Several gentlemen, in fact, have sent their agents to inspect this house, and these are the strangers you have no doubt noticed. Fortunately, however, your father's cousin, Sir Simon Heron, has shown an interest in your plight. I take it that you know your relationship to Sir Simon?'

The Herons are a close-knit family, much given to marrying amongst themselves, and consequently any pedigree of our ancestors appears very confusing. I had understood enough of the family history in my ten years, however, to remember the founder of our breed, one Christopher Heron, the fourth or fifth son of a Northumbrian gentleman whose main interest in life was pursuing cattle raids across the Scottish Border and blood feuds with his neighbours. Being a man of some sensibility, this Christopher Heron had tired of the primitive, bloodthirsty existence pursued by his father and brothers, and early left in search of greener pastures. By means which I had never really understood, but which fully attested to his intelligence, quick wits and talents, he had contrived to be friend and musician to that maligned monarch, Richard III, and also to rise high in the favour of Henry Tudor. By the time of his death, at a very great age in 1543, he had amassed a fortune, a knighthood, a place on the Privy Council, the lasting goodwill of Henry VIII (no mean feat in itself), and last but not least, a large estate in Suffolk, where on the site of a tiny priory belonging to the abbey at Bury St Edmunds he had erected the first buildings of the lovely rose-brick mansion known as Goldhayes Hall. His great-grandson Henry Heron indulged in what could only be called piracy with Queen Elizabeth's tacit blessing, and had been rewarded with a knighthood, court positions, plunder, and his second wife, a noble Spanish beauty named Catalina (the first, a young cousin called Isobel Drakelon, having died in child-bed). Henry, or Hal, and Catalina, (who with a tact rare in her race speedily anglicized both her name and her religion) produced five living children to supplement Elizabeth, the child of his first marriage. One of these, my grandfather Edmund Heron, had wed, perhaps for love, my grandmother Kate, a tough puritanical Yorkshirewoman; my dear dead father was the only surviving child of their union. Another daughter of Hal and Catalina, Magdalen, was from her earliest years wayward and wilful, refusing all offers of marriage – of which there were many, she possessing by all accounts great beauty – and her parents had been long resigned to her spinsterhood when, at the advanced age of twenty-eight, she suddenly produced a bastard daughter, and shortly after died, insane. The identity of the child's father remained forever unknown, but the babe, most inappropriately named Temperance by her mother, was reared at Goldhayes with her older cousins, Sir Hal's other grandchildren, and at the age of twenty-two married my father Matthew.

This Sir Simon Heron was one of those older cousins, and both my father's, and my mother's, first cousin. My grandmother, seeing that I had identified him, continued. 'He has exercised his right as your close kin to gain control of your wardship, for which God be thanked, for many of those who would have liked to have done so would have bled your estates dry before you were old enough to gainsay them, and married you to base kin, or even to themselves. However, I have known Sir Simon since he was in swaddling bands, and he is a man conspicuous for his honesty, integrity and godliness. He now has a brood of children your own age, and he feels it would be best if you were to join his household at Goldhayes to be reared with them, rather than living alone here with an ailing old woman your sole company. I think this a most excellent idea. You will naturally live on equal terms with Sir Simon's children, he is a very wealthy man, the house is most fine, and you will be able to have tutors for all the things which my failing eyesight prevents me from teaching you – French, music, dancing, sewing, all the accomplishments of a gentlewoman. Although he has now retired from Court because of his poor health, he still has many friends and contacts there, and there is even a chance that you might one day be offered a place in the household of the Queen or one of the Princesses. There is moreover the prospect of making an excellent match, for your portion will not be small, you are a considerable heiress, and you are not ill-looking, in an unusual way. You can rest assured that Sir Simon will not find you any but the best husband. Indeed, such is his care for you that he has sent his own coach to take you to Suffolk. It should arrive within two or three days – plenty of time to make all ready. You will have to leave your pony behind, of course, but Alice will go with you. Now, what have you to say?'

I did not care about Sir Simon, nor his fine house, nor

even his brood of children. The salient point was that I was to leave Ashcott, perhaps for ever, and in only two or three days. After all that I had lost, this was the final straw. I said, my voice loud with grief and fury, 'I'm not going! I don't want to go, I want to stay here!'

My grandmother had never had much patience with tantrums. She said sharply, 'Don't be foolish, child. It would be ridiculous for you to stay here all alone without your father and brother. At Goldhayes Sir Simon has five children living, four boys and a girl who is only a few months younger than you, and they will make you welcome, be your friends. In a year or less you'll think Goldhayes as much your home as this mouldering pile ever was. You'll have ample opportunity to get your nose into books, and sew fine stitches, and pick out a pretty tune on the lute or spinet, and it will all do you a great deal of good, for you've fast been growing into a hoyden. Now go to your chamber and con me that passage from Exodus; I wish to hear it before dinner.'

There was no arguing with Kate Heron. As I stared unseeing at my Bible, I pondered mutinously the prospect of Goldhayes and even, rashly, considered the possibility of running away. But I had to smile as I contemplated sneaking out of the gatehouse with a vagabond's bundle on my back. I realized miserably that nothing could prevent me from leaving Ashcott: my grandmother was notoriously implacable and once she had made a decision could not be moved by any tears, anger, pleading or promises. Even if I kicked and fought with all my strength, I would willy-nilly be placed in that coach. But for all these realistic thoughts, I could not face departure from the only world I knew, in response to this semi-divine decree, without a rebellious and unhappy heart. Until the coach's arrival, lurching down the hill, across the stone bridge over the river Swere and into the courtyard in an enveloping cloud of dust, I made my life and that of those around me a misery with my sulks and bad temper. So much so that my grandmother, giving me a farewell lecture in her parlour, was moved to say, 'The way you have behaved over the last few days, Thomazine, makes me almost glad to see you go. Now I know you have never been one to take advice gladly, and for that fault I blame your father's laxness, but I hope for your own sake you will remember what I have to say, and act upon it. The sooner you throw off your sulks and behave like the happy child you used to be, the better. No one will take kindly to you if you wear a fearsome scowl or act discourteously or in an ill-tempered way. You must go to Goldhayes, there is no alternative, and my advice is to accept it with a good grace and make life more pleasant for yourself and for everyone else around you. You will not otherwise find yourself liked, and in consequence will be even more lonely and unhappy than you are now. Do you understand me, Thomazine?'

For once, I did. With a great effort, I swallowed my pride and said meekly, 'I'm very sorry, Grandmother, and I will try to be better.'

For the first time since my father's death, my grandmother smiled. 'Good girl. Remember always what I have told you. You have many good qualities, but as in all children the Devil strives to gain ascendancy in you, and you must with God's help fight him. Be obedient and dutiful to your guardian, behave with humility and meekness, and throw off your pride and stubbornness – it ill becomes a woman. And above all, Thomazine, I want no reports of a hoyting girl. Do you understand?'

I nodded, but I knew myself too well already. I was no more capable of being meek and obedient than I was of changing my sex; however, I did love my grandmother, who was the last of my immediate family left, and I genuinely wished to please her. 'Yes, Grandmother, I will do my very best, I promise.'

'Good, Thomazine. Now, have you got everything you are to take with you?'

My clothes had been packed in a large iron-bound travelling trunk, although by the time I was out of mourning I would most like have grown too big for them. In a small bag which lay by the door I had another suit of black clothes, spare collars and cuffs, caps and linen, a night-smock and hair-ribbons and other necessaries: there were also a couple of chap-books with rhymes and tales to delight a child, a Bible, embroidery silks and needles and the sampler I had not yet finished, and a miniature of my mother. There were no toys; dolls did not interest me, and I had delighted more in games of Spanish-and-English with Edmund and the other children than in less active pastimes. There was also my fragile lute, made small enough to accommodate my childish fingers, in a separate case of soft leather. My grandmother checked through it all, frowning briefly at the chap-books, and then buckled up the straps. 'Well, you seem to have everything there. Now, it must be past eight, and it is time for you to go; the coach is ready and waiting.'

A liveried groom loaded my paltry baggage into the coach, which was vast and imposing in blue and silver, with the Heron arms on each door: silver heron on blue, the helm crowned by a prancing unicorn, and below the uncompromising motto inherited from generations of stubborn Borderers: 'No surrender'. Two handsome matched bays stood in the traces, and Alice's anxious face filled the window. 'Come along, little mistress, we should be long agone!'

My grandmother handed me into the coach. 'Now you must remember what I have said. Remember your duty to your guardian, who stands now in your father's place: and above everything do nothing that he would have been ashamed of. Do not forget to write and tell me how you go on. Goodbye!'

I leaned through the window for a parting kiss, and remained there, perilously balanced, as the coach drew away with much whip-cracking and shouting through the gatehouse, and turned left to make the long climb up to the Deddington Road. For as long as I could see her I waved to my grandmother's small black figure shrouded in dust; and even when we were climbing the hill hung out to hold in my memory my last glimpse of Ashcott, yellow and sleepy in the morning amongst the green grass and willow trees of the valley of the river Swere. Then finally it was lost to my sight as the coach drew on, and I sank back upon the padded seat and fought my tears.

It took ten days to reach Goldhayes, for the weather turned soon after we left Ashcott and the roads became sticky with mud, bogging the coach so that for a time we scarcely made eight miles in a day. Alice, despite being highly impressed by the luxury of such a conveyance, was very scornful of the mode of travel, saying that padded seats and horn windows or no, she would liefer make the distance in half the time on a horse and risk a soaking as stay dry, bored and sick in such a slow, lurching contraption. Every so often we had to get out so that the horses had more chance of hauling the coach clear of the glutinous mud, and my new black dress and neat white lace-edged apron suffered sadly, although the dried mud was brushed and beaten off every night by poor Alice in the inns where we stayed. I tried to be cheerful, swallowed my tears, rode once or twice with the coachman and made friends with the horses, but as Goldhayes drew inexorably closer, so my heart sank lower. We spent the last night at Newmarket, and I could scarcely sleep for apprehension, disturbing poor Alice, who since it was market day had perforce to share my bed, there being no other in the inn. In the morning, as we breakfasted, one of Sir Simon's grooms left on a post-horse to warn them of our coming. I picked moodily at the cold mutton and salted Yarmouth herring, crumbled my bread and flicked the pieces rebelliously round the room. Alice, clucking displeasure, herded me out into the coach, while the innkeeper's wife handed up a basket of provisions for our dinner. Then we set off, I with a heart as heavy and lurching as the coach, and Alice, oblivious, snoring in her corner, although how she could sleep in the swaying, hot and stuffy vehicle I could not imagine. My bones sore and jolted, I stared from the window at the countryside; the heath outside Newmarket, giving way to the sheep-downs around Kentford, and then, coming into Bury, the neat fields of corn and barley sprouting green in the May sunshine. People recognized the coach with salutes and smiles, or shouted cheery greetings to the coachman. Bury itself was a very fine and pleasant town of brick and plaster houses, with a wide square in front of the old abbey gateway, full of country people and gentry, animals and produce; another market in full cry. Alice, craning out of the window, directed me to look at the dancing bear, a sight which she doubtless hoped would take me out of my gloom. Once, indeed, I would have been delighted, but the bear was a mangy sad creature, chained up and prodded by his master to make him dance, and it only served to remind me of my own situation. Alice glanced at me as I bit back a sob, and then, the coach being stopped in the press of people, got out, shouting to the coachman as she did so. She shortly returned, bearing a sticky burden. 'Here you are, little mistress, that'll keep your jaw so busy you'll have no time to let it wobble before we get there.'

I took the gingerbread, still warm from sun, oven or Alice's hands, and munched my thanks through it. The coach edged through the crowd, out of Bury, through the East Gate and on to the Ipswich road. Then, after Eildon Wood, a sharp turn right, and down a narrow, winding lane scarcely big enough to accommodate the coach. Once a flock of sheep met us and the shepherd had to drive them round, up over the banks and through the hedges, a tidal wave of broad woolly backs eddying and baa-ing at the wheels of the coach. It made me at once both long for Ashcott, where sheep abounded, and feel more at home in this strange country of white- and pink-washed cottages and flint churches and small, shallow-folded valleys.

We passed a great house, half-hidden amongst trees, which the coachman told us was Rushbrooke Hall, the seat of the Jermyn family; a few scattered cottages and, here and there amidst the woods which lay drifted across the landscape, a grey church tower pointing humbly to Heaven. Then there was a very sharp turn to the right, and the coachman called that we were nearly there, and would see the house in a moment. Alice promptly thrust her head through the window, but I sat dumbly on the opposite seat, swinging my feet in their neat cork-soled shoes with the white rosettes, sadly muddied by the journey. I wished sorely for home, and my heart muttered resentfully against being transported hither and thither against my will, but I remembered my grandmother's advice, and knowing it to be good determined to make the best of everything.

Alice gasped as the coach swayed round a bend. 'Oooh! Oh, Mistress Thomazine, it's lovely! Much bigger and finer than Ashcott . . . oh, do look!'

'It's all right, I'll look when we get out,' I said through the last of the gingerbread. The coach rattled over the gravel and stones of the drive: then there was a different noise, hollow and echoing, as the wheels passed over the bridge across the moat. There was a final lurch as it pulled up in the courtyard, surrounded on three sides by the main body of the house and the two projecting wings added by my great-grandfather Hal, and on the fourth by the moat. The coachman opened the door and Alice tumbled out, bright-faced and smiling, and turned for me. 'Here we are at last, little mistress, journey's end!'

I scrambled stiffly after her and jumped down onto the gravel: and then stood and stared like an ignorant rustic at the house. Goldhayes, the jewel of Suffolk, had been built by Sir Christopher Heron a hundred years ago, and enlarged and embellished by his great-grandson: all in glowing rose-and-amber brick, strange to my Oxfordshire eyes, with a green copper-roofed turret at the end of each wing, falling sheer into the moat. The house faced south-west and the evening sun lay slanting on the blue-and-gold painted sundial above the porch, built in familiar mellow Cotswold stone. Around the dial was inscribed a Latin tag, which even I with my rudimentary knowledge of that language could puzzle out: 'I do not count the hours unless they are sunny ones.'

'Cousin!' I jumped, my dream of wonder burst, and looked round to see a man sitting in a chair, to which, I noticed with some astonishment, had been fixed a set of wheels. The blue-clad servant at his back pushed the chair towards me, and I realized that this must be Sir Simon, and that he was a cripple. 'Welcome to Goldhayes,' he said, and his drawn face, with the sharp eagle's nose a more pronounced version of my father's, and my own insignificant beak, relaxed into something approaching a smile. I remembered my training and sank into a deep curtsey. 'Thank you, Sir,' I said as I rose, and stopped, unable to think of anything more to say. The narrow dark eyes scanned me, from the neat child's coif to the tips of my ruined shoes. 'You must be weary after your long journey,' said my guardian. 'Come inside and meet your new family.'

I accompanied him, and the servant, under the sundial and into a dim cool hall which, though not as high as the one at Ashcott that was hundreds of years old and took up two storeys, was otherwise as large. A long, polished table, relic of the days when the family and servants had eaten together in this room, stood in the middle, a silver bowl full of new, blush-pink roses reflected in the shiny dark oak. Around it stood my cousins.

I had a confused impression of shy, impassive faces probably not dissimilar to my own. I curtseyed again, nervously, and stood with my hands clasped meekly behind my back to disguise their trembling, as Sir Simon spoke. 'And this is Thomazine, my dear. My wife, Lady Heron.' A plump, middle-aged, middle-sized woman in cornflower-blue satin smiled without warmth. I curtseyed again. 'My eldest son, Simon' – a tall dark gaunt boy of sixteen or so, with the family nose and a serious face – 'and Edward,' – a year or so younger, broader, with eyes blue instead of brown and a healthy outdoor glow to his skin – 'James, whom I regret everyone calls Jamie, in the Scots fashion,' – a boy of six or seven, breeched, with a look more of Edward than of Simon, a round childish eager face – 'and my only living daughter, Lucy.' A girl taller and plumper than I, round and pretty in peach taffeta with immaculate lace and apron and cap, stared at me solemnly as we curtseyed. 'And where,' said Sir Simon in weary tones, 'is Francis now?'

His family glanced at each other. 'Oh, there was some to-do about that dog of his,' Lady Heron began, without much concern. A door opened on my right and a boy came in, accompanied by a large and shaggy black and white dog of indeterminate ancestry to which I, brought up with animals, immediately warmed. This child was perhaps two or three years older than I, and quite unlike his dark brothers and sister, having hair of startling pallor in the dim light. He bade the dog sit, and then glanced at me and grinned. It was the first sign of real welcome I had had, and paradoxically made my chin wobble. I clenched my jaw on imaginary gingerbread and tried to smile back.

'Francis, where have you been?' asked his father, tapping long hands on the arm of his chair. The boy stood by the table, at ease and unintimidated. 'Oh, Drake got into the kitchens and Monsieur Harcourt wanted me to get him out because he had his eye on the rabbit carcasses. So I did.'

'If there is much more trouble with your misbegotten cur,' said Sir Simon, 'I will have it knocked on the head. It has been nothing but a nuisance since the day you found it. Now, apologize to your cousin for your late arrival.'

Francis Heron bowed low to me, his face quiet and his eyes, a smokey grey-green, alive with mischief and rebellion. 'My humblest apologies, Mistress Thomazine. Ever your servant.'

'Thank you,' I said, curtseying yet again. The dog trotted over to me and pushed a cold nose into my hand. Francis snapped his fingers at it and it returned to his side, panting gently, and watched with disfavour by Sir Simon. His wife looked round and said, 'Well, Thomazine, I'll take you upstairs and you can put on fresh clothes. You will share Lucy's chamber.' She turned and glided up the stairs on the right of the hall, stiff with carved balustrading. The house had a subtle, individual aroma to it; not the slightly damp dustiness of Ashcott but a fragrant smell of warm waxed wood, herbs and flowers and sunlight. I followed her, Alice behind me with the servant and baggage. Lady Heron paused at the top and looked back, smiling absently. She had once, obviously, been very lovely, with blonde hair and blue eyes: but the hair had faded, the eyes dulled, her skin sagging now and an unbecoming plumpness concealing the delicate bones of her face. She had a general air of indolence and soft living. 'Is this your nurse, Thomazine?'

'Yes, her name is Alice – Alice Jefferies.' Alice curtseyed as best she could, positioned halfway up the stairs and burdened with travelling bags. 'She's been my nurse for six years,' I went on, feeling that I ought to be more expansive.

'So nice to find a reliable servant. We have such trouble,' said Mary, Lady Heron, swishing off ahead of us down the long gallery, keys jangling from her waist with a deceptively business-like sound. I trailed behind her, gazing. The gallery ran the whole length of the house, great windows at either end and spaced along each side, lined with portraits where there were not doors or windows, and topped by an intricate plaster ceiling of a beauty I had never seen before. Judging from the sounds behind me, Alice was also lost in wonder.

The chamber I was to share with Lucy lay on the right, halfway down the length of the gallery. Lady Heron opened the door and ushered us both in. I had a confused impression of a window looking over some sort of inner courtyard, chests and cupboards, a large four-poster bed with brocade hangings drawn back for the day, and a fireplace neatly piled with logs. 'This chest is for your belongings,' said Lady Heron. 'Ring for my maid when you are ready, and she will show you down to supper. This chamber here is for your maid – she'll have it to herself, for I regret that I have recently had to dismiss my daughter's maid for misconduct. I am sure that Alice can look after you both. Supper will be served in half an hour.'

She went out. I sat on the windowseat and stared down into the little courtyard garden below, while Alice bustled round unpacking, and talking ceaselessly. 'Well, well, I knew it'd be nice but I never dreamed of a palace like this! D'you suppose the King comes here? It's grand enough! Did you *see* the tapestries? And the plate! Oh, little mistress, it's an ill wind as does no one good and it's brought us here, whatever's gone before, and you can't deny it's better than staying at Ashcott with only your old grandmother, good lady though she is, to oversee you, now can you? Oh, just look at your best apron, I've never seen such creases! You can't wear that, this one'll have to do; the lace isn't as fine but that won't notice and I can soon rub that little spot of mud away. What do your shoes look like?' I held them out for inspection. 'Tut, tut, those will never do. They're quite ruined. Best wear your kid ones with the black rosettes . . .'

I let her talk flow past me, as it was one of the last reminders of Ashcott that I still possessed: allowed myself to be undressed to my chemise, had the worst mud wiped and washed from my face and hands, and a comb dragged through my thick cloud of brown hair. Then Alice brought out fresh clothes, the black bodice and skirt, clean bib, coif and apron and a lace-edged neckerchief. I was decked out in them, directing arms here and there mechanically as ordered, Alice still talking, while I thought over and over of my grandmother's advice, and held my temper, and would not let myself weep. Then we were escorted down to supper, which was held in a large echoing room just off the Hall. There I met the remainder of the household above servile status: Dr Davis, the chaplain and tutor to the boys, a shrivelled old Welshman of forbidding aspect, black-clad, whose sole function seemed to be to act as a faded, sheep-like echo of his employer; and Mistress Bryant. She, I later discovered, was an impoverished relation of Lady Heron's, a large unattractive elderly woman, with big red hands and lank grey hair and a ruff, smelling powerfully of rosewater and underlying sweat. 'She will teach you and Lucy your stitches and dancing and all manner of other things,' said Sir Simon from the top of the table, as I curtseyed with a gloomy heart. And then, as the door into the hall opened, he added, 'Hullo, John! You're nearly come too late.'

The man thus addressed, with more warmth than I had yet heard Sir Simon use, shut the door and walked unhurriedly down the room towards us. He was big, with a broad, tanned face like a farmer's, and bright red hair turning grey and rusty with approaching age. He spotted my new face immediately, and smiled. 'Ah, so here's your cousin's little mawther.'

His accent was broadly Suffolk, like the coachman's, yet Sir Simon had addressed him as a friend and equal. Thoroughly confused, I curtseyed again to be on the safe side, feeling that I had done more of these this day than ever before in my whole life. 'Yes,' Sir Simon said, 'this is

Thomazine, newly arrived today from Oxford – John Sewell, who's been a good friend since we were at Bury School together and now runs the Home Farm for me. He has some brats of his own, they're always here and you'll probably see them tomorrow at lessons. Now, John, what news of that sick cow?'

The conversation turned to matters agricultural. I was served with thick juicy slices of mutton, with a fricassee of chicken, with bread and winter-stored apples and pieces of beef pie, and a syllabub to follow that was more delicious even than my grandmother's, and I wondered that my cousins supped as well on this, an informal occasion, as we had done at Ashcott on high days and holidays. At the head of the table, in the slowly gathering dusk, Sir Simon and John Sewell were deep in talk; Mary Heron ate greedily, pausing in her task now and then to address a word to her aunt. Dr Davis and Simon Heron were talking long of matters theological, and I saw the fair-haired Francis listening unobtrusively, his food somehow finding its way to his mouth without accident. Sometimes he glanced across at me, alone between Edward and Lucy, and smiled. No one else took much notice of me. When the meal was finished, I was relieved to hear Mary Heron say, her eyes elsewhere, 'I can see you falling asleep over your meal, Thomazine. You had best go up to your bed . . .' I took the opportunity offered and once more climbed the long stairs with a candle-carrying servant, and Lucy mute by my side. I dreaded the night.

However, when Alice had retired and the candles were blown out and we lay side-by-side in the great bed with the curtains drawn stiflingly, Lucy said, suddenly, 'Are you glad you came here?'

Caught off guard, I muttered, 'I – I don't know.'

'Well, I am,' Lucy said. 'I'm tired of all the boys, except Jamie, and he doesn't do needlework. I've been longing for you to come, ever since we knew. Can you sew, and dance, and play the spinet?'

'Well, I can sew a little,' I said, surprised by this

unlooked-for offer of friendship. 'And play the lute. I brought mine with me. I love music.'

'So do I,' Lucy said. She gave me a one-armed hug. 'I'm so glad you came. Did you think we were very frightening? You looked as if you did.'

'None of you smiled except Francis.'

'Oh,' Lucy said, 'Francis is different. But he can be just as frightening too if he wants to. He can be fun, though. When we can get away from lessons we have grand games in the Park. Simon and Edward are too old – or they say they are. Anyway, Simon likes his books. If he wasn't Father's heir I do believe he'd become a parson. And Edward likes horses, and hunting, and he can't wait to go to Flanders with Henry Sewell. But he's not as – as upright as Simon!'

'Who's Henry Sewell? Is he the son . . .?'

'Yes, Master Sewell who came to supper is his father. Henry's older than Simon, but Tom is the same age as Francis. He's nice, but he can be very annoying. Do you have any brothers or sisters?'

'I had Edmund,' I said, 'but he's dead.'

A sticky hand stole into mine. 'I'm sorry,' Lucy said, 'I forgot. We'll talk of something else. Oh, I know what I've been longing to ask you. Do you know the Forest of Arden?'

'The Forest . . . no, I don't. Why?'

'I thought it might be near you,' Lucy explained. 'You know . . . the Forest of Arden . . . where Rosalind went.'

I was completely mystified. 'Who's Rosalind?'

'Oh,' Lucy said. 'Don't you know *As You Like It*? It's a stage-play. By Master Shakespeare. Don't you know any stage-plays?'

'No,' I said, forbearing to say that I had never heard of Master Shakespeare. Lucy gave a wriggle. 'Well, you'll soon know lots. I've got nine already. Every time someone goes to London I get them to bring a copy back. When it's raining we act them, sometimes.' She giggled. 'We even got Simon to act, once. He made a very, uh, wooden Macbeth. But Francis is very good. He did all three witches and a different voice for each and it was quite frightening.'

A door opened and a candle gleamed through a crack in

the bedcurtains. 'Not asleep yet?' said the voice of Mistress Bryant, hoarse and scratchy like her grey grogram gown. 'Cease talking, you know what will happen if you don't. It's high time you were asleep. I shall not expect to hear any more from you. Good night.'

'Good night, Mistress Bryant,' we whispered in unison. The candle disappeared and the door closed. 'She has such sharp ears,' Lucy said softly, 'and the hardest slap you've ever felt. We'd best go to sleep. You must be very tired. Good night!'

'Good night,' I said, and snuggled deeper into the feather mattress and bolster, feeling suddenly happy. Lucy was my friend, Francis had seemed an ally, and I no longer felt alone. Contrary to my expectations, I fell almost instantly asleep.

My first weeks at Goldhayes passed very quickly. There was so much to learn and to accustom myself to. The house was vast, containing some seventy rooms of varying sizes from tiny houses of office squeezed inside the thickness of the walls to the great chambers, the long gallery and the hall, the chapel and the dining hall, and the library where we took our lessons. This was a high, light room on the ground floor at the end of the east wing, surrounded on two sides by the moat, which in the sun cast brilliant, dancing spears of light on the moulded plaster ceiling; it was hard to concentrate on the drone of Dr Davis's voice. In these summer days, we rose early; breakfast was at about seven o'clock, preceded by prayers, in which Sir Simon read a passage from the huge family Bible for the entire household who congregated in the chapel at the rear of the house. Then, lessons until dinner-time; stumbling dance-steps with Lucy, under the hard eyes of Mistress Bryant, or needlework. I was quick and neat-fingered, and found the creation of pattern or design in silk and cloth a pleasure. Lucy, however, seemed all thumbs, jabbed the needle everywhere except the right place, and on one occasion into her finger so that blood spoiled the work. Mistress Bryant was annoyed. 'You're too impulsive by half, girl! Why don't you think before you place the needle? Discipline and concentration are all you need. Now Thomazine here . . .' But Lucy sent me a quick rueful glance afterwards, to show she did not mind. And she was certainly better at the dancing than I, stepping with grace and flair to the music Mistress Bryant picked out with a heavy hand on the spinet, and so my superiority at needlework was no cause for jealousy. Not that there was any trace of it in Lucy's warm affectionate nature. When not under the hawk's gaze of Lucy's great-aunt, we learned from Dr Davis the genteel rudiments of French; to write a fine italic script, and to couch a letter in elegant phrases becoming to ladies of rank. Dr Davis had had trouble with Lucy, whose swift hand tripped over the letters and resolved itself into a rapid featureless scrawl, and whose elegant phrases were apt under pressure to reassemble into ludicrous patters. I, however, could see little point in a fine hand with attendant flourishes, so long as it was legible; nor in elegant phrases which took so long to remember and to write, and which seemed to me unnecessary when all that was required was to state one's meaning clearly and precisely. Dr Davis was sorely tried with us both. Moreover, I, having little patience with feminine accomplishments, apart from musical ones and my needle, had learned from Lucy something of the lessons given to the boys, and begged Dr Davis to be allowed to join them. Dr Davis, who had a poor opinion of the female sex, regarded me as he would a very small insect, and remarked that unbridled education had made enough mischief amongst those unsuited to it without their numbers being swelled by women. However, a few weeks at Goldhayes had restored most of my natural confidence and by cajoling and pestering him and learning as much as I could from books in order to impress him with my enthusiasm, I succeeded in winning him over. Lucy, fired by my example, demanded to join the lessons too. Though her interest in Greek and Latin was minimal, she did not greatly relish the prospect of a return to solitary lessons with Mistress Bryant. So, my mornings were divided between the two tutors, and the hour or so set aside for study before supper was devoted to practising music. I began to learn to play the spinet and virginals in earnest, to strum Lady Heron's lovely inlaid guitar, or to stroke chords on the dulcimer. In the quiet of the evening, after supper, my cousins gathered in the long gallery, and entertained themselves with music and singing, we children often taking it in turn to play a new piece, to share the singing of a round or to warble a ballad in our plaintive, uncertain trebles.

But the afternoons were free of lessons. Often we went riding or hawking, visited the Home Farm at the end of the drive, or with adult escort journeyed into Bury on market day. When it rained, which was not often that dry droughty summer, we stayed indoors, reading, playing music, acting in one of Lucy's plays, or arguing over cards or chess or backgammon.

But this was one of the fine days, in mid-July, when I had been at Goldhayes a little less than two months. The hay was not yet in; John Sewell prophesied no break in the weather for several days and advised holding off until the cut grass was fully ready. When the time came, every soul in Goldhayes save for Sir Simon and Lady Heron, Dr Davis who had arthritis and could not bend, and Mistress Bryant who suffered from megrims when exposed to the sun, would be out in the Home Farm meadows helping to gather in the thick lush Suffolk hay. I looked forward to it, remembering my enjoyment of haymaking and harvest at Ashcott. Today, however, there was little to do. The house was in turmoil, making ready for the arrival of Sir Simon's elder sister, Hannah, her husband Sir Roger Drakelon, their son and Great-Aunt Elizabeth from Yorkshire on an extended visit. Great-Aunt Elizabeth was a family legend. The daughter of old Sir Hal Heron by his first marriage, she was sixty-five and had reputedly been a woman of spirit and temper in her youth; age had neither mellowed her nor reduced her vigour. Her arrival would, by report of previous visits, mean an eye much too sharp for comfort upon our childish affairs. To judge by the feverish activity within the guestchambers, the servants felt much the same. Lady Heron was making a vague effort to supervise the operation, aided by her aunt, and had dispatched her younger children from under everyone's feet. Lucy had had a tearful quarrel with Jamie, involving large quantities of dust and rubbish removed from on top of and underneath the main guestchamber's four-poster; Jamie had received several chastising strokes from Dr Davis, whose duty this invariably was, and had taken his resentment off to the stables, where lived his white mice. Lucy, dust-covered and weeping, was ushered away by Alice for a wash and a change of clothes, and I was left to my own devices for the afternoon.

The sun shone temptingly upon the park. I gazed out through the long gallery windows, at the drive arcing away from the house; at the new fence erected alongside it to keep in the deer; at the hot still grass and the distant heat-hazed dark shimmer that was Piper's Wood. I ran down the stairs and across to the front door, panelled oak four inches thick, with bolts top and bottom and vast iron hinges wrought in curling patterns. I reached up on tiptoe, for I was not tall for my age, turned the ring handle and with a great effort pulled the door open. No one seemed to have heard the creak of iron; upstairs there were only the faint muted noises of sweeping and beating, mixed with anxious female voices. I pulled the door to behind me, ran across the courtyard, over the bridge, ducked under the fence and raced through the long grass, filled with a sense of happiness and freedom I had not known since before Edmund's death.

Then, suddenly, I nearly fell over Francis. H was lying on his stomach in the grass, his dog beside him. I missed him by inches as I jumped awkwardly over him, and landed heavily on Drake's shaggy plumed tail. The dog yelped in agony, and I fell over, burying my nose painfully in a grass tussock. Drake, in the manner of good-natured dogs, behaved as if it was he who was the offender and tried to lick my face and my stinging nose. Francis sat on his heels and stared at me. 'Can't you look where you're going?'

24

I had had little contact with Francis beyond those welcoming allying smiles, and brief discussions about lessons which had revealed the presence of some barrier between us, whether of shyness or hostility I did not know. I had an unwarranted feeling of kinship with this strange, wayward child who frequently got into trouble with Dr Davis for expressing contrary opinions or for sharpening his unchildish wits on the old cleric's slow brain and petty foibles, and this accidental meeting might well be an opportunity to scale the barrier, though how I did not know. I said, 'I'm sorry. Did I hurt Drake?'

'Drake doesn't seem to think so,' Francis said. 'But he always lets people take advantage of his good nature.'

I had found the place in the centre of Drake's spine which every dog, because it is the one spot they cannot reach, loves to have scratched. Drake shut his eyes, and wriggled in ecstasy. One hindleg began to scratch the air in rhythm with my fingers, and a corner of his muzzle wrinkled up to reveal an efficient-looking eye tooth. I looked across at Francis. Our eyes met and we grinned together. 'He likes you,' Francis said. 'He's a good judge of character. He hates Dr Davis.'

Smiles became laughter. I stopped scratching and Drake, rudely recalled to reality, got up and bounced round me, whining. Francis fished a leather-bound ball out of his breeches pocket and threw it, hard. Drake rushed after it. 'Aren't you with Lucy?'

'She and Jamie had a quarrel. Jamie threw dust all over her and he got a beating and Lucy had to be cleaned up.'

'Did she cry? If you spoil Lucy's clothes she takes it worse than if you've hit her. Where were you going when you fell over us?'

I said, 'Nowhere, really. I just felt happy, so I ran. I like running when I'm happy, and free.'

'So do I,' Francis said. 'A sort of celebration, when you feel so good you could run for ever and not get tired. Drake! Thank you . . . drop it!'

Drake dropped the ball and rolled a hopeful brown eye at his master. Francis picked the ball up and threw it again.

'That used to be a good tennis-ball. Now it's as pitted with toothmarks as cheese in a mousetrap. Why did you join our lessons?'

I was becoming used to these rapid shifts in Francis's train of thought. 'I – I think there's more to be had from Latin and Greek and things like that than from how to write a ladylike letter.'

Francis gave a hoot of laughter, his pale hair tossed gold and cream in the sun. 'I used to think all girls were like Lucy. Oh, I wish you'd always lived here, we could defeat Dr Davis, and Simon too, if we were together. Don't you want to be ladylike, though?'

Rejoicing in this new companionship, I said, 'Well, if it means beginning a letter, "I am most obliged to you for acceding to my desires and am very sensible of the honour you do me in singling me out for your attention," instead of saying, "Thank you for doing as I asked and taking an interest in me," no, I don't.'

'What of French, though? *Bonjour, Mademoiselle Heron, voulez-vous m'accompagner à la ferme, où il y a un nid d'un faucon dans un grand arbre, que je vais voir aujourd'hui.*'

I had followed all this with some difficulty, disentangling the meaning from Francis's exaggerated imitation of Dr Davis's accent. 'What hawk's nest?'

'It's in the big oak in the road by Home Farm, and Tom says the chicks are near to flying. It's only a kestrel, but Tom hasn't got a hawk and he wants to train one of them for his own, so we thought we'd try to climb up and get one. And you can see my new horse, too. Do you want to come?'

'Er . . . how long will we be?'

'It'll take five or ten minutes to walk there, that's all. Why?'

'Sir Roger and Lady Drakelon are expected for supper.'

Francis swore, while I gazed at him in surreptitious admiration for his fluency. 'I thought they weren't expected till tomorrow. It's not like Aunt Hannah to hurry on a journey – she likes to travel in state and comfort. Oh, she can go hang! Great-Aunt too. Is the house being turned upside down? I expect Mother wasn't best pleased at having to exert herself for once, even if she has got Aunt Margaret to help her.'

Because of the bustle in the house, we had spent, Lucy and I, a pleasant morning in the kitchen, under the genial eye of Robert Harcourt, the French master cook, learning how to make candied flowers and roots and fruit. Remembering this, I fumbled in the pocket of my gown and produced, slightly gritty and dotted with pieces of fluff, two sugared raspberries and four candied rose-petals. 'We made these this morning, as Mistress Bryant was busy. Want one?'

'I'm not sure,' Francis said, taking a rose-petal with suspicion, 'that I do. However, they look good enough . . . Ouch!'

'Perhaps that was one of Lucy's,' I suggested, 'she didn't quite succeed with one batch. Have you broken a tooth?'

'Not quite. I like the way you assume that because it was hard as stone it must perforce be one of Lucy's. It's fortunate she's good-natured.'

I gave him a sideways glance, afraid I had antagonized him, and received a grin in return. 'Don't worry,' Francis said, 'you're a strange little thing, but I like you well enough. So does Drake. Well, are we going to go and see that nest or aren't we?'

I said, my desire to cement our friendship getting the better of my wish to behave with decorum in my new family, 'They sent a servant on ahead and he said they lay at Newmarket last night and they'd be here by five o'clock, God willing.'

'As I said, Aunt Hannah likes to travel slowly. Around twelve miles in one day, and on good hard-baked summer roads too! When I can ride my new horse,' Francis said, with a kind of fierce longing all of a sudden undisguised in his light bantering voice, 'I'll ride twelve miles in an hour!'

'What's so special about your horse?' I asked through a candied raspberry that was soft and sharp under the hard crust of sugar. Francis said, lightly again, 'She's as black as nightfall and as beautiful as sin, she has Arabian blood and she's five years old. Now do you see?'

'The Saracen's Arabian too,' I said, referring to Sir Simon's and Edward's pride and joy, the young Eastern stallion brought from exotic deserts by land and water at vast expense to improve the family's horseflesh. 'And I haven't seen you mooning over him.'

'Unlike Edward. If that horse was human and female he'd marry him. That's what my mare is meant for eventually, of course.'

'To marry Edward?' I asked, all innocent. Francis doubled up with laughter. 'Ninnyhead! For the Saracen, to breed better horses than Sir Thomas Jermyn's. Father has always had a burning desire to surpass Sir Thomas in something.'

'Well, he has, hasn't he?' I said, remembering what I knew of the Jermyns of Rushbrooke. 'He has the lovelier house, and four sons, not just two. Anyway, why is she kept down at the Home Farm and not in the stables up at the house?'

'Because she's been ill. Father got her cheaply, for that reason, and she's been kept in the Orchard this past month and dosed up with all John Sewell's and Edward's best remedies. But when she's well enough, in a week or so, I'll be able to ride her. You can, too, if you like.'

'I'd love to, thank you. I love riding, and I had to leave my pony behind,' I said wistfully, 'and I haven't been given another yet, though Edward did promise. You are lucky,' I added, as a thought struck me, 'especially to have a horse as fine as that. Why are you allowed to have it, if it's to be used for breeding?'

'Because my old horse was too small for me, and because whatever else my father thinks of me, he knows I can ride well,' said Francis shortly, flicking a strand of pale silky hair out of his eyes. 'What about *your* father? What was he like? Did he like you?'

It was not something that I had ever thought about, any more than I had ever wondered about the sun's progress through the sky. 'Like me? Of course he did. Or he said he did; he used to laugh at the things I said. He used to tell his friends . . . he called me the nutbrown maid,' I said, remembering with a pang of sorrow the unthinking happiness that had been mine only three months ago, and had seemed so unchanging and secure.

'The nutbrown maid you are indeed – or a weasel, with that pointed little face,' said Francis. 'Do you favour your father, then, or your mother?'

'She died when I was born, so I never knew her. But I've seen her portrait, and she was like me, but beautiful.'

'Well, you might be one day, I suppose,' said Francis, eyeing me critically. ' "Item, one pair of lips, indifferent red . . ." '

I caught his note of cheerful mockery, and grinned. 'Indifferent pink, really. And eyes like – like blackberries!'

'No, sloe berries, and as sour usually,' said Francis. 'And you have the Heron look, you know, we're all very alike – have you noticed, that sort of look we all have . . .'

I had once heard my grandmother on the subject. 'Determined,' I said.

Francis laughed. 'Do I have it?'

'Yes,' I said, picking a straw of grass and chewing it thoughtfully. 'Yes, you're determined to have your own way in everything, too!'

'Determined to go and see that nest,' said Francis. 'If we stand here talking for much longer, it'll be dark. Where's that dog?'

Drake, it appeared, had made off after a rabbit. Faint barks of rapture echoed from Piper's Wood. 'We can't wait for him,' Francis said, and set off in the direction of the Home Farm, emitting the occasional ear-splitting two-toned whistle in the hope that his errant dog would respond. I trotted after him, the sun hot on my black gown, wishing that I could, as he had done, remove some clothes. He was clad at present in shirt and breeches, the former garment ventilated by a large tear exposing a back brown enough to suggest that he had often gone shirtless that summer. His doublet was tied round his waist by the sleeves, not a practice designed to enhance its condition, and he carried his shoes and stockings in one hand. Emboldened, I kicked my own footwear off as well, with the result that we arrived at the Home Farm as barefoot and dishevelled as vagabond children. John Sewell was in the yard, inspecting one of the small, ugly, dun-coloured cows that were everywhere in this part of the country, and his younger son was leaning against the wall of the house picking splinters out of the grey timbering and whistling through his teeth. I had some liking for Tom Sewell, with his hair as flaming as powdered ginger and face so scattered with freckles that you could, so Lucy teased him, scarcely set a pin between them. Although he excelled at mathematics and reckoning, and wrote a neat legible hand, he was not clever, nor hardworking, and was frequently made an example of by Dr Davis; but he had a quick wit and a ready ear for any possible jest. When he saw us enter the yard, he gave a whoop and trotted round to the gate, dodging between the piles of fresh and not-so-fresh cow dung with the ease of long practice. 'Hullo! Come to look at that nest? The chicks are surely nearly ready, you can hear them mewing if you listen below. They were late hatching, but it shouldn't be long now before they leave the nest, and if we can get up there we can see how many there are, and happen we can take one.' His bright teasing friendly eyes flicked to me. 'Why have you brought *her* along of you?'

'To see the horse,' said Francis. 'Let's do that first, before we go to the nest.'

'Why shouldn't he bring me, ginger-top?' I demanded, nettled. The most irritating thing about Tom was his fixed belief that women were of no practical use outside the kitchen or still-room. I knew what his answer would be – 'Well, you're only a *girl*, after all' – and was ready for battle. He did, indeed, open his mouth to speak, and then saw the appalling state of my garments. 'Christ in Heaven! What *have* you been doing, to get all drabble-tailed and slummocky like that?'

I looked down at my rent, grass-stained apron, at my filthy, scratched bare feet and the hem of my skirt which had trailed in a fresh pat of dung as we approached the farmyard. Tom sniffed pointedly. 'That smell nice and ripe, anyhow. Who'll buy my cow-turds, fresh-smelling and brown? A pleasant addition to any fine lady's aroma!'

'Tom!' his father bellowed, while the labourer holding the cow grinned behind his hand. 'Thass no way for any lad to go on, and in front of Mistress Thomazine too. Do I hear you do the like again I'll thrash the sauce out of you, good and all. If they've come to see Master Francis's horse, do you go and show 'em the brute, and not your cheeky ways. Good afternoon.' He turned to escort the cow to its field. John Sewell, despite his strange friendship with Sir Simon, retained a plain way of speaking, a lack of deference to those normally considered his superiors, that endeared him to a few and earned him the enmity of others. I knew already that Mary Heron despised him and grudged every moment her children spent with his: she had protested, with as much force as was in her nature, at the prospect of Tom and Henry sharing lessons with them, but Sir Simon was, on that subject as many others, quite unmovable. The memory of boyhood companionship and adult friendship, coupled with the fact that John Sewell had once saved Sir Simon's life when they were together on the disastrous Cadiz expedition ten years previously (my guardian despite this deed being left with a wound that had eventually crippled him), had spurred Sir Simon to offer to his friend and steward's sons the opportunities of gentlemen. The veneer on Tom was thin as yet, as his Suffolk speech showed, thinner than on his diffident, sensible elder brother, but such was his cheerful, thoughtless charm that at twelve years old it did not matter greatly.

'Don't you mind Father,' said Tom now, hopping over a pitchfork, 'you know what he's like, all bark and no bite. And he do say he won't hev that horse of yours here much longer, he reckon that's vicious.'

'Is it?' Francis asked. 'It's never been anything other than quite gentle with me.'

'Well, that near took a piece out of his arm yesterday,' said Tom. 'You should hev heard what he said, or rather *you* shouldn't, Thomazine, that weren't fit for no lady's ears. Do you mind that post!' He skipped neatly over it and, landing, turned a cartwheel in a blur of orange hair and green garments. 'I'll wager you can't do that, Francis.'

'Well, you're wrong,' said my new friend, and followed suit with not one cartwheel but two. I stood envious, for decency did not permit me to copy them – though at Ashcott, alone on the wide sheepwalks above the house, I had often practised such acrobatics and had even day-dreamed, wistfully, of putting my accomplishments to good use in a fair or troupe. But Tom's free comments on the inferiority of women had stung me deep, and there was no one else to see, so I bunched up my skirts, tucking them in my waistband, yelled at the two boys to get out of my way, and ran. I did two cartwheels and finished with a handspring and a somersault in mid-air. Only the landing spoiled it, for I tripped and ended on hands and knees. But the sight of Tom and Francis, open-mouthed, was more than sufficient return for any grazing or bruises.

'Jesus!' Tom, obviously, was scarce able to believe his eyes. 'Where . . . how . . . how in God's name did you do that?'

'She's a witch,' said Francis, grinning.

'I reckon she must be,' Tom went on, 'no girl could do that in a month o' Sundays.'

'Well, I did,' I told him, furious, 'and if you really want me to I'll do it again, and probably break a leg this time, and I expect you'd be glad, Tom Sewell.'

'No, no,' said Tom hastily, 'no, I didn't mean that, I meant . . . well, it were master good.'

Francis burst out laughing. 'Perhaps, Tom, if you stopped baiting her she'd be less concerned to prove herself a boy. Who taught you those, little cousin, and how did you manage to practise them? You must have been hard put to it to find enough time alone.'

'Oh, it was easy enough at Ashcott,' I said. 'And no one taught me. I saw some tumblers at a fair in Oxford, last year, and then I went up on the sheepwalks and practised till I could do what they could.'

'Well,' said Francis, 'you've beaten us both, for I know

full well I couldn't somersault like that, and I'm damn sure Tom can't, either. Teach me?'

Flushed and rosy with success, I said happily, 'Oh yes, I'd love to, but we must make sure we're alone and where no one's likely to watch, or your mother will throw a fit.'

'She would indeed – she's most concerned about your rough and rude ways, I overheard her telling Aunt Margaret so. She said that if it wasn't for your prowess at embroidery and music, and your application to your book, she would scarce dare let Lucy near you. And if she'd seen what you've just done, she'd banish you forever and pack you back to Ashcott.'

It was strange, for even an hour ago I would have wished for nothing better than to return to my home, but now of a sudden it was grown distant and shadowy, and my grandmother and father and brother were blurred figures, very far away. And Francis and Tom were here, vividly in the present, standing with me in the grassy path that led to the orchard where Francis's horse was kept, and I had won their respect and admiration and was utterly happy.

We walked down the last few yards of the path, stood by the gate and leaned our elbows on it. The trees hung green with the promise of apples and pears, quinces and plums. In the long grass a rabbit scuttled away with a flick of white tail, and something dark moved gently behind the bowed branches of a spreading and laden tree. 'There she be!' said Tom; and the black mare stepped thoughtfully into view, her small ears pricked to catch the sounds of our voices. Francis leaned his chin on his arms and stared at her, a small intent smile shadowing the corners of his long mouth. The horse stood still in the sunlight, ten yards away, her glossy hide afire with blue lights and shadows, and the breeze stirring the long, plumed tail and stroking and lifting the tresses of her mane and forelock. It was as if she recognized him, for she stepped delicately up to the gate, nodding her head, and blew gently down her nostrils. Tom, no respecter of beauty, pulled a handful of grass and held it out to her, and with a glint in her eye that might in a human have been mischief, she blew more violently and the grass was scattered, leaving Tom's palm empty.

'Let me try,' I said, tugging up a great arid handful: but with the same result. Francis looked at the horse, and she at him, as if they were sharing some private joke, then stopped, plucked a small juicy tuft and held it out. Delicately and cleanly, with the minimum of slobber, the mare took it from his hand and chewed it. Francis pulled her ears and patted her neck. 'Told you she was a one-man horse.'

'If you was an old woman, and she your cat, you'd be jallused of being a witch,' said Tom, his voice envious. He put up a hand, rather too abruptly, to pat the smooth shiny neck, and the horse flung up her head, showing her teeth, and then turned skittishly on her heels and trotted away, tail in air. 'Froward old horse,' said Tom. 'Come on, I'd like to see that nest.'

Reluctantly, we left the orchard, wriggled through a bare patch in the hedge to the left of the path, crossed a small field containing a somnolent-looking bull, giving him a wide berth, and emerged through the far hedge into the lane which led to the Home Farm and thence to Goldhayes. It was lined with thick bushes of elm and holly and oak – not so plentiful in this country the white-flowered hawthorn of Ashcott. In the hedge to our left stood a gnarled and twisted oak-tree, that had been mature when Agincourt was won, and had begun to decline before Kit Heron, courtier and Border reiver, came to make this gentle, unhurried country his home. It was reduced now to a huge knotted trunk, from which branches groped like crooked fingers, ten or twenty to a hand. 'There,' said Tom, pointing to a knot in the stoutest, highest-reaching branch.

We stared upwards, assessingly. To my practised eye, it was a difficult climb and one needing courage, for the nest, marked by the white splashes of droppings below it, was at least thirty feet from the ground.

'Well?' Tom demanded. 'D'you still think you can do it?'

Francis tipped his head back, and smiled. 'Look, see, there's one of them looking out! They're all but ready to go;

if we want one we'll have to get it now. Well, I'm game, Tom – what about you?'

'We can't both go up,' said Tom, 'someone's got to give a leg up, you coon't climb that first ten feet without that.'

'I could go up,' I said. The two boys turned and stared at me. Tom laughed. 'You! You coon't, not never! Girls don't climb trees!'

'You mean, Lucy doesn't climb trees,' I said, resisting the impulse to wipe the scornful leer off his freckled face. 'But I do. And I'll prove it to you.'

'Oh, no, you don't,' said Tom. 'That'd be a tidy bother if you was seen, and who'd get the blame? Us! Help me up, Francis?'

'Wait,' I said, 'you can't possibly climb down with a hawk in your hand, screeching and clawing and pecking as like as not. You'll need something to wrap it in.'

'Come on, Tom, admit it,' said Francis, 'she's right, you know, she really is. What do you suggest we use?' There was no patronizing note in his voice at all. I untied my maltreated apron and held it out. 'Will this do? You can bundle it up in that and tie the strings round it like a parcel.'

'Good idea,' said Francis, taking the proffered apron. 'Could you really climb the tree, do you think?'

'I've climbed harder,' I said, with a certain modest bravado; inwardly I was not so sure, but after Tom's remarks my pride would not allow me to retreat. Francis glanced round the deserted lane, making sure we were unobserved, and gave me a friendly, encouraging grin. 'Well, if you think you can do it I'll help you. Do you need a leg-up?'

'No,' I said airily, 'I can scramble up easily. You go first, Tom.'

Tom gave me a hunted, resentful glance. 'I don't want no part of this,' he muttered. 'Why can't she be like Lucy, a proper girl 'stead of all this here tree-climbing nonsense. I don't reckon as you ought to let her, Francis.'

'I don't think somehow I could stop her,' Francis said, grinning. 'Go on, Tom, I'll bend my back for you, and she can do the same for me.'

Despite the misgivings I was determined not to reveal,

the tree was sufficiently gnarled and ancient to make the task of ascending it a comparatively easy one. I climbed barefoot like a monkey, quick and nimble: my toes curled helpfully into knots and cracks in the bark, and I clung to the tree like a fly on the wall. Providing the more obviously rotten boughs were avoided, the profusion of twisted branches gave all three of us an ample choice of routes up towards the nest, and we climbed quickly, eager to reach our goal: I paused once or twice, but only to secure my skirts which, in my anxiety not to be left behind, had been tucked anyhow into my waistband. They still hampered me somewhat, so that I was the last to reach the sturdy branch that stuck out by the side of the hole where the nest was: but at least I had the satisfaction of getting there safely, and the sight of Tom's grudgingly respectful face, in addition to the exhilaration of swinging my feet in an airy void, with the ground some twenty feet below. Francis sat nearest the trunk and, leaning all his weight against it, peered round and into the hole. A furious keeking noise broke out. Francis grinned. 'There are three. Look, here's your apron, Thomazine. Spread it out on your lap and get ready to wrap it round the bird when I pull it out: and for God's sake hang on, both of you!'

We needed no second bidding, and Francis put his hand into the nest. The high-pitched screeching of the young birds broke out again, and than in a flurry of feathers Francis, swearing, hauled a furious, kicking young kestrel out of the nest, grabbed the apron from my lap and bundled it round the flailing wings and darting, vicious beak. Tom tied the knots and secured the heaving, squirming, soiled bundle over Francis's shoulder, and we hastily began the climb down, lest the bird escape before we reached ground. So intent were we on the descent that we noticed nothing below us, until at last as my feet touched the blessed, safe, broad ground John Sewell's voice said, close and angry, 'And what in God's name was you doing up there?'.

Francis and Tom dropped the last few feet and turned to face him. I myself was too relieved at being once more on

36

terra firma, unharmed, to be very much concerned. Master Sewell stood not three yards away, and beyond, his big bony brown horse was placidly cropping the grass verge; he had evidently been riding out to the village.

'Getting one of the young kestrels,' said Francis, unslinging the bundle from his shoulder. John Sewell cast it never a glance. 'I don't care a mite about that. But aside from what your father'll do to me if you kill yourself—'

'Is he likely to care much?' Francis demanded.

'Aside from that, what in the maim o' the flesh do you mean by dragging Mistress Thomazine up that there tree? Eh? Can you tell me that, Master Francis who thinks he know all the answers?'

Tom giggled nervously. His father rounded on him. 'And you, you sawny kite! Letting that little mawther climb that tree!'

I saw Tom's indignant face and felt it was time to intervene. 'If you please, Master Sewell, they didn't want me to go up, but I wouldn't be stopped. It wasn't their fault.'

'Well, then,' said John Sewell, 'you're as big a fule as they, maw. How old are you? Eight? Nine?'

'Ten, actually,' I said, bristling. 'Ten and a half.'

'Well, I'll give you this, you're a brave little maw, but you're a fule to climb that there tree. And what will Lady Heron say to all this, eh?'

'She won't like it at all,' I said, wondering with sudden apprehension whether he was going to tell my guardian. 'But my father didn't mind.'

'Your father let you go a-climbing trees? What in God's name was he a-thinking of? Happen he thought you was a boy.'

'No - but he often said I should have been one.'

At this, Tom sniggered. His father swung round on him with annoyance. 'Hold your tongue, you! Now, Mistress Thomazine, I doubt you'd like me to say nawthen o' this to Sir Simon or his good lady, eh?'

'I – I, no, I wouldn't, please, Master Sewell.'

'Then I'll strike a bargain with you, maw. I oon't say

nawthen about that, do you promise never to climb that tree again. Can you do that?'

I nodded gratefully. John clapped me on the shoulder. 'Thass good. Now, Master Francis, what's to be done with that poor bird?'

Faint, despairing screeches came from the bundle, which had long ago given up struggling. Francis said, 'It was to be for Tom. I have a hawk already. We were going to train it together, sit up all night with it, make a hood and jesses for it.'

'Well, you'd best take it back to the farm,' said John Sewell. 'And untie it from that old rag.'

'Thass no rag, thass Thomazine's apron,' said Tom. John roared with laughter. 'Thass lucky Lady Heron can't see you now, in't it? Now do you go along to the farm, and I reckon you'll find Joan's got suffen on the table for you. I'm a-going to Bradfield St George, and I'll be back afore supper. And don't you go a-climbing any more trees, mind!'

Very much relieved at having escaped so lightly, we walked back down the lane to the Home Farm, Tom carrying his precious kestrel. We collected our shoes from where we had left them by the gate leading to the orchard, and walked across to the ancient farmhouse, a small and crooked building, leaning on the new brick-built dairy for support, with tiny latticed windows and irregular grey oak beams and lumps in the plaster where some hamfisted previous occupant had tried his hand at pargetting. There, we sat in the kitchen while Joan, the housekeeper and, said the malicious, the widowed John Sewell's mistress, plied us liberally with her excellent food amidst the heat of the fire – it was her baking day – and chattered ceaselessly in broad Suffolk of local gossip. Listening to it happily with only half an ear, I was deciding that I liked the Sewells – their warmth, honesty and good humour – very much indeed. The elder son, Henry, who shared his father's and Tom's russet colouring and large build, but who seemed quieter and more sophisticated than either, made an appearance, dusty from his journey to Bradfield Tye, and was soon deep in conversation with Tom and Francis about the best means of training the young kestrel, now firmly fastened to a makeshift perch in the darkest corner of the barn. Munching warm apple pie and smoky ham and new steaming bread, I answered Joan's kind, inquisitive questions about Ashcott without a pang of homesickness, and for the first time a warm, comforting sense of belonging stole over me.

The time of relaxation ended abruptly. Joan, who had gone into a front parlour to find an example of her needlework to show me, came hurrying back with the news that a resplendent horse-litter, accompanied by several mounted men and women, had just come into sight. 'I reckon thass Sir Roger,' she said, breathless at the doorway. 'Thass their colours, in't it, red and gold. Ah, his lady must be wunnerful queer now, poor creature, to be in a litter. Thass only two year agone they was here last, though, and her didn't fare a mucher then. I doubt her's got long to live. Ah, she were the sweetest, prettiest lady you ever saw, Mistress Thomazine, when I was her maid, tall she were, and such hair, thick and black, and looked so well in they old farthingales. She wanted me to go along of her when she wed Sir Roger, but I didn't want to go to no furrin parts.'

'Just as well you didn't,' Francis said, grinning. 'She's not so sweet now, is she? Come on, Thomazine, we must go or we'll be in trouble. Where's my doublet?'

It was laid across a bench, scarcely recognizable for dirt, sweat and rips. Francis shrugged it on, slipped on his shoes, made an ineffectual pull at his stockings and pushed his hair out of his eyes. 'Thank you, Joan, that pie's one of your best.'

'That *were* one of my best, you mean, there in't nawthen left now, Master Francis, not a crumb. Don't they feed you, up at the house? Tom'd make two of you. And I oon't hear no talk agin Mistress Hannah neither, I'm not surprised her's turned bitter up there in that cold owd country. I oon't want to live there and thass a fact, and thass what I said to she, "Mistress Hannah," I said, "I bin happy with you five year but I in't a-going up there with you, thass not a Christian country up in they sheers," and thass as well I didn't for Sir Roger's a wicked Papist, and young Master

Dominic's bin bred up to it, with that outlandish Papist name and all . . .'

With winks from Tom and his brother, we made our exit at last, taking the front way this time through Joan's haphazard garden with salads and cabbage, lavender and marigolds, beans and lax, bursting-petalled roses all in the same undisciplined confusion as her talk, and on to the drive which led to the house. The litter and horses had not long disappeared round the corner ahead of us, and dustclouds lingered in the sun. 'If we take the short cut across the park,' Francis told me, 'we'll get there quicker, and then we can go round the back way without anyone seeing us. Then, we can put on fresh clothes and no one will be any the wiser – I hope! Come on, little cousin.'

We climbed over the deer fence and raced through the grass and clumps of bracken. I did my utmost, but Francis still had to wait for me. As I stopped to catch my breath, a distant, frantic barking made itself heard. Francis clapped his hand on my arm. 'Oh, Christ! Drake! I'd forgotten all about him. We can't leave him loose; father meant what he said about knocking him on the head. Sounds as if he's in the wood still – come on, we've got to find him!'

Tracking Drake down in the thick undergrowth was not easy; however, I finally spotted him in a patch of grass between tall banks of nettles and brambles. Shouting for Francis, I knelt by him and saw that he had caught his hind paw in a wire snare which had tightened round his leg as he struggled to free himself. Gently, I found the noose, surrounded by hair, mud and taut, swollen skin, and loosened it. As Francis ran up and dropped on his knees beside us, Drake leapt up, licking his face, whining with pleasure and pain mixed. I explained what had happened, and Francis frowned. 'Sit still, ridiculous animal, how can I see what's wrong? it must have been a poacher, after rabbits – see, we're on a coney-run, and I expect there's a burrow or two under those brambles. We've no need to set snares here, you see, there's a warren on the other side of the park gives us all the fine fat rabbits we could want. Yes, you stupid, witless dog, *sit*!'

Drake sat. Francis probed the injured paw with careful fingers. 'There's nothing there won't mend, so stop pretending you're hurt. I wonder what the time is?'

I glanced up towards the sun, which had dropped out of sight behind the trees. 'I don't know. Four or five o'clock, perhaps?'

'Maybe. I wish I had one of those little watches, then at least I'd know the rough time. Whatever it is now, though, it must be at least half an hour since they went past the Home Farm, and whatever happens we're going to be very, very late.'

'Was it worth it?' I asked, as we set off back again through the wood, Drake round our heels and limping when he remembered.

'For the kestrel or for Drake?'

'For the kestrel, really. Is it worth being in trouble for?'

'Well, I'd be in trouble already if Father knew I'd climbed that tree, and worse if he knew you'd followed me. But with luck John won't tell him – he's good that way, is John – and what my dear father's eyes don't see, his heart won't grieve over. Did you like my horse?'

Relieved at the change of subject, I said, 'Oh, yes, she was really, truly beautiful, wasn't she? What are you going to call her? She ought to have a grand name, something that no other horse will have, like . . . like Desdemona.'

'I'm not having anything out of one of Lucy's plays,' said Francis with decision. Like the rest of us, he knew his sister's collection rather too well. 'I'm going to call her Hobgoblin.'

'That's an evil name,' I said dubiously. 'That's what a witch would call her familiar.'

'I did think you a girl with more than the usual sense, but now I'm not so sure. You don't really believe in witches, do you? Only uneducated peasants believe in that sort of thing.'

'King James did and you couldn't say *he* was an uneducated peasant. Dr Davis does too, he said he saw some most notorious witches hanged once, when he was in the north parts.'

'King James and Dr Davis have one thing in common –

stupidity. All those witches he saw hanged, I expect they were just old poor widows, a little crazed with age perhaps, with a cat to keep them company and some skill with simples, until some credulous fool got it into his thick skull that they'd put a murrain on his cattle or turned his milk.'

'But they must have been witches,' I insisted. 'They had the Devil's mark, Dr Davis said.'

'If they had the Devil's mark, then so have you – that mole on your cheek might be taken for one. It's all nonsense, anyway,' Francis said, with thinly-veiled contempt. 'There isn't a Devil, so how can there be his disciples?'

'No Devil?' I cried in disbelief. 'Of course there's a Devil. The Bible – he's in the Bible. He tempted Christ in the desert, and lots of things.'

'You don't want to believe everything you read in the Bible – or in any other book for that matter,' Francis said. 'Or what Dr Davis tells you. I don't think he's yet realized that the earth goes round the sun, or that it's round, not flat. Perhaps the reason he's never been further than Lancashire is that he's afraid he'll fall off the edge!'

I giggled, glad to be off the sticky ground over which Francis's conversations always seemed to lead. For a moment, the solid foundations of my childish beliefs had quivered, and I had felt bewilderment and fear. I put theological speculations firmly to the back of my mind, and asked the question which my curiosity had been prompting all afternoon. 'How do you come to have Drake? No one else has a dog, except for the hunting dogs, and your mother's little Moppet.'

'Who could hardly be dignified by the name of dog at all. I found him,' said Francis. 'He was crawling in the muck of a gutter in Bury, someone had probably turned him out to fend for himself because they couldn't feed him. He couldn't have been more than five or six weeks old. I took him home and cleaned him up and called him Drake because it went so well with Francis. He's a grand dog, but not very obedient – my fault, I didn't train him for long enough – and he's forever getting into trouble. He chases sheep – he's meant for a sheepdog, you see, it's in his blood

– and he steals food from the kitchens and worries the deer, and though I've only had him nine months he's notorious as far as Stowmarket. He's good for hunting, though, and he's my friend, aren't you, old lad?'

Drake paused and gave a whisk of his tail. We were now making for the west side of the house, skirting round the spreading oak trees at the edge of the wood, hurrying through the long dry grass and thick bracken. In the distance, in front and to my right I could see the rose-red bricks of the house, sunlit, with here and there a glimpse of the brightly-hung litter standing in the front court. Praying we had not been seen, we slunk round the edge of the gardens on the west side, ducking below the line of the hedges, round the rear of the house, across the bridge over the moat and in at the stable gateway. I had thought it empty, but as we hurried across to the kitchen Edward, an unfamiliar sight in his best doublet and breeches, emerged from one of the stable doors with a bottle of horse-physic in one hand and a tattered volume, which I recognized as one of his favourite books of remedies, in the other. He stopped dead when he saw us and bellowed across the width of the yard, 'Where in the devil's name have you been?'

We stopped by the kitchen door. Edward hurried over, his broad sensible face anxious. 'Uncle Roger and Aunt Hannah have been here nearly an hour; everyone's been looking for you. There's going to be trouble, I can tell you. Father's in a bad humour, his leg's aching worse than usual, I reckon.'

'We've been at the Home Farm,' Francis said. I added, 'We went up the tree and got the kestrel for Tom!'

Edward's face grew long with astonishment. 'We? You don't mean to say that you went up it as well?'

'Yes, she did,' Francis put in, and added ferociously, 'and if you breathe a word of that to anyone, Ned my lad, I'll hang you from the rafters.'

'You've no cause to fear,' said Edward mildly, 'I'm not Lucy.' His sister was notoriously incapable of keeping a still tongue in her head. 'Anyway, supper will be ready in a quarter of an hour, in the dining-hall, always supposing you're allowed to have it. And the state you're in, the pair of you, it'll take all night to make you look respectable.'

'It might at that, if we don't hurry,' Francis said, grabbing my hand. 'Come on, child!'

Leaving Edward in the yard, we dashed together through the kitchen, chaotic as ever with preparations for supper, and up the winding turret stairs that gave the quickest and most private access to the first-floor bed-chambers. All seemed deserted; there was no sign of Lucy or Alice in the room we all three shared, so I retrieved my best clothes, the black-and-silver satin, from the huge carved clothes-press, and set about putting my appalling appearance to rights. Soon my filthy everyday clothes lay in an unpleasant heap which I kicked under the bed, and without a thought for the dirt on my legs and arms, donned fresh stockings and under-petticoats, slipped on my best shoes with their intricate rosettes, and wriggled into the top petticoat with a rustle of cool, gleaming, slithery black satin. The stiffened and boned bodice which went with it was not so easily dealt with. It was mightily uncomfortable, and after the loose-fitting waistcoat which I usually wore seemed a veritable prison. Moreover, it laced up the back and was almost impossible to put on without help. I struggled into it and wrestled with the laces for at least two or three minutes before giving up in disgust. I went to the door and called softly into the gallery, 'Alice! Alice, are you there?'

'I don't think she is – do you need help?' Francis asked, coming round the corner from his own chamber. It was one of the many advantages of being a boy that his clothes were altogether simpler to put on, and he was ready, his hair neatly combed and wearing his new suit of sea-green silk which sometimes matched the colour of his eyes. 'Black doesn't suit you, you know.'

'The laces won't do up,' I said, ignoring him. 'I'm ready except for that and my neckerchief and the apron. And my hair.'

'Very well, I'll help,' Francis said, slipping quickly into the room. 'Turn round, child, so that I can see.'

I turned obediently. Francis was quick-fingered and did the job speedily. 'Now the neckerchief. Does it button or tie?'

'It buttons, and I can do it myself,' I said, having no wish to appear a baby. Regardless, Francis buttoned it up under my chin and arranged it neatly over the neck of my bodice. 'Shall I do up your apron too, brat?'

'I can do that perfectly well, thank you,' I said indignantly. He watched in silence as I tied the apron, dragged a comb through my abundance of brown hair, pinned it roughly back and hid the tangles with the coif. 'Very well, Master Heron,' I said, lifting my skirt delicately to show the embroidered silk under-petticoat and the silver shoe-rosettes, 'wilt thou do me the pleasure of escorting me downstairs?'

'It's not only Lucy who likes stage-plays,' Francis said, taking my arm.

Our grand entrance down the main staircase was somewhat spoiled by the fact that our only audience was a maid sweeping up the mud left by the visiting party. We scurried through her accumulated dirt and fled to Sir Simon's chamber in the west wing. There we stopped, panting, outside the door, fighting to control our breathing, and Francis, motioning to me to be silent, applied his ear to the panels. In the quiet, I could hear an unfamiliar voice holding forth on the other side of the door.

. . . may have been indulgent to Simon and myself,' it opined, 'but he never let his indulgence run to allowing us to go gallivanting all over the countryside, consorting with all and sundry, when guests were expected, and then fail to arrive in time to greet them. Mind you, it is possible that Matthew's girl is to blame, I hear she more than a little favours her grandmother – Magdalen, I mean, not dear Kate, of course – and we all know what became of *her*.'

Mary Heron's voice came in, quickly. 'Now come, Hannah, I scarcely think that you are being quite fair. Thomazine is a charming child and I'm sure that there is an excellent reason for their tardiness. Now, Hannah, surely these excellent sweetmeats tempt you? Master

45

Harcourt is a rare cook, and sugared flowers are his especial skill.'

My guardian's elder sister was not so easily diverted from her path. 'You must forgive me for saying this, Mary my dear, but I do doubt the wisdom of letting them run wild, as you seem to do. Why do you not keep them at lessons after their dinner? Roger is most strict with Dominic about such matters, and now my dear son is a great comfort to me in my sickness.'

'A creaking door hangs long,' Francis whispered, 'she'll outlast us all, you see if she doesn't.' I smothered a giggle, having already heard at length from various sources of Lady Drakelon's tedious preoccupation with her health.

'Come, dear,' Mary Heron said, 'you're not ailing again, surely? You look the picture of health.'

We exchanged delighted grins. Hannah, at last diverted, strove to keep annoyance out of her voice and only succeeded in sounding more querulous than ever. 'I fear, Mary my dear, that you are very far from the truth. My physician assures me that my lungs are quite eaten away with a lingering consumption. That is why I have so high a colour, of course. Not a month ago he gave me at most a year more of life, and more likely half of that, but he also gave me this to take; I have a little by me, in readiness.' There was a pause, during which the bottle was obviously produced for inspection. 'Now this is indeed an elixir, Mary, and I've felt the proof of it in the short time I've been taking it. It has a most invigorating smell – try it.'

There was a violent fit of coughing from Mary. 'Yes, yes, Hannah – it does indeed seem very strong. What is in the mixture, to make it so, uh, good?'

'Part of the recipe I understand must remain a secret and Master Langley – my physician – only divulged the remaining ingredients on the strictest understanding that I was to inform no one. But you are of course welcome to hear them, and since you know a little of simples and remedies yourself you'll be more able to understand their use than I. Now, what did he tell me? It is some time . . . ah, I have it! A speck, no more, of dragon's blood, mixed with a larger

46

measure of powdered mummy, all the way from Egypt (the *expense*, my dear, you wouldn't believe) and a sovereign remedy to ease my cough and dissolve the clotted blood. There's also, I understand, part of a unicorn's horn, pounded into fragments and mixed with crushed pearls, but of that I'm not sure. Altogether, the mixture cost me a very great deal of money – Master Langley's a good physician and will be the saving of my life, I'm sure, but—'

'—We're like to starve in a ditch before your life is saved, my dear,' a new, masculine voice interrupted. Francis grinned at me. 'Aunt Hannah's not having the best of it. Uncle Roger doesn't often join battle, but when he does it's worth hearing. He's never been very forthcoming – well, not in Aunt Hannah's presence, anyway – but he's a kind enough sort, brings Lucy plays from London, that sort of thing.' He broke off and applied his ear once more to the door.

My guardian was speaking, his voice barely audible through two inches of oak-panelled door. 'Mary, where are those two? They are the only ones not here, and if we must sup without them I can assure you that they'll be punished most severely, if I have to do it myself.'

'Now!' Francis hissed, and knocked on the door.

There was a brief silence on the other side, and then Sir Simon said, 'Enter!'

Francis opened the door and we went in. Breathing hard with concentration, and intent upon proving that I was in no way, save looks, like my ungovernable grandmother, I made a perfect curtsey in a spread of black-and-silver satin. Out of the corner of my eye, I saw Francis put his all into a flowing bow. We rose slowly to face Retribution.

'And here, pat, they are.' The elderly, grey-haired lady regarding me with a penetrating grass-green eye must, I decided, be Great-Aunt Elizabeth. She was looking us over with a shrewdness which implied that she was well aware that we had been eavesdropping, and I quickly avoided her stare to glance about the room. It was placed at the south end of the west wing of the house, and was filled with evening sunlight from the windows on my right. On the white carved ceiling with the griffins and herons and unicorns and dragons – all the ingredients for Aunt Hannah's remedies, I thought irreverently – the reflections from the moat underneath the windows turned their frozen, endless dance into one that moved with joyous life. I felt that I could love this chamber, with its light and movement and the beautiful fantastic beasts spinning across the ceiling – but the place stank with the musty, thick odour of sickness. In one corner stood the great bed with the gruesome hangings depicting the demise of John the Baptist in unsparing detail, and beside it Sir Simon sat in his wheeled chair, unquestioned master of Goldhayes despite his illness. On one of the ubiquitous Turkey-work chairs, fruit of her own labours, his wife sat by him, her hands folded demurely in her lap, and her empty eyes fixed upon us. Francis's sister and three brothers were lined up by the south window, their faces turned gold by the sun, all looking as if butter would not melt in their mouths – but, in Suffolk idiom, neither would cheese choke them. Great-Aunt Elizabeth, who appeared to be as fearsome as the tales of her had told, was sat by the fire in deference to her age, if not to her health, which seemed robust. In the centre of the chamber were placed a middle-aged man with a pointed, grizzled beard and a resigned expression; an enormously fat woman, scarlet-faced and overflowing her chair squatly, like a replete toad (the resemblance being heightened by her huge ruff and taffeta dress in an unmatronly and unpleasant shade of green); and a boy of about Simon's age, startlingly good-looking save for the wilful, sulky downward turn to his mouth. These, I realized were Sir Roger Drakelon and his family. The wall of faces, watching us, was almost entirely set with stern disapproval.

'And what have you to say for yourselves?' inquired my guardian. Francis donned his most polite and apologetic expression and said, 'I beg your pardon most humbly, sir, but I forgot the time. Thomazine is not to blame.'

'You also seem to have forgotten other things,' Sir Simon said, staring us down. 'With Sir Roger and his lady your aunt, not to mention Mistress Graham, hourly expected, and your help required in the house – this applies in particular to you, Thomazine – with all this, you choose not to honour their arrival with your family, but to go running wild in the woods instead, dressed, if reports are correct, in a manner scarcely decent for cotter's brats and certainly not befitting your birth. What have you to say for your discourtesy?'

'I took off my doublet because it was hot,' Francis said, his head high. 'I am sorry if it was thought unseemly. Thomazine only took her shoes off.'

'When I want a tale of Thomazine's faults I'll ask her. It's plain you've led her into mischief. Where have you been this while?'

Francis played his ace. 'We were at the Home Farm, talking with Master Sewell. They have no clocks and time passed quickly. We only knew it was late when the litter came up the lane; then we came back as quickly as we could.' He turned to the centre of the room. 'Aunt Hannah – Uncle Roger – I apologize for our lateness, and hope you will forgive us.'

I had noticed from the beginning of my acquaintance with Francis that, whereas he clashed frequently with some personalities, who were irritated and angered by his easy half-insolent manner, others he could, when he chose, sweep along with charm and bravado. Aunt Hannah was of the former group, as her sour-as-verjuice expression showed; but Sir Roger, by the lift in his beard and a certain deepening of the folds around his eyes, belonged to the latter. 'Your apologies are accepted, both of you,' he said, a gleam of cheerful camaraderie in his smile. 'So now I must beg your father for mercy. Do they win a reprieve, Simon?'

My guardian was ever at a disadvantage in being a more tolerant man than, for reasons of policy, he wished to appear. He set his face into furrows of deliberation, while I, at least, waited in agonies of suspense. Finally, he spoke. 'Your pleas have been accepted, Roger. But remember this, you empty-headed pair – I'll not be so lenient next time, and I doubt your uncle will be there to intercede! Now go and stand with the others by the window, if you can be trusted to behave for five minutes at a stretch.'

We made our way over. I squeezed between Lucy and Jamie, where we could lean surreptitiously against the window-seat, and exchanged guilty grins with both of them. Jamie, his bright blue eyes round, started to whisper something, but was forestalled. 'You still keep your interest in stage-plays, Lucy?' Elizabeth Graham asked, her attention now fixed inexorably upon us.

Lucy, diverted by her obsession, nodded enthusiastically. 'Ooh, yes, madam, I know all of *'Tis Pity She's a Whore* by heart now.'

There was a deathly hush. Aunt Hannah had gone a prudish purple. Great-Aunt Elizabeth, on the other hand, was openly amused. '*All* of it, child?'

'Well, no, not really *all* of it, madam,' Lucy muttered defensively. 'But I know some of *The Duchess of Malfi* as well, and *Othello*, and lots more besides,' she added, brightening a little.

'All plays reeking of blood and murder and other foul and unnatural acts,' our great-aunt pointed out. 'No pretty comedies? No tragic lovers?'

'Oh, *Romeo and Juliet*, of course,' said Lucy. 'And Uncle Roger sent me *The Shoemaker's Holiday* and I know some of that by heart, too.'

An outraged stare directed by Aunt Hannah at her long-suffering spouse spoke eloquently of her ignorance of this generosity. Uncle Roger retreated into his beard. His formidable aunt, however, was thoroughly enjoying herself. 'The one also reeks of blood, and is moreover a fond and silly tale founded on somewhat unlikely errors of judgement, while the other can best be described as bawdy, can it not?'

Lucy, struck to the heart, turned a deep shade of red and burst out, '*A Midsummer Night's Dream* isn't bawdy!'

'On the contrary, I was under the impression that it was one of the worst,' Elizabeth Graham said. 'After all, it boasts a character named Bottom, does it not? No matter, child, I'm only teasing you. You do very well to read at all. Many boys of your age and station scarcely know their hornbooks, let alone read stage-plays, whether suitable or not.'

'I can read,' Jamie interrupted with pride. 'I can read in Latin too, and Greek, and count up to a thousand, and reckon as well!'

'James! Remember to speak only when you're spoken to!' his father said. 'I can't recall that anyone favoured you with a request for a list of your accomplishments. So hold your tongue until you've something to say that is neither boastful nor, remembering Dr Davis's last report of you, a downright untruth.'

Jamie did his best to look repentant and did not quite succeed. Mary sensed the pause and rose to her feet, ringing the small silver handbell that stood on the court-cupboard by the door. 'I think that supper will now be ready, and I'm sure most welcome after your journey. Shall we repair to the dining-hall?'

The supper spread before us was a feast far grander than any I had yet seen, even at Goldhayes. Monsieur Harcourt had excelled himself; the pastries were crusty and mouth-watering, the aroma of spices and cooked meat perfect, the fricassee of rabbit tender and creamy. It was ever a wonder to me that the Heron family, eating as they did, remained on the whole as meagre in build as their name would suggest. Aunt Hannah, who must have weighed all of eighteen stones, was one notable exception, and the burly Edward, solidly putting away slabs of succulent Goldhayes mutton, another. For my part, the exercise of the afternoon had had its effect, and I ate hungrily and with dedication.

On my right, Lucy took a quick look round between mouthfuls of pasty – we were at the bottom of the table, but even so her father disapproved of his children chattering over their food – and said, 'Uncle Roger's brought me another play.' Uncle Roger was her chief source of supply, but in view of Aunt Hannah's evident outrage at Lucy's revelations before supper, it was a source unlikely to be of further use. I tried to look interested. 'Oh, good. What's it called?'

'*The Tragical History of Dr Faustus*, by Kit Marlow,' Lucy said. 'I had a glimpse of it and it seems very good. Very exciting. Mmm, that was delicious, could you pass the rest of it?'

'You'll be as stout as Aunt Hannah if you're not careful. What's it about?'

'A learned man in Germany who sold his soul to the Devil in exchange for all the knowledge in the world. It's true, too.'

'It can't be true,' Francis said. He was sitting on the other side of Lucy and had been listening. 'There isn't any such person as the Devil, so how could he sell his soul to him?'

He said it a shade too loudly. All down the table there was lessening of talk and clatter of knives, deepening into silence. I felt the same cold unease that I had experienced earlier when Francis had talked of this. But now it was different, an opinion voiced in the hearing of his elders which could only cause deep trouble. For, as I had sensed, to deny the existence of the Devil was to deny the truth of the Scriptures and, by implication, the very existence of God Himself.

'Francis,' said my guardian, with a terrible quietness, 'do I hear you aright? You deny the existence of Satan?'

'Yes,' said Francis, standing up. He had gone very white and his mouth was set in a thin determined line. 'How can there be a Devil? If God is the creator of all things, and if God is good, then how can Satan have been created?'

Even I, hardly at ten years old well-versed in the finer points of theology, could see some logic in that. On my right, Lucy's and Jamie's eyes were near to popping out in horrified admiration for his daring. Sir Simon, however, was not so readily impressed. 'You blaspheme. I am not here to listen to a theological dissertation from an impertinent brat who has not the wisdom to understand the folly and wickedness of what he is saying. From whom did you learn this blasphemy? It was assuredly not from me; nor from Dr Davis here.'

That worthy cleric roused himself from the contemplation of his carp and assured the company, jowls quivering with indignation, that indeed Francis had not. 'I don't doubt but that he gleaned such lies from one or other of those atheistical books which I have had to remove from him in the past.'

'I didn't,' Francis said, defiant still. 'I thought it out for myself – not like some other people here, who only believe what they're told and haven't the courage to be anything other than sheep! *You* can't answer my argument, Father, can you?'

The silence was appalling. Lucy's small bright mouth trembled; her mother stared blankly at her husband. Young Simon appeared stunned, and Aunt Hannah's meat-laden knife languished in her hand. Of all the company, only Sir Simon moved. 'Francis, you will go forthwith to your chamber. You will stay there until I come to you. You will also receive a beating, the most severe that your tutor can administer, and you will meditate upon the evil of your ways without meat or drink, and locked in your chamber, until you repent. James will be moved into another room to avoid your contamination.' He paused, his mouth pressed like a vice, and then spoke again. 'My steward informed me, before your tardy arrival in this chamber, that your dog had been seen in the warren, having caught and half-eaten a young coney. I have warned you about that animal before. I have given orders that the dog be confined to the kennels and I intend, in view of your behaviour, to order further that it be knocked on the head. You may leave the table.'

Francis pushed the stool back, and replaced it with deliberation. He was trembling, but had himself well under control. He bowed with mocking exactitude to the assembled company and again to his father at the head of the table. 'I did not think you'd be so despicable as to punish me by killing my dog,' he said, his voice clear with hatred. 'It's hardly likely to make me change my ways to yours, or to improve my opinion of you. I hope you'll have learned more tolerance when we meet again.' And with that final shot, he turned and left the room.

chapter two

A bridge of unicorns

If thou be'est born to strange sights
Things invisible to see . . .
             (Donne, 'Song')

The rest of the meal was spent, at our end of the table, in a gloomy silence. Jamie ate with less than his usual gusto, and Lucy salted her pasty with tears. Francis had voiced in public his independence of mind and spirit, and nothing could be the same again. At the adult end, condemnations and recipes for punishment flew thick and fast, Aunt Hannah being particularly vocal and Francis's mother significantly silent. My ears strained to hear what was being said, and at the end of the meal I was left thankful that a beating was all Francis would suffer. His aunt favoured binding him 'prentice to some London merchant – 'That'll put an end to his evil thoughts; he'll be kept so busy for seven years they'll starve for want of nourishment. It's this idleness that breeds his dissent, Simon, you mark my words. I have always kept Dominic employed at his lessons or at exercise and you could not wish for a more dutiful child.' (I began to hate the smugly handsome Dominic.) Fortunately for Francis, his father had some acquaintance with the habits of London 'prentice boys and hastened to disillusion her. 'As for most of them, much of their time is spent in idleness, lewdness and stirring up trouble. It's very different from when we were young and Brother Henry was 'prenticed – it was not idleness killed him, but overwork, as you said yourself, Aunt Elizabeth. He was ever a sickly child, and only fourteen when he died.'

'If he's not to be 'prenticed, where is he to go?' Hannah demanded. 'It is plain to me he cannot be kept here in idleness. I would take him myself, but I fear my health would not allow it, and besides, I would be afraid for

Dominic. Not, of course, that he might be corrupted, but your Francis has a sly and deceitful charm which could cozen many, I'm sure, and Dominic is trustful to a fault. Why, not a month ago, I remember . . .'

I closed my ears to Hannah's ramblings and thought unhappily of Francis's fate. When supper was ended, and we had all left the table, Lucy and I slipped away to our chamber, united in our wish to discuss what was to happen. We sat on the windowseat and stared gloomily down into the courtyard garden below, shaded now from the sinking sun. Lucy wiped her moist eyes with a handkerchief. 'Poor Francis! Did you hear what Aunt Hannah was suggesting?'

'To bind him 'prentice?'

'No, before that. She wanted Father to have him beaten till the blood ran, every day for a week!'

'If she does that to Dominic I'm not surprised he never says a word.'

'Oh, he does, sometimes. She won't let him draw, you see,' said Lucy earnestly, 'he draws really well but Aunt Hannah thinks it's not an occupation for a gentleman. He hates her really, I think, though she thinks he's so good and dutiful. And I do, too. And sometimes,' she added, her mouth drawing together, 'I hate Father as well. I know Francis was very, very insolent, but he doesn't have to kill Drake, does he? Drake didn't do anything.'

'Except kill that rabbit. But if he has Drake knocked on the head, I think Francis will hate him for ever,' I said. 'How can we stop it happening?'

Lucy's fertile imagination bubbled over. 'I know! He's in the kennels, isn't he? Well, we'll go down now, and if the dog-boy isn't there we'll let Drake out and if he is there you can ask him something to distract him and I'll let him out while he's not looking!'

I disentangled this proposal and thought about it. My more practical nature soon discovered the flaw. 'What are we going to do with Drake when we've let him out? Set him free to kill more rabbits?'

Lucy's bright face fell. 'Oh. I hadn't thought of that. I

know! We can take him down to the Home Farm, I'm sure Master Sewell will keep him for us.'

'And it'll be dark by the time we get back,' I pointed out, 'and we'll be in as much trouble as Francis. Anyway, Master Sewell's done Francis one favour already today, and I'm sure he won't want to do him another.'

'What was that?'

I told her about the kestrel. Lucy's eyes grew round. 'How exciting! I wish I'd been there. He's really brave, isn't he, and so are you, just think, climbing all the way up that tree! You know,' she added, 'whatever happens to Francis it'll be a long time before we'll all be together to play games again, won't it? It won't be half so much fun without him. We must *do* something! Have you got any ideas?'

I had only one, and it seemed to me more impractical than any of Lucy's, but I put it forward with more confidence than I felt. 'Why don't we ask Great-Aunt to ask your father to save Drake? I'm sure he'd listen to her advice.'

It was Lucy's turn to pour scorn. 'That's a more crackpot idea than any of mine. *Great-Aunt*? You'll end up as mad as your grandmother if you're not careful.'

'Don't insult my grandmother,' I said, up in arms immediately. 'Anyway, I'm sure she'd listen to us. I think she likes Francis, and she didn't look very pleased when your father said he'd have Drake killed.'

'You don't know her,' Lucy said. 'She's an old dragon. Great-Uncle Gilbert had a feud with some family and she rode with him to get their casttle back, and took command when he was wounded, and killed two men with her own dagger. Uncle Roger said she's still known in Liddesdale as the Graham Battleaxe. She'd probably have us clapped in the cellars.'

'In chains, I suppose,' I said sarcastically. 'I don't think she'd do anything. I think she'd listen. Anyway, we haven't got anything to lose. I'm going to ask her, even if you're not!'

Lucy rose to the challenge. 'All right, I suppose it's

worth it for the chance of saving Drake. Come on then – but you start asking her!'

The Heron family and their guests had retired after supper to the coolest place in the house on this warm evening, apart from the wine and beer cellars – the eastern end of the long gallery. With the low sun laying pools of gold on the wooden floor, and all the casements of the big east window, with its band of stained glass and small square yellowish panes, open to the breezes, it was beautifully refreshing. My relatives had occupied more of the ubiquitous Turkey chairs and now clacked of the latest family gossip. Lucy and I emerged from our chamber and sidled up the gallery until we reached the stairwell. We stood by the banisters trying to look unobtrusive in a way which must have been noticeable, and waited for an opening in the flow of scandal.

'There's no doubt of it,' Hannah was saying, 'that man is a disgrace to the family and a sore trial to his brother. How he keeps his ears I do not know. As it is, he's seen the inside of Bridewell more than a dozen times. I've heard his father left him without a penny and I'm not surprised. Richard was an indulgent man but even he could not stomach being abused and called ungodly by his own son in his own house, and before his servants. He left him naught in his will but a prayerbook for him to scan till he mended his ways, and when the rogue had the impudence to come begging poverty he showed him the door and, I hear, has forbidden any speech or word of him at St Annis.'

Mary, forever fascinated by Heron gossip, got a word in edgeways. 'Have you heard the latest news of him?'

'Of Cousin Richard?'

'Who else?' Mary paused to savour her news. 'He's written yet another treasonous pamphlet!'

As the only 'Puritan' member of a High Church, if not Papist, family, Richard Trevelyan might not have been thus deplored had he not also made a habit of speaking out plainly against anything which offended his undoubtedly high principles. Kicked out of his Cornish birthplace first by his father and then by his elder brother, he now apparently spent his time in London, stirring up trouble, writing pamphlets and consorting with the more vociferous of the King's critics.

'Yet another?' cried Aunt Hannah, appalled. 'And what does he attack this time? Or is it another sermon on the virtue of giving a preaching licence to every rogue who likes the sound of his own voice?'

'It criticizes the King's rule without a Parliament,' Mary said, leaning forward in her chair with a rustle of dark green satin. 'And from what I hear it's packed with lies and slanders, not only about the King, but about the Queen as well. It was printed anonymously, of course, and suppressed almost immediately – I believe they threw the printer into jail and confiscated his presses – but in his last letter to us Rowland assured us that it was Richard's work. He was most enraged, I can tell you.'

I wondered how, if Rowland Trevelyan did not permit word of his erring brother to reach his ears, he had heard sufficient to pass the news on to his cousins. Aunt Hannah had evidently not noticed the inconsistency of her sister-in-law's gossip. 'And the usual ill-argued piece, I'll warrant. He will be clapped in jail for this sedition, I'll be bound, Mary. If he were other than our cousin, and a gentleman, I'd say he were best hanged.'

'Poor Rowland would die of the disgrace,' Mary said, with a shade of sarcasm. 'It's a shame indeed he's in poor health and unlikely to wed again, for there's only his little daughter between Richard and all the Cornish estates, and I'd not be surprised if Richard tried to buy her wardship should his brother die untimely.'

'Such wickedness!' Hannah sighed, clasping her fat white hands, jewelled on every finger. 'And how is Rowland's poor motherless little child?'

'Flourishing, I believe. With his last letter he sent a miniature of her; a very sweet pretty child, though she's scarcely nine years old yet.'

'I'd dearly love to see it,' Hannah said, smiling ingratiatingly. 'I've not seen the child since she was a baby, when we travelled to Cornwall to give Rowland our comfort. She was just like poor Zenobia, even then, with her fair hair and blue eyes. There'll be hearts a-plenty broken in Cornwall in years to come, I'll be bound.'

'Of course you may see it,' Mary said; she was never slow to show off the collection of curiosities and treasures which she kept in her hall at the end of the long gallery. 'I've others as well which may interest you, done since you last came to visit – there's a limner of skill works in London, and my husband brought him here last summer to do likenesses of us all. He's near as good at catching a face as is Van Dyck, who's done the big picture of the children in the hall. Would you care to come with me?' She rose, and the rest of the company did likewise and followed her and her lap-dog, Moppet, down the gallery towards her hall. Fortunately, Great-Aunt, who had stopped to flick Moppet's long silky hairs off her black bombazine, was last of all to pass us, and we waylaid her. As agreed, I spoke first. 'If you please, Madam Great-Aunt, may we talk to you for a minute?'

She stopped and looked down at our anxious beseeching faces. 'Well? And what's all this to-do? A most refreshing lack of ceremony,' Elizabeth Graham said drily. 'Has no one taught you to curtsey?'

Desperate to please her, we complied instantly. Astonishingly, above my meekly bowed head I heard the dry sound of laughter. 'If I know you children at all,' Great-Aunt said, still chuckling, 'you are only so prompt to obey orders when you wish for a favour! Come, get up and seat yourselves and tell me what it is – they'll not miss us for half an hour yet, I'll warrant.'

Hardly daring to breathe lest it should disturb our incredible good fortune, we rose with care and seated ourselves on a couple of plain oak stools. Elizabeth Graham reoccupied her chair, folded her gnarled hands and fixed us with a look that was almost benign. 'Well?' she said again. 'What's all this to-do?'

I hesitated. Lucy shot me an agonized glance, and I swallowed, lifted my chin and looked Elizabeth firmly in the eye. 'If you please, Madam Great-Aunt, it's about Francis – and Drake. Drake's his dog. We – we know he was terribly insolent to Sir Simon, and that's very wrong, but we don't think Drake should be killed, he only chased a rabbit and that's what all dogs do, why should he be punished for what Francis did, it'll only make him hate his father more and anyway, if he's locked in his chamber without food or drink until he apologizes, if Drake's killed he won't ever apologize!' I paused for breath and Lucy, emboldened, added, 'He might starve to death!'

'That would be nothing new. the common people do that every year after a bad harvest,' Great-Aunt said. She looked me over consideringly. 'Yes, you are certainly Magdalen's granddaughter, with your spirit and your lack of inches. Why do you feel, then, that I can save them? No doubt you've heard awesome tales of my wicked Border past – aren't you expecting to be clapped in irons for your pains, as your cousin so obviously is?' Lucy, suddenly under her stare, flushed and dipped her head. Realizing that the fates of Drake and Francis depended on me, I said, 'No, I just thought that you'd be the one to help. Lady Drakelon wouldn't and I wouldn't want to ask Sir Roger, and Lady Heron . . .' I stopped in confusion, and Elizabeth Graham supplied the missing words. 'Is not interested, I think you mean. Don't look like that, child, it's the truth. So you want me to help you. Do you think Francis and his cur are deserving of help?'

'Yes,' I said passionately, and stopped again. How to explain that behind the insolent defiance of a thirteen-year-old boy lay something to be valued and encouraged, something which I did not understand and yet by instinct was drawn to, like a moth to the bright burning of a candle? I searched for words which my childish brain would not supply, and at length, flushed with effort, muttered, 'It wouldn't do any good to punish him. It'd only make things worse.'

There was a silence. Lucy looked at me out of the corners of her eyes, miserably. I stared at Great-Aunt's face, anguished and desperate to win her over. The silence deepened, so that the voices of Mary and her guests came clearly down the gallery.

'You are right, of course,' Elizabeth Graham remarked conversationally. 'You seem to have got to know Francis remarkably well in such a short time – two months, is it, that you've been here? Very perspicacious of you, for he's no easy child to read. However, you're wasting your time with your supplications . . .' She paused, saw my face freeze with despair, smiled, and went on. 'For I've already decided to do something about Francis on my own account. I too think it a shame to destroy the dog, which is an animal of character. I have a solution which, I feel, will solve all problems – but I warn you, you may not like it. My only son, Sandy, who as you may know owns lands in Liddesdale on the Scottish Border, has two boys of his own – Gilbert and Malise, who is the younger and near to Francis in age. While Gib is perfectly happy riding around with his friends, Malise suffers from lack of companionship. He's not had a healthy childhood, and has been left much to his own devices, and mine – being altogether of a more intellectual turn of mind than Gib, who I fear will never aspire to anything more than farming. I think it would be an excellent thing if Francis were to return with me to Catholm for a space – at least a year, or maybe two, to be company for Malise. It'd do them both good, and neither he nor Drake could get up to much mischief, or come to much harm, under my supervision. Yes,' said Elizabeth Graham, thoroughly pleased with herself, 'an excellent idea. In one, to provide Malise with a like-minded companion to take him out of himself, to save Drake and Francis from further punishment, and to rid your father, Lucy, of a worrying problem! Then, by the time he returns, Francis will be ready to follow Simon to Oxford – I presume that's what is planned?'

'Yes,' said Lucy, 'it's Edward who wants to be a soldier.'

'But Francis is of a scholarly turn of mind – he's intended for a lawyer, is he not? I suppose that if he can concentrate that unruly mind of his into one narrow channel, as Simon does so well, then Oxford will be a suitable place for him . . . but I have my doubts. However, I shall ask Sir Simon to allow Francis to go North with us when we leave here in September, and he can then go on to Catholm with me from

Yorkshire. There's no need to contact Sandy beforehand, he'll be only too pleased to have another lad to get Malise out of the house. So – I think all your worries are over! How does it all suit you?'

While Lucy was stammering her effusive thanks, I sat still with my mind in turmoil. It did, as Great-Aunt said, solve many problems – but at a price. I would not see Francis again for a long time, two years or more, and our new-found friendship was unlikely to survive the separation. But the alternative was the destruction of Drake and all that it would do. I remembered Kate's philosophy and determined miserably to make the best of things. I joined my thanks politely to Lucy's, and the three of us went straightway to Sir Simon, arranging estate business with Harry Jakes his steward in his chamber, to ask him his permission for Francis to go north.

Lucy and I had perforce to await the outcome in the panelled parlour. We sat biting our nails, anxious for two entirely different reasons. Lucy, whose heart was generous and unstinting, wanted Francis to leave for a happier life at Catholm; I, against the inner logic of my nature, was wishing that a way might be found both to preserve Drake's life and to keep Francis at Goldhayes. But Elizabeth's tongue was persuasive and her arguments logical. She was vigorous and persistent and Sir Simon, although far from weak-willed, was sickly and anxious to get on with his business. In what seemed to Lucy and me a very short time, Great-Aunt emerged from the valet's room which served as an antechamber, a bowing manservant holding open the door. As it shut behind her, she fixed us with a beaming smile incongruous in that intimidating face. My heart sank, but I dissembled valiantly. 'Is Drake safe?'

'You've again forgotten to curtsey,' was Mistress Graham's answer. We hastily bobbed down and up again. 'Please say he can go, please!' Lucy begged, rather uselessly since it was not Great-Aunt whose permission was needed.

'Your father, Lucy, says that Francis can indeed go north in September, and Drake with him,' she said, to my bitter disappointment. Lucy's eyes opened wide, she danced forward and in a rush of peach satin embraced Great-Aunt's black bombazine middle, crying, 'Thank you, oh thank you, Great-Aunt!'

'Anyone would think that you had just escaped a hanging,' said Great-Aunt reprovingly, disengaging herself. 'Do behave with some decency, child, and not like a hoyden. And don't be so free with your delight, for there are certain conditions attached to this. Francis must stay in his chamber until it is time to leave for Catholm. He's already received a beating, but there'll be no more. Drake is to be confined to kennels, and exercised only on a leash. You may visit them both as you please, and you can rest assured, Lucy, that Francis will have food, plain fare but enough of it, so he won't starve. And he will be told that if, during the time between now and our departure for Catholm, he misbehaves in like manner to today's indiscretion, he will forfeit the journey to the north, and his dog will be knocked on the head. So restrain yourselves from encouraging him into mischief! Does that suit you?'

'Oh, yes, thank you, Madam Great-Aunt, how can we thank you enough!' Lucy cried, curtseying in her delighted agitation. Sorely irritated, I merely smiled stiffly and added my polite thanks. Great-Aunt looked hard at me, but continued, 'Whether or not your mother, Lucy, will be so happy, I cannot say. Come, we shall go above-stairs and see.'

We followed Elizabeth through the house to Mary's hall, where her pottery was kept and where she did what business she had with the local womenfolk and with her servants. Lucy's walk was more of a bounce; I followed decorously and sulkily, wondering why Sir Simon had acquiesced so readily to his aunt's whim. He was most likely glad to be rid of his troublesome son.

We entered Mary's hall with a cautious knock. She was still there, showing off her collection of curiosities to her guests and her children: pottery, miniatures and strange objects brought back from Eastern worlds by seafaring Herons, all displayed on heavy oak court-cupboards, the miniatures in beautiful gold and silver cases with the Heron arms engraved on the lids. Mary loved to be surrounded by beauty, and her hall was like a treasure-hoard beside the rather spartan, simple furnishings of the rest of the house. Her elegant, subtle clothes, her perfume and lap-dog and elaborately-dressed hair were also evidence of her love of luxury. She turned now as we came in, one of the miniatures open in her hand. 'Aunt Elizabeth, where have those children been dragging you? You shouldn't allow them to pester you!'

'No matter,' Great-Aunt said, waving a hand at us as we bobbed the required curtsey without, this time, having to be reminded. 'I had a most interesting talk with them, on the subject of Francis.'

'I've said it before, and I'll repeat it,' Hannah put in. 'The only way to control that child is with the strap. Beat him regularly and you'll have no more trouble with him, I'll be bound. Take my advice, Mary, it's the only way.'

'Well, beating seems to have no effect,' Mary said, still looking at the miniature. 'Can you suggest another way of keeping him under control? Never fear, Hannah dear, I can look after him somehow. Don't you think this an excellent likeness of Thomazine?'

I craned my neck to see the miniature which had come with me from Ashcott. The Oxford limner my father had engaged in the winter before his death had been uncommonly skilful, and had captured my childish features in startling detail: the narrow, pointed face framed by a thundercloud of thick, dark, unruly hair, in which my eyes and mouth seemed too large for any classic beauty. Any effect of childish innocence was entirely spoilt by my habitual glower. Mary put it down and picked up another. 'And here is the one I was telling you of; Rowland's little daughter. Meraud, she is called, a very pretty name and not at all in the common run, though I'm told that it's quite often met in Cornwall.'

'And such a pretty child, too,' Hannah exclaimed, peering short-sightedly at the miniature. 'Such lovely hair, and those deep-blue eyes . . . she'll be a beauty one day, I'll be bound. And possessed, no doubt, of a handsome fortune, if she's heiress to Rowland's wealth.'

'Yes, the house is not entailed as this one is, so she will get everything,' Mary said. 'Have you seen it, Aunt Elizabeth?'

'I cannot say that I have,' that lady remarked, taking the miniature. 'Ah, yes, as pretty as you say, though by the time she's grown the smallpox will like as not have changed all that. You would like to see it, children? I trust your hands are clean, and remember not to touch the surface of the paint.'

I took the miniature in my small brown paw, and turned it until the light was favourable. Lucy craned over my shoulder and Jamie left his place by the biggest court-cupboard, where he and the other boys had been standing, bored, fiddling with the unicorn's horn, and came to see also. The provincial limner had not been as skilful as the Oxford one, but even so her loveliness glowed from the flat paint. I looked with curiosity at the small, kitten's face, the pouting mouth and wispy, silvery hair, wondering what she was like, whether she was good or bad, clever or stupid, brilliant or dull; the miniature could not tell. I felt that no child as beautiful and serene as that could possibly exist, and was visited by a twinge of envy. I need not have bothered. As Lucy exclaimed with delight, her youngest brother withdrew, nose wrinkled. 'Huh, all that fuss for her? She's not as pretty as Lucy or Thomazine.' Lucy simpered, I grinned and Jamie, embarrassed by what he had said, turned a sudden and healthy shade of pink. Mary saw Aunt Hannah's open mouth and stepped into the breach. 'Jamie! I didn't ask you to speak, nor to move from your place, and I don't wish to have to admonish you again!'

Jamie, mouth sulky, stepped back. Great-Aunt, evidently reminded of her duty, took the miniature from me and handed it back, remarking as she did so, 'By-the-by, Mary, I have taken the liberty of suggesting to Simon that an excellent answer to the problem of Francis would be to send him to another household for a year or two, but not as a 'prentice. My son and daughter-in-law in Scotland have a boy of an age with Francis, who is scholarly likewise and destined for a university, and Simon and I have agreed it would be admirable for all concerned if Francis could spend some time at Catholm as a companion for my grandson. I think it probable that it will be good for them both; Malise needs a friend to encourage him to spend less time with his books and more time out-of-doors riding, shooting and so on, while Francis must surely benefit from contact with Malise's steady nature. All in all, I think a year or two at Catholm, under my watchful eye, and kept busy with lessons and healthful exercise, will change Francis out of all recognition. Well, Mary, what do you think?'

Mary, startled out of her usual abstraction, looked flustered and grateful. 'Why, yes, Aunt Elizabeth, it sounds the very thing, and I wouldn't hesitate, but . . . well, I've heard from your own lips tales of the Borders to make my blood chill. Murder, rape, plunder, all manner of thieving and villainy . . . won't he be in danger?'

'Danger? Nonsense! The tales you had from me,' Elizabeth Graham said cheerfully, 'were, I'm ashamed to say, fireside diversions more exaggerated than truthful . . . Moreover, when Scots Jamie came south and ordered Jeddart justice for all the reivers from the Debateable Land to Tyndale, all that sort of thing came to a speedy end.'

'Jeddart justice?'

'Hanging first, questions after. It was lucky I'd persuaded my husband to turn farmer, or he'd have been one of them. He died peaceful in his bed, a rare thing indeed in Liddesdale. No, Mary, nowadays our part of the Borders is peaceful and law-abiding. Indeed, I haven't seen a whisker nor a beard of an outlaw for many years. Francis is no more in danger at Catholm than he is here.'

'It all sounds very well,' Hannah declared, 'but I still say he'd do best as a 'prentice. A good master would soon knock the insolence out of him, don't you agree, Roger?'

'Humph!'

Jamie pulled at my sleeve and hissed, 'Is Francis going to Scotland then? For *good*?'

'Why don't you listen?' I said shortly. 'Of course he's going to Scotland, but only for a year ot two.'

'A year or two?' Jamie said, aghast. 'Why, that's a lifetime! Two years!'

'Fiddlesticks,' I retorted, the more angry because that was exactly how I felt myself. 'Don't be stupid, it's not so long.'

'I reckon that's the best thing for him,' Simon put in. 'With luck, he'll get the sort of discipline and hard work there that he's never had till now. I consider he's got off very lightly indeed, considering the measure of his insolence. Does he have no punishment at all?'

'He's to stay in his chamber until it's time for us to leave for Catholm,' Elizabeth Graham told him. 'And he's already received a beating, so I think he's certainly been punished. Anyway, life at Catholm will not be all beer and skittles by any manner of means. He will probably work very hard, helping my son with the farm; there's much hard work to do and I'll wager he'll ride further, faster and longer than he'll have done in all his life before. Oh, compared to Suffolk it will seem very primitive and hard, but not altogether uncivilized: my husband built up a small collection of books, and the local minister tutors the boys, as well as myself. Indeed, my daughter-in-law is devout and learned, and also undertakes some tuition in addition to our efforts. I think you need have no fears for Francis, for I can promise you he'll be well and safely looked after, and I myself will ensure that he gets into no mischief!'

Mary was nodding gratefully, glad to be rid of her burden. 'Yes, I'm sure you're right, it almost sounds too good to be true, the perfect answer to all our problems. And there'll be no need to advise your son of his coming, I take it. Things could not be better. Has Francis been told?'

To my horror, I had found myself dangerously close to tears. Desperate for a chance to get away before I disgraced myself, I said, curtseying, 'No, madam, he has not. Shall I go?' And before anyone could object, I removed myself hastily from the hall.

I ran along the gallery, wiping my eyes furiously on my cuff, and with Aunt Hannah's comments on my oddity and abruptness clearly audible. I paused in front of the great mirror, tidied myself to my satisfaction, and endeavoured to make the best of things. It was only for a year or two, after all, and my imagination, more down-to-earth than Lucy's, did not encompass the possibilities of Francis's sudden death or abduction by reivers. Also, I was beginning to feel ashamed of my selfish tears, for Great-Aunt Elizabeth with her plan had at one stroke saved both Francis and Drake, and provided for their possible future happiness. Filled with new resolutions of nobility, I knocked at Francis's door.

There was silence, then a voice thick with caution said, 'Who is it?'

'Me. Thomazine. Can I come in?'

'If you must.'

I opened the heavy door, apprehensively. Inside, Francis was lying on his stomach on the rush matting, reading a large leather-bound tome which I could not identify. He wore shirt and breeches, the former mottled unpleasantly with red. I had been beaten myself, and seen other children receive the same treatment more or less severely, but not as badly as this. Horrified, I put my hands to my mouth and stared. 'Come to gloat?' Francis said.

He was obviously in a difficult mood, as well he might be. I would have to tread warily. Abandoning ideas of expressing pity and sorrow, I grinned cautiously. 'Who do you think I am? Aunt Hannah? Is it painful?'

'Yes, very. Dr Davis has a heavy hand for one so shrivelled. He did, however, do me the kindness of salving it. I think that hurt more – it was one of mother's more unpleasant concoctions.'

I knew them well and smiled in sympathy. 'I don't know what she puts in them to make them sting so. Please, what are you reading?'

Francis twisted it round and turned back so that I could see the title-page. 'Brittannia?'

'By Master Camden, an antiquary. He went all round the kingdoms describing the counties and their histories and Roman inscriptions and so on. I'm reading what he has to say about the Scottish Border.'

I stared. 'How did you know that?'

'Oh, I called up my familiar and he told me what Great-Aunt's idea was. Have sense, infant. Is the door locked? No. I heard your voices – Lucy's, rather, hers carries some distance – and looked out to investigate. I found her vision of my future so intriguing that I'm afraid to say I eavesdropped.'

I made tut-tutting noises. Francis grinned. 'Which you're not above doing yourself, pest. Anyway, when you and Lucy had towed her downstairs like a pair of jolly-boats with a galleon, I went down to the library and got this book.'

'Didn't anyone see you?'

'Plenty of people saw me,' Francis said, annoyance showing through the sarcasm. 'Think, child. This place is crawling with people like maggots on cheese. How many in family are we? Nearly fifty, I think, not to mention the Drakelon entourage. It is impossible to go from here to the library and back without being seen by at least one of the sixty-odd people who live here. But they're not likely to tell my father. I wasn't seen by any of our family – they're all up here clacking over Mother's Dutch pottery and the unicorn's horn.'

'It isn't a real unicorn's horn,' I said, desire to be correct getting the better of me. 'Simon says it's the horn on the nose of some great fish, and it was sold as a unicorn's horn because it's twisted like a unicorn's and you can get more money for a unicorn's horn than a fish's.'

'Oh, you are a small-minded and literal little cynic, aren't you?' Francis said venomously.

'W – what do you mean?'

'Oh, you wouldn't understand,' he said angrily. 'You wouldn't understand about that or anything, you're just like Simon.'

'But . . .' I began, resenting the comparison. Francis, furious by now, went on, 'I don't suppose it's occurred to you or to my honoured and pedantic brother that sometimes it might, just might be better to think of it as a real unicorn's horn and that unicorns might exist somewhere in the world, than to do as Simon does and say it's only a fish's horn exploiting the gullible. Maybe unicorns are only a dream of the ancients, but dreams are good; it's dreams and imagination that make you human and different from horses and cattle and sheep . . .' In his agitation he had sat up too suddenly and now winced and relaxed, spreading hands in mock resignation. 'Oh, what does it matter? You couldn't possibly see what I mean.'

'But I do – I think,' I said, having guided my newly-trained mind through his rather elliptical argument. 'I'd much rather think of it as a unicorn's horn like the ones on your father's bedroom ceiling. I wish unicorns did exist.'

'Well, perhaps they do,' Francis said, sweeping an expansive arm. 'In the deserts of Africa or the forests of Muscovy or dancing in the mountains of Hy Brazil – imagine your unicorns! White, I think, with a sort of shine on them like watered silk, and horns of mother-of-pearl, and tiny mother-of-pearl cloven hooves like a deer's—'

'—And long, long legs like a deer's, or the Arabian mare's, and a mane and tail all rippling like the waterfall with the light shining through, in the tapestry in the gallery—'

'—And all made of water and light and ice and fire!' He smiled at me in triumph. 'How dare you say such a creature of wonder does not exist?'

'It does,' I said, and tapped my head. 'My unicorn's in here.'

'You do understand me,' Francis said. 'Now do you see? Simon can't imagine unicorns, or griffins or dragons or men with sunshade feet either for that matter, because he's closed his mind to it. That horn's a fish's horn and unicorns – well, there's no such thing, never was and never will be. But to us it's a unicorn's horn, a bit dull, maybe, but then the colour fades out of the mother-of-pearl when it's no longer on the unicorn.'

'Oh, does it have to be killed?'

'Well, I suppose some people might kill unicorns for the horns – they're proof against poison, did you know, so kings put powdered horns in their food and wine – but I think it'd be easier to find dropped horns. I expect they shed them every year and grow a new one, like a deer does. Anyway, we know it's a real unicorn's horn and there's always the possibility that if we get up *very* early one morning, even before daylight, and go out to the woods, we *might* see one – only a glimpse because they're very shy. But if you went alone they'd come to you and lay their heads in your lap to be stroked, just like Drake.'

'And their eyes would be beautiful – soft and dark and blue, and so wise and gentle,' I said, enchanted by the vision we had created. 'Grandmother had a book called a bestiary – she showed me pictures in that of a unicorn kneeling with his head in a maiden's lap, but I think I prefer our unicorns.'

'I did think I'd seen one once,' Francis said. 'I'd gone out very early to meet George Fowler, who's the warrener – we were going to try for some wild rabbits for a change, with his ferrets. I was going to meet him on the edge of Piper's Wood. It was so early the sun hadn't risen; the sky was just lit up, and there was one of those swirling low-lying mists and a thick dew. And I saw this silver horse, walking through the mist like a deer with very small steps, with a mane and tail like running water – and then the sun rose and lit up the horse all with fire and mist, and I couldn't believe the beauty. I was the same age as you, and it made me weep. Even when I saw it was only the Saracen, got out of his paddock for a stroll in the park, I couldn't quite rid myself of the feeling that perhaps when no one was looking he was a unicorn. With the mist round him it did look a bit as though he had a horn on his forehead.'

'Maybe he's enchanted and certain people can only see his horn at certain times, like fairy rings at midsummer.'

'Well, I'm still watching him and I've never seen – but there's always the possibility it might be true,' Francis said. He looked happier than I had ever seen him, all his defensiveness cast away. 'How strange it should be you to understand!'

'Why?'

'Well . . . when you first came you looked very unpromising, standing there in the hall in front of us all, and trying so hard not to cry. I felt sorry for you, but I thought you looked very grumpy and sullen.'

'I am.'

'That's as maybe. When you insisted on doing Latin and Greek with us I thought there must be more to you than met the eye. And you've a nice touch to the lute, too. My lady mother's lute is made of wood so fine it trembles under the strings. That's how all lutes should be played, with a delicate and light hand. Lucy plays hers as though she's wearing iron gloves.'

I snorted uncharitably. 'Your lady mother is rationing her supply of strings. If she breaks one more top course she'll have to do without till someone can order some more from London.'

'Lucy's too enthusiastic about everything she does, but I'd rather her than Simon any day of the week. But even she wouldn't understand; her mind's stuffed full of romances, and I should imagine Father will be in haste to betroth her before she fixes her heart on someone impossible. The only one of us betrothed yet is Simon, and that's not certain.'

'Who to?' I could not imagine Simon betrothed to anyone, much less married.

'To the daughter of a neighbour of ours over at Horringer. Have you heard talk of the Blagges? No? Oh, they're related to the Jermyns and they live at Horringer Hall – there's Ambrose Blagge and his second wife Margaret, and there are I think five children from his first marriage, and two or three the same age as you or younger, by Margaret. Simon's betrothed to Ann, the second daughter – she's the same age as he is, within a month or so, and it was all thought very suitable.'

'What's she like?'

'Nan? She'll make Simon a good wife. She's not very pretty, and she's shy and quiet, but she smiles a lot; she's got a turned-up nose – the whole family has – and her teeth stick out a bit. And her hair is very nice, a sort of dark gold and very long. I think she likes Simon, but Simon isn't very interested. It's his duty to marry her and that's that. I don't much care for the other Blagges, and old Ambrose is more of a die-hard than Father, and tight-fisted to boot.' He looked at me where I sat beside the book, my hands clasping my knees, and added with one of his abrupt switches of subject. 'Do you think Father will let me take the mare north?'

I had not thought of that, decided it unlikely and said so. Francis nodded. 'I know. I wonder if John Sewell would put in a word for me?'

'He might if Lucy and I persuaded him,' I said.

'Well, you do seem to have been remarkably successful with Great-Aunt. Honour has been satisfied all round, barring Aunt Hannah of course. And according to Master Camden, a good horse is a Borderer's first essential. He's very full of the wildness of the country and the savage and warlike nature of the people. 'Infamous for their depredations', he says. I'm sure they're not all now as godly and law-abiding as Great-Aunt would have us believe. There must be many still alive who've thieved cattle and set farms on fire and I'm sure they can't all have taken kindly to beating their swords into ploughshares. I think I shall enjoy myself up there with these uncouth cousins. It'll make a change from Goldhayes, anyway, and besides, if the Herons come from the Borders then all that's in our blood. Do you know what our motto is?'

' "No surrender".'

'That's what old Kit Heron made it. Apparently, there used to be two − that one, which they'd shout when besieged in their towers, and which he thought sounded much better than the other, which is just as appropriate for our family habits.'

'What is it?'

' "In moonlight is my gain and others' loss." Moonlight was just right for thieving.'

I grinned. 'I can see you riding out on Hobgoblin to fall on the English.'

'Perhaps I will. I've no objection if Cousin Sandy and his sons turn out to be reivers!'

* * *

And so I had perforce to reconcile myself to the fact that Francis's departure to Catholm was desired by almost everyone save myself. Certainly his parents seemed only too glad to wash their hands of him, and he himself welcomed the prospect of his freedom from them and from the restrictions of Goldhayes. However, there were still the few weeks left until the Drakelons' planned departure, and although he was confined to his chamber, reading or practising music, we were allowed to visit him as often as our duties and lessons would allow us. Sometimes he retired into his shell, assuming a remote and distant air reminiscent of his mother's, but which had nothing to do with arrogance, and I learned to let him alone in those moods. But occasionally he would ask me, perhaps with Lucy, to bring up lutes and viols and songbooks, and we would practise and sing together till our precious recreation hours were done. During those times our friendship flowered. We did not again build fabulous beasts out of words, but the magic of the unicorns lay between us like a bridge.

On the afternoons when I felt him barred to me, I had made a habit of sitting in the library, being then generally in melancholic and solitary mood. The windowseats could be made comfortable with a collection of cushions, and I usually slipped my shoes off and curled up amongst them with a book. Since coming to Goldhayes my reading matter had widened dramatically from the moral tales and religious tracts I had studied at Ashcott under my godly grandmother's eye. In the library here all manner of works, political, religious, historical, musical and poetical, jostled on the shelves. On the higher ones, where Dr Davis's rheumatism would not allow him to reach, lay the more interesting books: romances, translations of the lewder works of certain Roman poets, a fat volume of Chaucer, a well-thumbed edition of Boccaccio, books of travellers' tales and my greatest prize, a bestiary. On first discovering it, I had brushed off the dust, gently cleaned the binding so that the gold lettering sparkled, and read it from cover to cover in four afternoons, making dragons and wyverns and griffins in my mind as I went. Many times I dipped into it again, particularly appreciating the delightfully idosyn-cratic illustrations. One afternoon I was giving my absorbed attention to the phoenix, according to the author 'as big as an eagle: for colour, as yellow and bright as gold; (namely, all about the neck;) the rest of the body a deep red purple: the tail azure blue, intermingled with feathers among, of rose carnation colour: and the head bravely adorned with a crest and panache finely wrought' – altogether a most noble feast for my mind's eye. Wondering and fascinated, I browsed on, and could not resist a smile when I came to the mimic dog; not only did its portrait remarkably resemble a long-legged hairy sheep, but its description reminded me irresistibly of Drake: 'In wit and disposition it resembleth an ape, but in face sharp and black like a hedgehog, having a short recurved body, very long legs, shaggy hair, and a short tail.' Save for the tail (Drake's being a proud and lengthy plume), it was an exact picture, and I grinned appreciatively. But as I went on turning the pages, I became slowly and disturbingly aware of a feeling that I was being watched. As the hairs on my neck prickled in warning, I looked up and saw it was so.

'Hullo,' said Dominic Drakelon. 'Don't move!'

Despite my surprise, I managed to refrain. 'How long—'

'Turn your head back to where it was. Not quite . . . down a bit more . . . that's it. Are you comfortable?'

'Yes, but—'

'How can I do your head if you talk? Quiet and I'll do it quicker.'

My eyes on the bestiary and my mind on Dominic, I tried to be still. I supposed that he was drawing me, and was a little put out that he had begun unobserved while I was absorbed in the book. I wondered also at his manner, which carried all argument before it, and was a more palatable version of his mother's. I sneaked a sideways look at him where he sat, on one of the benches we used for our lessons, a piece of paper supported on a book on his knee and his hand moving swiftly with a piece or two each of charcoal and chalk. His hair was black and glossy, as Joan had des-cribed Hannah's as once being, his nose like Simon's rather prominent, and his eyebrows thick and pronounced. In brief, he was a more handsome version of Simon, with more grace, presence and, I felt, charm. His eyes, when they glanced up at me, were not Simon's sombre brown but a vivid and flashing blue. He was about sixteen, and I knew the maids thought him deliriously good-looking. I wondered if he would run to fat in later life, like his mother.

'It's all right now, you can talk.'

'Have you finished?'

'No, just your head. You'll see it when it is finished.' He spoke faintly patronizingly, as adult to small child. 'I'm sorry if I startled you. You looked very . . . appealing, sitting there in the windowseat. reading so heavy a book so earnestly, and you so young.'

'I'm ten years old.'

'Are you? I thought you younger.'

'People generally think I am, by reason of my small size,' I said with dignity.

'I stand corrected. You're my cousin, I believe?'

'Distantly. Your grandmother and my grandmother and grandfather were brother and sisters.'

Dominic was learning his lesson. 'It all sounds very incestuous to me. I've yet to work out the exact degrees of all our relationships. If our family didn't make a habit of marrying each other it would be easier. Tell me, Thomazine, what is your absorbing book?'

'It's a bestiary,' I said reluctantly. 'Nothing learned, it's not even in Latin.'

'If you did but know,' said Dominic with an air of confiding, 'how weary I am of works in Latin . . . even our religious observations are in Latin, our prayers, our unceasing devotions—'

'—You hear the *mass*?' I gasped, my Puritan grandmother's teaching rising to the surface.

'Oh, yes, we pay the standard fine for the privilege of being excused church in the village and then sit through Father Langdon's droning Latin and suffocating incense every day of the week. Then I have to confess every piddling little sin, real or imagined – sometimes I make them up to relieve the tedium. O father, I have sinned, I have most foully murthered my lady mother with her own remedies!'

Shocked and not a little embarrassed at this utterly unlooked-for outburst, for I had thought him as priggish as Simon, I searched about in my mind for something to say. It seemed that making me a confidante for emotional relations was fast becoming standard practice amongst young male Herons. 'Have you finished the drawing yet?'

'She'll murder herself, the silly woman,' Dominic said. I'm sorry, I can see I'm embarrassing you. I'm sure you understand what I put up with. You've only got to look at my mother.'

'It's all right. I don't mind. Can I move now? I've got a crick in my neck and pins and needles all down my legs.'

'What? Oh, yes, I suppose so. It's only a quick sketch, very slight of course, but I always seem to do those better than the ones I spend hours working over in paint.'

'I thought Lady Drakelon wouldn't allow you to draw – that's what Lucy said, anyway.'

'No, she doesn't, but she doesn't watch over me for twenty-four hours a day, nor does my father agree with her. There you are, do you think it's a good likeness?'

He certainly had a way with the chalks, suggesting my curled, absorbed posture with the minimum of effort. As for likeness to myself, I found it pleasing that my small, pointed, intent face with its slightly convex nose and over-large eyes was reproduced at once faithfully and with flattery. 'Yes, it looks more like me than that minature Lady Heron has upstairs.'

'I've been trying to think what you reminded me of ever since I first saw you, and now I have it! It's the trick you have of putting your head on one side when you're looking at something, and your slightly, uh, beaky nose and bright dark eyes . . . you're for all the world like a sparrow!'

'A sparrow?' I echoed dubiously.

'No, I mean it for praise. The sparrow's a bird so humble all despise it, but in reality there's none better, always cheerful and making the best of a hard life, unassuming and plain and with its own especial beauty, when you see it close to . . . yes,' Dominic Drakelon said, tilting my face up to the light with a long square-ended finger, 'that's you to exactness!' And his hands lightly caressed the planes of my face and lingered over my neck and shoulders with a touch that lifted the hairs on my spine. Thoroughly uneasy, I said, avoiding the intense blue gaze, 'I'm afraid I have to go and see Lucy now, I promised her we'd play bowls together.' I bobbed a hasty curtsey and turned. Dominic stopped me with a hand round my shrinking waist. 'Come, you're not afraid of me, Sparrow?'

In my anxiety to get away, there was no room for tact. 'No,' I said, 'but I don't like you very much. Thank you for drawing me. Goodbye, Cousin Dominic.' And I wriggled neatly out of his grasp and made a dignified exit.

Something in me made telling anyone, even Lucy or Francis, an impossibility. I merely ignored or avoided Dominic whenever I could, a course of action which aroused no comment, since I had never previously spoken two words together with him. However, I gave up going to the library, much though it hurt, preferring instead to seek quiet and safety in the chapel, which outside the hours of morning and evening prayers was almost always deserted. There was a sense of peace and of haven in that high, cool, whitewashed place that I came to value and cherish almost as much as the happy hours in the library of which Dominic had deprived me, and I sat there for many afternoons, generally crouched between two pews with hassocks between me and the cold stone floor, letting my mind rove free in thought and daydream, hardly any of it religious, and was undisturbed even by the curious Lucy, who was desperate to know where I hid myself when she most wanted to play with me. Perhaps because of this new refuge, my unease and nervousness dropped slowly away over the next week or so, and I walked and talked with Lucy, did Latin with the boys and played music with Francis, putting Dominic firmly to the back of my mind – although I could feel his eyes on me every time we were in the same room.

Until the morning when I was summoned to Sir Simon's presence. I had only just sat down in the library with Lucy and the boys, and was listening with half an ear to Dr Davis propounding the intricacies of Latin syntax, when one of the maidservants entered timidly and, under the disapproving gaze of the tutor, stammered that Sir Simon wished to see me, now, in his chamber. I had to leave and follow her through the house, running frantically in my mind over all my various misdeeds, and could not think of any transgression serious enough to warrant a summons of this nature. Still wondering, I was ushered into the chamber. Sir Simon was sitting at his desk, his hands clasped in front of him. On one side sat Sir Roger Drakelon, and on the other, the gross figure of his wife. Bewildered, I dropped into a curtsey and rose with my hand placed decorously over my apron to await their pleasure.

'Ah. Thomazine. You have been very prompt. Very well, Judith, you may go now.' As the maid left, Sir Simon added, 'This may take a little time, child, so pull up that stool.' I did so, grateful for the relief to my shaking knees. 'Now, I dare say you're wondering what all this is about. I can no doubt give your mind some rest by saying here and now that you've done no wrong and have nothing to fear. I – we – merely wish to discuss your future with you. As you know, you are a royal ward, under my guardianship, and the lands you're heiress to are quite considerable.' He ran through them all: Ashcott, the house in Oxford, the Yorkshire estates which would come to me on the death of my grandmother Kate, the Norfolk manors originally settled on my grandfather by Sir Simon's grandfather Hal. 'In all, you're worth upwards of £1,000 a year, which is a very considerable sum. There is also some coal on your Yorkshire lands which if mined would bring in a rich revenue. And your father had, as I have, considerable interests in trade and shipbuilding as well; in fact, he held a share of my yard at Ipswich, and owned two ships of his own outright, plying the Levant trade and to the Indies. All this is yours, held until your marriage by myself, and I have engaged various trustworthy men to oversee the manors and protect your interests. May I say that you're lucky indeed that I have been able to put up the very large sum of money necessary to purchase your wardship, for another buyer interested only in your estates would have let you run wild and neglected your education, whilst making every effort to milk your possessions dry before you came of age, and to marry you off to a lowly-born kinsman.'

'I'm very grateful to you, sir,' I said, since it seemed to be expected of me.

'I say all this to make it clear that I have acted throughout in your interests and that in return you have certain obligations and duties which are owing to any parent. With the guardianship of your person and your estates goes also your marriage. I have the right to bestow you where I please, and I don't deny that when you came here I had thoughts of marrying you to Edward, or even Francis. Simon has been betrothed to Nan Blagge for several years, and Ambrose Blagge and I have had an understanding since they were in their cradles that one day they would be wed. So Edward, or Francis, was intended for your husband, though I had some misgivings about your being married to a younger son, with your wealth. Moreover, Edward, though he's steady and reliable enough, has ever had soldiering in his mind and I fear a soldier's wife has a hard time of it. Francis . . . well, to be frank, I would be reluctant to place so much at his disposal so soon. If he's to make his own way in the world it will be the better for him. So you see that I was unhappy about finding a husband for you from my own sons.'

With all this talk of marriage, and duty, and seeing the impassive considering faces of the Drakelons, I could see the abyss yawning at my feet. I clenched my hands in my apron and tried to put Dominic's fierce appraising eyes, and the chilling touch of his hands, out of my mind.

'Well, I have now received from Sir Roger here an offer for your hand for his son Dominic. It seems he's quite taken with you, and is prepared to wait until you're sixteen or so and marriageable. Sir Roger and I have agreed that this is a very satisfactory solution, the more so as Dominic is the only son and will inherit everything. An added convenience is that your Yorkshire lands march with the Drakelon estates.

It is a very good match for you, far better than I'd originally intended, and I am very obliged to Sir Roger for his offer.' He tapped a bundle of papers in front of him. 'We have spent the past few days working out a settlement, and I have agreed to give you a small dowry, as well as your estates, as a token of my good will. There will be no formal agreement, as yet, and we've decided it would be best for you to remain here until your marriage to complete your education with my own children.' He smiled. 'I am told that you and Lucy are fast friends and it would be a shame indeed to tear you away from her before you'd been three months with us.'

'Let me make this clear, Simon,' Aunt Hannah interposed, her pale blue eyes fixed on me. 'I am not at all happy about marrying Dominic to this child. I would beg you to have a care for her education, for it's my opinion that she's sore in need of training and polish in the accomplishments fitting for a gently-bred girl. I understand she's quite expert in translating Caesar and Livy and Thucydides, but can she work fine stitches or sew a tapestry? Can she speak French, write a fair hand, cast accounts, play on the virginals? Is she capable of managing a household, of brewing simples and preserving fruit? I don't want a daughter-in-law who's a bookish recluse halfway to ruining her eyes before she's twenty. I want a girl who'll take on the running of Denby and relieve the cares and burdens that have done so much to destroy my health and happiness.' She coughed lugubriously. Sir Simon, catching my eye with unexpected sympathy, assured her that his wife was personally attending to many of those aspects of my education, and that Mistress Bryant was more than capable of dealing with the rest. 'And I understand that her needlework is exceptionally fine and that, if circumstances and her sex were different, she and her lute could shine in exalted company. She's of a more practical turn of mind than Lucy, and I myself can vouch for her sweetmeats! Moreover, my sister, she's very young as yet, and we have six years by our reckoning to mould her into your perfect housewife. I think you need not fear on that score.

Now, you look something overwhelmed, Thomazine. Have you anything to say? Don't be afraid to ask questions, for it's your future we are planning.'

I swallowed convulsively (for Sir Simon even at his most friendly was more than intimidating) and from somewhere dragged the courage I needed. 'If you please, sir, what happens if when the time comes I don't *want* to marry Dominic?'

There was a little silence. Sir Simon's face deepened slightly into a frown. He placed his hands, fingertip to fingertip, on the table in front of him, and stared over them at me as if boring his eyes into my heart. 'In a marriage, Thomazine, consent is everything. The bride and groom must go consenting to the altar. Therefore, in theory, if you do not wish to marry him, we cannot force you. We can, however, use all our powers to persuade you to see reason. And I think it fitting to remind you again that, as your guardian, you owe me the same obligations and duties as you would your own father, were he still living. You should acknowledge that I am acting in your best interests in this, and that you have a duty to obey me, as is ordered in the fifth commandment. I am aware that you are as yet very young, and that you may feel frightened or awed by the thought of marriage. I have some sympathy for you. But by the age of sixteen you should be capable of understanding that it would be extremely foolish, apart from the sin of disobedience, to have the impertinence to refuse such an eminently suitable match. Do you understand me, Thomazine?'

My mind was a turmoil of anger and rebellion, but I shut the lid firmly on my seething thoughts and spoke with calm. 'Yes, sir. I will do everything I can to please you and to follow your wishes.'

'Good girl. I know you for a child of some sense, and I'm sure you won't regret what we have planned for you. Now, you may return to your lessons – and have a care for your eyes!'

I made my obeisances to him, and to Sir Roger and Aunt Hannah, and made my way back to the library. All that morning my mind was tramping back and forth in rage, and Dr Davis had to call me to attention no less than five times – an honour usually reserved for Jamie or Tom. Even at dinner I ignored Lucy's appeals, frantic with curiosity, as to what had passed at my interview, and applied myself to swallowing the food, which turned to sand in my mouth and nearly choked me. As soon as grace was said, I made all haste upstairs to Francis's chamber, shaking off Lucy's persistent questions, and burst in on him without so much as a knock.

Francis was practising on the little silver flageolet which was his latest skill and on which he now spent more time than on his beloved lute. The bright dancing notes ceased abruptly as I tumbled into the room and stood, fighting tears of fury. 'Thomazine? I wish you'd knock. D'you want me to swallow it? And do me the favour, lady, of shutting the door.'

'I crave your pardon, sir,' I said viciously, and slammed it to. Francis looked up from the music, startled. 'What's the matter?'

'They . . . they . . .' I began, felt sobs coming and finished, 'they want me to marry Dominic!' And stood in the centre of the room, helpless, with the shameful tears pouring down my cheeks.

'What, now?' Francis fished in the slashed sleeve of his doublet and produced a kerchief, still clean and uncrumpled. 'Here, take this. What's so terrible about marrying Dominic? Alice thinks he's handsome enough for a prince.'

'Oh, Alice!' I smeared the cambric across my rumpled face. 'Alice is a stupid old chatterbox. I don't want to marry Dominic,' I added. muffled by the cloth, 'and they can't make me.'

'Look,' said Francis, 'I can't make head nor tail of all this. Come over here, and sit down, and calm yourself. Sobs and hiccups won't make your story any the clearer.'

Meekly, I folded myself down on a cushion, dried the last of the tears, and by concentration managed to get my breathing regular. Francis waited patiently till I was done. 'Now, tell me what's happened again, slowly.'

I gave a brief account of the interview with his father and the Drakelons, fighting down the anger which periodically threatened to overwhelm me when I thought of what this would mean. Francis heard me out impassively, his fingers performing little breathless tunes on the flageolet as it lay in his hands.

'So I'm to marry Dominic when I'm sixteen or so, and if I don't want to they'll force me to, I could see it in their faces!'

'In my father's face, you mean. Now, infant, you've a mind above the common run. Use it. How many years till you're sixteen?'

'Six.'

'Six years. Well, a lot can happen in six years. The plague may strike. You may be dead. Dominic may be dead. My revered father may be dead. Dominic may find someone he likes better. Anything could happen to change things,' my cousin said sweepingly, 'and even if nothing alters six years is a long time and you'll have every chance to get used to the idea.'

'That's what Sir Simon said.'

'Well, for once we're in agreement. Now look at me,' Francis said. 'You're behaving just like Lucy. What exactly is it about Dominic you don't like? It's not just the idea of marriage that so appals you, is it? It's marriage to Dominic.'

'N – no.'

'Oh, don't lie to me,' Francis said, 'I can see your face. Have you ever spoken with him? He's not so bad if you can forget his mother, and by the time you're sixteen he won't seem so much older.'

'It isn't that. I just don't like him. He drew me, when I was in the library reading, and I didn't know he was there, and . . . well, he . . . I thought he was a bit odd.'

'Tell me,' said Francis, gently for him, and I told him everything. 'He makes me feel all shivery,' I finished. 'I don't like the way he looks at me, or how he talked to me, and when he touched me like that, it was . . .' Stopping in confusion, I flushed. In my innocence, I had no words for, and no understanding of Dominic's attitude towards me, but my reaction was instinctive. Francis, older and more sophisticated than I, stared at me with his mouth compressed. 'I think I understand,' he said thoughtfully. 'It isn't right, not with you so young. At least you'll be out of reach till the wedding, if it ever takes place. You know, it may not happen, and if it doesn't you'll have wasted all your tears and anger for nothing.'

'Even if I'm not married to Dominic I'll be married to someone else whether I like it or not. Your father was thinking of Edward, or you, before Dominic asked.'

Francis snorted. 'You don't ask whether *we'd* approve, I note! I'm not sure I'd want to be wed to a hedgehog like you, all bad temper and prickles!'

I ignored him. 'I feel just like that poor bear I saw in Bury Market the day I first came here, pushed and poked and made to dance. Do this, do that, marry Dominic whether I like it or not – why can't I do what *I* want?'

'It might not always agree with what other people might want. If you wanted to set fire to the house, you couldn't be allowed to do that – or anything else that's dangerous to people or property.'

'But refusing to marry Dominic isn't dangerous.'

'Yes it is, because you might fall in love with a penniless vagabond who'd spend all your inheritance on drinking and dicing and cards, and then where would the family be without all your fine estates?'

'Just as rich, nearly,' I said gloomily. 'Francis? If it – if I – if they do try and make me marry Dominic, when I'm sixteen, and I still don't want to, will you help me and speak for me? I don't want to spend all my life married to someone I hate!'

'You'll probably run through four husbands before you're thirty,' Francis said cheerfully. He saw my indignant face and added, with sudden sincerity, 'Listen, infant, I've been teasing you. I will back you up, if they try to force the marriage through, and that's a promise!' He smiled vividly. 'A promise I mean to keep, unlike all the ones I make for my good behaviour. Remind me of it if you need it, won't you?'

'I will,' I said, 'though I hope I never do need it. Thank you.'

'My pleasure. And if I were you I'd do my best to avoid Dominic's company until they leave. No more sitting on your own in the library, however much of a bookworm you want to be.'

'Oh, I've found somewhere else,' I said unwisely. 'I go and sit in the chapel now.'

'In the chapel?' Francis grinned mockingly. 'I suppose you feel divinely protected there, but as it's a good plain honest Protestant place I don't think thoughts of sacrilege would give Dominic any pause for contemplation before he molests you again.'

I flushed, annoyed at his teasing. 'Well, he hasn't found me yet. Anyway, I like it there, it's peaceful and quiet and – and sort of watched-over, somehow – I feel safe there.'

'That place is just four walls and a roof, and as such is no more "watched-over" than the barns at the Home Farm,' said Francis, grinning and daring me to argue. I kept an unhappy silence and he added, 'Now, since you're here, shall we turn our thoughts to song? Can you manage my lute?'

Despite my resentment, I rose as ever to the bait. 'It's something too big for me, but I'll try. What have you been practising on that?'

'Jigs, dances, that sort of thing mostly. But I did try this . . .' He flicked over the pages of one of the books. 'That one, "What Then is Love?". Can you sight-read?'

'What do you take me for? You know very well I can. Play first, then sing?'

'If you like.'

We picked out the tune together, a little hesitantly on my part. I liked the mournful minor key of the piece, and the compelling, melancholy words. We sang them in harmony together, with my lute accompanying, and the spell of music wrapped round me once more, shutting out marriage and troubles and foreboding and sinking me deep into the power of the song.

What then is love but mourning?
What desire but a self-burning?

Till she that hates doth love return
Thus will I mourn, thus will I sing,
'Come away, come away, my darling'.

Beauty is but a blooming,
Youth in his glory entombing,
Time hath a while which none can stay.
Then come away while thus I sing,
'Come away, come away, my darling'.

Summer in winter fadeth,
Gloomy night heavenly light shadeth.
Like to the morn are Venus's flowers.
Such are her hours. Then will I sing,
'Come away, come away, my darling'.

Our voices, Francis's boy's treble clear and pure, my own throatier but no less accurate, mixed pleasantly enough. At the end of it, Lucy appeared, viol in hand, indignant. 'You said you were going to Mother to get some salve for a cut! I could hear you two singing in the hall, so I thought I'd come up and join you. Shall we try something more cheerful? I didn't like that mournful old dirge.'

Francis grimaced at me ruefully, and turned the pages in search of livelier tunes. I had to console myself with the thought that we would have other opportunities for talk and music, without Lucy's presence – but it was not to be.

That afternoon, strolling in the garden in the heat, Aunt Hannah suffered what she called a 'seizure'. It was in all likelihood nothing more than a touch of the sun, but Hannah was not disposed to take it so lightly. Prostrate in her darkened chamber, cooled with compress and infusion, she insisted on an immediate return to the cooler, damper climate of Yorkshire, and her husband, who had planned to stay longer, had perforce to agree with her, as he had done so often before, for the sake of peace – although I overheard him saying to his sister-in-law with some force that if the silly woman would only lace her corsets less tightly, and not insist on starching her ruffs to the consistency of steel plate, her health would suffer a dramatic improvement.

'Ah, but her life would then become so much less interesting,' said Mary, Lady Heron, sweetly, and Sir Roger Drakelon's laughter echoed appreciatively along the gallery.

So hasty preparations were made for their departure, and Francis's, and I had no more opportunity to talk with him. I grew more than commonly bad-tempered, until I recalled my grandmother's advice, ceased to pick quarrels with Lucy, Jamie and Tom, and set myself to making the best of things. I even managed a smile as we gathered in the front courtyard, early on the first day of September, to bid farewell to our visitors, and to Francis. It would be yet another fine day, with no threat of the break in the weather that Aunt Hannah was so anxious to avoid until she was safe back at Denby over dry roads. The rising sun was a red circle in the mist, and the dew lay thick and white on the grass. The riding-horses and Aunt Hannah's litter stood waiting; beyond the bridge the packhorses, laden with baggage, pulled at the drenched grass. There was a flurry of cousinly kissing and embracing, grateful thanks for hospitality given, presents exchanged. I received a tiny seed-pearl brooch from Dominic, which I made a mental note never to wear, and prided myself on not flinching from his kiss, so subtly hot it made me shiver. 'Jacob waited seven years for his Rachel,' said my prospective bridegroom, 'and I'll wait for my Sparrow likewise. I shall think of you often, Thomazine – may the waiting soon be over. Will you write to me?'

Not meeting his eyes, I said, 'If I have the time, sir.'

'You're young yet,' said Dominic, his uncomfortable blue eyes wandering over my face and leaving me now in no doubt that my youth was my chief attraction. 'Would that it were sooner! Well – till we meet again, my Sparrow, take care of yourself for me, and God be with you!'

'Goodbye,' I said with relief, and watched him swing gracefully on to his sturdy dark-grey gelding. Beside him

Sir Roger sat, or rather slouched, on his enormous hairy-footed horse which looked as though it had pulled a plough before being called upon to support its master's bulk. Elizabeth Graham had made it known that the day when she resorted to coach or litter would also be the day of her death, and in consequence was seated, a spare upright figure, atop a sleek brown palfrey. In contrast, Aunt Hannah, laid inelegantly in her litter, was fanning herself as she exchanged last-minute pleasantries with Lady Heron. And Francis, hat in hand, his face still over the excitement beneath, was enduring a final interview with his father in the porch. I made valiant efforts to catch some of the talk, but failed, and had perforce to stand miserably with Lucy and Jamie, my eyes fixed on the beauty of Hobgoblin, and my mind concentrated on not shedding tears. Sir Simon, in a fit of magnanimity no doubt caused by the enticing prospect of Francis's absence, had listened to John Sewell's suggestion and had confirmed that Francis could take the mare with him, on condition she was kept whole and sound and, on her return, used for breeding. So Goblin, her ebony hide glossy and her small ears pricked, stood a little apart from the other riding horses, held by a nervous stableboy, and stamping her neat black hooves as an occasional warning. Drake, his exuberance enhanced rather than suppressed by his long captivity, was tied to the drawbridge post and straining at his rope to catch Francis's voice as he bade farewell to his parents and to his brothers and sister. Lucy wept on his neck and was rewarded by a sarcastic comment. Finally, he turned to me, his eyes bright with laughter and overwhelming excitement. 'Farewell, little cousin. Don't look so sad, you'll find me again.'

'Keep safe, cousin,' I answered, taking refuge in formality. Francis laughed. 'Oh, yes, I will, and I'll keep Hobgoblin safe too. Don't worry, to you I don't make promises I can't keep.' He kissed me lightly and coldly on the cheek, as he had done to Lady Heron and Lucy, and whispered, 'Don't forget the unicorns!'

I watched as he climbed on to the Goblin, an excited Drake bouncing dangerously round her heels, on the end of his rope. Everyone waved and blew kisses; the horselitter started forward slowly under Hannah's bulk, crossed the bridge and swayed down the drive, Lady Drakelon's fat beringed hand languishing limply from the curtains. The other riders and the packponies followed it into the wreathing early mist. Francis looked back once, before they turned the corner out of our sight; and then they were gone.

chapter three

Return of a prodigal

He that loveth not his brother whom he hath seen,
how can he love God whom he hath not seen?

(1 John 4:20)

At first, the days and weeks dragged miserably. I was determined to enjoy life, but it was harder work than I had
expected, and I developed a capacity for burying my
unhappiness in books, which annoyed Lucy greatly. She
often complained, only half jokingly, how I had become
much less fun than before, and made a habit of involving
me will-nilly in any activity which her fertile imagination
could think up, from rewriting the rules of bowls on the
smooth turf of the green in the garden, to going hare-hun-
ting with Simon, Edward and the Sewell brothers. By
Christmas I had not forgotten Francis, but his absence no
longer left a gap in the busy round of my life.

The new year, 1636, brought changes. Simon, as had
long been planned, was sent to Oxford. He wrote that he
greatly appreciated it; there was ample opportunity for
hard work and serious thought, and he remarked with
disgust upon the considerable body of loose-living students
who, despite the multitudinous rules and regulations, ran
riot in the inns and streets of Oxford, to the detriment of
their studies and their health. Lucy and Jamie and I missed
him not at all, glad to be rid of him and his high principles,
which often spoiled our pleasures. We were sorrier to see
the departure of Edward later in the year, for volunteer
service with the Prince of Orange in the Low Countries.
Henry Sewell, who by that time was already in Holland and
had served for several months, was to take him under his
wing. I could not imagine plain, steady and dependable
Edward needing to be under anyone's wing, even that of
Henry Sewell, who was a much more reliable character than

his younger brother. Lucy, of course, feared for them both, and the regular letters, penned by Henry in his bold, uncompromising and inelegant hand, did nothing to allay her terrors, with word of disease, death and the appalling privations suffered by the local population on nearly every page.

With Sir Simon's three eldest sons, and Henry, absent, the four of us left at Goldhayes must have sorely tried the patience of our elders. Without Edward's common sense or Simon's censorious remarks to restrict us, we ran free, going much as we pleased in our afternoon recreation period. My riding improved beyond recognition, I found that I could almost equal Tom at running and jumping, and I acquired a most accurate eye with a hunting-crossbow. I filled my waking hours with learning, music and more riotous exercise, and to my very great delight grew four inches in a year.

To compensate for the loss of my cousins, my circle of friends widened considerably. We often visited the Jermyns at Rushbrooke, a couple of miles away, where Sir Thomas Jermyn had a large brood of young grandchildren, the eldest of whom, Robert, was a year or so younger than Jamie, and his fast friend. The younger members of the Blagge family, at Little Horringer, were also often at Gold-hayes, and we held frequent and cut-throat bowling matches on our green. I very much liked Ann, who was seventeen or eighteen, and who did not hesitate to concern herself with the affairs of those much younger than herself. She was evidently unhappy that the agreed match between her and Simon had not yet taken place, and feared that it never would, since her older brother Tom, now at Court, had suggested that she join him there as maid-in-waiting to the little Princess Mary, or even to the Queen. Of the other Blagges, Judith and Martha were then sixteen and fifteen and very frivolous; Ambrose and Henry, their half-broth-ers, contemporary with Lucy and Jamie and big, rough lads; while young John Snelling, son of Ambrose Blagge's second wife by a previous marriage, was shy and unassum-ing beside his boisterous half-brothers and giggling stepsisters, and teased unmercifully by us because of his stammering speech. And as if Blagges and Jermyns were not enough, there was also the Hervey family, three boys and four girls, whose mother was Sir Thomas Jermyn's sister; and the children of the widowed Lady Penelope Gage, a formidable Papist lady who periodically occupied her mother's house at Hengrave with her family. Amongst all these young people I found many friends, but no one to reach me as Francis had, no one to understand the unicorns.

We heard little of him during his years at Catholm. Cousin Sandy, whose spelling it took the entire family's efforts to translate, wrote occasionally to inform us that all was well, but we never had anything of Francis himself. At first I took this much to heart, but soon realized that I could expect no personal word from him. After two years had gone by, I found it hard to conjure up his face, but the memory of our talks was clear and vivid in my mind, and the bestiary became a talisman of his ideas, something which I read whenever I had the opportunity, and which I hugged to myself with secret delight.

Early in August, 1637, one of Cousin Sandy's letters arrived, sent not by the Post but actually delivered by one of the Catholm servants in person. It advised us that, as the agreed two years of his sojourn on the Borders were completed, Francis would shortly be dispatched home to Goldhayes. This seemed a little abrupt, but Sir Simon was at pains to remind us of the recent rumours of trouble in Scotland, and there was also the plan, of which we were all aware, for Francis to join Simon at Oxford some time in the new year, 1638. I thought no more, therefore, of the circumstances of his homecoming, preferring to immerse myself in happy expectation of that event, until my eyes were accidentally opened.

Sir Simon was in the habit of testing his childrens' educational progress at regular intervals and I, to my dismay, was not exempted from this monthly ordeal. Some three or four days after the arrival of Cousin Sandy's letter, the dread summons came, and I was ushered into his chamber after Jamie, whose unhappy face on his exit indicated that his learning did not match up to his father's exacting requirements. I had been trying frantically to recall some particularly irregular and annoying Latin verbs and was in consequence greatly relieved when Harry Jakes, the steward, hurried in with more urgent business, and I, a child of no account, had perforce to wait until they had finished. The immediate pressure removed, the verbs became clear in my mind at once, and I relaxed and allowed my eyes to wander. Sir Simon was poring over some huge account book, steward in attendance; his desk in front of me was littered with papers, receipts, calculations, lists, and, I was amused to see, a piece of paper on which Jamie had tried, and failed miserably, to recall those same irregular verbs. Beside it lay a letter, in the sharp hand which I recognized as being Great-Aunt Elizabeth's; I had not been aware of any recent correspondence from her, and so, my curiosity aroused, made an unobtrusive effort to read the parts not obscured by other papers.

> . . . feel it only right that you should be informed of this as a matter of urgency. I had not thought him to be interested in amatory matters, since he is after all only just fifteen, but it appears that the relationship with this girl has been going on for some time, under our very noses, and although I myself would be inclined to take a more liberal-minded view, and my son likewise, my daughter-in-law Grizel is most displeased and upset by it, and does not wish Francis to remain any longer at Catholm. The girl has been returned to her family, who are inclined to make trouble, despite the fact that she is, I would wager, no virgin innocent and probably the instigator of the affair — although Francis certainly showed no reluctance to be led astray . . .

I could read no more, and indeed would not have wished to, even had I been able. My cheeks burning, I hoped that Sir Simon noticed nothing as he eventually tore himself away from more important matters and tested my Latin, fortunately in fairly perfunctory fashion. I was not of course ignorant of the essential facts of life, but this astonishing revelation shocked and disturbed me in a way I did not really understand. I could in no way reconcile the strange but friendly child to whom I had seemed so close, with this stranger whose dalliance with, presumably, a servant girl, had obviously precipitated his sudden dispatch home. All my joy at his homecoming evaporated instantly and I spent many hours, whether in chapel, library or awake in bed at night, miserably pondering my secret: which seemed to imply an end to that exhilarating mental companionship we shared so briefly, two years ago.

We had word from Catholm that Francis, with an escort of two or three armed servants, would set out from Liddesdale on the first day of September, and all being well would take ten days to reach us.

Those ten days passed with agonizing slowness. My usual powers of concentration deserted me, and I lay awake at night wondering if he would still remember the unicorns or whether as I feared, he would have changed into one of those distant, languidly elegant young men particularly prominent in the Gage family; or worse still, be transformed by his reported experiences into the kind of pouch-eyed, sinister, dissipated rake that my Puritan upbringing had led me to believe was the form of any womanizer. I had held and treasured a memory for two years, and I prayed now that it would not prove to be vain illusion.

On the day set for his arrival, I was lax at my lessons, having failed entirely to sleep for most of the previous night. Lucy, Jamie and Tom were also excited and inattentive, and Dr Davis could only gain our concentration by threatening to keep us at our lessons for the afternoon as well. This sharpened our minds wonderfully, and we laboured industriously until dinner-time.

Over the meal, Lucy planned a welcome for her brother with her usual vibrant enthusiasm. Since the last thing that I wanted was to greet Francis in her company, and Tom's and Jamie's, I spent the hour making plans of my own. Lucy's idea was to ambush Francis at the Home Farm, so I had obviously to waylay him some distance before that, and would thus require some time. Accordingly, I ate very little of the food and, halfway through the meal, rose to my feet and made my excuses to Sir Simon and his lady, pleading sickness and a headache. Once out of the dining hall, I fled to my chamber, pulled off my plain dark-blue dress and substituted my new riding-habit. This I had made myself, over many weary hours, with Alice's help, and I was inordinately proud of it. Since it was more than two years since my father had died, I had been allowed to make it in a rich autumnal rusty brown, with a doublet cut like a boy's and a wide lacy collar. There was also a black felt hat and a glorious beech-red plume, seen by chance at Bury Fair and matching the cloth exactly. I arranged everything using my reflection in the window, and then stuffed a bolster down the bed, drew the covers up and closed the curtains round it, hoping that Lucy would not succumb to her normal curiosity. Then I made a hasty exit down the turret stairs and through the kitchens, stopping on the way to implore Monsieur Harcourt, who treated us children with expansive Gallic affection, not to say that he had seen me. The same promise had to be exacted from the stable-lad who helped me to saddle my pony Tamburlaine, and sealed with a handful of purloined raisins. I then mounted and set off at a gallop down the drive, hoping that everyone would still be in the dining hall and therefore unable to see me.

It was probable that Francis and his escort would come from Bury down the main road to Sudbury, and so on emerging from the drive by the Home Farm I took the narrow lane, not wide enough for a coach, in that direction. As I rode I ran my mind's eye over the surroundings of the Sudbury road, selecting a suitable vantage-point – one at a sufficient distance from Goldhayes to give me adequate time to greet my cousin, and with a good view of the road north to Bury. After a quarter of an hour or so, I arrived at the place I had thought best, led Tamburlaine to the stream sharing the roadway, and then tied him securely to a young oak bush growing stuntedly under its parent tree. The view of the road ahead would be considerably improved by climbing one of the trees, which was dying and therefore sparsely-leaved. The extravagant skirts of my habit were little hindrance; I gathered them up over one arm, exposing quantities of stocking and riding-boot to anyone who cared to view, and clambered up the tree to the first branch. It grew stongly and thickly outward, and I settled my back to the trunk, my legs side-saddle fashion over the right side of the bough, and fixed my eyes on the Sudbury road.

It dawned on me, after half an hour or so, that I might have long to wait. I had not come unprepared, and climbed down again to fetch *The New Atlantis* from my saddlebags, together with a couple of new-picked apples. Back on my branch, I tried to concentrate on the book, glancing up every so often at the road, but my heart was thumping and my palms sticky with sweat. I could not rid myself of the very real fear that this returning sophisticated, adult Francis would have forgotten all about his small scruffy cousin and the strange fellowship we had once enjoyed, and would instead have irrevocably entered the adult world in search of more mature, and physical, companionship. Thus transformed, he would doubtless be annoyed and embarrassed to have me strung once more at his heels. Growing certain in the conviction that I was about to make a fool of myself and an enemy of Francis, I wished desperately that I had not set out so impetuously, and only the thought of facing Lucy and the boys without Francis by my side kept me in the tree at all.

A small group of horsemen made my heart jump, but it was only a party from Horringer, taking the long way home from Bury via the excellent alehouse in Bradfield Combust, popularly known as 'Burned Bradfield' from some long-ago conflagration. I knew them all, and waved as they passed. Master Lucas, owner of Horsecroft and father of children my own age, stared disapprovingly at my unseemly position, and urged his horse on, his plain and sober garb matching his godly nature. Master Covell, on the other hand, waved cheerfully back and shouted, 'That's a strange bird sitting in that tree! What are you doing there, Mistress Heron?'

'Waiting for my cousin,' I called back, and watched them

jog off down the road, their spare-faced Suffolk servants at their back, before trying again to read my book.

Slowly, the sun dropped in the sky. Tamburlaine finished cropping the grass, and slept, one hind leg bent, under my perch. Clouds started to build up in the north, threatening more rain. I began to feel in my heart that Francis would not appear now, and was just making up my mind to accept defeat when four figures on horseback came in sight. I sat up instantly, my eyes straining, certain that it was him at last. The dark horse was assuredly Hobgoblin with her delicate walk, and proof came with the black and white dog which hurled itself out of the dust and raced, typically deaf to its owner's shouts, in pursuit of a rabbit. I fairly tumbled down the tree, rammed the book into the saddlebags, untied Tamburlaine, and scrambled into the saddle, remembering to brush off the bark dust. I spent some little time arranging my attire to my satisfaction before emerging from the shade on to the sunlit dusty road.

Instantly, to my immense delight, the figure on Hobgoblin put her into a gallop to carry them down the two hundred yards which separated us. I waited, heart pounding, as she was pulled up with a flourish two yards from Tamburlaine's placid nose.

There was nothing of the laconic, poetic, rebellious child I had known in this tall, broad-shouldered, spare young gallant in the elegant mud-splashed attire, and nothing either of my worst fears; although the mocking courtesy with which he removed his hat, revealing golden love-locks, and bowed to me from the saddle with a new casual grace, was more familiar. His voice had deepened into a man's, low-pitched and musical; he said, 'Greetings, Thomazine! You've not changed in the least.'

'I'll have you know I've grown six inches,' I said instantly.

'Three inches a year,' Francis said, amused. 'Are there any more of you?'

'Er . . . not yet. Lucy's planned an ambush for you by the Home Farm.'

'So you thought you'd put yourself in my way first? I see a blush. I also see large quantities of moss on your back.'

98

I swore softly and tried to twist round to see. Francis manoeuvred Hobgoblin so that he could brush it off. 'Where were you watching for me? Up that tree?'

'How did you guess?'

'The large quantities of moss on your back, which rather spoil the effect. I must say I prefer you in rust to black and silver. Well? Will you ride with me, lady? No doubt you're dying to ask a hundred questions.'

I put Tamburlaine into step beside him, delighted at the way in which we had slipped back into our old teasing talk as though there had never been two years' break in it. 'Well, yes, I am.'

'Drake! Drake! Damn that dog. Ever since we left Catholm I've been wondering why my father didn't have him knocked on the head after all. His major exploit to date has been purloining a complete goose, still live and kicking, from one of the inns we stayed at and burying the remains in the flour-bin. Added to which he's herded cattle uphill when they were being herded down, attacked Mistress Grizel Graham's tame Presbyterian minister, and taken his pound of flesh from Gib's well-covered thigh.'

I giggled as Drake appeared from the fields, rabbitless and panting, and scurried round the heels of the horses. 'Who's Gib?'

'He's your cousin, and mine. He's Great-Aunt's elder grandson. He's a good deal older than me – twenty now, in fact – and I don't much care for him.'

'Why not?'

'Because he thinks he's always in the right, and that he's God's gift to maidens to boot.'

'And I suppose,' I said, rashly probing, 'that you're well qualified to know?'

Francis gave me a very sharp glance, but did not rise to the bait. 'Perhaps. I suppose some find him attractive, for he's tall and imposing, if more than a little stout, and he has that real deep-red hair that Great-Aunt Elizabeth used to have. But his ladies are not the sort his mother would wish for his wife at all.'

'What sort of ladies?'

'Lewd women of loose morals – you'll find out one day, infant. Gib loves his pleasures, whether wine, women or song – he sings very well, by the way – and he'd rather be drinking and taking his other pleasures in the taverns in Hawick or Carlisle than looking after the farm and improving his relationship with his God. I fear Grizel is sadly disappointed in him.'

'Grizel's his mother, isn't she?'

'Yes, she's Great-Aunt's daughter-in-law, though she's more like her than her own son. Catholm,' said Francis with reminiscent amusement, 'is a thing rather common in our family – a household ruled by the women. Or it would be, if the two of them saw eye to eye.'

'Which they don't?'

'Which they don't. Great-Aunt, as you know, conceals within her stern exterior a sense of humour and a heart soft as butter. Grizel is granite all through. Her knees are bony with praying, she knows a large part of the Bible by heart I should think, and she's thrifty even for a Scot. But she was married to the wrong man, and produced the wrong sons, and it's soured her.'

I listened eagerly as Francis went on describing these unknown cousins, giving them life and colour; the lazy good-natured Sandy to whom Great-Aunt Elizabeth had improbably given birth, and his younger son Malise, obviously Francis's particular friend and Great-Aunt's favourite; and the other inhabitants of Catholm. But there was no mention at all of any voluptuous serving-maid, no talk of Francis sharing Gib's lecherous tendencies, and no sign at all in his face or manner of any such depravity; so that I began to wonder whether I had imagined the contents of that letter, and relaxed sufficiently to pay more heed to his words as he told me something of the more innocent pleasures of Catholm. 'Yes, we had grand times together, riding the hills and herding sheep and cattle and stalking the deer. The deer aren't like our own little fallow, they're big as your pony and the stags can gore a man to death. Everything at Catholm,' said my cousin, choosing his words thoughtfully, 'is bigger, and wilder, and more extreme, than at Goldhayes. The hills are high and bleak, fit only for sheep and birds, and covered in bracken and heather – desolate and lonely places to spend the night; which we did several times, at lambing, or after straying cattle, or in summer for the fun of it. The people in the farms and villages – well, they're poorer than any here; their hovels are mostly built of little more than grass and sticks, their animals share their beds for warmth in the winter, and the women grow aged at thirty – but the songs they sing would turn your heart to water, or send you out, in your mind, on an old Border raid with the Bold Buccleuch or Johnnie Armstrong or a dozen cutthroats with names like Gleed Tam or Halflugs Jock.'

'Eh?'

'Tom with a squint and Jock who's only got half his ears. The language they speak is strange to a Southerner's ears, quicker and with more music to it, but harder too. They found my Suffolk speech very amusing. And, by the way,' he added, reaching down to my saddlebags before I could stop him, 'what's this you're reading?'

'Oh, just a book,' I said uncommunicatively. Francis glanced at the title page. 'I see – *The New Atlantis*. Do my Lord Verulam's ideas intrigue you?'

'I find them interesting,' I said, with caution. 'It's not as long or as interesting, though, as the *Utopia*.'

'I agree with you there, even though Sir Thomas More was a notorious Papist. What do you read else? Plato? Stage-plays?'

'No, of course not! I like histories, and poetry in Latin and English and French, and Plato and Aristotle—'

'—In Greek?'

'Not usually, that's too difficult. In English.'

'You surprise me. What of theology, or travel? Do you read of far and fabulous lands? Sir John Mandeville, perhaps?'

'Not while I've got the bestiary,' I said, and stopped abruptly. Francis gave me a quick sideways look. 'You're blushing. Is your mind still full of unicorns? Don't worry, I've not forgotten. What bestiary is it?'

'I found it on the top shelf of the library. It's by someone called Topsell. It has a lot of pictures, and it's very interesting.'

'Have you discovered the Boccaccio yet?'

'I can't read Italian.'

'Just as well, he's not at all fitting for a maiden of your tender years. It'll be a sorry day when Dr Davis discovers the existence of all those top-shelf books – I've whiled away many a happy hour with them. Well, I've answered your questions till I'm weary, and now you can answer some of mine. What news is there of Ned?'

I gave him the latest news and gossip while we drew near to Goldhayes; the armed manservants from Liddesdale, old-fashioned in their leather jacks, following at a distance. As we took the fork up to the house, passing the Home Farm, there came a wild whooping noise from the outbuildings, and Lucy, Tom and Jamie galloped into the road, their ponies plunging and kicking, shouting a welcome. As we rode amongst them, Lucy spotted me. 'So you weren't really ill at all! I *thought* you were planning something!'

'Well, you were too, so I thought I'd go one better,' I responded, and watched her pull her pony next to Hobgoblin, the better to inquisition her brother. My own welcome was over, but at least my worst fears seemed to have been groundless.

Francis's reception at Goldhayes, however, provided some confirmation that I had not imagined the contents of Great-Aunt Elizabeth's letter. On his arrival he was summoned forthwith to an interview with his father, behind closed doors; but with the peculiar osmosis of Goldhayes, everyone was aware that Francis was being subjected to the full force of his father's rage. Lucy, naturally, was agog with excitement and curiosity, and plied me with questions and speculations as we strolled in the gardens waiting for Francis to emerge from his ordeal. 'What do you think has happened? Father must be very angry, I could feel it. Poor Francis, I wonder what on earth he's done?'

I of course had a very good idea, but I would have died rather than reveal the contents of that letter to Francis's prattling, romantic, innocent little sister. Feeling very worldly-wise and adult, I affected a casual attitude which was probably not dissimilar to Francis's own at that moment. 'I've no idea, and since he probably won't say anything about it, knowing him, I don't suppose we'll ever know. Anyway, what does it matter?'

Lucy looked at me with suspicion, and said, 'Are you *sure* you don't know?'

'Quite sure. He's probably just having his Greek tested.'

'Oh, pooh, you know as well as I do it's nothing of the sort. I'll ask him straight out when we see him,' said Lucy, with her usual excess of enthusiasm vanquishing common-sense: and fortunately did not quiz me further. I kept my disturbing knowledge utterly to myself, taking care not to hint again to Francis that I knew of the reason why he had been sent home, and tried to forget all about it. Since Francis himself and the rest of his family continued to behave as if nothing much out of the ordinary had occurred, this was an easy task.

Lucy, however, once come down to earth from her joy at his return and her curiosity as to the reason for it, was instantly aware of a change in him. She became notably reluctant to invite Francis to join at least the wilder of our games, and told me that it didn't seem right. 'He's so much bigger,' she said tragically, in the nightly stuffiness of our bed, 'and I can't ask him to do the witches or be Melancholy Jacques, not now, and he used to speak them so well!'

'I don't see why you shouldn't ask him,' I said, 'he isn't like Simon, he's not too dignified to join in even if he has grown up. I don't think it makes any difference.'

'Well, it does to me,' Lucy explained. 'I feel embarrassed. And I'm still dying to know why Father was so cross with him when he got home. I wonder what happened?'

'Well, he's not telling anybody,' I said, 'so I don't suppose we'll ever find out. And if he's going to Oxford in January we won't see much of him, so we'd better enjoy his company while we've got it.'

And so we did; and Francis, contrary to Lucy's fears and mine, evidently enjoyed ours, for children though we were, our talk and pastimes came as a breath of fresh air after Liddesdale, where the only people with pretensions to learning for miles around had been Malise and Elizabeth Graham. 'Not,' Francis said, 'that I'd despise anyone for lack of learning when they haven't had the chance to be otherwise. But it is good to quote a poem or make a literary allusion and not be received as if I'm mad!'.

So we talked, and made songs, and played bowls with the Herveys and hunted with the Blagges, and behaved with exact decorum under the refined and basilisk eye of Lady Penelope, who ever made me feel uncomfortable in her presence, and whose organizational abilities were a great hindrance to a free life. 'She'd make a grand general,' Francis said to me once on leaving Hengrave after a particularly regimented afternoon, 'but on the bowling green it's a touch out of place.'

'Sir William likes her.' Sir William Hervey, recently widowed, was evincing a strong desire to be organized.

Francis snorted. 'Rather him than me. That woman would reduce even Medea to a meek obedient sheep mouthing, "Yes, my lady, no, my lady," at any interval in her talk. I know my mother leaves much to be desired, but at least she's not Goldhayes' reply to Gustavus Adolphus!'

So the autumn drew on into winter. I was happy, whether arguing points of philosophy with Francis, learning with Dr Davis or singing and making music with family and guests in the quiet of the music parlour or the echoing splendour of the long gallery. Despite the three-year gap in our ages, never greater than at twelve and fifteen, Francis did not treat me as a child. Our minds met with delight and understanding, knowing no barrier of age or sex, as though we had each been born incomplete and needed the company of the other to be again made whole. Lucy remarked happily how well we accorded, and her mother uttered sly comments on our living in each other's pockets, eyed my growing body with what I now realize to have been a misgiving born of events at Catholm, and expressed her desire to pack Francis off to Oxford as soon as might be.

Towards Christmas my guardian suffered an attack of

the ague which was one of the relics of his part in the Cadiz expedition. Dr Despotine, summoned in haste from Bury, expressed fears for the worst in his comical Italianate English, and Simon was sent for. By the time he arrived from Oxford however, his father was improved and out of danger, although his health had been gravely weakened. So Simon remained to spend Christmas with us, and in those two weeks everything changed.

I had grown out of my old dislike for Simon. He no longer seemed the dull, pompous authority of my early years at Goldhayes. I could see now his basic kindness, his deep integrity and devotion to principle, and although myself decidedly lacking in some if not all of these qualities, could admire them in him. He was the only one of Sir Simon's children to lack any sort of charm, and his dealings with others were awkward and insensitive, but he did his duty, and his best, and if his rigid adherence to what he considered to be right earned him the dislike and enmity of some, it also won him the admiration and respect of many of his father's friends and tenants. I was fond of him, and more so of Francis, and could have asked for nothing better than their mutual friendship – and so it came as a sad shock to find the two brothers sharing a mutual antipathy. Francis, like the cat which will always lavish attention on those who dislike it, seemed to take a perverse delight in taunting his brother, and developed an alarming skill at bringing Simon to the brink of open quarrel and then retreating with a flourish. As with Dr Davis, his intellect ran rings round his bewildered, angry elder brother until I wished most strongly in my troubled heart that he could find a less dangerous and unhappy object on which to practise his wit. It was a great relief when, after Christmas, the two took their quarrel to Oxford, and Goldhayes lapsed once more into peace.

Soon after their departure, we received a letter from Edward. This in itself was occasion for astonishment, for Edward had only previously put pen to paper when forced by inexorable academic pressures. The creased, travel-stained missive was borne in triumph to Sir Simon's chamber, ceremoniously unsealed and read in Mary's soft, expressionless voice. The reason for this unprecedented event became clear; Henry had received a kick from an unruly horse and had broken a finger-bone, so was thus unable to write. Ned reported that, apart from this, they were both well, and had played their part in the taking of Breda the previous October. 'There is also one matter which will be of much interest to Master Sewell and to Tom,' the letter added. 'For among those taken at Breda was an Irish mercenary captain, one Conal O'Brady, and with him his daughter, a fair lady of sixteen or so, both much brought down by the privations they endured during the siege; whereof the captain shortly died. Now Henry will have nothing but marriage with the girl, though she be Irish and a Papist also, though he swears she will change her religion for him. Her name is Grainne, or Grania; she is tall and well-shaped, though thin, her teeth excellent and her conformation good . . .'

'Just as if he were describing a horse,' I said later to Tom. 'That letter was written more than two months ago, I expect they're married now. Will your father be angry, do you think?'

Tom considered, swinging his legs against the kitchen table, on which Joan was attempting to make a syllabub. 'I don't know. If she be a Papist, he might be.'

'I don't think that would make much difference,' said Lucy, mopping up with her finger and licking off the drops of thick white liquid spread over the table by Joan's too-enthusiastic use of the birch-twigs. 'Why does my syllabub always turn to butter, or curdle, and yours turn out so nice and yet we work to the same recipe?'

'Thass practice,' Joan said drily. Lucy went on, 'After all, Dominic's a Papist, and Thomazine's betrothed to him. Lady Penelope's a Papist, and Sir William Hervey is probably going to marry her. So why shouldn't Henry marry this Irish girl, what's-her-name?'

'It's different with me and Dominic,' I said. 'Dominic is a close cousin and anyway I don't think he'd make me become a Papist too. Uncle Roger didn't make Aunt Hannah a Papist. And in fact,' I added, carrying my examples to the highest in the land, 'the Queen is a Papist, and the King's as Protestant as you or I. So why should it matter if Grainne's a Papist?'

'That in't just her religion,' Tom pointed out. 'She's one of they Irish savages, don't forget.'

'I don't suppose *all* the Irish are savages,' Lucy said. 'And she must be beautiful if Henry wants to marry her. He's never looked at any of the girls round here, not even Sarah Greenwood.'

'And thass just as well,' Joan put in, still plying her birch-twigs vigorously through the thickening cream, 'that young maw will come to no good, you can be sure o'that. Thass a good thing our Henry's no fule, her be the best-looker for three mile round and that in't as if her be shy.' This was something of an understatement, as Sarah Greenwood, the eldest daughter of a poor but otherwise respectable family, was in a fair way to becoming the village whore. Joan continued. 'Thass no denying it, I woon't like him to wed a furriner, least of all a Papist, but there, if he be happy I don't mind. Did Master Ned say when they'd be a-coming home?'

'No,' I said, 'I think they like soldiering too much to be in any hurry to come back, even to show off Henry's new wife.'

'I reckon they'll be back quick enough when she be likely,' Joan said darkly. She added wistfully, 'And thass not so long since our Henry were a little mite himself. How the time do go . . .'

'I think it's all like a play,' Lucy said, her beautiful eyes misty and romantic. 'I can't wait to see her, she must be so lovely.'

But Lucy had perforce to wait a while to see Grainne, and in the meantime many other events contrived to make the days pass quickly. One brought me sadness, for we had word of the sudden death of my grandmother Kate, from the fever which was so common at Ashcott in its frequently flooded valley. Although it was now nearly three years since

I had seen her, her firm, upright figure had remained clear in my mind to guide me in some things, if not in others. Once more I had to wear sober mourning black and resolved, with a determination which scarcely outlived the next flight of Lucy's fancy, to behave less like a hoyden and more like the lady of quality which it was intended I should become.

Shortly after this news, my Ashcott maid Alice announced that she was to be wed, to one of the Bradfield Tye farmers. A new maid had therefore to be chosen, and Lucy, whose intimate knowledge of village affairs was a surprise to anyone who did not know of the long hours she spent gossiping with Joan at the Home Farm, suggested Hepzibah Greenwood. The Greenwoods were one of the poorest families in Bradfield Tye, the widowed mother attempting with the aid of hard work, the Bible and her eldest son Holofernes (invariably known as Holly) to keep her nine children from becoming a charge on the Parish. Hepzibah, or Heppy as we quickly began to call her, was a girl our own age, fortunately not in the least like her fly-by-night elder sister Sarah, and proved a delight. Possessed of an uninhibited tongue and a typically Suffolk sense of humour more usually seen in very old farmworkers, she provided us with many moments of laughter both with her wit and with her frequent social blunders. She proved quick to learn her duties from Alice: to dress our hair, to lay out our garments neatly, to wash and to iron and to starch, to speak quietly and in turn, to curtsey with dignity, to sew a straight seam, to darn and mend and embroider. However, the impact of all this knowledge proved somewhat superficial, for Heppy frequently lapsed from her newly adult dignity, most notably on the occasion when she mistook Nan Blagge's father (who affected very casual dress when in the country) for a serving-man and attempted to engage him in scandalous gossip about himself. It was not a mistake she made again.

What with the novelty of Heppy's arrival at Goldhayes, the celebrations attendant on Alice's marriage, the discussions in the neighbourhood about the ship-money (Sir

Simon had grumbled mightily but at length had paid his share), and the rumours of open rebellion in Scotland, the early months of 1638 passed quickly. It seemed not long since we had said farewell to Simon and Francis as they set off for Oxford after Christmas, and now in July they returned, bringing with them the first good weather since the spring.

It was obvious, even to Jamie, even before they had dismounted in the forecourt, that all was not well between them. Remembering their differences at Christmas, I could, I felt, have cut the atmosphere between them with one of the sharp polished swords hanging over the mantel in the dim, cool hall where we stood to greet them.

'Simon, my dear! How are you?' Mary drifted forward, Moppet at heel, her face shining with a kind of abstract pleasure. Simon, studious, dutiful, obedient, had always been her favoured son, largely because he was a credit to her. She pecked a kiss on both grimy cheeks, affectionately standing on tiptoe – Simon at nineteen was near two yards high. 'I do declare, you've grown still more! We shall have to raise the ceilings.'

Behind him, Francis leaned against the long polished table, his hand firmly hooked in Drake's collar, and raised a sardonic eyebrow. Mary glanced at him, her smile now rather transparent, and turned back to her eldest son. 'Your father presents his apologies for not being able to greet you; but Dr Despotine had to bleed him this morning, and will not permit anyone to trouble him till he has slept deeply. He hopes to be able to receive you both after supper, though.'

'I am most sorry to hear that,' Simon said, his face troubled. 'I've prayed daily for his recovery, at Oxford. May God grant him strength.'

'Dr Despotine was certainly very hopeful of it. Now, how was Oxford? Are you both working hard at your studies?'

'Yes, we both worked long and hard, but not necessarily

at our *studies*,' Simon said, with a sudden viciousness quite foreign to him. 'I contented myself with what my tutor set, but I am sorry to say, Mother, that Francis had other interests which occupied his time.'

Francis unhitched himself from the table, releasing Drake, who still frisked round him in ecstatic greeting (dogs were not permitted at Oxford, and the enforced six months' separation had gone hard with him). 'Not all of my time, brother, was spent in activities of which you disapprove. I also satisfied our tutor's requirements, remember. Hullo, infants, you're looking cheerful enough for a funeral.' He grinned at us, looking suddenly older than Simon, actually three years his senior; more mature, more graceful, more relaxed and assured. 'Thomazine, moi owd gal, I'd swear you've grown!'

I was puzzled but pleased at his use of the typical Suffolk endearment, the sort of thing an old farmer might say to his wife, or daughter, or horse, or cow; and I grinned. 'Don't sound so surprised, it's time I grew. I'm near fourteen now.'

'Well, you're still scarcely taller than Jamie. Aren't you going to greet us?'

There was then the usual round of family kissing, in the course of which I happened to catch sight of Simon's face, caught off guard as he stared at his brother. It wore such a look of hatred and disgust that I instantly looked away, the cold running all through me despite the day's heat. What could have happened at Oxford to make Simon feel like that?

Lucy had noticed it also, and she caught my eye with a look of bewildered anguish. Mary, too, seemed aware of the tension in the atmosphere and began to talk rapidly, leading the company towards the stairs. 'You'd best come up and change out of those travelling clothes. The floor's quite thick with dust already. I take it you've heard that Henry Sewell is married? Yes, and from all accounts she's even changed her faith and rejected all Papist practices lock, stock and barrel. Now, I'll send Dorothy down to order the supper; Monsieur Harcourt has done some mutton pasties, and there's a raspberry tart and syllabub. It will be in half an hour, in the arras parlour, I thought.' She glided up the stairs, pink and faded like an old rose in her calyx of green satin, and a whiff of rosewater scent. We all followed her; at the top I detached myself from my cousins and fled silently to the window-seat above the porch, where I had been sitting when I had first seen Simon, Francis and their entourage as they came within sight of the house. The book which I had been reading lay on the cushions. I picked it up, found my place and tried to concentrate on the words, but now, my mind disturbed and chaotic, my usual powers of concentration fell away and I could only stare at the lines, while the hatred in Simon' face as he looked at his brother swam menacingly before my eyes.

'A penny for your thoughts,' Francis said, from behind. I jumped, and the book fell off my lap and dropped, splayed out, on to the floor. My cousin picked it up, dusted it, and smoothed a crushed page. 'Golding's Ovid, I see. How learned you are, to read this for pleasure. Or were you reading it at all?'

I could feel my ears turning red and was thankful for the thickness of my hair. Francis, whatever his mood, was always too perceptive by half. I turned wide eyes up at him and said, 'Of course I was.'

'Liar,' said Francis, for once without malice. He sat down beside me on the window-seat and glanced out at the park. 'I noticed the crops are looking somewhat battered – how has the summer been here?'

'Wet, windy and stormy, till today,' I said, wondering whither this polite conversation was leading. 'You've brought the good weather with you.'

Francis gave me a quick smile and then stared abstractedly out of the window again. The vividness of his smile had given him an extraordinary look of Simon: reminded and spurred, I laid a brown paw on the green satin sleeve of his fresh doublet. 'Francis . . . what did happen at Oxford?'

He turned and gazed at me. I caught a wary gleam in his shadowy eyes, but had to continue. 'It's . . . well, I saw Simon looking at you in the hall . . . almost as if – as if he wanted you dead. I wasn't imagining it; Lucy saw it too, I could read her face, and I'm frightened. I mean, I know you've never really liked each other, but it's never been as bad as that before, has it?' I stopped abruptly and stared at the fine lace edging my apron, waiting for the explosion, and wishing that I could learn to keep my mouth closed. There was a long silence. Then Francis put his hands on my shoulders and shook me, gently. 'Thomazine, moi dear owd gal, when will you learn to keep your beaky little nose out of other people's business? What is it to you,' said my cousin, with a smile which stopped short of his eyes, 'what happened at Oxford?'

'Well, it means something to me if you and Simon kill each other!' I said angrily, and then, embarrassed by my outburst, added more quietly, 'I'm sorry, I shouldn't have said that. It must have been my imagination – please forget it.'

'It wasn't your imagination,' Francis said. 'But I'll forget it.'

Supper that evening, in the quiet comfort of the arras parlour rather than the echoing gloom of the dining hall, was nevertheless a subdued, strained affair. No one, not even Lucy or Jamie, said very much, although in their father's absence they were usually wont to chatter freely; and Francis uttered not a word. With Simon's grim eagle's face at the head of the little table, the atmosphere was oppressive enough, and I longed for the food to be finished so that we could rise. Sir Simon was still asleep, and it was not thought wise to disturb him, so after the meal was over we all repaired to the long gallery, lit fierily by the descending sun, and Mary took up her lute. I was glad, for it had always been my delight to submerge my troubles in music and singing, and my childish croak had of late improved to a passable alto. We sang songs and rounds for four and six voices, airs and ditties and ballads and madrigals until the sun vanished behind the trees of the park and a slow twilight crept the length of the gallery. Simon and Francis seemed to forget in singing whatever differences they had, their dark voices complementing the swooping sopranos of Mary and Lucy, my alto and Jamie's true piercing treble. I forgot everything except the intricate patterns of the music, until Mary stopped playing and said, looking at the darkening gallery, 'Shall I ring for candles?'

'Oh, no, not yet,' I said. 'Look at the sunset through the trees, like fire. Candles would spoil it.'

Lucy rose and wandered the length of the gallery to the wide north-west window at its end. 'Do come and look,' she called. 'It's so beautiful. It's as if the sky was burning.'

Francis, Simon and I went to join her. The sunset flamed through the leaves of the summer trees and lit the panelling and our faces with a golden reflected glow. The window was open, and all the park outside was quite silent, as if in respect for the incandescent glory in the sky. Below us in the moat, a single moorhen called softly.

'Well, you can ring for candles,' said Simon prosaically, and turned away. I saw Francis frown as if in anger, and said quickly, 'I'd like to go riding, now, out in the park. Wouldn't it be beautiful?'

'Oh, yes!' Lucy cried, her face lighting up. 'All of us – it won't take a moment to bridle the horses – we wouldn't need saddles, and it's not as if we need to change.'

'You're mad, you would break your neck for sure,' Simon said, a sudden suppressed longing in his face – he was very fond of his sister, and notoriously susceptible to her blandishments. Lucy took his arm and her advantage, smiling up into his face. 'Oh, Simon, do come with us! Please! You haven't been riding with us for so long, and you're not wearing your best suit. Let's have a celebration ride before it's too dark, it won't be dangerous if we're careful, and don't forget we all know every inch of the park.'

'That's as maybe, but I don't want to come home feet first on a hurdle.'

'Well, I'm prepared to risk it,' Francis said, excitement and mischief aflame in his eyes. 'And now, or it'll be too late, and too dark. Come on, brother – or are you so careful of your neck?' And he turned, pulling Lucy with him, to run down the gallery towards the stairs. Simon's long narrow mouth compressed viciously at the insult. 'No more than you!' he said, and followed at a brisk dignified walk. Certain that no good would come of this, I said to Jamie, who was looking expectant, 'Are you coming too?'

' 'Course I am!' Jamie shouted, and with a whoop chased after his brothers and sister, scattering music books and sending a spare lute string spinning across the polished boards in his haste. Feeling of a sudden far older and wiser than my thirteen and a half years, I exchanged resigned looks with Mary, and went in pursuit.

The stableyard was dark, the grooms at supper, and we found our mounts and bridled them ourselves, amid a great deal of laughter and confusion in which Simon was noticeably silent. 'A race!' Lucy said, breathlessly, dragging her little chestnut mare Zenocrate out into the yard. 'A race to the warren and back. What do you say, yes or no?'

'No,' Francis said. 'We'll have a chase.' He mounted Hobgoblin without aid of mounting-block, and they danced sideways out of the gate. Lucy and I followed, urging our ponies in pursuit; then Simon on his big bay gelding, wearing disapproval and reluctance and anger like a cloak, and finally Jamie, hampered by his round shaggy Bauble, and the too-large bridle Francis had unkindly handed him in the stables.

I had not believed that the so-familiar park could take on such a strange and wonderful beauty. The trees stood black against the lambent sky, crimson and scarlet, green and turquoise and deepest blue, a very rainbow in the west. I sat Tamburlaine, astride with my skirts all bunched up, and stared spellbound until Jamie passed me, and Francis, somewhere in the gloom ahead, shouted in a voice filled with joyous, wild, desperate laughter, 'Follow me! Follow me, who dares!' And we were off.

Never shall I forget that ride. Our horses raced blindly through the park, trusting to instinct to avoid rabbit-holes, fallen branches, unexpected tussocks and other notable hazards; we crouched over their necks, our faces lost in the flying manes, laughing with exultation and fear. Once, Francis rode straight into the deer, feeding quietly in the long grass, and for a moment as we followed him helter-skelter, we were jostled by startled, bewildered does and fawns with, here and there, thrown sharp black against the dying embers of the still-magnificent sky, the palmate antlers of a stag. Then, smelling man, they made off, galloping raggedly through the trees, and Francis reined in where they had been. 'We've had our chase,' he said. 'Now we'll have Lucy's race. Where to? The warren?'

'The warren!' Lucy cried, breathless and overexcited. 'And back to the house again. Are you all ready? *Go!*'

We must have had moon-madness that night. Crashing through the park, following my instinct and Tamburlaine's nose, I forgot all my worries and became a child again, thinking of nothing but the heady brilliant wildness of that ride, and afterwards could recall little of it save for the exultation; which drained abruptly away when Piper's Wood loomed like a great wall ahead of us in the gloom. It was like something watching me. Noises came out of it; Tamburlaine stopped of his own accord just at the foot of the trees, and I could feel his unease. Of my cousins there was no sound or trace, and I did not know where in the park I was. Loneliness and fear crowded in on me as the owls in the wood shrieked and hooted; I resolutely ignored them, turned Tamburlaine to the right and urged him along the edge of the wood. The pony refused to do more than a walk, and when, with a fearful screech an owl shot past us in a ghostly blur of white he panicked, rearing and plunging whilst I did my best to control him. As he quietened at last I slid off his back and took his bridle, talking to him softly and rubbing his nose while he stood and quivered. And then I heard voices.

I listened intently. They were too far away to distinguish words, but the general tone was another matter. With a cold feeling in my stomach, I tucked my skirts up into my waistband, took firmer hold of Tamburlaine and led him towards the sounds. It was obvious before we had gone twenty yards that it was Francis and Simon; also obvious that they were quarrelling. Careful to make no sound, I crept nearer, still leading the pony, until I was in a position to hear everything, and crouched in a nest of grass, straining my eyes to see.

'I've put up with you for nigh on seventeen years,' Simon was saying between his teeth, 'but slurs on my courage before our mother and sister can't be borne. For God's sake, man, what devil's got into you?'

'None that was not there always,' Francis said cheerfully. I could see him, outlined against the sky, sitting easily on his horse. Simon had dismounted and, judging by the noise, was striding back and forth through the bracken in his agitation. He paused, and said, 'And that is true, too. If it were not for the gross slander upon my lady mother, I would be inclined to wonder about your parentage. You're different, a stranger to us . . . Were you changed at nurse, to be so alien?'

'Undoubtedly,' Francis said sarcastically. 'I'm an elfin child put into this world wholly for purposes of mischief . . . my brother, are you not capable of taking a joke?'

Simon made a noise in his throat. 'A joke! A joke is it, to insult me as you did tonight? Is it a joke to profess atheism? To meddle with your foul experiments? To swim in the river in open defiance of the vice-chancellor's orders?'

'Ah, that was harmless enough!'

'Harmless, you say? One lad nearly drowned!'

'I should know, I pulled him out.'

'His death would have been on your conscience, if you possess one, so that it is fortunate you did. But is it so harmless to return to our rooms more drunk than sober two nights out of three, and you scarcely sixteen? To boast of lying with half the whores in Oxford—'

'—That's a lie, I'll swear it's only a quarter!'

'—and of cuckolding a godly and sober citizen and getting his wife with child—'

'That's a lie too, the child was neither his nor mine, and certainly he's worn horns before—'

'Be silent!' Simon roared, and all the birds flew startled out of the nearest tree and circled above their heads with a clatter of wings. 'Before God, you should be on your knees begging Him for forgiveness for your sins. Instead you laugh. What in Christ's name are you?'

'Only a man,' Francis said. Frozen with horror, I could

tell by his voice that he was taking a malicious pleasure in all this. 'Only a man who prefers to take his pleasures in this world, rather than store them up for the rather unlikely promises of the next . . . but tell me, who has been hurt by all of this? Have I killed, or maimed, or stolen, or deflowered some tender young maiden on false promise of marriage? Have I? Who complains against me?'

In a voice thick with rage, Simon said, 'I do. Against your sins, your viciousness, your blasphemy. Our father charged me with your care at Oxford, both material and spiritual, and it will be a sorry tale for me to relate to him tomorrow. As if that strumpet at Catholm were not enough, I now have to list all your depravities at Oxford as well . . . I have no desire to see you end in Hell, and nor has he.'

'That's out of more concern for the family name, I fancy, than for me.'

Dazed, I felt it was time to intervene before murder was done. Later, I would go over their words again and again, but as yet the full significance of what they had said had not sunk in, and my immediate duty was to break up the quarrel. I backed away, head down, pulling Tamburlaine with me, until I reached what I considered to be a safe distance. Then I called, loudly. 'Simon! Simon, is that you?'

'What?' Simon's voice had not lost its anger. I crashed noisily through the bracken and grass, pulling my skirts into decent folds around my legs. 'Simon?'

'Yes, I'm here. Who is it?'

'Thomazine, of course,' I said, arriving beside him, pony in tow. 'I'm glad I found you, I thought I'd lost myself. An owl flew past Tamburlaine's nose and he threw me,' I added, thinking that a reason for my undoubtedly disreputable state was needed, even though it would not be visible until we returned to the house. 'It was a lucky thing I landed softly in the bracken. Who else is here? Francis?'

'Yes, I'm here,' said Francis warily, and I wondered if he had guessed that I had been listening. I went on, hastily, 'I haven't seen Lucy and Jamie at all – do you think they've gone back to the house?'

'Probably,' Simon said curtly. 'The most sensible thing for

us to do too, I should think. It's quite dark and Mother might be worried. Whose crackbrained idea was this, anyway?'

'Mine,' I said, 'and you didn't have to come, either of you. Which way is home?'

'Behind you,' Francis told me. 'You can see the lights.' He turned his horse towards them and vanished with a soft rustling trot into the darkness. I was left with Simon; we both mounted in silence, and rode quietly after him. Neither of us, for our own good reasons, were prepared to indulge in much conversation. I was busy pondering this picture of Francis the wild-living student. Even at my tender age I was not particularly shocked, for my upbringing at Ashcott and at Goldhayes had not been particularly sheltered, I had seen my father and his cronies drunk and heard the village gossip about its amorous young men (and women), and my discovery of the letter from Great-Aunt Elizabeth about the girl at Catholm had in a sense prepared me for this development, but I still found it very hard to reconcile this sensual side of Francis with the idealist who had spoken of unicorns and played on the lute with mathematical passion. Then I bethought myself of the malicious child who had made subtle fun of his tutor and cooked mischief enough for an army of children, and wondered less. Simon's reaction I found more puzzling. He was notorious for his priggishness, true, but his rage and his condemnation of his brother had had a most untypical note of hysteria about it. I had not thought him so prudish a Puritan.

During the days that followed our sunset ride, I watched the two brothers closely, eavesdropped shamelessly and put my wits to work as to why their old mild antipathy should have suddenly taken this more serious turn. Over the weeks of their summer holiday, they circled each other like a pair of fighting-cocks, occasionally indulging in a seemingly mild exchange of words with a world of animosity beneath.

I saw with unhappiness Lucy's distress at the rift between her brothers, and justified my unseemly curiosity by the thought that, if I could only divine the reasons for their quarrel I would have a chance of effecting some sort of reconciliation. Quite what I, in my cheerful naïvety, thought that I could do to patch up so deep-seated an antipathy I do not remember, but my wish somehow to return matters to the old happy days of my first years at Goldhayes was paramount.

I avoided asking Francis any direct questions, wondering if he guessed that I had overheard that quarrel in the park. Simon, who considered himself the injured party, and whose skin was several layers thicker than his brother's, was given to dropping strongly worded hints about Francis's activities at Oxford, and from these, hearsay, eavesdropping and cunning questioning, I gleaned a little of what had happened.

Simon at Oxford had been a qualified success. He shone at his studies, a hard worker and an intelligent one, and among the more serious students his high principles and sincerely held beliefs made him respected and liked, if not loved; for Simon was not one to make friends easily and all too often retreated into a chilly, awkward formality with those he did not know intimately. However, his first two years at Christ Church convinced him, if he had needed convincing, of his own worth and righteousness. Then Francis joined him, the sun in splendour to Simon's cold moon, and proceeded to draw to himself all the scholars who had the least inclination to wildness. Simon had always rather despised his brother's ways, and it was a profound disillusionment to find that many of his friends and acquaintances preferred the 'worthless' brother, with his vices, brittle brilliance and spectacular imagination, to himself. His vanity and his opinion of Oxford alike received a stunning blow, and he began to regard Francis, who found time both to study effectively and to sample the town's assorted pleasures to the full, with a disgust and horror which rapidly turned to loathing. To my ears, the thinly disguised hatred with which he spoke of Francis's more repeatable exploits in Oxford was partly composed of genuine moral feeling and partly of envy, envy for the laughter and popularity which seemed to be Francis's birthright, and which made him the leader and instigator of a dazzling variety of student misdeeds while Simon pored over his books in their room. It seemed to me that this suppressed jealousy accounted for much of Simon's extreme attitude. I discussed the situation with Lucy at night, punctuated by her gasps of horror at Francis's doings, and she had her answer ready. 'What Simon needs is a wife. He's lonely, really, I'm sure,' said my cousin with the utter unshaken certainty of her thirteen years of worldly experience, 'and he wants someone to take his mind off Francis. Why, oh why, doesn't he marry Nan? They've been promised since they were babies.'

'Simon has to finish at Oxford first,' I pointed out, 'and then it may be too late; the last I heard, her brother had been promised the next place for her at Court with the Princess Mary or the Queen, and I expect then she'll make a better match, to an earl or someone like that.'

'I do hope she doesn't,' Lucy said. 'She loves Simon, I can see it in her face when she's here.'

'More fool her,' I said. 'Would you want to marry someone who'll love you out of duty? I wouldn't.'

'Nor would I,' said Lucy. She rolled over onto her back and clasped her hands behind her head. In the dim light filtering through the cracks in the curtains, I could see her eyes shining. 'I don't care what Father will say, I shall marry for love, like Juliet. I don't care if he's an earl's son or a cotter's; if he loves me, and I him, that'll be enough.'

I wondered how long this cheerful optimism would be sustained in the face of the kind of pressure I had glimpsed when told of my impending marriage to Dominic. Lucy was lucky, however, for as yet her parents had not bestirred themselves to find her a husband, although I gathered that they had once harboured vague thoughts of marrying her to Dominic, before he had taken a fancy to me. It would be best for them to hurry, for Lucy was rapidly becoming a beauty, and the combination of that, her birth and wealth and her irrepressibly romantic nature was an explosive one. However, I led her firmly back to the subject in hand. 'That's all very well, but what are we going to do about Simon and Francis?'

'I don't see that we can do anything, really,' Lucy said gloomily. 'Well, would *you* want to ask them politely not to hate each other? I value my life, personally.'

'Personally,' I said, 'I can't wait for them to go back to Oxford. These last weeks have been something of a strain. It's like living permanently in a cock-pit.'

Lucy giggled. 'I wonder what Francis will think of in Oxford next. I know he's turned Simon against him with all the things he's done, but Simon's a stuffy old bore, and I did like the story of when he smoked them out of dinner with his alchemy experiments.'

'I suppose,' I said with mock-weariness, 'we can be considered fortunate that he doesn't try them here. We'd have half the village thinking him a warlock.'

So a certain relief settled on us all when, in September, the brothers returned to the university and we could once more live at peace. When they did not visit us for Christmas, I was at once relieved and sorry. The brief letters which arrived by carrier or postboy, in Simon's stiff upright hand or Francis's swift, ornate and idiosyncratic one, gave no hint of any continuing enmity, but it was obvious that it could not have vanished overnight. At the thought of the summer of 1639 which lay ahead, my heart sank: but we were saved by help from an unexpected quarter.

It was a fine day for February, sunny and warm for the season. Lucy, Jamie, Tom Sewell and I had formed part of a hawking party in the rough ground bordering the River Lark by Rushbrooke, along with young Robert Jermyn, Nan and Henry Blagge and a sprinkling of Gages and Herveys. It had been a happy, carefree afternoon and now we wended our way home amidst jokes and riddles and laughter and snatches of song. As we came in sight of the

Home Farm, Tom stood up in his stirrups and said, 'Who's that?'

In the long road ahead of us, running straight down to the farm and the sharp left-hand fork into Goldhayes' park, was a little group of strange horsemen, riding wearily in the same direction as were we. 'Four men,' Tom said, shading his eyes, 'and a woman. Who can they be? That looks as if they've come far.'

Lucy, who was a trifle short-sighted, peered down the road. 'Edward and Henry?' she suggested, improbably.

Tom looked again and stared. 'Yes, it is, you're right! Look, thass Henry's hair I can see. Come on, let's catch them up!' He laid spurs to his horse and we all galloped down the lane towards them. It was indeed Edward and Henry, with their two servants and Henry's wife. There was the usual exuberant flurry of meeting, Lucy pressing her immaculate riding-habit heedlessly against Edward's dust- and mud-caked doublet and shedding tears of joy. When everyone had quietened themselves, we made as one for the Home Farm, to be greeted rapturously by Joan and John, and to partake of a liberal early supper. It was only then that we had a chance to exchange news and to take stock of each other after more than three years apart. Edward had left us a quiet, solid, diffident boy, very different from the confident, sun-darkened young man, strongly-muscled and loud-voiced, who sat on the old oak bench wolfing large mouthfuls of Joan's rabbit pie, and talking vigorously of his experiences in the Prince of Orange's army. Henry also had changed; self-contained as always, he followed the talk with a smile between his russet moustache and pointed beard, and there was a new man-of-the-world air about him that set him apart from the rest of his talkative, unpretentious family. No doubt to them the four of us were startlingly different – Lucy and I children no longer, outwardly at least, with our feminine contours (Lucy's fashionable plumpness being more feminine than my neat, slight figure) and elegant attire, Tom tall and deep-voiced, his Suffolk speech largely dissolved by his Goldhayes education, with an incipient moustache and a youthful clumsiness in his big bones. Jamie, although taller and broader, was the least altered.

And beside Henry, her long hand on his, sat Henry's Irish wife, and she was all and more that Edward had described. Like Henry, she said little, but her eyes followed us as we spoke, and there was a smile deep within them. I could at once understand why Henry had fallen so deep in love, for she was beautiful, white-skinned and slender, with a pure oval face, delicate features and long-lashed green eyes. She obviously paid scant regard to fashion, for her thick black hair was uncurled and too long, and her dress was of simple homespun, dark red, with a plain white collar. The reason for their return was evidently the fact that she was far gone with child. Why she had chosen Henry for her husband was less obvious, for to my naïve mind a girl so lovely could have had her pick of men, and Tom's brother was a man of plain appearance, unfashionably red-haired and freckled, simple in his tastes and humbly-born.

'But why,' Tom was asking, 'why didn't you tell us you was coming home? We could have made things more ready for you. As it is, I'll have to surrender my bed.'

'You can't think of nawn but your own comfort,' said Joan, who always took him too seriously.

Tom made a face at her and continued. 'But Lucy should be pleased, she's got a grand excuse now to put on her play in your honour.'

I closed my eyes and groaned inwardly, for our wet afternoons since before Christmas had been almost exclusively spent in rehearsing *A Woman Killed with Kindness*, and I was more than a little tired of it. Lucy, whose taste usually ran to more exotic works, had however been touched by the sentimental tragedy almost to obsession. 'Yes, that's a marvellous idea, Tom, we can make all ready in a few days and it would be a splendid welcome for you all,' she said now with enthusiasm. Edward tipped his head back to study the ceiling, the smoke from his clay pipe wreathing his dark head. 'Lucy, my girl, I refuse utterly to watch your infernal play. I'm sorry, but there it is. I've better things to do with my time.'

'Oh, please,' Lucy wheedled, putting her head on his chest and rubbing her cheek on the rough leather. Edward roared with laughter. 'Who's the most spoiled brat in Suffolk, eh? What do you say, Henry?'

Henry smiled. 'Well, I feel in need of some merriment after the sights we've seen.'

'But it's a tragedy!' Lucy wailed.

'Not when we act it, it isn't,' I said, *sotto voce*.

'The question is,' Henry continued, 'whether Grainne in her condition will survive the experience.'

'I said you'd come back when she was likely!' Joan said triumphantly.

'Also,' Edward added, 'there's the prospect of employment here, should we miss soldiering – I hear there's trouble with the Scots.'

'You can't fight Scots,' Lucy said indignantly, 'some of our cousins are Scottish.' Henry shrugged. 'They're in open rebellion against the rightful authority of the King – a short sharp lesson is all that's needed, although from what I hear the King's army is in no case to deliver it.'

'And the reason,' Edward pointed out, 'is patently obvious. They're jailbirds for the most part, pressed men or militiamen who scarcely know one end of a pike from the other. What wouldn't an army like ours do?' And the two were instantly deep in soldiering talk with an air of working familiar ground, Tom and Lucy gazing fascinated, and Jamie hanging on every word. I caught the Irish girl's eye, and she smiled. On impulse, I said, 'I expect you've heard it all many times before. Would you like to take a stroll in the garden?'

Despite Joan's look of horror at thus risking the unborn child (although since it had survived the journey from Holland it must perforce be tough), we rose and slipped outside to the sunny front garden bordering the lane, out of sight and smell of the farmyard at the back. Grainne was much taller than I, but unusually that did not make me ill-at-ease. She was, after all, only three years my senior, and I was drawn to her still friendliness. We stood on the neat gravel path, looking round at the clipped silver-grey lavender edging the flowerbeds, the snowdrops and Christmas roses and winter cabbage and the stout rosemary bush by the door, and Grainne sighed and said with happiness, 'It's so quiet in England, so beautiful, so untouched. I can't believe in the safety of it.'

'I think we take that for granted,' I said to her. 'Perhaps if we saw the troubles in Europe we'd be more appreciative of what we have here.'

Grainne said with quiet vehemence, 'I wouldn't wish anyone to see some of the things I've seen . . . If I were a man or bred to such things, it might be different, but I was reared in Cork with my mother, till she died when I was thirteen and my father came for me . . . and before my fourteenth birthday I had seen babies starved to death or disembowelled with their mothers, men killed or terribly wounded, villages and towns burned to ashes and the whole land laid to waste. My father could not understand why I never grew used to it. He thought he had done me such a great service by plucking me from my aunt's home in Cork to follow him to the wars, and it distressed him sorely that I begged him to take me back, unkind and hard though she had been to me, rather than be with him. And then he died, after Breda was taken, and I realized how much I had owed to his protection . . . Henry saved me from an unspeakable fate.' She shivered in the cool damp wind. 'I still wake at nights, sometimes, dreaming of the guns, and I can't believe I'll never hear them again.'

'You may wish for them,' I said, 'when you come to know us better. Tom Blagge at Horringer said he'd sooner live with a tribe of apes.'

'I would never wish for war here,' said the Irish girl. 'I want my son to grow up in peace and plenty, and know the joys of civilization rather than barbarism . . . Tom Blagge is the courtier, isn't he? Edward and Henry have told me a good deal about you all already. But I'm not accustomed to things courtly, and I've no patience with mincing, prinking gentlemen who can think of naught but the pattern and cut and colour of their next satin doublet – and so I think being a Sewell will suit me very well.'

'The Herons are not so different,' I said, rubbing a fragrant leaf of lavender between my fingers. 'We think more of ourselves, and perhaps with less cause – but I've never been to London or seen the King, and the talk here is of farming, or horses, or old-fashioned plays, or music, or whether Bradfield Tye will beat Bradfield St Clare at the midsummer football.'

Grainne smiled, a slow long warm smile which for the first time touched all her face, and gave to her rather cool, angelic beauty a look more human. 'Henry has told me of that too, and how the whole parish turns out to play, women too, and of all the splinting and bandaging needed after. I don't know if I'm looking forward to it.'

'And football is nothing to our native Suffolk game of Camp,' I said, laughing, 'the dead and wounded after a match of that can rival any contest of arms, especially if it's played with shoes on – that's called "Savage Camp".'

'Then I shall have to stock up my chest of medicines,' said Grainne, still smiling, 'and pray that it will be needed for nothing worse.'

And so Grainne, with her calm face and soft Irish voice, came to Goldhayes and became our friend; and is our friend still. Her presence had an influence of quiet, both upon us and upon the irrepressible Sewells. With grace and tact, she helped Joan with the domestic work at the farm, as far as her pregnancy allowed her, revealed to us a decided talent for singing and playing the virginals, and displayed an unexpected repertoire of Irish song, both in Gaelic and in translation, accompanying her own high, pure voice on her native harp. She was friendly, attentive and humorous, with a delightful way of ignoring some of the more ridiculous requirements of polite female behaviour. In particular, her habit of walking abroad alone, even in the last weeks before the birth, with her head uncovered in the coldest weather, and her simple unfashionable garb, excited comment amongst the locals. Half of them thought her admirable. The other half were of the strong opinion that, 'She dew fare t'be hully gatless, a-traipsin' around loik that, an' har loikely an' all.'

126

At Goldhayes, Mary was the only one who regarded her with disfavour. Refined and ladylike herself, she had little time for those who were not, and not even Grainne's love of music could redeem her. She was never downright rude, but she either ignored Henry's wife as much as possible, talked about her to her maids or her aunt behind her back, or made sly barbed comments to sour the atmosphere between them. But Mary had always set herself very much apart from us, preferring the company of her maids, her aunt and neighbours and friends such as Lady Penelope (her particular crony) or Mistress Jermyn, to that of her children or of her husband, so that her disapproval of Grainne was not as inconvenient as it might have been. Mary's husband, on the other hand, was much taken with Grainne (which may in part have explained Mary's hostility towards her) and she spent many hours by his sickbed, talking with him of matters philosophical, agricultural and horticultural, and describing the situation in Europe with the enthusiastic and often blood-chilling support of her husband and of Edward. It was these talks, led by Grainne, which first showed me that my guardian was not only the cold, dry, religious tyrant of my childhood, but also a man of wide knowledge and unexpected interests, who could display on occasion a wit I had scarcely known to exist.

Six weeks after her arrival, late in March, Grainne's baby was born. There had not been such an event in either family since the youngest of my cousins, another Henry, had been laid to rest nine years previously at the tender age of two days; and so the excitement was great. The Bury midwife and a team of capable local women were summoned, and Dr Despotine himself had advised Grainne as to her preparation for the birth. It became evident, however, that the baby's arrival would not be easy. Lucy and I, as unmarried gentlewomen, were excluded and spent a miserable two days in the parlour of the Home Farm, or at Goldhayes, awaiting news and praying that we ourselves, when our times came, would not suffer thus. Henry gave up his food entirely and hung around the farm yard shouting morose orders at the labourers whenever his anxieties got the better of him. In the end, when it became apparent that both mother and baby would most likely be lost, Dr Despotine arrived, breathing garlic and briskness over everything, and set to work. Not once during all that time did we hear Grainne cry out; the first that we knew of success was when, in the darkening spring evening, the faint cries of a distressed baby echoed thinly through the house. The child was a boy, rusty-haired like his father, and he and Grainne were weak but otherwise said to be progressing well. Just in case, the child was baptized the next day, and in gratitude Henry directed that he be called Jasper, for Dr Despotine. Edward was among the other godparents.

It was full summer before Grainne was quite recovered and could ride and walk freely as of old. She insisted on nursing the infant herself, in spite of custom, and young Jasper prospered greatly in her care. Henry was inordinately proud of his offspring, despite his small size, and became quite tedious with his conversations about the baby's rapid development. As Edward once pointed out, it was as though Jasper was the first child ever fathered by man.

In July, Francis and Simon returned from Oxford for the harvest, still with the thinly-disguised animosity between them like a wall. In six months, Lucy and I had become sufficiently well-acquainted with Grainne to apprise her of the situation between the two brothers, and Edward was similarly informed. For people so remarkably dissimilar, they agreed very well in their assessment of the problem. 'The harvest should keep Simon busy, and Francis apart from him,' Grainne said, her green eyes thoughtful. 'As yet, of course, I don't know either of them from Adam, but that seems the path of sense.' And Edward, with a cheerful smile, pinched Lucy's anxious cheek and said, 'Don't worry, sweetheart, as long as they don't have the time to be at each other's throats it'll be all right.'

In truth, that summer was good. Simon, forced by his

father's incapacity into the many tasks and duties required of a landlord and gentleman and farmer, involved himself in the work with his customary conscientiousness, and his habitual worried frown was due to the state of the weather or the price of corn rather than to the misdeeds of his errant younger brother. He was obviously glad of Edward's cheerful, steady assistance, and also was frequently seen in the company of Henry, whose quiet, deep temperament was in some ways very similar to his own. Henry's wife, however, rather took Simon aback; he had always had a soft spot for a feminine, intelligent woman but did not know quite what to make of Grainne, who was too independent and unconventional to be entirely acceptable.

Francis, on the other hand, took to her as I did, and the three of us and Lucy became fast friends, sharing our thoughts and our music and our sports until September, so that the dreaded quarrel seemed almost forgotten. When he and Simon returned to Oxford it was a sad parting, and filled with a sense of loss not only of Francis but of our happiness, I came shamefully close to tears. I saw Grainne looking sharply at me during the farewells; afterwards, when we were walking in the garden at Goldhayes, she said, 'You are very fond of Francis, aren't you?'

'Yes,' I said without thinking, 'we've always accorded well; we think alike . . .' I stopped, seeing her look, and added, 'No, I know what you think, Grainne Sewell, and there's no truth in it! He's like my brother, as Simon and Edward and Jamie are. Anyway, I'm betrothed to another.'

'Are you? I didn't know.'

'It's not a formal agreement, just an understanding. I forget it myself, often.' I shivered slightly. 'He's a cousin – Sir Simon's nephew in fact, and I haven't seen him since I was ten and he sixteen or so.'

'And did you like him?'

I stopped and faced her. 'No. No, I didn't. He had a way of looking at me . . . as though I was much older, as though he wanted to . . .' I flushed uncomfortably, and added, 'When he touched me, it made me feel cold inside. Do you think me foolish?'

'No, though in nearly five years he might have changed somewhat,' Grainne said, resuming her leisurely pace. 'When was the wedding arranged for?'

'I don't know. When I'm sixteen or so, I suppose. The intention was for me to complete my education here – if you can call it an education – and then to be wed. But no one ever mentions it, and I hope it's been forgotten.'

'So you don't want to marry him? What will you do if they try to force you?'

'Well,' I said, 'Sir Simon and his lady wife can hardly drag me screaming to the altar. I shall just refuse. There's little they can do to me, and whatever they do can't last forever. I'm a Heron, you see, and our motto is "No surrender".'

'It's Sir Simon's also,' Grainne said.

'I think I could outlast him,' I told her, with more confidence than I actually felt. Grainne studied my face. 'Yes,' she said at last, 'yes, I think you very probably could.'

But by the spring of 1640 it was fast becoming apparent that Sir Simon Heron would not live to see the year out. He grew daily weaker, but refused with the family obstinacy to die, and insisted on taking as much of an interest as possible in estate business, despite his very competent steward. When Simon and Francis came home from Oxford for their summer visit, it was plainly obvious that if they went back as usual in September they would not again see their father alive. For any other than Simon, who was shortly due to take his BA and would on his father's death be expected to assume the full management of the estate, the choice between his duty or a pleasurable scholarly existence might have been difficult; but Simon did not hesitate. He spent many hours with his father, discussing estate matters, and with the house steward and with John Sewell, and the only books into which he delved were those pertaining to matters agricultural. A letter was sent to their Oxford tutor apprising him of the situation, and in an atmosphere of gloom and resigned apprehension, Goldhayes awaited the death of its lord.

The end came late in November, a season even more stormy and wet than usual. Friends and neighbours had come to say their farewells in numbers which surprised me, for I had thought my guardian to be respected, but not loved. When the procession of Jermyns and Gages and Herveys, Blagges and Mannocks and Barbers and Barnadistons had departed, the family gathered dry-eyed around the bed to be with him at the end. The wasted grey face on the pillows looked utterly unlike the vigorous cripple who had ruled his children more strictly than he might have wished. He lingered two days, unconscious, before he died, so that the end came as a relief, both for his sake and for ours, and only Lucy wept.

Numbly, we emerged from the chamber, leaving the offices of death to be performed by Mary and her maids and village women. It was a damp and squally afternoon, and the drumming rain against the windows had been perhaps the last sound to touch Sir Simon Heron's senses. Dr Davis, ever eager to fulfil his role, was making strenuous attempts to offer comfort to the bereaved. At any other time, the sight of Lucy weeping on his shoulder, and being unctuously patted, would have brought me to laughter; even now, ill-timed as it was, I was hard put to it to suppress a smile.

'Mistress Lucy, take comfort, for he is with God,' Dr Davis murmured, his voice taking on a Welsh note as his emotions got the better of him. 'And surely you and he will meet once more, in Heaven, in the company of angels ... Do not fear, this is not the end for your father, for men such as he, wise and righteous in the eyes of the Lord, are assured of a place with Christ in heaven ...'

'Though why I can't think,' Francis said, his face alive with a casual delighted cruelty which seemed to stop my heart. 'And for Christ's sake stop snivelling, Lucy. You wouldn't do it if you didn't have an audience ...'

As Lucy jerked round, mouth open and the tears arrested in mid-flow, Simon stepped forward, his hand raised.

Francis dodged, quickly, his eyes holding his brother's. 'It's best to be cruel to be kind, you know. She'll make herself ill.'

Hastily, I plunged into the breach, aware of the shocked wondering eyes of the two servants in the corner of the anteroom. 'This is no moment for a quarrel, is it? Your father scarce departed . . . Francis, I want to talk to you.' And with a fervour born of desperation towed him out of the door and into the panelled parlour beyond. Mercifully, it was empty. Conscious of the muffled talk in the room we had just left, I faced my errant cousin and said angrily, 'I despair of you, Francis Heron! Why, oh why, do you do it?'

'Do what?'

'You know exactly what I mean! You used Lucy's grief to bait Simon, and insulted your father's memory with him hardly dead . . . One of these days,' I said, with my anger evaporating into sadness, 'Simon will lose his patience entirely and murder will be done. Is that what you want? Is it? Because if it is, it'd be better for us all if you went now to that window and jumped into the moat.'

The silence that followed my words was deafening. Francis stood in front of me, studying my earnest face. 'That's not what you want, though.'

'No, it is not! I want you to stop obeying whatever demon prompts you to sow discord and turn Simon against you. We all used to be so happy,' I said, feeling the tears prick my eyes and determined not to shed them, 'until you got it into your thick skull that it was clever and amusing to torment Simon, and since then it's all changed, can't you see! How can we all be friends when you're at each other's throats every time we're together . . . .' I stopped, not understanding the look on his face, and at that moment the outer door was opened to admit John Sewell, summoned from the farm when it had become clear that Sir Simon would not last the hour, and now arrived too late. Behind him were Henry and Tom, damp and muddy, and Grainne, her rain-darkened hood thrown back from her face. As the door was shut gently behind them, I said, 'I'm sorry. He died not ten minutes ago.'

A change came over John's weathered face, making it

heavier and older; he put his hand on my shoulder, slowly, and patted it. 'Aye, mistress, and I'm sorry too, the more so as we come too late . . . I reckon he was a right good man, and uncommon good to the Sewells, being as he did so much for my lads. And you, Francis, you've lost a father kinder than you know, though I doubt you think that now.'

I stared at Francis's still face, daring him to argue. My cousin, ignoring me, turned to John. 'My family is in here. I expect you want to see him, and I know Simon will wish to speak with you.' And they entered the antechamber, followed by the solemn Henry and Tom. Grainne caught my eye and said in a quick whisper, 'Were you having a quarrel?'

'Not exactly . . . just giving him a piece of my mind.'

'Giving Francis a piece of one's mind,' Grainne said, 'is like seeing water run off a duck's back. I won't ask why you were doing thus.'

'I'll tell you, one day,' I answered, and followed her into the antechamber.

So on the 28th November in the year 1640, Sir Simon Heron was laid to rest at the church of St Peter at Bradfield Tye, in the company of his ancestors and of his three children who had not lived beyond babyhood. The night was dry and the torchlit, solemn procession which accompanied him on his last journey was a most beautiful and impressive sight. Much was said amongst mourners and in the pulpit of his virtues and of the sorrow his death had brought. To my relief, Simon and Francis seemed to be going out of their way to avoid another such unseemly quarrel, and the row of black-clad, sorrowing young Herons at the funeral was almost as impressive as the torches and the mourners.

Although Christmas was approaching, there was little enthusiasm in the gloomy, black-draped house for any festivities. Simon, making the difficult adjustment from heir to head of the household, we hardly ever saw, for he was frequently absent inspecting his new possessions within Suffolk and further afield. Edward did his best on the farm helping John and Henry, but was visibly restless. The Scots wars had ended in ignominious defeat for the King, the English army which he had entertained thoughts of joining was unemployed, and he began to wonder audibly about a return to the Low Countries, without Henry but possibly with Francis, who showed no sign of returning to Oxford in the New Year. It was as well that Simon was too busy to take him to task, for Francis had no intention of going back to Christ Church, still less of proceeding to the Temple to commence training for a lawyer, and said as much to Lucy, Grainne and myself. 'For it's my own life, to dispose as I think fit, and I'll not be ordered to Oxford or to the Temple to fulfil Simon's wish to have me out of the way.'

I said dubiously, 'But returning to Oxford doesn't commit you to being a lawyer.'

'It commits me to a great deal of hard work, and I've got out of the way of book-learning. Besides, there's precious little of worth to learn. If you mention mathematics to most of them, they look at you as if you're mazed, and any meddling with alchemy is enough to brand you a sorcerer. If there's beauty in knowledge, they stifle it. Does my brilliant disputation in Greek, or Latin, on some pettifogging little trifle, like how many angels can be fitted on to a pinhead, make me a better man? I doubt it. Can't you see,' Francis said, with the same unusual urgency in his voice as he had had when he talked long ago of unicorns, 'can't you see that learning at Oxford is dead? What have I learned there to tell me of the marvels of Peru or the fruits of Virginia? What do I know of music or of painting or of science, save what I have taught myself from books? There have been other races and other faiths on the earth than the Greeks and Romans and Jews, but to hear them you would not think it. They do not allow wisdom to any but themselves and their classical favourites, who have mostly been dead for a thousand and a half years, and with few exceptions knew precious little about what they wrote. I can converse elegantly and translate Greek and Latin and Hebrew, but if you set me down in Rome or in Heidelberg or even in Constantinople, I could not ask my way. Our tutor is old-fashioned, and hates new ideas, or argument with his precious opinions. I have learned many things at Oxford which I value, but none of them from him, and I have made up my mind not to go back.'

'But what will Simon say?' I demanded; and Francis leaned back in his chair and said, 'Simon can go to the devil.'

'I think,' said Grainne slowly, 'that Simon could accept all of this did you not have to fling it in his face like a challenge.'

'I don't feel I have to make it acceptable,' Francis remarked. 'As I have said previously, my life is not his to be arranged by him. He's not three years older than me, and head of the Herons or no, he's not in a father's place.'

'But you wouldn't obey Father in this either,' Lucy said, 'I remember what you told me you'd say to him if he tried to force you to the Temple.'

'And what was that?'

'That you'd liefer go to Ned in the Low Countries,' I said. 'I remember that too.'

'Well, that still holds good,' Francis said, with the same mischievous look on his face. 'Edward has a yearning to go back, and I think he'd like my company. Simon will be glad to be rid of me and so, I suspect, will you.'

That, I thought, was as may be, but Simon had ever been loath to accept compromise, and I knew that Francis's departure to the Low Countries, however convenient it might be, would be seen as a challenge to his newly found authority as head of the household. My dilemma was acute, for I did not want relations between my two cousins to be strained more; but I could not wish either that Francis should meekly submit to his brother's demands. It was not in his character to do so, nor, in my own heart, could I desire it to be. I decided eventually, after some days of thought, that I would tackle Simon when the opportunity arose, and put forward the idea of Francis going to Holland with Edward as my own, knowing that it would thus be more kindly received.

Early in March, the first foals were born to Edward's beloved horses. Kept in paddocks next to the house, nourished with sweet hay and oats and fresh Suffolk grass, sheltered in dark, warm stables in times of sickness or inclement weather, they were more comfortable than many a cotter's family. I had always loved to go into the stables, listening to the quiet shuffling and munching of contented horses, feeling the thick warm aromatic atmosphere surrounding me, and particularly to watch the new foals with their long unsteady legs and wide curious eyes. So when Francis came to tell us that his own mare, Hobgoblin, had successfully dropped her first foal, I was eager to see it. 'What colour is it? Colt or filly?'

'Come and look for yourself,' Francis offered, and Lucy looked over her book and said, 'It won't run away, and one foal's much like another, and besides it's much too cold. I've got my fur tippet on now, and I don't want the bother of going out in a cloak just to cross the stable yard.'

'You sound just like your mother,' I said, grinning, 'but don't worry, Francis, *I'll* come to share your delight.'

Together we walked through the house. It was afternoon, and the kitchen was being cleared after the bustle of preparing the dinner. Monsieur Harcourt was making little animals out of sugar paste for some extravagant confection, and was unable to prevent Francis from tiptoeing up behind him and snatching a handful away, to the great amusement of the maids and scullery-lads. 'Master Francis! That is what you did when you were ten years old. What can you want with sugar-paste now?'

'Well, I suppose I can always eat it,' Francis said, tossing me two of them. 'There you are, infant, very appropriate; an owl for your wise eyes and a dolphin for your ridiculous smile. No, Monsieur, I do you the greatest compliment – would I take the trouble to steal them if they weren't well worth it? Thomazine, moi owd gal,' he added in the Suffolk voice he used to no one else, 'those are for eating, not for putting down my neck.'

'No, they're for your insufferable insolence,' I said, dodging him, owl and dolphin melting in my hand. 'Coward, stand and take your punishment!'

'No, I've more sense. Come on, brat, I thought we were going to see my foal.'

'Brat?' I said, as we shut the kitchen door with a rush of

mad March wind and stepped out into the stable yard, 'I'm a lady grown, and don't you forget it.'

'If I'd only your conduct to judge you by, madam, I would. Dear God,' Francis said, stopping so abruptly that I bumped my nose on his back, 'how old *are* you now?'

'Sixteen, sir,' I said primly. Francis whistled. 'Time does hurry past. It doesn't seem long since you were as small and unkempt and undisciplined as a stray puppy.'

'Nor since you were making a habit of perching up trees with a catapult and shying pebbles at the parson's horse.'

Francis snorted. 'I'd forgotten that. I got a royal beating for it, I remember, but it was worth it to see him trying to keep his seat, only to finish up in the ditch.'

'You,' I said, swallowing the last of the dolphin, 'were a menace as a child. You've not changed.'

Francis held the stable door open for me. As I passed, I neatly dropped the owl into the slash of his sleeve, and ran; only to be met with the solid bulk of Edward, armed with a scoopful of oats. We collided, tottered, and fell with a united thump on to the hard brick floor of the stables. Francis, grinning, walked forward, lifted the neat white kerchief I wore and dropped a glutinous mass of sugar paste into my modest neckline.

When we had all brushed off the straw, and I had given the paste to the big silvery stallion The Saracen, who had a sweet tooth, and wiped my sticky dress and neck with Edward's grubby kerchief, and we had quite done with our laughter, we went to see Hobgoblin and her foal.

At the other end of the stable-range, next to the coachhouse, was the separate stall for sick horse, mares with foals and the like, and here we stood by the door to look at its occupants. To my annoyance, I had to stand on tiptoe to see inside.

The stall, high with straw, was lit by a small window giving out on to the courtyard. The foal was still damp from its birth, and someone had rubbed it so hard with a cloth to get it dry that the soft smoky hairs of its coat stood out in little spiky whorls all over it. Like all new-born foals, this one seemed tiny beside the dam, all legs and head and no body in between, like a harvestman.

'He's a fine one,' Edward said approvingly. 'I always knew Hobgoblin's offspring would be good. Look at him, Francis, have you ever seen a better?'

'Rarely,' Francis said, a new delight in his face. 'Hobgoblin, my lady, you've done us proud this time.' The mare, hearing his voice, left the manger and stepped gently over, ears pricked, for his greeting. The foal, with great care, tried to follow, moved too quick, crossed his legs and sat down on the straw, looking ridiculously surprised. I laughed as he tried, and eventually succeeded, in getting up again and staggered across to his dam for a drink. 'What colour will he be? Black or grey?'

'Black,' Edward said, and 'Grey,' Francis added, instantly. 'He's got black points on his legs, and silver hairs in that foolish little mat of a tail, and I think he'll be grey like his sire.'

'I won't argue with you now,' said Edward, 'but I'll wager you my new saddlecloth, the purple one, against your red hawk's furniture with the silver bells, that in six months time he'll be black as midnight.'

'Done,' Francis said instantly, and they spat in their palms and struck them like the farmers making bargains at Bury market. 'What shall we name him, then? Midnight or Silver?'

'Midnight, of course,' Edward retorted, smiling, while I marvelled at the easy camaraderie between these very different brothers, and listened to the wailing wind in the roof, bringing the cold and the late unseasonable flurries of hard snow, and said, 'I know what he should be called.'

'What's that?' Edward asked, and I said, 'Boreas.'

My elder cousin looked at me blankly. 'Boreas? It sounds fine enough, but . . .'

'Boreas is the north wind, you ignorant old soldier,' Francis chaffed him, 'and I for one think it's an eminently suitable name. It's howling in the yard at this moment.'

I reached one hand through the high bars of the stall to

the foal, who sniffed it and gave it an exploratory lick. 'Hullo, Boreas! May you be as swift as your namesake.'

'Doubtless he will, neither of his parents are slow. What do you plan for him, Francis?'

'I don't know. You've got the Saracen's successor in mind, haven't you, that nice little chestnut three-year-old with the white face, so another stallion's not needed unless something happens to either of them. Geld him for a riding-horse, perhaps – I don't know. But not,' Francis said, reaching over beside me to pull the soft furry ears of the north wind, 'not, I think, to be sold. He's mine, I trust.'

'I relinquish any claim to him,' his brother said solemnly. 'Ah, Henry! Come and see our new foal.'

Henry Sewell joined our circle, a dusting of snow on his hat and cloak. 'That's foul weather for March, eh? Aye, that's a nice little colt, Francis. Give you twenty guineas for him?'

'Not likely, even at ten times the price. I'll need some horse to ride while Goblin is producing more marvels. How is Grainne?'

Henry's wife was expecting her second child in June, and had come close to losing it. 'Up, and baking, despite all Joan can do to stop her. You can't argue with Grainne,' her husband said, with fond resignation, 'nor would I want her any other way, but after the time she had with Jasper I do wish she'd be more careful of herself. The little mite's a one, though – most of what he say is just childish nonsense and prattle, but yesterday he told Joan she was pretty! She was something pleased, of course, and praised him and gave him a sweetmeat, and since then he's told everyone that, from me and his grandfather down to old Doll Mason who's eighty if a day and has no teeth. He'll be a lively one for the ladies in twenty years, I'll wager.'

'Like his father?' Francis suggested. Henry snorted. 'No finny! I do hear young Sarah's been making eyes at you now – that'll be your Jamie next, I'll wager. That wench han't got no shame. Pity, though, because the rest of the family's all right, and that Holly do a grand job keeping them all fed.' He blew on his hands. 'Like I said, thass master cold, even for the beginning of March. Any chance of a good hot mug of ale afore I go home? Oh, and by the way, if Simon's here I've a letter for him I picked up at the Angel in Bury this morning – come a long way, by the look of it.'

It had, indeed, and proved to be a missive of such importance that its contents were immediately the subject of a family discussion, Henry included, around a cheerfully blazing fire in the long gallery; a debate to which Grainne, walking over well-wrapped from the Home Farm in search of her husband, was also naturally admitted, despite Mary's faintly disapproving look. Written in a neat upright hand, it informed us that our Cornish cousin, Rowland Trevelyan, had died untimely but not unexpectedly from a wasting consumption of the lungs, leaving as sole heiress to his small but prosperous estate his fourteen-year-old daughter Meraud; and advised Simon to read the dying man's last missive, begging for the sake of the child and the estate to take good heed of the contents. Cousin Trevelyan's epistle proved to be a rambling, largely incoherent message, written to his dictation by the same steward who had sent the letter; the gist of it being a desperate plea for Simon to buy Meraud's wardship before her uncle Richard, the wicked pamphleteer, could lay his hands on the estate for his nefarious purposes.

'And bring her here, I suppose,' Mary said, resignedly. 'I doubt if Margaret and I have time to tutor her, and I don't really think she will wish to join your Greek and Latin lessons, Lucy. It certainly is not worth the bother of engaging yet another tutor or gentlewoman.'

'Why not?' Simon asked, looking up. 'I know that there have been various expenses falling upon us of late, but that is surely no reason for the poor child to languish alone in her mansion, Mother? She will do best here, with Lucy and Thomazine for company, and Cousin Rowland's steward seems from this to be a capable fellow – though I should have to go down there myself, of course, should I be successful with the wardship. Ah, Mistress Sewell, good day to you.'

'Good day to you all,' Grainne said. 'May I sit?' She

indicated a chair and Edward swiftly pulled it up for her. 'Please, pay me no mind . . . you were reading.'

'No,' said Simon, 'the letter is finished. We were debating whether or not to have yet another orphaned cousin to join our household.'

'She's fourteen years old,' Lucy said quickly, 'and her father has just died. I think Simon should bring her here to live with us.'

'At least she has no grandmother to leave behind, as I had,' I said. 'We'll make her welcome, won't we, Lucy?'

'Of course!'

'Naturally,' Simon continued, 'this will be a costly business, for her inheritance is not likely to be small – nearly as rich as yours, Thomazine.'

'We wards do not come cheap!'

'But I feel that it is in the interests both of the family and of the child that I act swiftly. It's fortunate I had already planned to go to London this week. I'll contact Sir Thomas Jermyn, or Tom Blagge, and we shall do our best to secure the wardship. As kin, we have sole rights for the space of one month, and more influence in the Court of Wards, I trust, than that scoundrel brother of Rowland's.'

'Ah, well, so be it,' Mary said, picking up her lute. 'I would not wish the girl to fall into his clutches, I must agree, for he sounds an unprincipled rogue, and a stirrer of sedition into the bargain. I would have preferred, of course, that poor Rowland should remain alive to care for his daughter himself, but as he is not, we must perforce do our duty.'

Grainne's smooth pale forehead creased with dislike. 'I am glad that the child is to be made welcome,' she said, shooting a glance at Lucy and me.

Mary picked out a little tune on the fine strings. Without looking up, she said, 'And your child, Mistress Sewell? Is he still fretful? I had just such a babe myself, I recall. Charles we called him, a taking child, who was born after Edward . . . he did not prosper either. Though the wet-nurse was excellent, he was ever too small, and cried continually. He was but two years old when the croup carried him off.'

Jasper was at this time just that age. Grainne said, with no apparent signs of distress at Mary's scarce-veiled malice, 'Jasper now does exceedingly well, madam. You would not think him the same child. It was breeding his first teeth that made him so fretful, and now that is long past he is feeding well, and growing fast. Yesterday he said his first proper sentence, and Henry was greatly amused.' She paused, and, prompted by the glint of quiet mischief in her eye and the similar look on her husband's face, I said, 'And what words did he utter, Grainne?'

'He was in the farmyard,' the Irish girl said, 'and fell over. I fear the language he hears from the labourers had made some impression on his tender mind, for at the top of his voice he shouted, "I falled in bloody turd!" You could not speak for laughing, could you, Henry, for quite five minutes?'

Later, when the expression of outraged sensibility had left Mary's face, Grainne and I dispatched ourselves downstairs to the music parlour, to collect some instruments so that more could join in with the singing and playing which Mary wanted. We shut the door behind us, looked at one another, and burst into laughter.

Grainne rarely laughed, and when she did it was with a quiet, infectious hilarity. I was less restrained, and it was several moments before I was able to rest my aching sides. 'Never before have I seen Mary repaid in her own coin! Not even Francis goes to that trouble!'

'I'm surprised,' Grainne said, still smiling, 'but he has been something subdued of late. I can see, however, from whence his malice comes. What have I done, to make her dislike me so?'

'It's not what you've done, I think, so much as what you are. She's never liked the Sewells, she thinks them beneath her, and you are too honest for her tastes. You all are. We Herons are more devious.'

'Except for Simon. He's too virtuous to be devious, but he is her favourite, I fancy. Edward has grown too rough and rude for her liking.'

'She can tolerate him. It's the children who are the most trouble to her she dislikes. Francis resembles her most of all of them, but he causes trouble, so she has no time for him.'

'I am certain,' Grainne said, 'that she was glad of her husband's death simply because he had been a burden to her; save that she then had the bother of arranging the funeral and the mourning!'

I snorted at this diabolically accurate portrayal of Mary. 'Actually, I think Simon did most of that. But you forget one thing – she looks so fetching in black, the bachelors of Bury will be beating a path to our door.'

Grainne grinned, but added, 'For myself, though, I was not glad of your guardian's death. He was that rare thing, a man of principle, and Suffolk will be the poorer.'

'I'd have thought,' I said drily, with a sober procession of Barnadistons passing through my mind's eye, 'that Suffolk was overstocked with men of principle, and a few the less would improve the place.'

'Men of principle not being comfortable neighbours? Agreed. Sir Nathaniel Barnadiston is a most worthy and godly man, but I for one would not wish to be of his household. Nor would I want to be of Harry Jermyn's.'

'You couldn't accuse him of being a man of principle!'

'Oh,' said Grainne, 'he certainly has principles. What they are, I shudder to think.' She picked up the required instruments and we made our laden way back through the house. At the foot of the stairs, I said reflectively, 'I wonder what this cousin Meraud will be like. None of us have ever met her.'

'You think she will be sent here, then?'

'When Simon is moved by family duty,' I said, 'he moves with more determination and thoroughness than anyone. The wardship will be bought and she'll be packed off here, just as I was when my father died, for the good of her soul and her education. I pity her.'

'Then you'd rather you'd never come to Goldhayes?'

I smiled. 'Oh, no. But I resented it bitterly for months. I'd been reared in an independent spirit, you see, and I took against being pushed hither and thither like a back-

gammon counter. I shan't be surprised if Meraud is similarly inclined.'

The next day, Simon rode to London. His original intention had been to inspect the family house in Covent Garden,
neglected for years due to his father's ill-health, and to visit
his friends at Court. Lucy had hoped that his wish was also
to see Nan, who had now been at Court for four months as
one of the Princess Mary's maids-in-waiting; but of this,
Simon did not speak. Now, he had also the task of securing
Meraud's wardship, and told us that, should he be successful, he would go straight to Cornwall from London to bring
her home. 'I shall write, of course, to tell you how matters
stand; but do not expect to see me for some time, mother.
Master Sewell will do all that is necessary for the running of
the estate, and you should also be of service there, Edward.'

'I daresay I can find the time,' Edward said cheerfully.
Simon continued, 'It is a great pity that I shall be so long, but
I have my duty to the girl, and I trust that you will be able to
manage in my absence.' His eye fell on Lucy and myself, by
Ned's side, and he smiled. 'If I were to send you gifts from
London, ladies, what would be your desires?'

Lucy's eyes grew round, for presents from London did
not often come her way. 'Ooh, Simon . . . I've wanted a copy
of *The Changeling* for so long, could you try and get it for
me? Please? Oh, thank you so much!'

Simon looked resignedly at me. 'And you, Thomazine?
Not, I trust, a stage-play also?'

'Oh, no . . . a bolt of velvet, or some such material, for a
new dress, will do me very well, thank you.'

'The colour must be sober, of course, but I shall do my
best,' Simon said. Mary, who had earlier given her son a
long list of requirements headed by a detailed account of
the Venetian glass he was to buy, said, 'I trust you will not
forget my wants, Simon?'

'Of course not, mother; I have the list here.' He patted his
saddle-bag. 'I shall take care to send everything here by
carrier before I leave for Cornwall. I should return with
Meraud in April, if all goes well.' He glanced suddenly at his
third brother, as if seeing him there for the first time, and

added, 'I will not see you then, Francis, will I, for you'll be at Oxford?'

Francis's grey-green eyes shone bright with sudden malice. 'If I choose to be, brother. I must confess I'd entertained other thoughts.'

For a moment Simon's cold dark eyes held his, and then his mouth compressed and he shrugged. 'I hope I do not see you, Francis. You have much work to catch up on, and your degree is due to be taken next summer. You know you are intended for the Temple, and you will make no lawyer if you do not learn to apply yourself.'

'And what if I do not wish to be a lawyer?' Francis inquired, tilting his head back to meet Simon's eyes, while I stood and silently begged him not to choose this moment of leave-taking to pick a quarrel. 'They're no better than the Papists of old, for they hold the key to wisdom all men need, and will only unlock the door for money. I have my own life to lead, Simon, not yours, nor my father's.'

There was a brief silence. Then Simon said, coldly, 'I will not see you, then, in April. Goodbye, Mother. The address at Covent Garden will find me, should the need arise. I trust it will not. Goodbye, and take care of yourselves!' And he turned his horse and, followed by his three servants, rode away down the drive.

At the end of the month, his eagerly awaited gifts arrived in a great wagon, delayed because of the bad weather, and for a time Lucy, Mary and I were kept very busy making up the bales of black or purple velvet and satin into new dresses, or unpacking the delicate glassware from its elaborate cases. All had gone well, Simon wrote; Meraud's wardship had been speedily purchased, and he was now setting off to Cornwall to bring her to Goldhayes. It was possible, given the parlous state of the roads, that he would be returning with our cousin well before the end of April. There was a disapproving final paragraph to the letter, telling of the disturbing news from London; the impeachment of Archbishop Laud, the continuing attacks by Parliament on the ministers and policies of the King, the surly behaviour of London 'prentice boys, and many other details distressing to my loyal and sober-minded cousin. Nothing was said of Nan Blagge, to Lucy's disappointment. At the foot of the letter, after the neat, stiff signature, a postscript added, 'I trust Francis has now betaken himself to Oxford.'

A vain hope, for Francis remained still at Goldhayes, mischievous and enigmatic and as ever good company, going with Edward and the Sewells on estate business around the villages and becoming liked by the Heron tenants – and their wives and daughters. Certainly Sarah Greenwood lifted her shabby red kirtle an inch or two to show her neat ankles, and simpered, and Francis, his eyes glinting, tossed her a daffodil with the dry comment, 'You'd best look after that flower, Sarah, for it's all you'll have of me!' Tom told the story later, with much laughter, and I wished that I had Sarah Greenwood's handsome face and bold, generous body, and wondered much that I did so, for Francis had shown no sign of indulging in his Oxford ways whilst at Goldhayes; she was nothing to him, and he, surely, was no more than a brother to me.

On the twentieth of April, the day when Simon and Meraud were expected to arrive according to my cousin's latest letter, there was ice on the moat and a rime of frost on the daffodils in the garden. I wore indoors my thick velvet dress with its layers of underskirts and a fur-lined cape and gloves. We spent the morning in the library, Lucy, Jamie and I, huddled close to the fire, studying and writing with stiff, painful fingers, wondering if the perpetual drip on the end of Dr Davis's nose would turn to ice. Before dinner, a well-wrapped Heron servant arrived to say that Simon, Meraud, the remaining servants, her nurse and luggage, could be expected before nightfall, having lain at Sudbury the previous night. Jamie, with all the indifference of twelve-year-old boys, said loftily that he did not, himself, see what all the pother was about, and didn't remember all this to-do when Thomazine had arrived in similar circumstances. Lucy reminded him vigorously that Thomazine, far from having to ride in all weathers, had had Sir Simon's own coach for her comfort, and moreover that he should feel sorry for the poor girl, orphaned and alone, packed off to join cousins she had never seen, and besides in the worst April weather anyone remembered.

'She should have waited, then, shouldn't she?' said Jamie, cheerfully insensitive. 'Anyway, it's been so comfortable here, old Ned never preaches sermons at you and he doesn't have Simon's piercing eye for sin.'

Despite myself, I had to laugh. 'I'll make you say that to Simon's face, young man, if you're not careful. Anyway, what happened to the Aeneid?'

'Burned if I had my way,' Jamie said rebelliously. He paused, and I saw conflicting emotions struggle on his wide, heart-shaped face, so like Lucy's and his mother's. Then he said, in an angry mutter, 'Dr Davis won't get it out of his head that I'm to take Orders! He says that was my father's wish, and Simon's too, but I don't want to a bit, why should I have to? If Francis can get away with not going to the Temple, then I needn't be a parson.'

Lucy and I exchanged glances over his head. Jamie went on, looking round to see if Dr Davis, who was growing deaf with advancing years, was still out of earshot. 'I wouldn't mind going to the university, except that all the learning sounds deadly dull, but I'm *not* going to be a parson, I swear it, never!'

I could see he had a point, for stuffing Jamie with theology was a course as likely to produce the desired result as teaching Hebrew to a monkey. 'Then what *do* you want to be?' Lucy asked unwisely. Jamie's blue eyes glowed, the floodgates opened and in a passionate, childish whisper we heard of his ambitions to be a soldier or a general in the Low Countries, 'for the Queen of Bohemia', Jamie said. 'I'll win back her kingdom for her, one day.'

We forbore to laugh, for our own dreams were themselves too real and beckoning to make mock of another's. I asked him what reading he had done. 'For,' I added, 'I never saw Edward without his nose in a military textbook before he went to the Low Countries with Henry. You can't just go off like that, you have to know something of what you're doing, or you're more of a help to the enemy than your own side.'

'Oh,' said Jamie, 'I've borrowed a few books from Ned and Henry, but there's one up there,' – he pointed to the forbidden shelf which carried the bestiary and the Boccaccio – 'It's rather old-fashioned but there's lots of battles and fighting in it.'

'What is it?' I asked, puzzled, and Jamie, breathing enthusiasm, said, 'The *Morte Darthur*.'

Lucy and I could contain ourselves no longer. As we spluttered over our books, much to Jamie's indignation, Dr Davis shuffled over, book in hand, his black gown and suit more than usually greasy. Since Lucy and I had left childhood, he had become increasingly wary of us, and treated us with gruff and uneasy respect. Shaking his head, he fixed us with a reproachful stare. 'Is there so much that is amusing in your Livy, Mistress Lucy?'

'No,' Lucy choked, her hands to her mouth, 'it was just something Jamie said.'

Dr Davis's manner changed at once. 'Master James, go over there, and continue your work where you cannot distract your sister and your cousin. No, not there; the table by the window.'

Jamie, scowling, went to the coldest spot in the room, sat down with exaggerated care and pretended to pore over his Virgil, whilst blowing on his hands ostentatiously and sending furious glances at his sister. Dr Davis continued talking. 'This cousin, Mistress Lucy, who arrives today . . . Do you know anything of her education? Will she wish to join us here?'

'I don't know anything,' Lucy said, 'save what was in my brother's letters. I understand she's had the usual education, reading, writing, accounts, sewing, music, French . . . I don't know if she'll want to join us here, or have most of her lessons with Mistress Bryant.'

'Ah, well,' said Dr Davis, with a pointed glance at me, 'perhaps she will not feel the desire to widen her knowledge as far as have you young ladies. Mistress Bryant will no doubt be glad to have a willing and receptive vessel for her skills.' He shuffled over to the bookshelf again and Lucy, in most unladylike fasion, addressed her tongue at his retreating back.

After dinner, it began to rain, and the wind beat it against the panes like the rattle of a drum. We all gathered in the long gallery, and engaged ourselves in energetic activities designed as much to drive the cold out of our bones as to practice our accomplishments. Jamie and Edward collected broadswords from the armoury and took them down to the western end of the gallery. To the unmusical clash of metal and Edward's shouted instructions to his eager pupil, Mistress Bryant and Mary picked out dance tunes on their lutes, while Lucy and I practised our galliards and voltas, and Francis amused himself throwing tennis balls for Drake to catch. The dog's nails scuttered over the polished floor, echoing the rain, as he lumbered in desperate elderly pursuit. He had never really recovered from being left behind with the Sewells whenever Francis went to Oxford, had developed a paunch, and became pathetically puppyish in his master's company. Occasionally he missed the ball and it rolled, accompanied by much cursing, amongst the feet of the sword-players, who accused Francis bitterly and with some justice of doing it deliberately. Despite our rather chaotic activity, we were all, with the exception of Mary and Mistress Bryant, eagerly anticipating the arrival of Meraud, and Lucy kept hurrying whenever she could to the windows to see whether she could espy the party's approach through the driving rain. On her umpteenth such excursion, her joyful shrieks rent the air. 'They're here! They're just crossing the bridge!'

'Well, I suppose we must go and welcome the child,' said her mother, without enthusiasm; and we all laid down lutes and swords and proceeded with haste down the wide stairs to greet Meraud Trevelyan on her arrival at her new home.

chapter four

Discovery

And now good-morrow to our waking souls . . .
        (Donne, 'The Good-Morrow')

As we came down into the hall, the great front door opened
on a crash of wind and rain to admit Simon, supporting a
tiny cloaked figure, and closely followed by a stout, ruddy-
faced elderly woman slung about with bags and baskets,
and an assortment of servants, similarly burdened. With
respectful care, Simon led the figure to the fire, where it
stood enveloped in cloak and hood, in a pool of fast-grow-
ing water. Outside, in the darkening courtyard, the lads
were leading the exhausted horses round to the stables for
welcome shelter and warm mash, and as the last of the
servants hurried across the threshold a gust of wind took
the door in spiteful fingers and hurled it shut. In the
sudden quiet, broken by the rain drumming on the windows and the water plopping from the travellers' clothes,
Simon said to the maid, 'For goodness sake, Jenny, get her
soaking wet cloak off before she develops a lung fever. No
doubt she is too exhausted to do it herself.'
    The Cornish maid, with a bobbed curtsey of acknowledg-
ment, obliged. While we watched with bright-eyed curiosity, she divested Meraud of the dripping cloak and hood
as reverently as she might unveil a bride, fumbling with
arthritic hands at the buttons and dragging off the heavy
garments to lay them in a sodden pool on the floor. All this
while, the girl had stood immovable and unspeaking, like a
player in some Court masque, waiting for her entrance,
until at last Meraud Trevelyan stood revealed, like some
glorious dryad lost among peasants, for us to gape at. She
was just fifteen years old, and beside her Lucy and I, though
agreed to be not ill-looking, were as nothing to her
loveliness. Her perfect, oval face might have been a painted

angel's, pale-skinned as milk, with vast sky-blue eyes, pathetically smudged beneath with the violet of exhaustion, a small straight nose and a full red mouth, rather like Lucy's but without Lucy's generous upward curves and dimples. Her hair, slightly darkened with rain, was a pale silvery yellow. She stood before the fire, utterly calm and self-assured within the protection of her beauty, and her wide blue eyes turned from Simon to the rest of us, in a huddle by the foot of the stairs. Lucy wore the same expression as she adopted when cooing over Grainne's son; Edward stood, legs apart, hand on Jamie's shoulder, his jaw dropped in admiration; Mary and her aunt had come as close to looking maternal as I had ever seen them; and Jamie's young open face was flushed with new-found emotions. At one crook of that small pale hand, I felt they might all have followed her through the gates of Hell, and was instantly consumed by jealousy. Only Francis, idly tossing a chewed tennis ball from hand to hand, a sarcastic smile on his face, seemed to have retained his sanity, and I was glad.

Simon took Meraud, very gently, by the arm and led her over to us. Her smart black riding habit, combining to perfection the rigours of mourning with the demands of fashion, trailed gracefully through the puddles on the floor, and I saw Mary sizing it up with a practised eye; evidently fashions in Cornwall were not so backward as was popularly supposed. 'Mistress Meraud Trevelyan,' Simon said, not as stiffly as his father before him had welcomed me, 'may I present you to my mother, Lady Heron . . . my brothers Edward and . . .' – a frown creased his face briefly – 'Francis, my sister Lucy, my youngest brother Jamie, my other ward Thomazine, who's lived with us for so many years she's like a sister to us all, and my mother's aunt, Mistress Bryant. Welcome to Goldhayes Hall, Meraud; I trust you'll be very happy here.'

'I am sure I shall, Cousin Simon,' Meraud said. Her slight lisp, and her charming care over her speech, were very pretty, as was her deep curtsey to us all. Simon, in courtly fashion, took her hand, bowed over it, and raised her back to her own diminutive level. I had been ready to like her and to sympathize with her position, since I had gone through exactly the same ordeal nearly six years ago, but somehow my generous impulse stuck in my throat when I saw her cool appraising eyes resting on us in a manner startlingly adult; reminding me that, despite her tiny stature and lovely childlike face, she was after all a maiden full-grown. I became suddenly conscious of all the faults in my appearance: the black gown which suited me as ill as her mourning became her, my rather angular pointed little face and light-brown skin, so unfashionable and so distressingly permanent, my wide mouth and large, rather deepset eyes under winged, uncompromising brows. Quite suddenly my jealous antagonism crystallized into real dislike. She's a spoilt, selfish, vain, artful, simpering little madam, I thought, soaking up admiration like sand soaking up ink. Encouraged by this, I allowed myself my most gracious smile.

Simon was receiving his mother's fond greeting, his head bent for her kiss. 'The glass, you'll be pleased to hear, arrived safe, only one piece broken and that can be mended. You see the girls wearing your gifts, and I can tell you, we've been glad of the velvet in this terrible cold, you'd hardly believe that it will be May in less than a fortnight. Now, Meraud, I expect you're exhausted from your journey, and you'd like to put on dry garments, I'm sure. If I may show you and your nurse (Jenny, is it? Is that also a Cornish name?) the chambers set aside for you, then you may come down for supper when you are ready, or if you wish you may have it sent up on a tray for you both . . .' And Meraud, escorted by servants and baggage, was whisked up the stairs, leaving us standing somewhat bemused in the hall.

Simon was the first to recover. As if emerging from a long enchantment, he removed his own cloak, handed it to his manservant, and favoured his family with a weary smile. 'Well, I am pleased to be home. It's been a long and exhausting journey from Cornwall, and Meraud, though she does marvellously, is not, I fear, very strong. It's been a worry, but at least we're safe home. Now, Ned, how are things here? I want to go over the estate accounts with you and John tomorrow, if I may, and discuss the farm too. I also want to ride round the village; if there are one or two tenants behind with their rents the sight of me may provide the incentive they need.' He stopped, and then said slowly and with emphasis, 'I shall also want to see you tomorrow, Francis. I shall desire some explanation of your disobedience.'

Francis smiled, but his face was pale with anger, and his eyes blazed green. 'You should thank me, brother, that this time no greater sin than disobedience lies at my door – though that's not for Sarah Greenwood's want of trying. Besides, what possible right have you to govern my life?'

'Every right,' Simon said viciously, 'as your want of conduct daily shows. I shall see you tomorrow, after breakfast. I am now going to change my clothes. Bring my baggage to my chamber, Adams.' Followed by his manservant, he crossed the hall in the direction of his father's chamber, which he now occupied.

As the door shut behind them, Edward said, 'What are you going to say?'

Francis grinned. 'I don't know. I'll think of something, I always do. Young Meraud was something of a surprise, wasn't she?'

'Wasn't she beautiful!' said Lucy in a rush. 'Like a maiden in a play or a romance.'

'Yes, she quite cast you in the shade,' Francis said unkindly. Lucy ignored him, and turned to Jamie. 'Didn't you think she was beautiful?'

Jamie flushed up to his hairline and muttered something in agreement. Lucy went on, 'And she looked so sweet and sad, standing there all lonely by the fire, I felt so sorry for her. I hope she does join in our lessons.'

'She looks too fragile for Latin and Greek and Hebrew,' I said acidly. Francis favoured me with one of his more penetrating stares, and then said, 'Do I detect a note of jealousy?'

Francis in this kind of mood always made me angry, largely because of the contrast between that and what I knew to lie beneath. I retorted crossly, 'Quite possibly you do. I've more reason than some to be jealous of such a beauty. No doubt it'll wear off in time, but it irks me sorely now to see you all agape like sheep!' And, furious with myself and with him, stamped off upstairs to the gallery, wishing that I could learn to control my tongue and my temper.

I had not gone half the length of the gallery, intending to gather up the lutes, when I heard footsteps behind me. Expecting Lucy, I turned and came nose to shoulder with Francis. 'What's the matter?' my cousin asked.

'You,' I retorted, and turned away. Francis grabbed my shoulder, painfully, and turned me round to face him again. 'What've I done to upset *you*?'

I stared at his long pointed face with the strange light eyes, framed by hair as pale as Meraud's. 'You've been your usual annoying self, cousin, and I've had a sufficiency for one day, that's all.'

'But there's no need for us to quarrel, no need at all. You should know me by now, I don't mean most of what I say.'

'Except when you say it to Simon. Perhaps you realize how unpleasant it is for the rest of us to have you two at each other's throats each time you meet – perhaps, to be charitable, you don't. But I'll tell you one thing – none of us feel we can take sides, and we're tired, Francis Heron, sick and tired of your stupid malicious provocation!' And I turned away once more, suppressing tears, to collect the lutes.

'You are jealous of her, aren't you?' Francis said, close behind me. 'You've no need to be, I'm not interested.' And as I jerked round, startled, he added easily, 'And nor are you as ugly as you suppose. Come on, come with me.' He took me by the shoulders and propelled me to the great Venetian looking-glass which hung at one end of the gallery, just outside Mary's chambers. Holding me squarely in front of it, my cousin said, 'Look at yourself. Are you ugly? Is that the form of hideousness?'

I stared wide-eyed at the reflection. No, I was not ugly, nor strictly beautiful, though I supposed grudgingly that some might find me attractive; but only myself, Thomazine

Heron, aged sixteen years and three months, brown of hair and eye, and scarcely five feet tall. I said, 'No.'

Are you as lovely as any Court lady?'

'I don't know, never having seen one.'

'You have, you know. What about Nan Blagge?'

I hesitated. 'Well, she's no beauty, but . . .'

' "No beauty, but . . ." That might be you too, moi owd gal. No portrait painter could capture any of your three hundred intensely annoying moods or expressions, or make you strictly beautiful according to convention without turning you into a wooden doll, but you've no need to worry, for there's more to beauty than a face. Now, lecture over – has your green-eyed hag disappeared?'

'No,' I said shakily, more disturbed than I cared to admit by this strange interview, 'but she's grown very thin and pale of a sudden.'

'Excellent. Forget her and Meraud, they're harmless to you. And don't damage those lutes, you're holding them as tightly as a remedy for the plague.' He turned and walked down the gallery to the stairs, and I stood and stared at his long black-clad figure with my mind in chaos. 'You've no need to be jealous, I'm not interested,' he had said, and there was only one thing he could mean by that. 'You may think I'm in love with you, you conceited, annoying, malicious, selfish bastard,' I thought on a wave of fury, 'but you're wrong. I'm my own person and beholden to no one!'

I was not surprised when Meraud, after the drama of her entrance into our lives, chose not to face us anticlimactically at supper and partook of a hot posset and broth in her chamber before retiring very early. Still in the throes of my anger with Francis, I sat between Lucy and Edward at supper and exchanged jokes and riddles with them alone, despite Lucy's significant conspiratorial glances from her third brother to me and back. Simon, like Death at the Feast, sat gloomily at the head of the table, refusing to recognize his weariness, and resisted all efforts to draw him into our conversation. I decided that I would not, after all, tackle him on the subject of Francis going for a soldier with Edward; not only was he in a black humour, but I had also come to the conclusion that Francis was not worth the effort. 'If he wants to go to Hell, let him find his own way,' I thought venomously, and left it at that.

The next morning, I regretted it bitterly. As usual, we breakfasted early, after household prayers, and then went about our morning tasks: Lucy, Jamie and I to the library with Dr Davis, Edward to the stables, Simon to his study, and Meraud with Mary and Mistress Bryant upstairs to Mary's own quarters, where her accomplishments were to be assessed. Francis, as was his wont, went to the music parlour to practise, and his impending interview with his eldest brother seemed forgotten.

Until, that is, I remembered that I had left an important book on the windowseat in the arras parlour on the western side of the house. Dr Davis clucked over my carelessness, but gave me permission to fetch it. Followed by the envious glances of Lucy and Jamie (the theology this morning was intolerably dull, and any break from it welcome), I left the library and made my way, taking my time, through the summer parlour, the dining hall and the great hall to the other side of the house.

Simon had chosen for his study a small room known as the garden parlour, since it opened on to the courtyard garden in the centre of the house. The window faced east, and the bulk of the house shielded it from the rising sun, so it got no sunlight and always smelt rather musty; moreover, there was no fireplace. However, it was not used as a passageway to anywhere but the garden, which was also accessible from the kitchen, and was thus comparatively quiet and isolated from the bustle of the house. The door to it led from the arras parlour, and as I entered that room I heard, rather muffled by the door, Simon's voice raised in anger. My missing book was still on the windowseat, where I had set it down so as not to carry it into the chapel that morning. The proper thing to do would have been to pick it up quietly and leave, but my curiousity got the better of me. I tiptoed to the windowseat, gathered up my book, and slunk closer to the study door.

'For God's sake,' Simon said, his voice rising higher in

pitch, 'when I tell you to return to Oxford I mean you to obey! You've never had much government, have you? Playing on the weakness of your crippled father, always creeping out of trouble, you've had it too easily in the past. You're not going to get away with it again, do you hear me? Either you return to Oxford and proceed to the Temple, or I shall bar this house to you forever.'

'You sound,' Francis said, malice and mischief jostling in his voice, 'just like a character from one of Lucy's plays. Are you sure that you want me to go back to Oxford? After all, without my brotherly keeper to watch over me, I can give free rein to all those pleasant vices you so detest.'

'By God, if you do, I'll . . .' For once, Simon's command of words failed him utterly in his fury. Francis went on, matter-of-factly, 'Face the facts, brother, there's very little you could do to stop me when we were together in the same college, and there'll be even less chance for you to dictate my pleasures, or the lack of them, from a distance of a hundred miles and more. There is nothing you can do, now or ever, to stop me going my own way, and I think you know it.'

'If I can't stop this vicious debauchery by any earthly means,' Simon said, 'I shall have to trust to Divine intervention to bring a halt to your activities, and pray God you'll repent before you roast in Hell . . . Dear God, you have the audacity to smile!'

I could imagine the expression on Francis's face only too well, and my skin crept. All the while his voice had kept quite calm and quiet, mockingly so, while Simon's climbed from anger to fury at his indifference. Now he said, 'I can't avoid it, the spectacle you're making of yourself, with your hypocritical disgust at antics that in anyone else's book wouldn't count for much . . . You give yourself away too much, my virtuous virgin brother. It's not your disapproval angers you so, is it? It's jealousy plain and simple, that you're too faint-hearted to go whoring as well—'

His voice, mocking and offensive, was cut off abruptly by the sound of fist meeting jaw, followed by a double clattering thud. I had heard that sound often enough at the matches at Bury Fair. Forgetting all caution, my heart banging with terror, I flung open the door.

Simon stood by the side of his desk, nursing his right hand, which was seeping blood, and staring down at the tumbled shape on the floor which was Francis. As I entered the room he turned to me a face white with shock and said, with real anguish, 'He forced me to do it. I could see it in his face. The things he said . . . I could not stand to hear them any longer. I hit him too hard, and he hit his head on the wall.'

'I know,' I said, thinking with a vague detachment that my voice was quite steady, although my whole body was trembling violently. 'I heard it all, I was listening. Is he dead?'

'I don't know,' Simon said. He seemed unable to move, and his hands were shaking. Impatiently, I dropped to my knees beside Francis and felt desperately for any signs of life. There was a lump already prominent on the back of his head, and a fair-sized bruise making itself obvious to spoil the line of his jaw, but he was breathing. I sat back on my heels, letting relief wash over me like cool water, and said, 'Why do you two quarrel so?'

Simon said violently, 'Do you think I wish to? I could easily have killed him in my anger. Do you think I want that?'

'It takes more than one to make a quarrel,' I said unhappily, aware of impending tears, and dragged the back of my hand across my mouth. 'Your attitude is as unreasonable as his, you know, if not more so. No, listen, because I think I'm right in this . . . Why can't you accept that Francis is *not* the same as you? Oh, he's just as pig-headed and obstinate as you are, and he's a Heron through and through, that's plain to see — and why you should be so upset by what he does at Oxford I really don't know, for he's not exceptional in that — but with all that he *is* different. He is not one to be led or governed or forced into acquiescence, he's his own self and makes his own rules, and I think you'd find, did you but take the trouble to look, that they're remarkably similar to yours in some respects. Anyway, what point is there in all this laying down of the law? He's not going to take any notice of your pronouncements, and the only effect is to make matters worse. He's halfway to hating you, I know, and he's not going to spare you anything when he feels like that. Why,' I went on, seeing Simon's eyes waver, 'why you can't just back down graciously off your high horse and agree to his going for a soldier or whatever it is he wants, I don't know, instead of making life so damnably unpleasant for the rest of the family.'

Simon seemed to grow smaller of a sudden. Wearily, still holding his knuckles, he turned and shut the door, which was still a little ajar. 'But, Thomazine, an insult like that . . . that can't easily be forgotten.'

'Yes, it can. Who knows of it, apart from us three? If you have the *will* to forgive and forget,' I said urgently, 'it can be done. Simon, please . . . not just for me, or for Francis, but for all of us.'

The uncalculated sentiment of my words seemed to soften him a little more. He came back to the desk and stood looking down at Francis's still, bruised face. 'Pray God I have done no damage . . . I've seen a man hurt in the head like this seemingly recover and walk away, only to die an hour or so later . . . Thomazine, I will forgive him, and endeavour to be friends, but he will have to apologize to me first for his behaviour. It would be unseemly and unfitting for me to let his words pass by unnoticed.'

Damn your stiff-necked pride, I thought, and said quietly, "And you also had best apologize for your violence, however provoked. As I said, it takes two to make a quarrel.'

Simon ignored that. He said, 'We had better make some attempt to bring him round . . . it would not be fitting to have any of this common knowledge.'

'With that bruise on his face, I'd have thought it would hardly be otherwise,' I said drily. 'He may have the spirit to brazen it out, but have you?'

Simon flushed. He crossed over to the court-cupboard, opened one of the top doors and took out a dusty, battered flask. 'Aqua vitae, I keep it in case of illness. It should bring him round; it's too strong for me to drink.'

With some difficulty, I lifted Francis's dead weight into a sitting position, his head against my chest. Simon knelt by us and put the uncorked flask to his mouth. There was a second's pause and then Francis's body jerked into a violent fit of coughing. Aqua vitae went everywhere, and the flask left Simon's grasp and dropped to the floor. Francis doubled over on to his side, gasping for breath, and I rather pointlessly patted his back. 'Oh, my God,' Simon said, his nose wrinkling with distaste, 'the stink of it is enough to raise the dead.'

'Jesus Christ,' Francis said, sitting up slowly, holding his head, 'what was that? Poison? My head's split apart.'

'You hit it on the wall, and it was aqua vitae,' I said. Francis turned his head cautiously. 'Ah, Thomazine. Were you eavesdropping again, or just conveniently passing by?'

It was my turn to flush. 'Just passing,' I lied, 'to collect a book. Hold yourself still, if you've a headache.'

'And an ache in my jaw,' Francis said with feeling. 'Brother Simon can certainly use his fist, he's got a hit like the kick of a carthorse. What will our dear mother say when she sees this? If, of course, she notices it.'

'What will you say?' Simon countered. Francis grinned, and then winced as he touched the bruise. 'Perhaps I knocked my jaw raising the lid of the spinet to tune it. No? It doesn't sound very likely, does it? Ah, I have it: I fell off my horse. That ugly nag Ned has found for me till Goblin's foal is weaned seems capable of any sin. He put his foot in a rabbit-hole and I came off, being accidentally kicked in the process. How will that do?'

'You haven't been riding,' I said involuntarily. Francis grinned again. 'No, true, but I'm going now. Summon a horse, for me, will you, brother, to be ready at the orchard bridge.' With difficulty, using the desk, he got to his feet, still rubbing his head, and went rather unsteadily out.

Simon and I stared at each other. I wanted to laugh at the sheer effrontery of it all, but said instead, to Simon's indignant face, 'You won't forget your promise, will you?'

'He's mazed,' Simon said, 'he must be. He'll kill himself
. . . Of course I won't have a horse ready. It's ridiculous to
ride in that condition.'

'You were the one who wanted all this concealed,' I
pointed out. 'So I should swallow your pride and order that
horse. If you can't, I'll do it for you.'

'Very well,' Simon said, with ungracious reluctance, and
stamped morosely out of the study. I decided to leave the
mess of aqua vitae for him to clear up, retrieved my book
from the floor and returned, still shaky, to the library.

The story of Francis's fall from his horse was received
without disbelief, particularly as the big, clumsy gelding was
known to have put his feet in rabbit-holes before. There
seemed to be no lasting damage, and the bruise quickly
faded. Simon said no more, however, about forgiveness;
there was still the same half-concealed animosity between
them. I looked in vain for the chance to acquaint Francis
with Simon's terms for peace, for my third cousin now kept
himself very much to himself and we only laid eyes on him
at mealtimes and, infrequently, of an evening in the gallery.
Moreover, the family's attentions were almost entirely
taken up with Meraud.

Our Cornish cousin's beauty opened doors that I had
never suspected to exist, and won even the most unlikely
heart. She did not stoop to our lessons with Dr Davis, but
spent her mornings with Mary, improving her needlework
and her music, and Lucy's mother was high in praise of her,
although her voice was not exceptional and she could play
but two instruments. Everyone praised her quiet, demure
seemliness, her devotion to her Bible, her pretty manners,
her good behaviour, her politeness, until even Lucy had to
admit that, sweet though the girl was, she was more than a
trifle weary of Meraud this and Meraud that. The male
members of the family were more uncritical. Simon was
unfailingly gentle, courteous and pleasant, showed her
over the house, and presented her with a little leather-

bound Bible for her own use; for Meraud, so it appeared, was of a retiring and religious nature. Feeling the iron of her vanity under the lovely velvet of her looks, I was highly sceptical of this trait, particularly since it endeared her to the godly upright Simon. Edward, generous in his own fashion, rode over to Horringer and purchased from Ambrose Blagge an outgrown pony belonging to his youngest son Henry. This he presented to her, and Mary added a handsome red leather harness and saddle, sewn with tiny silver bells, which looked very well on the pretty little dapple-grey horse. Meraud could not ride out in scarlet, but with her pale complexion and silver-gold hair she looked wonderfully fetching in black, and on her first ride won every susceptible village heart. Jamie, in the first flush of adolescent adoration, presented her with a falcon, a tiny beautiful merlin which it had taken most of his allowance to buy, and Meraud was properly grateful. Nothing was too good for her, in most eyes, no whim left unsatisfied. She was everywhere cosseted, indulged and generally treated like a particularly lovely and fragile piece of China pottery, and welcomed these attentions with grace and favour, like a queen receiving her dues from her subjects. With the rather superior attitude of those who think they see what their fellows do not, I found some humour in the situation.

One afternoon in the last week of April, I rode over to the Home Farm in between showers, to speak with Grainne, who was again unwell. There, at least, I would have some respite from Meraud-worship, for Grainne had not yet met the girl and, in her own fashion, was reserving judgement until she could inspect her for herself. Henry and his father were out in the fields, Tom had gone with Jamie, Meraud and Lucy to Rushbrooke, and Joan was making butter and had for once no breath to spare for gossip, so I mounted the narrow boxed-in stairs to Grainne's chamber, carrying a cheerful bunch of daffodils to brighten her day.

As I had guessed from his horse in the yard, Francis was there already. Grainne, warmly wrapped, was seated by the fire, with Jasper, now two years old, crawling happily at her feet, and my cousin was sitting on the floor talking to Drake, who was as puzzled by babies as he was by puppies, and looked thoroughly unnerved. As I entered, Francis glanced up and said, 'Hullo, not gone to Rushbrooke?'

'No, I couldn't stand to see all the Jermyns finnicking over her too,' I said drily. 'Hullo, Grainne, how are you? Perhaps these will bring a breath of Spring to you.'

'We do need it,' Grainne said, 'I see it's raining again. I dread to think of the harvest this summer if this weather keeps on. Oh, I'm very much better, thank you; I'm quite determined to see this child safe too, and there are only two months left now. Aren't those daffodils lovely! Thank you so much. Yes, do put them in the jug with the primroses, there'll be room there. Jasper!'

The little boy, giggling, had given Drake's tail a firm tug. The dog, thoroughly mortified, gave a yelp and retired to the opposite corner of the room, by the big four-poster bed. 'He's bored,' Francis said, lifting up the baby to stare into his face. 'Hullo, infant, how dare you pull my dog's tail?'

'Pretty,' Jasper said hopefully, an exploratory and appeasing grin on his face. Francis pretended to drop him, letting his hands slip and tightening them at the last minute. Grainne's son shrieked with laughter. 'More! Me want more!'

'You'll get more than you bargained for,' Francis warned, getting up. 'You take one hand, Thomazine, and I'll have the other. Do you know the old counting song our shepherds sing? Good. Now, start counting!'

'Unna, Tina, Wether, Tether, PINKIE!' I cried, and we swung Jasper up until his feet soared higher than his head and the bunchy skirts stood out stiff from the round waist. 'And again?'

'More!' Jasper gasped in between chuckles, and I started again. 'Up to ten this time. Ready? Unna, Tina, Wether, Tether, Pinkie, Hater, Skater, Sara, Dara, DIC!'

This time, Jasper left our hands altogether and flew up into the air. Fortunately, Francis caught him. Unafraid, he grinned at us; he was a very attractive child, with Grainne's grass-coloured eyes and the orange Sewell hair and a perpetual smile strongly reminiscent of Tom's.

'Go carefully,' Grainne said, smiling herself, 'he's the apple of his father's eye, that one, but he's forever in mischief. He's been lively all morning. Perhaps if I sing to him he'll sleep.' She took him from us and began to croon to him in a strange tongue which started a prickling at the back of my neck. Jasper pushed a thumb into his mouth and smiled cheekily. Slowly, his mother got to her feet and walked heavily across to the window. 'Listen, what do you hear, sweeting?'

The brief rain had stopped; faintly, in the woods, a cuckoo called. 'Bird?' Jasper said, questioningly. 'That a bird?'

'It's a cuckoo,' Grainne said. 'Shusha, little one, and if you're quiet I'll sing you a song about a cuckoo.' Softly, in her clear voice, she began:

> The Cuckoo is a pretty bird,
> She sings as she flies.
> She bringeth good tidings,
> She telleth no lies.
> She sucketh white flowers
> For to keep her voice clear,
> And when she singeth 'Cuckoo',
> Summer draweth near.

Jasper's small bright head drooped. 'Cuckoo,' he muttered through his thumb. 'Cuckoo. Pretty bird.'

Grainne, smiling, said, 'Here's a lullaby for you, and you must sleep.' Crooning gently, she walked up and down by the window.

> Sweet was the song the Virgin sang
> When she to Bethlehem was come,
> And was delivered of her son,
> That blessed Jesus had to name,
> Lulla, lulla, lullaby,
> Lulla, lulla, lullaby.

I joined in with her for the next verse, for the song was in one of our books of ayres.

'Sweet Babe,' quoth she,
'My son, and eke a Saviour born,
Who hath vouchsafed from on high
To visit us that were forlorn.
Lulla, lulla, lullaby,'
Sweet babe,' sang she,
And sweetly rocked him, rocked him,
And sweetly rocked him, on her knee.

'I think,' Francis said softly, 'that he's at last asleep.'

The baby, head laid in the crook of Grainne's arm, was quite quiet, his eyes closed, and his thumb fallen away from his mouth. Grainne walked over to the cradle which stood by the bed and laid him carefully within it. 'He always sleeps to that air, I don't know why. The tune is very pretty, perhaps it soothes him.' She tucked the blankets around the small hump in the cradle and returned to her chair, stretching painfully, her hands to her back. 'It's this damp weather affects me thus; I shall be glad indeed to see the sun. Francis has been telling me of Meraud. I understand that the sun and moon, not to mention Simon, Edward and Jamie, alter their courses in admiration.'

'But not Francis,' said my cousin, taking up again his place by the fire. 'Nor, I suspect, Thomazine.'

Grainne did not say, 'Why not?', but asked instead, 'What is there in her that you see and the others can't?'

'To be just,' I said slowly, 'I have to admit that I'm a touch jealous of her; she has everything, and in particular beauty. I was glad to hear her sing, for she's little better voiced than Mistress Bryant.'

'Who would make a starling sound sweet,' Francis said.

'So,' said Grainne, 'you admit jealousy. But there's more than that, isn't there?'

'Yet she can't be faulted,' I said. 'She is too perfect, too polite, too careful in her manners. Everything she does is correct. Yet I feel such ways are unnatural for her. I can't imagine her as anything other than seemly and demure, and yet I'm sure she is not usually so proper.'

'Wouldn't you be thus, in her position?' Grainne pointed

out. 'Mind you,' she added shrewdly, 'maidens with such beauty as a rule can rely on their fair faces to gain what they want, and do not have to make such efforts to be pleasant and seemly.'

I nodded. 'Yes, I'm sure you have it. At Goldhayes she's feeling her way into our hearts, carefully, giving nothing away; then, gradually, she'll appear in her true colours, and it won't matter because by then she'll have us all dangling after her.'

'But what, think you, *are* her true colours?' Grainne asked, and Francis said unhesitatingly, 'Vanity. And not only her particular care for her looks, either. The mainspring of Meraud is Meraud, and however pleasing she may appear, the only thing that matters is herself, and her own way. But judge for yourself, you'll meet her soon enough.'

'With all these slanderous portraits put into my head,' Grainne said drily, 'I doubt I'll be able to. And if she's been so decorous, careful you said, how can you know how she is?'

'There's no proof, of course there isn't,' I said. 'It's just, well, feminine intuition, if you like.'

'Not on my part, it isn't,' Francis pointed out.

'But,' I continued, ignoring him, 'her eyes are too cold, and her manner too – too graciously condescending for my taste. I've tried to like her, believe me, for her situation is so similar to mine, and I've every sympathy with the poor girl – but I can't. It's all artifice, I feel it in my bones, and I can't like her.'

'I find it rather amusing,' Francis said, 'to watch Jamie all besotted, the fool, following her with adoring eyes like a dog.'

'Not so amusing if she is as you say,' Grainne remarked. 'For she'll be looking for higher things than Jamie, and if he's not careful his heart will be broken young. Is Simon still betrothed to Nan Blagge?' Her voice and face were solemn, but her green witch's eyes danced. Francis burst out laughing. '*Simon*? Lord of Hell, I hope not. Meraud would lead him a dance, the little minx, once she'd looked him. No, the arrangement with Nan has never been broken, but as she's gone to Court I expect she'll marry elsewhere, to a title or into money. Her brother is just like her father, they both ever had an eye to the main chance.'

'A shame,' Grainne said, 'for I liked Nan, and she has a fondness for Simon. They'd agree well together, I feel. Listen! Is that *bells*?'

Through the ill-fitting windows came the sound of hooves, coming to a halt outside the garden gate. High and shrill and faerie above them was the music of harness bells. 'Speak of the Devil,' I said to Grainne, 'here is Meraud, so you can see for yourself.'

'How did you know? Magic?'

'Her pony has bells on its bridle, so that Meraud can have music wherever she goes,' Francis said, over his shoulder and halfway to the window. Grainne and I got to our feet and joined him. We all squashed together on the windowseat and stared out through the greenish glass with more curiosity than was seemly.

Below, Meraud was sitting her pony, looking round and up at the tilted, aged beams of the farmhouse. Every elegant line of her spoke a kind of resigned superiority. Jamie, who had never been anything other than a rough, noisy lad, was gracefully offering her his hand to help her dismount, while Tom and Lucy, smiling, hung on her words and young Robert Jermyn, who was ten and normally as boisterous as Jamie, held her horse with great presence.

'She may be a selfish and artful little madam, according to you,' Grainne said thoughtfully, 'but her influence on those two young ruffians appears to be nothing but good. Did you say her mother had died at her birth?'

'Apparently, and she was her father's darling.'

'So,' said Grainne, 'she was his only treasure, and no doubt she'd learned to twist him round her little finger before she left off hanging strings. Had her mother lived, or her father married again, she might well have been otherwise. I feel sorry for her, really, for it's not her fault she's been spoilt past all redemption – *if* all you say of her is true.'

Below us, Tom was leading his four guests into the house.

Seized with a sudden impulse, I said, 'Do you mind if we go, Grainne? I came here to get away from them, and I've had enough of Meraud for today; we did needlework this morning and Mistress Bryant's toadying was sickening to hear. "Meraud, your stitches are so fine, so invisible, your designs so beautiful, your work so neat . . ." Ugh! And for all that, I can sew as well, if not better.'

'Braggart,' Francis said. Grainne, grinning, added, 'No, I don't mind if you slink out before you've been here ten minutes. If I'm no more than a refuge from Meraud, you'd best go quick!'

Aware suddenly of what I had said, I hastened to apologize. 'Oh, Grainne, I didn't mean it to sound like that, you know I didn't. You do understand, don't you?'

'Of course I do,' Grainne said, her face aflame with laughter. 'Take the back stairs and go out through the back'us, and with luck you'll miss them. Come again tomorrow, and I'll tell you then what I make of her! And many thanks for the daffodils.'

'Accept them as a token of my most sincere esteem,' I said primly, and the Irish girl's quiet laughter followed us out of the room.

'Do you never watch your tongue?' Francis asked me, as we made our way, followed by Drake, through empty rooms to the back stairs on the other side of the house. 'Anyone less sensible than Grainne might have taken quite justified offence.'

'I wouldn't be as free with anyone but Grainne,' I retorted, nettled by his criticism. 'Much as I'd like to be, it doesn't make for comfortable living to tell the likes of Parson Eldritch that he's an obstinate old fool, or Ambrose Blagge that he's a self-seeking miser, or Jamie, for that matter, that he's giving his heart to a girl who may well be wanton. Not to many is the truth welcome, or harmless.'

'No, illusions are often best left alone. Do you remember the unicorns?'

At the foot of the dark, creaking old stairs, I turned and smiled. 'Oh, yes, how could I forget? I still carry them with me in my head. They're one of my most precious possessions.'

'While you can say that,' Francis told me as we crossed the kitchen to the 'back'us' and the outside door, 'there's hope for you, bad-tempered, blunt and unladylike as you are. Has the butter come, Joan?'

'No, that hasn't, Master Francis,' said Joan, her thin scarlet face, glossy with sweat, appearing round the buttery door. 'That do fare to be hully spoiled, that do, and I doubt that Goody Pearson's ill-wished that, and that in't for the first time, the evil long-nosed owd hag! Was that young Master Jamie's voice I heard?'

'Yes,' I said, 'but we decided not to stay, we'd be too many for Grainne otherwise.'

Joan, sympathetically, began on a long account of Grainne's fortitude whilst under such a strain. Eventually, we escaped into the yard, but only after Francis had been asked to put his superior strength into the making of the butter. It was sunny now, and the rushing clouds seemed thinner, but more showers were obviously approaching and the wind had not abated. 'Home?' Francis asked.

'Yes, we'd better, before it pelts down again,' I said, still nursing resentment, and at the same time, paradoxically, sadly aware that the barriers between us were still up, and probably more on my side than his. Our horses, Francis's raw-boned nag and my own Orlando, a smart chestnut, were tethered to rings on the side of the stable-range. 'Do you want my assistance to mount, Mistress Heron?' my cousin asked, with exaggerated courtesy.

I untied my horse, and put my foot in the stirrup; being angry with myself and with him, I said, shortly, 'Of course not!' Orlando, who was by nature skittish, laid his ears back and swished his long red tail, and then began to shuffle backwards whilst I, one foot in the stirrup and one on the ground, hopped beside him, trying not to fall over the ample folds of my riding-habit. Francis did not come to my aid, but stood helpless with laughter beside his own horse. 'Are you quite sure you don't want assistance?'

My anger suddenly dropped away, and I was breathless

with laughter myself. Determined not to fail, I tugged so hard on Orlando's bridle that he stopped in astonishment, and managed to scramble on to his back in the short breathing-space thus offered. 'Come, Master Heron, such a sluggard! Not mounted yet?'

'How can I follow such a graceful example?' Francis said, swinging up on to the gelding's back. 'You are such an, uh, elegant rider.'

'Flattery will get you nowhere,' I retorted. We turned our horses and, at a slow walk because of the thick mud and water clogging the yard, went out of the gate and on to the quarter-mile-long drive leading to the house, Drake ambling at our heels.

'Before you arrived,' Francis said, as we rode slowly side-by-side, splashing through the water and gravel, 'we were exchanging riddles, and Grainne has some I'll wager you've never heard before.' He paused temptingly. Since we were children, these had been one of the favourite intellectual pursuits of the Herons, and we had spent many a cosy winter evening in one of the warmer parlours at Goldhayes, trying to catch each other out with old riddles or inventing new and amusing ones. I said, 'Try me with them, then.'

Francis assumed the mock-solemn air customary with him when engaged in such trifles. 'Here's the first – an easy one, this. What's:

> As round as an apple
> As deep as a cup
> And all the King's horses
> Cannot pull it up?'

I waited a while, to keep him guessing, and then said, 'A well?'

'You've heard it before!'

I denied it vigorously. Francis grinned. 'Try another one, then, and if you get this one I'll know for sure you were as usual listening at the keyhole.

> White bird featherless
> Flew from Paradise,
> Pitched on the castle wall.

Along came Lord Landless,
Took it up handless,
And rode away horseless
To the King's white hall.'

I did not in fact know it, but it was fairly easy for one as well
versed in riddles as a Heron. I gave him a sidelong mischievous glance to match his own, and said after a pause,
'Not very seasonable, that one, is it?'

'Perhaps not,' said Francis guardedly.

'Snow, and the sun melting it?'

My cousin slapped his saddle in mock despair. 'How can I
surprise you? You've the knowledge of a sage. Is there a
riddle on earth you don't know, or can't guess?'

'I doubt it,' I said modestly. Francis sighed. 'Ah well, I'll
try again, and if you guess this one I'll give up.

What God never sees
What the King seldom sees
What we see every day.'

'Lord above,' I said, puzzling over it. 'You know, it's very
strange, the way the answer to a riddle seems so difficult if
you don't know it, but once you do then it's all so ridiculously simple. I can't think of an answer.'

'Then I have you at last, brat! Do you want more time?'

'No, I've thought of something, though somehow I doubt
it's the right answer. It's not money, is it?'

Francis grinned appreciatively. 'Shrewd guess, moi owd
gal, though as a matter of fact it's wrong; but it fits just as
well as the real answer.'

'Which is?'

'An equal. See, it is simple once you know. Have you any
to tell me?'

'None that you won't know already, I don't suppose.
Have _you_ any more to offer?'

Francis declaimed promptly:

'Tis strange, yet true
He's but a month-old man
And yet hath lived since the world began.

I had heard that one from Grainne before, and was mercifully quick with the answer. 'Ah, that's the moon, isn't it? No, I wasn't listening, I swear it, I had it from Grainne herself last year.'

'I'll believe you, for once,' Francis said good-humouredly. The sun was out, filling the side of his face with light, touching its fine-drawn lines, showing the relaxed curves around his mouth and turning the long, curling hair under his hat to gold. He looked happy, to my surprise, for such simple emotions were not usually associated in my mind with the complex, moody Francis whom I knew. Believing that now was the best moment, I said slowly, 'Francis?'

'What is it, owd gal?'

'You – you remember the day Simon hit you? Well, I talked with him, pleaded with him, to give up the quarrel. He was so horrified by what he'd done to you that he listened to me.' I glanced sideways and saw to my distress that all the finely balanced tension had returned to his face. Hating myself for marring the simple pleasure of the afternoon, I went on, 'He said – he *promised* me – that he'd forgive you and try to forget everything that had happened – he knows he's been partly at fault, but you know Simon, he won't admit it. But he wants your apology first.'

There was silence, above the slow clop and splash of our horses. Then Francis said coldly, 'What business is it of yours, madam?'

I flushed angrily. 'It *is* my business! It's the business of all of us who have to endure all the unpleasantness your stupid quarrel causes us.'

'But why you in particular, Mistress Long-nose?' Francis had never been this unpleasant to me, in all the years I had known him. Desperate, and feeling the abyss of unbearable hurt yawning before me, I cried, 'Perhaps because I'm the only one who dares, even though everyone else is unhappy too! Besides, I'm fond of you both, and I'm friendlier with you than with most. I—'

'In love with me, you mean,' Francis said, and the contempt in his voice was more than I could bear. 'No!' I heard myself shouting above the wind in the trees. 'Can't you even recognize a friend? No, no!' And unable to face him any more, dragged Orlando's head round and sent him plunging at full speed into the park, which we were just entering. Blinded by tears, impelled by the need to put as much distance as possible between me and the cause of my pain, I urged my horse to greater efforts. We flew through the trees on the edge of Piper's Wood, into the teeth of the wind and the new-falling, stinging rain, and I concentrated only on controlling the horse, letting the task numb my mind. Later, I might weep and grieve and succumb to thought, but for now I wished to forget.

But as I guided Orlando through the trees and bracken and tussocks, the thought woke and grew in the depths of my mind that he might, possibly, be right; and even as I tried to thrust the betraying thought down – for love was not friendship, nor did it seem to admit of friendship, only passion, and that was unknown and to be feared, and all those I had loved most dearly had died – even as I turned the idea from me, there was a fearful jolt, a crack like a gunshot and the sky and trees and grass spun like cartwheels before my eyes and turned abruptly to lights and pain and blackness . . .

There was rain on my face, and a cold wind numbing me, and I shivered and shook, and my head felt as though it were about to burst. Far away, and then nearer as full consciousness returned, I heard the laboured groaning breath of a horse in great pain. I opened my eyes, saw a grey scudding sky, and was promptly blinded by rain. Very carefully, holding my head, I sat up and opened them again. I felt sick. The grass and trees wheeled and then steadied. I was looking at Orlando, not three yards from me; he was attempting to rise, but fell back, with those horrible moaning breaths that wrenched my heart. His off-foreleg was obviously broken. I tried to get up, but my legs were too weak to support me. Nothing seemed broken, or even hurt, save for my head and a certain painfulness in my right arm and shoulder, but I was shaking and weak and winded from the shock of the fall. The rain fell harder, darkening my already damp skirts and shaking the grass and spotting poor Orlando's lovely hide. Laboriously, I got to hands and knees, ignoring my rebelling stomach, and crawled over to him. At my approach he quietened, and seemed glad to feel my hands stroking his head and pulling his ears, oblivious to the fact that it was I who had brought him to this with my thoughtlessness. Then I heard the brisk heavy tread of an approaching horse, turned my head, and saw Francis. At the same instant he saw us, altered course and set his mount at speed towards us. 'Dear God, what's happened? Are you all right?'

'I d-don't know, I think so,' I said, too relieved to see any face to think about our quarrel. 'I think he fell – a rabbit-hole or something – and he's in dreadful pain, oh, please, can you do something?'

Francis jumped down off his horse and took from its holster by his saddle the pistol he often, in these troubled times, carried with him. 'This is all I can do – is that all right?'

It was inevitable, and best. I nodded dumbly. 'Then get right out of the way; you needn't look,' Francis said. I gave Orlando a last anguished pat, painfully got to my feet, and without looking back, stumbled past him and under the shelter of a nearby tree. My legs trembling, I leaned my painful head against the rough bark and stopped my ears, hoping desperately that I would not disgrace myself, beyond all the other things I blamed myself most bitterly for, by being sick. There was a long, long pause, in which the drumming of my heart sounded loudest in my skull, and at last when the shot came I wept, for Orlando and for the breaking of an irreplaceable friendship.

Two hands fell on my shoulders, and very gently turned me round. 'Are you hurt?' Francis asked again. I had never seen the look on his face before, and could not interpret it. 'No,' I gasped, 'I don't think so, except for my head, I h-hit my head,' and fought to control my sobs. Francis stared at me for a moment, and I wondered what a picture I must make, and if Meraud had ever wept noisily like this, and then he said, 'Ah, my dear love, I cannot stand to see you weep,' and folded me into his arms. For a while, too glad of his shoulder and the gift of his comfort to pay full attention to his words, I stayed there, and then lifted my drowned uncomely face to his and said, unbelieving, 'Dear love?'

'I did say it,' Francis said, and for once there was no malice or mischief or deceit in his face, only the blessed relief of a secret long hidden and now at last shared. 'For that is what you are to me, my lady. You've loved me a long time, and been too afraid to admit it – haven't you? And I have loved you in like fashion, and been angry with myself for doing so, for it was one thing I thought I did not need.'

All the pain, and the jealousies, and the fearful-seeming complexities of my life fell away and it was as if everything was plain and clear and simple, where it had never been before, as if all the pieces in a pattern had suddenly been made whole for me to see them fully for the first time. I dragged my hands across my red eyes, and said, knowing it to be true, 'I don't believe it. Why? Why me?'

'Sit down,' Francis said. He pulled me down beside him, our backs against the tree. Water dripped from the branches on to our heads, unnoticed. 'Why you? I can't really explain. Can you understand – it's like being only part of a book, or a picture, or a piece of music, and searching for the person who's the other half, and without whom you can't be made whole. Like being in a foreign country, unable to make yourself understood, and then finding someone who can speak your language. You are my missing part, my soul's companion; I think I've known it ever since we made our unicorns that afternoon. Six years, sweetheart, is a long time to wait, with the missing part within reach.'

I said, shaken with delight, 'I think I've always known it too; I love all of your family, but you were always different, more important to me somehow.'

Francis smiled, and I had never seen him look happier. At last, it was easy to believe he was only eighteen. 'Moi dear, dear owd gal, I'm so glad I don't know if I can refrain from weeping . . . Most unmanly,' he added, with a glimmer of his usual sardonic manner. 'Why couldn't you unstiffen your overweening pride a trifle and admit your affections sooner?'

Laughing, I pointed out, 'I could say the same of you. I sat like patience on a monument, didn't I, and never told my love – not even to myself. But I think others have been less obtuse – Grainne had her suspicions, I know.'

'And before it had occurred to either of us, I reckon. Now listen, for you may not hear such words again from me; I'm sorry, sorry for what I said to you before. I've no excuse, sweetheart, except that I think you know that sometimes I am tempted to hurt most cruelly those whom I love the most.'

'If it led to this, what does it matter?'

'It could have led not just to Orlando's death, but your own. So it does matter, most deeply. Does your head hurt badly?'

'To tell truth, in the last few minutes I've hardly noticed. But, I've had a sudden thought, have you thought how strange it will look, to have both of us fallen from our horses in the space of two weeks?' I began to bubble over with laughter. 'You pretend it for a deceit, and then I have the foolishness to follow your example in reality!'

Francis began to laugh too, rather helplessly, and we clung together under the tree, dazed and bewildered by the turn our lives had taken, as though the earth had suddenly moved beneath our feet and changed all the world for only us to see. The rain died away again, and a gust of wind tore at our hair, mixing it brown and gold against the tree. 'Wilt kiss me, nutbrown maid?' Francis whispered below the rustle and sigh of the grass, and I nodded, unable to speak. As at last he took his mouth away, the sun came out and before us in the sky, slowly, colour by colour, faint at first and then growing strong and arching and glorious, a rainbow appeared, symbol of promises and delight. To stop myself bursting into foolish tears, I said, 'What of all the other women?'

'What other women? Oh, I see, the Oxford ones. So you *were* listening that night out here, were you? I thought you must have been. Youthful experimentation, they were, and nowhere near as numerous as Simon's fevered imagination would have you believe.'

'Simon hasn't got a fevered imagination. And what about the one at Catholm, who was the reason you were sent home?'

'How in God's name do you come to know about her? I thought that was kept very quiet. Apart from my parents, only Simon was told, the better for him to keep an eye on me at Oxford. So how did you find out? Eavesdropping again?'

'Er . . . I just happened to see the letter Great-Aunt Elizabeth wrote about it. It was on your father's desk.'

'So you've known all this time about my murky past . . . no wonder you were looking at me so strangely, the day I came home from Scotland. Well, I can assure you now, you needn't worry about that little whore; true, she it was who first initiated me into the lusts of the flesh, as Simon would probably call them, but I was not the first of her lovers – about the twentieth, in fact, for all she was only the same age as me – and I doubt very much if I was the last. Not exactly an affair of the heart, my relationship with Kirsty Armstrong, and soon forgotten; which will not in any wise be the case with you and me.'

Reassured, the ghost of four years' wondering laid at last to rest, I smiled at him. 'I did wonder why your embrace seemed so, er, practised. Now I know.'

'And how would you know a practised kiss from an inexpert one, my love? Or are you not as innocent as your wise and lovely brown eyes would seem to indicate?'

'Well,' I said, 'there was a certain air about it.' We had slipped back so easily into the old teasing banter, as if our discovery was too enormous to be looked at very seriously for too long. Francis laughed and hugged me closer to him. I rested my head on his shoulder, feeling strangely at peace. 'Then will you marry me?' I asked dreamily.

'*What*? My love, I am not the marrying kind. Of all things, so the fashionable young men would have us believe, the most tedious is a wife. A mistress is far more exciting. You'd make a good mistress, but a damn bad wife, for you're too lively and honest and unconventional ever to be tedious. Are you shocked?'

'Of course, sir – a seemly young maiden, scarce sixteen years old, cannot help but be shocked by such an improper suggestion.'

'Oh, yes? Where are your blushes, your downcast eyes? I see them not.'

'Begging your pardon, sir, but I am not Meraud.'

'A fact for which I daily give thanks.' Francis paused, and then continued more seriously. 'Marriage is an impossibility, though – Simon would never allow it.'

'He might, if you and he made up your quarrel and you gave some earnest of your friendliness towards him, and then asked him nicely for my hand.'

Drake came panting heavily out of the grass towards us, shook himself vigorously, looked at us and then, as if satisfied with what he saw, grunted, turned round three times and collapsed at our feet.

'Is that what you wish me to do?'

I looked round and up at him. 'Yes. More than anything, I want it. It – it seems to me that if you do truly love me, you could do no other. For me, and for your own sake too.'

Francis was silent, as if fighting off the last remnants of his hatred for Simon. Then he said, slowly, 'Very well, then, I'll polish up my halo and my wings and proffer my apologies. It'll cost me a deal in pride, mind you, but for you, my lady, I'll do even that.'

'I'm glad to know you'll sacrifice so much for me.'

'Ah, don't be so sarcastic! And you said that Simon is prepared to accept my humble repentance?'

'He promised me, and he'll have me to reckon with if he breaks it—'

'—I trust he's suitably alarmed at the prospect—'

'—but if you are truly sorry, he may well apologize to you!'

'And you'd give a world away to see it, I know. But listen, dear owd gal. Supposing all goes to plan, and Simon by some miracle gives his consent. Where, and on what, are we to live?'

> Come live with me and be my whore
> And we will beg from door to door,

I misquoted cheerfully. Francis cuffed me very lightly on the shoulder. 'Be serious, infant, and listen. I'm a third son, I've little learning, no property beyond a share in that shipyard and some minute manor near Ipswich, and my only skill is with the lute. Wandering players went out of fashion years ago. How shall I keep you in the style to which you are accustomed?'

Wondering how he had forgotten, I said, 'But I have Ashcott, and a house in St Aldate's parish in Oxford, and an estate in Yorkshire, and a share likewise in that shipyard, and four manors in Norfolk, and two ships plying the Levant trade besides . . . Shall we not find those sufficient?'

'And if my pride will not allow me to live off my wife's property?'

'Then we beg from door to door,' I said. '*Will* your pride not allow you?'

'I don't know. If it meant not having you otherwise, I think I could swallow it, though it would grieve me sore to go through the world not leaving my own mark on it somewhere. It's strange,' Francis remarked, tilting his face to look at the rainbow, fading in the sky, 'but for years I've been telling myself that I was not made for love, of that sort anyway, and industriously cultivating my natural detachment, and now that I have ceased to fight, and have duly surrendered, I can't imagine how I ever thought myself above it, or afraid of it. Is it the same with you?'

'Yes; and besides that I feel *safe*, like being by the fire on a cold dark night with the wind and snow howling outside, but excited too. I almost want to climb the tree and shout it out for all to hear.'

'No,' Francis said quickly, 'we must keep it secret for a while, so don't succumb to that temptation.'

'Because we want to win over Simon first?'

'Yes. He'll probably take it kindest if we gradually accustom him to everything first. So don't, as you value your life, tell Lucy – you know what she's like. And don't let Meraud know either. I've seen her eyes everywhere, she's sizing us all up, I'm sure, assessing friendships and quarrels and love affairs too, to turn them to her own advantage no doubt. She'll have her meddling little finger in all our business, given the chance, so don't let her. It will be difficult to keep it secret, but we must make every effort to, or it may ruin everything. And there's another thing.' His arm tightened round my waist. 'Dear though it may cost me, I shall make you neither lover nor mistress till we are safely wed, for nothing would spoil our case more than getting you with child!'

'Such self-control,' I murmured, at once relieved and, obscurely at the back of my mind, disappointed.

'Self-preservation, actually. Do you wish Simon to show me the door with the command never to darken it again, and hide your shame by marrying you to someone else? I know I don't. You look very serious of a sudden.'

Sudden anguish twisted my heart, I turned again to face him. 'We have forgotten – there's one thing will spoil our case for sure, and there's no way out! I'm not betrothed to you, but to Dominic!'

There was utter silence. Then Francis said quietly, 'Oh, God. So you are. There's been no word, has there?'

Aunt Hannah, much to her amazement, had succumbed to her numerous imaginary ailments two years previously. 'Perhaps it was thought to be unseemly so soon after his mother died. And his father sent him to Spain and Italy, afterwards, and as far as I know he's there still. Maybe,' I said with brave optimism, 'he'll find some dark-eyed madonna more satisfactory.'

'Than the rather unhealthy lust – for that is what I think it was – of a sixteen-year-old boy for a child of ten? I trust so. But it's a matter that will have to be thought on most deeply, for a betrothal can't lightly be brushed aside, not at any rate by such as Simon.'

'It being a matter of family honour. No one could be more devoted to that cause than he, yet the history of the Herons is not, to say the least of it, respectable; as I've heard you say yourself.'

'It wasn't an argument which carried much weight with him, as I remember. But that's probably why he is so anxious to uphold what respectability and standing we have got. So we must tread very, very carefully. There must be no inkling of our plans. If the question of your marriage to Dominic is raised, you must refuse to consider it. Simon will think you highly unreasonable, but you must resist him, and as he's susceptible to feminine wiles you have an excellent chance, with your sweet owl eyes and dolphin's smile, to persuade him at least to postpone the dreadful day. Of course, there's a good chance that Dominic will have lost all interest in ancient passions and will seize the chance to break it off altogether. And if the worst comes to the worst,' Francis said, his grey-green, reckless eyes holding mine, 'I shall pack my bags and you yours, and we shall tiptoe out of Goldhayes at dead of night and ride north to Catholm to be wed. Lucy would be delighted.' He bent his head and kissed me again.

A long time later, breathless and shaken by mutual passions I at least had never suspected to exist before that day, we drew apart reluctantly, lest they overwhelm us. Around us, the light was beginning to fail, the wind dropping and clouds now covering most of the sky, leaving only a shred of blue here and there to remind us of the vivid sudden sunshine of the afternoon. 'We must for home,' Francis said, 'before a search party is sent out. Do you feel ready to ride pillion?'

'I still feel very unsteady, but that's not from the effects of the fall. Oh, my love, have we dreamed all this, to wake from it tomorrow? Or is it real?'

'It is real, as real as you or I or this tree,' Francis said softly. 'I can't quite believe it either – and all our hopes and happiness so finely balanced, to fall at the slightest touch. So much hangs on what we do now, I almost fear to move – but we must.' He got to his feet and pulled me up. 'My nag will easily carry two, especially if the pillion is as light as you, but it'll be uncomfortable without a proper pillion pad. You shouldn't mind too much, though – it'll be one time when you're able to hug me close without occasioning comment.'

I laughed happily as he took up the reins of his horse, Drake frisking round his feet in hopes of some attention after such long neglect, and said, 'It *will* be difficult to keep everything secret, but if all depends on it then we must do so.'

Francis reached his hands down to pull me up behind him. 'Ah, but there are some who'd say that such a clandestine relationship gains added spice with the fear of being discovered.'

'But too much hangs on this for that to be true,' I said. 'But I would dearly love to tell Lucy, and Grainne, and Edward, for I'm sure they'd wish us well.'

'Tell Lucy, and the whole county will know all in the space of an hour. Not wise, sweetheart. Besides, her delight, when all is finally revealed, at having such a romance under her very nose will know no bounds.'

'Likewise her annoyance, at not having suspicioned it sooner.'

'There you have her wrong – you're wishing on her your own nature,' Francis said affectionately. 'My sister has what you are striving for, and what I must learn to pursue – a warm and generous heart. The Lucys of this world know little jealousy or meanness, and they give fully with both hands. Would there were more.'

'But she must learn that life is not one perpetual romance.' The horse, doubly burdened, had left Orlando's stiffening body on the tormented ground, and was striding through the thick wet grass and thistles and bracken towards the distant house. Slowly and lightly, it began to rain again. Francis smiled, looking over his shoulder. 'Would you unburden her of her illusion? I wonder who she will fall in love with. Whoever it shall be, I hope he will be suitable in position and character, for nothing less than love for life will do with Lucy, and she faces great trials should the object of her affections be some penniless vagabond – or worse, one who does not return her love.'

I laid my head against the back of his damp, bark-rubbed doublet. 'Lucy would win even one such as that in the end, she has the Heron determination.'

' "No surrender"? But we surrendered to each other in the end.'

'The Herons have determination, and also common sense. When we see the inevitable, we give way gracefully.'

'Lucy would not, I'll wager, were it a question of love. Ah, there is the house – they've lit some candles already. It must be very late.'

'And still you have no pocket-watch to tell the time!' I said.

'It will be about half after six, for the sun's not yet set. We were perhaps an hour and a half beneath that tree.'

'Time passes very quickly, when you're happy.'

'I've never spent time better,' Francis said.

I smiled. 'And to think it all began with a quarrel. It's an ill wind blows no good.'

'But you've lost your horse because of me – what shall you do now?'

'No – it was because of me he died. I shall ask Edward for another,' I said.

Francis went on, 'But not so good a one that you grow fond of it, for my betrothal gift to you shall be Boreas.'

I sat up straight behind him. 'Boreas? But you were going to keep him for your riding horse.'

'Well, I've changed my mind. He shall be yours. Of course, you won't be able to ride him for two or three years yet, but if you can wait that long there'll be no better horse – particularly if Ned and I have the training of him. You'll be the finest-mounted lady in all Suffolk.'

Delighted, I offered my thanks. 'No matter,' Francis said, waving them away. 'You named him, so in spirit he was yours already. Now you have him in reality. Don't let *him* break his leg in a rabbit-hole.'

We reached the driveway, and followed it through a gate in the deer fence, over the moat bridge and into the front courtyard, now in deepening shadow. The rain was falling heavily, and Francis jumped off and lifted me down. Weak-kneed, I clutched at him for support, feeling suddenly exhausted and sick and shaken. 'What is it?' Francis asked, and I said, 'Nothing. Let's get in out of this rain.'

We hurried into the porch, leaving the brown horse standing disconsolately on the gravel, chewing at one of the little knots of herbs and flowers set into the court. Francis said, 'One kiss before going in – no one will see us here.' The embrace was enough to make me yet more dizzy, and Francis opened the door and propelled me into the warmth and comfort of the hall. Almost immediately, as I stumbled to the fire, shivering in my wet cold clinging garments, Heppy came ßying down the stairs, her blue maidservant's skirts bunched up to show most of her calves. 'Mistress Thomazine! What's happened?'

'I fell off my horse,' I said weakly, 'he put a foot in a rabbit-hole and I was thrown. Master Francis found me, or I'd be lying there still.'

'We did wonder where you was,' Heppy said, her broad freckled face wrinkled with concern. 'Mistress Lucy and the others come back an hour agone. We thought you must've gone a-hunting or suffen.' She felt the sleeve of my riding-habit. 'My God, thass soaked! Do you go upstairs now, mistress, and I'll have they clothes off of you. You fare to be grey as a ghost.'

'Oh, Heppy,' I said, embarrassed by her overflowing concern, 'I can manage without too much help.' And then, betraying me, the room began to go round, my legs gave way and I fell suddenly into darkness.

I woke to warmth, and the faint music of the birds on the roof of the courtyard garden. Opening my eyes, I could see the blue sky through a gap in the bedcurtains. My head's fierce throbbing had faded to a hardly noticeable ache, but my right arm was stiff and painful. I remembered very little since my faint in the hall; a dim confused idea that I was being carried somewhere, and a lot of bother and talk, in which Mary's voice had been prominent, were all I could recall. I turned my head to look at my arm. There was a bandage around it, and I guessed that someone had bled me. Considering that I had felt so ill the night before, I now felt remarkably relaxed, and refreshed, and warm. I yawned and stretched, and rolled over to see Lucy, sitting on a chair by the bed with a book. She jumped up, smiling broadly.

'Awake at last, sluggard! It's an hour or so until dinner. Would you like some brought up to you?'

I sat up, gingerly, feeling happy and light-headed. 'Yes, I'm very hungry, but I'll come down for it. I've only fallen from my horse, not been injured for life.'

'But you might have been,' Lucy said. 'Francis told me what happened. Wasn't it lucky he found you!' She eyed me closely. 'And poor Orlando, to break his leg like that. You must have been going at a terrible speed.'

'Yes, it was all my fault. I didn't think of what might happen.'

'Well, you'll have to have another riding-horse, won't you, but Edward's already said he'd be dubious about letting you have one of his precious stock if you're going to ride it like that.'

'I shall *never* ride any horse so thoughtlessly again,' I said. 'It was horrible. Francis had to shoot him to end his suffering, and just leave the body there.'

'It always seems such a shame to kill a horse merely because its leg is broken, for if I broke my leg it would mend easy enough, but I suppose it must be done,' Lucy said. 'Grainne said you were at the farm yesterday, but left before we arrived. She sends her good wishes, and renewed thanks for the daffodils. Did you ask Wat for them?' Wat was the head gardener, as old and gnarled as his apple trees, full of Suffolk lore both wise and foolish, and a jealous guardian of the plants in his care.

'No, they were growing wild by the moat, so I helped myself. How did Grainne find Meraud?'

'She seemed quite cool,' Lucy said. 'You could see Meraud didn't think it was much of a place – well, it isn't, is it? But she liked Jasper, and Jasper said she was pretty, so that was all right. Oh, and I have most remarkable news for you! Simon and Francis have patched up their quarrel, they're friends now!'

Amazed, I stared at her; for, despite everything, I had not dared to hope that Francis would proffer a reconciliation so soon; nor that Simon would so readily accept it.

'And well you may look startled,' Lucy said. 'So was

everyone else, and none more so than Simon, by the look on his face. In fact it's a great pity you were stupid enough to faint, for you'd have liked to have seen it, I'll wager. We were just sitting down to supper, and Francis was late; he came in with Drake and instead of sitting he went straight up to Simon and held out his hand, and said . . .' She paused, trying to remember. 'Yes, I have his words exactly. "I have done you many great wrongs, Simon," he said, "and caused you much hurt, and I am most grievously sorry, and hope that in future we can all be friends." So we all sat there, hoping, and I had my fingers crossed for him, and Simon just looked frozen with surprise, as usual – and then he smiled suddenly, and held out his hand too, and offered *his* apologies, and they sat down most amicably. I declare,' Lucy said, 'I almost felt like weeping. And amicable they've been ever since. Pray God it lasts!'

'It seems almost too easy,' I said, 'it can't be possible, surely, to wipe out years of insult with a handshake?'

Lucy wagged her head at me. 'The trouble with you, Thomazine Heron, is that you can't believe good news. *I* think it will last. Simon always keeps his word, and Francis – well, for once he even *looked* sincere.'

With an effort, I imagined the scene. At least, I thought, this proves that the events of yesterday were not some glorious but insubstantial dream. Lucy leaned forward, confidingly. 'And I've a good idea why he's changed so suddenly. I've been waiting to ask you, Thomazine – what were you and Francis doing in the porch last night before you came indoors? I was in the library and I saw you. What were you doing?'

I felt suddenly sick at heart. Lucy was no more capable of keeping a secret than of ceasing to breathe. I strove to eliminate dismay from my face, and forced myself to say levelly, 'Doing what? What do you mean?'

'You know!' Lucy said triumphantly. 'I saw you, don't deny it! You were *kissing* him, weren't you? How long has that been going on for?' Her eyes glowed.

I said, 'Only since yesterday.'

'I don't believe it. I *thought* you were both behaving oddly, but I never in my wildest dreams thought of *that*.'

'Is it such an unlikely combination?' I asked, nettled.

'He being six foot and blond and you five foot and brown, yes,' Lucy said mischievously. 'Are you in love with him?'

'Don't be such a romantic little fool!' I snapped, feeling my flush betray me. Lucy beamed. 'Oh, yes, you are, aren't you? I must say, I like the thought of your being my sister-in-law.'

'Who says we're to be married? I'm betrothed to Dominic Drakelon, after all.'

'Oh, that. Well, I'm sure that can be put aside, he's never shown much interest,' Lucy said, eliminating my husband-to-be with an airy ease which I deeply envied. 'Anyway, now Simon and Francis are friends — I suppose that's why Francis wanted a reconciliation? I *thought* there must have been some hidden motive — now they're friends, there's nothing to stop Simon giving Francis permission to marry you, is there?'

'If you go to him now and tell him about us,' I said, 'it'll undo all the good and they'll be enemies again. We'll have to make Simon accustomed to the idea gradually.'

'Why ever should I tell him? I can keep a secret. Moreover,' said Lucy, whose faith in the universal generosity of human nature was, like Jamie's, unshakeable, 'I don't understand why that should start the quarrel over again.'

'You can't keep a secret,' I said. 'You know you can't.'

'What of it? You have nothing to hide, have you? You love each other,' Lucy said, as if that was the answer to everything. 'It would be nice if you married.'

My patience was rapidly wearing thin. 'I'm too young, for a beginning.'

'No, you're not. Juliet was only fourteen.'

'And what happened to her? Oh, Lucy, don't be so silly. Why should I marry Francis after a kiss or two? I'm not the first he's kissed, after all, and I don't suppose,' I said cynically, 'that I shall be the last. But Lucy, please, please don't tell Simon! Or anyone else, for that matter.' I shook her to drive the point home. 'I mean this, Lucy, most seriously – I really do. Please, please, *please* don't tell.'

Lucy looked startled. 'Well, if you feel like that . . . All right, I promise, on my honour, I'll try not to tell anyone.' She hugged me. 'Isn't it exciting?'

'Yes, isn't it,' I said caustically. Lucy released me and, pouting, got off the bed. 'Very well, if that's how you feel, I won't say another word. Shall I call Heppy for you? She's in her chamber.'

'I am perfectly capable of calling her myself,' I said, setting my feet on the rush matting. 'Lucy, dear Lucy, can you take a hint?'

'Oh, you are mightily bad-tempered today. I hope love doesn't strike me that way,' Lucy said cheerfully. 'You will be coming down for dinner, then? I'll see you there.' She swept out in an arch swish of skirts, head high. I glared at the door, and them summoned Heppy.

The village girl, with many exclamations of sympathy for my fall, helped me don my clothes and sat me on a stool to dress my hair. I wondered if she had heard anything, but a look at her broad and open face, innocent of any assessing, interested gaze, convinced me she had not. 'Master Francis carried you upstairs,' Heppy said, knotting my back hair into its bun, 'and Lady Heron bled you. Thass a lucky thing he found you, in't it? We was all wholly scared you was a-goin' to die.'

'Well, I didn't,' I said, relaxing. Heppy teased my unruly hair into neat curls along my forehead. 'Thass raining still, terrible weather that is still, Holly don't think nawthen's a-going to grow this year.'

As Heppy's brother was notorious for his utter pessimism, a philosophy of life in his case entirely justified by past events, I took little notice of this. 'Is that done, Heppy? Can I see?'

Heppy held a little hand mirror to my face. 'That look nice, Mistress Thomazine. You'd never think you'd ha' been ill. That suit you, that white face.'

I did indeed look somewhat pale, but my excited brown eyes stared joyously back at me in a face made suddenly attractive by happiness. Wholly satisfied with my appearance, for almost the first time in my life, I thanked her and fairly danced out of my chamber.

The first person I saw was Simon, examining a portrait of his notorious great-grandfather, Sir Hal, with a frown on his face. He looked up as I entered the gallery, and smiled with a quick vividness that reminded me of Francis. 'Good morrow, Thomazine. Lucy told me that you were quite recovered, and I resolved to escort you downstairs, if you will do me the honour?'

I overcame my irritation, for, I knew, his pompous style of speech was only the result of an awkward and basically shy nature. Francis could never be awkward. 'Of course, Simon; you do me honour.'

Simon looked down at me from his considerable and ungainly height. 'You gave us some cause for anxiety, last night. Had my lady mother not been so skilled, I really fear that you might have been very ill. It must have been quite a serious fall; Edward tells me that your horse's leg was broken in several places. A great shame, for he was a good riding-horse, and worth more than kennel-meat.'

'It was my own fault entirely,' I said. 'I rode him too fast, and without a care for the rough ground. I must apologize to Edward, for he was so pleased to have found Orlando for me, and he's always upset when a good horse is destroyed.'

'However, he will surely see that you have learned your lesson from poor Orlando's misfortune. I have no doubt that he already has another horse in mind for you. I can tell that dinner must be nearly ready; Master Blagge and Ambrose and Henry are our guests, and we should go down.'

I took his arm and we proceeded grandly down the stairs. In the hall at their foot, seated in the bay window, were Lucy and Edward, evidently indulging in gossip. As soon as she saw me, Lucy turned a guilty shade of red, and Edward stared at me with a new and inquiring interest. It was easy to guess what Lucy had been imparting to him. I fixed her with a basilisk stare, and her colour heightened.

Simon, oblivious, said, 'I have told Thomazine, Ned, that you are willing to provide another horse for her, to replace Orlando.'

Edward came over, big and stocky beside Simon's gaunt length. 'Only if she can promise me she won't ride this one to death as well.'

'I shall never,' I said firmly, 'ride any horse in such a way again. I've learned my lesson, Ned.'

Edward's bright blue eyes looked straight into mine. 'This is your last chance, Thomazine – there'll be no more fine and spirited riding-horses for you should this one be lamed or injured. I'll give you one of John's Punches instead!'

We all laughed. Lucy, avoiding my eye, said, 'Why don't you give Thomazine that roan filly? She's lovely, and she has a good turn of speed.'

'I did want to breed from her,' Edward said, 'but there's time enough for that, she's but five years old. Yes, she'll do nicely for you; gentle little thing, but she'll jump anything if you let her. I'll take you down to the farm to see her later.'

The seal set on my delight, for the rest of the day I sailed on air. Francis and Simon, whilst not as yet bosom friends, seemed on the best of terms. I was introduced by Edward to my new horse and took to her at once; a pretty young mare, about fifteen hands, with a silvery mane and tail, and her iron-grey coat flecked with white hairs. From her colour I named her Chalcedony, and rode her back to her new quarters in the stables at Goldhayes, delighting in her willingness, her smooth gait and her swift gallop.

On the ride home a strange little tune with words to match had arrived in my head from nowhere, and when I had seen Chalcedony fed and rubbed down, I retired to the music room, not bothering to change my habit, with quill and paper and lute to work it out more fully. It was not long before the door opened to admit Francis, grinning fiendishly. 'Aha! Trapped you at last!' he said, leaning against the door. 'What are you doing, owd gal?'

Beyond a secret exchange of smiles, I had had little contact with him all day, and was beginning to disbelieve all that had ever happened the previous evening. 'Making a song,' I said, poking at the paper with my pen. 'It came into my head and I had to write it down before it vanished.'

Let's hear it, then.'

'It's not gone beyond the second verse.'

'That's no matter, we can make some more together.'

I looked at him reluctantly. Francis grinned again. 'Don't tell me you've turned shy!'

'Very well,' I said, taking up the lute. 'But don't say I didn't warn you.

> The Western wind may blow, my love,
> The Eastern wind may whine,
> And I will ever go with thee
> Till bitter end of time.
>
> The Southern wind will blow, my love,
> The Northern wind will whine,
> But never shalt thou go with me
> Till bitter end of time.'

'That's a trifle melancholy, isn't it?' Francis queried, as the last sad notes faded from the air. 'Is it addressed to me?'

I flushed. 'No. I told you, it came into my head from nowhere.'

Francis smiled suddenly, and all my doubts were dispelled. 'It's as strange as some of the songs I learned in Scotland. What think you of this?' He came over to the stool where I was perched, appropriated my lute, drew up a stool of his own, sat down, and began quietly to sing:

> The men in the forest, they once asked of me
> How many strawberries grow in the salt sea?
> I answered them back with a tear in my e'e,
> How many ships sail in the forest?

As the echoes of his low, clear voice died away, I shivered at the strangeness of it. Francis said, 'It's a verse they sing with a song you must already know – "The False Bride". The one that begins, "Oh, I saw my love to the church go, With bridemen and bridemaidens she made a fine show." '

' "And I followed on with a heart full of woe, For she's

191

gone to be wed to another," ' I added. 'I like that, that new verse, it enhances the melancholy and – and eeriness.' I drew my stool closer to his and laid my head against his arm. 'So you and Simon are reconciled.'

'I expect Lucy told you. My pride was well and truly swallowed last night, but it was worth it. So the first part of our plan has succeeded – may the rest go as easily. You know, my love, when I saw you this morning you outshone the sun, such was your happiness, and I could barely restrain myself from hoisting you on to my horse and riding forthwith to be wed. Being in love suits you.'

'Lucy thinks it makes me bad-tempered. Oh, Francis, she saw us, last night in the porch, and put two and two together.'

'And no doubt made it twenty. Has she married us off yet?'

Despite my anxiety, I had to laugh. 'Not quite. She was overjoyed. I was very firm with her, but I don't think somehow that she will resist temptation. She may already have told Ned; that's all right, I suppose, but once she starts there's no end to it. I told her about Grainne's New Year gift, if you remember, and Grainne herself knew what it was from six different sources before Christmas.'

'I'll talk to her,' Francis said, in a voice which boded ill for Lucy. 'I can be quite frightening, when I allow myself. Now, since we're here, let's forget Lucy and her peccadilloes and sing our cares away.' He grinned suddenly. 'I've been wanting for a long time to speak this to you – it's Master Shakespeare's, I add, and not one of my own. Listen.' His arm round my shoulders, he shut his eyes and solemnly declaimed:

My mistress's eyes are nothing like the sun;
Coral is far more red than her lips red;
If snow be white, why then her breasts are dun;
If hairs be wires, black wires grow on her head.
I have seen roses, damask'd red and white,
But no such roses see I in her cheeks.
And in some perfumes is there more delight

Than in the breath that from my mistress reeks.
I love to hear her speak, and yet I know
That music hath a far more pleasing sound;
I grant I never saw a goddess go.
My mistress, when she walks, treads on the ground.
   And yet, by Heaven, I think my love as rare
   As any she belied with false compare.

Spluttering and speechless with laughter, I jerked away from him, full of mock indignation. Francis gave me one of his solemn sidelong glances, which sent me into fresh fits. After a second's pause, he joined in and we leaned together, helpless with amusement.

'I'm glad you can laugh,' Francis said, holding me close. 'Some ladies would be mortally insulted.'

'Lucy, for example? Meraud, for sure. Do I, when I walk, tread on the ground?'

'Most certainly you do – you'd fall headlong, else. I will grant you that your breath does most emphatically not reek—'

'—I'm heartily glad of that!'

'—and your voice is most pleasing, when it does not shout, but you, my lady, are no common or garden beauty. You are just yourself, and I love you – is that sufficient?'

'With such sufficiency, what need have I of more?'

'Some would court you with false words and flattery. You may not look for those from me, so if you wish them you must go elsewhere. Master Shakespeare has the happy knack of putting my feelings and thoughts into his words, and if you'll be patient with me there's another of his sonnets makes a mirror for my thoughts of you.'

'You know so many, and by heart?'

'I had little else to read, at Catholm. Hear this, and mark it well, my love.' Utterly quiet and serious, he spoke the lines of the sonnet, and my heart grew warm to hear them:

Let me not to the marriage of true minds
Admit impediments. Love is not love
Which alters as it alteration finds,
Or bends with the remover to remove.

Oh no! It is an ever-fixed mark,
That looks on tempests and is never shaken.
It is the star to ev'ry wandering bark,
Whose worth's unknown, although his height be taken.
Love's not Time's fool, though rosy lips and cheeks
Within his bending sickle's compass come;
Love alters not with his brief hours and weeks,
But bears it out even to the edge of doom.
    If this be error, and upon me proved,
    I never writ, nor no man ever loved.

Shaken and humbled, I said slowly, 'My love, I am not worth this . . . you make me afraid.'

Francis's pale eyes shone into mine. 'Afraid of what, lady? Afraid of love? You are drowning, sweetheart, do not struggle. Do you love me?'

'Until bitter end of time.'

'Then that is all you need. The rest will follow. Thomazine, we are those true minds, and between us there will be no parting, *whatever* may happen. Don't you see? Though we may be a thousand miles apart, you will always travel with me, as I will always go with you. Do you still doubt me?'

'No, no more.'

'That's to the good, for I've seen love and disbelief in your eyes now for a day. This is now no dream, for our souls are waking.'

'I know. I've ever been one for doubts, for I can't accept good fortune at its face value. That's what Lucy said.'

'Lucy in her way is as wise as you in yours. Shall we sing, since that is the purpose of this place? A round, to start with, I think.'

' "Rose",' I suggested instantly. As good as his word, Francis picked out the tune on the lute, and began. I waited until the end of the first line, and then started on the second part. The tunes blended perfectly:

Rose, rose, rose, rose,
Shall I ever see thee red?

Aye, marry, that thou shalt,
When thou art dead.

'Eureka!' said Edward, unexpectedly learned. He shut
the door behind him. 'I thought you must be here when I
heard you singing "Rose". I've been meaning to find you
alone all day.' He looked at us as we sat together on our
stools, and my heart sank. *What's* all this I hear about you
two from Lucy?'

Francis's eyes met mine. I said carelessly, 'Oh, nothing,
nothing at all.'

'Well, Lucy didn't seem to think it nothing,' Edward said.
'In fact, she could hardly contain herself.'

'I told her not to breathe a word!' I said furiously. Francis
laughed. 'If you beg Lucy to keep a secret, that's merely
spice to the telling of it later.'

'Then it *is* true,' Edward said. 'The wind's been blowing
some time in that quarter, hasn't it? Why did it have to be
secret?'

'Use your wits, Ned!' Francis told him. 'She's betrothed to
Dominic. One whisper of this to Simon, and not only would
she be wed to him before the month was out, but most likely
my quarrel with Simon would break out again. We must
tread very warily, and our case won't be helped by Lucy
blurting out our affairs to all and sundry.'

'But it's six years or more since the betrothal,' objected
Edward. 'And though Aunt Hannah didn't like the plans, I
know, she's been dead two years now and there's still been
no approach from them. Surely it's all been forgotten?'

'There was a settlement drawn up, and though nothing
was ever signed, it was all agreed and arranged,' I said. 'You
know what Simon is – he'd feel honour bound to follow his
father's word.'

'But surely you can approach him, ask him to set it aside.'

'Not yet,' I said. 'He has to grow accustomed to liking
Francis first, hasn't he?'

'You do seem to have thought things out very
thoroughly,' Edward said, considering. 'And I suppose you
are wise to go carefully, knowing Simon, though you can

rely on me to put in a good word for you, should you need it. And you both have my heartfelt good wishes. I'll leave you two turtledoves to your cooing now – and I promise I won't breathe a word into anyone's ear.'

'I hope your word's better than Lucy's,' I said severely. Edward laughed. 'I'll seek her out and give her a good brotherly talking-to.'

'I was going to do the same,' Francis said, 'but another voice to add to mine will make it more forceful yet. That sister of ours needs it. She can't live all her life imagining her friends and relations as characters in some stage-play or romance.'

'She has some idea that *Romeo and Juliet* is appropriate to our case,' I said, shuddering. 'I sincerely trust not, I don't want this to end in a welter of death. Fare thee well, Ned, and don't hesitate to speak your mind to dear Lucy. I could cheerfully drop her in the moat.'

'I will if she tells Meraud,' Francis said, with a note in his voice which made me look closely at him. But his face was laughing, even if his eyes were not.

chapter five

Rumours of war

And there went out another horse that was red:
and power was given to him that sat thereon to take peace
from the earth, and that they should kill one another.

(Revelations, 6)

Lucy, suitably chastened by two separate lectures from her
brothers, for the first time in her life sealed her lips and let
our secrets go no further. In consequence, during the first
half of the year 1641 we allowed our love to grow and
flourish, taking comfort and delight in each other and in
the meeting of our minds and hearts. Simon, who was ever
blind to all but the obvious, and who was frequently absent
in Ipswich or Bury or London, was easily kept in ignorance,
and his ebullient youngest brother likewise. Grainne took
one look at us, on the next occasion she saw us together, and
knew, and was amused to point out to us that she had long
divined that we were intended for each other. But beyond
her, and Lucy and Edward, our secret did not go, and nor
did anyone seem to guess.

In June, rather earlier than expected, Grainne's second
baby was born. A girl, named Hester for Henry's long-dead
mother, she had Grainne's black hair and presented a startling contrast to Jasper. That young man was delighted with
his new sister, but whether from mischief or a genuine wish
to be helpful, was discovered in the early hours of one
morning attempting to force dry salt beef, purloined from
the larder, down his month-old sister's throat. Her screams
had woken the entire house; when questioned as to the
wisdom of such action, Jasper's defence had been, 'But
Mama, Hess was hungry!'

'He'll come to a bad end, that one, he's got an answer to
everything,' Grainne said the next day, after recounting me
the story. It was July, and hot, and haymaking time at the

Home Farm. As was the custom, the young people of Goldhayes had turned out to help the Sewells and their workers, and tonight there would be a splendid supper at Goldhayes for all, from Simon and John down to the meanest labourer and the barefoot, ragged children who swarmed about the fields, often of more hindrance than help. In deference to the recent birth of the baby, Grainne was excused all work, and now rested in the shade of an oak tree on the edge of the field, whither I had repaired for a respite from raking hay. Jasper, sunnily scarlet-haired, was working his way along the hedgerow, gathering flowers with a total lack of discrimination, and his little sister lay sleeping in Grainne's lap. We sat together in the peaceful shade, and watched the distant workers proceeding implacably along the other side of the field. I could pick out John Sewell, supervising the loading of the cart; Henry, with another, perched on top of it distributing the hay as it was pitchforked up by the men below, including the four Heron brothers and Tom; and the women and children raking the lines of cut hay into more manageable piles ready for loading. Lucy, Heppy and Meraud were among the latter, Meraud recognizable by her smallness and the silver halo of her hair.

'I must confess, I did not think her capable of so demeaning herself,' Grainne remarked. 'She told me that she had never been allowed to join in the haymaking at St Annis.'

'I suppose she was keen not to appear the odd one out,' I said. 'To do her justice, she works as hard as I – harder, in fact, for she's taken no breather yet.'

'But she does not do it for enjoyment,' Grainne said. 'Jasper, my sweeting, what *are* you doing?'

Jasper had overbalanced and fallen squarely backwards on to his well-padded seat. Uncaring, he waved a flower at his mother, and shouted unintelligibly. Grainne wagged her ears with her hands, to his huge delight, and then turned back to me. 'She seems to me to have improved somewhat. Do you think that the free-and-easy ways of Goldhayes have unbent her seemly nature?'

'I think she has relaxed a little,' I said. 'She still has that superior air about her, as though we were none of us quite good enough to consort with her. But I don't suppose, if the tale of the poor girl's childhood is to be believed, that it's her fault; in fact, I think she's more to be pitied than condemned, for it's her father made her what she is. Yet I still dislike her. Her manner irritates me, and I can't trust her, for I feel in my bones that she has little concern for anyone but herself.'

'Time will be the judge. I think you're wise, though, not to let her into your secret. Where has that child disappeared to now? Jasper? Jasper!'

'I'll fetch him,' I said, scrambling to my feet. Jasper was the wandering kind and, for so young a child, capable of covering an astonishing amount of ground in less time than one would think. He was not in the hedgerow, but there was a trail of cornflowers, like broken pieces of sky, leading through a narrow gap in the hedge and out into the road which led to Bradfield Tye. Being small has some advantages, and I was able to squeeze in pursuit where the taller Grainne or plumper Lucy could not have done. Jasper was standing squarely in the middle of the road, surrounded by cornflowers, and still clutching one in his small sticky paw. The other pointed at the horse and rider standing in front of him. As I scrambled to my feet, the child turned a vast smile on me and said in tones of rapture, 'See, Thomazine! Horse!'

The stranger riding it did not bother to remove his dusty, tall-crowned hat. 'Good day to you! That is a fine child you have.'

I dropped an impeccable curtsey, so that he could see, despite my disreputable and hay-spangled garb, that I was no peasant. 'No, he's Mistress Sewell's son, and much given to wandering. I apologize if he's blocked your way.' I walked over to Jasper and took his hand, at the same time making a covert inspection of the stranger as he sat his tired horse. Although I had never laid eyes on him before, there was that about his long face and pale hair which reminded me strongly of someone. Then I knew; he had Meraud's cold, assessing, untrustworthy blue eyes.

Confirming my guess, the stranger said, 'Can you tell me, mistress, where I may find Goldhayes Hall? I have ridden from London to see my niece, who is in Master Heron's wardship, and I have met with no one to give me the way.'

'You need go no further,' I said. 'Master Heron and your niece are haymaking in that field, and I can call them across to see you; or you can go up to the house and await their return, for Simon's anxious to have the hay in while the sun lasts, and his welcome may be a little lacking if you speak with him now.' I looked up at the lean, quiet face, and wondered if this self-contained middle-aged man was really the Richard Trevelyan who had gone to prison for his seditious beliefs. I had imagined some fiery, crop-haired fanatic full of fine Biblical phrases, and the reality was disconcertingly different.

'Am I right in believing you to be Temperance Heron's daughter?' Richard Trevelyan asked suddenly. 'You greatly resemble her.'

Startled, for I had not been aware that he and my mother had ever met, I said, 'Why, yes I am . . . I am Thomazine Heron, and I presume you are Richard Trevelyan. But . . . I feel it's only fair to warn you that my cousin's welcome may be less than enthusiastic. He has a deep sense of honour, and he is strongly loyal to His Majesty; we have many friends at Court.'

'It was not he I came to see,' Richard Trevelyan said, 'but my niece. I mean no disrespect to you or to your cousin, but I had it in mind to satisfy myself that she was well, and happy, in her new home. I am sure that he will not refuse to let me speak with her. Moreover, he may, if he cares to ask questions of me, discover that the opinions of my youth have mellowed somewhat, and that we may on many points find ourselves in agreement. Besides, having come fresh from London, I have news and information I feel he should hear.'

I looked into his face, rather dubiously, wondering what to do. In the end, I said, 'I think it would be best if you went up to Goldhayes and announced yourself there, to await Simon's return. I could tell him of your arrival now, and give him some time for any ill feeling to subside, for he sometimes needs a little time to become used to unpleasant facts or unwelcome news. I mean no offence, cousin, but it's for your good.'

Richard laughed. 'You have summed up your cousin very shrewdly. mistress. I will take your advice gladly. How may I reach the Hall?'

I gave him the directions, and added, 'Lady Heron, who is Sir Simon's widow, will receive you; should she question your arrival, I should say that Simon approves it.'

My cousin gave his thanks and bade me farewell, and I stood in the middle of the road, with Jasper clutching my hand, and watching him ride gently off in a lazy cloud of dust towards Goldhayes. I found his manner, with its overtones of patronizing flattery, almost as annoying as Meraud's, and wondered how Simon would receive the news of his arrival.

'Who?' that worthy demanded, leaning on his pitchfork. '*Richard Trevelyan*? Are you certain?'

'Of course I'm certain,' I said, Having delivered Jasper back to his mother, I had gone straight across the field to tell Simon of his visitor, and on seeing his sunburned, outraged face was wishing I had not. 'He told me himself. He wants to see Meraud.'

'And where is he now? Simon asked, looking round the hot field as if Richard Trevelyan, armed to the teeth, was about to spring murderously out from behind the cart. I said innocently, 'I sent him up to the house. I thought you'd not wish your business interrupted.'

'Not by the likes of him,' Simon said. 'If he were not my cousin I'd turn him away. I wonder he dares show his traitorous face.'

'He's not at all as I'd imagined,' I said. 'He seemed quite civilized. And he said he'd modified his opinions somewhat.'

'He would need to change them completely to find any favour with me,' Simon said angrily. 'I wonder if Meraud feels the same. I expect the poor girl does. I wonder how she will receive the news?'

'Ask her,' I said bluntly.

But Meraud, summoned from her labours, stood small and still before us, her rake held firmly, and her lovely delicate skin flushed and reddened by the sun, and exhibited pleased surprise. 'Uncle Richard here? Oh, that is good. I haven't seen him for so long.'

Simon, astonished by this warm reception, said, 'But I thought your father had forbidden him to set foot in his house.'

Meraud's face broke into her sunny, charming, empty-hearted smile. 'Yes, but that was a long time ago, when I was very little. Father was often away from home, and then Uncle Richard used to visit, sometimes. He wasn't so bad as Father thought he was, and he was always very nice to me; he used to bring me lovely presents from London, that I had to hide from Father.' She smiled again. 'I'm sure you'll get on well with him, Cousin Simon, for I'm certain his only wish is to be friendly.'

'Why then did your father hate him so?' Simon asked. Meraud shrugged her small square shoulders, while the sun shone blindingly through her hair. 'I do not know, Cousin Simon. I think it was something to do with politics. It all seemed a great mystery to me, and somewhat stupid.'

'Then you've no objection to his visit?'

'Oh, no, of course not,' Meraud said. 'Why should I have? He was always so nice to me.'

So that evening, there was a stranger at our haymaking supper. The dusk was banished from the dining hall with a hundred brilliant candles, and the great long table loaded with dishes. Below the salt, trestles and benches had been added for the labourers and their families, and above it the five young Herons, myself and Meraud, Mary and Mistress Bryant, the Sewell family in its entirety from John to Hester, and Dr Davis, sat on chairs and partook of Monsieur Harcourt's dainties and delicacies in the coolness of the huge room. The wine and beer were passed freely round, and when all had eaten and drunk their fill, one of the labourers who boasted a fine singing voice rose, as was the custom, to regale us with a few songs. Mary pursed her lips;

the spoilt daughter of a rich merchant had never become used to the rustic customs still adhered to by the Herons. Sam Potter was young and just married; he was a big man with melancholy brown eyes, and chose his songs to match. Amid cries of 'Sing up, Sam!', 'Happen your Bess has taken all o' your strength!' and similar ribaldries, he worked his way through 'The Three Ravens', all thirty verses of 'Lord Thomas', 'The Riddle Song', and ended with a long and monotonous ballad of Robin Hood. Then the musicians in the company were summoned, the diners rose and we all repaired to the hall, which had been cleared for dancing. This celebration, along with the Harvest Horky and Christmas, was an opportunity for the Herons to enjoy, if only for a short time, festivities in conjunction with their tenants and workers. For form's sake, Mary took a seat at the side, to watch with bored, sophisticated eyes as her children mingled with their inferiors. We danced all the old country dances till we were sweating and breathless, and even Simon seemed to be enjoying himself, although he was put to great efforts to escape the shameless attentions of Sarah Greenwood. In the middle of the laughing, joyous mob of gentry and labourers, I spotted Richard Trevelyan, smilingly attentive, dancing with Meraud.

'Shall we retire to the garden?' Francis asked me softly. 'It's damned hot in here, and I'm longing for a breath of night air.'

'I'll come out a little later,' said Grainne, overhearing, 'and no doubt some more of us. Master Trevelyan wishes to speak with us all in peace and quiet, so I've heard from Simon, and the walled garden has been suggested. So be warned!'

'We'll take proper care, my chaperon,' I said, laughing, and followed Francis out of the door to the western side of the house. The cheerful sound of pipes and fiddles and drums followed us ever more faintly as we slipped hand-in-hand through the deserted parlours to the orchard room, from which a door led to a little wooden bridge across the moat to the walled and other gardens, and to the orchard.

The orchard room was cool and smelt of long-vanished

apples, which were stored here in the autumn on the empty wooden racks round the walls. Francis opened the door and the night air touched with cold and welcome fingers my hot head, swimming from sun and dancing and rich food and wine. We leaned on the rails of the bridge and listened to the soft rustles of the ducks as they searched the unseen water below us, and felt the flick and whisper of the bats flying and darting round the walls of the house. Then we made our slow way down to the walled garden, opened the gate, and passed through it. All the scented flowers there, lavender and sweet damask roses and gilly-flowers and stocks, poured their perfume into the still gloom. In a further corner of the garden, under the old wall, an arbour had been made from a rough wooden frame trained over with honeysuckle. With this end in mind, we wandered down the gravel paths, between fruit trees and hedges of box and lavender, finding our way more by memory and instinct than by sight. Far away in Piper's Wood the owls screamed and hooted, and nearer the music from the revels in the hall, faint and clear, had struck up the familiar riotous notes of the Brawl.

'I'm glad we're not there,' I said, in the circle of Francis's arm, 'For I declare I would have dropped in a dead faint after one more dance. Anyway, out here it's more pleasant by far, in the cool. Why Heppy should think the air harmful I don't know – what could ease my sunburn better?'

'A swim in the moat?' Francis suggested mischievously. 'I can arrange that, should you desire it.'

'I would rather stay safe and dry with you, love. Unlike you, I cannot swim.'

'Then I'll spare you, for I've no wish to see you drown. Unless I tied a rope round your waist, and hauled you in hand-over-hand.'

We had reached the arbour. A month ago, in June, the honeysuckle had been in full bloom and the scent almost overpowering in the hot sun. Now there were only a few late blossoms, high up and fragile, their pale trumpets dropping their fragrance into the night. We sank gratefully on to the rough-hewn wooden seat within the mass of woodbine, our arms round each other, worn out by the work of the day and the dancing of the evening.

'There's a flower still, up there,' I said, throwing back my head to look at it. 'I think I can reach it.'

'Wat would have your head,' Francis said lazily. The head gardener regarded his plants more highly than his own children, and any unauthorized pruning was in his eyes equivalent to murder.

I got to my feet and reached on tiptoe for the flower. Francis snorted with laughter. 'Too small?'

'No!' I said furiously, and jumped for it. A couple of green berries and a handful of torn leaves, and one trumpet, were all my reward. Francis, chuckling, came to my rescue, reached up a long lazy arm and plucked it. 'A flower for your hair, my nutbrown maid?'

But all the sweet-smelling trumpets came off and dropped to the dust, and I stared down at them shimmering in the gloom, oddly sad. And then, in one of the fruit trees, a nightingale began to sing, and I lifted my head to listen.

'A vastly overrated bird,' Francis said in my ear, very softly. 'But all lovers dream of a nightingale while they embrace, so why should not we?'

As we kissed, at the top of the garden someone started to sing in a pure, high voice, of a beauty to compare with the nightingale. I knew well the tune, and the words, and yet tonight they seemed charged with a sorrow that sent a chill all through me, as though the singer were not of this world:

Dear, if you change, I'll never choose again,
Sweet, if you shrink, I'll never think of love:
Fair, if you fail, I'll judge all beauty vain,
Wise, if too weak, more wits I'll never prove.
   Dear, sweet, fair, wise, change, shrink, nor be not weak,
   And on my faith, my faith shall never break.

Earth with her flowers shall sooner Heaven adorn,
Heaven her bright stars through Earth's dim globe shall
   move:
Fire heat shall lose, and frosts of flame be borne,
Air made to shine as black as Hell shall prove.

Earth, Heaven, fire, air, the world transform'd shall view,
Ere I prove false to faith, or strange to you.

But it was only Grainne's way of heralding her coming, so that we would not be surprised. The nightingale fell silent, and I could hear faint voices coming down through the dark. Grainne's feet crunched on the gravel, and presently, still humming, she came to the arbour. 'Hullo, I thought I'd find you here. The others are all coming down – shall we sit over there?'

An old gardener in Sir Hal's time, more than thirty years ago, had made a little grove of four apple trees and a lawn and bank covered with chamomile, and here we sat on the sweet-scented mounds, illuminated by the rising half-moon. 'Did you like my song?' Grainne asked.

'It was beautiful,' I said, 'I love Dowland's tunes, though they all seem to be melancholy ones.'

'I agree,' Grainne said, 'and somehow the sadness adds to the beauty. Do you know what Master Trevelyan wishes to say to us?'

'I have no idea,' said Francis. 'Personally, I find the man too close in manner to his niece for my comfort, but he seems most unlike the figure of terror conjured up by family gossip. And to my mind, he has his thoughts in the right place, unless he's changed them altogether.'

Lucy slipped into the grove with a frail candle and an escort of blind enchanted moths and midges. 'Isn't it lovely out here! So cool. My head's been splitting all day with the sun.' She put the candle down and folded up beside it, smiling. The rest came after her, spoiling the solitude; Jamie with Meraud trailing demurely beside him, prim and proper again in her black; Simon, with Edward his burlier shadow; the Sewell brothers, cheerfully arguing about dance steps; and last of all, looking somewhat out of place amongst all these young people, John Sewell and Richard Trevelyan. It was crowded in the grove, and there was only the one candle; the shadows were long and flickering and deep behind us, over the chamomile and the gnarled tree-trunks.

'You have news from London, Cousin?' Simon asked. His initial coldness towards Master Trevelyan was gradually thawing as it became apparent that our Cornish cousin would not dream of murdering us in our beds, and far from being an uncouth fanatic was courteous, quiet-spoken and friendly.

Before Richard could reply, Jamie interrupted eagerly. 'Did you see the Earl of Strafford's head cut off?'

'Be silent, or you'll be sent back to the house,' Simon snapped instantly. 'This discussion is not for ignorant children, so hold your tongue.' With a touch of embarrassment, he turned again to Richard. 'Tell us what you have to say, Cousin. You'll have an attentive audience.' He cast such a basilisk stare at his youngest brother that I felt that, at the least, was certain.

Richard Trevelyan looked round at our intent faces, a faint smile touching his lips. 'I do not know how much you know of events in London. or whether you subscribe to some newsletter, and therefore much of my news you may have already.'

'We are fairly well acquainted with events,' Simon said. 'I've been to London several times since my father's death, visited friends and neighbours at Court, and so on. One of them offered to use his influence to win me a place at Court, but that I had to decline.'

'You never told us that!' Lucy cried indignantly. 'Who offered it to you? Why didn't you accept it?'

'It was Tom Blagge offered it, and I did not accept it because I felt it to be too soon. Before I abandon my responsibilities and hie me to London in the services of the King, I must ensure that my estates are solidly based and capable of being run for long periods without my personal supervision. I beg your pardon, Cousin, I fear that we are sadly ill-mannered and past all hope of redemption, and I trust that you are able to accustom yourself to our style of discourse.'

Cousin Richard laughed, and said, 'I am very used to argumentative talkers, and you need not fear that I would take any offence, for in my experience the more undisciplined the talk, the more of worth is said. However, that is as maybe. I gather, then, that you are well-informed as regards political matters? You see, I bring you a warning, which you may or may not choose to believe, and I feel that perhaps if you know of events in London you may take more heed of what I say.'

'A warning?' Henry said, his amber eyes gleaming suddenly. Richard Trevelyan held up his hand. 'I will come to that shortly. But first of all, I feel I should explain how I came to change my opinions. As you know, I was hot against the authority of the King and of his ministers, in particular the bishops who sought to impose their rituals on us all and feared and hated the godly. I have been imprisoned for my writings, and have made myself unpleasant in my brother's house, and stirred up rebellion and discontent amongst the people of London.' He paused, looking round, holding his audience. 'That is, until, with my friends, I went to see the Earl of Strafford's trial. I was – we all were – hot for his blood, thinking him a black and bloody tyrant, trampling on the ancient laws and liberties of the people. And there he sat in the Hall of Westminster, no terrible tyrant but a little shrunken gouty old man, with a fur coif and a warm cloak to keep out the chills of March; a man harried beyond all deserving. There were many such as I, who came to howl for blood and left filled with pity. I could not forget him, and I was filled with unwilling admiration for him, for, sick man or no, he defended himself with brilliance. It became obvious to me that the case against him was very weak, and that the force of law lay with his arguments. And the Parliament who impeached him claimed the law to be on their side. I can tell you, I wrestled long at nights with what I heard at the trial, for it is hard to disavow those beliefs which have long guided one's life, and to deny them even after long thought seems like a betrayal of oneself. But the Lord was with me, and guided me through my struggle and showed me the way to the true path of righteousness.'

I saw Francis's face crease in a momentary frown. Unnoticing, Richard Trevelyan continued, his voice deepening. 'I no longer desire revenge or bloodshed of any kind, whether it be the flogging of my erstwhile friend Lilbourne, or the losing of Strafford's head. The Lord our God hath shown me that he is not terrible and merciless, but just and forgiving with all men; one whose disciple could say, "Forgive them, for they know not what they do." Vengeance belongeth to the Lord, and it is not for us to usurp his place. Should Tom Wentworth be deserving of punishment, it is the Lord who should undertake that task, not his self-appointed deputies and the minions of Pym. I am not one of your Presbyterians, Cousin, nor am I a follower of Laud, or of the Bishop of Rome. I follow the dictates of the Lord, who speaketh in mine own mind and heart, and He does not desire the execution of an old man, however deserving of death, on a trumped-up charge influenced by the mob. I am no longer in association with Pym or my former friends. I saw at Strafford's trial his implacable hatred for that broken man revealed for all to see, and I wondered, for what ends does he thus persecute the King's servant? And the Lord gave me the answer. It is Pym, not Strafford, who is the tyrant. It is Pym who manipulates the law for his own ends, and commits treason and murder in its name. He is a man more implacable and set on his course than ever Strafford was, and that course is set irrevocably for collision with that of the King, with no turning back for either, however much they may appear to yield or compromise. And that can only mean one thing, sooner or later – war. And I will have no part in war.'

There was a little silence. No music, now, from the house, only the distant noise of the happy, tired revellers, going home oblivious as their world reeled about them.

'War?' Simon said sharply. 'We live in the seventeenth century, Cousin, rather than the fifteenth, and times are not now so barbarous.'

'But it has now gone too far. Pym is bent on having his Commons rule England according to his desires, and the King will not easily forget that he and they and the London mob forced him to kill his dearest and most faithful servant, as surely as though his own hand and

theirs had lain on the axe. Believe me, war is certain now,
and the only matter for doubt is the date of its beginning.'

We digested this in silent shock and disbelief. Then,
Henry leaned forward, the light of battle now glowing
unhidden in his face. 'And for whom then will you fight,
Master Trevelyan?'

'For no one,' said Richard. 'The Lord has shown me that
the path of violence is not the path of righteousness, and
that those who would walk with God must also walk in
peace. I do not deny that others may not feel as I do, and
that many of them are good and godly people, but I will not
take up my sword in any cause, however rightful I deem it
to be, for war can only lead to terrible sufferings.'

'You've a right to your beliefs, of course,' Henry
remarked, his voice cool. 'For myself, I believe that the time
must come in many disputes when mere words are no
longer enough, and should the quarrel between the King
and his Commons come to that pass, I shall not be slug-
gardly in offering my servicers. Soldiering is my trade, and
my sword has grown over-rusty during the past few years.'

'If war does come,' Jamie said eagerly, 'can I fight?
Simon, can I? I've always wanted to go to the Low Countries, but if there's a war here that will be just as good. Please
can I fight?'

Richard's face hardened abruptly, his hand shot out and
gripped the sleeve of Jamie's doublet. 'Listen, child! If you
had gone to Holland and Germany with your brother and
his friend, you would have seen horror and suffering and
killing enough to last you the rest of your days. I have been
in Germany, and I have seen what a Civil War can do. None
of you, except for Edward, and Henry Sewell, can have any
conception of what it is like, and I can promise you that your
disillusionment will be bitter.'

Jamie's eyes stared back, wide and startled in his freckled
face. 'What horror? It can't be wrong to fight for a just
cause, can it? I would fight for the King, as I would for the
Queen of Bohemia and her kingdom.'

'Ignorant little fool,' Francis muttered beside me, 'he's
been reading too much Malory.'

'Pray God that such a thing does not come to pass in England,' Grainne said unexpectedly. 'I too have seen war, Master Trevelyan, for I followed my father and the Prince Cardinal's army from fourteen years old, and I thought when Henry brought me here that England was a haven of peace and tranquillity. You do not wish to see that peace shattered, and neither do I.' She cast a considering look at Henry, who shrugged. 'It's my trade, sweetheart, like it or no, and if war comes here I won't shirk my duty . . . but I confess I dislike the thought of it as much as you do. Happen it won't come to that, for we're a sensible people, not like you wild Irish, and our swords have for the most part been beat into ploughshares these two hundred year agone. We're not a fighting race, any more.'

'Unless we feel that a cause is worth the fighting.' Francis said. 'And King and Commons are of like mind in that, I think. The question is, if it does come to war, which of us will fight – and on which side?'

Tom laughed disbelievingly. 'I don't believe a word of that, I really don't. War? Here, in England? It's ridiculous. Can you imagine our lads taking up their pitchforks or trying to hold a musket? The militia musters en't more than a common joke, more an occasion to get drunk than a proper drill. We – we just aren't *ready* for any war!'

'Well,' Francis said, 'just assume that war has broken out, and that you have to choose – not to fight, or to fight for one side or the other – which, Tom?'

Tom flushed unbecomingly, and stared at his shoes.

'Simon?' Francis said, an eyebrow lifted. His eldest brother stared at him with a suspicion of the old hostility on his face. Then he shrugged, smiling awkwardly. 'I? I would fight for the King. I think you will know why. It is the duty of every loyal subject to support the Lord's anointed ruler against those rebels who would infringe and usurp his power.'

'I would fight for the King, by your side,' Edward said. 'But more because I know something of soldiering than for any other reason. I don't concern myself over much with the subtleties of politics.'

'Pym,' Francis said drily, 'has all the subtlety of a runaway bullock.'

'I agree he's not made much secret of what he's about,' Richard remarked, 'but whether he acts from self-interest, lust for power or from a genuine concern for the common weal I do not know. The King, on the other hand, seems to me to be less open. I think some moderates feel that he has in his mind adopted a compromising course. I am convinced myself, however, that our High and Sovereign Lord King Charles loves compromise as he loves the Plague, and he is a very stubborn man – as is his opponent. So I came here to give you warning of the storm I feel lies ahead of us, and I trust that my words have not been taken amiss. I hope that I have by doing thus given you the time you may require to make any preparations, should you desire to fight; and that I've made some amends for my past opinions and behaviour.'

'Your warning has indeed not been taken amiss,' Simon said, and his voice carried as much warmth as I had ever heard in it. 'On the contrary, you've thrown a great light on my mind, Cousin. Despite our knowledge of events, I had not thought matters to be at such a pitch, and I respect and value your judgement in this. We can make ready, now, for His Majesty will need help if he's to crush any rebels, and should all nevertheless work out peacefully, we shall not have lost anything by being prepared for the worst.' He stretched his arm across the candlelit circle to Richard, sitting opposite, and the two clasped hands. 'I regret, Cousin, my previous error of judgement,' Simon said, smiling. 'I thought you a traitorous fanatic, and I find you no such thing. My apologies.'

'My apologies also,' Richard said gravely. 'For I also find you not as I had thought you to be.'

'And what was that?' John asked. Richard laughed. 'Courtesy forbids me to tell you. But, I must say, I did not think Goldhayes an environment suitable for the upbringing of my favourite niece.' He glanced at Meraud, and the girl said, 'Your only niece, Uncle Richard.'

'But still my favourite,' Richard Trevelyan said, and the

look of tenderness on his face was touching, as though she was the daughter he had never had.

During the weeks that followed our garden discussions, it became apparent that Richard Trevelyan was rapidly winning for himself a place at Goldhayes, if only because of Meraud's obvious delight in his presence. Perhaps because of his kinship with, and close resemblance to her, I found it hard to like him, although he was always pleasant enough, and soon dropped the slightly patronizing manner which his less experienced niece still held to. As with Meraud, I felt guilty about my dislike of him, and wrestled long with my conscience, coming at length to the conclusion that my feelings against him were not so much dislike as distrust.

'I can't help wondering what he wants of us here,' I said to Francis. We were out hawking in the park, and Meraud's merlin had refused to return to her fist or to the lure. It was now sitting in the lower branches of a stout elm tree, with a ring of would-be catchers – Lucy, Edward, Robert Jermyn, young Ambrose Blagge, Tom and Meraud herself – fuming impotently beneath. Francis and I had withdrawn to a little distance, holding the others' horses, to watch the fun.

'You don't like him, then?' Francis asked. He had taken off his doublet in the heat and sat Hobgoblin, whose foal had now been weaned, with one leg hooked over the pommel of the saddle. The haymaking and the heatwave had turned his fair skin through all the shades from red to golden brown, and his new tan looked unfamiliar against the white of his shirt and his sunbleached hair. My own arms, I saw, looking down at them resting on the decorous purple of my mourning riding-habit, were positively swarthy. I thought of my Spanish great-grandmother, and smiled to myself. Lucy had it from Judith and Martha Blagge, and they in their turn from Nan, that London ladies of fashion thought of nothing but the whiteness of their skins, wearing chicken-skin gloves at night to that end, and Lucy had since gone about out-of-doors well shaded in a hat and veil. I felt my hair hot on my shoulders in the pleasant sun, and was glad I was no lady of fashion.

Jamie, being chivalrous, was about to ascend the tree in pursuit of the merlin. My eyes on him, I said, 'Not so much dislike as distrust. He seems so honest, so frank, so godly, that I can't help but think that it may all be false. And can someone who's been imprisoned for his beliefs, and held to them for so long and suffered for them; can that person *really* change all overnight? My love, I smell hypocrisy.'

'I must confess I detect a whiff or two myself, but perhaps that's only what I'd like to believe. His godliness sticks in my craw, but to my mind he's sincere in that. I'm not so sure of his politics, though. They're sound enough to Simon and his like, now he's changed them, but I preferred them before he did, if you take my meaning.'

'Would you support Pym, then, if there was war?' I asked, with the spectre of Herons fighting on opposing sides rising before me. And Francis said, 'If I was free, yes, I would, for I think he has the right of it. With Pym there is a chance for the people to regain some of their former freedoms; with the King, nothing.'

I resisted the temptation to embark on a political argument. 'What do you mean, "if I was free"?'

'What I say. I'm not free to choose to fight for Pym, for if I did I'd lose all hope of ever winning you from Simon's grasp, would I not? Don't look like that, owd gal, for it's a sacrifice made gladly.'

'But if you believe Pym is right, that's no sacrifice, that's betrayal!'

'I don't really believe Pym is right, I believe he is the lesser of two evils. If I believe that anyone has the absolute right of the argument, it will be the man who champions the common people; who allows each man and woman from Papist to Anabaptist to worship as they please, or not to worship at all; who says that each and every man rich or poor should have a voice in the affairs of state, and won't restrict electors to a few wealthy gentlemen or fat burghers whose only interest is in keeping and expanding their riches at the expense of the poor and the landless.'

214

Words rose in my throat, and died. I thought suddenly of the Greenwoods, in desperate poverty and struggling against great odds; of the beggars who sometimes came to the kitchen door for scraps; of the vagabonds I had seen whipped at the cart-tail out of the parish, of the people Francis had once described who lived in Liddesdale in hovels made of mud and grass; and the abused and pathetic dancing bear whose plight had seemed to me, at ten, so similar to my own. I had thought myself ill-used, but how much more to be pitied were these. I saw the unfairness of it all, that so few could hold so much wealth and land while the rest of the people groaned in poverty. Even as these compassionate impulses overwhelmed me, my clear cynic's brain was marshalling the usual arguments for property and the *status quo,* but, beside the ideals I glimpsed in Francis, they looked mean and petty.

'Your silence usually means disagreement,' Francis said, eyeing me quizzically. I shook my head. 'No, no, it doesn't. I – I'd never realized it before, I think, how many people are poor.'

'And it took merely a few words from me to provide that revelation? For shame, Thomazine, you're as unconvincing as Cousin Richard.'

I flushed angrily. 'Yes, it did. *You* may not believe that, Master Cynic, but it's true – I'd never seen it before, and now I do, I see the injustice of it all, but I don't think we can do anything about it.'

'Not now,' Francis said, 'but if war does indeed come, we may find that circumstances change. In chaos, it is comparatively easy for such ideas to take hold.'

I stared at him, glimpsing the terrors that civil war could bring to our stable, complacent, unmoving and peaceful little world. Then I quoted, slowly, my eyes holding his, ' "And there went out another horse that was red: and power was given to him that sat thereon to take peace from the earth, and that they should kill one another: and there was given unto him a great sword." Francis, I love you more than I can say, but tell me truly, is that what you want?'

'If in the end it brings justice, yes,' said Francis, with the clear-eyed idealism I found so chilling. I spread my hands round the sunny, peaceful scene, the heat-haze shimmering the wood, the distant tower of Bradfield St Clare's church, sun-dried yellow grass and dusty blue-green trees, butterflies of all hues dancing around us, the heavy scent of grass and ladies' bedstraw, all glorious and immeasurably dear. 'Look, look at this, it's all so fine – would you spoil it all, and bring suffering and death, for an idea?'

All the tension went out of his lean, taut body, and he smiled, vivid in the sun. 'To tell you the truth, lady, I don't know what I want. I desire too many things – you, and justice for the oppressed, and Goldhayes, and my freedom. I can't have them all, I know. Perhaps it will never come to war, and I don't know if I shall be glad or sorry.' He turned his head towards the tree, down which Jamie was climbing laboriously one-handed, the merlin clasped firmly to his bosom. 'He may be sorry, so will Edward and Henry, but Grainne will be glad. I respect her judgement almost as much as I respect yours, my love, and as you are both so firm for peace, I may yet be persuaded.'

The summer lingered long that year, and was kind and warm till the days shortened into October. Lucy and Meraud and I laboured in the still-room and brew-house and kitchen, bottling and preserving, making ointments and salves, and brewing the good October ale. We helped pick and store the apples and pears and nuts from the orchard, and in the salting down of beef and pork from the Autumn slaughter, and had little time to talk of politics and of the slow-gathering clouds about our small, sunny fields. Lucy, with her faith in human nature, refused to believe that war was likely. 'I can't credit it,' she asserted stoutly. 'English people are too *sensible*. And besides, as soon as harvest-time came round everyone would leave the armies for home and then they couldn't fight, could they? Why should anyone want to bring war to our lovely peaceful country, just because of a few plaguey old bishops?' she added. Not being of a fanatical turn of mind herself, she was quite unable to understand why anyone should want to fight for what seemed to her such trivia.

Meraud looked at her sideways, slyly, but kept her own counsel. Lucy went on sorting apples into those fit for eating or storing, preserving, and feeding to the horses and pigs. I said cautiously, 'It's not just because of the bishops. There's trouble in Scotland too, don't forget, and the King's had to go there to try to settle it. And however much he concedes to the Commons, they seem to demand more of him.'

'And of us, too,' Lucy said. 'Did you hear about Parson Eldritch? A band of busybody Puritans out of Bury came to demand that the Doom be painted over and the rood-screen hacked down, and when he refused they abused him for a Papist scoundrel and Constable Keele had to intervene. Heppy told me this morning.'

'She told me too. Orders of the Parliament, apparently. I'm glad Parson stood his ground,' I said, 'for I like that Doom, old-fashioned and Papist as it is, and the screen is too beautiful to destroy so wantonly. Lucy, are you really thinking of what you're doing? You're put a rotten apple with those for eating!'

'My mind was wandering,' Lucy explained. 'Yes, I know these are troubled times and all the rest of it, but I really can't believe that men could go to war over it, not when they've got all the horrors of the German wars as an example of what could happen.'

'Simon would,' I said. Of late, he had been in the habit of holding forth on the evil plots and wicked demands of those opposing the King, and had recently, very embarrassingly, entered into a most heated argument with Sir Nathaniel Barnadiston, one of the Members for Suffolk, on this subject. The worthy knight had been Simon's guest, had left in a fine rage, and had not deigned to speak when encountered a few days later by Simon at Bury Market. If the normally courteous, dutiful Simon could behave thus with his guest, his father's honoured friend and a man many years older than himself, then he was certainly capable of fighting for his chosen cause.

As the year 1641 drew to its cold and frosty close, matters grew worse. The King returned from Scotland in high spirits, convinced he had quieted the Covenanters and brought about a new alliance between himself and them, and was greeted by a Grand Remonstrance, drawn up by Pym, which listed all Parliament's grievances against him. Hideous tales of the sudden uprising in Ireland had spread like wildfire through the country, so that Grainne began to draw sidelong glances from those who did not take kindly to her unorthodox ways. One Member of the Commons had had the unprecedented audacity to demand that Parliament choose the commanders of the Trained Bands, and Pym himself told the House that the King should henceforth be surrounded only by those whom Parliament should choose. With each fresh piece of news from London, Simon grew more angry, and Richard Trevelyan wore the faintly self-satisfied air of one who had been proved right against all odds. In the villages, and in Bury, talk buzzed in the taverns, ale-houses and market-places, and wild rumours of Irish invasion flew from mouth to mouth until all of us, deprived of hard facts, were fit to start like restive horses at the sound of the church bells.

Francis, like Meraud, kept his own counsel, avoided political argument and poured cold water on the more lurid rumours current in the villages. Just as his acute perception of character had led him unerringly to the deadliest insults, the most provoking mischief, so now could he choose the words most likely to soothe the fears of the old goodwife afraid of being murdered in her bed, or point out to the suspicious that Grainne Sewell, far from being a Papist savage, was civilized, a devoted wife and mother, and attended church of a Sunday. Often I rode with him, but we were always aware of potential gossip and made a habit of asking Lucy or Jamie or some other friend to accompany us. The strain of hiding our affection was becoming great; even in such a large house as Goldhayes opportunities to be alone together were rare, and, with the shortening of the days and worsening weather, becoming rarer. Sometimes we could find an empty chamber where we could embrace briefly, or walk in a private part of the garden; Grainne did sterling service and often contrived to ensure we were not disturbed on our visits to the farm; but it was becoming increasingly difficult for us to hide our love and to contain our feelings and desires. Not unnaturally our tempers became short and we picked quarrels with each other or with Lucy or Jamie. Looking back, it seems astonishing that more people did not guess. Mary in particular I feared, for years ago she had packed Francis off to Oxford to avoid this very thing, but she was increasingly unaware of her children's doings, and often absorbed with her own friends in her chambers or at Rushbrooke or Hengrave. Moreover, her sight was beginning to fail, and our speaking glances passed unnoticed, since she was fortunately far too vain to wear spectacles. Simon, notoriously obtuse when it came to things not placed immediately in front of his nose and thus forcibly brought to his notice, appeared happily oblivious; perhaps the fact that in more innocent times Francis and I had frequently enjoyed each other's company blinded him to the fact that the quality of our enjoyment had changed.

But in December the summons I had been dreading for so long finally appeared. Brought by a muddy, tired servant in red and gold livery and speaking an almost incomprehensible dialect, its arrival was sufficient to have me brought from my lessons in the library to face Simon in his study.

I had seen from the windows the arrival of the servant, and had recognized the livery. So had Lucy, and her round worried eyes did little to boost my morale. When Tom Sewell (who had lately put his quick and legible hand and skill with numbers to good use as Simon's secretary) brought word that my cousin wished to speak with me at once, I rose with a thumping heart, well aware of what lay in store, and walked with a lifted chin through the house, desperately planning my strategy. There was but little time in which to do so, and I did not have Francis's cool quick brain to consult, for he had gone with Edward to Horringer to look over some likely yearlings of Ambrose Blagge's. Nor did Tom help; he knew of the contents of the letter and with broad winks and sly comments was attempting to give me some hints. 'I reckon you'll soon be a bride, eh, Thomazine? There's a fine husband somewhere for you, I'll be bound . . .'

Once I had found Tom's cheerful insensitivity amusing. Now, however, I said with suppressed fury. 'Oh, hold your tongue, Tom Sewell, I've little stomach for your jokes today.'

Tom, maddeningly, only grinned the broader. 'Do you guess, then? Not to your liking? Joan reckon he's the best-looking of all your family.'

'That's saying little enough,' I commented, 'it's the female Herons have the looks, in this generation at least.'

'Thass true enough,' said Tom. 'You and Lucy and Meraud, prinked up in the fashion, would turn heads even in London; mark my words, I know.' He had been to the City but twice, with Simon on business, and was fond of acting the man of the world. Often I wondered how two so different as he and Henry could be brothers, save for their great similarity in looks. I also wondered how Simon could put up with Tom ever at his elbow – but Simon, like his father, was curiously tolerant where the Sewell family was concerned.

'I have her!' Tom announced, opening the study door with a flourish. I rustled past him, plain and sombre in my purple stuff gown with the full sleeves and high-waisted, basqued bodice. Simon, also plain and sombre in the mourning he and his brothers and sister would wear for some years yet, rose from his desk with his rare, vivid smile. 'Ah, Thomazine. Come and sit down. Tom, go and get a flagon of Rhenish and a couple of cups – we've some reason today to celebrate!'

'Aye, sir,' Tom said, gave me a wink, and closed the door behind him. I heard his heavy tread receding, and sat down on the proffered chair. Simon remained standing. 'Did that young rapscallion give you some indication of why you've been so abruptly summoned here?'

Despite my sick feeling and the taste of sand in my throat, I could not suppress a smile. 'Yes, he did. I gather that Cousin Dominic has recollected our betrothal.'

It was the wrong line to take with Simon; the smile faded, and he became his usual chilly self. 'Yes. You may have seen the servant who brought the letter. Shall I read it to you?'

'If you wish,' I said. Simon sat down, cleared his throat, and picked up a single closely written sheet. I listened with growing despair. The letter was not actually from Dominic, but from his father, reminding Simon of the betrothal, saying that his son had but lately returned from his travels in Italy and Spain, and now wished at last to wed. The fact that since Lady Drakelon's death the house at Upper Denby had been lacking a mistress to run it, was an additional reason for the timing of the proposal. If all was agreed, Sir Roger and his son would travel to Goldhayes in April, when the roads should be easier, to celebrate the wedding; after which they would escort me back to Yorkshire to begin my life as mistress of Upper Denby Hall.

'Well?' Simon asked, looking up. 'I daresay you thought this would never arrive. Is all agreeable to you?'

I swallowed, not knowing what to say or how to say it, to soften the blow he had never expected. Finally, I raised my head to meet his eyes, seeing them widen in horrified astonishment as I spoke. 'Simon, I don't wish to marry Dominic. Not yet, at any rate – not so soon.'

'Don't wish to?' Simon demanded. 'Thomazine, what in God's name do you mean? This marriage has been arranged for more than six years, and you want more time? You're nearly seventeen, you're fully marriageable; why should more time be needed?'

'Lucy isn't wed yet, nor even promised.'

'None suitable has yet been found, though I've had some few offers. But my father arranged this for you when you were but a child, and you agreed it then . . .'

'I did not have the courage to say no,' I broke in. 'I didn't know what it would mean, to marry Dominic.'

Simon stared at me with suspicion. 'What is so amiss,

then, with Dominic? Are your affections engaged else-where, without my knowledge?'

'No, no, you don't understand,' I said, desperate to throw him off the scent. 'How can I in conscience wed him? He's a Papist, through and through.'

It was obvious that this was an objection that Simon had never thought of; equally obvious, from his comically open mouth, that it was an effective one. Exhilarated by the success of my spur-of-the-moment excuse, I pressed my advantage home. 'I'd never been happy about such a mar-riage, but I couldn't say so to your father, nor to Sir Roger . . . I was but ten years old, Simon, and not long at Goldhayes, and I did not know you all so well. But you must remember,' I went on, 'I've been bred a Protestant, my grandmother came from a Puritan family, and my step-mother was also inclined that way; not to mention my nurse, who's of good Banbury stock . . . Simon, I was bred to hate and fear Papists, and I cannot now so easily forget it!'

Simon leaned forward, a frown of concern between his strongly-marked straight brows. 'To be frank, Thomazine, I find this surprising. Why have you not mentioned this before?'

I flushed under his fixed stare. 'To tell truth, I thought it had all been forgotten . . . also, it seemed impertinence to repay your father's kindness with a refusal in such manner. He was so concerned to make me aware of my duty in this that my objection seemed of no account.'

Simon did not move, but frowned deeper. 'It is not of no account, but I did not think that you felt very strongly about such things. It does not seem like you to do so.'

Curse your unusual perception, I thought, but made my answer, my brain working feverishly the while. 'In truth, since I left Ashcott, my childish beliefs have relaxed, and in my religion I think as you do – but that does not prevent me from feeling that marriage to a Papist, and to rear my children in that faith, would be very wrong. It goes against all I have been taught.'

'But, Thomazine,' Simon said, his voice gentle and per-suasive, 'times have changed. Fifty years ago, in the Old

Queen's time, Papists were indeed a threat and a menace to our lives, but you could not say that now. They are peaceable, retiring, anxious to conform in all save their religion. You could not say that such as Lady Penelope were a danger to the State, nor does the fact of her religion deter Sir William Hervey from wishing to marry her. My father's sister was reared as good a Protestant as you or I, yet she did not demur at marriage with a Papist, and Sir Roger never attempted to convert her to his own religion.'

A knock announced Tom, with a tray of wine, glasses and cakes. Seeing our solemn faces, he placed it on Simon's desk, bowed, sent me a hideous grimace, and retired without a word. Simon looked at the glasses, and then at me. 'What say you, Thomazine? I shall be most unhappy to communicate your wishes to Sir Roger and Cousin Dominic; but I cannot but respect your misgivings, and I wish it were otherwise. It's possible, of course, that Dominic is not as hot for his faith as is his father, and in the event of Sir Roger's death might well turn Protestant – I do not know. In that case, of course, all our difficulties would be resolved, but it is such a slender hope that I fear I shall have to cast around for another husband for you. Are you quite sure that you do not wish to marry him?'

He looked so resigned and unhappy that I was torn between my jubilation at the success of my excuse, and my sympathy for his shouldering of yet another responsibility. I said, putting a remarkably sincere note of anguish into my voice, 'Oh, Simon, I wish that I did for your sake and his, but I can't, I can't marry a Papist, it goes so much against all my beliefs. Simon, you do understand, don't you?'

Simon was always so temptingly, pathetically easy to deceive. With a weary, sympathetic smile, he rose and came round to offer me his hand. 'Yes, Thomazine, I do . . . I could most heartily wish it were otherwise, and I trust that you will tell me should you change your mind . . . but I shall have to write to Sir Roger, and that will not be easy, to dash the expectant bridegroom's hopes.'

'I will help you draft it, if you like,' I said. 'It would be a pity to waste the wine and cakes even though there's nothing to celebrate – shall we sample them?'

And so, fortified by Simon's best Rhenish and Monsieur Harcourt's delicious cakes, we composed together the letter of refusal. Far from antagonizing him, my excuse seemed to have made him more friendly towards me than he had been before, as though the supposed discovery in me of strong religious principles had forged a bond between us, all based on deception. I began to feel most disquieting pangs of conscience.

Francis, true to himself, suffered no such qualms. I had no chance to tell him of my interview until the afternoon, when we were riding over to the Home Farm. My brief resumé of Sir Roger's letter and our subsequent conversation sounded, even to my dishonest ears, most despicable. Francis laughed. 'You have the most uncommon quick wits, owd gal. What prompted you to seize on the one excuse not to marry Dominic that would appeal to Simon's better nature?'

'My worse nature,' I said.

'Are you turned scrupulous all of a sudden? Think on it; you don't want to marry Dominic, do you? You want to marry me, Heaven help you, and we've already decided that it will entail a certain amount of deceit – and what's more, we agreed we could do no other. So why your scruples now?'

I kept my eyes on the familiar curve of the driveway, littered with the dead leaves and mud of winter, and shivered inside my fur-lined cloak. 'I don't really know. Partly, I suppose, because I feel guilty about deceiving Simon in such a way; he seemed so pleased to find such unlooked-for sensitivity in me, and it was all untrue. And also I've got grave misgivings on another score. When – if – he finds out how we've led him a dance, won't his anger be the worse? Aren't we doing ourselves a disservice?'

A glance at Francis's carved, pale profile as usual revealed very little. 'Then we shall have to make damn sure he doesn't find us out, shan't we?' he said after a while. I sighed, recognizing the frayed edge to his voice. 'But that's becoming more and more difficult. Sooner or later *someone*

– be it your mother, or Dr Davis, or Meraud, or Simon himself – is going to come upon us locked in each other's arms in a corner of the garden, or some such place, and our secret will be out with a vengeance, and then what? As like as not you'll be forbidden the house, and I will be packed off to Upper Denby as soon as may be, religious scruples or no.'

'You seem to be arguing against being locked in each other's arms at all,' Francis remarked. 'I was merely hinting at an arrangement with, say, Grainne, for us to meet at the farm for our snatched embraces, and at no other place. But I'll tell you something, my love. For two pins I'd carry you off with me to Catholm now, for a clandestine wedding, and let the rest of our family go hang themselves.'

'That would lead to all sorts of complications, not the least of which would be to incur Simon's lifelong enmity. Do you really want that? I don't, nor do I want to be barred from Goldhayes forever. I want to have you, *and* them!'

'But one day,' Francis said, 'if all this drags on too long, you may have to make the choice. How much longer do we wait? When do we start drawing Simon's attention gently to the fact that we hold more than a cousinly affection for each other? If he runs true to grain, he wouldn't realize until someone told him, and then he'd be enraged simply because he hadn't noticed it earlier.'

'I suppose, then, we must wait until an opportunity presents itself to tell him,' I said dubiously. 'Perhaps he would not then take it so amiss. if you were to make, say, a formal offer for my hand.'

'That's all very well, but have you considered something else? There's every likelihood of Cousin Dominic arriving hotfoot at the gate, eager to prove that Papists possess neither horns nor tail.'

'But he'll still be a Papist – he's not likely to change that now, or at any rate not until Sir Roger dies, and since I had the luck to hit upon that excuse, I'll stick to it. And seeing Dominic again will only confirm me in my resolution. There was something about him,' I said, feeling again his devouring blue stare amd the cold touch of his hands, 'that I didn't like, and didn't then understand. But I think he looked at me as you do now, but with less . . . warmth in it. Rather as Meraud looks when she sees something she wants.' I shivered, not only from the cold. Francis smiled, brilliant with mischief. 'And there's our answer, then! Should your ardent suitor arrive unlooked-for, you can contrive to throw Meraud in his way. It will serve her well, of course, that she with all her guile should be so used!'

I laughed, but his smile vanished quickly. 'This is no subject for levity, really. If he is like Meraud in that look, is he also like her in going to all lengths to obtain what he wants? Do you remember at the fair, when she took a fancy to the bolt of satin that Judith Blagge had already bespoke? She tried to persuade Jude to have another colour, and when that failed she coolly paid the merchant more than he was asking, though Christ knows that was enough, simply to snatch it from under Jude's nose. If Dominic is as she is, which, remembering his mother, is likely, the merest suspicion that he has a rival will be enough to ensure that he never rests until he has you, by means fair or foul.'

'But he shall *not* have me,' I said, setting my chin. 'He cannot force me, if I will not have him. I am yours, my love, forever – nothing will shake me in that!'

Francis looked at me, with a smile that turned my heart to water and raised a blush to my face. 'And I yours, lady, till bitter end of time. But I wish I shared your confidence that everything will end well. We are here, and alive, and all is real and not from one of Lucy's plays.'

'But if we are within a play, let us be Beatrice and Benedict,' I said, 'and not, pray God, Romeo and Juliet.' And I forced a laugh, not wishing to acknowledge, even to myself, the cold clutch of fear within me.

But the matter of our love, and of Dominic's proposal, paled into insignificance beside the news which reached us from London in January. For what was any passion, when set beside the threat of civil war and the losing of a kingdom? The King, doubtless aided and abetted by his wife, whom even Simon regarded with faint suspicion, had over-reached himself, and attempted to arrest those members of Lords and Commons who had been most trouble to him. By some means or another – the name of the Countess of Carlisle, confidante both of the Queen and of Pym, was mentioned – his plan had been betrayed and when he arrived at the House with soldiers at his back, his quarry was already safely hidden in the city. Having failed in his attempt, the King stood revealed – however provoked – as the instigator of aggression. He had played into Pym's hands, and in the resulting tumult was forced to leave London. The ferment in that city spilled over into the surrounding countryside. The privilege of Parliament had been breached, and the talk was of nothing else. Rumours of Irish invasion, of French armies coming to the King's aid, of Papist risings, flew from ale-house to ale-house, losing nothing in the telling. Local Papists, including Lady Pen-elope and Dr Despotine, were abused in the streets of Bury, where itinerant preachers whipped up hatred against all who owed allegiance to the Bishop of Rome. I wondered whether this sort of feeling was current in Yorkshire; even if it were not, Dominic would not be safe if he were to come south to persuade me into marriage, and Simon, recogniz-ing the fact, wrote again to him advising him against any visit until anti-Papist feeling in Suffolk had died down. So from that quarter, at any rate, I was saved, for the county showed no signs of returning to a peaceful existence. In the clothing villages of the southern valleys, around Lavenham and Sudbury, discontent at the slump in the cloth trade spilled over and thousands threatened to march on London to present a petition calling not only for measures against Papists and the King's policies but for positive action to avert the starvation which loomed over the poor, and bid fair to destroy the peace of the county. Indeed, three of their number presented themselves at Goldhayes, as at other great houses, requesting support, to be told by Simon that whereas he sympathized with their plight, he would not lend his name to attacks on his lawful sovereign. He said it coldly, and I saw the black, bitter looks of the men as they left. It was plain that most of Simon's neighbours, rich and poor alike, did not share his support for the King's policies. Edward, more attuned to the mood of the people, and mindful of his European experiences, took once more to carrying a pistol unobtrusively at his saddle-bow, and Simon, Francis and the Sewells followed his example.

One afternoon in late February, Sir Thomas Jermyn rode over to Goldhayes. Now retired from Court, on account of his gout, he kept in close touch with affairs of state through his eldest son Thomas, who was a groom of the Prince of Wales's bedchamber. With him he brought his grandson, Jamie's friend Robert, and a pretty, youngish woman in widow's black, whom he introduced as Mistress Newton. It transpired that Sir Thomas, an imposing, bearded man of nearly seventy, not long widowed, was to be wed to Mistress Newton as soon as the banns were read, and we were all invited to the feast. Simon called for wine and cakes and sweetmeats in celebration, and after his mother had escorted the bride-to-be to her own chambers to view her curios, the talk turned to politics.

Sir Thomas, who had as usual partaken abundantly – he was reputed to have the strongest and most capacious stomach in all England – belched and leaned back comfortably in his chair. 'There's no doubt His Majesty needs help now more than he's ever done. This is no Scots War, to be patched up with words and promises; the quarrel runs too deep for that. As I see it, war is the only course before us.' He laughed. 'Were I younger, and with fewer responsibilities, I'd be hastening now to the King's side; as you should be, lad.'

Simon, fixed with a pointed stare, flushed and said clearly, 'I do not intend to shirk my duty, sir. When the King calls his loyal subjects to arms, I will gladly join him, but while there is still a chance of a peaceful solution I do not intend to act precipitately and risk all to no good purpose.'

'Very circumspect, no doubt,' said Sir Thomas, with all

the wisdom of his fifty superior years. 'Very wise. But have you considered, Simon, that the King's call to arms may well come too late for you to join him?'

Simon looked puzzled and aggrieved. 'How so, sir?'

Edward leaned forward. 'I think I grasp your meaning, Sir Thomas. In the event of war, this county would be largely hostile to the King, and anyone attempting to raise troops or arms in his service would be speedily set upon.'

'You have the right of it,' said Sir Thomas. 'I have left the King's service, and my only desire now is to enjoy a peaceful old age with my bride, but that has not shielded me from abuse from those who should know better their place in life. Only yesterday I was accosted in Bury by some rogue of a weaver who accused me of being a Papist, one of the King's evil counsellors, and a godless cavalier, and then went on to describe my younger son . . . I will not soil the ladies' ears with such expressions. Suffice it to say that his words were such that I was able to have him clapped in the pillory for his impudence. I like this not, that the people should behave thus to their superiors; the Old Queen would not have tolerated such sedition.' He fell silent, staring into the fire, back to the days of his youth when all seemed to him now golden and peaceful, and ordered according to the laws of men and nature. Lucy, who was no respecter of silences, said quickly, 'Sir Thomas, what do you advise my brother to do?'

Sir Thomas, called thus abruptly back from contemplation of the past, smiled fondly at her pretty, eager face. 'What is your brother to do with you, my dear, not spoken for and you a great girl of sixteen? You'll be soon breaking all the hearts in Suffolk, no doubt; I note that John Snelling languishes already.' (Lucy grinned, for the sheep-like adoration of Ambrose Blagge's stepson was a constant source of amusement to her.) 'But to do with war, your brother must wait until war is certain, but before war is declared. Then, Simon, you must gather your tenants in as much secrecy as possible, and make good your escape to the King before the countryside can be raised against you. Unless you can count on sufficient loyal men to protect you from the people's anger, and can steel yourself to use force against unarmed countryfolk, you must not draw attention to yourself. Do your recruiting quietly, bring your horses up to condition, look to your arms, but do not make any attempt on the militia arsenals, or you'll bring the countryside down upon you like an overset hornets' nest. They're ripe for rebellion, particularly to the south, and you'll as like as not be clapped in Bury Gaol for your pains.' He looked round at our wide-eyed, solemn faces: Simon and Edward, Francis and Jamie and Robert, Lucy. Meraud and myself and, his face impassive and disapproving, Richard Trevelyan. 'Well? I know how little notice you young people generally take of the wise words of an old soldier like myself, so I won't take offence if you should entertain other plans.'

'No, Sir Thomas, indeed not – you've said exactly what I have thought ever since this trouble broke,' Edward told him, with warmth and a touch of relief. He had patently been wondering how best to put his ideas across to Simon, notoriously unreceptive to notions suggested by anyone of his own generation or not of his station. 'I've felt all along that we are too greatly outnumbered in Suffolk to do any good here. If we raise troops, we must take them to the King. Making proper provision for the safety of Goldhayes and Mother and the girls and Jamie, of course.'

'Why, will we be in any danger?' Lucy asked. 'Surely that's impossible.'

'In Germany, neither age nor sex nor beauty nor birth would save you from horrors which even I don't wish to think on,' Edward said grimly. 'It's possible the pattern will be repeated here – the Queen has gone to the Low Countries for help and may well bring back a mercenary army. And we've all heard what has happened in Ireland.'

'The Irish are for the most part little better than savages,' Simon said impatiently. 'I cannot conceive that our solid Suffolk peasants, however moved by hunger or misplaced religion, would attempt to murder innocent gentlewomen in their beds.'

'Or maybe not only murder,' Edward said.

Meraud gave a little shudder. 'But if we are not safe here, where can we go?'

'You'd be more than welcome at Rushbrooke,' Sir Thomas said, smiling in avuncular fashion. 'Mind you, it's no more defensible than Goldhayes – both houses may be moated, but cannon would make short work of our soft brick and fine large windows.'

'But Ashcott is defensible,' I said without thinking. Sir Thomas, clearly surprised that a female should entertain any military thought in her head beyond fears for her own safety and that of her menfolk, turned to me and said, 'Ashcott, Mistress Thomazine? Where is that?'

'It's my house,' I said. 'The house where I was brought up. It's in Oxfordshire, on the road between Oxford and Banbury. It's old, like a little castle, and it has a high wall around it, and in the winter the valley floods and surrounds it with water like a moat. The walls are about three yards thick and it has a deep well, and I should think that it would make a good fortress.'

Edward slapped his thigh. 'Ah, Thomazine, why didn't we think of that before? Your little castle, of course – fine strategic position – well, finer than this house, anyway – defensible . . . how big?'

'Not very big, but there are lots of outbuildings, barns, stables . . . my grandmother was always complaining that the courtyard was more like a farmyard. I should think it would hold out against a siege for quite a long time,' I said, rather pleased that my impulsive suggestion had apparently been taken seriously by a professional soldier.

'And the countryside about? Would they be friendly?'

I thought back to the people I had known so long ago. 'Well, Banbury is very Puritan; it's a byword for it in those parts. But Sir Henry Wilmot's house is at Adderbury, and he's a King's man, I should imagine.'

'Yes, I knew him at Breda – a good soldier, if not so worthy a man.'

'And the people at Ashcott – there aren't very many of them, but they'd be friendly, I expect. They'd remember

231

me, give us provisions. They might be glad of a garrison, for their own protection, and better a Heron garrison that'll have a care for them and my house and lands, than some others, whether for King or Parliament, who'll have no such scruples,' I said.

'Really,' remarked Edward, looking at me with new respect, 'you have the makings of a soldier under all that mass of hair!'

'My father said I should have been a boy, and I was forever playing Spanish-and-English with my brother.'

'Well,' said Simon, 'it seems as though Ashcott might profitably be garrisoned for the King. However, I'd thought of raising a troop of horse, and that will be of little use cooped up in a castle.'

'No, but it could be usefully employed in raids on enemy territory,' Edward said, his enthusiasm rising. 'We could perhaps leave a small force at Ashcott, and then take the larger part of the troop to join the King.'

'And where exactly do you propose to raise your men?' Sir Thomas asked. 'I know I'd have little hope of response from Rushbrooke, at any rate in the village; the farmers and labourers would be reluctant to leave the land, particularly if you tried to recruit near to harvest time. The household – well, that would be another matter, but if you take too many of your grooms and servants you leave Goldhayes with few able-bodied men for the protection of the ladies.'

'But we won't be here,' I protested. 'I for one want to go to Ashcott.' As Simon looked his astonishment, I added, 'It's already agreed we'd be safer there, with a force to guard us, than left behind here in a house wide open to attack, with a rebellious countryside, and with no menfolk to give protection either to us or to the house.'

Silence. I wondered if anyone could guess the real reason for my desire to go to Ashcott – that I did not want to be left behind while those I loved went to war, and that at Ashcott there was a greater chance of being with Francis, or hearing news of him, than at Goldhayes.

'You would not be short of friends here,' Sir Thomas

said. 'I am sure that should occasion arise, we would be only too glad to give you shelter at Rushbrooke, and Ambrose likewise, particularly since Simon is betrothed to his daughter . . . when is the wedding to be, lad?'

Simon did not like being addressed as 'lad'. He said stiffly, 'I do not know the date. Ann is at present with the Queen and the Princess Mary in Holland, and I do not know when I will next see her.'

'You'll doubtless be reunited when you join the King,' Sir Thomas said imperturbably. 'But to return to our discussion . . . the house must indeed be looked after. Perhaps it would be prudent to make your estate over to your mother, or some other responsible and neutral person, before you leave; that may discourage depredations by those who take exception to your support of the King.'

Simon frowned. 'My mother is a very responsible lady, but I feel that such a burden would be too much for her . . . she is, almost, an unworldly person.'

It was not the word I would have used to describe the vain, sophisticated, pleasure-loving, lazy Mary, but I could see what he meant.

'I would not fight,' said Richard Trevelyan's quiet, unassuming voice. Up till now, he had only been a listener, and Simon looked round, startled, as he went on. 'It is a burden I would be glad to shoulder on your behalf, to stay here for the protection of your house and your lady mother, for I do not wish to fight in any war which sets father against son, brother against brother, as this one will. Moreover, I flatter myself I still have some influence with my erstwhile friends in London, and I might be able to use that to ward off attacks on Goldhayes, whether military or financial.'

'It is indeed a heavy responsibility,' Simon said dubiously, 'and one which I would not wish you to bear alone . . . I should feel happier were I to nominate a group of trustees to whom I could make over my estates, so that the burden could be shared. John Sewell is one name that springs to mind . . . you, and my mother. Sir Thomas, would you also be one?'

As Sir Thomas, seemingly pleased at the offer, expressed

his willingness to help, I glanced at Richard Trevelyan. Was I imagining the look of disappointment which crossed his face? I did not think so, and it did nothing to increase my confidence in him.

In the next weeks, Simon plunged himself and his brothers and the Sewells into a frenzy of activity; as if he had been waiting for such a discussion to confirm his own plans before taking action. He visited the little old man in Bury who had acted as his father's lawyer, and had drawn up for signature the papers transferring ownership of Goldhayes and all his estates to John Sewell, Richard Trevelyan, Sir Thomas Jermyn, Ambrose Blagge and Lady Heron. Edward had all the horses brought up from pasture to be corn-fed into condition for war, and toured the villages with Francis and Tom and Henry, visiting all the able-bodied men who would be likely to join a troop. Many of them, in any case, would follow their landlord whichever cause he espoused; the finer points of politics were beyond them, as indeed they were beyond Edward. A few visits to Mother Pryke's squalid ale-house, dignified by the name of the 'Sunrising' and a tatty painted sign hanging alongside the customary bush, were enough to distinguish the genuinely enthusiastic from the dubious and the downright hostile without any form of inquisition, for the affairs of King and Parliament were much discussed, if not fully understood. As Sir Thomas had expected, the enthusiastic were those young enough to entertain thoughts of going away to war, and not yet old enough to have family responsibilities. Many were able to supply their own horses, for the village was well stocked with tenant farmers of the better sort, but for those who could not, Simon was buying in horses from friendly gentlemen round about, taking care to choose known Royalist sympathizers. Almost all of the household were keen to go, and here Simon, or rather Edward, could pick the best horsemen, the eager young grooms and farmworkers, leaving the older servants for the protection and maintenance of the house. Wat the gardener was most insulted at not being chosen, protesting that, despite his sixty-odd years and severe rheumatics, he could still bestride a horse as well as he had forty years ago.

Not unnaturally, Simon was not keen to escort his women-folk through a possibly hostile, war-torn countryside to a fortress he had never seen, and I thought at first, in desperation, that I would have to dress up as a soldier in order to go to Ashcott. However, Grainne, most emphatically, assured Simon that she would follow Henry, come what may, with her children; that she was used to war and desired nothing else but that Lucy and I should accompany her. Simon wavered, and when Meraud added her pleas, his resistance collapsed. I had not expected her to want to follow the drum, but she was unshakeable in her desire, and already quite capable of twisting Simon round her little finger. I was highly suspicious of her motives, and not for the first time wished that Simon would make haste to marry Nan; for Meraud was now just sixteen and her deceptive, diminutive stature, which led so many to thinking her still a child, disguised a sophisticated and entirely adult young lady who, I felt instinctively, would stop at very little to achieve her desires.

Edward and Henry collected up all the military equipment they could lay their hands on, from Goldhayes and the Home Farm, from the assorted tenants and from the militia arms stored in Bradfield Tye church. Ambrose Blagge donated some rusty swords, an ancient fowling-piece and some dilapidated bits of armour, while Sir Thomas Jermyn, in the first flush of newly-wed generosity (the nuptials had been celebrated in March), presented Simon with a magnificent pair of snaphaunce pistols of the latest London pattern, which he said he had intended as a gift for his younger son Henry – 'But as the young villain is fled to foreign parts, and not likely to return for some time, I thought that you could put them to better use, lad.' And Simon, too overcome with delight to take exception to the 'lad', had flushed deep scarlet and stammered his thanks like a twelve-year-old. All the weapons were arrayed in the armoury next to the hall; items ranged from Sir Thomas's pistols, a dozen fowling-pieces and a score of carbines, through swords of varying types and in widely different states of repair, to hunting crossbows, yew longbows half a century old or more, a tilting helm three times that age, and an arquebus.

'And the armour!' Jamie said in an awed whisper. 'King Arthur himself might have worn that helmet.'

'He probably did,' said Francis drily. 'There's two inches of rust on it. What have you got there, Ned? Great-Grandfather Hal's piratical broadsword?'

'I wouldn't be surprised,' Edward said, putting it down on the table. 'Well, I must say, a finer collection of useless and outdated weaponry I've yet to see. I don't even know what some of it is for. And how old Goody Simmons got hold of that tilting helm I tremble to think.'

'She told me that Sir Christopher had worn it at Court tourneys, and when he grew too old gave it to her grandfather. I suppose it's possible.' I picked up the list that Edward had made of all the usable equipment. 'It all sounds very impressive, anyway. Eighteen carbines, fifteen pairs of pistols, thirteen wheel-lock, one matchlock and the snaphaunce pair; ten muskets, all matchlock, twelve fowling pieces, five with rifled barrels. fifty-eight assorted swords and daggers, twenty score of musket balls, the same each of carbine and pistol balls, moulds for their making, wadding and powder-flasks in quantity if not in quality, twelve pikes, thirteen halberds and two pole-axes, fifteen pike heads requiring shafts, eighteen steel backs, twenty-one steel breasts and fourteen steel gorgets, all needing cleaning, thirty-three buff jerkins in varying states of repair, nine military saddles and a dozen kegs of gunpowder.'

'They have been left in the stables, for obvious reasons,' said Edward. 'Add to that list the swords, pistols and muskets being repaired by the blacksmith, not to mention the stack of armour needing cleaning and repainting. Then we've managed to obtain fifty-eight horses, with promises of ten more or so - though some of those aren't fit to pull a plough, let alone carry a trooper – and their trappings, and we've enough for a sizeable troop.'

'And men? How many do you think we'll get?'

'We don't know exactly. Many have shown willing, but of course if the call comes close to harvest-time we may have few to answer it at all. Sir Thomas has said that he knows of several servants and young men at Rushbrooke who'd be willing to join us. but Master Blagge was less forthcoming – it appears he's been making inquiries on behalf of Tom, who had the same idea in mind. Ambrose and Henry of course are very keen, and even your lovesick swain, Lucy, is talking of nothing but war.'

'John Snelling?' Lucy said. 'He doesn't look like a warrior to me.'

'Well,' Francis said, striking an affected pose, 'I don't suppose I look like a warrior either, but I have every intention of becoming one.'

'No,' I said, grinning, 'I can imagine you commanding a troop, you've the voice and presence for it. John, though he's a good enough fellow, has neither – the battle would be over before he could spit out the order to charge!'

'Stammer or not, he's very pleasant,' Lucy said, 'but there's no need for those sly looks, Thomazine Heron, he's not for me.'

The door opened and Meraud entered with a rustle of the dark purple satin which had been wrested so neatly from Judith Blagge. 'Hullo! Good heavens, this is a collection, Ned! You'll be the finest troop in the King's army with all that at your disposal.' She smiled charmingly at the three brothers, and I wished that she could make up her mind which one of them she was after. Edward smiled indulgently at her. 'No, we won't, for there's not enough to arm everyone as I'd like; they'll all have a sword, of some sort, but there aren't enough firearms to go round, nor buff coats nor armour. And to buy up what we want in Bury or London would be to make ourselves conspicuous, so we must make shift ourselves or do without. The blacksmith is doing splendid service.'

'And if I have to patch up one more torn, greasy, smelly, worn-out buff jerkin,' said Lucy, with some feeling, 'I think I shall scream! Heppy and Thomazine are doing most of it;

I don't know how you *can*, Thomazine, I really don't. But then you always have been good with your needle.'

'I can keep a thimble on my thumb,' I said. Meraud sighed. 'I too am weary of it, but there are only three more, I thank God. And it is good to think that our work may save our men from hurt.'

Francis grimaced at me, behind her back. Meraud went on, 'There's one thing puzzling me, Ned – who is to have the command? Will it be you, or Simon?'

Edward, embarrassed, shuffled his feet, Jamie leapt in, tactless as usual. 'It *should* be Edward, or Henry Sewell, they've both fought in the Low Countries. But can you see Simon fighting under them?'

'It is quite right and proper,' Edward said, indignant. 'Simon is the head of the family, when all's said and done. Henry and I will organize stores, quarter, that sort of thing, and offer advice where we think fit, but Simon will be in command. He's the one with a head on his shoulders, and some understanding of politics, and he's the one the men will follow. I'm just a soldier.'

'I wish there was a place for me,' Jamie said, wistfully. 'I'm almost fourteen, after all, and you weren't much older when you went to the Low Countries.'

'I was sixteen when Father sent me, not thirteen and a half, and I had Henry to watch over me, and some knowledge of what I was about,' Edward pointed out, without rancour. 'You fulfil none of those conditions. When you can control a restive horse, obey orders without question, fire a pistol accurately, use a sword intelligently and know your cavalry drill, *then* I'll consider you, but not before. But you may come to Ashcott.'

After this conversation, it became noticeable that Jamie spent many long hours with his nose buried in military textbooks, training his new horse, and practising his sword-play with anyone who could spare the time. He would also have practised with pistols, but Edward, mindful of the precious store of powder, forbade it.

*   *   *

As the year marched on, we realized that war, if it came, might not be so soon. Events seemed to move with agonizing slowness, and yet day by day the rift between the two parties grew deeper. Simon, having done all he could by way of preparation, fretted and chafed at the indecision. When the King, after spending some time in his palaces around London, journeyed northward towards York in March, he halted at Newmarket, and Simon and Edward went to see him. They rode there and back in a day, travelling unobtrusively across country, a journey which struck me, and Sir Thomas, as foolhardy. They were, they said, waiting for an audience with the King when my Lords Holland and Pembroke arrived with the text of Parliament's answer to his rejection of the Militia Bill, by which they had hoped to have command of the armed forces. The King, said Simon, had been justifiably brisk with their impudent declaration, and had sworn not to relinquish control of the militia for one hour. His former courtiers had returned to London, and hostility between the two parties seemed absolute. Simon's deeply sincere protestations of loyalty, following hard on the heels of this, had apparently greatly impressed His Majesty, and the King had listened with interest to Simon's military plans, the while bemoaning the tragic circumstances that had led to the imminent outbreak of war, and expressing a wish that more of his subjects could show Simon's loyalty. However, he urged my cousins to wait until hostilities had been formally declared. 'For,' he told them, 'there are still many honest men on both sides who desire only peace and goodwill, and we may yet effect an end to this sorry struggle.'

Simon, it appeared, entertained no such thoughts. He returned from Newmarket unusually elated and inspired, and made miserable company throughout the spring as he waited restlessly for the final moves which would herald war. Amongst other things, he dispatched Edward to inspect Ashcott, and to report on its suitability for a garrison. After two weeks' absence, Edward returned, full of ideas for ditches, bastions and fortifications; but admitted that the curtain wall's condition left something to be desired, that the house itself was neglected and in need of repair, and that my bailiff, William Tawney, was an idle sort of fellow, with a shrew for a wife, and had taken to living, with her and their five children, not in their allotted gate-house but in the smaller rooms of the main house. 'But,' said Edward, in his capable, reassuring way, 'you needn't fear for your house, Thomazine. I've kicked 'em back to the gatehouse, brats and all, and ordered repairs to the worst bits of the wall. The major work will have to be done when we arrive there. I'd thought of diverting the river to make a moat, or even installing sluices so that we can flood it at will to discomfit any besiegers, but though I saw something of that in Holland I'm no expert – now, if only we had one of those Dutch engineer fellows who've been causing such a stir up in the Fens . . .' And he spent several nights poring over the maps and notes he had made. Francis showed, to my surprise, a greater interest in this than in other aspects of military activity, and I often saw him, Edward and Henry, blond, brown and red heads bent over their plans, discussing lines of fire, sluices, falls of land and so on with animation and ingenuity. But in my mind's eye I saw also the peaceful, stolid peasants of Ashcott, dependent on their few cattle and sheep and the grazing which Edward plan-ned to flood, probably in high summer to the ruination of the hay, and wondered with a cold chill what we would bring with our soldiers and guns. With luck, Goldhayes might be spared the ravages of war, but for Ashcott, my childhood home, no such respite. In my more sober moments I regretted ever suggesting it as a garrison.

As spring advanced, so did the course of events. The King held court in York, gathering the Royalist gentry in the north to his side. The hideous stories spreading from Ireland gave credence to rumours of Papist-Irish invasion, and it was widely believed that the King intended to go to that country not to quell rebellion but to lead an army of rebels into England. But he showed no sign of doing so; instead, using the Duke of York as a decoy, he attempted to capture Hull. Only slightly checked by failure, the King next struck at the Parliament (who had all along placed great reliance on legal arguments to justify their declarations) by ordering Lord Keeper Littleton, with the Great Seal, to join him at York. On 27th May, the Commons, in retaliation for this blow, issued a declaration stating that the King, deceived by evil advisors, was making war on his Parliament, and that in consequence loyal subjects had no option but to obey the commands of Parliament alone. Three days later, the first day of June, the Houses issued their ultimatum, demanding amongst other things control of all military and civil offices of importance, and of fortresses. It was now obvious that war was imminent, and Simon, at long last, could act. In those last days at Goldhayes, the uncertainty lifted and the way ahead now clear, if heavy with foreboding, he seemed a different person – almost happy in this frenzy of activity. By contrast, Francis grew more thoughtful, amd I could sense, although he did not confide in me, that he was having second thoughts; but I knew better than to pry.

Edward and Henry had had all ready for some time. The horses had been corn-fed and worked up into hard condition. Saddlery and harness had been checked and oiled and repaired, and two light four-wheeled carts made ready to transport all the baggage which could not readily be carried on pack-ponies. They had decided that this arrangement would be swifter and less cumbersome than using one of the cripplingly slow farm wagons, customarily drawn by four of the solid chestnut Suffolk Punches in tandem. Arms were in good repair, checked and stored in the stable-loft amid the last of the previous year's hay. The glorious day when we had helped to gather it in, free of the threat of war, seemed another world. A quantity of weapons, bullets and powder had been set aside for the defence of Goldhayes, should it prove necessary. Most of the baggage had been packed or made ready – chests full of clothes, books, linen and other necessaries, bandages, remedies and medicines, such things as bedding and jewels, pewter tableware for our use and the gold and silver plate, made from the plunder of Spanish treasure ships, for the financing of the King's forces. There was ready coin to finance our journey and to pay the soldiers – Edward had advised his brother of the necessity of regular and sufficient pay to prevent the troops from deserting forthwith to their homes, and Simon, who was more ready now to accept advice from his soldier brother, agreed. We could not be burdened with too much baggage, for the sake of speed, so took no hangings, furniture or pictures. Valuables left behind were entrusted to Mary and Richard Trevelyan, and Simon advised that they be hidden at the first sign of trouble. In a house as large and rambling as Goldhayes, there were plenty of places. We had also packed food of the preserved sort, cheeses, wines and ales, salted meat and spices, bottled fruits and sugar and sweetmeats. Nothing, we were sure, would be left behind.

So, on the third day of June, Simon, Edward and the Sewell brothers and Francis rode out in the drizzle, visiting those who had shown an interest in joining the troop, and tempting those who wavered with the promise of regular pay. All had had training of some sort in the militia, sketchy though it had been, and a handful had even seen service in the Scots wars, or abroad. At the very least, they knew one end of a pistol from another, and could all ride; a fair number had horses of their own. They were in the main servants, grooms or craftsmen, the local husbandmen and cottagers being reluctant to leave their soil with the new-growing summer crops. In all, we could muster sixty-one armed horse, forty or so from Bradfield Tye and Goldhayes, and the rest from Rushbrooke and round about; enough, perhaps, to leave a small garrison at Ashcott when the rest went to join the King. The rendezvous was set at Goldhayes, an hour before dawn on the fifth of June, and the recruits were ordered to present themselves with horses and equipment, if any, and food for two days' march.

On the day before this, Sir Thomas called to wish us good fortune, as did Ambrose Blagge, and Simon escorted the two of them around our stableyard. Sir Thomas, limping heavily from his gout, looked around the home paddocks behind the house, filled with glossy, fit horses, the stableyard piled with chests and bags and bundles, ready to be slung on to the pack-horses, the carts covered with canvas which contained our powder and shot, spare weapons, and bulkier baggage. Inside, the beautiful plate and candle-sticks, flagons and ornaments, had vanished from buffet and table and court-cupboard, to be replaced by pewter and pottery.

'I wish I were fifty years younger,' Sir Thomas said, his eyes gleaming. Ambrose Blagge, a thin pinched man who always drove a hard bargain, muttered something about a waste of money under his breath, but gave Simon good wishes readily enough.

That night we slept little, despite our exhaustion. Lying in the big bed I still shared with Lucy, the curtains flung back so we should not stifle in the heavy and humid air, I dreamed uneasily of Francis, of battles, of Ashcott, and of my grandmother, four years dead, directing us under siege. It was a relief when I awoke to Lucy's shaking. 'It's three o'clock! An hour and three-quarters till dawn, so hurry!'

I fumbled sleepily into my riding-habit and followed her downstairs. In the kitchen the fire was burning cheerfully, candles were lit, and Monsieur Harcourt and the kitchen boys were distributing ale, cheese and cold bacon and bread to the assorted company; Sewells, Herons, servants and a few already of our prospective troopers. Grainne was there too, a grey tinge to her face, for she was two months gone with child, although for the sake of following him she had as yet managed to conceal this fact from Henry. She was perched on the edge of the kitchen table, holding Hester, now a year old, who was looking round the crowded room with solemn tawny eyes. Beside them sat Jasper, in a state of high excitement, his legs sticking out from underneath his ample green serge petticoats, eating a large hunk of the hard cheese known as Suffolk Thump. Now well past three years old, he had lost most of his baby fat after some childish ailment, and was an alarmingly bony child, tall for his age and with huge green eyes circled with blue bruised shadows. He talked precociously, with a facility and charm that spoke of growing intelligence, and rarely cried, but there was something ethereal and elfin about his fragility, so unlike his father's, and Grainne's love for him had a hint of desperation about it. I took a tankard of ale and some bread and bacon from a kitchen boy and joined them. 'Hullo, Grainne. How are you feeling?'

'Not well,' Grainne said, 'but it will pass. I'm more concerned that Henry will discover my condition and keep me here. I'd follow him to the ends of the earth, but I'll settle for Ashcott – I can see that's as far as I'll get, for a while at any rate. I wish the baby wasn't coming just now.'

Francis appeared from somewhere, in his old buff coat with his basket-hilted sword clanking at his side. 'Good morrow to you, ladies, and to you, Master Jasper. If you're not careful, you know, you'll turn into Suffolk Thump.'

Jasper's eyes opened wide. 'Oh, no, I won't!'

'What have I told you, infant, about speaking with a full mouth?' Grainne asked.

'Sorry,' Jasper said, looking sideways at her with a small guilty smile. Grainne smiled sideways back and her son, swallowing his mouthful all at once, said again, but anxiously, 'I won't turn into a cheese, will I, Mamma?'

'Goose,' Grainne said, hugging him with the arm that was not holding Hester. 'Of course not. But even if you did, then a Suffolk cheese is the best kind of cheese to turn into.'

'I don't want to be a cheese,' Jasper said seriously. 'Master Francis, do you want to be a cheese?'

Francis considered, his face equally serious. 'No. You might eat me.'

I grinned at Jasper's delighted giggles. The casual, charming affection which the intellectual Francis gave to Grainne's children never failed to surprise me. Then, seeing what he carried under his arm, I asked, 'What is your book?'

'Praissac's *Art of War*. It's Edward's copy, hence its well-thumbed look. I have also in my bags Dr Donne's poems, some music, my flageolet and a copy of the *Morte Darthur*.' He grinned wickedly. 'Someone has to teach Jamie how to fight with a lance in full armour!'

'It's not necessary – he's already very competent with a broadsword, according to Henry,' Grainne told him. 'You'll have him in your troop if you're not careful. Where are your colours, by the way?'

Simon was to captain the troop, with Edward as his lieutenant, Henry his quartermaster, Tom as a corporal and Francis entrusted with the colours. Once flown at the masthead of Great-Grandfather Hal's privateer ship, named with his usual conceit 'Great Heron', these had been cut down to the two-foot square demanded of a cavalry standard and mended and re-embroidered by myself and Meraud, as the most competent needlewomen – Mary with her short sight declared herself unequal to the task. Now the silver heron on blue would head our troop, with the motto 'God and the King' painted below it in letters of gold, and fringed all around in golden tassels filched from a grandly upholstered chair.

'Over by the door,' Francis said. 'I know Simon thinks it's a signal honour to carry the damned thing, but I'd as lief have my hands free to use my sword and pistol.'

'Hush!' I warned him, as his brother and captain entered from the dining hall, spurs jingling, sword slapping in its sheath, and his unhandsome face graven in its now-familiar worried frown. The kitchen was filled now with recruits, almost all of them men and boys familiar to me from my years at Goldhayes: Holly Greenwood, who had left the farm to his seventeen-year-old brother Elijah, standing talking to Ben Harper, the blacksmith's elder son; Heppy flirting with the head groom, John Skinner, who was twice her age and more; Daniel Keele, a weaver and last year's constable, swapping crude stories with the parson's young nephew, Jonathan Eldritch, who was an orphan and lived with his uncle. Simon looked round at the crowd, down at his new and highly unreliable watch, and picking up a wooden trencher, rapped the table with it.

The talk took some time to die down. Simon waited until there was total silence and then consulted the paper in his hand before calling the roll of volunteers. Astonishingly, with two exceptions, one a waverer and the other a hen-pecked man with a Parliamentarian wife, who had been keen enough in the ale-house, all were present, and only one or two had mislaid or forgotten to bring items of equipment. Giles Mede, a big thoughtless man with a reputation for jokes verbal and practical, tried to make believe that he had forgotten his horse, a tactic which brought roars of delight from his fellows and a chilly light to Simon's eye. They were grown men all, and the excitement of going to war had reduced them to the simplicity of children. The quality of Simon's rebuke took some of the hilarity from their faces; they listened in shuffling silence as he lectured them on military discipline ('Orders must at all times be obeyed without question'), pillaging and looting ('It will not help the King if our troop is lost through attack by irate countryfolk'), pay ('Two shillings a day for troopers from me, and maybe more when we join the King's army'), and our destination; Ashcott first, and then York or wherever the King might be. The marching order was then given: Simon, the two trumpeters, and Francis with the colours, followed by half the troop, then the baggage, the munitions and spare horses and women and children – Grainne, Jasper, Hester, their maid Betty, myself, Lucy, Meraud, Heppy and Jamie. Bringing up the rear would be the other half of the troop, with Henry and Edward. Simon repeated the order twice, to make quite sure. 'Have you any questions? Good. Listen for orders on the march and in battle as you have done here, and we'll do well. Now, those who have all their equipment, that is, horse, saddle, bridle, sword or rapier, pistol or carbine, and food for two days' march; those who have all those, mount up outside and wait for your orders. The rest report to me and you'll be allocated equipment.'

About forty men converged, talking and laughing, on the door to the stableyard while the others queued to receive weapons from the selection laid out on a trestle table in the corner, presided over by Edward. Henry was outside, supervising the mounting and distribution of surplus horses, and above the bustle his voice was clearly audible even in the kitchn. Francis's eyes held mine. 'Well, that's it. We march to war. I hope you're practised with a pistol, Thomazine.'

'Perhaps more than they are,' I said, with a nod of head towards the confusion outside. 'And is "march" the right word?'

'It has a deceptively military ring to it, I agree. I must take up my allotted position, and you yours, and we may not see much of each other on the march, but I wish you well, in the middle of all that rough soldiery; and remember, my love, that many will be watching who are less simple and more observant than Simon — so your speaking eyes will have to say less.'

'I will remember,' I said, and we all went out into the stableyard, dim and horse-filled. Light was flushing the eastern sky, but it wanted half an hour till dawn and the torches in their iron brackets round the yard did little to help. Horses jostled and neighed, strange figures muttered and swore terrible oaths. Somewhere by the gatehouse, Henry had descended to abuse in the attempt to instil order. I thought of troops and companies all over England, being gathered without even professional help, and fighting, and did not know whether to laugh or to cry. Chalcedony, my sweet roan mare, was tethered to the dovecot; I had ordered it thus so that I could be sure of finding her. A stablelad helped me mount, and then held her head while I stroked her neck, trying to calm her restiveness, and to calm myself. I wanted to weep, for no particular reason, save that it seemed that this moment was like standing in a doorway; light and safety, all the old familiar world of my childhood behind, and in front, the dark unknown. And there was only one way left to go.

'You look very serious,' Jamie said, his heart-shaped enthusiastic face peering up to mine. 'Isn't this exciting! I *wish* I was riding with the troop; I'm old enough, the Queen of Bohemia's children fought at Breda when they were my age.' It was a well-worn argument and I had little patience. 'That's as maybe, but they were princes and well looked after, to make sure they took no hurt. Have you got everything? Because that's the signal to leave.' I had thought I had heard the notes of the trumpet above the noise, but neither trumpeter could yet be described as competent, despite long and excruciating practice, and I was not sure. However, the men seemed to be filing one by one out of the yard, their officers' shouted orders barely rising above the clack of hooves and the blurred noise of many moving horses. I could hear them being formed up in some sort of order outside the gatehouse.

Tom Sewell rode over to us. 'I trust you han't forgotten the marching orders, you two? Everyone else is outside and the carts are going. Just remember that we must keep together for our own safety, in case we should meet hostile troops. Now Henry want you outside right away, and don't forget – no straggling!'

'No, sir, Master Corporal Sewell, sir,' I said. Tom grinned and turned away. We rode out under the gatehouse behind the carts.

It seemed an age, and was half-light, before we were ready to move off. Miraculously, our fifty-nine men were in some semblance of Simon's marching order, ranked five or six abreast, twenty-nine in front and thirty behind, and the baggage-train in the centre. Behind us all those staying at Goldhayes sent up a cheer which raised the pigeons in a clap of wings from the dovecote, their feathers lanced with the red light of dawn. I looked back, once, and saw the house in the trees as a dim outline all ablaze with lights. I would not set eyes on Goldhayes again for four years.

part two

'Cold reality'

Our castle's strength
Will laugh a siege to scorn.

(Shakespeare, *Macbeth*)

chapter six

Ashcott

The right true end of love . . .
(Donne, 'Elegies': 'Love's Progress')

Our journey to Ashcott took just under a week, and by the end of it I was weary; weary of riding at a stiflingly slow pace, enclosed by sixty boisterous children in the guise of grown men and soldiers of the King; weary of the rutted, mired roads, squelchy with unsuspected quagmires and potholes deceitfully filled with thick mud up to four feet deep; weary of the seemingly endless rain and chilly June wind which knifed through my thick cloak. Simon, under the mistaken impression that any inn, however squalid, was more suitable and comfortable for his womenfolk than the barns full of hay that were the soldiers' nightly quarters, thus ensured us many disturbed nights plagued by small invaders, despite our weariness. Only one incident brought a respite from the dogged endurance to which I at least was reduced, and that was after the only night when, no inn fortunately within reach, we all stayed in the one barn. The following morning, Jasper discovered a kitten sharing his nest in the hay, and the farmer's wife, delighted by the little boy's enchanting manners and the picture child and kitten made together, let him have it for a groat. The gingery little cat, whose fluffy fur matched the colour of Jasper's hair exactly, was named Orange, and found a basket to ride in, much to the delight of the soldiers, who had adopted Jasper as their mascot, letting him ride at their saddlebows and hold the reins of their horses. To all this unmilitary conduct, Simon at the head of the column was happily oblivious, although I had the classical precedent of Caligula in mind, should he appear with objections. The kitten, securely battened down in his covered basket, rode in one of the carts, and was fed by his small owner at every stop, with food ranging from cheese to salt pork and milk-soaked bread.

Two days after this, we reached our destination at last. As the road grew more and more familiar, and the town of Deddington approached, my tiredness was evaporated entirely by the rush of nostalgia and excitement that each remembered landmark brought. I was delighted to be asked to guide our little troop around Deddington, so as not to give undue alarm to the inhabitants, and was still buoyed up with self-importance and anticipation when we emerged from the tiny lane on to the main road, which ran broad and rutted between Deddington and Adderbury. The latter village lay across the Swere valley to our right, struck with sudden afternoon sunlight that brought its spire and trees to vivid gold and green against the grey-blue northern sky. I felt a pang of nostalgia for these lovely Oxford valleys, steep-sided and broad, but no sense of homecoming any more. I realized suddenly that only Goldhayes could give me that now.

'Well, we're nearly there,' Simon said. 'There seems to have been a considerable quantity of rain fallen; the road's little better than a mud-slick down the hill.' He turned, halting his horse, and held up his hand. 'Take care, men, the ground's very slippery here!' Too late, for one trooper, reining in his horse, did it too abruptly, and the animal lost its footing and slid three yards on its rump before struggling to its feet. The unfortunate rider, red-faced and sweating with mortification, had to endure the laughter and jeers of his companions. Scarcely had the column got under way again, with rather more care than before, picking their way down the edge of the road where it seemed to be less dangerous, when there arose sounds of uproar from the rear; the crash of breaking wood, screams and neighs from injured or frightened horses, and shouts of alarm. Simon jerked his horse round, almost colliding with mine in his haste, and I followed suit.

The reason for the noise was soon apparent. One of the horses drawing the second cart (fortunately that containing provisions and personal baggage and not the powder and shot) had fallen, breaking the shafts and entangling the other horse in the traces, and behind them, obviously, another horse had also gone down. With a sick heart I recognized it as Henry's excitable bay gelding. As Simon, riding as fast as was safe, reached the spot, Grainne knelt, her clothes dragged unheedingly in the mud, beside her husband. Some of the more quick-witted men began under orders to free the cart-horses, and I dismounted and ran across to Henry. His horse had fallen on him, and obviously its death-throes had caused more damage than the fall itself.

'Get that carcass off him,' Simon said, as a dozen willing pairs of hands clustered to help. 'Carefully, now . . . roll it off gently . . .'

Grainne, her hair brushing Henry's face, was holding his hands in hers, as if by that means she could transmit courage and relief from pain. 'Ned was right,' he was muttering, 'the brute should ha' been shot years ago — for Christ's sake, Trooper Pryke, thass not a bale of hay you're shifting, you sawny gatless fule . . .' He broke off, gasping, as the horse's body was finally pulled and rolled off his legs, his relapse into Suffolk dialect an indication of the severity of the pain. 'Where are you hurt?' Grainne asked him, and then, although he had said nothing, went on, 'Yes, it's your leg — your right leg, the left is sound.'

'Tried to get clear, but I didn't quite manage to do it,' Henry said, on a clenched breath. His face was grey and sweating with pain, the only colour the fierce vivid orange of his hair and eyebrows and beard. 'That was an awkward fall — think it fare t'be broke.'

'Trooper Skinner!' Simon shouted, and the head groom, a tall thin man who had some reputation as a bone-setter, appeared from the ring of curious, concerned faces and knelt beside his quartermaster. 'Aye, that fare to be a bad 'un. I can make a goo o' setting that, but I doubt that'll set short. I'll need a straight owd bit o' wood, and suffen to bind it with . . .'

Simon pulled off the blue silk and tasselled sash which he wore and handed it to him. 'Will that do?'

'Aye, sir, that will. Now, we're a-going to need a hurdle or suffen like that, for to carry him on. He can't ride i'the cart, not like that.'

'Simon,' I said, 'we can have that from Ashcott.' From the way he looked at me when I spoke, I could see that he had all but forgotten my existence. 'If I ride ahead – with some of the troopers – and tell them we're coming, I can get a hurdle and another cart – we always had plenty of each.'

'An excellent idea,' Simon said with relief. 'Cornet Heron? Take six men and escort Mistress Thomazine to Ashcott. Bring back a hurdle and a cart, and tell them to make ready to receive us. We shall be two nights there at the least, I imagine, so doubtless food will have to be arranged.' He glanced at Henry, who up till now had organized the feeding and quartering of our troop, and would do so no longer. He lay still and taut under the gentle, searching hands of the bonesetter, and only the set of his mouth and the white-boned clenched hands betrayed the fact that he was conscious. 'And make all the haste you can,' Simon said.

'Yes, sir,' Francis assured him. He was standing by the carts, and I realized suddenly that his had been the clear concise orders that had directed the disentangling of the fallen horses. He turned, picking out the half-dozen men he needed. 'Troopers Eldritch, Pryke, Shoosmith, Garner, Thomson and Harper, with me. Mount up, and have a care for your horses on this ground!'

A Rushbrooke man held my stirrup for me as I mounted Chalcedony. I guided her through the throng of mounted and dismounted men, sparing a grin for Jamie, white-faced as he watched Skinner at work, and for Jasper who was staring at the scene with huge serious eyes from his nurse's arms. Francis was waiting for me, his men at his back, and together we rode down the hill. It was the first time since leaving Goldhayes that we had had a chance to talk, even though, with an audience of six, we would have no opportunity to do other than chat of commonplaces.

'Will he be all right?' I asked, speaking of Henry. Francis

considered, his eyes on the road ahead as Hobgoblin minced delicately through the grass. 'I don't know. A break such as that rarely mends straight, and I've seen gangrene set in on a couple of occasions, in Scotland. He may lose it altogether; at the least, I fear his soldiering days are over.'

I thought of the vigorous, athletic Henry, crippled perhaps for life. Words seemed inadequate; to cover my feelings, I pointed. 'There's our road, there, by the clump of bushes.'

The sun came out in floods of colour as we turned down the Ashcott lane, under tall arching elms. Long and straight it ran down into the valley, and now the land on either side of it was mine. I leaned forward in anticipation as we followed it down, peering through the leaves, until suddenly the lines of trees ceased and Ashcott lay revealed. Despite our need for haste, the thought of Henry's hurt like an ever-present spur, I drew rein for a moment, staring down at the house which for the first ten years of my life had been my home.

Ashcott was built of the same golden Cotswold stone as Deddington, Adderbury, Banbury and all the towns and villages round about. It lay close by the river Swere, with willows and water-meadows all around it, at once its beauty and its curse, the source of the ague which had carried off my grandmother and many another villager. It was much, much smaller than I remembered, just a Hall with a stone tower at one end, squat and thick, a timbered and stone one at the other, and a crumbling wall, ivy-covered and derelict, flung round it. The gatehouse, stone with a half-timbered upper storey, its two huge wooden doors propped drunkenly open, guarded the only entrance to the courtyard lying in front of the house, and as I stared a small boy emerged driving two or three bony-looking cows.

'You mentioned something of its rustic charms,' Francis said drily. 'I hate to denigrate your castle, my girl, but it appears to me to be close to falling down. One well-placed culverin shot would bring the lot about your ears.'

'I hardly think so,' I said, giving Chalcedony's reins an indignant twitch. 'The walls of the west tower are nigh on twelve feet thick, and the mortar's sound yet. It's the curtain wall is in bad condition, I know, but Ned did say that repairs had been put in hand.'

'It looks to me as though Edward was wrong – or duped. No doubt your rascally bailiff has done himself mighty well.' We had reached level ground, approaching the bridge over the river, and he urged his horse into a trot. 'And what chance of feeding sixty men from this place, even for two nights?'

By now somewhat annoyed at his teasing derogatory manner, I snapped, 'Every chance, I should think, we can always kill a fatted calf.'

'Not one of those,' my cousin said affably, pointing to the cattle we had seen earlier, now grazing on a threadbare strip of land between the road and a fenced-off meadow. 'They don't seem to have recovered from the winter yet, do they? Oh, well, no doubt we can lay our hands on five loaves somewhere, and the river might provide two small fishes.'

Despite myself, I grinned. The small boy, stick in hand, stood by the roadside to watch us pass. He was perhaps nine or ten years old, with a thatch of mouse-brown hair, no stockings, and feet thrust into worn leather shoes much too large for him. I cast my mind back to William Tawney's five-fold brood, and said, halting my horse, 'Hullo, Jack.'

The boy stared at me, astonished. 'How – how did you know my name. mistress? I've never seen you before.'

'I remember you well, though you were but three years old when I left. I'm Mistress Heron – Mistress Thomazine Heron – and I've brought a troop of soldiers for your protection, and mine, for I'll be living in the house again. They'll need food, for sixty of them, and some kind of stabling or pasture for their horses, and beds – but that can wait. Jack, do you want to earn a shilling in my service?'

The child's eyes, already round and brilliant as they studied the soldiers, grew larger still. 'Ooh, yes, mistress, what must I do?'

'There's been an accident on the Adderbury road, a man hurt, and we shall need a hurdle and a light cart. Have you those to spare?' The unruly head nodded. 'Then can you find your father, tell him that we are here, and ask him to get them for us as soon as may be? My friend is grievously hurt, and needs help urgently.'

'He's in the courtyard, mistress, mending the wall,' the boy said breathlessly. 'I'll tell him!' And with a last delighted glance at the six solid Suffolk troopers, turned and ran down the road to the gatehouse, his shoes slapping loose against his heels.

'I can see I shall have to take care,' Francis remarked, with a sidelong glance at me. 'You seem to have made a conquest. How did you know his name was Jack?'

'Well, he's one of Will Tawney's children for sure – they all had that wild hair and those freckles. And Master Tawney had but three sons – two nearly of an age with me, and one little more than a baby when I left Ashcott. Thus it's easy – he's too young to be George or Young Will, so he must be Jack.'

We had by now almost reached the gatehouse. Seen from close quarters, Ashcott appeared even more dilapidated than at first. The curtain wall, where not cloaked with ivy, showed weathered, flaking stone and powdery mortar, patched here and there, glaringly, with fresh. The gates had evidently not been shut for many a long year, although I remembered that my father had insisted on the nightly ritual of their closing. They were propped open now with lumps of stone. The gatehouse itself was not above seventy years old, but lumps of plaster had fallen off to reveal the laths beneath. Two lights in one of the upstairs windows were broken. With a sinking heart I rode into the courtyard beside Francis, wondering how my much-vaunted 'safe' castle walls had looked to Edward's professional eye.

The courtyard had changed little since my childhood; a large irregular piece of beaten earth, pecked over by a few scrawny fowls, with strategic stepping-stones over the worst of the mud. The barn and stable range, built precariously against the inside of the curtain wall, were marginally more decrepit than I remembered, and my grandmother's prized herb garden, adjoining the kitchen outbuildings, had been reduced to a damp struggling rosemary bush and a few pathetic clumps of sage. At the point where the curtain wall joined the west tower, a ladder had been propped against the stones and a workman was perched halfway up it, trowel in hand, mortaring the wall. At its foot, the boy Jack stood, pointing at us, and a man turned, shading his eyes against the sun, to study us. As we drew rein, he approached.

Will Tawney had been my father's steward, and the natural choice to look after the estate on my behalf. But his virtue, his kind, easy-going, diplomatic nature, was also his chief fault, for it made him a lamentable man of business, and I could still remember my father's anger when he discovered that, far from ending the contract with a Banbury man who had supplied rotten meat, Tawney had placed further orders because he felt sorry for the man, who had an ailing wife and seven children. It seemed probable that Ashcott's condition owed much to my bailiff's cheerfully indolent ways.

He had changed little in seven years. Still the same, round, short man with a straggly beard and red cheeks, but with rather less hair than before. His face cleared of worry as soon as he was close enough to recognize me. 'Mistrss Thomazine! After all these years! It's good to see you back, mistress, good indeed! My Jack said it was you, and I wouldn't believe him, but now of course I know you. You've grown so like your mother, poor dear lady.' Pausing for breath, his eyes slid past me to Francis and the troopers waiting at my back. I said, with as little fuss as I could muster, 'There will be a troop of horse to be fed and sheltered here for a night, possibly two – I trust that you can arrange something. But that can wait for now, what's more important is that we need a hurdle to carry an injured man; his horse fell on him on Deddington Hill and his leg's broken, if not worse. Have you any to hand?'

Will Tawney closed his mouth, which had been agape ever since my reference to feeding a troop of horse, and pointed to the barn. 'Yes, Mistress Thomazine, there's a stack of 'em in there. Jack! Come and help me with the hurdles!'

My bailiff, I now remembered, was not one to do anything with a great deal of bother. It seemed no time before a suitable hurdle was extracted from the pile, and less before a small cart, with shaggy pony to pull it, appeared led by the younger of Jack's two surviving sisters, Sue, who had been a tiny baby when I left. By now, the entire Tawney family, plus at least half of the villagers, had gathered in the courtyard to gape. To my surprise and delight, many of the older folk came up to bid me welcome, with happy smiles and cryptic utterances such as, 'Now at last we'll see things done,' which spoke volumes for my bailiff's stewardship. Many of them I recognized, house servants, parents of my playmates, the warrener who had shown Edmund and me the use of a bow and arrow, the groom who had guided me on my first pony. I found myself surrounded by a group of excited people, introducing themselves, children and neighbours, and asking most kindly after my welfare.

'The cart's ready,' Francis said, appearing already mounted above the edge of the throng. 'We must away. Will you stay behind then, and arrange everything?'

'I'll try!' I said, laughing, and waved him out of the gatehouse, the soldiers and the cart with the hurdle placed inside it following after with a crowd of eager children. Then I turned to Will Tawney. 'I must speak to them all — where? Ah, I know! The mounting-block!'

This stood by the hall doorway, mossed over from disuse. Disdaining my bailiff's hand, I scrambled up to balance uncertainly on the top. It was the first time I had ever spoken in public, and the fact that my audience were by and large my tenants made me additionally nervous. My hands clenched at my sides, I spoke loudly. 'Good people, I am most glad of your welcome, and in these troubled times you've given me fresh heart and courage.' I paused, to a ripple of sycophantic cheering, for thought, and then went on. 'I am here, with my Heron cousins, for my own safety, and for yours. If there's to be bloodshed between the King and his Parliament, it's best that people and property be protected. My cousin and guardian, Captain Heron, has raised a troop of horse for the defence of His Majesty. He and they have escorted us here from Suffolk, and in a day or two they'll depart to join the King in York, leaving some trained and armed men for the defence of this house. We shall need your help to feed them, and so I ask that, if any of you have any surplus of corn or stock, please bring it to the kitchen here. You'll be paid at market rates, and there'll be no thieving or forced loans. We are engaged in defending you, and the King, from the actions of violent and unscrupulous men, and we have no wish to quarrel with the people of this village. Should any of my cousin's men misbehave in any way, I suggest you address your complaints forthwith to him, and the offender will be speedily dealt with. Now, I thank you all for your welcome, from my heart, and I pray that we may work well together. God save the King!'

'God save the King!' thirty or more broad Oxfordshire voices shouted, hats were flung in the air, and several willing hands assisted me from my precarious position. I was rather pleased with my little speech, though any noble ring about it was borrowed from Simon, and it had certainly spread an aura of goodwill. People crowded around me, promising sacks of wheat or flour, pigs and fowls, nets of cabbages and barrels of home-brew. It took me some time to direct all these to bring their goods to Ashcott as soon as possible, and when the crowd had dispersed a little I turned to Will Tawney. 'I would like to see the house, of course, and we must make ready for the night. The men can make shift in the barn, but we'll need beds for the officers – half-a-dozen of them – and for myself and my cousins.'

'My wife will speak to you regarding that, mistress – she holds the keys to the linen presses, and knows the working of the household better than I do. The estate's my concern, now.' He opened the great main door, and we entered Ashcott's hall. High, dusty and echoing, it loomed above us, the great hammer-beam roof hung over our heads in the gloom. The windows were long and narrow, high-placed, and the sun shafted through them in great dust-filled golden beams to lay pools of light on the stone floor, the high table, the fireplaces and the cupboards and presses along the walls under the north-east windows. My father, a quiet family man, had never dined with his servants and household in the hall, but had taken his meals with wife and children in private, and in my memory the hall had only been used for the periodic manor courts and harvest celebrations. It had a gaunt, unused look and smell to it, but I ran a quick eye over the trestles and boards stacked against the wall and said, 'We'll all sup in here tonight, Will, there's space enough.'

'Very good, Mistress Thomazine.'

I walked over to the high table, filmed with silvery dust. 'And someone must be set to dusting and cleaning . . . I know there's not much time, and notice is short, but this table is filthy. Were you not warned of our coming?'

Will Tawney mumbled something about not realizing it would be so soon. I guessed that he had preferred to hope that we would never arrive to disturb his peace. As we continued around the house, the neglect it had suffered was laid bare before me. I took note of dusty, musty rooms, of rotting hangings that had taken the moth, of damp plaster and furniture set as if on purpose to catch rain through broken windows. About halfway round, we came upon sudden frenzied activity; Mistress Tawney with her elder daughter and a gaggle of village girls and women, frantically sorting linen and bedding, shaking blankets and raising clouds of dust. I exchanged wary greetings with Will's wife, who had in my childhood often let me feel the sharp edge of her tongue, and of whom I had stood in some awe, and friendly grins with Doll, her daughter, who was a year or so older than I. Then I asked to see the kitchen and still-room.

Mistress Tawney stiffened, her eyes on her husband's face, and then left Doll in charge, with admonitions to 'see those lazy girls do their share of the work,' and escorted me down to the kitchen in a rigid, disapproving silence.

The kitchen building was a large, single-storey structure built of wood and tacked roughly onto the foot of the east tower. The bakehouse, still-room, dairy and other offices had been added to it and the curtain wall at various times. The house had been uninhabited now for the four years since my grandmother's death, save for the Tawneys' illicit tenancy, and the ubiquitous film of dust lay over hearth and spit and table. The still-room, where once Kate Heron had instructed me, and where I had spent many happy hours brewing potions and simples, was in a sorry state, the walls mossy and mouldy with damp. All the equipment, bottles and pestles and stills, was there, but the contents of the jars had long since reduced to sticky residues of indeterminate colours. I was glad for Henry's sake that our baggage contained a stout chest full of medical supplies. Making plans in my head for the still-room's refurbishing and restocking, I turned to Jane Tawney. 'And what stores are there? When Master Heron – Master Edward Heron – came in the spring he left instructions that salt meat and cheeses and flour and beer be bought.'

Mistress Tawney's gaze rested smoothly on my face. 'I regret to say, mistress, that it has not been done. We were unable in these troubled times to procure sufficient for your cousin's needs. The money he left was put to good use on the repairs he ordered.'

Or slipped into your pocket, I thought. But without proof, nothing could be voiced, only suspected. It would be well to keep a very watchful eye on the Tawneys, Jane in particular, for I could not imagine her lazy, pleasant husband cheating his late employer's daughter of anything; although to avoid his wife's tongue he might well turn a blind eye to her activities.

'That's a matter will have to be rectified soon if we're to live here for any length of time. Also, we must lay in a stock of provisions that can be stored for months without harm, in case we have to withstand a siege.' I saw her eyes widen in alarm, and added, 'But there's small chance of that. My cousins hope that all this will pass without bloodshed. It was thought that I and my cousins, Mistress Lucy and Mistress Meraud, and our friend Mistress Sewell and her children, would be safer here, in case of war, than at Goldhayes. There is to be a small garrison, a dozen men or so, left here for our protection, so you need not fear. Also, Mistress Sewell's husband is the one who has been hurt in the accident on the hill – he'll be left here to recover, and he's a professional soldier, so we'll be doubly safe.'

Mistress Tawney's eyes were still doubtful as she turned away to the window, which looked on to the courtyard. 'They have arrived, mistress. No doubt you will wish to greet them.' And as we walked together out of the still-room door into the sunlight, relief was writ plain on her sharp, handsome face. No doubt that my brief questions had struck to the bone.

The courtyard, from being filled with country people, was now crowded with soldiers, more filing under the gatehouse. In the midst of them, four men bore a hurdle which they set down with great care before the main door. Grainne knelt beside him; as I came up I saw that he was unconscious. Skinner's face, grave and anxious, hung above them. By the gatehouse, Edward was getting the troop to dismount in something approaching order. Simon, obviously attempting to conceal that he was at a loss, was looking round and up at the Hall. As soon as he saw me, Jane Tawney at my back, his face cleared. 'Ah, Thomazine, is all well?' His sidelong glance at the walls revealed his fears. I said quickly, 'Yes. The villagers are bringing some supplies in. I said you'd pay for them, I hope that was in order. The men may safely be accommodated in the barn, and the horses, or some of them, in the stables, and there'll be beds in the house for the officers and us.'

'Excellent,' Simon said, with a last, still-suspicious glare at the fresh mortar slapped anyhow on the crumbling stone of the curtain wall. 'Is this Mistress Tawney? I am Captain Heron, mistress, and I trust you have been looking after our interests.'

Jane Tawney curtseyed. 'Yes, sir,' she said with unwonted meekness. 'Now if you will excuse me, sir, Mistress Thomazine, I must return to oversee the women.'

It was several hectic hours before our troop was finally installed to Edward's satisfaction: the horses bestowed in the stables or in the horse lines hastily erected across a corner of the courtyard, the men's gear in the barn where they would sleep, the ammunition cart alongside the farm wagon in the barn and the baggage cart unpacked and the contents stacked in a corner of the hall. Meanwhile, I had been housewife for the first time in my life, assuming a role not normally assigned to unmarried girls. Fortunately, I had Grainne at my side to advise and suggest, and I was properly grateful, although she had insisted on accompanying me, saying that Henry was sleeping sound after a small draught of her precious laudanum. Her eyes were shadowed with worry, and I guessed that she wanted something to do, to keep her mind from dwelling on Henry's condition. Accordingly, we went through the domestic quarters like a purge, giving orders to our own two maids, and to the women and girls under Jane Tawney's eye, and trying to make a start at setting four years of neglect to rights. We finished in the kitchen, where Tom, sorely tried, was attempting to collect the offerings of food and to give out payment in return. The cheeses, of varying stages of ripeness, the sacks of flour and bunches of salads and nets of cabbages, coneys from the warren in a still-warm, furry heap, and other inanimate objects presented no problem, but the livestock was another matter. When we entered Tom and two of the three troopers assigned to help him were attempting to coax a dilapidated but still vigorous fowl from its perch on top of the smoke-jack, just out of their reach. The third man, harassed almost beyond endurance, had one arm around a struggling, naked piglet and the other clutching two more hens by the feet; from his crouching positon on the cold stone floor he was also attempting to keep a watch on the little bag of coin on the kitchen table. A half-dozen of villagers, riotously amused, stood and watched and offered uncouth suggestions.

'Light a branch and touch up its tail feathers! That'll move it, right enough!'

'Drop a noose over its scrawny neck!'

'Throw salt on its tail!'

'Get your pistol and shoot the bugger – oh, begging your pardon, Mistress Thomazine.' The last speaker, a young man I vaguely recognized, had the grace to blush, and I the wit to hide my smiles. 'If there's some unground corn,' I suggested, 'tempt it down with that.'

This simple stratagem was enthusiastically and successfully adopted. Tom, red-faced, speedily excuted his vows of vengeance and wrung the necks of all three birds. I suddenly realized that the afternoon was cooling into evening and that there were nearly eighty mouths to feed. Seized with panic, I looked wildly round at the neglected, dirty kitchen and at the unpromising tableful of foodstuffs. 'What's to be done with all this?'

Grainne gave me a friendly, encouraging grin. 'Something quick, I think . . . I see there's been bread brought, and cheese. We can set someone to baking for tomorrow; for tonight cheese and bread and some of that cold salt pork, and the bacon and beer, will be sufficient. And we can put the fowls in a broth with some of the vegetables; I see there are onions, and a goodly bunch of herbs – that'll do nicely for the seasoning, and with the wheat and eggs and milk and our raisins, we can boil up frumenty for breakfast.'

'You seem used to cooking for large numbers,' I said, bedazzled. Grainne shrugged. 'I've followed in an army's train before. You soon learn what to do with the most unpromising materials. But one thing's for sure, we won't make anything of this without help. Corporal Sewell! Would you find a half-dozen likely village girls and boys for us? Your supper depends on it.'

The village girls and boys were found, and brought, and I spent the rest of the afternoon sweatily in the kitchen, coaxing the new-made fire to rights, trying to make sure that our helpers did as they were asked, and thankfully, if a little guiltily, left the organization to Grainne. It was several hours of hard work before we were able to send the message that supper was ready, and the men filed into the hall to sit at the trestles and eat their broth and cheese and bread, and sample the ale brought from the village and from Ashcott's own cellars. By then, I was so tired that I could barely lift spoon to my mouth, but managed to stave off sleep for long enough to receive the news that Henry had woken, showed no signs of fever, and had demanded a hearty supper.

'When he tastes it, he'll wish he hadn't,' I said to Grainne, and the shadows lifted from her face with her laughter.

The only ones who did not, I hope, sleep like the dead that night were the men Simon had posted on sentry-duty. Before I tumbled gratefully into the musty bed I was to share with Lucy and Meraud – we would not be so crowded once the soldiers had gone, and I was thankful, for I did not relish the prospect of sharing my dreams with Meraud for more than a night or two – I pulled my night-rail over my chemise and walked over to the window. Behind me, the two girls and Heppy, who was to sleep in a truckle bed in the corner, were making ready for bed, folding clothes and brushing hair, talking quietly. I laid my elbows on the sill and stared out into the soft warm night. The window was open and the breeze gently laid velvety fingers on my weary face. The moon was full, and high, drenching ice-white light on the land, barred with the dense black shadows of the trees. An owl hooted, mournfully, in the distance, and was answered by another much closer. I breathed in deep the quiet and peace and beauty of it, unable to believe that men would ever shatter the scented calm of the Oxfordshire night with guns and bloodshed, or pour in hostility down the silver ribbon of lane from the Deddington Road. Below me, in the courtyard, two men on guard-duty conversed softly, and one of them struck flint and lit a pipe, his square bearded face suddenly and redly illuminated by the flame: Edward, the officer in charge for the first part of the night. Leaning out further, I caught part of their talk, full of spavins and forelegs and fetlocks, and grinned to myself; what with that and the sentry on the ramparts, who was strolling up and down whistling 'Bonny Sweet Robin was all my Joy', no scene could have possessed less of a mlitary atmosphere.

I felt a presence at my side, and looked round to meet Meraud's wide blue eyes. 'It's so calm and still,' said my Cornish cousin, leaning her elbows likewise on the sill, her silvery hair made yet paler by the moon's light. 'It will be a fine day tomorrow, I think. Are you glad to be home?'

Startled, I turned fully to look at her, expecting her usual condescending stare, and met only an apparently genuine interest. Feeling uneasy, I shook my head. 'No, I can't think of Ashcott as my home, not now. Goldhayes is my home, where I belong, not here. Oh, I love it here, but it's not where my heart is.'

Meraud's delicately arched eyebrows rose, and I realized that I had said too much; and with that realization blushed rosily and guiltily. Quickly I turned back into the room, hoping that she would not notice. Meraud stumbling upon my love affair with Francis was the last thing I wanted.

I was too tired to waste sleep worrying about it; we all four in that chamber slept like the dead in our musty sheets and damp bedding. The next morning dawned so glorious and sunny that all unpleasant thoughts were impossible to live with for long. The dew lay thick in the courtyard, the cocks crowed long and joyously, and in the woods on Coombe Hill and by the Deddington Road, cuckoos chimed in counterpoint. In the kitchen, we boiled up frumenty for breakfast, poured beer into leather jacks, cut hunks of bread and slabs of cold bacon, and sang and whistled as we worked. After the meal, there was more to be done, baking and roasting and mixing, seemingly without end, until I began to see the sense in Edward's talk at last night's supper, about supplies being utterly essential to any army. 'The side that's well supplied with food, and equipment, and organizes its victualling thoroughly,' he had said, 'is the side that'll win in the end, in this war as in any other. Soldiers won't win battles on empty bellies, without bullets or going barefoot. So you may grumble about your long hours in the kitchen, my sweet coz, but it's work as vital as firing guns or marching in formation.'

Vital it might be, but I was glad when dinner-time came; for we had prepared the evening meal as well, and so the afternoon could be left free. The soldiers had spent the morning in drill, in the meadow by the river (Simon had promised compensation for the flattened, bruised hay crop) and since it was the Sabbath were excused further activity for the afternoon. I had it in mind to revisit some of my old childhood haunts along the valley, and suggested to Francis that he come with me, knowing full well that it would be our last chance to be alone together before the troop left in the morning. Lucy and Edward agreed to accompany us, and could be trusted to keep a still tongue and turn a blind eye should our ways chance to part.

We crossed the courtyard, threading our way between men playing makeshift bowls on the bare ground, or nine men's morris in the shade of the ramparts, passed under the gatehouse and out on to the road, Drake scampering round our feet in happy expectation of a walk. The dust rose in little puffs under our feet and above us the sky was a glorious butterfly blue, cloudless and shining with heat. Lucy wore a white kerchief, hat and gloves to shield her from the sun, but almost as soon as we emerged from the gate she was complaining of the heat, and desiring shade. 'How can you moan, Lucy?' I asked her. 'The best and sunniest day of the year, and you complain of the heat!'

'It's all very well for you,' Lucy grumbled, 'your skin is as dark as a Moor's already, so the sun can't touch you. Still,' she added, with one of the mercurial changes of mood so typical of her, and Francis, 'you're right, it is a glorious day. Just listen to the cuckoos!'

But Edward and Francis, strolling on ahead, drowned them in song of their own. The strains of a soldiering air, brought back from the Low Countries and now popular with the men in the troop, rolled back to us, and with a rueful glance at each other, Lucy and I joined in the rousing chorus:

When cannons are roaring
And bullets are flying
He that would honour win
Must not fear dying.

'That's no music for a peaceful walk in the country,'

Lucy said, picking up her skirts and running to catch them up. 'Here, let's sing this instead.' A little breathless, she sang an old favourite:

Oh, the lark in the morning, she rises from her nest
And she mounts up in the air with the dew all on her
    breast:
And like a merry ploughboy she whistles and she sings,
And she goes home in the evening with the dew all on her
    wings.

We all took up the song as we drew near the little bridge over the river. Here grew the rushes which thatched the cottages and, dipped in tallow, lit them of an evening, and also meadow-sweet and forget-me-nots, buttercups and ladies' smock. Lucy, still singing, started to gather some of the flowers; as one song ended she began another, a plaintive melody of which two lines lingered echoing in my mind:

Oh, love it is a killing thing —
Did you ever feel the pain?

We strolled on up the hill, in and out of the dappled flickering shade of the tall elms, and about halfway to the top, I led my cousins off on a small path to the right, which meandered through the sheepwalks above Ashcott, and would finally emerge at Barford St Michael, nearly two miles away. The side of the hill stretched in front of us, thickly grassed and flowered, broken by a few trees and bushes; and below us Ashcott sat golden and sleepy, shimmering and dancing in the heat like the butterflies weaving and darting in their perpetual galliard around us. Above us, more and thicker trees promised shade, and Lucy cast a longing glance at them. 'Is it possible to die of heat? I think I shall, if I don't have a chance to walk in the cool for a while. Would you mind, Ned?' She turned a coy, meaningful look on me and Francis which made me long to push her down the slope. 'I don't suppose you two would mind being left alone, either.'

'You'll leave us quick enough,' Francis said, 'before I set

my dog on you.' He turned to the faithful Drake, who had followed his dust patiently all the way from Suffolk, and who now lay panting hotly in the grass. 'You hear me? Kill!'

Drake rolled an eye in his direction which plainly said, 'It's too hot for me to bother.' Lucy grinned. 'What a fierce dog you have, brother. Don't worry, we'll go. We're out of sight of the house now, so no one will see we've split up. Don't be back too late!' With a simpering wave, she picked up her skirts and set off up the hill. Edward snorted. 'She wants a strap taken to her, little minx.'

'I wouldn't put it past her to have a telescope concealed about her person, the better to spy on us,' Francis said, laughing. I called up the hill at her retreating back, 'I hope you step in a sheep-turd!'

'Now I know you're no lady,' Edward said, affectionately reproving, and followed after his sister. We were left alone with Drake and the sizzling grasshoppers.

'Drake, you're a failure,' Francis said, glaring at his dog. 'Come on up, owd lad, it's not time for a rest yet.'

I took his arm as we walked on through the pasture. 'Do you feel uncomfortable? As though something were expected of you?'

'Well, when I throw myself passionately at your feet I'll make damn sure Lucy isn't watching. What that girl needs is a love affair of her own, to take her mind off ours.'

'Who with? Tom? Or some dashing captain of the King's army?'

'Some sour-faced Puritan in the Parliament's, more like. Lucy is like you in that respect; unexpected and perverse.'

'You can talk.'

Franis stopped to remove his doublet. He tied the sleeves round his waist, as he had done when a boy, and I remembered so clearly the afternoon of our first acquaintance, when I had been ten and he thirteen, on just such a glorious day as this. I smiled to think of it, and Francis smiled back. 'What are your thoughts, my lady?'

'The day of the kestrel's nest. Seeing you wear your doublet like that reminded me.'

'Will you then remove your shoes and stockings? Or are you now too modest?'

I grinned. 'I've no wish to tread on a thistle – or in a sheep-turd, for that matter. Modesty takes no part in my reasons.'

'So say you. Where are you leading us, owd gal?'

I had taken his hand and towed him off the path and down the slope a little way. There was, I remembered, a hollow, partly screened by bushes, where we could sit unseen even by Lucy's curious eyes. It was nearer than I had thought, and we all but fell into it, Drake entangled in our feet. Laughing, Francis sat down, glancing round at the grass and hawthorn bushes, thick with sweet white blossom and humming with bees, which suddenly formed our horizon. 'Admirable, Thomazine. What did you and your devilish little brother do here? Torture your captives?'

'Actually, we used to burn them at the stake. No, I used to come here when I wanted to get away on my own. Edmund never found it, and it wasn't he who was devilish – it was me.' I sat down beside him, thinking back, seeing the small bright-haired boy who had always followed me, the domineering older sister. 'I must have been a despair to my poor grandmother. My father just laughed, and said I'd mend my ways as I grew. I still feel guilt, for Edmund and for Father.'

'Why?'

'It was my fault they died. I insisted on playing with the village children. There was smallpox in one family; I caught it, and gave it to them. I lived, and they died.'

'You look so woebegone, I feel you'd almost prefer they lived, and you died. I'm glad it was as it was, so that I could have you. Would you want to have lived all your life without me, incomplete?'

'No,' I whispered. Francis put an arm round my shoulders and drew me close. The sun shone hot on our faces as we kissed, long and slow, with somewhere at the bottom of my heart a new note, born of farewell. Echoing it, I became aware as our lips separated of a skylark singing rapturously, somewhere in the arching blue void above us. Francis threw his head back to seek it, a half-forgotten smile on his face, and I watched him, absorbing this picture of him to hold to in the empty days ahead; the careless way his pale bright hair fell to his shoulders, struck all sparkling silver by the sun behind him, the outlines of his face, the clear line of his nose and wide mouth and straight eyebrows and shadow-green, far-set eyes, all rimed by the vivid light. I saw, too, the long relaxed line of his body, the thin clever hands and the eager, mocking, individual life within him, and love and fear caught my throat together, so that I could scarcely breathe. I thought suddenly of Henry, a sturdy oak to Francis's slender ash, yet cut down without warning; and a dreadful picture came slyly into my mind of Francis dead, or maimed, or dying, on some terrible field of battle. Aware of a change in me, Francis dropped his gaze from the sky to my face. 'What is it, love?'

'Be careful, Francis, oh, be careful,' I whispered in despair, 'don't let yourself be killed.'

His eyes rested steadily on mine. 'I'll certainly do my best to prevent it – within reason. Being too careful of one's life, however, doesn't make for a good officer. Nor will it make me beloved of Simon. He'd no doubt leap at the chance to think me a coward. And the devil of it is, I probably am.' He smiled wryly into my eyes. 'People like Ned, all stolid professionalism, are the brave ones. They haven't the imagination to be craven. It's soldiers like me, who've never seen a shot fired in anger, and who can imagine all too clearly the consequences of a collision with cannonball or musket-shot, who make the cowards.' He stared down at his hands, lying still on his knees. 'How will they look on the eve of battle? None so steady, I'll wager.'

'It's not so much being frightened, though,' I said. 'I mean, I don't suppose Edward knows what being frightened is. So he's not being brave when he marches stolidly on, is he? He's just doing his duty. It's the ones like you – who are frightened but *still* go on; they are the ones with true courage.'

'And what makes you think, O my wise Thomazine with your owl's eyes and dolphin's smile; what makes you think that I will go on, and not run away? I think,' said Francis reflectively, 'that I might very well run away.'

'No, you would not,' I said, looking him full in the face. 'You wouldn't have climbed that tree for the nest, or answered back your father, or followed your own ideas and heart all the years I've known you, if you were going to melt away like snow in summer at the first sound of gunfire. But just don't, please, don't do anything stupid.'

'Don't worry,' Francis said, 'I won't. I'll do what I think is right, according to circumstance. I would not die needlessly, to leave you alone, neither of us having known each other completely.'

I knew what he meant, and it took me a second, no more, to make up my mind. There was silence on the hillside, except for the lark, and we were alone and unseen. And such was my feeling that we must snatch and keep and hold as much as possible, in case it might be denied to us for ever, that I could throw all caution and modesty to the winds. Deliberately, I loosened the ties on my bodice and placed the long, tasselled ends in his hands. 'You won't leave without knowing more of me,' I said.

Francis took a quick sudden breath, in surprise and delight mixed, and then gathered me into his arms and held me close. 'No,' he whispered into my hair. 'No, little love. What if I were killed, and you left to bear a child alone?'

I pulled back to look at him. 'I could stand the shame of that – if there is any shame. And you would not die with your love unsatisfied, and I'd have something left of you to give me comfort. I don't want either of us to be left with nothing, with not even a memory of you as my true lover.'

Francis smiled. 'Put like that, persuasive lady, how could I refuse? And it has been such a long time, waiting for you.' He pulled me back against him, and we kissed with a new urgency and sweetness that turned my bones to water and made me dizzy with a fresh, sensual delight. Gently, he undid my laces and his hands explored me, lighting the fires within us both that had been too long suppressed.

There was no shame in this pleasure, it seemed as natural and inevitable as sunrise, and I drowned myself unhesitatingly in the poet's 'right true end of love' – forgetting all save that I was Thomazine and he was Francis, and my desire for him was the equal of his for me.

And then Drake, somewhere just above us on the hill, barked, sharp with warning, and then again, more urgently. Someone called, too close, and we sprang apart as if each had burned the other. I became aware of reality, of the intruders on the hillside, of Francis's rueful, annoyed smile, of the fact that my bodice was unlaced and falling off my shoulders, that my neckerchief lay crumpled where we had been, that there was grass in my hair and bits of buttercup in my stays and that I had all unnoticing laid myself down on a thistle. Suppressing a mad hysterical desire to laugh, I said, 'You'd better help me – it's bound to be Lucy!'

'I'm not sure I want to help you – you look utterly delightful half-naked and I've half a mind to let you emerge thus – or leap upon you with renewed passion.'

I could hear Drake trotting off through the grass to greet whoever it was on the hill. Francis abandoned his moment of teasing and with quick, deft fingers rearranged my chemise and stays, laced up the bodice, repinned my neckerchief and, with a flourish, removed a spray of sweet-scented pink clover from between my breasts. 'You look almost decent. Well, since Drake has broadcast our presence far and wide, we'd better reveal ourselves. I'll kill dear Lucy, and her unbounded curiosity with her.'

Giggling weakly with reaction to such a stunning anticlimax to our moments of passion, I stood up to face whoever it was approaching.

It was not Lucy, or Ned. It was Meraud, with Jamie a few paces behind her, his hand in Drake's collar. Her eyes widened in surprise, and then a kind of quick, malicious amusement crossed her face. It was plain that she had guessed at once what we had been about, and had jumped to a conclusion that we had been prevented from reaching, because of her arrival. 'Hullo, Francis, hullo Thomazine. I thought it must be you, because of Drake.'

Jamie, I could see from his unsullied face, had come to no such conclusion. To keep him in ignorance, despite Meraud's uninnocent guess, I said quickly, 'We were watching for the skylark. Listen, you can hear it now.'

Jamie gazed upwards, his movements a faint shadow of Francis's earlier, a smile on his lips. 'Yes, look, I can see it. See, Meraud? Over there, above the hawthorns. Such a small brown thing, to make all that song!'

Meraud glanced once, then turned away to walk up the hill, her face faintly and malevolently triumphant. Francis and I looked at each other, then followed her uneasily. Jamie walked behind us, whistling in untuneful imitation of the lark. His was not the sort of mind that jumped to malicious conclusions; and besides, he was used to seeing Francis and me together for no more than companionship. I thanked God that he, at least, was as yet too innocent to see that it was no longer just companionship that bound us close.

'Do you remember that skylark mother had in a cage in her chamber?' Jamie pursued, unheeding of our silence. 'That never sang a note, not once all the time she had it, till she let it go because it wouldn't sing – and *then* it sang. Like the trumpets of Heaven, you said.'

'They have to be free, to sing,' said Francis, surreptitiously picking bits of grass out of my hair. Meraud, ahead of us, glided through the grass as if nothing had happened, as if this was just another ordinary afternoon walk, but I knew now that our precarious secret was safe no longer, and that even if she concealed it now, she might well reveal it at some later moment when it would suit her best. My heart chill within me, I walked back to Ashcott with them, and the skylark, an unceasing heartless torrent of song, seemed to mock all my hopes and desires and turn them to nothing.

*   *   *

The troop left at first light the next morning, bound for York. We all stood in the courtyard to bid farewell. By the gatehouse Heppy was talking earnestly to her brother Holly, a sturdier, fairer, masculine version of herself, unheeded emotional tears shining through her freckles, handing over some good-luck charm to turn the bullets from him. Lucy, also close to tears, had a big bunch of new roses, thick with dew: Maiden's Blush and the White Rose of York, the tight-packed cabbage roses and the small fantastically-striped petals of Rosa Mundi, the Rose of the World. The dozen or so bushes, tangled and neglected in a sunny corner of the courtyard, had been almost denuded. She gave one to each of her elder brothers, to Tom and to Jonathan Eldritch and anyone else standing near. Grainne stood, with Jasper by the hand, talking to Edward; she would not now have to say farewell to her husband, and perhaps for that reason the shadow of parting seemed to lie less heavily upon her. Behind her, near the door, Orange darted at shadows, patted the flickering grass-stems, and swirled like a small flame around Meraud's seemly purple skirts.

I had nothing to give him, except myself, and that had been denied to us. I stood irresolute by Grainne's side, afraid as ever of the moment of parting, which no matter how loving seemed always to leave behind a forlorn, unsatisfied taste. I stared round at the new day, the silvery dew and azure sky and the cool fresh promise of fine weather. The men were ready, mounted in formation of some kind, the cart harnessed and waiting. Lucy, having divested herself of her roses, was now bestowing parting kisses on all who were entitled to them and some, to Simon's evident disapproval, who were not. A sudden memory of a line in one of her plays came to me; I turned, plucked a sprig of rosemary from the tattered bush below the Hall windows, and went over to Francis. He held, rather gingerly, one of Lucy's roses in the hand which did not grasp the standard, and its sweet heavy scent coloured all the air between us. He smiled at me, and my heart melted. 'In all this rash of cousinly kisses, who will notice another?'

'No one, I hope,' I said, 'because this I doubt will be just a cousinly kiss.' But it was, all the same, and left me with a desperate unsatisfied yearning for what we had so nearly had. To hide my grief, I held out my sad sprig, and quoted, with a touch of my old sardonic humour, ' "There's rose-mary, that's for remembrance; pray you, love, remember." '

'For ever,' he said simply, and tucked the sprig inside his doublet, keeping the rose in his hand for display. 'It's a herb used in wedding garlands, so that's good fortune.'

And also at funerals, I thought, but did not say so. Simon's voice telling Lucy impatiently to have done with her farewells, broke roughly in. Francis took my hand briefly. 'Remember this for yourself; that whatever happens, I will always be with you. "Parting is such sweet sorrow" – who said that?'

'Juliet.'

'Ah. I was ever of the opinion,' said my lover drily, 'that she knew little of what she was speaking about. There's no sweetness in this, my love. Remember to kiss Edward, and Simon too, or your salutations to me will stand out like a rose in winter.'

'I don't care if he knows now or not – if Meraud has guessed, I should imagine the rumour will come to his ears in time.'

'But be circumspect, all the same,' Francis said, and his eyes were not circumspect at all. 'And now, my lady, "Since there's no help, come let us kiss and part." One day, you know, I will cast off other men's words and salute you with a voice of my own. But for now, if you'd know my thought of you, read in Dr Donne – ."Oh my America – my new-found-land." '

I said my farewells to Edward, and to Simon, and to Tom, and then drew back to watch with the others as the troop filed out of the courtyard, looking ever for the blue-and-silver standard above the dust. Lucy and Meraud waved, and the Tawney girls blew kisses, until they were almost out of sight up the hill, between the elms and the thick frothing lines of cow-parsley hemming the road.

And then they were gone, and we were left alone, to wonder which of them we would never see again.

As Francis had bade me, I read in Dr Donne, but could not finish the poem.Grainne found me, in the little bare stone-walled parlour in the east tower, sitting in the window-seat unable to check the tears that had blinded me to the book open on my knees. At the sight of the Irish girl, who had never given vent to such displays, I felt ashamed of my unwonted emotion, took several deep breaths and wiped my face with my sleeve. Grainne, without comment, handed me one of her neat plain handkerchiefs that I had seen used to mop Henry's brow or wipe spilt food from Hester's face and waited until I had calmed myself. Then she said, 'It's Francis, isn't it? Do you fear he will be killed?'

I nodded. 'But it's not just that . . .' I raised my eyes to her thin, calm, understanding face, and not for the last time yielded to the impulse to unburden myself to her. Stumbling, I attempted to convey some idea of what we had felt the previous afternoon, and of the terrible sense of loss which had hung over me ever since. In my friend's face I read no shock or condemnation. 'I know exactly what you mean,' Grainne said, with one of her quick smiles. 'But there's no need to justify yourself, no need for shame. There never is, to my mind, any discredit in giving yourself to the man you love above all others. Had Henry not been able to marry me immediately, I'd have thrown myself at him as passionately as did you at Francis.' She turned to look speculatively out of the window at the courtyard twenty feet below, and the two sentries, part of the ten-strong garrison left behind, playing dice in the dust under the gatehouse. 'I am almost glad that Henry broke his leg. At least, selfishly, I am spared the agony of waiting for news. I was never able to understand why one of my father's friends said that war fell hardest of all on the women. Now, I know.'

'Yes, it's the not knowing that's worst,' I agreed. 'And no possibility, or very little, of letters being carried. It would be weeks before we heard of battle or death, if ever.' Feeling dangerous weakness creeping over me once more, I gritted my teeth and added, 'For two pins I'd disguise myself for a lad and go with them. I'd far rather face the guns in their company, knowing what was happening, than wait here in tortured ignorance. I came here thinking there'd be more chance of news at Ashcott than Goldhayes. I think I was mistaken.'

'Well, I'm very glad you came,' Grainne said. 'I would run mad here on my own, had Henry gone away too. He knows now about the child, and he'd not have allowed me to drag about in the army's tail with a baby expected. Nor, knowing how ill I've been with Jasper and Hess, would I wish to be a burden to him. I'd have stayed here, on my own, with two babies and the Tawneys for company, and I dare swear Mistress Jane would have driven me to the bottle!'

I grinned. 'She's never been sweet, but she's more vinegary now than I remember her. She's of Puritan stock, more unbending than most, and I don't think she relishes our light hearts and our Cavalier politics. She'll be an uncomfortable companion, should we ever find ourselves besieged.'

Henry made a remarkable recovery from his fall. Within a week of the troop's departure, he was instructing Trooper Pryke, the son of a carpenter, in the making of a pair of crutches, of stout elm with a horsehair-stuffed pad to wedge under each arm. On the day of their finishing he had himself carried downstairs and, the weather having once more turned cold and rainy, could be seen, and heard, stumping round the Hall with increasing speed and dexterity, the rhythmic thumping of the crutches interspersed with horrible oaths as something jarred the injured leg. Jasper, utterly fascinated, took to hopping round on one leg in imitation. Jamie seized his opportunity while Henry was still comparatively immobile, and at every available moment pumped him for military talk and discussion. Henry, who was good-natured, patient and a surprisingly apt teacher, took this monopolization of his time in fine spirit and could frequently be seen acting as drill sergeant not only to the ten soldiers of our garrison, who were undergoing an intensive course in the use of the musket and of marksmanship, but also to Jamie, his sturdy thirteen-year-old frame bowed under the weight of a musket nearly as long as he was, and to Jasper, proudly armed with a stick.

Of course, all this military play would be of little use unless the fabric of the house was improved, and before June was out a proper mason was summoned from Deddington to complete the repairs half-heartedly begun by Will Tawney. The courtyard now echoed to the brisk tap of workmen's hammers, the sawing of wood as the gates were repaired and properly hung, and the rip and swish of the blurring, clinging ivy being torn down from the outer walls. For a man, however tough, not yet recovered from serious injury, Henry's energy seemed boundless. He thought of everything, oversaw everything, and the rap of his approaching crutches (or Jasper's skilful imitation of them) was enough to send everyone in the castle scurrying about their business like an overset ants' nest. But he was overtaxing himself, and in the quiet of evening, resting by the fire with his wife and children and our cluster of young Herons, his exhaustion showed.

News both local and national came to us from a variety of sources: alehouse gossip, carriers who spread information and topical pamphlets and news-sheets in the inns of Deddington and Adderbury, and local gentry like Colonel Wilmot at Adderbury House, or Mr Oldys, the vicar of that town, who was a rabid King's man of a loud and violent disposition at odds with his calling, and much disliked by his sober parishioners. We heard of the chaos caused by the King's issue of Commissions of Array to his Lord Lieutenants; many of these, with more valour than discretion, chose to read the call to arms in the market places of towns not inclined to their cause, and often found themselves violently set upon for their pains. Closer to Ashcott, the Earl of Northampton, from his lovely house at Compton Wynyates, was organizing the raising of a regiment, and by some miracle as yet avoiding a direct confrontation with his

Parliamentarian neighbour, Lord Saye, an ancient and wily politician known to his enemies as 'Old Subtlety'. The castle at Banbury was being repaired by the townsmen under the direction of him and his crony, Lord Brooke. It was suddenly very plain that Ashcott, unlike Goldhayes, would occupy no quiet backwater in this war, if war it proved to be. Henry, mindful of the dangers, used some of our store of coin to organize a network of watchers in the villages round about, but particularly in Deddington and Adderbury, who undertook to bring us instant word of any troop movements in the area, whether hostile or friendly. It was an Adderbury man, muddy and out of breath from his hasty two-mile walk down to Ashcott in a continuous depressing drizzle, who brought us the news, late in July, of a confrontation four miles outside Banbury between the Earl of Northampton's forces and those of Lord Brooke.

Henry was able to get about on horseback now, or with a stick; Skinner had done an excellent job of setting the break, and it seemed that, apart from a slight limp, his recovery would be complete. Our life at Ashcott had settled down into a busy, rather nervous routine, which did not give me the time to take notice of the dreary nagging ache of missing Francis. Since neither Grainne nor I trusted Mistress Tawney, we had overseen the victualling of Ashcott for ourselves. The storerooms and cellars were, if not full, at least well stocked, and Grainne had taken the kitchen into her own hands when it became apparent that Jane Tawney's sour nature had overspilled into her cooking. In the high cool gloom of the hall on Saturday, 30th July, we sat at our dinner, family at one table and soldiers and servants at the other, until our talk was rudely disturbed by the entry of Trooper Shoosmith, damp and excited, and the Adderbury man beside him. 'Sir! This 'un say he hev news for you.'

Henry's tawny eyes gathered spark and fire. 'Have you, indeed? Speak up, man!'

The Adderbury man, controlling his breath, said, 'If you please, sir, I have, and I've come to you straightways, soon as I heard . . .'

'Get on with it!' Henry said, his usual patience and good temper falling off him like a sloughed skin. Our informant, flustered, took a huge breath and gabbled. 'It was the ordnance, sir, six pieces of it, sent up to Banbury for the defence of Warwick Castle and Lord Brooke.'

'Fat lot of good it'd do him in Banbury,' said Jamie cheerfully. Henry looked at him and then at the Adderbury man, and both quailed. 'You make little sense. Explain yourself.'

'I am,' said the informant, with a touch of defiant temper himself. 'The ordnance reached Banbury yersterday, and Lord Brooke rode all last night from Warwick to escort it. He'd a hundred men or more with him, so the guns must be valued highly. There's powder and shot with them as well, I understand. Well, someone sent word to my Lord of Northampton, and he raised the trained bands and went to meet them. And there they stand, sir, out on the Stratford road, and neither will give way to the other; my Lord of Northampton looking very angry, and waving the King's commission and saying he must have the ordnance, and his men with pike and musket at ready; and Lord Brooke as stubborn, will not yield up the guns to him, and *his* men ready to give fire likewise. All the Banbury folk, and people round about, are coming to Lord Brooke's aid, but Colonel Wilmot won't let the Adderbury men go, and they're mightily enraged.'

'Does Lord Northampton require help?' Henry demanded. The other man nodded. 'Aye, sir, he does, for he's only got two troops of horse and the same number of pikemen and musketeers, and they're only militiamen and the heart's not in them; they can see Lord Brooke's men mean to fight them if they must. And so Colonel Wilmot bade me come here and bring back what help I could.'

Henry stood up, casting his mutton-bone to the floor. 'You'll get all the help we can muster. Jamie! Stir off your arse and rouse the village. They don't need weapons, cudgels and pitchforks will do if necessary. Men! Be mounted and ready with all speed!'

In an instant, the hall had all but emptied. Grainne and

Lucy and Meraud and I sat looking at each other across the mass of half-eaten food. Hester, who was a solemn, rather wilful child, had got down from her bench and with great concentration was gathering up every scrap of spilt food and stuffing it into her mouth. Betty, the nursemaid, hastily picked her up and admonished her. Above the child's sudden roar of anger, Grainne said wryly, 'I suppose we'd better go and bid them farewell.'

'I pray God Lord Brooke's men are not as warlike as they seem to have appeared,' Meraud said, touching accurately on Grainne's vulnerable place – Henry's safety. My palms itched to slap her, but instead I rose and went to the door. Our garrison were feverishly buckling on swords, saddling horses or checking pistols. An idea struck me, and heedless of the drizzle and mud, I ran across the courtyard. 'Henry! What about us? Are you leaving anyone for our defence?'

'Trooper Edwards and Trooper Pryke,' Henry said. 'We won't be gone long, I shouldn't imagine.' With his glittering eyes and eager face, like a hound that scents its quarry after the chafing boredom of too long a wait, he seemed a different creature entirely from the patient teacher initiating Jamie into the arts of war. 'Mount up! Form up in double file outside the gatehouse!'

Grainne appeared at his side, her hair silvered with rain. 'You won't leave without saying goodbye,' she warned him. 'Besides, Jasper wants to sit on your horse for a moment.'

'All right, you young rascal, do you come up here . . . Are you marching to war with me, think you, or will you reckon to stay at home and look to your mother?'

'I'm coming with you!' Jasper said, his voice sqeaky with excitement. 'Oh, no, you're not,' said his father. 'You're a brave little mite, but your mother wants you more, I reckon. Up you come!'

I held Jasper in the saddle while he wriggled and waved and pointed imaginary pistols to the sky, and I prayed silently that the war he took such innocent delight in would not leave him orphaned. Behind me, his parents were locked in a last quick embrace that increased the permanent ache of my longing for Francis. Then I lifted Jasper down

283

to allow Henry to mount, and waved as he joined his men outside the gatehouse, just as Jamie panted back from the village with seven men and boys, all that even his enthusiasm had managed to rouse There was a brisk argument with Henry, who was evidently witholding permission for Jamie to go with him, and then the troops and villagers set off through the steady misty rain for the main road, leaving a disconsolate Jamie standing gazing yearningly after them.

The shock of their abrupt departure had a subduing effect on all but Jasper. All day we attempted to drown our worries in household chores, but we were all on edge and I lost my temper with Lucy over a missing skein of thread and reduced her to tears. The only happy soul was Jasper's, as he dragooned Jamie into playing soldiers with him, and stretched our nerves to screaming-point every time he accompanied the firing of his imaginary musket with a piercing shout of 'Bang!'

At dusk, when Jasper had been at last calmed down enough to be put to bed, the villagers returned with their news. They had arrived on the scene of the confrontation to find a parley going on, and had joined the supporters of the Earl of Northampton, who were by now far outnumbered by those of Lord Brooke. And there they had stood all afternoon, while the two leaders haggled and swore at each other, and finally agreed that the ordnance should be carried back to Banbury, and that Lord Brooke should give the Earl three day's notice of removal, and the Earl should do likewise of any attempt by him to capture the guns. So back the six pieces had gone to Banbury, the people had dispersed and the excitement seemed over.

'But it's my bet,' said George Abbott, the warrener and friend of my childhood, 'that the Earl will make another attempt on the cannon, and that's why he wanted Master Sewell to stay with him for the moment. I should think he's glad of soldiers like ours – you should have seen the crew he had with him! Scarcely knew one end of a musket from the other, and most of 'em were scared as rabbits; he'd just told 'em they were to go and see a piece of ordnance, and the poor sods thought they were going on a day's training. It was a fair shock to them to find themselves looking down the muzzles of Lord Brooke's muskets, I can tell you!' He grinned. 'So the word is that Lord Brooke's off to London, to consult with his friends in the Parliament, for he daren't stir a foot without their advice, and that's why he didn't make any move against us, though he'd more men, and they knew their business better than ours by the look of 'em. And my Lord of Northampton has gone back to his mansion, and taken Master Sewell and our troopers with him, and when you'll see them again I know not.'

'All I can say to that news,' I told Lucy later, as we settled ourselves for the night, 'is that I hope the zealous men of Banbury don't take it into their heads to use their precious six pieces of ordnance against us. With a garrison of two troopers, my fat bailiff and his sons, nine women and girls, and two babies, we'd be lucky to fire a shot against any besiegers.'

'I expect they won't let the guns out of their sight again, in case the Earl attacks,' Lucy said optimistically. 'All the same, I feel rather naked and unprotected, don't you?'

'Speak for youself – I've got my chemise on.'

'Oh, Thomazine, this is no time for joking,' said Lucy earnestly, her cheerfulness suddenly withered. 'I wish Henry hadn't gone. I don't like being here on our own.'

'If he'd thought there was the slightest risk of attack, he wouldn't have left us thus,' I said with more confidence than I felt.

All the next week we waited. The rain lifted to give a fitful sun some small chance to shine. With Henry absent, Jamie abstracted some of the precious powder and fell to perfecting his marksmanship with a fowling-piece, shooting from the west tower at wooden target posts at varying distances. The irregular, unexpected crack of his gun set our nerves further on edge, but I was both surprised and pleased to find, on inspecting his targets after all the powder had been expended, that long practice had paid off and that he was a

285

tolerable marksman. Jamie, one step nearer joining the army in earnest, glowed with pride and walked with a pronounced swagger perilously akin to Colonel Wilmot's.

The men and women of Banbury had spent that week fortifying their castle further and putting their defences in order, and on the Thursday, 4th August, we were informed that a large contingent of men had marched in from Northamptonshire to join them. Then the Earl sallied forth again from Compton Wynyates. The Northampton men, apparently fearing that their homes would be attacked, withdrew on the Saturday and left Banbury largely unprotected, and those country folk who took up arms to come to the town's aid were quietly intercepted by the ring of Cavaliers in the lanes around it and told that all was over, there was no ordnance left in the town, and that they had better return home – which they did.

'He's a clever man, I reckon, that Earl,' Henry said, regaling us with all this on his eventual return. 'Those country people swallowed it all, hook, line and sinker. No more trouble from *them*. And he had informers in Banbury, so we knew what was being planned almost as soon as it was decided, and they'd been told to spread rumours about the town of the huge forces about to overwhelm it. And he'd put three pieces of ordnance on Crouch Hill, commanding the place for all to see and cower at. Sunday night, this was. Then we judged it time to move on the town, and when they'd word of our coming, most of the townspeople fled before us. Then in the morning we sent for a parley, and after not much persuasion they let us into the town and the Earl spoke with Colonel Fiennes. So beset the poor Colonel was by rumour that he fully believed all our arguments, and besides Banbury was quite filled with our horse, and we'd threatened to fire the town if he would not hand the ordnance over. So, not having much choice in the matter, he did. Whereupon my Lord decided to march forthwith with the ordnance to the reduction of Warwick Castle, and I reckoned it time to take my leave.'

'But I still don't understand,' said Lucy for the twentieth time, 'how did you get a cannon *and* another ten men from him? By wizardry?'

'By a bargain. I am to watch Banbury for him, in case the honoured Colonel takes it into his head to march out in pursuit of him, and to offer harassment to arms, soldiers and supplies coming to Banbury past our door. Colonel Wilmot is trying to organize a regiment of his own, and besides, his house isn't defensible, as this one is, or should be. So we are to be the thorn in Banbury's flesh, in return for ten men and a falconet.'

The gun stood beside us in the courtyard, black and deadly. Henry's strong, veined hand stroked it affectionately, as if it were a kitten. 'A lovely thing she is – more for show than for actual destructive effect, though. These things make a fine loud noise and a devilish amount of smoke, but against a city wall they're hully useless – the shot only weigh one and a quarter pound. They're of more use against a man. The shot would pass right through him – if you managed to hit him, that is.'

'Very much a hit and miss affair,' Jamie said, sniggering. Henry grinned. 'Aye, that's the difficulty, with ordnance as with ordinary muskets – to find a way of hitting the target. To do that, this wedge, here, is thrust under the breech to raise the muzzle. The further that go up, the further will the shot travel. But to get your range, unless you're a skilled gunner, you must first fire the piece, and see where the ball lands. Only then can you judge whether to point the gun more to right or left, or raise or lower the muzzle.'

'There's not much shot,' said Jamie. 'Couldn't you squeeze any more out of his lordship?'

'His lordship had more squeezed out of him than he wanted to give, as it was. I doubt Warwick Castle is a bigger fish than Ashcott. Anyway,' said Henry, giving the gun a final loving stroke, 'at the sort of range I'd think of using it, from the ramparts or to defend the gate, hail shot is more effective. Musket balls, nails, bits of drainpipe, even stones if you're desperate; they'll inflict a good deal of damage.'

I shuddered, thinking of the destruction such a weapon could wreak in a confined space. And in the next few days

Henry underlined my dislike of the gun's powers by gathering together piles of such things in baskets in the barn. I had no real idea of the horrible wounds that rusty nails or jagged pieces of metal propelled from a gun could cause; but a vivid imagination.

The gun took up all of Henry's time now. He had the Deddington mason back to construct a sloping ramp of stone up to the walkway around the curtain-wall, so that the gun could be easily dragged up and down; and a broad platform at the end of it to accommodate the falconet, its recoil, and a team of gunners. He was training two of the troopers (not Northampton's men, who were less quick to pick up military matters than our own two Suffolkers) in the drill and use of the cannon; and the courtyard frequently echoed with shouted commands and abuse as Troopers Jackson and Shoosmith got into inextricable tangles with ladles, wads, worms and linstocks. The rest of the garrison, occupied in beating out slow-match or making musket balls in a home-made furnace by melting down bits of drainpipe, listened with undisguised hilarity; an attitude which faded to respect when Henry allowed his team actually to fire the thing. By this time, after three days of intensive training, they were almost proficient, and Henry timed them after a fashion by using an hour-glass, estimating what fraction of the sand had descended between the first shout of 'Order your piece to load!' and the ear-shattering roar of the firing. 'That in't bad,' he said, as we all peered over the ramparts to see where the shot had landed; in a clump of bushes a couple of furlongs away on the hillside opposite, with a white tangle of split wood to mark the spot. The men of our garrison, gathered with us on the ramparts, raised a cheer of surprised approval.

Having instilled into Troopers Shoosmith and Jackson the rudiments of gunnery, Henry turned his attention to his womenfolk. We were taught, through one weary August afternoon, how to load muskets without blowing them or ourselves to pieces. Lucy proved of little use in this, being as in needlework too careless and hasty, apt to forget the difference between priming powder and ordinary gunpowder, or in which hand to hold the slow-match. Henry, evidently preferring to lose patience rather than persevere and risk Lucy blasting Ashcott to the heavens, dismissed her fairly quickly. Grainne, Meraud, Doll, Heppy and I were more trainable; we loaded matchlocks and snaphaunces and wheel-locks until supper-time came and our fingers were weary, but we had achieved some degree of skill. Henry would not let us touch his own pistols, bought in Holland and of a design quite unlike any other I had ever seen; instead of ramming powder and shot down the muzzle of the weapon the barrel unscrewed at the breech and the charge and ball were placed inside. The barrel was moreover rifled like a fowling-piece; Henry explained that this made the pistols much more accurate. 'You can't be certain of hitting with a musket anything that's more than thirty or forty paces distant. But with a rifled barrel giving the ball a bit of spin through the air, you could sit up on the ramparts and pick off men as you chose, to a much greater distance. Those half-dozen fowling-pieces we brought from Goldhayes will come in very handy in a siege, and of course they've got English locks, which makes them very much safer and more reliable than a matchlock. The locks on my pistols, though, are proper French flintlocks. Beauties, these are, and I don't reckon there's more than a score like them in all England – so I'm loading them myself, in case you don't screw the barrel on straight.'

Meraud sat on the topmost step leading up to the ramparts, a cool August wind ruffling through her silvery hair, and lifted up a pistol, two-handed, to point it at the Hall door. 'See how my hand shakes! I could never hope to hit a man unless at point-blank range – this is much too heavy for me to grip it properly.'

'You'd have to rest it on something,' I said, trying the other of the pair. 'My wrist must be stronger than yours – I can just manage to hold it steady with one hand, but I couldn't hold it in position for long. They ought to make lightweight pistols, especially for ladies' use.'

Meraud shuddered delicately, and put her pistol down with exaggerated care. 'Pray God we never have to use these dreadful things against human beings.' She turned bland, wide eyes upon me. 'Sometimes, Thomazine, I feel that you positively revel in this terrible war.'

A touch guiltily, for I was despite myself fascinated by all the weaponry and talk of tactics that formed our daily environment, I said, 'No, I don't. And there's no war yet, nor likely to be, if all that happens is on the level of Lord Brooke and the Earl of Northampton abusing each other in front of their lesser brethren on the Stratford road.'

Even as I spoke, one of the sentries raised a shout. 'A body of armed men! Coming down from Milton way!'

Henry laid his precious pistol down on the step beside me and sprinted up, past Meraud, and round to the corner by the west tower, which afforded the only clear view to the north without ascending the tower, where the sentry was stationed. Below us, men leapt to close the gate, but Henry's voice stopped them in their tracks. 'Hold still! It's the Earl of Northampton's men!'

I craned my neck to see them, but could distinguish little more than a cloud of dust and a waving colour above it, a quarter of a mile off and moving at a steady trot down the long shallow hill from Milton. Henry returned past me, his limp less pronounced than I had yet seen it, to yell orders at the garrison lounging in the courtyard. Before our impressed eyes, the half-dressed, lazy men became in the space of a couple of hectic minutes a neat double file of smart soldiers, one each side of the gate, to greet the Earl's men as they rode in.

There were only a dozen of them, on matched chestnut horses that put our rag, tag and bobtail to shame, arrayed in coats of green with backs and breasts and pot-helmets gleaming black. For the first time I beheld properly-equipped troopers, and felt almost ashamed of our little garrison in their old buff coats and doublets of every shade of blue, the colour which Simon had preferred for his troop. Nor were the ten men we had had from the Earl much better clad. Above the heads of the troopers a plain green damask colour flapped gently.

'That means they're the Colonel's troop,' Jamie hissed to

me, as we stood in the courtyard to watch. 'From the Earl's own regiment, most like, and not trained band men like the ones we got for the garrison.'

The leader of the men dismounted and exchanged bows with Henry. They then stood in deep and animated conversation, while the troopers sat their beautiful chestnuts and looked round at our shabby domain and amateur soldiers with a bored, supercilious air that made me long to inform them that the worth of a soldier was not always to be gauged by the newness and expense of his uniform.

At length Henry broke off and turned towards us, his face gleaming with the light of battle. By my side, Grainne's slender hands clenched together in her apron, and I heard her soft whisper. 'Oh, no!'

'We're to attack Banbury tomorrow,' Henry said, an unholy light in his golden-brown eyes. 'That'll give Colonel Fiennes and his round-headed crew something to remember us by. The Earl knows I'm a Low Countries man – he was at Breda, though I never knew him well – and he wants me and the pick of the garrison to be with him. We're to ride to Compton Wynyates now, and on to Banbury before dawn.'

'To leave now?' Grainne said, and in her face was only a kind of wry resignation, hiding the deeper pain. 'Ah well, as a soldier's daughter and a soldier's wife I know what must be done, must be done . . . Who will you leave us?'

'Four or five Suffolkers, and the trained band men – they'll do well enough. There'll be no danger from Banbury; they'll have sufficient to do fighting our attack, but don't go a-jaunting into Deddington, or knocking on Colonel Wilmot's door,' said Henry cheerily, 'or stray alone in the fields, just in case. Stay close to Ashcott. If we can take Banbury, it'll be a fine blow for the King's cause, and one of the first and most telling to be struck, so wish us fortune, my love, and God speed.'

He kissed Grainne, and Jasper and Hess who had run out to see the soldiers, and turned to give orders to his men. Once more we stood to watch, caught in a never-ending circle, as soldiers clattered busily out of the gate and out of our sight, and into danger; the only difference being that this time they turned north, towards Milton and Compton Wynyates, ten miles away. We watched until they could no longer be discerned beyond the brow of Coombe Hill, and then with resigned and heavy hearts returned to the house.

What little remained of that day, August 17th, passed unbearably slowly. The remaining soldiers, bored, and resentful of being left behind in the charge of Tom Shoosmith, whom Henry had picked as the most intelligent and resourceful of our men to take temporary command in his absence, dozed in the barn or sat on the ramparts with at best half an eye on the roads they were supposed to watch. They obeyed Shoosmith's orders sullenly and seemed disposed to mutter behind his back – probably only the thought of Henry's return kept them from open mutiny. It was in a very uneasy state of mind that we got to bed that night, ready to cry havoc at the slightest disturbance, and woke with thumping hearts and sweating bodies at dawn. As we broke our fast on cold meats, cheese and small-beer, I took one look at Grainne's green, exhausted face and felt sick myself; she was so obviously afraid, more than ever before. Jasper and Hess took their mood from us and were fractious and bad-tempered, quarrelling over a piece of meat and both exploding into tense, angry tears. Grainne's eyes met mine with a faint shadow of her usual smile. 'We'd best busy ourselves today, or else I think we'll surely run mad.'

So once more the day of waiting stretched before us, and I wondered, if we were like this now, what would happen if real war enveloped us? Nor was Grainne, who after all was the one with most cause for anxiety, helped by Lucy's tragic tear-filled eyes or Meraud's frequent prayers for the soldiers' safety, harping on our nerves with a gentle deadly unerring finger; nor by my own frayed temper. So we threw ourselves into work, scouring and cleaning with Heppy and Jane Tawney and her daughters, and managed to keep our jokes and laughter on the right side of hysteria.

*   *   *

In the afternoon the sun came out and, glad of an opportunity to escape from the fraught atmosphere within the house, I went into the courtyard with Doll Tawney to see what could be done with the remains of my grandmother's herb garden. The pleasant, unaccustomed warmth combined with Doll's cheerily ribald and disrespectful conversation to distract my mind from its anxiety; so that when it came, the hail from the man on the ramparts was a most abrupt and unwelcome recall to reality. 'There's a rider coming! From the Deddington road!'

I leapt to my feet, scattering earth and weeds over Doll, and ran to the wall and up the steps, hauling my skirts up to reveal rather more of my legs than was seemly. The sentry called, as I reached the top, 'Open the gates! Thass Trooper Reynolds!'

I stared at the distant figure belabouring his weary horse, and a cold weight settled on my heart, heavy as stone. There was the creak and groan of the gates being opened, and I turned and ran down the steps. So it happened that I was the first to meet Reynolds as he rode in under the gatehouse; and as I beheld his agonized, desperate expression, I knew the worst. He reined in his horse and slid down, grey-faced. 'Mistress Thomazine – where's Mistress Sewell?'

'She's inside – what's happened, for God's sake?'

'We was beat off from Banbury, but thass nawn – Master Sewell's bin hit, as we came off; we didn't think as that was too bad, but as we was a-gettin' into Adderbury, he swounded, and now the surgeon say as thass suffen bad, he can't last long, and he want Mistress Sewell, and the little mites as well, an' quick.'

Despair in my heart, fighting tears, I fairly flew inside, shouting for Grainne, while Reynolds organized horses for us. She was in the parlour upstairs, dusting the carved stone mantel; as I burst in, she turned a white desperate face to me, the lovely green eyes huge and dark with strain, and knew before I spoke. 'It's Henry, isn't it? Is he dead?'

I had no time to choose my words. 'No, not yet. He's at

Adderbury, and he wants you, and the children. The horses are being made ready now.'

'Thank you,' Grainne said, took a deep breath, and laid the duster down. She gave me a faint hollow smile, and added, 'Please . . . come with me, and Lucy and Jamie if you can get them. I'll find Jasper.'

In not more than five minutes we were riding hell-for-leather out of the gate, turning north-east to ride to Adderbury across the fields. Jasper rode before Trooper Reynolds, his face a mixture of excitement and nameless fear. Hester, clutched in Jamie's too-tight left arm, howled with a crimson crumpled face for her mother, but Grainne was ahead of us, riding like one possessed, leaving all her calm dignity behind in this last despairing ride to be at her husband's death-bed.

They had taken Henry to one of the inns in Adderbury; I never knew its name, for we had no time for noticing such matters. Our troopers were gathered outside, as if on guard, and several villagers with hostile faces hovered near. As we dismounted, someone shouted, 'Death to the ungodly!' and there was another cry, which I pray Grainne never heard, as she was already inside the door, of 'There goes his whore!' Jamie, his face red with barely suppressed tears, turned with fists raised, and I had to drag him inside before he could be set upon.

It was dim and cool in the inn, the windows set wide open in the sun. A respectable, efficient-looking woman who must have been the landlady led us to a chamber above stairs. Outside it stood a tall, gaunt man in a stained russet doublet, talking to Trooper Jackson. At sight of us both men brightened, and the tall man hurried forward to greet Grainne. 'Are you Mistress Sewell? Yes, you come in time, but it will not now be long; the ball has entered the lung, I fear, and we can do little for him.'

Grainne nodded, and then opened the door. Behind me, Hess, clutched in Reynolds' arms, set up wailing again. I turned and relieved him of his wet, noisy burden, and taking a white-faced Jasper by the hand, followed Grainne into the room.

It was small, curtained and dim. The heat was oppressive, and I thought could have done no good to the wounded man in the bed. What lay under the embroidered covers, breath bubbling in his throat, seemed no longer the brave, bright, vigorous Henry. My eyes filled with tears; I wondered how Grainne could bear this, the cruellest agony of all that could befall her, to lose thus the man she loved above all else. As I entered, a frightened-looking girl in the plain cap and apron and blue dress of a maidservant hurried out, a stained bowl in her hands.

'Grainne?' Henry said, on a laboured whisper. 'Ah, and thass Hess I reckon, I . . . can . . . hear her . . .'

His daughter's wails suddenly stopped, on a hiccup. She twisted strongly in my arms, tears drying rapidly. 'Dada?'

'Kiss your father,' Grainne said, her voice kept gentle and normal. I knelt by the bed and held Hester close so that Henry's grey lips could brush her cheek. A glint of the old humour appeared in his eyes. 'Poor owd . . . Thomazine, she's dreepin' wet . . . Where's Jasper?'

Jasper, all eyes, came to the bed. Grainne had explained to him, very calmly and clearly, that his father was not well, and wished to see him; and the child had seemed to accept without question. Now, he wriggled from my careful hands and scrambled on to the bed. 'Why aren't you well, father?'

'Some . . . fule hit me,' Henry said, trying not to wince as the thin arms wound round his neck and he was solidly kissed. 'Make it better,' Jasper said, seriously, sitting back. 'I rode on Reynolds' horse, I did, father. Is that blood?'

Whatever dressings they had put on Henry's wound were inadequate. There was blood on Jasper's hands and on the coverlet. He looked down at his father and his face crumpled suddenly with fear. I quickly lifted him off the bed, and Henry whispered, 'Look after you little sister, lad . . . Goodbye, Thomazine . . . thank you.'

I could take no more. Lucy, her face gaunt but tearless, grabbed Hess and followed me from the room. For the children's sake, we held back our grief, and stumbled down the stairs and into a small parlour silently shown to us by the landlady. Hess started to cry again, and Lucy jiggled her gently up and down, talking softly to her, holding off her own tears by absorbing herself in the child. In a little while, the door opened and Jamie came in, accompanied by the landlady and a tray of cakes and mugs of ale. She set them down on a table in front of the open windows, looking out on the bright scented sweetness of her garden, and without a word went out. We sat looking wretchedly at each other, while Lucy soothed Hester.

'I'm glad Meraud couldn't be found in time,' I said, breaking the taut silence between us and raising a startled aggrieved look from Jamie. 'I wouldn't be able to stomach her false prayers, not here.'

'How can you say that, Thomazine?' Jamie demanded hotly. 'She is deeply sincere in all she does and thinks.'

So that's the way the wind blows, I thought angrily, but Lucy leapt quickly into the breach. 'This is no time to quarrel, is it? Have some ale, there's enough of it for all of us.'

Jamie gave me a last glare, and then handed mugs round. Hess, after a cake which partly occupied her stomach and more abundantly besmeared her face, fell damply asleep in Lucy's lap. Jasper sat on an enormous box chair, completely dwarfed by it, and clasped both hands round a mug of ale which I had half-emptied for his use. Looking at his great strained eyes over the rim of the mug, I wondered just how much of all this he understood. Even if he had no understanding or experience of death, his mother's agony had probably reached him. But he was quiet, too quiet, and did not cry, and ate his cake tidily, picking up the crumbs from his lap and popping them into his mouth.

After a long time, we heard slow, heavy footsteps descending the stairs. It was by then growing late, and the setting sun shone full into the window, turning Jasper's hair to fire as he sat, dozing now, in my lap. Jamie stood by the hearth, his finger desultorily tracing the coat-of-arms carved on the mantel. As the steps reached the parlour door, I raised my head to look at Lucy, feeling sick with sorrow, and saw that she was still holding back her tears, but with difficulty. I was glad that, on this occasion at least, she håd suppressed her usual noisy dramatics for the sake of Henry's wife and children.

The door opened, and Trooper Reynolds stood there, his face in its grief a mirror of our own. 'He's dead,' he said softly. 'A few minutes agone. The landlady hev sent for a woman t'come and lay him out. She say you'd better stay here for the night. She in't no lover o' the Cavaliers, but she won't turn us abroad. An' I reckon, beggin' your pardons, that one o' you ladies had better go up to Mistress Sewell. She's a-takin' it suffen hard.'

I saw Lucy's look of agony and said, 'I will.' Gently, I got to my feet, and laid Jasper in Jamie's arms. I felt afraid of what I would see, of having to bear Grainne's grief with her, but I could not deny her my presence if that was what was needed. Up the stairs I walked, slowly, bracing myself, and then quietly knocked at the chamber door and went in.

Henry lay in the bed, his eyes decently closed, the blood a damp dark stain over the coverlet. Beside him, Grainne knelt, his hand still clasped in hers, and her face hidden. I could imagine so strongly how her grief must tear her heart, as it would mine if it were Francis lying there instead of Henry, that my eyes filled and for a moment I faltered; then, setting my will, walked round the bed to the other side, and laid a hand gently on my friend's shoulder. 'Grainne?'

For a moment she did not move. Then she turned her head and saw me. It was all I could do not to weep aloud at the sight of her face, and the despair in her eyes. I gently unclasped her hand from Henry's limp, still-warm one, and said uncertainly, 'You – you must come downstairs now . . .'

'No,' said Grainne the calm, the unruffled, the sensible, 'no, I must stay with him . . .' She was shaking now uncontrollably, her eyes bewildered. 'I can't believe it, I can't believe he's dead, I feel he's so close, so near . . . Oh, God, what shall I do?'

I could only hold her close, weeping myself, as she vented her grief against the coarse purple serge of my oldest dress; feeling beneath my sorrow the strangeness of it all, that I who had always looked to her for support in times of sorrow or trouble should now be the one to offer comfort. For a long time we knelt together on the floor by the bed, until Grainne raised her head and gave me a drenched, valiant smile. 'You're right, we must go down now . . . thank you, Thomazine.' Stiffly she got to her feet, removing the tearstains with her sleeve. 'Do I look reasonable? I've no wish to frighten the children. And I must explain to Jasper, he must be quite bewildered.'

'He's been very good,' I said. Grainne leaned over the bed and kissed Henry's forehead once, gently, in farewell, and then walked softly from the room.

We buried Henry Sewell the next day, in the churchyard of St Mary's in Adderbury. Within the church lay the members of my own close family, commemorated by a terse tablet on the wall of the south aisle: Matthew Heron, died 8th April, 1635, aet. 32; Temperance his wife, died 7th January, 1625 (the day after my birth), aet. 22; Jane, his second wife, died 22 December, 1632, aet. 30; Matthew, his son, died 4th March, 1633, aet. 3 months; Edmund, his son, died 6th April, 1635, aet. 7; Katherine Heron, relict of Sir Edmund Heron, Knight, of Ashcott in this parish, died 16th February, 1638, aet. 57. During the service within the church, sitting by Grainne's side trying to stop Hester's wriggling, I thought much of those six people who had shaped by their presence or absence the first ten years of my life; but more of Henry, from whom it seemed Grainne derived much of her strength, so that now, numbed and bereft, she seemed almost like a sleepwalker. She sat white and unmoving as the fiery vicar, Master Oldys, extolled Henry's devotion to the King, his valour and sacrifice, the despicable and warlike habits of the Parliament's adherents (most notably Lord Brooke and Lord Saye and Sele), which had led to this tragedy, a noble young man foully murdered and slain . . . and so it went on, while Henry's family and friends and troop sat beneath it, and I at least wondered what cause was worth such grief as had now overtaken us.

Then we followed the bier, with its white-shrouded burden, out to the churchyard, and watched silent as the red Oxfordshire earth was shovelled upon Henry Sewell, a Suffolk man of humble birth but a far from lowly heart, whom I had never really known and understood as I did his friend Edward, but who had given all he had for our protection and for the King's cause, and deserved all our respect, and sorrow, and love; now given in full measure to Grainne. After that first agonized flood of grief she had not broken again, only retreated far within herself, too far for even her children to reach her. Lucy and I had looked after Jasper and Hess the previous night, washing and putting them to sleep in a little truckle bed in Grainne's lonely chamber before retiring ourselves; and in the morning dressing them, putting milk pap into Hester's greedy mouth and answering Jasper's bewildered questions: 'Why won't my father come back? Where has he gone? Why won't mother talk to me?' It seemed hardest of all to cope with Henry's children after what had happened to their father, but having them ever on our minds helped to lessen the sharpness of our own sorrow.

When all was over, we rode back to Ashcott, to a very depleted garrison. All but one of the Earl of Northampton's trained band men, and more seriously three Suffolkers, had taken the opportunity to desert us. The remaining Earl's man, a huge and cheerful blacksmith from Stratford, explained why he had chosen to stay; 'I've a girl in Stratford proving troublesome – fact is, I've got her into trouble, and she's halfway to being a shrew already, so I've no mind to wed her, or have Parson nagging at me to do it. It's her own fault anyway, taking advantage of me after the church-ale – I was so drunk I didn't notice her tongue, nor her ill-favoured face!'

So there were eight men in our garrison now, and I began to grow anxious. Open, large-scale warfare now seemed inevitable, with the raising of the King's standard at Nottingham four days after Henry's death. And with only eight men and no officers to guard us, Ashcott seemed laid open to attack. Despite the fact that Simon had deemed less men than these sufficient for our protection, without Henry's competent energy we were as helpless as a dismasted ship in a storm. Shoosmith was a worry, too. He had all Henry's enthusiasm and energy without any of his common sense and knowledge of military tactics and discipline, and he had a ready and eager disciple in Jamie, who would have been off to Banbury at an hour's notice to avenge Henry, had not Grainne made it clear that she desired no vengeance and despised those who did. My instinctive feeling was that we must lie as low as possible, for if we made ourselves too much of a thorn in Banbury's flesh, and brought the might of Lord Brooke down upon our dilapidated walls and sparse garrison, then we would not withstand him for long. I managed to communicate some of my anxieties to Shoosmith, and he listened politely, but made it plain that warfare was men's work, and that however worried I might be about our depleted garrison, it was really none of my business. As was becoming increasingly frequent, I lost my temper. 'And I suppose you'll tell me that it's none of my business if I'm turned out of doors from my own house because you've been rash enough to provoke my Lord Brooke's wrath? None of my business if I'm raped or abused by Parliament's soldiers, who I doubt very much are as godly as they're made out to be? I'd have you remember, Trooper Shoosmith, that you were all left here by Captain Heron for our protection – *not* to play the hero and have us all attacked and murdered or worse, for the sake of covering yourself with glory!'

Trooper Shoosmith seemed as startled as a cat who suddenly finds the mouse biting back. 'Why, mistress, I han't . . . it wouldn't . . . I in't got no wish to put you in danger, thass for sartin!'

'Well, don't,' I snapped, my voice chilly with anger and suppressed fear. 'Or I'll order you back to Suffolk and leave us defenceless – and probably safer.'

I must have conveyed an authority I had never previously possessed, for Shoosmith appeared now to give up any thoughts of taking on Lord Brooke and Banbury virtually single-handed, and concentrated on perfecting the defence of Ashcott, which was, after all, his primary duty. I had entertained fleeting thoughts of going back to Suffolk, where, from what little firm news we could garner, open warfare was a good deal more distant. But Henry had ultimately given his life for us and for the King's cause, and it seemed despicable to cast aside so lightly all that he had worked for and poured his energies into, so I never mentioned it. I did ask Grainne, some weeks after Henry's death, whether she would not prefer to return to Suffolk with the children. She looked at me in some astonishment. 'Back to Suffolk? I had thought of it, but it would seem disloyal to Henry, and besides you are too much my friends for me to desert you now. Anyway, I doubt if I could bear with Joan's chatter for very long without one of you on hand to translate it!'

It was the nearest she had come to making a joke for a long, long time, and I was heartened. Heartened, too, by Sir John Byron, a tireless champion of the King's cause, who was giving a great deal of trouble to Lord Brooke and the worthy citizens of Banbury, and thus inadvertently diverting any warlike intentions they might have had towards Ashcott. Even the news that, after occupying Oxford, Byron had been driven out of it again by Lord Saye's Bluecoats and Master Hampden's regiment, and pursued west towards Worcester by them and, it appeared, upwards of two hundred country people, did not much cast us down. After that, Oxford was occupied by the two Parliamentarian regiments, and the area seemed exclusively under their domination.

It was too much to hope for, that we should remain forever unmolested. Situated as we were, not a quarter of a mile from the main road between Banbury and Oxford, sooner or later some Parliamentary commander, perhaps Old Subtlety himself, would wake up to the fact that here, in a prime position, was an ill-guarded fortress to be had for the taking. And sure enough, one grey, rainy morning in late September – the 21st, and Jamie's fourteenth birthday – one of Henry's Deddington informers rode in, on a damp and muddy horse, to say that a detachment of Lord Saye's troops was in the town, and a party was even now preparing to ride down to Ashcott. It seemed that no attack was planned as yet, and that this would be just an exploratory parley aimed at ascertaining our strengths, weaknesses, and political opinions. 'I thought I'd best ride down and tell you, sir,' said the Deddington man, looking expectant, and I had to run inside to furnish Shoosmith with the necessary crown to give him. When he had plodded off homewards, his horse's hooves sucking and squelching in the mud, I said, 'I suppose we'd better shut the gates.'

Shoosmith nodded. In the past few weeks he had become used to accepting suggestions from myself and Grainne in particular and also from Jamie, as to matters concerning Ashcott's defence, and since my outburst had treated us with a good deal more deference and respect. I realized suddenly now, with the cold rain stinging my face and turning my hair under my plainest lace-edged coif to limp brown hanks and scattering dark spots on my blue dress, that Grainne and I were as good as in command of Ashcott, and Shoosmith our intermediary and adviser. It was at once a heady and a frightening thought.

Jackson and Pryke were heaving the great gates shut and Jamie leapt between them to drop and slide the huge iron bar into its sockets. Feeling very much safer, although Lord Saye's men were nowhere in sight as yet, I looked round the people under the shelter of the gatehouse arch; the three Suffolk men, Jamie's breathless excited face, Grainne composed and thoughtful, Lucy brilliant-eyed and afraid, Meraud solemn. 'Well,' said my blonde cousin, 'what shall we do?'

'Well, we shan't hand over Ashcott without a fight,' said Jamie eagerly, plainly spoiling for just that.

'I don't think a fight will be necessary,' I put in. 'I'm sure we can think of some reason why we shouldn't hand the castle over to them, not just yet at any rate. And *if* the King's army is now making for Shrewsbury, *if* that man you saw yesterday in Adderbury spoke truth, Shoosmith, then when they march for London, they'll pass quite close to Ashcott, and we can perhaps ask for reinforcements, or even get a proper garrison, if the war drags on longer.'

'From what else that Adderbury man said, they troops in Oxford fare t'be a proper poor lot,' Shoosmith said. He had gone to the town the previous day to gather news and buy in provisions. 'Thass all Lord Saye can do to howd 'em in, and they fare to be more concerned with burning Popish books and frightening owd parsons than fighting. Happen we won't have to do more than sit tight and say no.'

Jamie's face dropped; he was longing to put his marksmanship into practice. Lucy said, 'When they come, who will speak to them?'

'I will,' I said, with more confidence than I felt. 'It'll preserve the appearance of neutrality if they see a woman on the walls. And the soldiers must keep out of sight – can you clear the courtyard, Shoosmith? – and we must try and pack away all the evidence that they've been here – that pile of cannon shot and those drainpipes don't help the illusion.'

'Nor does the cannon,' said Meraud, her eyes travelling to the falconet, canvas-covered against the rain, in lonely shrouded splendour on its platform. 'Can it be hid, too?'

'If we're quick,' Jamie said. 'I'll get the ropes!'

For the next few minutes the courtyard presented a scene of indescribable confusion as seven of the eight soldiers – one had been dispatched to the tower to watch for any movements – scurried about carrying into the obscurity of the barn armfuls of the one-and-a-quarter-pound iron shot for the cannon, or shafts for pikes and the sharpened stakes known as swine-feathers. Ropes were fastened to the falconet and, with several soldiers and Jamie hanging on to them as counterweights, it was allowed to run gently down the ramp to the courtyard and manhandled into the barn. This was already piled high with suspiciously military-looking equipment, hastily masked by canvas and a strategically-placed cart, and the doors firmly shut on them. I prayed that an inquisitive Parliamentarian officer would not have the opportunity to stick his nose inside, or our careful pretence would go for nothing. As we shut the barn doors the shout went up from the tower. 'Soldiers! From Deddington way!'

My heart pounding, I picked up my damp skirts and ascended the slippery steps to the ramparts. Below me, the soldiers were quickly vanishing into the stables, where there were upwards of fifteen horses to keep silent, or into the basement room at the bottom of the tower where our muskets and powder were stored. If trouble threatened, they could offer protection by firing through the narrow windows, or from the roof. Grainne had sent Jasper back into the house, just in case, but she and my cousins stood at the foot of the steps, ready to appear in my support should occasion arise.

Peering cautiously over the ramparts, I could see a small body of horse coming haphazardly through the mud and rain towards the gate. I counted fifteen of them, looking thoroughly miserable, their heads lowered against the wind, which blew keenly down from Coombe Hill into their faces. They came up to within twenty or so paces from the gatehouse, and halted at an order from their officer. This gentleman could not from any vantage point, least of all my own, be taken seriously as a leader of a cavalry troop, being short and extremely fat, and moreover perched atop a very large, bony grey horse. He squinted up through the raindrops at the gatehouse and then dismounted, walked forward and hammered with his fist upon the gate, demanding entrance in the name of the King and Parliament in a voice so high-pitched that I was hard put to it not to laugh aloud. If this was the best that Lord Saye could send against us, then we were fairly safe. He stepped back, and I ducked down, keeping them waiting for a minute or so, and then rose to my rather insignificant height. One of the troopers gave a rude whistle, and the officer's eye rolled round towards me. He bowed with a flourish and repeated his request in less peremptory tones. 'I regret to trouble you, mistress, but I am ordered by my commanding officer Lord Saye, to enter this house and in the name of the King and Parliament impound any weapons, arms or plate which I may find within it; and to place therein a garrison for your protection and that of the countryside around you from the enemies of Parliament.' He looked at me expectantly. My confidence rising as I realized that this man seemed little more than a fool, I said, with the same elaborate politeness, 'I regret, sir, that I do not intend to open the gates. The only grown man within is my bailiff, for the rest we're women and children only, and I have heard sufficient of the practices of all soldiers, whether of one side or the other, to fear for our safety should I let you in. I will not open, not for you, not for my Lord Saye, nor for the King himself should he pass by.'

The officer, plainly rather taken aback, began again. 'Mistress, I am empowered by Lord Saye, who holds the Commission of both Houses of Parliament, to enter the house known as Ashcott, in the parish of Adderbury, and to secure any arms and plate hidden within it in defiance of their orders. You must open the gate, madam.'

'I will not,' I retorted, by now thoroughly enjoying myself. 'I will open to no soldiers until men I can trust be found to protect myself and my cousins and the children. Nor can you make me open, unless you wish to incur the odium of all right-thinking people loyal to your cause by making war on defenceless women and children.'

The officer's mouth opened and closed again. His round face ruddy with impotent anger, he shouted up, 'Where, then, madam, are the troops reliably reported to have been placed in the house by the Earl of Northampton?'

Damn. I thought quickly, and then retorted, 'They're precisely why I will not open the gates. I've never seen a sorrier, more ill-disciplined crew,' I added mendaciously, feeling now that I had the advantage not only of height and position, but of intelligence and calmness. 'They deserted a month or more ago, taking many of our possessions with them. There are within my friend Mistress Sewell, who's recently a widow, and her children; my three cousins, two of them ladies and the third a boy of fourteen; two maids, and my bailiff Will Tawney and his wife and family, and we do not wish to be molested, robbed or abused by soldiers of any kind, whether they be of the King's party or of yours.'

For a moment, seeing the scarlet indignant face below me, I wondered if my bluff would work; and then, with a most ungodly oath, my inquisitor mounted his horse with some difficulty, dragged its head round and trotted off through the wet back towards Deddington, his men trailing dispiritedly behind. At once, Grainne, Lucy, Meraud and Jamie raced up to join me; we stared at their disconsolate retreating backs in delighted disbelief. Even Meraud was well-disposed towards me, speaking admiringly of my courage and resource until my head was much swelled with self-importance. 'Well,' I said, cheerfully, as we descended to the courtyard to report to Shoosmith, 'that was easy, wasn't it? I reckon that's the last we'll see of them!'

As it happened, it was, though not due to any action on my part; Lord Saye recalled all his men to Oxford, where the billeted troops were demanding more pay, and shortly mutinied. For the rest of the month, therefore, we were saved from that quarter; Lord Saye swiftly took coach to his castle at Broughton, despairing of controlling his unruly men, and those left in Oxford fought drunkenly with each other in the streets until finally rounded up at the beginning of October and dispatched to join the Earl of Essex's army at Worcester. We rested a little easier now, until news came that a regiment of foot – the Earl of Peterborough's – had been placed as the Banbury garrison. They, however, had little local knowledge and did not seem to be aware of the potential danger at Ashcott. Jamie, flaunting all the military theory he had learned from Henry, said that Essex, whom he referred to in an off-hand way as 'Old Robin', had made the mistake of spreading regiments around the countryside in garrisons like Banbury, and thereby weakening his main army; and that to move against or garrison Ashcott would be likewise weakening Banbury. So we relaxed a little during the first weeks of October. Grainne, now growing great with the child Henry would never see, seemed to ail less than was usual in her pregnancies and spent much time sewing, reading, and playing gently with her children and Orange. The horses were let out to pasture in the wet fields by the river, and the scant grain from the meagre, rain-soaked harvest was threshed and stored in the raised brick granary in the corner of the courtyard. News-hungry, we sent Will Tawney or one of his sons every day to Deddington or Adderbury to gather what we could, usually without much success. It appeared that the King had left Shrewsbury with a sizeable army, amongst whom must surely be my cousins and their troop, and it seemed fairly sure that they were advancing towards London, though at a snail's pace both by virtue of the immense quantities of baggage and the artillery train, and the appalling weather. It was later rumoured that Essex had left Worcester in an attempt to block his path. One of my grandmother's most treasured possessions had been a volume of John Speed's maps, and Jamie spent many hours poring over them, wondering when and where battle might be joined, if at all.

On Saturday, 22nd October, Will Tawney's eldest son was sent off to Adderbury, as usual, with Doll riding pillion and an order for the Adderbury blacksmith to make some pikes. To Deddington, where it was market day, went Will, his wife and a cart to bring home the provisions and supplies we were in need of. With them went Jamie, Shoosmith and Reynolds, unobtrusively armed, in case of ill-intent by marauding soldiers or country people. They should have returned by three o'clock. At four, George Tawney and his sister came back from Adderbury, fairly alight with news; it was all round the village that the King's army was about to fall on Banbury, and would be quartered around the town that night before attacking the following morning. There was apparently no sign of Essex's army, and it seemed that Banbury must fall; which had set one part of Adderbury in a panic, and the other, much smaller, part dancing with delight. I resolved that somehow word should be got to the

King of our predicament, and a request for a proper garrison made, but did not know who could take it. If Essex's army was in the vicinity, it would be rash indeed for just one or two soldiers to deliver the message; if Simon could not be found to add weight to our pleas, the word of a common soldier would probably count for little, quite apart from the difficulty of understanding their broad Suffolk. A letter might be sent, but if it fell into enemy hands would prove more dangerous to us than sending no message at all.

My thoughts were interrupted by the arrival, precipitately, of the missing party who had gone to Deddington. The cart rocketed into the courtyard, urged on by a sweating Will Tawney, and hard on its heels in a spray of mud came another cart, larger and drawn by two horses. It was piled with barrels and covered by roped canvas, and on the seat perched Jamie, his face flushed and wild with exultation. Behind thundered Reynolds and Shoosmith, the former leading Jamie's horse. They leapt down and hurled the gates shut, while the rest of us ran into the courtyard from house and tower and barn to demand what was happening.

Jamie sprang down from the cart and raced up the steps to peer over the walls. 'There's no pursuit!' he called. 'They've given up! We've done it!'

I stared at the carts, at Will supporting his white-faced wife, at the broad grins on Reynolds' and Shoosmith's faces. 'Would someone tell me what the *hell* is going on?'

Jamie took the steps two at a time and landed with a flourish at my feet. 'We've captured an arms cart that was bound for Banbury!'

'What?' Grainne demanded. 'Is that it?'

'Yes,' said Jamie. 'Look at it! Muskets, and powder and pikeheads and shot – just what we need!'

'We saw that in Deddington as we was coming home,' Shoosmith explained. 'That was Master Jamie's idea, to have a goo at it. I reckon Master Sewell would've been proud of the lad. The driver was having a mug o' beer in the Red Lion, and them guards with the cart wasn't looking, sawny fules, call theyselves soldiers! So Master Jamie leapt off of his horse atop of the cart and lashed up the horses and off he drove, along o' Master Tawney in the other cart, and me and Reynolds dealt with them soldiers. There was only three of 'em; we winged one of 'em and onsensed another with our pistols, and the third fell under his horse, and he was trampled on suffen terrible.'

'Well,' I said acidly, 'I hope you've acted rightly. If the King decides against attacking Banbury, then it's quite likely we'll be attacked by them to get their powder back. I expect half the town saw this, and knew who you were?'

Jamie, looking a little crestfallen, admitted that, yes, there had been a certain number of onlookers, and no shortage of people to tell the injured troopers the identity of their assailants. I told him of the King's presence at Banbury, at which he brightened somewhat, and finished, 'You'd better pray that Banbury's attentions are engaged elsewhere for the next week or so, or we'll doubtless find ourselves besieged by them, and then not all that cartful will be of much use against half a regiment or more, and proper ordnance.'

'But if the King takes Banbury, then we'll be safe,' Jamie said, on the defensive. 'And Simon will probably come to see us, and then he'll arrange for a proper garrison. So it *was* a good idea, because Banbury hasn't got the arms we took, to use against the King!'

'I doubt it'll make much difference to a big garrison like that,' Grainne said. 'But can we rely on Simon coming to us? Anything can happen if Banbury is stormed. And Essex's army must be somewhere near— they may catch up with the King's army before they can take Banbury.'

'I don't reckon, from what I've heard o' that Banbury lot, as they'll put up much of a fight,' said Shoosmith. 'Ripe for mutiny, most of 'em, like they soldiers in Oxford, demanding more pay. The King's army fare t'be best, I reckon, and they've got his nephew, Prince Robert or whatever his name be, that's a proper fighter, if you can believe what they say on that there Worcester business.'

'So,' Jamie said, dismissing the Earl of Peterborough's men with a gloriously airy wave of his hand, 'you've no need to worry, Thomazine, really you haven't. We've got the powder and arms, and the King and the Prince will have Banbury by this time tomorrow.'

But I did worry, and so did Grainne. That evening, I went up to her little room and helped put the children to bed, and to listen as fascinated as Jasper to the stories of Irish kings and heroes that she always told him at bedtime. When both children were asleep, we sat in the tall-backed chairs by the softly flickering fire, and talked.

'Jamie takes it all very lightly,' I said, 'and so does Shoosmith, but I don't feel inclined to believe them, even if they do claim superiority of sex and knowledge.' Jamie had been very scornful at supper of Lucy's anxieties, dismissing them as women's fears.

'They know little more than we do,' Grainne said drily. 'And I have never really believed that women are necessarily inferior. We may not possess the physical strength of men, but I cannot believe that in any other way we are weaker.' She smiled at me. 'Certainly, you seem to be stronger in matters of common sense than all the male members of our community put together!'

'Jamie, I can tell, thinks I'm unwomanly and fast becoming a shrew. About the latter, I think he's right.'

'Well, someone needs to speak to him and his military friends forthrightly,' said Grainne. 'If it turns out that Banbury is not so easily won, or if it is relieved by the Earl of Essex, their hotheadedness may yet see us turned out to make our own way to shelter.' She paused, staring into the fire, and then said, 'Someone must get word to Simon that we need help, and quickly too.'

'They would not go,' I pointed out. 'They're too confident of their own abilities and the King's and besides, I have a sneaking suspicion that they're of the opinion it's unmanly to show common prudence.'

'Would that Henry were here,' Grainne said, her eyes staring bleakly into the fire. 'He knew what he was doing – I pray the garrison of Banbury do not.'

'If our fat friend of Lord Saye's is anything to go by, they don't.'

'There's bound to be at least one man of resource and foresight,' Grainne said. 'And he may move against us quickly, both to seize our supplies and to remove our threat to their security. People in the villagers can tell him how weak we are, if necessary, and Jamie has proved conclusively that we are not a defenceless group of women and children; and are therefore legitimate prey in time of war.'

'And what if, at the worst, Essex arrives, engages the King's army and defeats them?'

The silence was broken by the gentle rustle and crack of the flames. Grainne reached forward and placed another log on the fire; in the sudden flare of light and sparks her face showed clear, calm and thoughtful. 'There's nothing for it . . . *someone* will have to find Simon, tomorrow.'

I knew with sudden clarity what was to be done. 'Not the men, because they won't go . . . Will Tawney's useless; he'd go to Oxford by mistake, or stop in an ale-house . . . Jamie wouldn't . . . Lucy would think it a great adventure, and probably get abducted, or lose her way . . . and Meraud would think it far too hoydenish, and trust her safety to God . . . and you are with child. So, it must be me.'

Grainne's beautiful eyes met mine. She said softly, 'Would you do it? You have a stouter heart than the rest, it seems.'

'No . . . just common sense, and a feeling that I cannot trust anyone else to do it right,' I said, grinning. 'I'll go tomorrow, while everyone else is at morning prayers, and I'll take some pistols just in case of any danger.'

'Take Henry's,' Grainne said. She smiled again. 'I often feel as if he is standing beside me, giving me strength, and never more than tonight. He would not mind; in fact, he'd be glad, I know. I'll show you how to use them.'

She rose and brought from a chest in the corner the long case containing the pistols, and for half an hour or so I practised unscrewing the barrels, dropping in the shot and an imaginary charge, aiming, and pulling the trigger. There was a little chinking heavy bag of shot to go with them, a horn and measure for the powder and even a mould for making more of the correct-sized shot oneself.

Much moved, I thanked Grainne from the bottom of my heart for her generosity, but she shook her head, saying again that Henry would be glad. As I left her chamber, I felt humbled, for I had still my true love to go to, and indeed the longing to see Francis again was overwhelming me, drowning out all thoughts of fear and a far more potent motive force than my concern for Ashcott. But she, in the words of that mournful ballad, now had ne'er a one; but would watch over his son, while he was growing.

chapter seven

The red horse

When cannons are roaring
And bullets are flying
He that would honour win
Must not fear dying.
   (Anon: 'When Cannons Are Roaring')

After saying goodnight to Grainne, I went first to the kitchen to purloin some food, and then to my bed, but could not sleep for the thoughts tumbling in my mind. A combination of excitement, fear and longing made me feel physically sick, and when I did at last fall into slumber it was an uneasy one, filled with dreams of violence and shameful, delightful images of Francis, his arms around me and his soft, mocking, loving voice in my hair. It was as well I was not given to talking in my sleep, or Lucy would have heard much to enlighten her. As it was, she looked curiously at my green, haggard face. 'Did you sleep at all? You were very restless.'

'Sorry,' I said, 'I didn't sleep much. Did I disturb you?'

'Hardly at all,' said Lucy, who always slept like a log and woke looking delightfully refreshed. 'You look as if you could do with some more sleep, though.'

I saw the opening I had been looking for. 'Well, I think I'll stay in bed for a little longer. I really don't feel well enough for prayers, or breakfast, so don't bother to bring anything up for me.'

Lucy looked more suspiciously at me. 'You don't feel sick, do you?'

'No, I'm not with child, Mistress Long-nose, nor have I cause to be,' I snapped with what I hoped was peevish bad temper, only partly feigned. Lucy grinned. 'Don't worry, I was only teasing. I know you're a lady of unimpeachable

313

virtue.' And escaped smartly out of the door before I was able to aim a pillow at her.

Sunday prayers, led by Will Tawney since Henry's death, always took at least half an hour. I quickly got out of bed and dressed warmly in my thick mulberry-coloured riding-habit, collected the case of pistols and bag of food from their hiding-place under the bed, drew on my cloak and hat and gloves, and slunk down the stairs. I was concealed from the people gathered in the hall by the screens, but the tap of my boot-heels on the stones seemed sure to be noticed. At the bottom, my heart banging as if it were the men of Essex's army behind that panelled screen instead of my cousins and friends, I paused for a second and then scurried into the parlour on my right, through into the tower parlour and out of the little ancient door, worm-eaten and strapped with huge squeaking hinges. The courtyard was empty except for the inevitable chickens. I glanced up at the tower looming above me, on top of which stood the sentry, and then with the precious case of pistols and the food in my arms ran across to the stables.

Most of the horses were out at pasture, but the old chestnut who pulled the cart, my own Chalcedony, Lucy's and Jamie's horses and one or two others were there. Feverishly I hauled my saddle from the rack at the end of the building. It was heavy, an effort to carry, and more still to lift it on to Chalcedony's back. All thumbs in my haste, I buckled the girth over the mare's calm flanks and fitted the bridle over her sleek sweet head, thanking Heaven that she was placid by nature, despite the long days cooped up in the stable's gloom on hay and oats. I fastened the straps, prepared to lead her out and then realized that I had nowhere to put the pistols. There was a pair of holsters strapped to a saddle on the rack: I ran back to get them, Chalcedony's ears swivelling to follow my progress. As I unbuckled them, wondering at my nervousness (for surely I had nothing to fear from anyone at Ashcott, you might think I was escaping from prison), the door swung open and shut and Jamie's voice said, 'What *are* you doing?'

I gasped and whipped round to face him, the holsters in

my hand. Jamie gave an uneasy laugh. 'I thought I heard someone creeping out and thought it must be you . . . Why do you look so guilty?'

I walked towards my horse and began to buckle one of the holsters to a strap on the saddle. Jamie came over to me, and saw the pistols. 'Thomazine! Those are Henry's!'

'Yes,' I said wearily, 'Grainne gave them to me. I'm going to ask the King for a garrison.'

Jamie's blue eyes, so like his mother's and sister's, fairly bulged. 'You! But you're only a girl! What if you meet with Essex?'

'From what you yourself said at supper last night,' I pointed out, 'he shouldn't be within fifty miles of Banbury, so I should be safe enough.'

'But you can't go on your own! Unprotected . . . You don't know what might happen!'

There were times when Jamie's deep sense of chivalry grew tedious. I looked round the saddle for somewhere to fix the other holster and failed. 'I have these. And I don't think anyone would find it easy to ravish me.'

Jamie flushed at my bluntness. He said, 'Then I must come with you.'

I stared at his soft, heart-shaped face, very much like Lucy's, and at the shining, fervent eyes. The idea appealed to me; it would certainly be safer than going alone, and no less effective.'That's a good idea,' I said. 'But hurry, before prayers are finished, I don't want to have to face Shoo-smith.'

Jamie gave me a bright, conspiratorial grin, and ran for his own tack. He was more efficient than I, and was soon ready, putting a proper military saddle on his horse, and taking charge of one of the pistols. Then he ran over to the tower and returned with a small quantity of powder. Care-fully, we loaded the pistols and placed them in our respec-tive holsters. Then we led our horses out, opened the gate, and walked through the gatehouse. With a great sense of relief and overhelming, mad excitement, we mounted and turned our horses' heads for the Banbury road.

We passed through Adderbury, turning curious heads of

those few already about. It was cold, and our breath smoked cheerfully in the bright air. Above us the sky was blue and shining, the dreadful September rains having given way to this crisp frosty October morning. After Adderbury we halted to discuss our route. It was perhaps three miles or more to Banbury, and we had no wish to be caught up in any fighting.

'If they were quartered north of Banbury last night,' Jamie said, 'then it'd be best to take a big sweep round the place and search the villages like Hanwell and Wormington. We'll at least have news of the army. But there's Lord Saye's garrison at Broughton; we'll have to sweep very wide to avoid that.' He dismounted and scratched a map with a stick in the crusty, frosted road. 'Here's Banbury, and this is us. Now, if we take that track running off to the left there, we'll come to Milton, and Bloxham, and avoid Broughton, which is there!' He stabbed viciously with the stick. 'Pity we didn't think to go the Milton way in the first place, but still. Come on, then!' He mounted and we trotted down the track.

It being a Sunday, we saw very few people: one or two ploughmen, keener to finish their work than to obey the customs of the Sabbath, or, as we neared Bloxham, men and women from outlying farms and hamlets making their way to church. They assumed we were on the same errand, and waved cheerfully.

The road that Jamie said we must take skirted round Bloxham, with its famous spired church, 'Bloxham for length', as the rhyme went. The necessity of giving Broughton a wide berth meant that for several miles we had to ride due west before Jamie decided that it was safe to turn for Banbury. By this time both the sun's position and the hollow feeling in my stomach told me that it was past noon. We halted our horse under the shade of a tree by the roadside and ate in the saddle. I had provided generously just for myself, but half a meat pie, with a thick coffin of pastry, a hunk of bread, some cheese and some apples were inadequate when shared between two. Jamie dismounted and risked injury to procure a hatful of blackberries, wet and ripe on a sunny bush. Then we continued on our way, feeling more at ease in this empty, peaceful countryside, between hedges bearing hawthorn berries and hips like glowing scarlet lanthorns, as if hung out in celebration of our passage. Most of the people of this area, generally of a godly persuasion, spent the Sabbath quietly within doors, and we saw no one.

And then, very distantly, I heard a curious sound; a flat 'crump' as though someone were beating a giant carpet. It came again, and again, somewhere to the north of us. I reined in Chalcedony. Jamie had also heard it; his eyes turned excitedly to mine. 'Listen! It's gunfire!'

My heart jumped, but I said, as calmly as I could, 'The siege must have begun.'

'Fiddlesticks,' Jamie said cheerfully. 'Banbury's over there.' He waved an arm to our right. 'This comes from the north, listen. There must be a battle.'

My heart finally sank. 'If Essex's army have come up with the King's, then they won't be able to attack Banbury, and Banbury will be able to attack us.'

'Well, we'd best hurry!' Jamie said, eyes shining. 'Or we'll miss it! Come *on*, Thomazine!' And he laid heels to his horse and made off over the sheepwalks by the road, towards the distant battle. After a second's hesitation I rode in pursuit. Now I saw the madness of our expedition with a bitter clarity, and even more so the insanity of the two of us, a boy just fourteen with more heart than sense and a girl, however determined, only three years older and all of five feet tall, riding straight into the thick of a pitched battle between two great armies, each numbering thousands of men, in the hopes of finding just one individual. But I would not leave Jamie alone; it was my doing that we were here, and I could not desert him. And besides, I might see Francis . . . and again that awful vision that haunted my nightmares, of searching for his body among the slain of some dreadful battlefield, rose in my mind, and I urged Chalcedony on in Jamie's wake, following the sound of the guns in the north and not having the slightest idea of our destination. After riding for some distance hell-for-leather across the sheepwalks, we came suddenly to a road, not a humble country track but a broad, well-used highway stretching north-west, towards the gunfire.

'I know what this must be,' Jamie said, reining in breathlessly. 'I'll wager my life it's the Stratford road. It must be somewhere here that the Earl of Northampton and Lord Brooke had that confrontation. We're not far from the battle now, the guns sound much louder. Are you still with me?'

'Yes,' I said, 'but go slowly. If we run into fighting we may be killed before they realize what we are.'

As we went on towards the sound of the battle we began to see other people also evidently making for the scene. Some of them seemed just curious country folk. Others, more rapacious in appearance, I did not like the look of. 'I expect they've come to pick up what they can,' Jamie explained, in a know-it-all way incongruous in one so young and untried. 'That sort wait until dark and then strip the dead, and the wounded too.'

One of the pleasanter-looking men, in a shepherd's smock and old felt hat, his dog trotting by his side, told us when we asked that the fighting was in the Vale of the Red Horse, around the village of Kineton, and that an excellent view could be had from the top of Edgehill. He himself had come to see the battle in case anything had happened to his son, who had joined the Earl of Northampton's Foot. He seemed confident that his John would be easily found amongst the thousands in the army. Amusement at his naïve hopes was quickly tempered by the thought that our own journey would probably be equally fruitless.

The sun was sliding down towards dusk when we came to the slopes of Edgehill. Below us the ground fell away abruptly, steep and uncertain, with rough grass and bushes merging into the flat valley which stretched for miles to the north and west of us. All along the ridge stood little groups of spectators. Quite near us there was a large knot of horsemen, some dismounted, some still in the saddle; evidently, from their fine clothes and armour, part of one of the armies, guarding someone important. A countrywoman near to us, seeing my interest, pointed. 'That's the King's own troop o' horse, and those two boys sitting down, watchin' the battle . . . the Prince o' Wales and the Duke o' York.'

Jamie's eyes swivelled briefly from the scene below to study the princes, who were younger than he, and apparently part of the army; and then returned to the battle. Clouds of smoke drifted over the fields below us. At the foot of the hill, almost directly beneath, was a small village, houses and enclosures and gardens. 'Radway,' said my informant. 'I live there, *when* it's not being used as a battlefield. King and Parliament! Each as bad as the other, turning honest folk out o' their homes to fight a battle. I'd ha' stayed, mind you, but when I heard them guns I came up here quick. I'm only a poor widow keeps an ale-house, but no cannon-shot'll make an end of *me*, sure as my name's Bess Marston.'

I peered at the battlefield. The smoke, from cannons or muskets, obscured much, but I could see clearly the great tangled mass of foot-soldiers struggling perhaps half a mile or more away, to the right of where we were standing. I looked hard but could discern no evidence, save for one or two groups here and there, of any cavalry. This could only mean that the Royalist troopers had chased their opponents from the field, for if the opposite had been true then surely the hill where we stood would have been littered with fallen cavalry, and we would have met fugitives. I uttered a brief prayer in my mind for the safety of Francis, and sat down in the cold grass with Jamie to watch. Up here, with the clear sky, the sun shining redly in our faces, a soft westerly wind stirring in our hair, and above all the calm and silence common to hilltops, it was hard to believe that scenes of slaughter were being fought below us. The cannon had more or less stopped firing; only the occasional puff of smoke and the delayed distant thump of the explosion marked where pieces were still being used. Faintly, far off above the gentle rush and rustle of the wind in the grass, came to our ears the cries and crashes of the battle. It was an experience at once beautiful and terrible in its implications, that we could watch rampant death thus calmly, as if at a play. It did not seem real.

Wounded men were beginning to make their way up the steep hill, on foot or supported by comrades. The Prince of Wales, his brother and their escort had disappeared, presumably gone back to their quarters. The sun sank behind the distant western hills, outlining them fierily in the autumn mist. It began to grow chilly, and I wrapped my cloak about me, shivering from cold and fear. Surely, I thought, if anything had happened to Francis I would know, I would feel it, feel the severance of the ties that bound us invisibly together. But I felt nothing, only a weary, cold foreboding.

It was growing late, too dark to see much at all, when the King's men returned up the hill. One group of foot-soldiers, trailing stained, battered pikes, with a weary officer at their head, almost bumped into us. Jamie spoke quickly. 'Can you tell me, sir, where are the horse?'

The officer swore. 'Nowhere, lad. God only knows. Not where we wanted them, anyway.' He peered into Jamie's young, anxious face, and added less brusquely, 'Who d'you want? I've a friend in the Prince of Wales's Regiment, and a cousin in the Lifeguard. I might know 'em.'

Jamie said, 'Captain Simon Heron – I don't know his regiment.'

'Heron? No one I know of,' said the officer. 'Sorry, lad,' he added, looking at Jamie's suddenly drooping shoulders. 'I don't know him. You'd best be home to your mother.' And he stumped off, his exhausted pikemen straggling behind him.

'Well,' I said, 'we can't go back. Not now it's dark. Where are the cavalry usually stationed in a battle?'

'On either wing, and the foot in the middle,' said Jamie. 'So if we move to right or left we may meet some, you mean? Let's try.'

So leading our horses, we made our stumbling way north-east along the ridge, meeting with soldiers coming up, and country people slipping down to hunt for friends or strip the dead. Many of the foot we saw were wounded, and few had time or energy to answer our questions, reeling from tiredness and injuries. And then, suddenly, miraculously, there was a face we knew; John Snelling, Tom Blagge's stepbrother and Lucy's admirer from far-away days of peace in Suffolk. By now, fires were being lit here and there along the ridge and his long beaky face leapt suddenly to my notice in a group of officers feeding a fire with brushwood. Forgetting all decorum or caution, I shouted, 'John! John Snelling!'

Startled, he looked up, and saw me. His jaw dropped. 'M-my God, Thomazine Heron! W-what in Sweet Jesu's name are you d-doing here? And Jamie t-too?' In front of the curious stares of his brother officers he ran over to us. Jamie said, 'We're looking for Simon. Do you know where he's likely to be?'

'He's in P-Prince Rupert's regiment,' John said. In the months since we had seen him, he had changed from a scrawny, shy youth to a brisk, confident officer, though his old stutter was still there. 'Blue coats, on the right, they w-were. They charged f-first, rode right over the enemy, but I've seen n-nothing of them since. G-God, it was l-like Hell must be d-down there, for us. W-we were hard put to it to know w-what was happening to the rest of the regiment, l-let alone the horse.' He looked at our anxious faces. 'B-but why in God's n-name did you c-come? The d-danger . . .'

I explained quickly. John frowned. 'You'd b-be unlikely to get m-many m-men for a g-garrison, but you might be l-lucky, a few w-walking w-wounded, perhaps . . . L-look, you can't carry on on your own, I'll c-come with you. W-we'll f-find him, or get news of him; the whole army's to w-withdraw to this p-position, and though T-Tom's already g-gone b-back to the village where we w-were this m-morning, I d-don't think Simon will l-leave his men so readily. We'll f-find him.'

So, with the welcome help of John Snelling, we went from fire to fire, seeking news of Simon or his troop. Soon the presence of horses, tied to bushes, in makeshift lines, hobbled or turned loose, indicated that we were amongst the cavalry. Almost immediately, a florid young officer in froth-

ing lace and wide boots, who did not look as if he had
exerted himself any more than he might have done on the
hunting-field, extended a languid hand in response to
John's questions. 'Captain Heron? Yes, my dear fellow.
That fire over there.'

By now, I was wearier than I had ever been in my life,
barely able to lift one foot after another, and Jamie was in
like case. John, who had fought a battle that day, must have
been suffering similarly, but did not show it, I knew how
fortunate we had been to meet him, out of all Tom Blagge's
regiment, for he had ever been good-natured and helpful
beyond the common run, and no one else would have done
as much for us. Now, as we stumbled towards the fire, I
thanked him profusely, remembering guiltily all the times I
had made fun of him behind his back or to his face, and was
waved away. 'It w-was all I c-could d-do, Thomazine, after
all, and I m-must say it w-was v-very courageous of you to
c-come here, though foolhardy. Yes, I c-can see Simon, so
you're safe n-now, but if I c-can help you again, in any
w-way, you know where I am . . .' and he melted away into
the dark. Suddenly fearful of our reception, Jamie and I
looked at each other and then squared our shoulders and
stepped firmly into the circle of firelight.

The expressions of amazement which greeted our arrival
were, to say the least of it, comical. Jaws dropped, eyes
bulged, men struggled to their feet. I saw all the familiar
faces; Eldritch, Tom Sewell, Skinner, and the men who had
escorted us from Suffolk, in smart blue coats, their unbuckled backs and breasts and helmets piled on the ground
around them. But, look as I would, I did not see Francis, or
Edward; and there was no colour planted by the fire, as
graced other troops. A dreadful fear clutched my heart, but
I had to conceal it. I turned to Simon, who was looking at us
as if we were apparitions. 'Dear God! What in Christ's name
are you two doing here?'

I was a little tired of hearing variations of this. Jamie said
quickly, 'Don't be alarmed or angry, please. We've come
because of Ashcott. We need your help.'

Simon lost some of his astonishment, took our arms and

steered us a little distance away from the troopers, calling to one of them to make our horses secure. 'What do you mean?' he demanded, and through the fog of tiredness and worry I realized that he thought that Ashcott had been taken. Quickly, I explained about Henry's death, the depletion of our garrison, and our worries about Banbury. 'Can anyone be spared to go back with us?'

Simon's face was sombre. 'Poor Henry. He was a good friend and a good soldier, and all of us are the poorer for his death. I shall see that his widow and children do not lack for anything . . . men spared for a garrison?' He sighed. 'I do not know. I shall have to ask the Prince, see if some can be sent back with you . . . it won't be many, but it should protect you until we've dealt with Banbury. There's every likelihood, though, that we will deal a swift blow now at London, since the field is ours.'

'Then the King has won?' Jamie demanded. Simon nodded. 'Yes, though the losses have been heavy, amongst the foot in particular . . . but we drove their cavalry from the field, so I think the day is ours, although more could have been done . . . so many opportunities wasted . . .'

I said, hardly daring in case the reply struck my heart, 'Where is Edward? And Francis, and the colour?'

A cloud came down over Simon's face. He said shortly, 'I do not know. The troop was split up in the pursuit of the rebels towards Kineton. The Prince managed to rally some men; I and some of these troopers were with him, and the rest rode on, to loot and pillage at their will. They are probably scattered over the countryside.'

It did not seem like Edward, ever calm and sensible, to ride hell-for-leather in pursuit of the enemy, in defiance of his commander, but I said nothing. It was probably quite true, and he and Francis would be somewhere else on the hillside, or making their way back as darkness fell. There was no reason to worry, but I did.

'Have you got any food?' Jamie demanded in his outspoken way. 'I'm ravenously hungry.'

Simon laughed mirthlessly. 'No, I'm afraid you'll have

to go without. We have had little to eat since yesterday, and what we had got has just been shared out.'

'Oh,' said Jamie, his face fallen. Simon gave him a brief vivid tired smile that reminded me heartbreakingly of Francis. 'Never mind, you two, you've done well and bravely, though it was a mad exploit to come for us in the thick of battle.'

'We didn't know it was a battle, till we heard the guns,' I explained. 'And by then we'd gone so far it didn't seem right to turn back. Simon, please . . . can I sit by the fire?'

The soldiers, cheerfully welcoming, made room for us, inside the warm, glowing circle. I held my hands to the blaze, revelling in the heat. Tom Sewell tossed some more wood into the flames, and turned to us. 'Hallo, you two. What's been happening at Ashcott?'

Once more we told the whole sad story of death and desertion, and at the news of Henry's untimely end, the weather-lined faces around us showed signs of genuine sorrow. Mutters of 'Thass a proper shame,' and 'He was a master good 'un,' reached me. I felt sorry for Tom, who had bowed his head in grief; all his usual ebullience drained away, and I wished that the news could have been broken more tactfully, away from the curious, sorrowful eyes of the troop. Abruptly, Tom got up and walked off into the dark, and Simon left us to follow him. I heard their voices distantly, and quickly turned back to the fire. One or two men were already endeavouring to make themselves comfortable for the night on the cold ground, muffling themselves in their cloaks against the frost. Jamie, beginning to be heavy-eyed, drooped against me, but I would not be able to sleep without knowing what had happened to Francis. I stared into the fire, while from another group close by came the familiar strains of Edward's song:

> When cannons are roaring
> And bullets are flying
> He that would honour win
> Must not fear dying.

The tune brought back vividly that bright June day at

Ashcott, the last calm before the storm broke, and my longing for Francis grew so great that I clenched my fists and closed my eyes. I heard Simon return with Tom, and sit down with weary grunts. Slowly, heavily, a horse was approaching; I could hear its stumbling, shuffling gait across the rough grass. Something made me open my eyes and look up; and I saw Francis. He stood just outside the main circle of firelight, hatless, his hair darkened with sweat and a streak of blood across his face; beside him, head down, utterly weary, his black mare Hobgoblin; and across her back, someone's body.

He saw me at once; his eyes widened in surprise, and a brief unguarded smile crossed his face for a moment. Then Simon glanced his way, and leapt to his feet. 'Cornet Heron! Where are your colours?'

It was, I thought, typical of Simon that his first concern was not for the safety of his brothers, nor for the apparently lifeless and anonymous form draped over Hobgoblin's back, but for the honour of his troop. Francis said, his voice toneless and curiously slurred, 'Don't worry yourself . . . I still have them, they're under Trooper Greenwood. I couldn't support him and carry them as well, so I took them off the pole.'

'Is that Greenwood?' Simon demanded, his voice rough and sharp. 'Is he alive?'

'He was,' Francis said. 'He's been poleaxed.'

Several men lifted Holly's limp form off Hobgoblin's back, and laid him on the ground near the fire. Skinner bent over him, putting a blade of grass to his lips, feeling with gentle hands the back of his head. He knelt back on his heels and said to Simon, 'He's alive, sir, and his head's not broken. He'll probably come to himself quite soon.'

'Thank you, Trooper Skinner. Make him comfortable for when he wakes,' Simon said. He swung round on his brother. 'I think you had better explain your over-long absence, Cornet Heron. Where are Lieutenant Heron and the remainder of the troop?'

Francis's heavy eyes rested for a long moment on his brother's face, as if he did not understand the question. He was visibly swaying on his feet. He looks drunk, I thought, and sounds it, too, but he can't be. Simon's eyes narrowed suspiciously; he opened his mouth to speak, but Francis forestalled him. 'Lieutenant Heron is dead,' he said, and his mouth twisted with a dreadful, bitter amusement. 'For the rest of the troop I can't answer; they're probably carousing on stolen beer.'

'Dead?' Simon demanded, in disbelief, and his façade cracked suddenly. 'Edward, killed? In God's name, how?'

Francis, still standing, more or less, put his arm across Hobgoblin's withers to steady himself. 'We went after the troops to try to bring them back. They were in Kineton by the time we'd managed to catch up with them, looting the baggage and killing wagoners. There were several other officers trying to beat them off and bring them back, but it took a long time. On our return a troop or more attacked us; they came through a gap in the hedge. I saw Ed – Lieutenant Heron fall, and rode to help him, but he was dead already.'

'Are you sure? How can you be certain he was dead?' Simon said, in his grief and anger unable to believe it. Francis's eyes flickered, then he said coldly, 'There's not much doubt when a man's shot through the head.'

For a brief agonized moment there was silence around our fire, all eyes on the two brothers locked in this strange and unnecessary battle of words, that on Francis's side seemed as in the bad days of old calculated to infuriate his brother. Beside me, Jamie gave a little sob and buried his face in his hands. Simon said, 'Did you make no attempt to bring away his body?'

'No,' Francis said. 'The enemy were everywhere; it would not have been long before they'd have come upon us, though we were partly screened by the hedge . . . and besides, I'd found Trooper Greenwood alive, and my horse could barely carry both him and me, without taking Lieutenant Heron's body as well.'

'So you left him there,' Simon said, his voice thick with sorrow and a vicious, unreasonable anger. 'You left him there for his body to be stripped and abused . . . you should have taken him and left the trooper behind – he would not have come to harm—'

'In this frost?' Francis asked. He did not, I realized with a shock, seem to be aware of the consequences of taking this unconciliatory attitude. 'He'd have died before morning, of the cold. Better a living man here and a dead one out there, sir, than two corpses.'

Simon's fists were clenched white-knuckled at his sides. 'And then what did you do? By the look of you, you've been imbibing steadily ever since. Do you know, Cornet Heron, of the penalties for being drunk?'

Francis stared at him for a long, dragging moment and then grinned foolishly. His voice even more slurred than before, he said, 'Drunk? God, I wish I were . . .' and then abruptly pitched forward on to his face in the grass. Horrified, realizing that something were very wrong, I half rose to my feet. Simon had frozen, staring down at his brother. It was Skinner, quicker than all of us, who reached him first, turning him over, his hands gently probing and searching as they had done for Holly. Dreadfully afraid, my heart thudding, I sank back on my heels and watched. At last, Skinner glanced up at his captain and said, 'He's hurt, sir, and lost a good deal of blood by the look on it . . . thass a proper bad cut in his arm, and he's taken a thrust in the side as well, though he don't fare t'be a-dying of it . . . Thass a-bleeding bad, hev we anything to stop it?'

As he had done for Henry once, Simon removed his sash, avoiding Skinner's gently accusing eyes. Several of the troopers did likewise. For a moment, he stood looking down as Skinner made pads and bandages and ripped the cloth; and then, too proud to make apology, turned and strode off into the night. On impulse, I retreated into the semi-darkness at the edge of the firelight and pulled off one of my innumerable petticoats, which would, I felt, make a better dressing than the sashes. Skinner received the bundle of soft Holland with an appreciative smile, and there were one or two ribald comments, *sotto voce*, from the men. Francis lay sprawled in the grass, his closed uninhabited face lit with deceptive health by the glow of the fire, and the thick bloodstains marring his shirt and less obviously the new blue of his coat, the colour of Prince Rupert's Horse. I held down the tears that had seemed close ever since I had first heard of Edward's death, and said to Skinner, 'Can I do anything?'

'No, mistress,' said the one-time head groom. 'I'd look to your little cousin, that's took him proper bad.'

Jamie was struggling with tears, being comforted rather uneasily by Tom Sewell, whose own grief for his brother was also near the surface. Reluctantly, I left Francis and knelt beside his young brother. 'Oh, Jamie, hush now, hush, it won't bring him back.'

'I know,' Jamie hiccupped, tears gleaming redly down his freckled cheeks. 'But I can't believe it . . . not old Ned too! I'll kill the man who murdered him, I will, I swear it, if I ever find him. When can I be a soldier, when?'

'To get yourself killed too?' I said softly. 'You owe it to Lucy and your mother, to keep out of it.'

'Mother! She wouldn't care if we lived or died, would she?' Jamie muttered, with a quite alien cynicism. 'But none of you will stop me, I *will* be a soldier and avenge them if it's the last thing I do!' He burst into fresh, angry tears against my shoulder, and I put my arms about him and hugged him, feeling the last of my hoydenish youth slipping away to leave me as old and wise as time. What Grainne said was true, I thought, it's the women and children who suffer in war; they are left behind to grieve their lives long, while at least for most of the men it is over quickly. At least Ned did not suffer. The slow tears, for him and Henry and for all the men of both sides whose hideous, distant groans and cries came up from the too-aptly named Vale of the Red Horse, trickled down my face into Jamie's hair.

I must, we both must, have slept in the end; for I woke cold and stiff-limbed when the first light of dawn flushed the sky. Someone, Tom perhaps, had settled Jamie next to me, under our cloaks piled one on the other for double warmth, and pillowed our heads on a pile of bracken. Gingerly, so as not to wake him, I sat up, stretching my cramped limbs, shivering in the cold air, and wishing vainly for food. All around the grey smoking heap of our fire lay the troopers, huddled together for warmth amidst the shuffling, heavily breathing bulks of their horses. I looked about for Simon, but could see no sign of him. Next to me, a freckled nose and a mop of orange hair above a thick frieze cloak were all that could be seen of Tom Sewell. Someone the other side of the fire grunted, stirred and sat up, wincing. It was Francis. Forgetting Jamie, I leapt to my feet and ran across, dodging feet and bodies, to kneel beside him. 'How are you?'

'What in God's name are you doing here?' Francis asked, with a marked lack of originality. 'Joining Rupert's horse? He'll never put up with your petticoats, you know.' He chuckled. 'Apart from being damnably cold and stiff, and having a pain in my side like a red-hot stitch, I do very well, thank you.'

'I was worried,' I said, though looking at his grey face and over-brilliant eyes did not do anything to lessen my anxiety. 'I'm glad you're better.' The thought of twenty-odd pairs of ears, all possibly listening surreptitiously to our conversation, was proving remarkably inhibiting.

Francis was exploring his injured left arm with cautious fingers. 'Our Roundhead friends have very sharp swords. Who bandaged me? Skinner? I thought as much – he's used enough to bandage a horse. Hullo, Jamie.'

Jamie sat down beside me, rubbing his red-rimmed eyes and yawning. 'Hullo. Are you better?'

'It looks as if I am,' Francis said, 'since the world is not now circling round me, and I no longer feel quite so lightheaded. The effects of loss of blood seem to be strangely similar to being drunk.'

'Simon thought you were,' Jamie said, with an uneasy snigger. 'Tell me what happened,' he added, eyes gleaming. 'Tell us about the battle.'

I could see that Francis did not want to talk about it, but quietly he obeyed. 'There's little more than what I told

Simon last night. We charged the enemy horse, and they broke and ran, and most of ours rode loose-reined in pursuit. The Prince, who's well named the Devil, halted two or three troops, and half of this one, and Ned and I went after the rest to bring them back. If we'd succeeded in gathering all the horse together again, we could have re-formed and fallen on the enemy foot from the rear, and then the battle would have been ours, conclusively. So we did what we could in Kineton, but it was an hour or more before we'd rounded our men up and were ready to return. There were perhaps five troops of us, all riding back together, and then a group of Roundhead horse burst through a gap in the hedge beside us and fell on the rearmost troop, which was ours . . .' He paused, his shadowed bleak eyes gazing at the dawn, gathering the strength to go on. 'I saw one of them aim his pistol at Ned, who was fighting another of them off with his sword – our pistols were all discharged. I rode Goblin at the one with the pistol, but too late to stop him firing it. I ran him through, and then went to Ned. He was lying in the grass under part of the hedge, but before I could get to him I had to fight off the one with the sword. He it was gave me these, before I killed him. Then I could get to Ned, but it was too late; he must have died straight away, and there was nothing I could do. There were no living Roundheads near, the fighting had moved away a bit and it was getting dark. I saw Holly lying close by, so I went over to him and found he was still alive.' The soft, deceptively unemotional voice paused again, and I glanced at Jamie, seeing not tears but a white, set, intense face. Francis continued. 'It took me a long time to get him on to Goblin, he's not exactly a lightweight. By the time I did manage it, it was dark, there was no one living left around us, and we had to make our way back across the battle ground. I could see the fires on the hill to guide my way. That's all there is to tell, Jamie – do you like war so much now you've seen it?'

'I'm glad you killed the man who shot Ned,' Jamie said fiercely. 'I'd have done it, somehow, if you hadn't. Hey! Here's Drake!'

A shaggy black-and-white bullet hurled itself into Francis's arms and began to wash his face frantically. Fearful that more hurt might be done, I set my hand to his collar and hauled him off. Francis, holding his side, said in between gasps, 'Thanks, Thomazine. You infernal animal, have a care! I tied him to one of the ammunition carts for the duration of the battle, and I'd forgotten all about him, yes, I'm afraid I did, you old rascal. It's a good thing somebody thought to release him.'

'Do they mind you having a dog in the army?' Jamie asked, as Drake licked his master's hands and pounded his tail joyfully over the grass. Francis grinned. 'Well, Simon's not very keen, but as the Prince himself has a dog ever at his heels – a fine big white dog it is too, much finer than you, you moth-eaten old carpet – he can't say too much.'

'The Prince has a dog?' Jamie said in surprise, and then, 'What's he like, the Prince I mean?'

Francis's eyes travelled past his brother's shoulder and he grinned again. 'You'll see him soon enough. He's approaching now, with Simon, and the dog, whose name, by the way, is Boy. Keep a hold on Drake, we don't want a fight.' He got stiffly to his feet and added loudly, 'Rise up, men, for the Prince!'

With an alacrity which suggested that most of them had been awake already, the troopers scrambled to their feet, straightening coats and breeches, folding cloaks and brushing off grass. One or two who had presumably made off to relieve themselves ran hastily back. By the time Simon and his companion arrived, everyone was standing neatly around the fire looking as alert as was possible after a night spent in the open. The precious colours, creased and stained, had been found a new pole which looked suspiciously like a broken pikestave, and as the Prince approached Francis took hold of the staff and dipped it in compliment.

The Prince overtopped even Simon by perhaps three or four inches, quite the tallest man I had ever seen. It was a shock to see how young he was, probably near Simon's own age, and with the kind of fierce dark good looks that would have set Lucy's romantic heart racing. He came striding over the grass towards us, Simon and the huge white dog at his heels, and I had a vivid impression of enormous, contained energy beneath the elaborate dress and velvet cloak, on which bits of grass indicated that he too had spent the night on the hilltop.

I curtseyed deeply, and Jamie bowed as best he could with one hand firmly grasping Drake's collar. 'Your Highness,' Simon was saying, 'may I present my cousin and ward, Mistress Thomazine Heron, and my youngest brother, Master James Heron.'

'I have heard of your brave ride from Captain Heron,' said the Prince. In accordance with his height, his voice was deep and strong, with a foreign intonation reminding me that his father had been German. 'It was well done, for a boy and a woman, through dangerous country.'

'We had Master Sewell's pistols, Your Highness,' Jamie explained, 'and he taught me to fire them before he was killed.' He added in a sudden rush, 'Since my brother Edward was slain yesterday, Your Highness, there must be a vacant place in my brother's troop in your regiment, and I would very much like to enlist as a volunteer, or – or anything!'

The Prince looked down at Jamie, with his soft untried face and scant five-foot-three; still obviously a child, despite his broken voice. Amusement and approval twitching his long mouth, he said, 'How old are you, Master James?'

'Fourteen years and a half, Your Highness,' Jamie said, overstating his age by five months. Simon frowned. 'You seem to have mistaken your age, Jamie; if I remember rightly, your fourteenth birthday fell last month.'

The Prince gave a short bark of laughter. 'In either case he is too young, I regret to say. But in a year or two, Jamie Heron, it'll be a different story. If we're still at war, present yourself with your horse and arms, and there'll be a place for you.'

Jamie's eyes glowed with delight. 'Oh, thank you, Your Highness!' he cried, more overwhelmed than I had ever seen him. I felt it was time to intervene; plucking up my courage, for the Prince was by far the most exalted person I had ever encountered, I said, 'Your Highness, is there any chance of obtaining a small garrison for our house? We feel in great danger, from the Parliament men at Banbury, from Lord Saye and others.'

'Captain Heron has already told me why you sought him out, and has impressed upon me the parlous state of your defences,' said Prince Rupert. He gave me a smile that quite won me over. 'And how could I refuse a lady so small and yet so valiant? There are few men I can spare you; and they will be those with sickness or wounds that are not serious, but nevertheless would not endure the swift march to London which I trust will be speedily put into execution. Of your cousin's troop you may have Cornet Heron and Trooper Greenwood, and three troopers from the Duke of York's troop, all with their horses and arms, and what powder and shot can be loaded on to a spare horse. More than that I cannot give you, I fear, but I trust that it will be better than nothing; and I shall endeavour to arrange that the garrisons at Banbury and Broughton be speedily reduced.'

So Francis was to come with us to Ashcott! Delight informing my face, I curtseyed deeply. 'Your Highness, I am most grateful for your kindness, and I am certain that the men will make all the difference to our garrison. We shall all rest easier in our beds for your generosity.'

'It was the least I could have done for so courageous a lady,' said the Prince, and I could have sworn, Royal blood or no, that he was a trifle embarrassed. 'Ever your servant, mistress.' And he turned abruptly and strode off through the little knots of troops dotted about the ridge, the dog Boy still following faithfully.

'My God, Thomazine, you appear to have made some impression,' Simon said in astonishment. 'He doesn't usually pay much attention to women.'

Feeling very smug, and hugging my happiness to myself, I said, 'Perhaps now he will. We're not as weak and feeble as you imagine, you know. And I've got what we asked for.'

It seemed little enough when the men were assembled. Holly Greenwood, with a fresh bandage haloing his homely face, was suffering from a sprained and swollen right wrist in addition to his battered and aching head. I did not like the look of Francis, who was very white about the mouth but ignored any pain with typical Heron stubbornness. The three from the Duke of York's troop were an ill-assorted group: two of them pleasant young men of quality, both with good horses; one had received a pistol ball through the arm, the other several serious cuts about his thigh, which I remembered Henry as saying was the most vulnerable part of a cavalryman's body, unless wearing full armour. The third was an exquisite young gallant with a fashionable court drawl and a beautiful moustache; he had no discernable wound. Bowing over my hand, he introduced himself as 'Robert Radley, ever at your service, madam.'

Disliking him somewhat unfairly on sight, I said, 'Are you to come with us? I understood from His Highness that we were to have sick and wounded men.'

'Alas, madam, I am to be numbered among the former,' said Radley. 'I suffer from an, uh, unpleasant but all too common ailment not unconnected, I fear, with the unhappily inappropriate quarters which, as a gentleman volunteer, I am forced to inhabit.' As my startled mind began to run over several highly embarrassing possibilities, he added, 'I am told it is a form of ague, madam, which strikes whenever the weather is cold or damp, and which leaves me prostrate in a fever for three or four days together.'

('In truth,' said Charles Lawrence, one of his brother troopers, to me later, 'he proved so damnably incompetent and argumentative that his Lieutenant has seized the opportunity to be rid of him.')

By the middle of the morning we were ready to return to Ashcott. By now those officers and men who had gone to seek warmer accommodation for the night had returned, so that most of the King's army stood upon the hillside, and there was much confusion as officers attempted to reform their troops and companies. I had walked to the edge of the ridge to see the battlefield below. Somewhere, perhaps by that very hedge I could see running along to my right towards Kineton, lay my dear cousin Edward, abruptly wrenched from life by a rebel bullet, and destined, unless Simon could order it otherwise, for a common grave on the field; friend and foe, officers and men, mixed in the final companionship of death. I could see, even from this distance, that numbers of dead were strewn about the field, interspersed with living, moving figures searching for those wounded who had survived the bitter night. Beyond, the Earl of Essex's army could be seen, once more drawn up in battle array, waiting ominously. It would be best to be gone.

Simon had told Francis of Henry's death and the situation at Ashcott, of which of course he had been ignorant; and had placed him in charge of the garrison. 'Remember that you are there not only for the protection of the women and other civilians within its walls, but also to hold it for the King; and the Prince has accordingly given you a commission as lieutenant in this troop and authority over the garrison at Ashcott, to take in arms and supplies and do what harm you can to the cause of our enemies.' He passed his brother the precious scrawled piece of paper, with the bold signature 'Rupert' at the bottom. Then he turned to Jamie and me, already mounted and waiting. 'I am grateful to you for coming, you two, foolhardy though it may have been, and I wish you a swift and safe journey and an unmolested sojourn at Ashcott. If it proves possible, I shall write to you to see how you go on.' He paused, and added, 'By the way, Thomazine, I've just remembered; there is in the Lifeguard of Foot our cousin and your betrothed, Dominic Drakelon, fighting in his father's company. I have not yet heard how they fared in the battle, but should they prove to be safe, I shall send them your regards.' And before I could protest that he knew very well that Dominic was no longer my betrothed, he said, 'You'd best be off, Lieutenant. Mount and away! Godspeed, Thomazine and Jamie, and good fortune.'

We left the battlefield and retraced our path of the previous day. It did not take long – fortified by food bought on the way from a sympathetic farmer's wife, we rode through

Bloxham and Milton and came at last down Coombe Hill in the late afternoon sunshine, to find the gates of Ashcott flung open in welcome. I dismounted stiffly, and Lucy's arms flung round me nearly knocked me over. 'Thomazine! Oh, thank God! We were so worried, even when Grainne said where you'd gone. And Jamie with you too, we thought he must be. Oh, thank God you're both safe!'

'Is there no welcome for me, little sister?' Francis asked from behind. Lucy released me so abruptly that I almost fell over and turned to embrace him. 'Francis! Why are you here?'

'Don't you want me to be?' said her brother. 'Uh, let go, will you? I've not come back unscathed.'

'You're hurt?' Lucy demanded. 'Where? How? You must come inside right away and Grainne will look after you.' The implications suddenly dawned on her. 'But if you're hurt there must have been a battle. Is – is everyone safe?'

Francis took her shoulders gently. Lucy, looking up, read her answer in his face and gave a little gasp, putting her hands to her mouth. 'Who? Who is it? Who's been killed?'

'Ned was killed yesterday,' he said, quietly. Lucy stared at him and then burst into a great storm of tears. Behind her Heppy, despite her delight at her unexpected reunion with Holly, put her apron to her face and started to weep also.

'Who is it? What has happened?' Grainne asked of me; she had only just emerged from the house. Lucy was weeping abundantly all over Francis's chest while the Ashcott people and the soldiers stood around, embarrassed and curious.

'Ned was killed,' I told her. Grainne's face creased with distress. 'Oh, God, no – not Edward as well! How – has there been a battle?'

I explained as concisely as I could the events of the previous day, both for her benefit and for everyone else's. Meraud was dabbing picturesquely at her eyes, and suddenly the full extent of our loss took hold of me, as it had not done before, and I wept exhausted tears into my hands.

Grainne, of course, took charge of this pathetic and

lamenting crowd. Heppy was dispatched to organize an early supper, and arrange for beds for the extra men. Then we were all guided inside the house to warm ourselves by the great fire in the hall, and to let the three most seriously hurt sit down. Jane Tawney reluctantly brought in water and old linen and Meraud, Lucy and Grainne ministered to their injuries.

Throughout all this time I had had no word with Francis. It was as if, with Edward's death and his new command, he had deliberately shut himself apart from me. But now, with Lucy unbuttoning his doublet with more vigour than gentleness, and Meraud piously exclaiming over the sword-gash that raked his left arm from elbow to shoulder (and which I could hardly bear to see, so much did the knowledge that I had nearly lost him for ever frighten me), he caught my eye and gave me a warm, resigned smile with such love in it that despite all our griefs and pains and exhaustion it made me ridiculously happy, so that I could have circled dancing round the hall.

Over supper the battle was fought yet again, for the benefit of Shoosmith and the others, employing saltcellar and knives and pieces of bread for the regiments, and I closed my eyes and tried to imagine the confusion and noise and the wild, exultant terror of fighting that lay behind Francis's impassive description, augmented by the more excited stories of the other four. Radley in particular attempted to dominate the discussion, correcting what Francis had said without apology or explanation, or pointedly interrupting Holly, a mere yeoman's son, whenever he dared to speak. But little by little the story of how Ned had died, of the confusion in that dusk skirmish on the fringe of the battle, was dragged out of Francis again, and I saw Lucy's great eyes shining with tears and admiration, and heard Holly's laconic Suffolk voice saying, 'Well, Master Francis, I'm known as one who allus believe the wust, but thass one good thing hev happened to me, what you did,' and knew from Francis's eyes that his fear that he would not be able to master his imagination had at last been exorcised.

Halfway through the meal, one of the other troopers, a thin young man with a Warwickshire accent named John Hewitt, complained of feeling ill. Meraud, sitting next to him, felt his brow and announced that he had a raging fever; the wonder of it was, I thought as he was bustled, feebly protesting, straightway to bed, that none of the other soldiers showed similar signs. A short sojourn at Ashcott, with the floods which almost invariably afflicted it in winter, would doubtless alter that.

In the night the wind got up and it began to rain. Listening in my bed to Lucy's delicate snores and the intermittent drum of rain and leaves on the window, I felt sorry indeed for the soldiers of either army who were probably somewhere out in this cold, windy, rainy night. Nor did the morning bring much better weather; a grey, scudding sky and heaps of sodden leaves in the courtyard greeted us when we rose. I would in happier times have liked to have gone riding, feeling the wind in my face, in freedom over the sheepwalks, but if attack was expected, it would be foolish to venture beyond the walls. But feeling in need of something – to taste the wind, to take part in the weather, to see things from afar – I slipped away after breakfast and went up the tower.

It had been a favourite place of my childhood. We had enjoyed mad games, Edmund and I, Spanish and English fighting with sticks on the stairs, my skirts hoisted above my knees for ease of footing, or standing on the roof dropping bits of moss on unsuspecting people in the courtyard. Every step up the narrow spiral staircase with the arrow-slits letting knife-edges of wind through that whipped my hair across my face, took me further back to the child I had been, and still was deep inside, despite the veiling skins of love and grief and experience; so that I eventually burst laughing on to the rooftop, to meet the Autumn wind.

I truly had not known Francis was there; we almost collided, hurled by the gale into a breathless embrace, and even when he had done kissing me I was held within his arms as if he would never let me free. 'And what were you doing here, waiting in ambush?' I demanded.

'Watching. You can see more from here than from the walls. And I heard you coming up, and thought I'd surprise you.'

'Which you certainly did. How is your arm today?'

'Well enough, I thank you, lady,' said my beloved, proving it by hugging me closer. 'Are you sure we can't be seen from up here?' I asked anxiously.

'I don't *care*!' Francis yelled recklessly at the sky, and swung me round so that my feet left the ground and one of my shoes flew off and landed by a battlement. With a grunt of pain, he dropped me abruptly. 'I was wrong about my arm. It hurts damnably.'

'It's your own fault,' I reproved him as I hopped in pursuit of my shoe. 'God, what a wind! Don't you want to do something mad – like horses when they've the wind in their heads?'

'Or take wings and fly from the tower; in this gale and with your skirts I'm sure you could go some distance, and it would certainly put any besiegers to flight.'

'Or you with your cloak,' I said, sitting down to put my shoe on. As I dropped below the level of the battlements, the wind was cut off abruptly, and my tormented hair ceased to sting my face. Francis sat down by my side, leaning his back against the stone battlements with a suppressed sigh. Looking at the lines round his mouth, I said, 'Are you *certain* you're all right?'

'Positively,' Francis growled. 'If you don't cease fussing I shall throw over all thought of marrying you; you're fast becoming a second Aunt Hannah.'

I giggled; then a thought struck me, and I said, 'Simon told me that Dominic was in the Lifeguard. Did you see him?'

'Occasionally,' Francis said. 'He's a fine figure of a man in his red coat and gold lacing – are you sure you don't wish to marry him?'

'Quite sure,' I said. 'Did he make any mention of me?'

'No, but he described at great length the charms of various easy-going ladies he'd met with in Italy. Perhaps your face and figure, lovely though they are, would now seem insignificant beside all that opulence. I pray they do; or that he has met with some godly Puritan pikeman on the battlefield. I'm not being totally biased, my love, when I say I didn't entirely like him. And besides, after all that experience in Italy, he may well have the pox.'

'And how can I be sure,' I inquired sweetly, 'that after your sojourn at Oxford you have not?'

'You take my word for it,' Francis said. He added, 'And talking of suitors, that Radley should be steered from Lucy before she realizes how beautiful his barbering is.'

I snorted, but pointed out, 'Who are you to dictate whom she may or may not look at? Anyway, I don't think she's quite so empty-headed as you say. But when she does give her heart, oh then beware, for she's like all of us and will do nothing in small measure.'

'Least of all in love,' Francis said. He leaned back and tipped his head to look at the sky. 'I can't believe that Edward is dead, nor Henry. Of all of us they were the two I'd have thought least likely to have been killed; they were too full of energy to be so easily laid low. On the surface Grainne takes it calmly, but I can see in her eyes how she grieves.'

'She is stronger than I could be,' I said. Francis did not seem to be listening; he went on, almost to himself, 'I'd always wondered what it would be like to kill a man . . . Until I slew the one who shot Ned, I'd not known how it would be – like putting your sword through a sack stuffed with straw, till the blade jars on bone . . . That would not raise him from the dead, but at least it was quick. You know, I rode over the place where the greatest slaughter was, I suppose where the standard had been, and in the dark Goblin could not find her footing between the corpses, and some moved and groaned under her hooves . . . I would have stopped, had it not been for Holly, and that I didn't think that once out of the saddle I could get back in it again. Do you remember, my wise lady, when you warned me of the rider on the red horse? Never was a place more aptly named than that one.' He sat, hands clasping his knees, staring across the tower roof, and clumsily, with a sudden unwonted shyness, I put my arms around him, hoping to afford him some measure of comfort. We sat there a long time without speaking, while the wind gusted above us; until at last Francis disentangled himself, gently, and stood up. 'Since I'm here to watch for the enemy, and moreover in command of this garrison, then I'd best do it.'

'Which way would they come, if they did?'

'Hard to say. If they come from Broughton, or go that way from Banbury, then down Coombe Hill from Milton; if not, then from the Deddington road. Either way, we'll have some warning, but not enough.'

'We might have more,' I said, and told him about Henry's network of informers. Francis grinned. 'Good old Henry seems to have thought of everything. Christ, I wish he was with us now. I've had the story of the falconet from Shoosmith, and very impressive it looks too on its little platform, though I doubt it'd do more than scare off a few ploughboys.'

'It makes a most satisfactory bang and great clouds of smoke, but Henry, I must admit, didn't think it would be of much practical use.' I leaned my arms on the top of a battlement and stared into the wind, my eyes stinging; and then grabbed Francis's arm. 'Look, oh look! What's that, on the top of Coombe Hill?'

A small figure had appeared on the horizon; a man on horseback, perhaps half a mile away. As I watched, more appeared, on foot; scores and scores of them, it seemed, with in the middle what seemed to be a couple of carts. In horror, transfixed, I saw our doom approaching.

'Shut the gates!' Francis bellowed down into the courtyard. One or two startled white faces were briefly turned up to us, and then as he repeated his order, ran to obey. 'Make sure all the women are inside the house,' he said, and ran for the stairs.

I went down after him faster than I had ever done in my life, and at the bottom had to stand aside for Radley and Pryke, running up with a brace of fowling-pieces each. Behind them, carefully, came Reynolds with a small barrel of powder and several bags of shot slung about his person. I ran out into the courtyard, where there was remarkably little confusion. The gates were safely barred. Holly and Shoosmith were manhandling the baskets of stone-shot. and cannon-balls up to the falconet, and Jackson was assembling the tools of the gunner's trade, ladle and linstock and wad and match. Jasper stood in the middle of the courtyard, staring round-eyed, Orange wrapped round his feet. I ran across and took his hand. 'Come on, Jasper, we must go inside.'

'I want to watch the soldiers!' he protested, but I scooped him up, grabbed the kitten by the scruff of its neck and hurried into the hall, closing the door firmly behind me. Once safe, I put Jasper down and ran to warn everyone of the approach of the enemy. I was overtaken by young Hewitt, risen from his bed and hollow-eyed and flushed with fever. 'Are we being attacked, mistress? I must go out to the walls!'

'Lieutenant Heron told me,' I lied firmly, 'that you'd be of more use to him in here. Take a fowling-piece from the armoury below the tower and go up to the other tower and cover our north front so that we may not be surprised there.' That part of the house, the back of the main range of buildings including the hall and the west Tower, was guarded only by a ditch, an embankment and a field, and although any attacking body would probably attempt to force the gates rather than try to scale the walls of the actual house and climb in through the hall windows ten feet above the bottom of the ditch, it was better to be safe than sorry. I pointed out the position of the armoury, and then once more went to look for my cousins and Grainne.

They were gathered in the kitchen, and Lucy was standing with Doll Tawney on a bench and peering out of the window into the courtyard. As soon as I entered I found myself facing a barrage of questions.

'Where have you been, Thomazine?'

'What's happening, for God's sake?'

'Oh, mistress, thank God you're safe!'

'I saw you taking Jasper in hand,' Grainne said, 'for

which many thanks. Come here, sweeting, and you can have a lick of the spoon . . . is it the enemy?'

'Apparently so,' I said. 'Is everyone here?' My eyes swept round; Grainne, Hester, Lucy, Doll, and Heppy. 'My mother and Sue are cleaning in your chamber, mistress,' Doll said. 'Mistress Meraud is reading in the parlour upstairs, and Betty's putting some linen to rights. But my father and young Jack've gone over to Barford to the mill.'

'Then they'll have to stay there,' I said. 'They were warned not to go . . . Where are your other brothers?'

'On the ramparts with the soldiers,' said Doll. 'Master Sewell did teach them how to fire a pistol, but knowing them it won't have had much effect . . . oh, mistress, what about the village?'

'They'll have gone to Milton if they've any sense,' I said. 'What's happening, Lucy?'

Her nose was pressed to the high greenish-glassed window. 'They're all on the walls. There's no firing but everyone has muskets at the ready; Francis is standing up, he's talking, I can see his mouth moving. He's stopped, and all our men are cheering – listen!'

Faintly through the glass we could hear the sounds. 'What do you suppose is happening?' Lucy asked, turning.

'I expect the enemy have summoned us to surrender,' said Grainne. 'And Francis has presumably told them that he will not – probably in rousing terms, hence the cheering. Now they'll fight.'

I looked up at the flimsy beams of the kitchen roof. 'Wouldn't it be best to go back to the main part of the house, until we know better what's happening? If they have got cannon, we're not very well protected here. And we'll know better what's happening, and be able to help.'

So, rather subdued, the five of us and the two children made our way back to the hall. As we did so, the first crack of musket-fire assaulted our ears. Doll's sister, eight-year-old Sue, appeared running, squeaking with terror, and as soon as she saw us burst into frightened tears.

'Go along with you!' Doll scolded her. 'Afraid of a little bit of musket fire? You should be ashamed of yourself. Now sit down there at the table and start tearing up that old cloth to make bandages.' She gave me and Grainne a broad wink and shooed the child over to the hall table, where the pile of old linen, too far gone to be mended, had been placed by Betty for just this purpose. As the rest of us crowded to the windows looking out to the courtyard, an ear-splitting bang rattled the beaded glass and set our ears ringing. Francis had ordered the falconet to be fired.

Hester immediately burst into huge terrified roars. Jasper, ridiculously fatherly, put his arms round her. 'Come on, Hess, don't cry, 'sonly the gun, it won't hurt you. Come 'n' talk to Orange, look, he's scared too.' And he led his little sister over to the cupboard under which the kitten was cowered with flattened ears and puffed up tail.

'Thank God for him and Doll,' said Grainne. More musket fire savaged the end of her words. I peered out of the window nearest the door. Directly opposite stood the gun platform, with the two troopers, Shoosmith and Jackson, feverishly reloading, the latter holding the linstock, with its smouldering match, in readiness for the next firing. The wind tore through his thinning brown hair and forced him to cup his hand round the match to protect the spark. To the right, where the wall curved round to the tower, three soldiers knelt at regular intervals with muskets or fowling-pieces propped between the battlements. I recognized Edwards, and Holly Greenwood, and the third man from the Duke of York's troop, Charles Lawrence, who despite his badly wounded leg was apparently making a valiant effort with his fowling-piece. Up on the tower I knew were Radley and Pryke, and the ailing Hewitt covering our north side from the other tower. To the left of the gun, in the stretch between it and the gatehouse, I could see Francis, kneeling and sighting along his gun, and one of our Suffolkers, Matt Jenkins, beyond him. Craning my neck I could just see Girling's elbow; he was crouched on the little angled stretch between the kitchen and the gatehouse. Presumably those men who were not in view were positioned in the gatehouse itself. A thought struck me; where was Jamie? Withdrawing from the window, I demanded this of Lucy.

'I don't know,' said my cousin anxiously. 'But he was out in the yard earlier, helping to beat match or something, so he may still be there.'

'Well, I can't see him – unless he's in the gatehouse,' I said. At that moment, the falconet fired again, and a cloud of smoke was whipped across the courtyard in a sudden leaf-blown gust of wind. Into the ringing silence which followed the explosion, I said, 'I'm going out to see what's happening.'

'No!' Lucy screamed, clutching at my sleeve. 'You'll be killed!'

'Rubbish,' I retorted. 'There's danger only if they've got cannon, otherwise it's quite safe unless I go dancing on the ramparts.' And I shook her off, opened the door on a rush of wind, and stepped out. The sound of firing was immediately much louder and clearer, a sharp cracking sound. I walked across to the steps and was about to ascend to the ramparts when Francis saw me, put down his gun and, keeping low, made his way along the walk to a spot just above where I was standing. 'What's going on?' I called above the wind and the firing.

Francis glanced over the ramparts and then turned back to me. 'Very briefly, they called on us to surrender in the name of Parliament and the King – a grand piece of hypocrisy, that – and I refused. Whereupon we begun firing at them before they could take cover. Young Jamie – he's in the gatehouse, if you were wondering – he's accounted for one of them, and one of the men on the tower has got another. They've retreated behind the hedge bordering the other side of the road, and they've just begun to return our fire. They haven't any ordnance as yet, though there's some goodly ammunition supplied, by the look of the carts they have with them. So if you want to come out and help us – reloading, carrying powder, anything – then for the moment you'll be quite safe. There'll be food needed before long, and water – no excuse for any to stand idle. Can you organize them for me?'

'Of course!' I returned, feeling the excitement taking

hold of me in answer to the spark in his eyes. 'How many of them are there?'

'I don't want to worry you, but too many for comfort. A company or more, between fifty and sixty men. So hurry! If we can hold them off for long enough, the King's army should relieve us.'

I raced back to the hall with my head full of plans. Once inside, with a scattering of leaves rustling across the floor, I faced the female part of the garrison. Jane Tawney had appeared with more linen, and Meraud was listening to Lucy's urgent description of the siege with a frown across her face. I said, 'They've no ordnance, so it's safe for us in the courtyard. Francis – Lieutenant Heron – wants some of us to go out and reload for the men, carry powder and so on. There's also food and drink to be organized. Meraud and Grainne and Heppy and I can do the reloading. Doll, will you come out too and help where you can?'

'Gladly, mistress,' said Doll with a cheerful grin.

'I'll organize the victuals, then,' said Lucy. 'And Mistress Tawney and Sue can help.'

'Betty, look to the children,' Grainne added. 'Take them somewhere out of sound of the gunfire if you can. My chamber is no good, it looks on to the courtyard, and so does mistress Thomazine's.'

'You may use mine,' Meraud said generously, and Betty disappeared with the two children in tow, patently glad that she was not to be asked to do anything more hazardous. With a quick, breathless, half-fearful look at each other, the five of us who were to reload went out into the courtyard.

For the rest of that morning we laboured; loading and re-loading the muskets and fowling-pieces, replenishing powderhorns, and dragging baskets of stone, left over from the repairs to the wall and the building of the gun platform, to the gatehouse, where Jamie and one of the Tawney brothers hauled them upstairs to the chambers above, to be dropped on the enemy's heads should they come too close. A cauldron of water was simmering with gentle menace over the fire in the tiny kitchen on the ground floor, and a selection of leather buckets stood beside it. 'Boiling water, stones, hot ashes, anything will be effective,' Jamie explained.

At noon the hall door opened. Lucy and her helpers emerged with baskets of food and a barrel of beer, and set the latter down in the courtyard whilst they went round the walls, bent double, to distribute the food so that there should be no break in the firing. I cautiously peered over the ramparts and saw that the enemy were still ensconced behind the hedge, where there appeared to be a good deal of activity, though to what purpose could not be distinguished. There were perhaps a dozen or so musketeers returning our fire, and as I crouched there a bullet, with a whine and a crash, slammed into the battlement beside me, throwing up dust and stone splinters which grazed my cheek and hands.

'Why don't they advance?' I asked Holly, who had come to see if I was safe. He shrugged. 'I don't know, mistress. If they did, happen we'd be overrun, being as they fare t'be too many for us. Happen they don't know as we're so weak, like.'

'Not so weak,' said Charles Lawrence, on his other side. 'We've accounted for five of them now. I think they're afraid of the falconet, though all it's done is send shot over their heads. Ah, there's one showing his round poll too high!' He aimed the fowling-piece carefully, sighted, and fired. 'Got him,' he said with terse satisfaction, and, handing me the gun to reload, picked up another. With blistered hands I dropped the shot into the muzzle, rammed it home, and measured out the powder into the pan. Suddenly there was the distant crack of an enemy musket, followed by a choked cry from the wall next the gatehouse. With sudden terror I twisted round and saw Jenkins on his knees, swaying, his hands to his neck and jets of scarlet spurting between his fingers; then he crashed backwards, on to the barn roof, slid down in a track of blood, and dropped to the ground out of my sight. Doll put down the bags of shot she was carrying from the barn and ran back to his aid. With suddenly uncertain fingers I closed the lid of the powder pan, crawled to the steps and as soon as I was below the level of the ramparts ran down and across to Jenkins' body. Even as I reached him the breath gurgled in his throat, his limbs twitched convulsively and he was dead. Doll, her hands running red where she had vainly tried to stem the flow with her fingers, pulled off her apron and laid it across his face. The first of the garrison was killed; how many more would there be?

Between us, not without difficulty, for Jenkins had been a sturdy man, we somehow half-carried, half-dragged the body to the hall. I could not let myself consider that this had been a few minutes ago a living, breathing, intelligent man, as alive as now were Francis, or Doll, or myself: in the same way as I never when preparing a pheasant for the table could let myself think of the living bird in the glory of its flight.

With the help of Jane Tawney we laid Jenkins in the tower parlour, and I left Doll and her mother to make the corpse tidy. They had stronger stomachs than I. I slipped cautiously out of the hall door, half-expecting to see another body crumpled on the ramparts or sprawled on the ground below, but a quick glance along the walls showed everyone in place, still firing intermittently as rash members of the enemy showed too much of themselves. Obviously our attackers, to have any hope of taking the castle, would have to advance right up to the walls and break down the gates. They could, I reflected, always wait for darkness, but might not have the time.

Shoosmith and Jackson were reloading the falconet. I saw the latter lay an incautious hand on the breech of the gun and snatch it off, swearing. A sudden memory came back to me, of Henry expounding the practice of gunnery at supper one night. 'You can't get more than eight or so rounds an hour out of a gun, and then when it's too hot you must let it cool, or you risk that bursting,' he had said. But the gunners had evidently forgotten that; the falconet had been fired steadily, once every ten minutes or so, ever since morning, and so absorbed were Shoosmith and Jackson in their task that they were about to fire again.

I believe I shouted something; I saw Jackson standing back, and turning inquiringly towards me, as Shoosmith put the linstock to the breech of the gun. With an earshattering roar, the falconet exploded in a cloud of dust and hurtling lethal metal.

I suppose I must have been flung backwards. Fortunately, the rosemary bush prevented me from being hurled into the wall of the house, and I was too far away from the scene of the blast to have been hit by any debris. Dazed, I struggled weakly out of the bush, and stared at the place where the gun had been. There was only a haze of dust and a pile of twisted metal and shattered stone where the blast had demolished part of the wall. On the ramparts I could see, running a panicstricken eye over them, Holly struggling to his knees, and Charles Lawrence staring, bemused like myself, at the wreckage. Edwards, the nearest to the gun, lay on the steps, dead or injured. The only other one on the ramparts had been Francis. He was standing upright, in full view of the enemy musketers, gazing down at the torn bloody rags sprawled across the barn roof, that were all that was left of our two gunners. A flying shard had grazed his forehead and sent a thin thread of blood trickling down his face, which under the powderstains and dust was perfectly white. As I stumbled towards them, he called, 'Thomazine! Stay where you are! It's no sight for you.'

I stayed, my stomach heaving. Fortunately, no one else had been near the gun; Grainne was stationed in the gatehouse, where it was comparatively warm, and Meraud had picked up the shot Doll had put down when Jenkins was killed and had gone up to the tower. Heppy was reloading for Girling and both had been far enough away to be safe. From the tower and the gatehouse our fire was continued with remarkable cool-headedness, I thought, if they had seen the carnage on the walls.

At a shout from Francis, Charles Lawrence and Holly removed their cloaks and laid them across what was left of the gunners. Lawrence limped down the steps to examine Edwards. I saw the eloquent shake of his head, and then his shout of alarm as a musket ball sang past Francis's shoulder.

As if remembering where he was, my cousin dropped down below the battlements, took up his fowling-piece again and began to load it. Lawrence half-carried Edwards to the bottom of the steps and then returned to the walls. I realized that I would have to pass that dreadful scene if I was to carry on loading for them: and I could not. I stood, shaking, trying to summon the courage, and Heppy came running up to me. 'Mistress Thomazine! You can't stay here! Do you look at yourself, and your face is bleeding suffen terrible, do you come inside along o' me.'

'I can't,' I said, 'they need us to reload for them.'

'Not with your hands a-shakin' like that,' said Heppy practically. 'Do you come in and sit down a moment.' She took my arm and pulled me, unresisting, through the hall door, sat me down on a bench and dabbed at my face with a piece of linen. 'And don't you goo a-thinking on they poor men, mistress.'

'I can't help it,' I said. 'One minute they were there, alive, and Jackson was looking to see why I was shouting, and the next . . .' I shuddered. 'Heppy, we can't hold out forever; what if the King doesn't come? What if the castle is taken?'

'He'll come for sartin,' Heppy said, with as much optimism as her brother usually had pessimism. 'Thass jest a doddy little scratch, Mistress, you oon't be marked.'

'What in God's name does my face matter when four men have died for us already?' I demanded with a bitter anger, and walked determined back out into the courtyard. Heppy gave a shrug and a wry grin and followed.

I was able after all to go back on to the walls, keeping my eyes firmly averted from the stained heaped cloaks on the roof. As I joined them, Holly gave me a grin the echo of his sister's, and Charles Lawrence raised his hand in salute. I liked Charles, whom nothing seemed to ruffle. He said now, 'They've taken heart from the gun bursting. If you look carefully, mistress, you'll see they've moved a couple of carts up, and a wagon they must have taken from the village, to give them more and closer cover. They've got something planned – ah, look, see, it's a ram!'

From behind the hedges appeared an extraordinary contraption; a long tree-trunk, slender but quite capable, I thought, of demolishing our flimsy gates. It was slung on a rope cradle between two carts, and the men who were to wield it crouched in the carts or between the straining horses, trying to conceal themselves as best they could from our musket-fire. At once Charles aimed, steady-handed, and pulled the trigger, and a figure dropped like a stone from between the horses and vanished under the wheels of one of the carts. Holly aimed likewise, for the horses, and wounded one of them; with a scream it reared up in the traces and was hastily cut loose to stumble out of the way. Slowly, inexorably, the ram drew closer to our gates, and we had not the firepower to stop it.

And then something was shot from the window of the gatehouse, something bright and flaming that left a great plume of smoke arcing behind it, and sank with a thud and a sudden burst of flame into the front of one of the carts. 'My God!' said Charles, leaning further than was safe between the battlements. 'That was a fire arrow!'

I glanced down the line of the ramparts and saw that George Tawney and his brother had taken Francis's place on the walls, and that Francis himself was nowhere to be seen. Another arrow soared from the window and plunged into the belly of the other cart. Sheets of flames and screaming men erupted from it; evidently it had been filled with straw. The horses were running amok, kicking and plunging, trying to escape from the flames harnessed firmly behind them. One cart was pulled one way, the other a different one; the tortured, smouldering ropes snapped and the ram was deposited squarely upon the ground twenty yards from the gatehouse, while the carts, both furiously ablaze, were pulled by the frantic horses along the length of our walls for us to shoot at as we would. One eventually overturned and the other came to a halt by the village, according to Pryke, who told us afterwards that it barely missed setting fire to the cottages. The Parliament men retired behind the hedge to lick their wounds and to think of a more orthodox method of forcing the gate.

By now it was approaching dusk, and with the dying of

the day the wind had also died, bringing us only fitfully the smell of the charred carts. Charles Lawrence wiped the sweat from his face, leaving a damp pink smear across the dirt. 'Well, first round to us, I think. Whoever's in command of them certainly has ingenuity, but I feel Lieutenant Heron is a match for him in that.'

Jamie came scampering up the steps to us, casting never a glance at the hidden remains of our gunners congealing on the barn roof. 'Did you *see* that? Wasn't it good? It was Francis's idea; he wrapped a crossbow bolt in pitch and rag and set light to it before he shot. Lucky thing your father kept hunting crossbows, Thomazine.'

'They were my mother's; she was a huntress to emulate Diana, he always said.' I shivered in the sudden chill; the sky was clearing, and bright and sparkling in the southern sky, the evening star had appeared to promise fine weather on the morrow. 'Have they given up, do you think?'

'For tonight, Francis says. Look, you can see behind the hedge, they've lit a fire. I expect some of them will be quartered in the village. There's a watch to be kept all night, of course, in case they try any tricks; we'll be ready for them if they do!'

Slowly, flexing my weary blistered hands, I got to my knees and stretched my arms. Grainne's voice of calm and sanity came from below. 'Thomazine? You're under strictest orders to go at once within doors; Jamie too.'

We crept, bent cautiously double, down the steps and walked across to the hall door. Francis had emerged from the gatehouse and was directing what remained of our garrison, allotting sentry-duties, and organizing the tidying of the gun-platform and the removal of the bodies of Shoosmith, Jackson and Edwards. I lifted the latch and gratefully entered the dim normality of the hall. To see it just as usual, with the long tables and benches dark shapes in the gloom, lit only by one hesitant candle, was to feel that all the events of the past few hours had been nothing but a bad dream from which we had only now awoken. But if I glanced out of the window I would be able to see the wreckage of the gun, and the decently shrouded bodies now laid out in the courtyard. Deliberately, preserving the illusion, I did not look out.

Francis left three men outside on the first watch, and Lucy and Heppy took them out their supper. The rest of us ate in the hall, now less fitfully illuminated, and our talk ran on the siege and on what the enemy would try next. Radley was of the opinion that they would attempt a night attack, and waxed eloquent on the dangers of being unprepared until Heppy and Betty grew pale and clutched each other.

'If you'd care to take over the command, Trooper Radley,' Francis said, leaning back in his chair and gently turning the wine-cup between his long fingers, 'then I'm perfectly willing to resign it.' And Radley, after some justificatory bluster, retreated into silence. After that, it was an uncomfortable meal, with every ear strained to catch the first sounds which might herald attack. Nor, when I eventually crawled into my bed, did the night prove any more relaxing. Lucy had been in good spirits all day, playing the beleaguered heroine, I had thought unkindly, but now her fear was hardly concealed, and it would not take much for her brave facade to crack. So she, Heppy and I huddled together in the one bed for comfort and warmth, but it was a long, long time before I slept. Mercifully, my dreams did not, as I had dreaded, repeat that terrible moment when I had seen Jackson turn towards me in answer to my warning, only to be blown to pieces a few seconds later; but my slumber was not a peaceful one.

We woke at first light and looked out of the window on to an unchanged courtyard and the men on watch in positions unaltered from those of the previous night, save that these were different men, Francis among them and distinguished by the pale hair drifted around his shoulders. There had been a frost, and the courtyard was sparkling silver with it; every stone and blade of grass outlined in white fire, the men's breath like plumes of smoke in the still cold bright air. We had to rub frozen ferns from the window-panes before we could see out, and there was ice in the ewer of water in which we had washed before going to bed. The fire was quite dead, and Heppy set about clearing it with her usual cheerfulness, just as if there were not sixty-odd Parliament men waiting beyond our gates. Lucy and I helped each other to dress, putting on our warmest clothes and with chilled fingers dragging a comb through Lucy's sleek black ringlets and my own cloud of hair, wood-brown and unruly. I could not keep myself from wondering where we would be at this hour tomorrow – here, performing the same office for each other, with hearts lightened after the lifting of the siege? Or emerging from haystack or ditch after being ejected from Ashcott? Who would be living, this time tomorrow, and who would be dead?

'Ow, you pulled,' said Lucy, with a little less than her usual good humour; and I apologized for my inattention.

Breakfast came and went, and no imminent attack seemed in the offing. One or two groups of men could be glimpsed behind the shielding hedge, but they were careful to keep out of range of our marksmen. The sun rose higher, and filled the courtyard with brilliant yellow light and blue frosty shadows. Imperceptibly the atmosphere inside Ashcott relaxed. Radley and Pryke, back on the tower roof, could be heard singing a bawdy song in remarkably good harmony – surprising, their new comradeship, since Radley, the gentleman volunteer, had so plainly thought himself superior to Pryke, the carpenter's son. In the gatehouse, surrounded by ready-loaded fowling-pieces and smouldering match and muskets, Reynolds and Jamie were swapping jokes. 'Did you hear the one about the gentleman who had an Irish servant? He asked him to bring a half-pint of claret and a half-pint of ale, and the man bought back a pint mug telling him that if he drank through the ale at the top he'd reach the claret at the bottom.'

'I'm not sure I should laugh at that, being Irish myself,' said Grainne to me as we stood by the door of the gatehouse, watching Jasper and Hess playing with Orange in the sunshine. The scene was one of deceptive tranquillity, but just then the calm was shattered by Jasper's screech of pain. 'Mother! Mother! Orange scratched me, I was only playing and he scratched me!' Grainne, with a rueful glance in my direction, briskly escorted her bleeding and unhappy offspring within doors, while the garrison, whose state of nerves were unequal to the strain of such interruptions, breathed again and returned to their watch. After a quick glance at Hester, who was now gathering stones together in the dust with her usual concentration, I ascended the steps to the ramparts.

'Very quiet,' said Charles, taking a swig from the leather jack beside him. 'That fare t'be too quiet,' Holly corrected, with his usual gloom. 'I reckon they be plotting suffen. There han't bin no sight nor sound o' them, no nawthen at all. Thass too quiet.'

'Not with them up there,' I said, nodding my head up to the Tower, from whence snatches of cheery song assailed my ears. 'I hope they're watching as well as singing.'

'I could do with some singing myself,' said Charles, leaning comfortably against the battlements. 'Let's match 'em, show 'em we can do better – do you sing, mistress?'

'I in't singing,' said Holly disapprovingly. 'That fare t'be suffen duzzy, to go a-doing that. Happen it'd take your mind off of what *they're* a-doing.' He turned firmly and fixed his eye on the hedge. Charles shrugged. 'The longer they wait, the better chance we have of being relieved. Their commander must be a lack-wit, to come out here with sixty valuable men when his own garrison's threatened, and waste a day on us. For all he knows, Banbury's taken.'

'Or may not be,' I said, 'the Prince was all for ignoring Banbury and Broughton and making a lightning march on London. If he's done that – and we don't know he hasn't – if he went by the quickest route he'd not go within miles of here, and then our ingenious enemy has all the time in the world to plan his assault.'

A wild yell and a crack of musket fire from the tower proved that they were at least alert. 'They're moving!' Radley's voice bawled down at us, broken by another report as his companion fired in his turn. Charles snapped into position with astonishing speed, considering his relaxed casual mood of a moment before. No thought in my head but a burning desire to see what was happening, I peered between the next battlements, heart banging against my ribs, and saw men bursting from behind the hedge and running towards us. They were each carrying something bulky and apparently quite heavy; I stared bewildered until the first of them stood their burdens upright on the ground and crouched behind them, provided at once with a screen and a rest on which to prop their muskets. The first bullet whipped over my head, and I hastily dropped out of sight as Charles and Holly opened fire in return.

'Thomazine!' Francis yelled from his place further down the wall. 'They're making an assault! Get down and get inside before you're hurt!'

'But reloading—' I began indignantly. My true love forestalled me. 'Get inside! *Now*!'

Resentfully, I crawled down towards the steps. Doll, her skirts hoisted above her ankles, was running for cover. Francis turned back to fire; and Charles said into the crackling air, 'What in the name of God is that?'

Francis was not looking at me. I plunged back to my original position and stared over. A couple of men were running from screen to screen, carrying something large and black shaped rather like a tall-crowned hat. Charles aimed his fowling-piece and fired; his cursing announced that he had missed. And then the men had vanished out of our sight, into the sheltered space below the jutting first storey of the gatehouse.

Francis whipped round, his voice in its urgency echoing across the courtyard. 'All of you, get inside! Now, for your lives!'

Holly and Charles scrambled helter-skelter for the steps, their guns and shot and powder clasped close. I followed them, bewildered and afraid. Francis came up running behind me. 'I thought I'd told you to get inside! Do it now, or you'll be killed!'

I reached the bottom step and turned. 'What is it?'

'A petard. They'll fix it to the gate and blow it to pieces, probably within two minutes. Now *run*!'

Stumbling, I obeyed. In the gatehouse, Jamie's white face could be seen at an upstairs window, mouth open, protesting. 'Can't we drop—?'

'Do you *want* to be blown to Kingdom Come? Reynolds! Get him down, *now!*'

The face disappeared abruptly, and ten seconds later Jamie emerged from the door, propelled by Reynolds, both laden with weapons. I hurtled through the open door into the hall, seeing startled women's faces, and Holly and Girling and Charles manhandling one of the cupboards over to the door to block it. Jamie, Reynolds and Francis arrived hot on my heels; Francis hurled the great door to with a crash that shook the glass, and wrenched the bolts home, top and bottom. 'Get under the tables. When the petard blows it'll shatter the glass. Reynolds, go and secure the other door by the tower, and cover that. Put your musket stock through the glass to fire through, if the explosion hasn't done it for you. Jamie, go up to the tower, take the shot and powder and a couple of muskets, and support those two. Tell 'em what's happening, and when the gate's gone keep the courtyard under as heavy a fire as you can manage. Girling, leave that and go and cover from the kitchen – that's the only other door, isn't it?' I nodded breathlessly. He went on, his face bright with a kind of desperate elation. 'Is everyone accounted for? Hewitt's upstairs, who's here? . . .' He glanced round the women and children cowering behind the tables, Grainne and Jasper, Doll and her sister and mother, Meraud . . . The far door opened and George Tawney and his brother entered; they had been covering the north side since daybreak. Then my stomach churned within me, and I said on a small terrified note, 'Grainne, where's Hester?'

Utter silence, save for our frightened breathing and little Sue's sobs. 'There!' Holly cried, pointing at the window.

Outside, the courtyard was bright and still and clear, a small vivid picture through the glass; calm before disaster. Across our vision strolled Orange, tail erect as a flag, and behind, pursuing with unsteady, single-minded concentration, came Hess.

In a flash, I was at the door, straining back the bolts and clawing at the latch. Grainne was with me, to reach the top bolt that I could not; Francis shouted something as we hauled open the door and ran into the courtyard. Grainne screamed 'Hess!' and the child turned her head briefly and then wobbled on, her hand outstretched within an inch of Orange's flaming tail.

And then the petard exploded.

As when the gun had burst, I was flung backwards, but with far greater force. I must have lost consciousness for a few seconds, and came to myself on the ground, my eardrums ringing and dust in my eyes, on my dress, choking me. I remembered Grainne – it was all I did remember – and struggled on to all fours, dust and debris dropping from my clothes, crawling towards where she had been. As the sunshine filtered through the haze I saw the tiny scrap of dust-clogged fur that was Orange, hurled many yards by the explosion; and beyond was Grainne, kneeling, all that could be seen of her a bent black head, black dress, and a white apron all sifted and scattered with dust and bits of wood and plaster as she cradled Hess in her arms. Then a yell of 'For Parliament and the King!' echoed from sixty throats, as the enemy musketeers trod hotfoot through and over the wreckage of the gatehouse and poured into the courtyard.

I knew then that if they opened fire, or if the few behind us did likewise, then we would be killed for certain, caught in the crossfire. In the few seconds left to me, I believe I prayed, feeling a great yearning terror that Francis and I should thus be torn asunder after all my fears – 'Oh God, no, don't fire, don't kill me, don't kill him . . .'

Francis ran past me; he hurled his sword away and stood in front of Grainne, his hands empty and his head bare, haloed by the sun with a ring of fiery dust. 'Hold your fire!' he yelled, 'we surrender!'

I stared, seeing the musketeers lower their weapons, the dragoons put up their carbines. A man of middle height, with straight mouse-brown hair framing a brown, ugly, wide-mouthed face walked forwards, stooping to pick up Francis's discarded sword. My cousin went on, more softly, a kind of despairing resignation woven somewhere into his voice. 'As commander of this garrison in the King's name, I surrender it to you, and ask for quarter for all within the walls.'

One by one, incredulously, our troopers emerged, weaponless, to stand in the courtyard. I could ignore them now; Grainne and Hess and I were safe, saved from sure death by Francis's surrender, not only of the castle, but of his honour. Obstinately, I crawled over to Grainne. She was rocking backwards and forwards, crooning something; but all I could see of Hess was a small pink hand, curled limply like a wilted flower against the smudged black of her mother's gown. Chilled to the bone, I shook Grainne's shoulder. 'Grainne! Grainne! Is she hurt?'

Slowly, unwillingly, my dear friend laid down her burden in the dust. The round tawny eyes, so like Henry's, were open on nothing, the bright rosy face drained of all colour under the dust; and on the soft curve of her temple was a great bloody mark where some piece of debris had cracked her delicate skull as if it were made of glass.

'She was living when I took her up,' Grainne said, her eyes fixed on the small dead face. 'She breathed still, and saw me – I pray God she saw me – oh, Hess, little one, you were too young to die in battle . . . how shall I tell Jasper?'

A shadow fell over us. Someone coughed, embarrassed. I looked up, shaking with grief and anger, and beheld a very sturdy solid Roundhead sergeant, twisting his hat in his hands. 'Excuse me, mistress – Captain Ashley wants you to go inside now.'

I gestured at the dead child. 'So hastily? Surely he can leave her mother to grieve for a moment longer?'

'It's not safe, madam,' said the sergeant, not meeting my eyes. 'The men are ripe for mischief; they've lost twenty of their number killed or wounded by your garrison, and some of them, mistress, if I may be frank, would have the clothes off your back, given the chance, aye, and you on your back, too, most like. I'll take the child, shall I, madam?'

Grainne gave him a small, meaningless smile and rose to her feet. The big man stooped and gathered Hess into his arms. Grainne had closed her eyes, and the mark on her forehead was hidden against his breastplate, so that it seemed she was merely asleep in the deep puppyish slumber of the very young. Grainne turned to me, her eyes distraught, and I took her hand, and we followed him in.

The hall floor was covered in glass, wrenched from the window-panes by the force of the blast; it crunched under our feet. In one corner all the women and children were wailing together, Betty crying that she did not want to be ravished. In another corner, by the big oak table, the remaining members of our garrison stood, silent, stunned, relieved. And in the middle of the hall, the sun striking reddish sparks from her hair like steel on flint, was Lucy, white-faced, eye to eye with the brown-haired man who must be Captain Ashley. 'We are *not* going! Not for an undisciplined rabble who've invaded our peace and killed our friends . . .' Her gaze travelled over his shoulder to the sergeant and suddenly tears flooded her face. 'Oh, no, not Hess! Not her as well . . . Why the children, why is it always the children? . . . You men and your wars,' said my cousin with a new and bitter defiance, 'you'll not have done till all of us are dead.' She slid past him and went to take Grainne's other hand, and with me helped her to a chair. Captain Ashley came to us. Looking up, I saw his face hovering above us; a kind, humble, serious, ugly face, with deep grey eyes and lines of weather about his mouth. He might be thirty years or less, it was hard to say. He said softly to Grainne, 'Madam, what can I say? I am most desperately sorry, if I could have foreseen this I would never have begun at all . . . to have lost your husband, I hear, and now your child . . .'

'No, it's not your fault,' said Grainne. 'It's no one's fault, save for the fools who involved us in this coil in the first place. So if there is anything to forgive you for, then I forgive you – it wasn't your fault.'

'But I shall always have it on my conscience, shall always feel responsible for what has happened,' said the captain. 'If there is any reparation I can make, anything I can do, you have only to ask and it shall be done.'

'Then let us all go,' Grainne said. 'The soldiers as well,

they're our friends and servants and brothers. If you intend to fortify this place for the Parliament, then it may well have to suffer another attack, and I do not mean to risk my other children, and my friends.'

There was silence. Lucy stared at her with drenched, miserable eyes, for this was the opposite of what she had just demanded. And Francis, bareheaded, reserved, said into the quiet, 'That will be our request, Captain. To go free, whoever of us may wish to leave, with carts and baggage and horses and weapons, to wherever we may choose, severally or together.'

Whatever had been the captain's original intention regarding us, it had now altered. Hester's death had laid Ashcott open to him, but it had also laid a duty on him, to honour Grainne's wishes, and I knew at once that like Simon, but more humanely than Simon, he was a man who set great store by duty.

'So be it,' he said, a brief sorrowful smile lightening his seriousness for a moment. 'I will write you a pass will carry you wherever you wish to go, within the authority of Parliament; without it, you will I trust also be safe. Who among you wishes to leave, and where do you want to go?'

Suffolk was a possibility that leaped to mind, but I thought of Grainne, six months gone with child, and young Hewitt, delirious upstairs, and Charles and Francis also hurt, and knew that it was too far. 'I have a house in Oxford,' I said. 'Would that do, Lieutenant Heron?'

Francis threw me a quick appreciative smile. 'It will do well, for the moment. Who wishes to come to Oxford?'

Grainne, of course, and Betty, Lucy and Meraud and Jamie, and Heppy, and all who remained of our garrison. Jane Tawney said, 'My husband and I stay here, sir. Mistress Thomazine may rest assured that her property will be looked after while garrisoned for the Parliament.'

Captain Ashley wrote out the pass on the hall table, with borrowed quill and ink and paper; for four ladies, two boys, two maidservants, Lieutenant Francis Heron and seven troopers. Then we were given an hour in which to make ready. I stared down at the pass on the table with the neat signature at the bottom: Daniel Ashley, Captain, Earl of Peterborough's regiment of foot, and wondered whether we would have had such kind usage from any other Roundhead captain.

It was arranged between Francis and Ashley that the remains of our four killed men should be interred in Deddington as soon as possible, by the Roundheads; we were in Adderbury Parish, but it seemed unlikely that Master Oldys would oblige the hated Parliament men by burying those they had slain without a fight, verbal or otherwise. Pryke, the carpenter's son, with sorrowful hands made a little makeshift box in which the remains of Hess could be decently laid until we reached Oxford and could direct her proper burial. 'For I'll not face Oldys again, even for the sake of laying her by her father,' said Grainne. 'If there is a Heaven, and Henry with all his faults has gained entrance, then she will surely be with him there.'

After the allotted hour, we were ready to go, gathered in the courtyard under the sullen, jealous eyes of Ashley's men, who had been thwarted of their plunder and were now clearing the wreckage that the petard had caused. One cart held our baggage, as much as we had managed to gather together in the time: chests of clothes, books, musical instruments, the last of our money, a basket or two of food; the other contained only Hester's pathetic little coffin. All was ready, Captain Ashley conversing with Francis as the latter sat his beautiful black Goblin, speaking of the admirable defence he and the garrison had made, and Francis in turn complimenting him on his ingenuity with the ram and the petard, as if twelve of Ashley's men and four of ours, and Hess, had never died in the struggle for Ashcott, my own castle and the charming, golden, peaceful home of my childhood.

And then, echoing again that earlier, dreadful moment, Lucy looked round from atop her horse and said, 'Where is Jasper?'

Grainne's green eyes swept the courtyard and came to rest, with fear, on my face. Captain Ashley was undeniably to be trusted, but his men were not, and what they could do to a boy, however precocious and valiant, three and a half years old, did not bear thinking about. I kicked my legs free of stirrup and pommel and slid down from Chalcedony. 'I'll look for him. He's probably wandered off somewhere.'

'I'll look in the house, Mistress Sewell, I saw him there last,' said Betty, and ran as fast as her stout legs could carry her for the door, Ashley's lieutenant following her to offer assistance. I glanced round the courtyard, at kitchen, barn, stables, granary, well, and made first for the nearest, which was the barn.

The deep dim light within made it hard to see anything. A smaller door had been cut in one of the larger ones to admit a man when it was unnecessary to open the main doors, and I stepped through this and left it ajar to let in some light. Jasper had always liked this place. It was probably here that Hess had been, unnoticed, before that last fatal pursuit across the courtyard, and I knew that the piled hay was an irresistible draw. Calling softly, I moved towards it. 'Jasper? Jasper, are you there? We're going soon, and we don't want to leave you behind.'

Silence, I looked around; and then a small sound made me glance up. Half the barn had had a loft made in the rafters for apples and grain-sacks, reached by a ladder. And over the edge of the loft, peering down in the gloom, Jasper's small elfin face came into view. I gasped with relief. '*There* you are! However did you get up there? Can you get down?'

Jasper said nothing, only stared at me. Then, abruptly, his face vanished. I muttered an oath under my breath, dragged the ample skirts and petticoats of my riding-habit over one arm and began, awkwardly, to ascend the ladder. Made by William Tawney, it did not look sturdy enough to support Jasper's weight, let alone mine, and at any moment I expected to feel the crack and sickening jerk of a rung breaking under my foot. How the child had got up, God alone knew, or for what reason.

I reached the top, trembling with nerves and effort, and gratefully put my weight upon the trustworthy boards of the loft. Apples and pears lay on slatted shelves to my right, vanishing into the gloom, and to the left were sacks of grain and flour, stored up here out of the reach of damp and vermin when the granary grew full. By one of these Jasper was kneeling, bent over something laid on the sack, talking to it softly in a way that prickled the hair on the back of my neck and sent gooseflesh running along my skin. For what he had there, I saw in the dim light, was the corpse of Orange.

I had not heard of grief and shock overturning the wits of any child so young, but I feared for Jasper now. Slowly, quietly, so as not to frighten him, although he had known and loved me from his birth, I tiptoed up to him and knelt down by his side. 'Jasper, my poppet, you must leave the kitten now, and come down with me. Your mother wants you.'

No answer from the child. I tried again, striving to keep my voice normal and level. 'Jasper, Orange is dead. He can't hear you now, he's dead.'

'No!' Jasper screamed. 'He's not dead! You won't take him away, you won't, you won't!' And he snatched the kitten up and clutched it to his black-clad chest; above it, his green eyes blazed hotly at me, distraught and bewildered after so much loss. From somewhere came a small, suffocated squeak, and momentarily distracted I looked round for mice where no mice could be. Then I held my hand out gently to the boy, saying gently, 'Please, Jasper, put him down and come down with me to your mother.'

'No!' Jasper cried again, struggling backwards, still on his knees, clutching his precious burden still tighter. There was another squeak, and unbelieving I stared at the bundle of fiery fluff, seeing a small, pink-padded, desperately scrabbling paw. 'Jasper, for Christ's sake put him down before you crush him to death! Can't you hear him crying?'

Jasper stared down incredulously. His hands relaxed, and Orange's indignant head, all owl-round eyes and flattened ears, popped up from behind his arms and shook itself. With a wriggle and a scratch, he extracted himself, stalked a pace or two away, and began to wash the thick dust from his once-beautiful fur. Jasper's face split into a huge, glorious, joyful smile. 'I *said* he wasn't dead!'

'That cat will have to be renamed Lazarus,' I said. 'Are you coming now, or shall we leave you both behind?'

Suddenly obedient, Jasper snatched up Orange again and trotted with me to the ladder, the kitten struggling furiously. I was racking my brains for a way to get down when a welcome voice called up from the doors. 'Thomazine! What are you doing? Have you found him?'

'Yes, Jamie, I've found him – can you come and help us down?'

My youngest cousin came to the foot of the ladder and stared up. 'What's he got there? Not another kitten?'

'Not another, but the same old Orange. He can only have been stunned by the explosion, and Jasper had the sense to see it and raise him from the dead,' I explained, looking down at the boy and the cat as if to reassure myself that he was indeed alive and it was no figment of our imaginations. Jamie whistled. 'Well, I should think that's about five of his nine lives gone at one fell swoop. Well done, Jasper, now let's get you down.'

He took the child while I was left with the twisting, angry kitten. We emerged from the barn to amazed looks; I had not been the only one to assume that Orange was killed.

Grainne stared at the cat who had, indirectly, caused her daughter's death, and then smiled at her son. 'Well, who'd have thought it, sweeting? Put him in the cart and ride with Betty – I'm glad he's safe.' And looking at her worn, bleak, smiling profile, I knew that she meant it.

One by one, picking our way through what remained of the gatehouse, we rode out of Ashcott, the scene of hope and destruction, of love and delight and sudden death, and turned towards Deddington and the Oxford road. The villagers, curious and solemn, lined the track to see us go, and some waved and commiserated with us; but Francis rode past them, his face utterly still and set, without turning his head to see once again the scene of his failure. Behind him came Radley and Pryke, similarly impassive, heading the women and children and carts and the litter; bringing up the rear were Girling and Jacobson, the Northampton-shire blacksmith. Of all of us, only I looked back, half-expecting to be transformed to a pillar of salt like Lot's wife, seeing the little sleepy castle, almost, were it not for the wrecked gatehouse, untouched by the dread hand of war. The tawny banner of Essex, the Lord General, flew insolently from the tower against a suddenly black northern sky, illuminated with the brilliant clarity of sunshine on the brink of rain. Tears welled in my eyes as I thought of all that our surrender might mean, and of the bitter price we had paid for Ashcott, most particularly Grainne; and then, resolutely, I turned my face towards the Oxford road.

It wanted an hour to noon when we left Ashcott, in blazing sun with sixteen-odd miles to go before dark. Accordingly, Francis set a brisk pace, and as the miles rolled away behind us I began to hope cautiously for a night spent under a proper roof instead of in ditch or barn. But within an hour, before we had gone five miles from Deddington, the sky turned dark and threatening, grey grim clouds hung above us, a cold wind whipped at our cloaks and a curtain of rain drove towards us from the north. Fortunately, we had our backs to it, so it was not as unpleasant as it might have been; but before long we were all soaked to the skin, drenched and shivering. Then the rain swept south to Oxford, leaving us to struggle on through mud and puddles in a fitful sunshine that did nothing to warm or dry us, despite the steam rising from our wet garments, as if, said Charles with a gleam of mischief in his eyes, we were a travelling laundry. He was the only one who was at all cheerful; Francis, with a face like stone, had not spoken to anyone for hours, not even to the damp and miserable Drake at his horse's heels; Grainne was silent, grieving for her child; Lucy had rain and tears mixed, drying on her face; Meraud's mouth moved soundlessly, presumably praying; and even Jamie was cast into the depths of gloom. By the time we came within sight of the towers and spires of Oxford, glowing gold against a thundercloud in the last of the sun, we were exhausted, hungry and in the last stages of despair. It was Wednesday, one of the days of market, and the broad street of St Giles, lined with trees and houses and the fair college of St John, was thronged with country people with cart and wagon and packhorse, hastening to be home before darkness fell. They looked curiously at our wet, bedraggled convoy, and made way for us with a resentful alacrity which suggested that their previous experience of soldiers had not been pleasant.

The north gate, with the prison known as Bocardo, barred our way; to the right, the town wall ran round towards the castle high on its mound by the river Isis, and to the left were the houses lining the wide street which led to the parish of Holywell. The gates were open and apparently unguarded, people passing through freely; we joined the crowd, pushing against those making their way out of the town, but it was too much to hope that a group such as ours would enter unmolested. Of a sudden two citizens in ill-fitting breast and back plates, and pot helmets, brandishing a pike apiece, stepped threateningly into Francis's path, while another strung a chain across to block our way. 'Halt! Where d'you think you're going?'

For a moment, Francis said nothing; then, as if recalling his mind from a very great distance, told them, 'We're going to a house in St Aldate's parish . . . escorting these ladies.'

'You're soldiers!' said one of the pikemen, on a note of discovery. Charles cast his eyes heavenwards, and there was derisive laughter from the jostling, hindered crowd. 'Aye, Harry, that's what men with swords and breastplates and pistols generally are these days!' someone called out rudely, and another voice, closer at hand, added *sotto voce*, 'More than you can call yourselves.'

'Whose soldiers?' asked the other pikeman, rather more alert than his companion. 'King or Parliament?'

Francis, I could see, was beyond any subterfuge. 'King,' he said, his voice curiously hoarse, and at once shouting broke out, some yelling, 'Let them through!' and others demanding that we be forthwith clapped in the castle. The pikemen looked at each other; I felt that if they had not had pot helmets, they would have scratched their heads.

'What d'you reckon, Dick? Do we let 'em through?'

'I dunno – there ain't many of 'em, and they're a sorry enough crew. Hey, sir, what house in St Aldate's? I know the parish well enough, my sister lives there.'

I felt it was time to intervene. I did not know what was wrong with Francis, but he seemed to have been robbed of the power of speech, and was staring blankly at the citizens. I pushed Chalcedony past everyone, excusing myself to the people crowding round, and addressed myself to Harry and Dick. 'It's my house we're going to – in Pennyfarthing Street, on the south side; a good big house built of stone, with two gables.'

'I know that one,' said Dick. 'That's the one old Widow Gooch lives in, her that's a bit touched in the head. But I thought she'd leased that house from one o' the colleges – did you know any different, Harry? No, I thought not, you don't know nothing, do you?'

Cheers from a section of the crowd, who seemed to know Harry of old. He grinned round at them amiably; the whole thing seemed like a performance, put on for the benefit of the people of Oxford, and at another time might have been amusing, but now my frustration seethed up. Fortunately, I could remember the Widow Gooch, who was certainly somewhat peculiar in her habits, and whom I had once reckoned to be a witch; she was some poor relative of my stepmother, Jane Willoughby, and my father had solved her want of a roof over her head and his desire for someone to look after his second wife's Oxford house by installing her as housekeeper. Since his death and my removal to Suffolk, she had resided there alone. I said, thinking back ten or more years, 'I can tell you of her, if you doubt me – she's a little grey-haired old lady, always wears black. She keeps chickens in the kitchen and loves them as if they were her own flesh and blood.'

Dick gave a shout of laughter. 'Aye, mistress, I can see you know her.'

'And moreover,' I continued in what Lucy had once

called my 'great lady' voice, 'we have this day been turned out of our house by soldiers, and this lady behind me has lost both her husband and her little daughter to them, and we have not come twenty miles to safety to face your obstructiveness. So would you please, please let us pass, before we drop dead of weariness before your gates?'

There were murmurs of sympathy from the women in the crowd, and more cries of, 'For God's sake let 'em through, simpletons!' Someone else, more practical and less altruistic, added, 'I for one want to get home before midnight.' A lone voice from the back yelled, 'The strumpets have only got what they deserve!' and was instantly set upon by half-a-dozen men more sympathetic to our case. There seemed to be quite a brawl developing. Dick and Harry looked at each other, at me, and grinned. 'All right, mistress, you can pass, and all your men with you.' The chain dropped, and with a cheer and a creaking and lurching of carts and litter, we were through the gate and into the broad sweep of North Street.

'Thank you,' said Francis to me. 'Is the Widow Gooch as terrifying as she sounds?'

'No, but she's touchy as well as touched. I was always told she'd never been the same since her husband died, but I wonder if there ever was a Master Gooch.' I glanced at him, taking my first good look at him since we had left Ashcott, and saw the heavy, brilliant eyes, dark-circled, and a face blazing with fever. I said, horrified, 'You're not well! I *thought* there was something wrong.'

'Don't fuss, Aunt Hannah,' Francis retorted, and set his jaw to control the wave of shivering that shook his body. On the other side of him, an earnest countrywoman was asking if he had been at Kineton Fight and if he had seen her son, and Francis turned away to reply. At once several more people jostled our horses, asking for news or, in the case of the ghoulish, inquiring what had happened to us. Exasperated at Francis's stubbornness, I set my face in a mask of bad temper and said not a word. Still escorted by a curious crowd, we came to Carfax, where the four main streets of Oxford met, and continued south in the growing dusk down Fish Street. Now I could recognize landmarks from the times when I had spent days in my stepmother's house, and with my brother Edmund had known the area round about, and most particularly the more generous kitchens, like the backs of our hands. There was the Blue Boar, on the corner of New Lane to my left, and after it on the opposing corner John Henslow's house with the Racket Court behind it, where my father in his youth had worked off his excess energy as a student at Christchurch. The walls of that collage loomed up beyond it, and opposite stood the church of St Aldate's and just before it the welcome, dearly familiar shapes of the houses of Pennyfarthing Street. We had reached our destination at last.

chapter eight

Pennyfarthing Street

Now if thou would'st, when all have given him over,
From death to life, thou might'st him yet recover.
(Drayton, 'Sonnets')

Our bedraggled, weary little procession followed me around the church and into the road that ran behind the house. There was the high wall bounding the garden, interrupted by a wooden gate, large enough to admit a cart or a small coach, and I leaned stiffly from my saddle and hammered on it with my fist.

'There can't be anyone to hear, can there?' asked Jamie, dismounting. He walked up and added his own tattoo to mine. Out of the tail of my eye I saw some of our escort dismounting or sliding down from their mounts, stretching their legs gratefully. Sudden panic, a feeling which only afflicted me when in the last stages of exhaustion, took hold of me. What if the Widow Gooch really had gone mad? What if she refused to let us in, or kept us waiting for hours, or called for the Watch?

'All right, all right, no need for that noise, I'm coming.' A testy, croaking voice fell into the silence following Jamie's last, most desperate battering. There was the sound of a key being turned, then the gate opened very, very slowly and a white-coifed head glimmered round it in the gloom. The sky was heavy and threatening with the approach of another storm, the rumblings of it already whispering menacingly in the distance, and the tense air around us only added to the prickle on my spine at the sight of the Widow Gooch, of whom I had been a little afraid with a thrill of childish, superstitious, almost enjoyable terror. She peered from one man to the next, muttering to herself, and then said, 'What d'you want? We've had enough of soldiers, first Byron ripping down the Botley Bridge, then brawls at

Carfax . . . What d'you want, I say? Speak out or I'll call the Watch.'

I heard all along the street the creak and scrape of windows and doors and shutters being opened as curious neighbours looked out to see what was amiss. 'It's me, Mistress Gooch, Thomazine Heron; Mistress Willoughby's stepdaughter. We've travelled a long way, and we're tired and hungry and some of us are hurt – will you let us in?' I was unable to keep the pleading note out of my voice, but ordering the Widow about had ever been as effective as asking the tide to stop flowing.

'Eh? Mistress Thomazine?' The Widow peered further round and up at me. 'Get down off your horse, lass, so that I can see your face.'

Slowly, numbly, I dismounted, feeling a wild desire to laugh; for the second time that evening we were caught up in the same sticky toils of nightmare, unable to gain an entrance through someone's stupidity or suspicion. Whatever the soldiers of both sides had done in Oxford, it had certainly left its mark. I walked right up to the Widow, who took my chin in a hard grasp and turned my face to the last remaining light. 'Aye, you could be, though you've not grown much, have you? Little skinny thing you used to be, all eyes and hair, and as lively as an imp from Hell . . . What was your father's name?'

The question, slipping out with sudden sharpness, caught me unawares. 'Matthew Heron.'

'When did he die, and what of, and at what age?'

'On the eighth day of April, 1635, of the smallpox, and he was thirty-two,' I said, annoyed. 'Is that sufficient for you?'

'Yes, though I'd know you more by the tone of your voice than by your face,' said the Widow Gooch with malicious satisfaction. 'Yes, I'll let you in, as it's your house, but what about all these? Who are they?'

This was the final straw. I said, barely controlling my voice. 'They are my cousins and some soldiers, some of them hurt. Would you kindly let us *all* in, before the storm breaks?'

'And what am I to feed them on?' the Widow demanded,

holding fast to the gate as the first big, sparse drops of rain slapped the ground. I had never felt in my anger and weariness and frustration more like hitting someone; but at that moment I saw out of the corner of my eye Francis slump forward over Hobgoblin's neck. Lucy gave a shriek and dismounted in a flurry of skirts to rush to his side. 'Francis! What's wrong? He's fainted – help get him down, Jamie!'

As Jamie and Girling lowered the long, limp form to the ground and bent over him, I said to Mistress Gooch, 'You see? I said some were hurt – and like to die if they're left out in this all night, for we've nowhere else to go.'

Grudgingly, muttering, the old woman pulled the gate back. 'They can put their horses in there with my old nag, there's not much straw and precious little hay but that can't be helped. Get some more from the Blue Boar if you're needy. Come up to the house when your horses are settled and I'll have some food ready; poor fare, but if you want more try the Blue Boar. And lock the gate, lass, we can't be too careful these days.' And with those words of welcome turned and stumped slowly back up the path through the little garden to the house.

'My God,' said Charles, suddenly appearing at my side, 'she's like a fugitive from Macbeth.'

'Thomazine!' Lucy cried, clutching my sleeve, 'Francis is ill, he has a dreadful fever. We must get him indoors quickly!'

'There's certainly no point in standing idle,' said Grainne. 'I'll make sure the horses are housed – you could help, Charles. You go in with Francis, and take Jasper too. The cart can wait till tomorrow to be unloaded, but I would like – I would like Hess to be brought in.'

With no help from the Widow Gooch, somehow our tired, dispirited, ailing band organized it all. The horses were crammed, a dozen of them, into a stable intended to hold half that number, and with enough hay for two, although oats were available as well and duly squandered. The carts were drawn up in the little yard, and the pathetic box that was Hester's coffin carried carefully inside to be laid in the best parlour, looking onto the street. And as gently as possible, Francis and Hewitt, both feverish and unconscious, were carried upstairs by the strongest men, and laid in two separate chambers; Hewitt's the one over the street entrance, and Francis in a cosy little room on the top floor, the only one on that level to boast a hearth. 'Don't like the look of either of 'em,' said the Widow, peering into the silent faces as they were carried laboriously past. 'Ripe for death, both of 'em. Sure it's just wound fever, and not the plague?'

'Quite sure,' I said, staring dazed with fear at Francis's dragging golden head as he was transported up the steep stairs, Drake whining behind. 'And I don't think a sixteen-mile ride in rain did either of them any good.'

The Widow, hearing the break in my voice, peered into my face. 'Sweet on one of 'em, are you?'

'No,' I said, too quickly – would I never learn? – 'but he's my cousin and I'm very fond of all my cousins.'

'Oh, aye, your magnificent Heron cousins,' said the Widow Gooch with rich scorn, but she patted my shoulder. 'Don't you fret, lass, I know a bit about fevers and sicknesses, and I've some skill with simples – saved you once, as I remember. Don't worry, we'll make them both well for you.'

'More likely kill them both,' said Grainne to me later, when the Widow was upstairs making chambers ready for the night with Betty, Heppy, Jamie, and Girling and Jacobson, who were the only men, seemingly, to have any energy left. Charles Lawrence looked so pale that I feared he would be the next to succumb, and the wound in his leg had reopened and was bleeding sullenly. Radley could apparently only muster the strength to stir the bubbling pot of broth sitting over the kitchen fire. Pryke had the beginnings of a streaming cold, and his throat was so sore he could barely speak; he sat as close to the kitchen fire as he could, shivering, and Holly was next to him, attempting to dry his doublet and stockings after being caught in this latest downpour which now battered the closed, shuttered windows. The candles in sconces and sticks and holders shed their golden, shifting light on the big kitchen and on the bedraggled, exhausted people in it: on Grainne, cutting wedges off loaves of new bread and on Meraud's lovely, intent face as she spread them liberally with butter and laid them on pewter plates; on Lucy, wiping dust-covered bowls which had been resurrected from some cupboard where they had lain since my father's death; and on me, carving a joint of cold bacon with hands that seemed numb and useless as Grainne spoke. 'My chest of medicines is in the baggage cart; if the Widow Gooch's nostrums do no good, I have some remedies of my own which may help.'

'What's wrong with them?' Lucy cried, flinging down the last bowl (fortunately made of pewter) as if it were personally responsible for her brother's collapse. 'Francis seemed all right, and so did Hewitt at first. Is it some camp fever?'

Grainne gave me a long steady look, sending me strength, before she answered. 'No, I don't think so. Hewitt's probably got an inflamed wound, sending poisonous humours to heat his blood, and it may be the same with Francis, but not only that; did you hear his voice? With him it may be the lung fever.'

It was uncommon for anyone, even young and strong as Francis was, or had been before Edgehill, to survive that. I stared at her, my brain numb with shock, and yet not really surprised; as if I had known all along that he was more seriously ill than it appeared, but suppressed my knowledge to the bottom of my mind. Lucy gave a strangled sob and burst out, 'No, oh no, not another, I couldn't bear it, after all we've lost!' She turned her agonized face to Meraud, who was nearest, and like a sister the blonde girl took the taller, dark one into her arms and stroked her hair, saying, 'Don't worry, dear Lucy, please, with God's help and our nursing he'll recover.'

I gazed for a moment at the little scene, dry-eyed, at Meraud's soft, smug, unctuous face turned towards Lucy's buried head, and then, overwhelmed with grief, and anger, and helpless exhaustion, turned abruptly and went out of the door into the passage which led to the front door. Once out of the kitchen my anguish was given free rein; I leaned my head and hands against the dark panelling and wept.

After a while I heard the kitchen door open and close. I opened my eyes and began to wipe my face with my cuffs. Grainne said quietly, 'Don't give up hope yet; I nursed my father through the lung fever, once, and he survived both it and my care.'

'Grainne,' I said, giving her a watery smile, 'you're really more than we all deserve. I don't know what we'd do without you, I really don't. You're our rock, and it isn't fair.'

'I'm not concerned with things that aren't fair,' said Grainne, studying my face. 'Only about things that are right. I don't know what I'd do without a Heron to support, though,' she added with a glimmer of her old slightly acid humour. 'Shall we go above stairs and see what has become of the invalids?'

Hewitt's chamber was large, bare and dusty, with a huge old-fashioned carved bed hung with shabby curtains. It had been my father's room, and I remembered, painfully, lying on that same bed with Edmund on lazy Sunday mornings, listening to his stories or assimilating the rudiments of Latin or Greek or history or astronomy, for my father had possessed at least a little knowledge of any subject you could care to mention. Now in place of my father's blond bearded head and sturdy, robed figure, lay Hewitt's brown curly hair tossing from side to side on the pillows, muttering. Grainne turned back the bedclothes to inspect the dressings on his arm. 'Well, at least they've been changed, and efficiently too; the Widow has some skill, it appears.'

'She nursed me and my father and Edmund that last summer,' I told her. 'They sent for her and she came from Oxford in some carrier's wagon and did her best, but she could only save me. I don't think I've ever really forgiven her for not being able to cure them as well, which is very unfair. She's a good-hearted soul, once you get used to her ways.'

'But I can see why you thought her a witch,' said Grainne, replacing the blankets. 'There should be someone sitting with each of them the clock round, for safety.'

'Do you think Francis will die?' I demanded urgently. Grainne lifted her honest eyes to mine. 'I don't know. You never do, with that particular sickness. I can't hold you out any false hopes, I can't make you any promises, save that we'll try our hardest.' For a moment anguish twisted her face. 'I know what it is, to lose the man you love. I would not wish that on you for anything. But it'll mean long weary hours of watching, and above all the ability to stay calm.'

'Better not to let Lucy near him, then,' I said, feebly joking. 'What about Hewitt?'

'If no infection develops in the wound, he'll live. If it does, then he loses his arm, or his life, or both. Nursing wounded men, and I have done it often enough, is not a very satisfying or happy task, for too often they die,' said Grainne, bleakly. I took her hand and we stood for a moment, united in sorrow and fear and friendship, then softly left the room and went upstairs.

The Widow was standing by Francis's bedside, looking down at him, her hands full of old dressings. Even from the doorway I could hear the fast, painful rasp of his breathing, and gripped Grainne's hand again.

'Always said he'd come to a bad end,' said Mistress Gooch as we came hesitantly up. I stared blankly at her, for I was unaware that they had ever met before. The Widow gave a small, witchlike cackle of laughter. 'You didn't think I knew him, did you, lass? But I do. Full of charm, he was, bright-haired young student with all the world — and half of St Aldate's women — at his feet. He used to bring 'em here, sometimes, and slip me a crown or two when he did, so as his brother wouldn't know. All sorts of women, respectable some of them, and others no better than they should be.' She cackled again. 'Has that turned your heart from him, lass? Best to do it, for he'll break it else.'

'It was a long time ago, and he told me some of it,' I said, keeping calm with an effort. Francis had never revealed this, and it had somehow a foul taste to it to use my house thus, though at the time nothing had been further from his thoughts than loving me.

'How is he?' asked Grainne, and the Widow's sharp blue

eyes swivelled to her face. Hastily, glad of a respite, I introduced her. 'This is Mistress Sewell, a very dear friend. Her husband was killed two months ago and her little daughter died this morning' (Was it only this morning? That terrible moment seemed a lifetime away) 'when the siege ended. She has some skill and knowledge of healing.'

'She's very young for it,' said the Widow, studying Grainne, who answered calmly, 'I followed my father in the imperial army for two years in the Low Countries. It afforded me some practice.'

'Hmm. Well. You'll be useful, if that's so. He's got the lung fever, though of course you knew that already, Mistress Sewell. Needs a lot of care, does that. The other lad will be all right in a day or so, for his wound's not gangrenous, but Master Francis Heron will be lucky if he's up before December – if he lives that long.' She gazed at me, as the slow helpless tears found their way down my cheeks, and suddenly grinned, revealing a near-perfect array of yellowing teeth. 'Don't take on so, lass. I can see he's your sweetheart for all I've tried to dissuade you, and he's a strong lad. We'll do all we can, and never mind an old woman's sharp tongue, it doesn't mean half of what it says.'

The Widow had indeed a kind heart, for all that night she kept watch by the two sickbeds, and I doubt if she slept, even though she had made herself up a truckle-bed in Francis's chamber. The rest of us, too weary even to do proper justice to our supper (Jamie, indeed, fell asleep over his), crawled into whatever bed had been arranged: Lucy, Meraud, Heppy and I crammed into the small rear bedchamber behind Hewitt's; Betty and Jasper in the bigger room the other side of his, normally the Widow's; Jamie and Charles and Radley in one of the little fireless chambers on the top storey; Holly, Pryke and Girling in the other, and John Jacobson, the Northamptonshire blacksmith, on a straw mattress in the kitchen, surrounded by hens. And Grainne, whose strength during that long terrible day had seemed beyond the human, had calmly gone into the front parlour, where Hester lay in her coffin on the table, with a candle at each corner lighting the rough wood and bent nails, to watch over her all night. Lucy had protested, but the Irish girl shook her head. 'No, it's the last thing I can do for her and I will not shirk it for the sake of one night in a cosy feather bed.' And, shamed, Lucy had fallen silent. After supper she and I went with Grainne for a little while, to kneel in silence and pray for a small soul whose harmlessness had not, in this new and violent England, protected her from a sudden and terrifying death.

I looked in again at Francis before finally going to bed, and was foolishly delighted to be received with a flash of the old wit. 'Ah, Thomazine. Now I know the vultures are gathering.'

There was no one else in the chamber, save for Drake on watch at the bed's foot. Mistress Gooch was downstairs administering a sleeping-draught to Hewitt. I sat on the bed and kissed him, smiling hugely. 'Do you feel better?'

Francis coughed, a dry hacking sound. 'No. And I've enough to do repelling that loathsome old witch without having to fend you off as well. Were you worried?'

'Yes,' I admitted, not liking to say as I stared at his hot, dry face and listened to the sound of his breathing that I was still very anxious. 'And you mustn't call Widow Gooch a witch, she's very kind really, and she's very skilled.'

'Yes, she changed my dressings with all the skill of a practised torturer,' said Francis with a faint grin. 'So skilled was she that I passed out with the pain.'

'Well, I'm glad you've at last acknowledged that you've been hurt,' I pointed out. 'Ignoring something like that is the best way to make it worse. You've been pretending you're in the best of health ever since the battle, and now your chickens have all come home to roost with a vengeance.'

'You'd best get off that bed or you'll take an infection as like as not!' Mistress Gooch said, coming in briskly with a little silver vial and a pewter cup. 'Now, Master Francis Heron—'

'Lieutenant,' Francis said, 'I'm no student now.'

'Gown for a buff coat, eh? All the young men at Christchurch are the same, and some of the tutors and divines as well. Now, this'll grant you a night's sleep – young Hewitt's like a baby at this moment, dead to the world – but there's not much of it, so you won't be getting it often. But doubtless you'll be able to think on your sweetheart to give you pleasant dreams.' She winked at me, with a bawdy good nature under the irascible exterior that it was impossible not to respond to.

'So she's not deceived,' said Francis ruefully. 'Strange, Thomazine, and you so practised in trickery.'

'Don't you go on at her,' said the Widow, carefully pouring drops from the vial into the cup of water. 'She's a lass of spirit, but she's weary to the bone – they all are, and not a word of complaint from any of 'em, and Mistress Sewell will do herself no good by sitting all night by that poor little corpse, nor the baby neither. When's it due?'

'December or January, I'm not quite sure which,' I said.

'Poor little orphan. The little boy's a good stout fellow, for all he's wedded to that damned cat,' said Mistress Gooch. 'Can't have that in the house, piddling all over the place and making a stink. Stable's the place for that, I'll put my foot down tomorrow. I've spent a lot of time keeping this place decent and no cat is going to make it like a pigsty.'

'Or a chicken coop,' said Francis, straight-faced. The Widow glared at him. 'Your tongue was ever your undoing. I could tell you some stories, lass – but I won't, they're not fit. Now sit up and drink this.'

The exertion left him coughing and gasping for breath, so that it was some little time before the draught could be swallowed. Then, all the veneer of cheerfulness drained away, he leaned back against the pillows, eyes closed, breathing so harshly and with such difficulty that I stood rooted with fear. Widow Gooch gave me a little push. 'Kiss him goodnight, lass, and be gone to your bed, it's high time you were.'

I bent and dropped a brief kiss on the hot forehead, remembering with a pang of grief and foreboding the identical gesture with which Grainne had said farewell for ever to Henry. Francis's eyes opened briefly. 'Wish . . .

your bed . . . was mine,' he whispered with a gleam of amusement, and then seemed to fall asleep.

'Go on,' said the Widow, fairly pushing me from the chamber, 'I'll watch over him, don't fret yourself. But you'd best be prepared,' she added in a whisper round the door as I stood irresolute at the head of the stairs, 'he's going to get much worse afore he gets better.' And with that comforting speech shut the door in my face.

I did not sleep very well in the crowded bed – all four of us packed in it together – and tossed and turned for much of the night, my feet cold and unable to move very much for fear of sticking an elbow or leg into Lucy, who was next to me, or of falling out the other side. But despite being clogged with fatigue, heavy-eyed and yawning, I was able to rise with the first grey light of dawn and to dress with Heppy's help, and go below stairs to inquire after the invalids with an apprehensive heart. Mistress Gooch, lively as her own hens even after a sleepless night, was piling hot frumenty into a bowl when my tentative head appeared round the door, and she had set the huge brown-bearded Jacobson to cutting bread and laying out the table for breakfast. She gave me an encouraging smile. 'This is for Master – Trooper, I beg his pardon – Hewitt. Woke ten minutes ago, cool as a summer salad, and demanding something to fill his stomach. All he wanted to set him to rights was a good night's sleep.'

'And my cousin?' I asked. The smile faded. 'Worse, but it's to be expected. It's not got a grip yet, and when it does he'll be in a high fever, raving, not knowing where he is, and coughing blood. Don't let that alarm you, when it comes – I've seen many such. Then after some days, if all goes well, the fever will go down, he'll sleep naturally and soon be his old devilish self again. If not . . .' She shook her head significantly. 'I don't believe in hiding the truth, lass. But there's hope, for I've nursed several with this sickness, and seen more recover than die.'

I went with her up to Hewitt's room, to watch him wolf down the broth and frumenty and coddled eggs that the Widow considered suitable for an invalid, and then up the flight of stairs to Francis. He sprawled restlessly in the bed, eyes closed, and did not respond to my greeting, although Drake in bewilderment pushed his cold nose into his hand and whined. Immeasurably sunk into despondency, I returned to the kitchen and partook of a breakfast which turned to sawdust in my mouth, while our household was organized by Mistress Gooch. We were severally dispatched to buy provisions for ourselves and for the horses, or assigned kitchen duties commensurate with ability or age. Charles Lawrence, with a kindness that I found very touching, took Grainne's place of vigil beside Hess, and Grainne herself, with the Widow, went out all in black to find the incumbent of St Aldate's, or a churchwarden, to arrange for her child's burial. Meraud and I were to bake some bread, the ashes already heating the oven to this purpose, and Lucy went upstairs with some sewing to sit with her sick brother.

But I had no stomach for baking bread, nor for any household tasks, nor even for eating. Only Hester's burial in the St Aldate's churchyard that afternoon, with no pomp or ceremony save our grief, seemed to infringe on my own fear and anxiety. My world shrank rapidly during the next few days to the little room on the top floor with the blazing fire which could not stop Francis's shivering, and the syrup of violets which did not lower his fever, and the villainously-smelling concoction of mustard and pennyroyal which did nothing to ease his continual cough or painful breathing. We took it in turns to watch, day and night, Lucy, Meraud, Grainne, Widow Gooch and I, and I spent many weary anguished hours in the hot, scented room hung with sprigs of rosemary, listening to my lover's restless body and the rambled speeches of a delirious mind. This was the most painful of all; sometimes I listened hot-faced to words of love or desire addressed to me or sometimes, obviously, to some other lady who had consorted with him in the past. At other times he relived old quarrels with Simon or his father, or the siege, and once, so vividly it drove me from the room with my hands over my ears, the battle which had put an end to the brother for whom he had never really admitted his very deep affection. What was worse was the knowledge that I was not the only person to listen to his ravings; I did not mind Lucy, or Grainne, or even the Widow Gooch hearing the heart and soul of one usually so reserved laid bare, but Meraud was another matter. If I could have excluded her, I would, but I really had no excuse that did not sound vindictive or spiteful, and had to endure the look of speculative amusement in her eyes whenever she emerged from the sickroom. Whatever impression she had gained of our relationship on that far-distant June day on the hill above Ashcott was now, obviously, amply confirmed.

The news that the King had taken Banbury and Broughton Castle passed by us almost unnoticed. Even the triumphal state entry of the King with his sons and all his army into Oxford, three days after our own arrival, was marked little except as the source of much noise disturbing the uneasy stuffy peace of the sickroom, as the King and his court invaded Christchurch amid the cheers and drums and trumpets of his welcome. Only at dusk, when the noise had dwindled into the laughter and chat of the townspeople making their way home after the spectacle, did the realization come to me of what this would mean. Soon, Simon would come to seek Francis out and demand an explanation of Ashcott. When had Banbury and Broughton been taken? I strained my mind back as I peered over the rent petticoat I was mending, catching the last of the light, since our wax candles were in short supply and tallow too foul-smelling for a sickroom. On the twenty-seventh, it had been, Thursday, the day after we had surrendered Ashcott. I could imagine how that would look to Simon, and how it would be one more score to be added against Francis's name.

A knock at the door heralded Lucy, bright and windblown with her dark hair in great tangled ringlets round her glowing face. 'I've been outside to see the show.' she explained in answer to my look. 'It was so fine, all those soldiers, and I saw the King and the Prince of Wales, and Prince Rupert too!' She clasped her hands enthusiastically. I said in low, caustic tones, 'It's no good, Lucy, he's quite ineligible.'

'You mean, I am,' said my cousin. She went over to the bed where her brother lay in an uneasy doze, shedding her gay outdoor mood like a cloak. 'Is there any change?'

I stared unhappily out of the little window in one of the two gables that topped the front of the house. Opposite, the rooftops and chimneys of Pennyfarthing Street humped against the dim grey evening sky. 'No, no change. He's been sleeping, if you can call it that, for some hours now. Did you see Simon, too?'

Lucy's white face turned, startled. 'No – I'd forgotten! He's in the Prince's regiment, isn't he – what colour uniforms do they wear?'

'Blue coats.'

'There were *some* blue coats, I think,' said Lucy doubtfully. 'But I couldn't see anything very well, and Jacobson trod on my foot.'

Despite the empty hopelessness inside me, I chuckled. 'Have you still a foot?'

'Just, but no thanks to him,' Lucy said, 'he must weigh all of sixteen stone.' She sat on the bed and gently stroked the lank hair away from Francis's face and mouth. At once he turned restlessly on to his side. 'Thomazine! Is that you?' His hands clutched at the pillow, and his voice was hardly recognizable. 'I'm here,' I said, as I had so uselessly said for the last three days, and got up and went to sit beside Lucy. 'That's it, owd gal,' Francis muttered indistinctly. 'Can't think why I love you, all eyes and hair she said, and a scold to boot . . . your hair's like a shadow round your head . . . kiss me, love . . .'

I did, with tears disfiguring my face, and he took my hand and held it while he drifted back into restless sleep. Lucy's round helpless agonized eyes looked into mine. 'Oh, Thomazine, how can you bear it?'

'I can't, very well,' I said, dragging my remaining hand across my eyes with a snuffle. 'What does he do if he calls for me when Meraud's there? What does she do? Listen, and pretend she's me?'

'I'm sure she doesn't, don't be silly,' said Lucy. 'It's strange for me to have to comfort you when you're fanciful, isn't it? The Widow's making something good and hot for supper, so go downstairs and eat, please, Thomazine, for me? And for Francis? You've been up here since morning. I'll watch now until bedtime, so make sure my supper comes up, I'm ravenous. Go on, Thomazine. If anything changes I'll call you, you know I will, I promise.'

'All right,' I said reluctantly, and with gentle fingers extracted my hand from Francis's, despite his muttered half-conscious protests, and went downstairs.

The next day brought no improvement. To the weather, yes, with high white clouds puffed up like ships in the breeze, and in the street children laughing and yelling with the wind in their heads, chasing the flickering, bouncing brown leaves up and down and round as they gusted from house to house like a whirlwind . . .

I pulled myself together with an effort, and turned from the window to my sewing. So restless had Francis been the previous night, as the fever mounted, that Widow Gooch had given him some of her precious laudanum, and he lay now in a heavy unnatural stupor, the harsh gasp of his breathing filling the room. Below me the house was quiet, for with the exception of Hewitt and Charles Lawrence, the troopers had gone in search of their regiment. There was none of them I could really trust to give any fair account of Ashcott, not even Holly, who in his quiet way had transferred any allegiance he owed to anyone to Francis, who had probably saved his life; and certainly Radley, without even any real malice, would most like present a damning picture quite casually. How to explain to Simon that the only way to save Grainne and myself had been to surrender? But of course, I reminded myself, to Simon it would not seem the only way; he would have ordered the men on the tower to fire, dragged us behind a bush or back inside, and let the defence proceed. You could argue with Simon that it was an impossibility until you dropped dead with fatigue, I knew, but he would never (not having any knowledge of the real situation), never believe you.

It was hopeless. I put down the endless, tedious sewing (ripped lace on one of Lucy's cuffs this morning) and laid my head in my hands and wept. Half a year ago I would have considered myself a strong-minded young woman who did not usually indulge in the luxury of tears, but now they seemed always near the surface, my strength worn down by grief and anxiety and weariness.

Suddenly there came a mighty pounding on the street door, so that the little diamond-leaded window jumped and rattled in its frame. Heart racing, I leapt to my feet and squeezed round the little table to the window, straining my neck in an effort to see who it was. The window, once opened, could not be shut without a struggle, and I did not intend to try. All I caught was a glimpse of swirling black cloak before the door was shut behind the visitor. But I knew who it was.

I sat down, and listened with a heart full of dread. Even from up here I could hear that there was an argument going on, could recognize the Widow's normally low voice raised in anger, interspersed with Simon's familiar harsh tones. Then Lucy joined the fray, her high clear impetuous words reaching even up here. 'You can't go willy-nilly up there, Simon, he's ill!'

Despite myself, I crept to the door, and with a last look at the still-sleeping Francis, opened it a crack.

'Ill, is he?' Simon's voice said viciously. 'Or skulking cowardly where he thinks he's beyond my reach?'

'He's very sick, with a fever,' said the Widow. 'And not like to live long, if you go up there like a charging bull, young man.'

Simon had never been able to cope with that sort of familiarity from those he felt to be his inferiors; even with the Sewells, lifelong friends, he had been uneasy. In his present rage, his reaction was predictable. 'By God, old woman, I'll brook your impertinence no longer. Get out of my way!'

'Simon!' Lucy shrieked. From the sounds, I guessed she was clinging to his arm or possibly, knowing Lucy, his feet. The Widow was hurling unintelligible abuse that the whole street could probably hear. Into the din, Grainne's voice cut low and cool and clear like water. 'Simon, I really wouldn't go up. Francis is very sick indeed, of a fever, and wouldn't be able to answer your questions even if you hurled them at him all day.'

'Well, I have no intention of taking your word for it,' Simon said nastily. 'Let go, girl, or you'll be hurt! I said, let go!'

A scream from Lucy and then the thud of his approaching feet up the first flight of stairs, followed by Lucy's urgent pleas and Grainne's more coherent voice saying, 'Simon, you'll regret this later.'

I was not afraid of Simon. I retreated to the door, suddenly and overwhelmingly angry, and stood in the opening with one hand on each post, braced to meet his fury, and Drake crouched behind me, hackles raised. He came bounding up the stairs, two and three at a time, his face dark and suffused with rage, and stopped with a jerk when he saw me. 'Thomazine! What are you doing here?'

'Watching over the sickbed,' I said coldly. 'Simon, you're being ridiculous. Ungovernable rage is not now the fashion, nor is it seemly. And I'm not going to let you in till you've calmed down, because he's asleep and I will not have him disturbed.'

Simon's dark angry eyes glared into mine. He stood on the second stair down, his hand on the banisters, breathing hard; below, I could just see Lucy's and Grainne's anxious faces peering round the curve in the staircase. For a long moment, our eyes held, and then his dropped. 'I apologize,' he said stiffly. 'I wished to make sure that he was genuinely ill. If that is the case, I will come in quietly. What is his sickness?'

'Lung fever. The result of ignoring the wounds he

received at Edgehill, and riding sixteen miles in rain from Ashcott,' I said. 'I'm not blaming you, for if he dies it'll be his own fault, but just don't give me any pretext to fasten guilt on you, for I'll do it just as readily as you do it to him.' And I stood aside to let him enter.

Simon stamped up the last two steps, recollected himself, and walked more quietly into the chamber. He stood for a long time by his younger brother's bed, noting as I did the flushed, sunken face, the dark-ringed eyelids and dull, tangled hair. The expression on his face was unreadable. At last, he turned away, grim lines around the thin, pressed mouth that was a less flexible version of his brother's. 'Satisfied?' I asked.

'For the present,' said Simon, oblivious to my sarcasm. 'Later, when he has recovered, he will have to account for the surrender of Ashcott to his comanding officer – and also to me. We will probably leave Oxford in a few days, to march on London. If God grants we take the city, then the war will end quickly and it is quite possible that all this will be forgotten. If not . . .' He shrugged. I said slowly, 'Simon, have you heard how Ashcott was surrendered?'

'Yes, Mistress Tawney told me when we retook it. A detachment of foot and horse, with a couple of pieces of ordnance, was sent to Ashcott when we received intelligence that it had been taken. It surrendered at the first firing of our cannon.' He coughed. 'I regret to say, Thomazine, that they had been remarkably thorough in removing articles of value, so Mistress Tawney said. Doubtless they will turn up in Banbury sooner or later. Meanwhile, the Tawneys are still in residence, and a garrison has been left. You are therefore free to return, should you wish.'

I shook my head. 'No. We were given the choice of staying by Captain Ashley – was he in command when you retook it?' (Simon indicated that he was not.) 'But we refused. We couldn't face a siege again.'

Simon looked me up and down, suspiciously. 'Very well. Since it now lacks even the basic comforts – I believe several of the beds have been taken to pieces and carted away – you are probably wisest to remain here. The King has always had a great affection for the University – certainly our welcome yesterday was most encouraging – and should by any evil chance the war continue, he is quite likely to return here, and it is possible that the headquarters of his army will be here. Should it fall out thus, not only will you all be much safer here than anywhere else, but Francis and the other two troopers will be able to rejoin the regiment when they are fit – or in Francis's case, to face an inquiry.'

'Simon,' I said urgently, 'did Mistress Tawney tell you? He couldn't have done anything else. The gate was blown up by a petard, and—'

'Because the gate is destroyed, it does not mean that the house itself is indefensible,' said Simon's logical, cold voice. 'I understand there were men posted on the tower. He had only to hold out for a further day, to have been relieved. It is plain that he was either unnecessarily pessimistic, or disgracefully concerned with his own safety. In view of my knowledge of his character, I incline to the latter reason. I apologize for any unseemly behaviour, Thomazine. Good day to you.' He bowed briefly, turned on his heel and went out, leaving me seething and sick with rage and despair in the middle of the floor. As if from a great distance, I heard the clatter of his feet down the two flights of stairs, the brief rumble of his apology to his sister, Grainne and the Widow, and then the crash of the door slamming and faintly, through the closed window, his booted feet and jingling spurs echoing down Pennyfarthing Street towards Christ-church.

Although the King did not leave Oxford for another five days, Simon did not return. But none of us had much strength or thought to spare for that eventuality, for it became increasingly likely as the days spun out that Francis would by then be dead. Day after day, the fever continued its grip, the coughing grew worse and, as the Widow had prophesied, brought up blood, while his breathing became more and more tormented. There were five of us to nurse him, although Grainne by reason of her pregnancy and the presence of Jasper was perforce able to do little, so Mistress

Gooch, Lucy, Meraud and I bore the brunt of it. Although Dr Clayton, Master of Pembroke and an eminent physician, lived just round the corner in Fish Street, the Widow stubbornly refused to call him in. 'Probably tell us to force live toads down his throat or something. I know them doctors, all great promises and grand speeches. Kill more than they cure, more like, and charge a fancy fee for it too.' And though I had very different memories of Dr Despotine, who had saved Grainne and Jasper, I realized that he was the exception and that the Widow was very probably right.

The King left for London on November 3rd, a Thursday, and in the house in Pennyfarthing Street we did not even know. Francis had now been ill for a week, and we all realized, but did not admit, that if the fever did not break within the next few hours he would die. As I supported the thin shoulders and held his restless head so that more of Mistress Gooch's preparations could be poured down his throat, I willed him not to die with a silent desperation, sending my pleas from my heart to find his, wherever it might be. 'I will always go with you,' he had once promised me, and now as I laid him back on the pillows, all his body racked with coughing, and wiped away the blood-stained froth gathering at the corners of his mouth, I prayed that somehow I could transmit to him some of my own strength and will him back to life, even from the edge of death.

'Go on, get some sleep,' said the Widow, using brute force to get me away from the bed, for all she was no bigger than I and at least forty years my senior. 'Mistress Meraud's here, now go down to your chamber. You'll do no one any good to wear yourself into a fever as well as him.' And she pushed me out of the room as Meraud entered, with a bundle of fresh linen for the bed and another bottle of the Widow's special cough concoction. Dazed with fatigue and helpless terror, I wandered down the dark stairs, candle in hand, and into the chamber that I now shared only with Lucy, Meraud having moved into the one that Hewitt had occupied during his illness. I had just enough wit left to lay the candlestick down on a table away from the bed, and then I collapsed on top of the embroidered silk coverlet, still fully clothed, and fell instantly asleep.

Someone was shaking me. I muttered, 'Leave me alone!' and tried to turn away. 'Thomazine, wake up, for God's sake!' said Meraud's voice in my ear, and a candle flame suddenly shone brightly into my face, making me blink. As memory returned, I sat up abruptly, almost knocking the candle out of her hand, and gripped her arm. 'What is it? Is it Francis?'

'He wants to see you,' said Meraud softly. 'You'd best go up quickly.' And her eyes followed me to the door as I leapt off the bed and ran full-tilt up the stairs, knowing I went to face his death. I burst into the room, jerking the Widow's coifed head round. She was sitting on a stool by the bed, a cloth in her hands, and a three-branched candlestick stood on the table by the tightly-shuttered gable window, throwing its soft guttering light on to Francis's gaunt face. As I came up to the bed, his eyes opened, very wide and dark in the dim light, and he smiled. 'Hullo, owd gal.'

'Hullo,' I said, and stopped, unable to say more. The Widow gave me a startled glance, and Francis, slowly and with much effort, lifted a hand and traced the tracks of my tears down my face. 'Hey, what's this for, my dear?'

'There's no need for it,' said Mistress Gooch. 'The devil's been cheated of his own for a while yet.' And I realized with a sudden glorious leap of my heart that the hand that gently touched my cheek as I leaned towards him was cooler, and wet at last with perspiration, and that, although very weak, he was his own self again. 'I . . . wanted to see you . . . before I slept,' Francis whispered, dropping his hand back. 'I understand from Madam Witch here . . . that I might live . . . to plague you further . . . so I thought you'd best be informed.'

'Hasn't stopped her tears, though,' said the Widow, as I sat halfway between laughter and weeping, holding his hand. 'Nor your tongue either, Lieutenant. Sleep's what you need, so settle down under the sheets and say goodnight to your lady.'

'It's a pity,' said Francis, as we made him comfortable, 'that when she's come so close . . . to sharing my bed, I'm too weak . . . to take advantage of it.' As I giggled, suddenly light-hearted with euphoria, he added, 'Give me a week or so . . . it'll be a different tale . . . good night, little love, and sweet dreams.'

He was asleep almost at once, and, hardly able to believe it, I listened for a while to the faint, steady, easier sound of his breathing. The Widow fixed me with a sharp glance. 'What did you think when you came in, lass? Did you think he was dying?'

'Yes,' I said. 'Yes, I did. Meraud told me to come quickly, and I assumed the worst.' I laughed weakly. 'Is he really going to recover? Really?'

'He is, if nothing goes amiss. It'll take a long time before he's fit for soldiering, but he'll do. I don't much care for your little Mistress Meraud,' said the Widow abruptly, 'and that's a fact. Artful she is, and too sly by half for my liking. It's my belief she told you to make haste like that deliberately to make you think he was dying. And I've seen her listening to some of his rambling with a thoughtful sort of look on her face, like she was remembering it all for no good purpose.'

'What purpose?' I asked uneasily. 'What could she do? She knows already about me and Francis, she thinks we're truly lovers.'

'And are you, eh?'

'No,' I said. Mistress Gooch cackled. 'But I'll wager it's not for want of trying. Don't you worry about her, she's only a young lass when all's said and done – how old? Sixteen? Though mind you, they say that Borgia woman started young.'

'I don't care about Meraud,' I said. 'He's the one that truly matters, though everyone here is dear to me – and you, Mistress Gooch.' And with a sudden impulsive gratitude worthy of Lucy, I hugged her small wiry body. 'You've saved him for me, and I don't think I can ever thank you enough.'

'Ha, that's not much,' said the Widow drily. 'That makes five now I've nursed through the lung fever, and only two I've killed. It's his own strength you should thank. Now go and get some rest, it must be all of three o'clock, and I'll make up the truckle bed in here should he need me.'

I woke late the next morning, but not as late as Francis; not until close on supper-time was I able to go upstairs with a bowl of steaming broth for him. He had slept peacefully for fifteen hours, and woke at six o'clock demanding nourishment, so the Widow said. 'We'll have him strolling the garden within the week.'

'I doubt it, somehow,' said Francis, told of the anticipated brevity of his convalescence. 'It's as much as I can do to turn my head. But I'll be glad to get back to proper food instead of this pap. What is it, beef?'

'Mutton broth, with onions, peas and barley,' I said, putting a steaming spoonful into his mouth. 'Very nourishing, according to Widow Gooch.'

Francis swallowed it, coughing. 'You . . . enjoy all this, don't you? Admit it, owd gal, you're glad to see me weak and helpless.'

'No, I'm not,' I said, searching with the spoon through the thick lumpy liquid for a piece of mutton. 'You nearly died, you know. For a week your life was despaired of, and it's Madam Witch, as you so unkindly call her, that you have to thank for your life.'

'Were all those revolting potions I can remember being poured down my throat of her devising? Then she richly deserves the epithet "witch". Devil's brews, those were, but this is better - just.' He swallowed another mouthful, and added, 'Did I imagine Simon's visit?'

I stared. 'You were asleep! How could you know?'

'I can remember you and he shouting at each other . . . but very vaguely and far off, like a dream . . . so he did come? What happened?' He broke off in a fit of coughing, and added, 'You'd best give me all the news, and let my voice rest.'

So, in between feeding him the rest of the broth, and wiping off the results of my unsteady hand, I apprised him of all the events of the past week or so, finishing, 'The King's army marched yesterday for Reading and so for London, and all our troopers went with them save for Hewitt and

Charles Lawrence, whose leg still hasn't healed. Simon hasn't shown his face here again.'

'I doubt he'd dare to! I wonder what will happen,' Francis said thoughtfully, his eyes resting on me, alone unchanged in the gaunt wreck of his face. 'If the King takes London, then the war is all but over, and I should think Simon is right when he says that in that case Ashcott will be forgotten. But if Essex . . . gets to London first and faces the King again, it's hard to predict who'll be the loser . . . My bet would be, the King, in which case he'll either fall back here or to some other strong city – Bristol, perhaps – or possibly try at London from some other direction, maybe Kent or Essex.' He closed his eyes briefly, and then went on in the same strained husky voice. 'The one certainty in all this is that Simon . . . will never forgive me Ashcott. He might in time accept that I left Edward's body on the battlefield and saved our humble Holly instead . . . but to him Ashcott was thrown away cowardly . . . he'll never forget it.'

'He doesn't know the truth.'

'If he did, he wouldn't understand . . . He'd most like have stood there and watched the two of you die . . . three, for I thought Hess was still alive. No castle or cause or battle on earth,' said Francis with intensity, 'is worth the loss of you or of Grainne. It is not worth Hess, either. How does Grainne now?'

'Well enough, considering, I don't honestly know what we'd do without her – she's been a friend beyond price. And she does all this whilst still grieving for Henry and Hester. I could never have her strength.'

'I hope you'll never need it,' said Francis. 'I must thank her . . . and the Widow . . . and I suspect I must also thank you, for some half-dreamed memory tells me you were often with me . . . My poor love, your face tells its own story, all shadows under your eyes. Did I hear you telling someone – Simon, was it? – that if I died it would be my own fault? So I must present my apologies for putting you to so much grief and trouble.'

'It doesn't matter. Nothing matters now, if you get well. I so nearly lost you,' I said, hugging him, my head on his shoulder, 'that every other worry pales into insignificance. I had a glimpse of what it would be like on my own, and I'm decided on it – we must be wed, Simon and Dominic notwithstanding. If you'll have me, of course.'

'How could you doubt it? There's not been a day since that April when I haven't thought of you with longing. I want you, far more than I've ever wanted anyone else, and there've been enough of those.'

'I know – you brought them here, didn't you? The Widow told me.'

'And you'll still have me? No doubt she managed to imply a veritable procession. In actual fact there were three, none of whom I wish to remember . . . suffice it to say there's more than one worthy Oxford citizen who'd attack me on sight . . . but understand me, my dear, dear owd gal, that's in the past, and gone for ever. All my love is now concentrated in you, I want to love all of you, your mind and your body and even, God help me, your prickly temper, as I've never loved before. Do you believe me?'

'Oh, yes,' I whispered, shaken by the passion and longing in his face. 'Oh, yes, I believe you, and it's the same with me. As soon as you're recovered, we'll be wed.'

'A marriage of true minds . . .' Francis said, his voice fading, and kissed me. 'And pray for a victory at London.'

We had November; a dark stormy month, with snow and rain and gale, draping the garden sadly with drenched dead leaves and making it difficult to walk abroad in cloak or cassock-coat without being blown before the wind like a ship in full sail. It was the middle of the month before Francis was strong enough to leave his chamber and join us in the parlour or kitchen downstairs; and even then he still was deathly pale and short of breath, and the light seemed to shine through his hands, giving him a strange, transparent, almost angelic look of fragility. But cosseted by Lucy and the Widow, kept firmly within doors and stuffed with red meat, he grew daily stronger. In the wet afternoons we would sit lazily by the fire in the front parlour where Hess had once lain, listening to stories of army life, embellished and corroborated by Charles Lawrence, still unable to sit a horse; Hewitt had a while ago left to rejoin his regiment somewhere near London. We now made no secret of our love, although as yet neither of us had made any mention of our marriage plans; those could wait until Francis was fully recovered and, as he put it with a glint of lechery in his eyes, able to do justice to me. Two or three days before he first came downstairs, news had come of great victories at Brentford, and all the Oxford air had trembled under the assault of the joyful bells, although the bonfires also lit in rejoicing seemed with the wind to be in a fair way to burning the city down. So for a few days we believed that the King's cause and ours alike were ripe for triumph. But the Royalist army got no further than Turnham Green; as Charles put it with a ponderous, ill-timed pun, the trained bands 'turned 'em green'. We did not laugh then, nor when the King fell back from London, to linger with his army in Reading. Although now with a deep fear at the back of my mind, that even at so late a stage something would come to block our happiness, I did my best to be cheerful and unconcerned. On the first dry, comparatively warm day we all walked abroad to see the defensive works in progress at Magdalen Bridge, on the way back stopping at a little dim apothecary's shop so that I could buy the raw materials of the Widow's depleted medicine cupboard; bunches of pennyroyal, dried and aromatic; feverfew and the fantastically expensive laudanum and Peruvian Bark. And as we were about to leave, Francis jogged my elbow and directed my gaze upwards. 'Look.'

Hung above us in the dim, cobwebby ceiling, was a unicorn's horn; and though to anyone else it might have seemed a dusty and undistinguished deceit, to my love-dazzled eyes it shone in the gloom with its own faint, ethereal radiance. I emerged into the sunlight with a new hope lightening my step, and Francis's words still softly in my ears like the echo of a sea shell: 'When we are married, my lady, I'll buy you a unicorn's horn for our chamber, to remind us ever that imagination and reality can still coincide.'

Somehow, Simon had obviously written to Goldhayes during some pause on the army's march, for towards the end of November came a travel-stained missive from Richard Trevelyan, addressed to Mistress Lucy and Mistress Thomazine Heron; at the Widow Gooch's house in Pennyfarthing Street in the city of Oxford. It was the first news from Suffolk we had had for nearly six months, and we pored over it. The county was apparently in turmoil, everywhere soldiers being raised, trained, or marched hither and thither. The Sheriff had demanded that Mary yield up all the weapons in the house. 'He went away with two brace of pistols, a fowling-piece of Master Sewell's, and your poor brother Edward's crossbow,' Richard wrote, 'and would have taken more, had he been able to find any. It is now common knowledge here that your brothers have gone to the King's army, their tenants also, but the men that now rule us can do no harm to the estate within the law, it being safe in our hands, and we pay all their infamous taxes and Assessments with a sorry heart; knowing it is for Goldhayes' sake and yet that our coin may buy your brothers' deaths.' He offered his condolences to us and to Grainne, and told of the death of Jamie's friend Robert Jermyn, Sir Thomas's oldest grandson, of a fever in October. I had expected Jamie to take this news hard, sharing as he did Lucy's emotional nature, but to my surprise he accepted it calmly, as if it were almost an anticlimax after the experiences and losses of the past few months. Thus was the war already hardening us.

The last but one day of November was Charles Lawrence's birthday, and as he would come of age he was determined to, as he put it, cheat the times and celebrate with some style. From his home in Warwickshire, where lived his widowed mother and three young sisters, came a cheery letter borne by a carrier, which when opened proved to contain epistles from all his sisters, down to the youngest aged eight, as well as a kindly note to Mistress Gooch thanking her for taking good care of her son. With the letter came a small wooden chest which yielded a pair of fringed embroidered gloves, a book of homilies – 'That's from Sarah, she's of a godly turn of mind,'– a rather crookedly-knitted pair of hose from Jane, who was ten, and a reel of linen hemmed with huge stitches, apparently a bandage. 'And that,' said Charles, laughing as he unwound it, 'must be Peg's contribution. She's no seamstress, even allowing for her youth. And here at the bottom, cunningly concealed . . .' He drew out a leather bag which looked heavy and chinked promisingly. 'This will buy a royal feast for everyone in the house – we Lawrences don't stint on hospitality!'

So the kitchen was piled with provisions bought by Heppy and Charles, Lucy, Meraud and myself on our forays out to the market; carp and capon, mutton and rabbit, cream and eggs and butter and, the final touch, a gallon of sack and a gallon of claret obtained from the Blue Boar at the iniquitous price of a crown a gallon. It would be such a supper, said the Widow, sitting in her kitchen nursing on her lap a sleek-feathered, bright-eyed, chuckling hen, as had not been seen since my stepmother's first husband had died; despite a certain lack of freshness in the carp, a purchase for which the unfortunate Lucy was responsible, as the Widow reminded her. 'Some people don't know a fresh fish when they see it. Nor a stale one neither. I suppose they was always fresh from your own stew-pond before, eh? Well, you're a town-dweller now, lass, and a nose for bad fish is the first thing you'll have to learn.' But her admonishments were given, and taken, in good spirits, and not even the distant sounds which heralded the return of the King and all his army from their failure at London, could intrude on our merriment. 'Well, at least we have a little time before we must take up the military life again,' said Charles, with a lingering glance at the lovely Meraud which she did not fail to notice. 'Let tonight be merry, at least – a farewell party, as well as my birthday supper.'

We were in truth a happy company in the front parlour that evening, with the cold banished by the glowing fire, and the dark put to flight by a dazzling array of candles, and our varying forebodings at the army's return firmly submerged in a lavish display of food and wine, paid for by Charles's mother. Jasper had been put to bed with Betty to watch him, and Heppy and the Widow brought in the steaming dishes, arranged the bulbous earthenware wine-bottles on the side-table, placed the rose-scented finger-bowl in the centre of the table and left us for their own repast in the kitchen. I had tried to persuade them to join us, but the Widow averred she was too old for the company, and Heppy insisted on staying with her. Nor did the fact that we had all had more or less of a hand in the preparation of the meal lessen our enjoyment; indeed, I had a treasured memory of Jamie, with all the address of a swordsman, slicing lemons and horseradish for the fish sauce. His efforts had successfully drowned any lack of freshness in the carp, the mutton was cooked to perfection in its spear-mint sauce, the capon was succulent, fat and tender, and the wine strong and fragrant. Too strong, perhaps; two cups were enough to set my head swimming, and when Charles came round to refill it I had to place my hand over the rim. Jamie, brilliant-eyed and flushed, accepted a third measure despite what was evidently a severe kick under the table, administered by his sister. 'A toast!' said Charles, standing at the head of the table and doffing his hat. 'To Mistress Meraud Trevelyan, the fairest of all the ladies in Oxford!'

Meraud blushed prettily, and lowered her eyes with a fine show of maidenly modesty, As I dutifully drank her health with a sip of the last of my wine, I saw Francis's eyes blazing vivid green upon me. Like Charles, he was more than a little drunk, both with wine and with the last hectic gaiety before the realities of war could again intrude. 'I wish to propose two toasts,' he said, getting to his feet, cup in hand. 'The first to a lady who's been such a comfort to all of us, despite her own grief, as we do not deserve. To Grainne, our love and our thanks!' And as her health was drunk, I saw Grainne's beautiful eyes fill suddenly with unaccustomed tears.

'And the second toast?' Lucy demanded, as Charles refilled the empty cups with a none-too-steady hand. Francis laughed and turned, bowing, to me, his face alive with love and wine and delight. 'The second toast is to the lady there who will shortly, I trust, become my wife – Mistress Thomazine Heron!'

'Mistress Thomazine Heron!' Charles and Jamie repeated, and my health was drunk while Lucy got up with a squeak of pleasure and came round to hug me. 'Oh, Thomazine! At last! After all this time! Oh, I'm so glad, now we'll be truly sisters.'

'After all this time?' I asked. 'It's been eighteen months, you know, not eighteen years.'

'You've kept it very dark, you know,' said Jamie, waving a finger at me. 'I never knew.'

'You never did notice much,' said Lucy. 'I guessed straight away.' She sat down, eyes dancing, and selected one of Mistress Gooch's delicious candied fruits, all a-sparkle with sugar, from the dish in the middle of the table. 'When will it be?'

I looked at Francis, who grinned and sat down, pouring himself more wine. 'As soon as may be, war or no war.'

'I wish you luck and joy,' said Grainne. Charles got to his feet again, with tipsy uncertainty, and raised his cup. 'So here's to the happy couple! May they have a long life and much delight together, both in bed and out of it!'

Francis reached across the table and took my hand as congratulations rang in my ears. 'Don't look so solemn, my lady.'

'How can I help it? No one becomes Lucy's sister-in-law with a light heart!'

There were roars of laughter, even from Lucy, who could not always be relied upon to take teasing in good part. More toasts were drunk, to the King, the Queen, the Prince and even to the absent Widow – 'May her chickens keep her warm at nights,' said Charles, 'for it's certain no one else will!'

Amid the laughter which greeted this rather unkind remark, the hammering on the street door cut like the beat of a drum. We fell abruptly silent, staring at each other. The kitchen door opened and shut, and we heard on the other side of the panelled wall the shuffle of the Widow's feet and her muttering. 'Who's that?' Fine time to call of an evening!' The bolts were drawn back with a reluctant crash. 'Who – who's that?' Jamie echoed, thickly.

We had our answer almost instantly. The door from the passage was hurled open, bringing with it an icy draught from the street which blasted the candles and drew a great gout of smoke from the fire. Simon stood there, very tall and full of menace in his black doublet, black breeches and swirling black cloak. We stared at him, our faces aghast, as his quick hostile glance took in the remains of our repast, the spilt wine and empty bottles and half-full cups, and digested their implications. Simon, notably abstemious himself, had ever been roused to disgust by any drinking to excess, and his reaction now was predictably extreme. 'My God, what's this? I heard the noise of your drunken carousing from Fish Street.'

'Itsh . . .' Jamie swallowed and tried again. 'It's Charles's birthday.'

His eldest brother stared at him, his face hard. 'Get up.'

Jamie got up, unsteadily. Simon said, in a voice thick with suppressed fury, 'When your elders and supposed betters try to debauch you in the future, you will refuse. Understand? Now go and douse your head in water. Go!'

Jamie, weaving slightly, stumbled from the room. Simon turned to Grainne. 'I'd not have thought it fitting, madam, for you to be present at such a gathering, so soon after your bereavement, and in your condition.'

'I was unaware,' said Grainne, her gaze as chilly as his, 'that my doings were any concern of yours, Simon. Now would you kindly shut the door and sit down?'

The door crashed to. Charles got up and indicated Jamie's vacant place. 'Sh – sit there, Captain Heron.'

Simon gave him a glance that stopped him in his tracks and sat him down abruptly. 'I have not come to join in your debauchery. I am shocked beyond measure to see you make such a spectacle before my sister and my wards, all of whom are of tender years. I have come to hear Lieutenant Heron's explanation of why he basely surrendered Ashcott in defiance of his commission from His Majesty.' He turned to

Francis, who was watching him with drunken, bright-eyed malice. 'Yes, I can see you've returned to your old wine-sodden ways again, brother. Now, if the wine hasn't fouled your tongue, explain yourself.'

I could see that Francis was going to say something unforgiveable, and leapt in with speed. 'Simon, he had no choice. If he hadn't both Grainne and I would have died in the crossfire. You see, Hess—'

'I didn't tell you to speak, Thomazine! This can't possibly concern you!'

'But it does!' said Meraud's sweet, soft, treacherous voice. 'She and Francis are lovers, after all.' And as the appalling silence threatened to stretch out for ever, added, 'Didn't you know?'

I had thought that I was not afraid of Simon; but now, seeing the look on his face, I trembled as a deer before the tiger. He swung round on Meraud. 'How long has this been going on for?'

'I don't know, exactly,' said Meraud primly. 'But for certain he tumbled her at Ashcott in the summer.' There was now a distinct, lascivious note of triumph in her voice, but Simon in his fury did not notice it. 'My God! You, of all people! Did you lie together?' And his dark, inimical eyes fixed mine. 'No!' I cried in horror, but even as I spoke blushed guiltily with the memory of that distant, sweet, anguished day. Simon took my heightened colour for guilt, and his face twisted with disgust. 'So he's taught you to lie as well as debauching you, has he? Don't deny it, madam, I can see your guilt writ plain on your face. I've trusted in your innocence all these years, and now with your betrothed ready to claim you, you betray him and me by fornicating with my own brother . . . You're no better than a whore!'

Francis leapt to his feet and hurled the contents of his wine-cup full into Simon's face. Lucy screamed as her eldest brother, the liquid darkening his doublet and staining his collar, threw off his cloak and ripped his sword from its scabbard. 'You'll answer for that!'

'It's no more than you deserve,' Francis said. He was more angry than I had ever seen him, his face white with it and his eyes glittering green. He was not wearing a sword; Charles with fumbling fingers drew his own and tossed it to him in a flash of light, and Francis caught it neatly. Drink had not apparently had much effect on his reflexes. Grainne, moving awkwardly in her last month of pregnancy, got up as if to go between them. 'For God's sake, Simon, are you mad? Put up your sword, this is neither the time nor the place for it, and besides you've an unfair advantage.'

'Why?' Simon demanded viciously. 'Because he's too sodden with drink to hold a sword? If that's unfair it's his own fault.'

'I warn you,' said Francis, smiling wolfishly as I had never seen him before. 'Don't underestimate me, dear brother; no one knows better than you how much practice I've had at holding my drink.'

Simon's sword snaked out wickedly, and Francis parried. We had stood rooted round the table, until at that first clash of metal Lucy screamed, and screamed again. 'Simon! Francis! Oh, God, stop it, make them stop, make them stop!' She made a rush for them, and Charles grabbed her roughly and hauled her back against the wall by the fireplace. Grainne and Meraud joined her; only I remained by the table, staring at all my worst nightmares, my most terrible forebodings, enacted before my eyes, as the two brothers, both tall and lean, one blond and graceful and half-drunk, the other dark, awkward and utterly sober, circled the space between the table and the door.

'Simon!' Grainne appealed again. 'For the love of God, stop this insanity! Do you *want* to kill him?'

Simon's answer was a sudden attack which drove Francis backwards against the table. A wine-bottle rocked and fell, staining the fine damask tablecloth with a pool like blood. Lucy screamed again, as Simon's blade descended, but Francis ducked and dodged neatly out of the way, the sword slicing the edge of the tablecloth where he had been, and turned in his room to the attack. In normal times, he was more than a match for Simon's sword-play, but drink and his recent illness had obviously, as Grainne had seen, given Simon the advantage. His attack only lasted a moment; soon his elder brother was pressing him backwards towards the wall, the crash of metal on metal reaching a crescendo, and in his face, plain for all to see, the intention to kill. I broke free of the shock which had paralysed my limbs, seeking only to stop the fight. Francis's attention wandered for a second as I moved, and the bright lance of steel flicked across his face, leaving a red carved line along his cheekbone. 'Not so attractive to the ladies now,' said Simon, cruelly; and I snatched up his discarded cloak and hurled it across their blades.

It succeeded better than I had hoped. Both swords, muffled by the heavy flying folds of material, were wrenched from the brothers' hands; and they stood, breathing hard, facing each other. At that moment, the door opened behind Francis and two troopers, whom I did not recognize, rushed in, pistols in their hands. 'Take that man!' Simon said violently, and his hand shot out to indicate Francis.

'By God, you shall not!' Charles, moved out of his stupor for the first time, made a lunge for the nearest soldier, knocking him off balance as he cannoned into him. The man's pistol exploded in a crash and a great acrid cloud of powdersmoke. At the same instant, Francis picked up the silver candlestick standing by the little table by the door and hurled it at the other trooper. The man dropped his pistol and clapped his hands to his smashed face, and Francis ducked down, wrenched his sword from the clinging folds of Simon's cloak where it lay like a black pool on the polished floor, and vanished through the door. With an oath I had never thought to hear on his lips, Simon grabbed the fallen, undischarged pistol and with the unhurt trooper careered in pursuit. Their feet crashed down towards the kitchen; we heard above the moans of the injured man the double slam of the back door as quarry and hunters disappeared into the garden. Almost immediately there came the muffled report of a pistol-shot, and Lucy, her face the colour of lard, slid to the floor in a dead faint.

When the Widow appeared in the doorway, the room was in utter chaos: chairs overturned, wine bottles and cups spilt, the candlestick dented in a corner and the pervasive sharp smell of powder everywhere. Lucy lay in a tumble of black skirts on the floor, Charles attempting to revive her by splashing water from the fingerbowl on to her face; Meraud was mopping the blood from the trooper's nose and mouth with a napkin dipped in the same bowl; Grainne holding the discharged pistol and Simon's sword firmly by the fireplace. My legs having given way, I had sat down on one of the few chairs still upright, feeling sick and dizzy. 'You'll be pleased to hear he got away,' said Mistress Gooch. 'They're still after him, though. Who's hurt? Mistress Lucy?'

'She fainted,' said Grainne. 'The trooper had a candlestick in his face. Wherever that pistol ball went, it did no harm to any of us.'

'Thank you, Charles,' I said, my voice surprisingly steady. Charles, remarkably sobered, grunted. 'The least I could do. Dear God, what an end to a merry supper! Is he mad?'

'Who? Simon? No – I'd always thought him quite sane,' I said, and shivered. 'But he has a blind spot where Francis is concerned – always has had.'

'More than a blind spot,' said the Widow. 'Mad hatred is apter. Well, we'd best put some order into this room, and get Lucy to her chamber.'

Lucy moved, her face still grey, and shouted suddenly, 'No! Stop it, please, for God's sake, stop!'

'It's all right,' Charles said, his face concerned. 'It's all over. He's got away.'

Lucy sat up, her eyes staring with terror. 'But I heard a shot!'

'Missed him by a yard,' said the Widow with satisfaction. 'Now come on, lass. It's all over, all quiet. Heppy'll take you upstairs while the rest of us put this shambles to rights.'

Lucy, still shaking, was guided upstairs by a wide-eyed Heppy. The trooper, his nose swollen and broken, his eyes already blackened and his mouth split and leaking blood, was dispatched to the kitchen. Dizzy and still weak and trembling, I joined the others in righting chairs, carrying plates and mopping up the spilt food and wine. The pistol-ball was discovered embedded in the panelling above the mantel, too deep to be readily extracted. It did not take us long to remove all but this evidence of the supper and the fight. The room as we left it seemed impossibly normal after the intense drama that had been enacted there not half-an-hour before.

The kitchen, too, was warm and quiet as usual. Jamie, snoring, was laid out on the same straw pallet in the alcove by the fire that Jacobson had occupied. Weakly, we sat on the benches around the big scrubbed table and the Widow made mugs of mulled ale with roasted apples frothing at the top of each one. 'Tankard of Lambswool's always the best thing to set you to rights. Yes, Master Lawrence, I know you've had more than enough tonight, but this'll do you no harm.'

Heppy came in and reported that Mistress Lucy had fallen asleep, and that Jasper had slept through it all, though Betty had been in a fever to know what had happened. 'Thass a proper terrible thing, Mistress Thomazine. Who'd hev thought such an evening would've come to that? I pray as they don't catch him.'

I did not like to think what Simon would do to Francis should he be captured, and took a sip of warming apple-scented ale instead. It was as much as I could do not to choke over it; only an hour ago I had been so happy, rejoicing that at last Francis and I were to be wed, and now it had all gone horribly, dreadfully amiss. I knew as I gazed through blinding tears at the faintly smug smile on Meraud's lovely face, that I would never, never forgive her for what she had done.

A knocking came from the front door. We exchanged wide-eyed glances, as nervous as a herd of deer. 'I'll go,' said the Widow, and got up and went out. We heard the bolts drawn back and the tramp of feet, and then Simon stood in the doorway, his collar still stained with wine and his hair wet and dripping from a sudden rainstorm. He looked round at our hostile faces and then said, 'He has escaped us for the present. I apologize to you for the scene which I was forced to enact in front of you.'

'Forced!' said Grainne, with a look on her face that would

have quelled anyone less eaten up with pride and hatred. 'Have you any notion, Simon Heron, of how despicable your behaviour has been?'

Simon ignored that. He said, 'Where is Lucy?'

'She fainted,' said Grainne. 'She is now asleep upstairs.'

'And Jamie?'

'Sleeping it off in the corner,' said the Widow. 'There's no harm done there.'

'No harm done . . .' Simon's face for a moment bore an extraordinary mixture of revulsion and anger and bitterness. Then it passed, and he turned his head at last to me. 'Thomazine, I wish to speak to you. Now.' And he turned on his heel and walked back down the passage to the front parlour. For a moment I sat there, clutching my mug of Lamb's Wool like a talisman, staring at Grainne as if she could give me the strength I needed to face Simon's rage. She gave a barely perceptible nod of her head, and, with a desperately thundering heart and legs which shook beneath their enveloping skirts, I rose and followed Simon to the parlour.

He was lighting candles as I entered. The room seemed untouched by the drama, but the smell of stale food and wine and burnt powder still prickled my nostrils. I shut the door behind me and stood, my hands locked together to still their shaking, stiffened to meet his anger. Silent and deliberate, my eldest cousin lit the last candle with his taper, blew it out, and turned to face me. With a shock, in his harsh face I read no anger but sadness and reproach. 'Thomazine, how, how could you?'

Anger I could have dealt with, but not this, not so easily. I said hopelessly, 'I love him. He is part of me. You couldn't understand how much . . .'

'You betrayed our trust,' said Simon. 'Mine, and Dominic's. A betrothal is as binding as marriage. While you were promised to him, you were seduced by my brother, taking advantage of your innocence and tender years.'

'No!' I cried. 'No, it wasn't like that! He didn't seduce me, he didn't want to, he wanted to marry me—' My voice shook, but I swallowed and carried on, '—but I offered myself.' Better to have Simon think me a whore than to see yet another score against Francis. Simon stared at me, his face frankly disbelieving. 'You can't seriously expect me to swallow that tale, Thomazine. You don't know what's he's like, you didn't see him here when we were students. I'll swear no woman was proof against his lecherous charm. I thought he'd left that behind when he came back to Goldhayes – I never dreamed that you of all people would succumb to his blandishments. I suppose as before he weaves seductive dreams of love to woo you?'

I flushed, defensively. 'Simon, I tell you it was not like that. We loved – love each other, truly, and I'm as certain of that as I am of my own existence.'

Simon laughed, a derisive humourless sound which raised my hackles and my despair alike. 'You have been taken in, Thomazine, gulled most thoroughly. Remember that he is a third son who of his own volition has thrown away all hopes of bettering himself through hard work, and has now obviously fixed his hopes on your money and property. He no more feels love for you than he can fly.'

I knew then that nothing could shake Simon's belief in his brother's villainy. He had ever been one to trust only in what he wanted to believe, and just as previously he had trusted my innocence when the true facts had been obvious to the perceptive, so now he had fixed his mind firmly on Francis's supposed transgressions to the exclusion of all else. I said, my voice threaded with despair, 'It's no good, Simon, you've always seen only what you want to see. I could argue with you until Kingdom Come and present all the proof you wished and it would still be of no use . . . Please, promise me you won't harm him?'

'What I did was in the heat of anger. You need not fear that I will kill him, if that's in your mind, not now. But by God, if he tries to seduce you again it'll be a different tale,' said Simon. He crossed to the mantelpiece and stared up at the panelling, all marred and splintered where the bullet had struck it. 'I can have him imprisoned if he dares show his face here again.'

'What in God's name for?'

'Cowardice in surrendering Ashcott.' He ticked them off on his fingers, the roll-call of doom. 'For that alone he could be shot. Striking his superior officer. Desertion.'

Shocked at the rank injustice, I cried, 'But it was you forced him to desert, as you call it. If it wasn't for your stupid hatred he'd not have fled. And Ashcott – he did it to save Grainne, and me. It was how Hess died – we'd have been caught in crossfire and killed for certain if he hadn't surrendered. We owe him our lives and you call it cowardice!'

Simon turned, weary and implacable, to face me. 'You always defended him to me. I wondered why.' For a second his fists clenched at the betrayal. 'Tell me, for how long has this been going on?'

'Since the spring before last. But Simon, it's not true that we were ever lovers . . .' and saw that I had said and revealed too much in my earlier talk. There was no chance now that he would believe me. He said, 'Are you with child?'

I flushed indignantly, at the same time remembering my distant, foolish hopes. 'No, I am not, and no cause to be!'

'Then,' said Simon, pursuing an earlier train of thought, 'you lied to me when you told me that you did not wish to marry Dominic because he was a Papist. It was because you were infatuated with Francis.' He spoke the words with contempt. 'My God, he's corrupted you so thoroughly, hasn't he? Fornication, falsehood, treachery, drunkenness . . . I'm not sorry I called you whore, for it seems I was not mistaken. You will be lucky to marry Dominic, now, after your shame.'

'I don't wish to marry Dominic, not now, not ever!'

'Well, you can be certain you will not marry Francis,' said Simon angrily. 'I'll see him dead first, the drunken, womanizing craven. This whole business has sickened me, the viciousness under my nose, the trust I placed so mistakenly in both of you – and not one of my family or so-called friends saw fit to inform me of the stink in my own household, though they must have known.'

'Jamie didn't. Nor did Meraud, till Ashcott,' I said. Simon swung away from me. 'My sister, my mother, Mistress

Sewell . . . thus does the corruption spread. It shall be cut out, this canker. Thank God Meraud told me!'

'She did it to spite me,' I said, aware that my words sounded like spite themselves. Simon smacked his fist against the table. 'Spite? What reason for spite can that quiet, sweet-tempered child have against you, save what you yourself have done to offend her? My God, you disgust me. Get out now, before I am tempted to use violence against you. Go on – out!'

I fled, defeated by a prejudice and hatred that I had never expected to exist, even in the prudish Simon. In the passage outside stood the Widow, blatantly eavesdropping; without any thought at all I flung myself at her and sobbed my heart out on her bony chest. The parlour door opened and closed; there was a pause as Simon evidently stared at us, then the Widow spat at him with a rich, boundless contempt, and without any word he went out. The door slammed behind him with a crash that shuddered the house, and he was gone.

Mistress Gooch led me upstairs, and gave me laudanum to quieten my hopeless, hysterical tears, and tucked me in beside the slumbering Lucy as if she were the mother I had never had. Then she sat beside me, lit eerily by the one candle, holding my hand as my exhausted weeping finally stumbled to its end, and sleep crept up. 'Don't worry, my dear. I know what he is to you, and what you are to him, and it's plain to me that brother of his can't recognize true love when he sees it. Probably because he's never known any himself, he's secretly jealous of what you have with Francis. But we'll do something, try to persuade him; somehow we'll make it come right.'

'I suppose he *is* jealous,' I said, as the treacherous peace of approaching sleep relaxed my limbs and gave to all the events of the evening a deceitful distance and unreality. 'Lucy said once, oh, a long, long time ago, that he needed a wife . . . perhaps that would mellow him . . . and he's never liked Francis anyway . . . but I think another part of it is being deceived by us. It's as if he's angry with himself because he never noticed, because we gulled him as thoroughly as Francis is supposed to have gulled me. You don't believe that, do you?' I stared up into her kind, witch-like, sharp-nosed face. 'You don't believe it's all lies, that he's only after my money?'

'I don't,' said the Widow. 'I've seen his face when he looks at you, and that's no lie. It's plain you were made for each other.'

'A marriage of true minds . . . but so many impediments,' I whispered drowsily. The Widow released my hand and got up. 'Now that's enough for tonight. You'll wake Lucy in a minute. Go to sleep and we'll do what we can in the morning.'

But in the morning I woke with a sore throat and tickling nose, sure harbingers of a head-cold, and the Widow took one look at me and told me to stay in bed. By afternoon I was sneezing, shivering and feverish, and when Simon appeared with Dominic I was asleep, and they had to go away without seeing me. Everyone in the house was very kind. The Widow made broth and hot ale and tore up an old sheet when I ran out of handkerchiefs. Lucy went out with Jamie, hang-dog and full of headache, and returned with a book, rather battered and with cut pages disclosing that it was second-hand, which proved to be a volume of Master Shakespeare's sonnets. She did not know whether to be sympathetic or offended when I burst yet again into foolish tears. Grainne, who never caught colds, appeared with Jasper and Orange, and the antics of child and kitten brought a weak smile to my face, and for a little while made me forget my troubles. Orange had disappeared under the bed, and Jasper was trying to extract him, when the Widow came in, a disapproving look on her face, carrying a huge bunch of Christmas roses, with their white waxy petals. 'Not from Master Francis,' she said. 'From your other suitor, and he hopes to call on you tomorrow, if you're better.'

411

'Well, he won't see me,' I said wildly. 'And he's not my suitor; I won't ever marry him, I refuse to!'

The Widow put the Christmas roses down. 'No one's going to make you if you don't want to, not even that prejudiced oaf who calls himself your guardian. Though this Captain Drakelon – funny name, foreign-sounding – I've never seen such a good-looking young man.'

'I know what he's like – I've been betrothed to him since I was ten.'

'But prefer your cousin, eh?'

'This one's my cousin, too.'

'Does no good, all this cousin marriage,' said the Widow, arranging the roses in a little chased silver bowl. 'Your own parents were cousins, I heard tell – both Herons. Weakens the blood – seen it in chickens, brings out the faults. You'd be better off without either of 'em.'

Jasper emerged dustily from under the bed, a squirming Orange held firmly to his bosom. 'They're pretty. What're they?'

'Christmas roses. Not true roses, mind, but a kind of hellebore.' She turned to me. 'Do you want me to send Captain Drakelon away when next he comes?'

'Send who away?' Jasper demanded, looking from my face to the Widow's. His mother said, 'Nothing to do with you, poppet, and next time you ask a question remember to say please. Now go downstairs and let that poor cat out before it bursts.'

Jasper trotted out, having to put down Orange before he could reach to open and close the door. When he had gone, I said wearily, 'I don't know. I wish Francis would come back.'

'He won't,' said the Widow bluntly. 'Your chivalrous cousin has left a trooper on guard at the door. Half the street thinks we've got the plague and the other half is convinced there's a fortune in plate in the attic. Young Charles has gone out to look for him, but there's no sign. He's gone to ground in one of his old haunts, shouldn't wonder, but I don't know where they are. His brother does, I expect, so he won't stay hid long. Well, are you going to receive the fine Captain, or no?'

'No,' I said, and sneezed.

But I had forgotten how persuasive Dominic Drakelon could be. The next morning I was up, better but still cold-ridden, and sitting in a chair by the chamber fire, reading. I heard the knock on the street door and leapt to peer out of the window, but was too late to see any more than the top of the trooper's sturdy pot helmet as he stood outside, gawked at by children to whom a soldier was still a comparative novelty. I could hear the Widow's voice raised in argument and braced myself to meet Simon. But the quick footsteps up the stairs were not Simon's. I barely had time to realize it before the door burst open and there, filling the space of it, and bowing flamboyantly, was Dominic.

He was bigger, broader, in every way. He wore the brilliant scarlet coat of the King's Lifeguard, with glorious intricate lace falling from his collar. His red sash was fringed with gold and the scabbard of his sword was elaborately decorated. His black hair fell in immaculate glossy ringlets to his shoulders, a thin moustache cut a dash above his mouth, and his eyes were the same vivid compelling blue that I remembered.

Meraud's eyes. Feeling breathless and sick, I rose to my feet and curtseyed. With conscious gallantry, my betrothed raised me up, his lips brushing my hand as his eyes devoured my face. 'Well, I'd seen the promise, but never thought to find such beauty as this! My sparrow, you have grown ravishing!'

I was well aware of my streaming eyes, my reddened nose and swollen face. I said drily, 'It's not possible to be in looks with a head-cold.'

'I was desolated to hear of your illness, my love, and pray you will soon be recovered. I resolved to call upon you as

413

soon as I heard you were in Oxford, and Simon gave me his leave to pay my addresses to you. I apologize for disturbing you now, but I could not bear to wait longer, and we have much to discuss.'

I stared at him, wondering how he had the effrontery to call me his love. Then, recollecting my manners, I said, 'Pray sit down, sir. I fear you are acting under a misapprehension. Simon cannot have told you; I do not wish any more to marry you.'

For a moment something like anger flashed across Dominic's face, so quick I doubted I had seen it. Then, he said, 'I have heard the whole sorry tale of your terrible experience from Simon. You are not the first innocent to be taken in by a flattering voice and winning ways, nor will you be the last, and I care not a rap for anything that has happened before now. All I wish is that, as has been long agreed between us, you become my wife with all speed. You'll be safe then from wagging tongues.'

'It was agreed between your parents and my guardian, and I had no part in it, nor was I old enough to understand the implications. And I have no time for wagging tongues,' I said angrily. 'I'm sorry, Dominic, I will not marry you, betrothal or no betrothal, and neither you nor Simon can force me to the altar. And that's an end to it.'

Dominic stared at me in disbelief. 'My God, that rogue must have truly wormed his way into your heart. Well, I swear by Mary Mother that you shall forget him and marry me of your own free will – if it takes five years or five days, by God I shall replace him in the end.' And he took two strides forward, gripped my shoulders where I stood rigid with fury by my chair, and bent his head to kiss me.

Drake had not left my side since Francis's disappearance, suffering Orange and Jasper so that he could be near me, as if he understood that Francis had been dear to me too. Growling, he leapt up from the fireside and rushed to my defence. Dominic's lips had barely touched mine as I frantically turned my head to escape him, when Drake sank his teeth into his stockinged leg. With a yell, my betrothed sprang back, kicking out in a frantic effort to dislodge the

414

dog. Laughter bubbling in my throat, I plucked the silver bowl from the table and hurled its contents, water and Christmas roses, full on to Drake's head and all over Dominic. The greying muzzle opened, Dominic hopped backwards with all dignity utterly vanished, and I grabbed Drake's collar before he could renew the attack. 'I'm sorry. He must have thought you intended me harm. I think you'd best go.'

My cousin bent to examine his injured leg. The exquisite silk stocking was utterly ruined, both by toothmarks and by the slow-welling blood. 'That's Francis's dog, isn't it,' he said, rage plain in his voice. 'It should have been knocked on the head years ago, and by God if it tries that again I'll do it. Make sure it isn't here when I call next time.' And, limping, he made his exit with as much of his lost dignity as he could muster. 'You can be sure there won't be a next time,' I called after him, a parting shot I could not resist, and then, unable to contain myself longer, I hugged Drake and burst into wild laughter, which he must surely have heard as he went down the stairs.

The next time he called, Charles blocked his way implacably, telling him I did not wish to see him, and he had perforce to go away. I found Dominic's behaviour very strange, this sudden violent attention after all the years of silence, and it worried me. I had wondered childishly long ago at his manner, and now I suspected that he might be a little unbalanced.

Tom Sewell paid a call to offer his condolences and sympathy to Grainne, ruffling Jasper's hair and pulling Drake's ears. It was from him that we learned that Dominic's father had just been reported dead, a prisoner after Edgehill Fight, mortally wounded in that dreadful tangle around the royal standard. So he was now Sir Dominic Drakelon, lord of Upper Denby Hall – 'If there's anything left of it,' said Tom, who seemed to have the same taste for army gossip as he had had for Goldhayes talk. 'Rumour has it he's lost everything to Roundhead plunderers. No wonder he's turned so ardent, Thomazine – not only did his father by all accounts urge him very strongly to marry and secure the

inheritance, but your fortune, that must be a proper power-
ful lure.'

'Strange then that Simon supports his suit so strongly,' I
said 'since that's the self-same reason he's disgusted with
Francis's wooing.'

'Yes,' said Tom uncomfortably, as embarrassed as ever by
awkward situations, 'but the two are entirely different.
Dominic's been betrothed to you for years, yet you went
behind his back and Simon's to dally with Francis. And
besides, Dominic's got some prospects and an inheritance,
however plundered. Francis has nothing.'

'I think it's time you went, Tom,' said Grainne calmly. 'No
one wants to hear that sort of talk at the moment, I'm afraid
– feelings are running too high. It's all we can do to keep
from laying violent hands on Simon.' And she firmly
pushed a bewildered, unhappy Tom from the house.

On the Sunday we walked the few yards to St Aldate's
Church, and listened to Master Bowles, the rector, expounding on the sins of rebellion and the duty of obedience to
King and parents alike. It was not what I, at least, wanted to
hear, but my anger was forgotten when we emerged into
the cold blustery December day to hear even from the
church door the sound of the Bellman, Oxford's dis-
seminator of news and proclamations. We hurried to listen,
joining the crowd around him as he stood in the street at
Carfax, by the beautiful fountain where we drew our water
in common with the other townspeople, and boomed out
the news that the King required all horses in the town, with
the exception of troopers' animals, to be brought that afternoon to St Giles' Fields, where the best would be taken for
the King's army and payment made.

Lucy looked at me in dismay. 'Oh, no, not our horses!
They're bound to take mine, and your Chalcedony,
Thomazine, she's so beautiful.'

'Good thing, I say,' said the Widow as we made our way
disconsolately back to Pennyfarthing Street. 'Do nothing

416

but eat their heads off to no good. Stable's full enough with 'em all.'

'There are only eight,' I said, 'and two of those belong to Charles and Francis, so the Goblin's safe, at least. And I don't think they'll take the grey cob, Mistress Gooch, he's too old and fat and slow. It's our riding horses they'll want.'

'You could say Chalcedony was a trooper's horse; I don't suppose they'd know any different,' said Jamie. 'But my Stag, and Grainne's horse, and Meraud's, and yours, Lucy – they're all Goldhayes horses, and valuable! What would Simon say?'

'He'd say it was vital to help the King's cause, even with such a sacrifice,' Grainne pointed out. 'But I doubt if Ned would have said the same.'

We were silent, thinking of Ned who had bred or bought all the horses in that stable, save for Charles's and the Widow's grey cob. In the end, I said reluctantly, 'Simon's sure to notice if they're still there. And there's always the chance that they may not take them all.'

So that afternoon, we put headcollars on the five horses who had carried us so faithfully from Suffolk, and joined the crowds progressing similarly up North Street, jamming through the gateway under the Bocardo, and out towards St Giles' Fields. The tack we left behind, having no mind to give that up as well. Lucy, hugging her cloak around her in the wind, was close to tears, and I also felt a foolish pricking behind my eyelids as I looked at Chalcedony's gallant flecked head, her proud tail and sweet-natured dark eyes. She had become mine at the same time as I had fallen in love with Francis, and to give her away seemed like a denial of my feelings, a symbol of the ending of our love. I thrust such ominous thoughts to the back of my mind, and wondered instead, as I saw a fine grey colt being led sullenly by, whether my beautiful Boreas, left behind at Goldhayes an unbroken yearling, would also be taken, but to serve the enemy cause.

The fields around St Giles' church were thick with horses, ranging from sturdy feather-legged carthorses. slow of speed and kind of eye, to dancing overbred riding animals, although more of the former sort than the latter. 'It reminds me of the horse-fairs at Northampton,' said Charles, looking round at the busy crowd and the jostling horses. 'There must be four or five hundred here.'

We joined a huge group of waiting owners and horses. On another part of the field groups of cavalry officers watched each animal as it was trotted past. Those who were rejected, the lesser number, returned jubilantly with their animals to the town; the unlucky ones either accepted their loss with as good a grace as they could muster or, more frequently, could be seen arguing furiously with the implacable officers.

Someone jogged my arm as I stood with Chalcedony, my eyes still ceaselessly searching the crowd for Francis. I turned, startled, and saw a grimy child of about ten or so with lank brown hair and no shoes. He thrust a fold of paper into my hands, and disappeared into the crowd. No one had seen him; Chalcedony's bulk shielded me from the others. Instinctively secretive, I furtively unfolded the paper and stared down with a wildly leaping heart at Francis's quick, flamboyant scrawl.

'Dear heart, if you would marry me still, rise at midnight tonight and meet me at the back-gate with what you might need for a long journey. Bring the Goblin and another horse for yourself. Do not worry, all else is arranged. Tell no one,' and at the bottom, simply, 'Yours forever. Francis.'

With trembling hands I tucked the paper inside my glove. So he had been somewhere in that crowd, guessing perhaps that I would be here this afternoon, and had used that child as his messenger. I wondered where he had been hid for the last five days. But it did not matter; what mattered was that I would be free, free of Dominic and Simon and the prospect of a forced marriage that was repugnant to me, and at last free to be with Francis, in spirit and body and mind, and to marry him. I did not care where he intended to take me, although I guessed Catholm; it was enough that he would come for me, and take me away.

So dazed was I with excitement that I did not really mind when our turn came to lead out our horses and all but

Grainne's ugly, long-backed old mare were taken. The soldiers tried to give us promissory notes; Charles, who was ready for this, insisted on cash, and eventually his arguments and threats won the day. We returned to Pennyfarthing Street with only one horse and a leather bag of silver coins, less than the horses' value but better than a worthless piece of paper.

I had left Chalcedony with hardly a backward glance.

That evening I could scarcely eat, and by pleading a return of my cold escaped early to bed. Before Lucy came up to join me, I had packed some linen and an old dress into a cloth bag which could be attached to a saddle, and tucked into the bottom a handful of the money from the horses without a qualm. After all, it had been paid for Chalcedony, who was mine. Then I stuffed the bag under the bed, laid out my riding habit on the top of the clothes press, covered it with the Turkey carpet, stripped to my shift and scrambled into bed. Sleep, of course was impossible, but I lay still with my eyes shut, rigid with tension, while Lucy tiptoed round the room, making ready for bed, both she and Heppy taking ludicrously elaborate pains to avoid waking me. At last, the candle was blown out, Lucy snuggled up beside me, and she and Heppy in her truckle bed were soon fast asleep.

I thanked God that neither of them was easily woken. I lay stiffly, listening for the chimes of the lantern clock in the back parlour; and on the stroke of a quarter to twelve slipped quietly out of bed. Lucy did not stir, nor did Heppy. With fumbling hands I buttoned up the doublet of my riding-habit, hooking on the skirt, pulling on petticoats and stockings. Then with fumbling terrified fingers I picked up my boots and gloves and hat, and the bag from under the bed, and crept noiselessly from the chamber. So far, so good.

I tiptoed down the stairs. avoiding the third from top and the bottom one, both of which creaked, and slipped into the kitchen. The fire still lit the room with a faint red glow, although it had been banked up to last all night. Beside it the hens perched on the cupboard and on the handles of spit and saucepans. I sat down on the bench, scarce daring to breathe lest they be disturbed, and pulled on my riding boots and my gloves. The folded paper was no longer there; for a moment I panicked, and then relaxed. I could remember removing my gloves in the street on the way home, and if it had fallen out then was hardly likely to do harm trampled into the mud. Very carefully, I lifted the key to the back gate from its nail by the fire, and slipped out of the back door.

I got through the garden more by luck than judgement, for the clouds were thick and black and I could see nothing. But I had made sure that afternoon that the right saddles and bridles were laid out where I could find them, and also a lanthorn with flint and tinder. I shut the stable door, breathing in the warm aroma of horse, and found and lit the lanthorn. The four heads turned inquiringly towards me, and I prayed they would not make a noise. From the straw where I had tied him a few hours before, Drake leapt up, tail lashing with pleasure, and whined pleadingly.

'Ssh, old boy! I've a deal to do before I can let you go,' I whispered, patting him, and set about saddling Hobgoblin and Charles's chestnut gelding. I did not like taking Charles's horse, but I hoped he would understand, and as a trooper would be issued with another. One day, I vowed, I would repay him.

At last I was ready. I unhitched both Goblin and the chestnut and led them to the door, then I released Drake and with the reins and his leash wrapped round my hand, doused the lanthorn and opened the stable door.

Outside it was bitter after the warmth of the stable, and I shivered with cold and excitement. I made my way by touch to the back gate, the two horses following noiselessly on the soft ground, put the key in the lock with only a little fumbling, turned and opened it. There was a ring somewhere on the outside wall; I ran my hand along the rough stone, located it and loosely knotted the reins and Drake's leash to it. Then I crept back, shut the gate and locked it, pushing the key underneath. If by some disaster Francis did not come, I could retrieve it and let myself back in.

I heard, very quietly, a footstep. A darker shape loomed up out of the darkness. I would have known him anywhere, and with a suppressed sob of relief flung myself into his arms. We kissed with joyous hunger: then Francis lifted his lips away and said very softly, 'I knew you would come . . . there's a barn where we can hide till dawn, then we can slip through the gates. Are you sure no one knows?'

'Quite sure,' I whispered, trembling in his arms – and then suddenly, everywhere, giving me the lie, there were running footsteps, and torches abruptly thrust from round the street corner, illuminating us brilliantly as we stood stock still by the horses. Drake barked frantically and rushed forward, but I had tied him too securely and he fell back, choking. Francis said, 'It seems someone knew!' and pushed me towards Hobgoblin, wrenching the reins from the ring.

'Take him!' Simon's voice yelled, and half a dozen troopers with swords and staves in their hands rushed at us. Francis had his own sword out, and slashed at them like a madman, trying to win a space for me to get to the horses. I was grabbed from behind and screamed, kicking and struggling like one possessed, but whoever had hold of me, his hands gripping my arms, was too strong for me. Nor did Francis have any chance against six. One of them knocked the sword spinning from his hand with a blow of a stave, and then they were on him, kicking and beating him into submission around the clattering, startled horses, whilst Drake barked futilely and I kicked and screamed, powerless to do anything.

'Enough,' said Simon, coming forward, the two torchbearers on either side of him. The troopers reluctantly withdrew, rubbing bruised knuckles and putting up their staves. I did not recognize any of them, and doubted whether any of our Suffolk men could have been brought to do such a thing. Francis lay in the mud by the gate, unconscious, the blood and bruises already marring his face, his arms spread wide. Drake, whining in his throat, wriggled on his belly past the restless horses and tried to lick his hand, but the rope checked him.

'He is a coward and a deserter and we have moreover caught him in the act of abducting my ward by deceit,' said Simon. 'Take him to the castle, on my authority and the Prince's, and make sure he is kept close.'

Two of the troopers lifted the heedless bedraggled body of my lover and slung him, none too gently, over Charles's horse. I stared, too numb with horror to do anything, as they disappeared into the darkness; then saw Simon's furious twisted face looming towards me, and fainted.

When I came to myself, I was not in my own bed, but in one of the top floor rooms. I could see, in the daylight leaking through the warped shutters, that it was empty. For a moment I wondered how I had got there; then I remembered everything. Francis was a prisoner, and Simon would make sure he was charged as a deserter and with the supposedly needless surrender of Ashcott. And for either of those two 'crimes', I knew, he could be shot.

I stared at the bare whitewashed plaster walls. Surely Simon could not do such a thing to his own brother? But even if he regretted his hasty action, once the wheels of military justice had started to turn, it might very well be too late.

I leapt out of bed. Someone had undressed me, but it was my deep blue everyday gown that lay on the end of the bed, not my riding habit. I ran barefoot in my shift to the door. It was locked.

For a moment I could not believe it, then anger washed over me and I pounded on the stout oak with my two fists. 'Hey! Let me out!'

In a flash, I heard footsteps running up the stairs, then Lucy's voice, breathless, said just the other side of the door, 'It's all right. Mistress Gooch has gone for a locksmith, he'll be here soon. Are you all right? What happened?'

I ignored her questions. 'What do you mean, a locksmith? Where's the key? Who locked me in, for God's sake?'

'Simon did,' said Lucy. 'And he's taken the key with him, and then not an hour ago he rode out with Prince Rupert's regiment, and foot and dragoons as well, thousands of them, going to Thame. We were at our wit's end, for no one knew how long they'd be gone, and then the Widow thought of the locksmith. But why has he locked you in? What happened last night? All we knew of it was a great noise in the street behind the house that woke us all up, and then Simon came marching in carrying you, with a face like thunder, and demanding to know where there was a chamber you could be put on your own. So we said this one, and he just carried you upstairs and told Heppy to undress you and lay out your clothes, and when she'd done that he locked the door on you, pocketed the key, and marched out without another word. And we've been in a fever to know what happened ever since. Was it something to do with Francis?'

I told her everything, from the note thrust into my hand at St Giles' Fields to that last appalling moment when I had seen Francis taken off to the castle. As the story unfolded, her gasps of excitement turned to exclamations of horror; when I had finished, she said nothing for a long time, and by the sounds I knew she was weeping. At last, rather muffled, she said, 'Oh, God, poor Francis. And poor you. It must have been terrible, to think you were free together at last and then to have Simon and his men attack you. Did they hurt him badly?'

'I don't know, they wouldn't let me see,' I said, and then with a violence which surprised me, Lucy cried, 'I could kill Simon! Why, why, oh why does he have to be so cruel? Can't he *see* how stupid and ridiculous he's being? Everyone here thinks the same; Jamie wouldn't speak to him last night, and the Widow looked at him as if he was something that had crawled out from under a stone, and Charles went off this morning to join his troop saying he thanked God he wasn't in Simon's. I shall miss Charles,' she went on inconsequentially, 'he's been so kind. And still Simon can't see or understand that he's done anything that's in any way wrong, or out of the ordinary. or despicable. He thinks it's his bounden duty to have his own brother dragged off to prison like a common criminal. I hope he rots in Hell!'

I waited till her sobs had died down, and then said, 'What puzzles me is how he found out about our meeting. Unless

423

he was having Francis watched and followed, which seems a trifle far-fetched even for Simon, the only way he could have found out is by somehow getting hold of that note. And I couldn't find it when I looked for it last night – I thought I must've dropped it in North Street yesterday.'

'And someone picked it up and somehow gave it to Simon or one of his men?' said Lucy. 'It doesn't sound very probable.'

But I remembered, suddenly, Betty slipping out of the house the previous evening, on an errand for Meraud that I had paid little heed to, so excited had I been by the prospect of reunion with Francis. 'I think I know who,' I said with deep bitterness, 'and if it was her then it's highly probable. Why does she bear such a grudge against me?'

'Meraud? Oh, don't be ridiculous,' said Lucy. 'You've got as much of a blind spot where she's concerned as Simon has for Francis.'

'I think after she revealed all to Simon at Charles's supper, I'm entitled to have reservations about her. You have to admit, it was exceedingly well done.'

'Ye-es,' said Lucy, sounding dubious, 'yes, that was a bit strange. Ah, here comes the locksmith!'

As the Widow escorted my deliverer up the stairs, I hastily pulled on my gown, trying to hook up the bodice without assistance and getting into something of a tangle. 'Don't worry, lass, we'll soon have you out of there!' the Widow called, and sure enough it was only a few minutes before the delicate metallic probing noises from the lock ceased and the door swung triumphantly open. Before I could move, Lucy burst into the room and embraced me, lavishly. 'Oh, poor, poor Thomazine, you're so cold! Your hands are like ice, and there's no fire in here, oh, how could Simon have been so cruel?'

The locksmith's eyes were fairly popping out of his head at this. Whatever tale the Widow had spun him, it had not involved deliberate incarceration by callous guardians. But I was in no mood for circumspection. I tore myself free from her clinging, affectionate hands and said, 'Whatever I suffered, and it wasn't much, how much worse must Francis have fared? Lucy, come on, we've got to go to the castle and get him out!'

'Break your fast first,' Mistress Gooch warned, putting her hand out to detain me as I rushed to the door. 'Or we'll have you keeling over in the street. He can kick his heels for an hour more.'

So I snatched a hunk of bread and cheese, standing in the kitchen, while Mistress Gooch paid the locksmith out of our store of coin, enhanced by the disposal of our horses, and Jamie and Meraud plied me with questions about the previous night. By now certain that it had been Meraud who had betrayed me, I had the greatest difficulty in keeping my hands from her face, and answered her inquiries in curt monosyllables which made Jamie eye me with a puzzled, annoyed expression. Then, united in our purpose and indignation, we left Grainne, now periously close to her time, in charge of the house, and set off for the castle.

Oxford Castle had once been a great stronghold, scene of the escape five hundred years ago of the Empress Matilda across the Thames, all in white in a snowstorm to deceive the besieging forces of the wicked King Stephen. As told by my father, it had been a tale to stir the blood, and for months after I had taken on the role of the Empress in our games, while my long-suffering brother had perforce to play King Stephen. But Matilda would not now have recognized her fortress; sadly decayed, the towers dismantled or crumbling, it had degenerated into the county gaol, with a permanently erected gibbet on which common criminals kicked away their lives. The war, however, seemed to have given it a new lease of life, and the sound of mallet and hammer and chisel greeted us as we walked down Castle Street towards the main entrance. Workmen were erecting scaffolding, replenishing stone or mixing mortar, and the two soldiers on guard at the bridge seemed more interested in watching others working than in impeding passage in and out of the castle. We could have passed through freely, but Lucy, thoroughly on her mettle and thus unusually emboldened, went straightway up to them. 'I wish to visit a man held wrongfully in the castle. Could you kindly escort me to your commanding officer?'

The men gazed at her, from the soft dark folds of the hood encircling her enchanting face, from which glossy wisps and tendrils of hair escaped, to the sweeping hem of her best mourning gown and the neat kid shoes glimpsed beneath. Lucy gave them her most brilliant smile, and their faces postively sweated with admiration. Finally, one of them said, 'Which prisoner would it be, Mistress?'

'He was brought in last night,' Lucy told him, flushed all over again with indignation. 'And for no real offence, just a private quarrel. There's been a grave misunderstanding somehow, and we wish to see it rectified at once. So if you will just escort me, and my friends . . .'

'I know the one you mean, madam,' said the older, more responsible-looking guard. 'And there's no mistake about *him*. A proper rogue, by all accounts, deserter and traitor and debaucher of young women.' His gaze upon Lucy sharpened, and my cousin said hotly, 'I'll have you know he's my brother!'

'Ah,' said the soldier, evidently not believing a word of it. 'But I don't think it will be possible, madam. Orders were that he be kept close confined, being particularly dangerous – not that he looked in a state to be dangerous, mind you.'

Lucy's eyes widened. 'Was he hurt? Badly? I must see him! Please take me to your commander, at least – he could be dying in your dungeons at this minute!'

'No need, madam,' said the soldier. 'Here he comes now.'

Through the gateway strutted a short, fat man, in middle age, with flowing lovelocks and an overweening air of his own importance. A couple of soldiers followed at his back. The two on guard stiffened into salutes, and the elder hailed him. 'Sir! There's a lady here wishes to speak with you about a prisoner.'

The officer approached us, and bowed with a flourish.

Lucy again produced her best smile. 'The prisoner is my brother, sir, brought in last night after a sorry misunderstanding. I trust you will now see him speedily released.'

If she had thought to carry him along with her confidences. she had sadly misread his character. 'I regret, madam,' said the officer smoothly, 'that the prisoner – Lieutenant Heron, was it not? – is to be kept close until his trial, and I have had specific orders not to allow him any visitors, parcels or other privileges which may make it easier for him to escape. In particular, I was instructed not to allow him any *female* visitors.'

'You mean I can't even *see* him?' Lucy demanded, and there in the midst of her dramatic indignation I saw her eyes suddenly spill over with genuine tears. 'But he might be dying in your filthy cells . . . please, sir, I beg of you, let me see him, just to make sure he is safe.'

'I regret it from the bottom of my heart, madam, that I am unable to help you, sister to the prisoner or no,' said the officer, and with another bow prepared to continue across the bridge, Jamie, his chivalrous soul touched to the core by such callousness, stepped boldly forward. 'Since no ladies, not even my sister, are to be allowed to visit my brother, may I be permitted?' And his hand touched the officer's, and I heard unmistakeably the chink of coin. The Widow caught my eye and gave me a broad encouraging wink. In a few seconds, Jamie was being escorted inside the castle, and we, the despised females, were left to kick our heels on the bridge in full view of the curious.

'Even if we can't see him freed, we can put our minds at rest,' said the Widow, after a while. 'Look, don't worry, lass,' she added to Lucy, who leaned pallidly against the side of the wooden bridge, her hands gripping the splintery rail. 'Blind spot he may have, but your brother's not a monster. He may well come back from Thame or Aylesbury or wherever it is they've gone, full of remorse and good intentions. Give his anger a chance to cool off, and he'll be more reasonable.'

I doubted it myself, knowing how Simon was incapable of admitting he was in the wrong, but it was never very difficult to make Lucy believe what she wanted to believe. Her face brightened, and she turned expectantly towards the gatehouse. Mistress Gooch nudged me. 'Good thing I thought to bring a guinea or two, eh? Dear me, the corruption of these army men!'

Despite the despair weighing my mind, I grinned. 'A sorry thing for us if they weren't. Did you put the idea into Jamie's head, to ask to see him?'

'No, lass, he thought of it himself, and I gave him the guinea to grease his way in,' said the Widow admiringly. 'He's not such a fool as he seems, your Jamie, is he? Once he grows out of this chivalrous nonsense, mooning after that hard-faced little blonde bitch, he'll be a man to reckon with.'

'Like Edward,' I said, recognizing it suddenly, the similarity of temperament, the unthinking strength and enjoyment of life whatever the pitfalls and dangers. 'Like his brother who was killed at Kineton Fight. Sometimes I think how different things might be if Ned was still alive. He put a check on Simon; he was always so sane, so cheerful and reasonable.'

'And now he's gone, His Prudishness can give full rein to his obsessions,' said the Widow thoughtfully. She looked across at Lucy and Meraud standing together on the other side of the bridge, dark head and silver bent together as they talked. 'And what d'you suppose she's after? Or, should I say, who?'

'Simon,' I said, glad of any scandalous backbiting to take my mind off Francis in the castle. 'He's the wealthy one, after all.'

'You think so? I'm inclined,' said the Widow, thoughtfully picking a splinter off the handrail and pitching it into the cold rumpled waters of the moat, 'to think her one of those women – young as yet, of course, but the fault's plain for all to see – who'll pursue anything in breeches. Now Lucy is the same, but she's not serious, nor's she selfish; she can no more help flirting than she can breathing. The other one, that's all artifice, and to purpose. Ah, Mistress Meraud, you look cold. Why did you not bring your warmer cloak?'

Meraud gave us a quick, measuring glance, as if she knew

who the subject of our conversation had been, while I suppressed a rather hysterical snigger at the Widow's beautifully sarcastic hypocrisy. 'I did not think the wind would chill so, nor that we'd be refused entrance and left to stand in the cold. How long will he be?'

'However uncomfortable we feel,' I said angrily, 'it must be far worse for those imprisoned.'

'But they're common criminals, and doubtless used to it,' said Meraud, cool and hostile, and I saw the dislike in her face and was suddenly smitten with astonished indignation. Why did she hate me? Why had she, young as she was, seemingly done her best to wreck my life and Francis's? And the answer followed hard; because from the beginning we had both shown our dislike for her, and for little more reason than intuition. I remembered how once, questioned about her calm affection for her supposedly wicked uncle, she had revealingly replied, 'He was always very nice to me.' In a flash of humiliating self-knowledge, I saw myself as I must seem to her, an ill-tempered, selfish, intolerant bitch. No wonder she hated me, as I in her position would hate. And now I had made an enemy of her, it was too late, and we were both forever cast in the moulds we had made for one another. In my mood of misery and self-hatred, I might almost have begun to weep, but at that moment Jamie emerged from the bowels of the castle and strode up to us, his face scarlet and blazing with angry tears. 'It's no good,' he said, as we clustered round, 'it's no good, they won't set him free, he's there by order of the Prince himself and not all the gold in England would persuade them to incur his wrath.'

'Did you see him?' Lucy demanded, bursting with the questions I was too afraid to ask. 'Is he hurt? Where are they keeping him?'

'Yes,' Jamie said, and glancing round at the avid faces of the windswept passers-by, dragged a hand across his eyes and made a stubborn effort at composure. 'Yes, I saw him. He was in some filthy cell with about thirty other men, criminals and prisoners of war all herded together, with just one tiny barred window and straw on the floor and rats . . .

and the stink – I've never smelt anything like it, I wouldn't keep *pigs* in a place like that!' he finished wildly.

Lucy pressed her hands to her face, clenching her fists so hard that her knuckles gleamed white. 'Oh, God, he'll die there! Was he much hurt?'

'His face was all bruised and he'd two black eyes,' said Jamie. 'Simon's men weren't very gentle. One day I'll kill him for all this, I swear I will! He must be a monster!'

'But he's only doing what he thinks to be right,' said Meraud, and Jamie rounded on her with such a look of fury that she flinched. 'And what's right about hounding his own brother into prison to face a possible firing-squad simply because he's committed the unforgivable crime of wishing to marry his ward? You're as prudish as he is, you mealy-mouthed little puritan!'

'I think,' said Mistress Gooch, a hand on his arm, 'that we'd best go home before the whole of Oxford learns our business.'

'I don't care if the world knows it!' Jamie said, stalking out of her reach down towards the outer gate. Meraud burst into tears, the first that I had ever seen her shed, and Lucy at once put a comforting arm round her. Sick and sore at heart, I walked ahead of them, my own tears struggling to be shed, oblivious of the wind and cold and the nudging stares of soldiers and townspeople.

It was not far to Pennyfarthing Street. I was too shaky at the knees, and too conscious of my pride, to run, so Jamie was there before me, standing at the step, evidently torn between sparing Grainne the effort of answering his knock, and the blow to his dignity dealt by cooling his heels at the door waiting for the Widow to arrive with her key. The wind had driven his hair into wild dark peaks and tangles all over his head, and through the strands across his face his wide blue eyes stared back at me, haunted. I felt suddenly desperately sorry for him, cushioned from reality for so long, and now brought brutally face-to-face with it. He no longer looked very much like Lucy; in his grief and fury he had now more than a little resemblance to Simon.

'Where's Meraud?' he demanded, as I approached.

'Following, rather more slowly. You've upset her somewhat.'

'It's no more than you've done in the past yourself,' Jamie muttered ungraciously. 'Women! You're more trouble than you're worth, all of you.'

'And where would you be without us?' I pointed out. Jamie gave me a feeble grin, a dreadful travesty of his usual cheerfulness. 'I'm sorry, Thomazine. I just didn't know what it would be like, I'd no idea . . . I suppose I'd imagined a little whitewashed cell, rather like Sir Walter Raleigh's in the Tower . . . I've been very naïve, haven't I?' he finished, with a rueful twist to his mouth that reminded me with a pang of Francis.

'You said he was hurt . . . how badly?'

'Well, his face looked as if it had been trampled on, and he said his ribs felt in like case. But he seemed . . . indifferent to it, somehow,' said Jamie. 'Do you remember how he used to be when he'd been punished when we were children, going into his shell like a snail and not taking any notice of anything? He was like that. He didn't even seem particularly pleased to see me, and he didn't even thank me when I slipped him the last few crowns to buy himself some decent food.'

I could well believe that Francis in such painful and humiliating circumstances would thus withdraw into himself, but the aggrieved note in Jamie's voice showed how little he really knew his brother. I said, 'Did you have any conversation with him at all? Did he mention me?'

Jamie cast a quick look up and down the street and then bent his mouth close to my ear and whispered, 'He said, "Tell Thomazine to remember Catholm, and make sure you do it while no one else is listening." He was very emphatic.'

'Is that all?' I hissed back, aware out of the corner of my eye that Meraud, Lucy and the Widow were now in sight at the other end of the street. Jamie nodded, his face puzzled, obviously dying to know what it meant. I understood well enough, but knew better than to enlighten him. 'Thank you,' I said, 'and Jamie, please, keep that a secret between us

– don't even tell the others, any of them, that you had a message for me, let alone tell them what it was. It could be very important.'

Jamie gave me a conspiratorial grin, reminding me of the day when we had unawares ridden to Edgehill, and banged his fist on the door.

The rest of that day was a nightmare. Only the Widow, bustling about organizing meals and baking and shopping, was anything like her usual self. Meraud sulked, casting reproachful glances at Jamie whenever he caught her eye; it was not so easy now to forget her real age. Lucy was white and strained, and burst into a flood of tears whenever anyone said anything to her that could in the least be construed as criticism. Jamie, very conscious that he was the man of the house, stalked about with outsized dignity and refused to apologize to Meraud. Grainne, once the details of Francis's captivity had been conveyed to her by Jamie, angry all over again at his eldest brother's iniquity and injustice, retreated into a white-faced, thoughtful silence.

And I? I lost my temper at the slightest provocation and joined the Widow in feverish activity which echoed the frantic workings of my mind, desperately seeking for some way to overcome its frustration and impotence. Perhaps we could contrive a way to get Francis out of the castle, some daring and implausible means of escape, but when Simon came back, that would be impossible. I discounted any chance that my guardian would have changed his mind; I knew him too well for that. It was beginning to seem as though Francis was right, despite my desperate efforts to prove the contrary, and that in Catholm lay our only hope. I had instantly understood what he intended to convey in that brief cryptic message; that at Catholm we would be safe from pursuit, and that if he could contrive to escape from custody he would not attempt to snatch me romantically from the lion's jaws, but would make his way to Liddesdale to await me. It would be easy enough for me to announce my intention of returning to Suffolk to disarm suspicion, and then change direction *en route* and head north, perhaps with Grainne or even Jamie but if necessary by myself . . . I tore my thoughts away from visions of a reunion on the side of some bleak Scottish fell, and reminded myself that first, Francis had to be extracted, or extract himself, from the castle.

That night I dreamed that I too was in prison; the hot foetid air, thick with the smell of sweat and rotting straw and more unpleasant aromas, the stifling, suffocating, helpless feeling of being shut in, enclosed, with no way out and no escape, locked in forever to rot. In my dream despair lay on me like a great weight, crushing down initiative and hope and resolution, rendering all down to a vast invincible apathy. Then a rat ran across my face, and I sat up, screaming. At once Lucy was there, clutching me, calling my name, asking me over and over again what it was, had I had a nightmare?

'Yes,' I said, feeling the horror breaking out again in my mind as I recalled it. 'I dreamed a rat ran over me. I'm sorry – did I frighten you?'

'I only thought the Lord General was attacking the house,' said Lucy, trying to hearten me without much success. 'That rat must have been the bedclothes.'

The curtains parted, and I said, 'Oh, Heppy, it's all right, I had a nightmare, that's all. Go back to sleep.'

'I can ask Mistress Gooch to make you up some of her potions, that'll put you back sound asleep,' Heppy offered, but I declined, and she softly drew the curtains and padded back to her truckle bed. Once more we settled down into silence. Lucy rolled over and her quick breathing lengthened into the rhythmic sounds of slumber. I lay awake, staring into darkness, and felt myself become aware as never before of his presence, in the room with me, around me and inside me, offering his comfort. I knew that in some strange way he had also woken abruptly, at the same moment, and that the feelings and sensations that had haunted my dream had been his. Lying desolate in the night, I sent him my love and my hope, to lighten his heart, and then at last, without my knowledge or intent, sleep claimed me.

The following day was much the same, all of us strained

and on edge. Jamie made another attempt to visit Francis, but this time his slipped coins were spurned and he was sent away with a humiliating tirade about bribery and corruption ringing in his ears. Again we were helpless and impotent against the implacability of Simon's vengeance, combined with the stupidity of officialdom. And still Prince Rupert and his men did not return, and we did not know whether to be glad or sorry that we were spared Simon's company.

And that night, dear God, I dreamed again, even more horribly and vividly than the night before. I was running, pursued in the dark, and the rain and wind caught at me, and then something knocked me from my path with the force of a hammer blow, down into water. I remember even now the fear, the helplessness as the waters closed over my head, and I fought in vain for breath, struggling weakly until hands grasped me and Lucy's voice said, with real concern, 'Thomazine! Thomazine, don't worry, it's all right, it's only a nightmare!'

I found I was cold, and sweating, and shaking all over. The bedclothes had not clogged my face, they were pushed well down the bed. I did not know then what made me burst into uncontrollable sobs while Lucy held me, patting my shoulder and clucking ineffectually like a distressed hen, and Heppy fetched the Widow and one of her potions, and together they made me swallow the foul-tasting liquid between my gasps and hiccups, and sat by me until drowsiness overtook me and drained away my grief, leaving only a great emptiness around me and inside my heart and within the depths of my soul as I drifted helplessly into sleep. I did not know the reason then, or could not face it; even when I woke from a heavy, unrefreshing sleep and felt again that numb, uncaring emptiness around me, I could not accept what I knew in my heart to be true. I allowed myself to be dressed by an anxious, garrulous Heppy and led downstairs to the cheery firelit parlour with the pistol-ball still firmly embedded in the panelling; I sat and stared at a book without reading it, ignoring the hushed whispers, the puzzled and anxious looks of my friends, and waited for the news that would surely come.

As the lantern clock in the other parlour chimed ten, there came a knock on the front door: a heavy, subdued knock. I heard, dully, the Widow's quick tread in answer, then Simon's voice and hers, muttering together in long conversation, and then Mistress Gooch saying suddenly, loud with anger, 'I'll leave to you the task of telling her, lad, and I hope you're proud of all you've done to bring her grief!'

The door opened, and closed, and Simon stood there, tired and mud-splashed, his hat in his hands, and his face twisted and strange with a new, unaccustomed, unlooked-for sorrow. He stared at me miserably, in a way that another, earlier Thomazine might once have found amusing, but now meant nothing to me, except as confirmation of my fears. He said slowly, not meeting my eyes, 'Thomazine, I . . . I am most truly sorry . . . I . . . I . . . it was never my intention to let this happen, I . . .'

And I said what I had known since that nightmare, when my lover drowning had reached me in his last agonies, and my own life had also ended.

'Francis is dead, isn't he?'

chapter nine

A killing thing

Nae living man I'll love again,
Since that my lovely knight is slain.
Wi' ae lock of his yellow hair,
I'll chain my heart for evermair.
         (Traditional Scots ballad)

Since Simon did not seem to have heard me, I repeated my flat statement. 'There was no need to tell me. I know it. Francis is dead.'

Simon stared at me in astonishment, his jaw dropped. 'You know? How in God's name do you know?'

'I guessed,' I said tonelessly. 'Tell me . . . how did it happen?'

Simon seemed immobilized by my unemotional reaction. To him, grief meant his own angry sorrow, or Lucy's habitual flooding cries and lamentations. I could see that he was incapable of understanding that terrible dead wasteland where nothing mattered, and nothing was to be cared about, not even his death, because it was his life that mattered and that was over, finished, ended, gone forever. As my mind had wandered aimlessly through its new, bleak and featureless landscape, I had thought of killing myself; I believe I might have done, had not the thought of what Francis would have said to such a spineless deed prevented me.

'How?' I repeated. Simon, twisting his hat round and round in his hands, stared fixedly at my shoulder. 'I only know what I was told by the guards . . . He . . . he had apparently bribed one of the turnkeys to let him out of the castle, by the mill. He had to get across the river somehow, and the mill was guarded. He tried to run past the sentries; I don't quite know what happened . . . one of them saw him and fired his musket. He saw Francis fall from the bridge into the river and disappear. We have searched for his body, but there's no trace of it; however, it seems certain that he is dead, probably trapped under one of the mill-wheels. It could be months before he is found.' He raised his haunted, desperate eyes to mine. 'Believe me, Thomazine, before God I swear I did not really mean him harm. I . . . you know how his conduct had angered me, I was consumed with hatred, insane with it, I must have been mad . . . I – I don't know what I had intended to do. Perhaps have him transferred to another regiment, or cashiered, I don't know. I hadn't thought very much about it. But I swear, before God I swear it, I did not intend his death!'

'We all have to live with the consequences of what we do,' I said bleakly. Simon's eyes held mine for one brief, further moment, then he bowed his face in his hands and sank to his knees. I thought at first that he was praying; then I saw that he was weeping. Muffled, he said, 'I have no right to ask for your forgiveness, or his. I can only ask to share your grief.'

The simple dignity, so unlike Simon, touched my heart where nothing else would have done. I knelt beside him and put my arms awkwardly round the shaking, buff-coated shoulders and laid my head against his. For the moment, my weeping was done – I could not share that. But through my bitter, lonely, oh how lonely desolation, I could sense his own remorse and recognize that at last, at what terrible cost, Simon was learning that he was not invincible, infallible, eternally in the right.

At last he could calm himself, and raised his ravaged face to mine. 'Did you truly love him?'

I knew the line his reasoning was following. 'Yes,' I said, 'yes, we loved each other beyond anything . . . do you think I don't care? Now he's dead I care about nothing, nothing at all, I can't weep . . . I wish I could. I can't really believe that he's dead, he seems so close in my memory, but in my heart there's nothing, no presence, nothing at all, so I know he's gone.'

Simon stared at me with a look of such appalled bewilderment on his face that I realized he thought I had run mad. I got to my feet and turned away. 'I'm sorry. It's very difficult to explain . . . I had a dream last night . . . It was as though I shared his death.'

'I'm sorry,' said Simon inadequately, also rising. 'I – I wouldn't blame you if you spat in my face, but you have not. Thomazine . . . if there's any way I can assuage your grief, tell me. I will do all I can for you. You aren't with child?'

'I told you before,' I said, 'we were never lovers, so there's not likely to be a child – would that there was. But it's too late to make amends, Simon. He's gone, and not even you can raise the dead.'

'I'm sorry,' Simon said again, futilely. 'I am so very sorry. I have made terrible mistakes, errors of judgement. I have committed the grievous sin of self-righteousness, and it is not I who has paid, but Francis, and you. If I could raise the dead, I would, and you would be married tomorrow.'

All of a sudden the enormity of my loss overwhelmed me, the bitterness and tragedy and stupid pointlessness of it all. It need never have happened, that was what broke my empty uncaring calm, and I wept into my hands and then into Simon's smelly buff coat, on and on as if I wanted to sob my life out with my tears.

At last friendly hands guided me upstairs and laid me on my bed and put hot possets to my lips, and I suffered this help and manipulation as if I were a wooden toy, and did not heed their entreaties and condolences and sympathy. I could tell, in a casual detached sort of way, that they feared for my sanity. And when the tears had at last run dry, I lay unmoving on the bed, locked within my own mind and memories, where the shadow and ghost of Francis still existed.

I do not know how long that state lasted, but it must have been several days before I again accepted food and drink, and then only because my rebelling body overcame my mind. It was brought by Meraud, who sat on the bed and fed me with a spoon until I took it away from her and did it myself, for I was after all not that weak. Then she smiled, a genuine friendly smile, and said, 'That's better, Thomazine. Now I know you'll recover.'

'I don't have the plague,' I pointed out. Meraud flushed and looked down at her small hands. They were trembling, I saw. She said through her falling silvery hair, 'Thomazine, I have a confession to make, and an apology. It was I who told Simon you were meeting Francis by the gate that night. I saw the paper fall from your glove in the street, and I picked it up. I thought you might want it, and then I looked at it and saw what it said, and I . . . I . . . I didn't approve. So I gave it to Betty and she took it to one of Simon's soldiers. As soon as she'd taken it I wondered if I'd done right, I regretted it after but it was too late . . .' She turned her great blue eyes towards me, sparkling with unshed tears, and I said, 'Why? In God's name, why did you do it?'

'I didn't like you,' said Meraud, with the simplicity of a child. 'And I thought you were lovers, and it all seemed so deceitful and sordid and ungodly. It didn't seem fair to Simon or to Cousin Dominic, it was all so low and horrible . . . but not as horrible as what happened in the end.'

'No,' I agreed with bitterness. Meraud went on, painfully. 'If I'd thought for a moment of what might happen, I'd never have done it. Thomazine, oh, Thomazine, I am sorry, so terribly sorry . . . will you forgive me?' she added timidly. 'And be friends?'

It sounded like the aftermath to some petty girlish squabble. The earlier, complete Thomazine might have found some amusement in it. I thought she was genuinely full of remorse, but had no faith in promises of her good will hereafter; however, I clasped her hands in mine, generously. 'Yes, Meraud, I forgive you . . . and now perhaps we can forget all this stupid enmity, it's brought sorrow enough.'

'Oh, yes,' said Meraud delightedly, and kissed me with innocent flourish. 'Now we can be friends, and forget.'

But there would be no forgetting Francis. My loss of him was ever present in the silent empty spaces of my heart and the numbness inside my head, so that nothing could now amuse me or touch me because he who had shared so much with me was gone, and I had no hope of ever finding another.

What made it worse was Drake, who followed at my heels like a bewildered bereft shadow and guarded me with such ferocity it was obvious he feared that I too would vanish. And the little bundle of clothes and books and the silver flageolet so sweet and high, that I could draw no music from, and Hobgoblin patient and docile in her stall, waiting forever. And all the songs heard whistled in the market or sung thoughtlessly in the street, once just sad songs but now everlastingly charged with grief almost past bearing. 'Oh love it is a killing thing – did you ever feel the pain?'

No one else talked about Francis to me; the subject seemed by tacit agreement to be avoided. Grainne understood, though, and often we went walking, two black-clad bereaved women in the cold little garden, and talked about our lost lovers. But she at least had Henry's son, and another soon to be born; I did not even have a night of love to remember.

After a decent interval, as Christmas approached, Dominic renewed his attentions. At first I refused to see him, but he seemed to be ever on the doorstep, and Lucy and Jamie, glad of anything to lighten the gloom and guilt pervading the household, fastened on to it as a joke.

'Your suitor's here again, Thomazine!'

'More Christmas roses!'

'A pair of gloves this time!'

'Why don't you marry him?' said Lucy, once, quite seriously. 'He's so handsome, he looks so fine in that lovely red and gold, he's rich and a baronet and you'd be Lady Drakelon!'

'For someone who's always sworn she'll marry for love, you're very mercenary,' I pointed out.

'No,' Lucy said earnestly, 'it's just that, well, it'd help you forget. I mean, it's not being *unfaithful* to Francis, is it? And you can't go all your life long wedded to his memory, can you?'

'No, but I'd rather be married to a memory of Francis than to a flesh-and-blood Dominic.'

Then it was Meraud, clasping her hands and swearing that if I spurned him she'd cast her line at him herself.

'You're welcome,' I told her. Meraud looked surprise at me. 'You can't be indifferent to him! He's . . . he's like something from a play!'

I was not indifferent to Dominic – there was something about him that both attracted and repelled me. If it had not been for Francis, I might have accepted him with a show, at least, of pleasure. But Francis had shown me what love could be, how two minds could be as one until at last wrenched asunder by death, and now to accept any less seemed like a betrayal of him, of me, of love.

But they were all very persuasive. Even the Widow put her oar in with gusto. 'Now don't you be finicky, lass. Fine young man like him, soon get you swell-bellied, and that's what you need if you ask me, a child to look after.'

I smiled weakly. Women often died in childbed; my mother had, and my stepmother. Perhaps it would be best if I did. But to lie in the same bed as Dominic, to have him touch me, do the things that I had shamelessly asked Francis to do . . . that was true betrayal. And yet it was the necessary price to pay for a child – and once the Widow had put the idea into my head, I realized that I did indeed want a child, a delightful boy like Jasper perhaps, worth all the indignities and pain attendant on his conception and birth. There was nothing else to do with my life, now.

Simon came to add his voice to the chorus. 'I fully understand that you are reluctant to wed, so soon after his death, but he is very keen, desperate even, to marry you, and he loves you, Thomazine.' He coughed. 'Of course, in view of the circumstances I would be more than generous with your settlement and dowry—'

'In other words, you'll buy my forgiveness and forgetfulness,' I said with scorn, and regretted it a second later as I saw from his face that I had really hurt him. I turned away to walk across the parlour, my hands twisting and turning with my thoughts. I would have to bear Dominic's presence in my bed and at my board – but there might be a child on which to base my emptied life. It seemed a denial of all that Francis and I had avowed – but he was dead and gone, for certain although no one had ever found his body, and whether in Heaven or in Hell I knew not, since he seemed neither saintly enough for the one nor evil enough for the other; only himself. And I had to acknowledge that what Lucy had said was true; I was still alive, nearly eighteen years old, and I could not forever remain celibate because the man I had loved was dead.

But not so soon! I thought, and then realized that there would be no respite from this continual, gentle, well-meaning pressure from all sides. If I sent Dominic away, he would not be so easily discouraged. I could well imagine him still on the doorstep a year hence, Christmas roses in his hands. And if he retreated, there would be others in plenty to take his place – I was after all an heiress, even if, 'all eyes and hair', not much of a beauty. I saw in my mind's eye a procession of earnest godly sober young men, without a spark of wit or imagination or freedom or rebellion, and thus thoroughly approved of by Simon. I could not face it. My numbness was slowly dissolving, and I cared a little, now, about my future, and the people I would share it with, and the children I would – might – bear.

But I did not like Dominic.

I was tired of arguments, of resistance, of pressure. I wanted peace now, after the last terrible months. At least if I were married to Dominic I would not have to face any procession of earnest suitors at the door, would not have to undergo the continual urging and teasing, might have a child.

I remembered Grainne saying to me, a week or so previously, in the cold garden, 'Whatever you do, Thomazine, I can't make up your mind for you. But do remember – all this tragedy has been made totally unnecessarily by thoughtless people who plunged into action without thinking of the consequences. So please, whatever you do, before you do it, think first.'

But I have thought, long and endlessly, my feelings going round and up and down like a turnspit dog.

Better the devil you know than the devil you don't.

I may have children.

I want peace, a haven. He loves me, Simon says. I don't like him, but time might change things.

I would not be parted from the other people I love.

Francis, wherever you are, I shall love you for ever. I shall bring up any children I have in your image, to think and argue and love and make music and puns and riddles, to have a sense of humour and proportion. Forgive me. I am so very tired. 'Once I had a sweetheart and now I have none – Once I had a lover, and now he is gone.' My heart will ever be in your keeping, but I have lost you, and now I have to make the best of what is left to me.

I turned to Simon, tears in my eyes for what I was going to do.

'Yes,' I said. 'I will marry Dominic.'

Everyone was delighted, none more so, of course, than Dominic. Slightly appalled at what I had done, I suffered his overwhelming attentions with a bemused feeling of astonishment that I should be the object of such devotion from two so very dissimilar men.

Dominic, of course, as everyone was forever pointing out, was breathtakingly handsome in a flamboyant, vivid way quite different from Francis's thoughtful, slightly mocking, fallen-angel face. He filled a room with his presence, the force of his personality, his large gestures, his smile and dash. He obviously had a huge opinion of himself, and there was a whole-hearted enthusiasm in his attack on whatever happened to obsess him at the time, which was very

443

endearing – except when, as in my case, you happened to be the object yourself. Before I knew where I was, the wedding was fixed, for four days before Christmas, that being the earliest date for which Dominic could obtain a licence. Meraud had to move out of her chamber, which had been my father's, and squash in once more with Lucy and me whilst the other was arranged for Dominic and myself, with fresh paint and new hangings. Meraud and Lucy would be my bridemaidens and Jamie and Tom Sewell my bridemen, whilst Jasper, too young to be anything other than deliriously excited at the prospect, was to precede me into the church bearing the customary cup containing a sprig of rosemary.

I felt like the eye of the storm as all the bustle of preparation whirled round me, the still centre. I could not quite believe what I had committed myself to: the marriage I had been dreading for seven years. It seemed unreal, as if another Thomazine were being married on the twenty-first of December to Sir Dominic Drakelon, Captain, of the King's Lifeguard of Foot. But the date rushed inexorably closer, and the favours were sewn on my dress, which Dominic had insisted should be of a good, gay colour, 'For I'll warrant you're as weary of black as I am.' So it was orange-tawny velvet, in the new long-waisted style, with narrow cuffed elbow-length sleeves and a low bodice fastened across the jewelled stomacher with gold cords. It was the dress of which I had always dreamed, a dress to give me beauty, and when I wore it to check the fit, the reflection in the little mirror which Lucy held up and down so that I was able to see myself in sections, only served to add to my sense of unreality. This gorgeous, sophisticated, lovely young woman with the cloudy dark hair and bitter, haunted eyes, bore no relation to the Thomazine, plain-speaking and lacking airs and graces, which I felt myself to be.

The ceremony itself passed by, in a blur of laughter and colour and hysteria, all seeming to be happening to somebody else. Early in the morning, I was dressed by Meraud and Lucy, jabbering their approval of my appearance like a pair of starlings; and Grainne, still laden and gross with her unborn child, now so imminently expected that she had been advised not to attend the wedding, stood quietly in the background with the circlet of pearls which would adorn my head. They left my hair loose, and combed free of its usual tangles into a thick glossy mass hanging halfway down my back. The final touch was to ensure that the favours had been sufficiently loosely sewn all over bodice and sleeves and skirt, and I could remember the crush and flurry at my maid Alice's wedding as they were plucked off, to be worn in the hats of all the young men. All good-hearted, bawdy fun, but my heart would not be in it, for always I had the thought when I looked upon my bridegroom, that with any justice in this world, another man should have stood in his place. But it was too late for that, as I walked to the church with my cacophonous escort of musicians (for Dominic was determined to do everything in as fine a style as possible, given the circumstances), and the proud Jasper bearing his silver-gilt cup with a solemnity of carriage more appropriate for a much older child. It was very cold but not, luckily for my tawny velvet, raining as had frequently been the case that month.

The church was dim and cold. Our breathing plumed like smoke in the raw morning air. There were few guests, mostly brother-officers of Dominic and Simon. I caught sight of Robert Radley and Charles Lawrence, and so far forgot my new, sophisticated shell as to send them friendly grins. And at the head of them all, the guest of honour, Prince Rupert himself.

I could tell by the gasps behind me that Lucy and Meraud were overcome with awe, but we proceeded up the aisle, rather more slowly, and so I came to my groom and the altar. Dominic in all his finery of scarlet and gold was enough to take the breath away; and I found myself wondering what I would have thought of him had Francis not become my own true love.

The words of the ceremony, spoken by Master Bowles, rolled sonorously over my head; '. . . to have and to hold, from this day forth . . . till death do us part.' And I promised mechanically to love and honour and obey my husband, and could not really believe that it was happening to me.

There was a sermon, in which St Paul's views on marriage were vehemently promoted, and then we drank wine together from the mazer-bowl, and everyone trooped out of the church again to return to Pennyfarthing Street. I saw that despite the short notice of the wedding, Dominic had managed to provide his friends with a lavish array of embroidered gloves, each one a riot of fringes and colour and beading. I had had no time to make gloves for my bridemen as was the custom; so Tom and Jamie had pairs from a local glover that had looked very fine, but now seemed poor specimens beside Dominic's.

The little house was very crowded for the bridal feast. The two downstairs parlours were filled to overflowing, and the Widow had had to send out for two neighbours' wives to come and help serve the food. I noticed that the Prince, although he joined rather self-consciously in the joking and bawdry, drank very little and seemed both physically and mentally out of place amidst the noisy crowd of young English officers. The favours had been torn from my dress as we left the church, and now there was a bunch of ribbon – white, carnation, blue, silver or gold – in every man's hatband. There was no room for dancing on a grand scale, but the three men who had accompanied me so unharmoniously to the church struck up again in the corner, fortunately almost drowned by the flow of talk and the toasts to the bride, the groom, His Highness, the King, the Queen and all their children, and anyone else thought appropriate. The noise was deafening, and combined with the wine to give me a fair headache, so that I began to long for the peace of the bedchamber upstairs, with its huge carved bed and the hangings embroidered by my grandmother Kate, many years ago, and most unsuitably depicting Europa carried off by the Bull. I had often wondered whether she had felt that this sorry tale bore some relation

446

to the manner of her wooing by my grandfather. The thought of it now was enough, surprisingly, to bring a faint smile to my face, despite the fact that Europa's unhappy situation was in some ways rather akin to my own.

'You look very lovely,' my husband (how strange and elderly the word sounded!) said, his blue eyes dropping from my face to the revealing curves of my neckline and lingering there. I wriggled in my seat like an uneasy child, and took a goodly gulp of wine to cover my embarrassment. I felt as if I should be able to laugh at this nervous maiden, who had always prided herself on her self-assurance, and was now reduced to the kind of foolish giggles she had always heartily despised in others; but I could not. The situation I was about to face, peaceful bed or no, was too alarming for laughter. I asked myself, bitterly, why I had allowed myself to succumb to everyone's blandishments.

Some time during that long, noisy, drunken day, they cleared the larger parlour and with much elbowing and laughing we engaged in an apology for dancing in extremely cramped quarters. The Prince led out the blushing bride and promptly cracked his head on one of the stout beams barring the ceiling. Robert Radley, the worse for drink, led out Lucy and fell flat upon his face. Simon, with a superhuman effort, disciplined his temper and confined himself to ordering the recumbent cavalier removed to a place less inconvenient for the dancers. Seeing his rigidly suppressed disgust, I was glad that at least a wedding was the best of all excuses for a riotous celebration, and that the so-thoroughly-approved-of bridegroom was the most riotous of all.

There was in consequence a fearful scramble when the time came to unfasten my garters. The Widow had told me to untie them discreetly beforehand, so that some decorum could be preserved, but I left it too late and accordingly found myself on the floor at the bottom of a heap of my bridemen, all attempting with drunken hilarity to get their hands far enough up my skirts to untie my garters. Finally, Lucy and Meraud were able to haul Tom and Jamie off me, and I was escorted, giggling weakly, up the stairs to the bridal chamber. There I was disrobed with a lot of laughter as we hunted for the pins which, if left in my clothes or kept, would bring bad luck for me, and for Lucy and Meraud, no marriage until Whitsun. We had thought all of them found, until Meraud pricked her finger on one as she laid my tawny velvet on the clothes-press, and then they had to hunt again to make sure.

'Because the last thing you want is any more bad luck,' said Lucy, and swooped triumphantly on the last one. 'Can you remember how many we put in, Meraud? We should have counted them, I knew we should.'

'About a score,' said Meraud. 'No pins left in your hair?'

I ran my hands through the thick loose tangle. 'None. There were few to start with, only to hold the pearls.'

'Then you'd best put this on,' Lucy told me, advancing with the beautiful embroidered and lace-fringed shift draped over her arms. I slipped out of my old chemise and stood for a moment, virgin-naked for the last time, and then ducked my head to put the wedding-shift on.

A great eruption of noise, swelling up the stairs, announced the imminent arrival of my groom. Standing there in the middle of the wide cold draughty floor, the rush matting tickling my feet unpleasantly, all my stupid wine-flown hilarity dropped abruptly away; and at the thought of the coming night, of Dominic's leering, assessing eyes and cold hands, I began to shake. Lucy, who knew me so well, said quickly, 'It'll only take a moment or so to make him ready, and then he'll be here . . . quick, into bed!'

I scurried in between the chilly, scratchy sheets and lay rigid, my teeth clenched to stop them chattering. Lucy sat on the bed beside me, her pretty dark head bent attentively to mine like a listening bird, as sounds of rowdyism came brutally through to us from the chamber next door where Dominic, with further liquid refreshment all round, was being made ready for bed. I stared up at the warm-hearted, romantic cousin who for years had been my friend and confidante, and who now, bright-eyed with sentimental tears, whispered, 'Good luck! And don't dwell on the past!'

Only the fear of making a fool of myself, and a feeling of inescapable doom, prevented me then from making good my escape. But I had, literally and metaphorically speaking, made my own bed, and now, with a vengeance, must lie in it.

The door opened, and I jumped, but it was Grainne, emerged from her chamber where she and Betty had been putting a boisterous and over-excited Jasper to bed, and now come in her turn to wish me good luck. As Meraud and Lucy moved quietly about the chamber, tidying and folding and laying clothes away, she gave me a friendly, encouraging smile, and said softly, 'How goes it with you?'

I had never been able to lie to Grainne. 'I'm frightened,' I said. 'And just realizing what I've done.'

Grainne sat on the bed with the clumsiness of the heavily pregnant. She took my cold clammy paw between her thin warm fingers and said, 'I remember how frightened I was. I had seen so much of man's abuse of woman, and it seemed impossible that there could be any other method but rape. Thank God Henry taught me otherwise. May you have as much joy in your husband as I had in mine, and have him for far longer. God grant you peace and content after all your sorrow.' And she dropped a sisterly kiss on my cold cheek, got up and went out, leaving me foolishly wiping away my tears, overcome by so much warmth and goodwill which I had never, in all years amongst my cousins, quite felt in my deepest heart that I truly deserved.

Scarcely had she left when the abused door crashed open to admit Dominic, wild and glittering drunk in his night attire, accompanied by his two scarlet-clad groomsmen and followed hotly by what appeared to be nine-tenths of Oxford, wine-flown, singing, bearing the sack posset for the bride and groom. I lay in the bed with the coldness and rigidity of death, as Dominic thumped heavily down beside me and planted a wine-laden kiss on my mouth, while the company drank our health with a noisy abandon which must have assaulted the ears of Fish Street if not Carfax. Finally, there was the flinging of the stocking. Lucy and Meraud, giggling, perched on one side of the bed holding my silk bridal stockings, and Dominic's two uproarious groomsmen on the other side with his. The Prince, his head bent to one side by the lowness of the ceiling, gave the signal as guest of honour, and the two girls and two men flung the stocking backwards over their heads. Three of them missed, but Lucy's landed square on Dominic's chest, and a scream went up, 'Wed before long, mistress!', and an outbrust of clapping and congratulation. Then Lucy, a pleased and rosy pink, gave me a final kiss, retrieved the stocking and retired with the rest of the company with a last rush of good wishes and bawdy encouragement. The curtains were swished shut around the bed with an ominously final sound and the noises of revelry grew fainter as the guests returned below stairs to continue the celebrations.

The full and final loneliness of my position smote me with renewed terror. Dominic held the posset cup to my lips, and I drank the warm thick sweet liquid, aware all the while of his greedy eyes, already in imagination stripping the smock from my tense body and devouring the virgin flesh within . . . I upbraided myself sternly for these morbid fancies, but unusually it did not work; my teeth clacked against the cup and Dominic withdrew it and placed it on the table beside the bed. He drew the curtains again and smiling turned to me. 'Are you afraid, my little bird, my little sparrow? So small you are, so small it seems your bones will break at a touch, and yet so dauntless and stubborn . . .' Slowly, his hands stroked me, unlacing my chemise, slipping it down from my rigid shoulders like some terrible lost travestied echo of that afternoon with Francis, oh so long ago. I was too overcome with – what? fear? – to show any maidenly modesty; like the helpless rabbit, I could not look away from my predator's eyes. And I saw that he enjoyed and savoured my helplessness, this defeat of a girl who had always prided herself on her stubborness and independence. He bent his head and kissed me, and for an instant my body overcame my mind and I had a glimpse of what I could enjoy, if I did but let myself, without thoughts of betrayal – and then his full weight was upon me, bearing me down upon the heaped pillows so that, crushed, I could scarcely draw breath. And, fatally, I panicked; fought and twisted and struggled like a woman raped, not a bride on her wedding night. I was wiry and tough for a girl of my stature, and for a moment, as he was taken off guard, I half got free, not scrupling to claw and scratch and even to sink my teeth into his hand as he tried to regain control. At that he lost his temper and slapped my face with a force which made my head ring, and stilled my struggles. Dazed I lay as he took his revenge, not caring how much he hurt me, so that all I really remember of my deflowering is the pain and my sick angry despair and disgust that I should be so used, and the thin bitter thread of thought, 'Francis would not have done it thus.'

At last, his pleasure exhausted, he rolled heavily off me and almost at once began to snore with the uncouth abandon of the drunk. For a while I lay rigid, staring into the dark, too sick and shocked to weep, aware only of the grinding pain between my legs and the aches all over my body which tomorrow would be bruises. I wanted to creep from the bed and wash myself; I felt ill and unclean and defiled, but I did not dare move in case the same thing should befall me again. At last, cautiously, I painfully disentangled the bedclothes from my limbs and slipped between the curtains. The fire was still glowing and I huddled beside it, warming myself; my chilled soul nothing could touch. Then I washed scantily with the icy water in a jug on the clothes-press, and at last gathered the courage I needed to return to the bed. I hugged myself, shivering, under the covers as far away from my husband as I could get, and at last, sore and weary, fell asleep.

A terrible noise woke me with a jerk; like a cat in its death-throes, it shrieked below our window. For a moment, I truly thought that murder was being done, then I discerned a tune somewhere half-strangled in the middle of it, and realized that, according to custom, the three musicians of yesterday were serenading us at break of day. It was unfortunate that the fiddler, who had apparently neglected to tune his instrument, was also still suffering from the quantities of strong beer he had imbibed the day before.

My husband had, it appeared, no ear for music. Smiling broadly, he leapt from the bed in his nightshirt and flung open the window, fern-patterned from the icy night. At once the music ceased and a faint chilly cheer rose up. I heard the chink of thrown pennies, his thanks and the good wishes of the musicians, the thump of the window shutting. The curtains flicked aside and Dominic stood looking down at me, huddled in the furthest corner of the bed. He said, in his abrupt way, 'Did I hurt you?'

To say yes seemed like an acknowledgement of defeat, so I defiantly shook my head, feeling my body throb and ache. Dominic frowned. Then he climbed in beside me and took my cold unresisting paws. 'I did hurt you – don't deny it. I can see the bruises on your arms.' He looked down at his own hands briefly and then back into my face. 'I am sorry, most desperately sorry. I was somewhat wine-flown, and I forgot.'

That I was not one of your loose Italian women, I thought, but did not say it.

'But let's forget that now,' Dominic went on, and his hands slid over me as before, his voice soft and urgent and beguiling. 'It won't happen again, I swear it. Oh, my sparrow, you are mine at last after all the waiting, and I want you so much . . . I'll treat you as you deserve to be treated, with all gentleness.'

I sat unmoving as he caressed me with new, careful hands, and kissed me, and laid me down and made love to me with consideration and an almost touching respect. If he had done that first, then all might have been different, but now the brutality of the previous night lay like a wall around me, and my heart sheltered within, guarded by bitterness, untouched and resentful. It was too late, nothing could be so easily mended by kind words, and the knowledge that I had with my hysterical panic brought all this on us in the first place added guilt to my sullenness.

When he had done with me, he leaned on one elbow and looked me in the face and must have seen that all this gentle wooing was too late and in vain. He had my body, true, but my mind was still my own, and my heart still in my dead lover's keeping. And in revenge for my ill-usage, I took a sullen, childish pleasure in defying his blandishments, and let him see my contempt for him.

His mouth tightened, and he raised his hand viciously, and then thought better of it and flung himself out of the bed. I heard him pacing the room, hurling wood upon the fire, splashing water, and rejoiced that I had hurt him as he had hurt me.

It was an inauspicious beginning to a marriage, the groom's ardour turned to fury by the bride's rejection of him, both for an act of violence she had herself provoked, and for something he could in no wise be blamed for – it was not his fault he was not Francis. During the day he was often absent on military affairs, seeing to the lodging, training and well-being of the soldiers of the garrison under his command; the nights were different. He tried every way to win me: presents, gentleness, fine words, flowers, but my Heron pride and stubbornness defeated him. In my heart of hearts I might at last have accepted him as husband and lover, instead of the violator of my self, but I was too eaten up with pride and resentment to capitulate, and in the end, from sheer frustration, he began to behave like the brute I had labelled him.

Thus, as with Meraud, I had looked on a person with prejudice, and created an enemy in the mould I myself had made. It is not a time in my life of which I can be proud.

On the eighth day of January, Grainne's baby was born. It was the first time I had been present at a birth, by consideration of my wedded status, and it shook me to the core;

especially when, at the end of a long, terrible, agonizing day in which Grainne had suffered more than I ever wished to, the Widow Gooch held out to her the wrapped screaming bundle that was her daughter and Henry's, and said cheerfully, 'Well, that was an easy one, wasn't it? Like laying an egg.'

Grainne gave a gasp of painful, hysterical laughter. The midwife was gathering the soaked sheets for washing, the room was filled with the thick sweet stench of blood and birth. 'Easy?' I said, fighting nausea.

'Compared with the other two, yes,' said Grainne. She looked down into the tiny crumpled face, clashing hideously with the thin strands of wet orange hair stuck to the bony scalp. 'Look at that, will you, it's the print of Henry, that hair.' Her hand gently traced the soft curves and creases round the button mouth, for a moment refraining from protest at this new cold expanded world. 'Little Henry, he said, if it's a boy, and Henrietta for a girl. Henrietta she shall be. No beauty, is she?'

'New-borns never are,' said the Widow busily. 'Henrietta for her father, eh? Poor little mite, brought orphan into a cruel world.' She looked round at me standing dazed by the bed. 'You look pale, lass. Too much for you, eh? Well, we'll soon have you breeding by the look of you.'

'I hope not,' I said, only half-joking as I thought of my own body, neither so broad nor robust as Grainne's (though God knew she was slender enough), similarly rent and abused. And yet I wanted children, and to see the look on Grainne's face as she smiled down upon her daughter only confirmed my desires.

In the third week of January, it turned colder still, and snow fell thickly, lending a silver enchantment to the streets and gardens of Oxford, providing the perfect background for the brilliant scarlet and gold of the Lifeguard officers, and the glowing velvets and satins of the men and women of the Court. Each morning I woke to a pale and brilliant world, snow-light on the ceiling and frost-ferns riming the windows with delicate lace; and my husband's baffled, angry face as I yet again resisted his charm. When Prince Rupert asked for a detachment of Lifeguards to help in the storming of Cirencester, Dominic was one of the first to volunteer, and on the 21st January we watched them ride and march out of the city towards the West. My only feeling was one of relief; I do not know what his were. Perhaps he hoped that military glory was the key to my heart, or more probably he just wished to escape for a little while from a situation which had become intolerable.

I did not tell him, before he left, that I believed I was with child. It was too soon to be sure, but I felt certain of it and hugged my secret to myself with childish delight, and looked long at Grainne's children, wondering what mine would be like.

Those weeks without Dominic were good ones. We went strolling in the quadrangle at Christchurch, revelling in the ogling of the young gallants, or descended in one glorious leap from adult dignity to indulgence in wild snowball fights with Jasper and other children and young people. Officers came calling, paying extravagant court to Lucy and Meraud, with bows and poems and once an unharmonious consort under Lucy's window at crack of dawn – *that* suitor won no favour. The Widow was highly amused. 'She was the one flung the stocking hit your man, wasn't she? Married within the year, she'll be.'

'No, I won't,' Lucy said, overhearing. 'I shall marry for love, and as no one has yet presented themselves I shall remain single until they do.'

Jasper, who was at the stage of picking up adult conversations, announced that he would marry his mother. When we had explained the impossibility of this, he turned his dazzling smile upon Lucy and said, 'I'll marry you, then.'

'I'll be no one's second choice,' Lucy retorted, grinning. 'If Thomazine has a daughter one day, you can marry her.'

Jasper was not interested in hypothetical possibilities and stalked off to tease Orange. The Widow gave me a sharp glance, noting the faint flush which had betrayed me when Lucy had talked of my child. Later, she cornered me in the kitchen and said without preamble, 'Breeding, aren't you?'

'What? Me? No, of course not!' I said. 'Whatever gives you that idea?'

'I know the look,' said the Widow. She counted off on her fingers. 'September or October, eh? Quick work – if it's his, of course.'

'Of course it's his,' I said. 'Who else's could it be?'

'You know. It's what a suspicious mind would think,' said Mistress Gooch. 'You and your Francis sharing a house all November. They'll jump to conclusions soon enough, and forget that you also shared it with me, Mistress Sewell and her brood, your cousins and that young Charles for good measure, not to mention Heppy and Betty. That sort always ignores inconvenient facts.'

'Well, they can for all I care,' I said. 'If I am going to have a baby, it's unquestionably my husband's. I know that, and you do, and everyone else whose opinion matters.'

'Including Sir Dominic?'

My gaze shot back to her face. 'Of course. He knows I was a virgin when I married.'

'Yes, in his heart he may, but is he the same breed as your fine and hasty cousin Simon, ready to believe the worst and ignore the voice of reason? Don't think I haven't got eyes to see, lass,' said the Widow, sitting down on a hen-free stool. 'He used to come here sick with love for you. Since you wed him, he's gone about like one in the grip of despair. It's not my place to pry, or tell you how to mind your marriage, but I'll tell you one thing, it's not his fault he's not Francis.'

I dropped my eyes from her sharp gaze. The Widow went on, 'If I was you, lass, I'd start afresh. Make up your mind to love him. Welcome him back with open arms and be as a wife should. After all, he's your husband, for life, for better or worse – and you made certain promises on your wedding day that I'd wager you haven't kept.'

Guilt and shame crept from the back of my mind and

bore me down. I felt my eyes smart with tears. The Widow got up and put a motherly arm about my shoulders. 'I'm sorry, lass, but it had to be said by someone, and I can see you agree with me, don't you? Just remember what I said, and mind, it's not fair to him if you don't – you didn't have to marry him, after all, and once you've done it you must accept it with a good grace, or you'll end by putting him in despair.' She gave me a little push. 'All right, lass, my preaching's done. Let's get this capon plucked, eh?'

So with a newly humbled heart, for I knew her advice to be utterly sound, I awaited Dominic's return, feeling almost eager. We heard of the successful storming of Cirencester, on the second day of February, and five days later stood in the streets, with the rest of Oxford, to watch the prisoners brought in.

It was a bitter cold day. Lucy and Meraud and I, swathed in our warmest cloaks and escorted by a ruddily glowing Jamie, huddled in North Street to watch them go past. They had arrived the previous evening and been lodged in St Giles' and Magdalen churches – chill hard beds at the best of times. Now, even the strongest of them looked half-dead from cold, hunger and exhaustion, unshaven, their clothes ragged and bloodstained, many supported by stronger, unwounded comrades. As they passed, some Royalist-minded souls hissed and booed, but the majority of the crowd were silent or muttering angrily, a swelling growl of protest as they saw that the prisoners were bound with cords. I stared at the haggard despairing faces, so like the ones who had defended Ashcott or fought at Edgehill, men who were in no wise different from the soldiers I knew, save that they had committed the cardinal sin of fighting for the wrong side, out of conscience or duty or desire for regular pay, just as Simon's little Suffolk troop had done.

And for that, dear God, they were led through the streets of Oxford bound and on display like criminals. There were very many of them, a thousand or more, and at the rear came the carts and litters full of the worst wounded. It was as these, most pathetic of all, rumbled slowly past us, that

Lucy clutched my arm wildly. 'Look, oh look! Isn't that Captain Ashley?'

It seemed very unlikely – what would he have been doing in Cirencester? But I looked obediently in the direction Lucy indicated. 'There, sitting in that four-wheeled cart with the bay horse. See? It *is* him, isn't it?'

How she had recognized that unshaven, feverish, bandaged face amongst all the others I still do not know. I was hard enough put to it to distinguish the Captain Ashley I had briefly known, even when told where to look. But if you examined him closely enough, it became probable, and final confirmation was provided as Lucy pushed her way to the front and his face, as he stared dully at the crowd, suddenly lit on hers with recognition. He made no sign with hands or voice, but as the cart rolled on slowly down the street, his eyes turned to hold our diminishing figures until other wagons and bodies interposed.

'We must do something!' Lucy cried, her eyes anguished and aghast. 'Did you see him, he looked ready for death, and he'd only a shirt against the cold! We can't leave him like that! Where are they going?'

'To the castle,' said Jamie, his brow perplexed. 'But why do you want to do anything? He's one of the enemy.'

'The castle?' Lucy's voice went up in a frantic squeak that turned curious heads to look at us. 'But you know what that's like, you've seen it when . . . when F-Francis was in there. If they lock him up in a room like that he'll die!'

'I still don't see why you should be so concerned,' Jamie protested. Meraud began some speech about loving one's enemies, but Lucy cut in more simply. 'He was good to us at Ashcott. He needn't have been so kind to us. And doesn't that ask for us to be kind to him, in our turn?'

'That's all very well,' said Jamie dubiously, 'but how can we put your high and mighty ideas into practice?'

'You're so *slow*!' Lucy cried in feverish irritation. 'We can at least take him food, try to bind his hurts, make sure he isn't abused. Let's go home now, and make up a basket to take.'

458

It was half an hour or more, however, before the crowd had dispersed enough to let us return to Pennyfarthing Street, and Lucy was in a fret of impatience that set me wondering. She even bullied Mistress Gooch into helping her gather medical supplies, bandages, and food, and a spare doublet of Dominic's was shamelessly purloined behind my back and stuffed into the basket before I could object – if I had wanted to. Grainne, her green eyes amused, pointed out that flint and tinder might also be of use, and Meraud contributed a Bible – 'For he had the look of a thoughtful and godly man.' Jamie, still peeved at this lavishing of attention on the man who was supposedly our bitterest enemy, turned at last to Grainne and said, 'What do you think of all this? You've more reason to hate him than any of us.'

'Why? Because he was the cause of Hester's death? You know very well that it was an accident, and could not have been prevented, and he grieved very much for it, and was kind to us above his duty. You cannot in all conscience,' said Grainne, gently rocking her new child asleep in the warm cradle by the kitchen fire, 'paint a man as evil and beyond all aid simply because he happens to disagree with your politics. That's the reaction of a child, not an adult.'

'There's a good many children in this land, then,' the Widow observed acidly, packing bread and half a capon pie in the basket. 'Well, that's it then, Lady Samaritan. Are you going to the castle on your own?'

Lucy looked round the company. Grainne, not yet churched, could not go with her. Jamie looked mutinous; Meraud pleaded tiredness. I met the Widow's eyes. We nodded, and I said, 'I will, and Mistress Gooch as well. Then she can dress his wounds, if they let us see him.'

So once more we made our way to the castle in the damp cold air of February, the dirty snow still staining the streets and dropping in fat wet lumps from roofs on to unwary passers-by. At the castle the scene was chaotic. Many of the prisoners had not yet been bestowed and stood in miserable groups around the courtyard while the strongest of them were being promised a finer, more successful future fighting for the King. It took an hour or more of diligent questioning, slipped crowns, and Lucy's dizzying charm, before we finally gained access to one of the tower chambers wherein some of the officers were held.

It was a big, bare room, innocent of any comforts save a few verminous straw pallets strewn about. Light entered thinly through two small lancet windows, too high to look out from. There was a hearth in one wall; at this a young man more hardy than the rest was endeavouring to make a fire from straw and sticks which looked like part of a jackdaw's nest. The other men, upwards of a dozen, lay or sprawled about the room, too far gone with hunger and fatigue to do more than turn their heads at our entrance. The harassed turnkey, totally flustered by the drastic swelling of the numbers in his charge, seemed so relieved to have some of the burden of care taken from his shoulders, however briefly, that he gave us no time limit. We stood in the middle of the cold room and stared round, suddenly daunted by the fact that we could not in conscience give aid to Captain Ashley and ignore the rest.

'Captain Ashley? Is he here?' Lucy asked, her eyes searching the room. For a moment no answer came, then the man at the hearth, blowing lovingly on the starveling flame between his cupped hands, said without turning, 'He's in the corner under the windows, mistress, and you'll get little sense out of him.'

We negotiated the sprawled, bandaged limbs and gathered around the still figure propped against the wall. The sight of his gaunt, stubborn face, blurred with five days' growth of beard, reminded me in its illness of Francis when he had lain sick unto death – the same grey pallor and shadowed, sunken eyesockets. Lucy bent, her eyes bright with tears, and said gently, 'Captain Ashley?'

At the touch of her hand on his arm his eyes opened and stared bewildered into our faces. 'Mis-Mistress Heron, surely? What are you doing here? It's no place for you.'

'We've come to help you,' Lucy said firmly. 'We saw you in

460

the procession and we felt we must do something. Where are you hurt?'

'I'm not the worst,' the Captain whispered. 'There's a lad over there with his leg ripped to shreds – look to him before me. But you shouldn't anyway – no sight for a lady – why should you want to do anything for me?' He began to cough, harshly, and we glanced at each other. 'If you don't get him out of here,' said the Widow in her croaky whisper, 'he'll go the same way as Francis, and in a place like this he'll die for certain.'

'We must get him out of here,' Lucy hissed urgently. The Captain heard her. 'Not . . . going . . . to give . . . parole,' he said, his voice coming in hoarse gasps as he fought to control his breathing. 'Not going . . . to desert my . . . friends.'

The man who had been lighting the fire came over; he stood over the prone figure and said, 'Dan, did you hear? If you don't give parole and go with your friends, you'll die.'

'What . . . about young Thomson?'

The other prisoner's eyes flicked to a boy lying curled up in his cloak on one of the pallets. 'He'll do. He has no fever, and his leg's nowhere near as bad as you think. Now for God's sake, man, give in and see reason. What would I tell Kez if you died in here when you could have been saved?'

Silence. The Captain's eyes closed in defeat. I guessed that his resistance had never been more than a token effort, anyway – the last protests of an unselfish man against inevitability. I wondered who Kez was – sister, wife? His hands carried no ring, but that of course meant nothing. And I began to hope very much, for Lucy's sake, that he had no wife.

'But will they let us take him away?' Lucy demanded. The Captain's friend turned to her, taking in the details of her face, her hair, the sleek folds of her black dress, mourning for two brothers. He smiled. 'I should imagine, mistress, they'd be only too pleased to be rid of a mouth, particularly a sick one like to die without care. And they wouldn't want him to die, once they discover who he is.'

'Who?' Lucy asked, staring down at the exhausted face.

'Cousin to Pym,' said the prisoner, 'and also my wife's brother, but that counts for little with the men who'll arrange any exchange. What matters is, they think highly of him at Westminster, and so he's worth a great deal to our Royalist captors.' He glanced round at us and added, 'If I may be so bold as to ask, what is your interest in him?'

'We knew him when he was part of the Banbury garrison,' I said tactfully. 'Then we saw him in the street being brought here, and felt we had to help.'

'If we can take him to our house,' Lucy added, 'we'll leave you the things we brought to share amongst yourselves.'

'And the sooner we get him out of this draughty old heap the better,' said the Widow, looking round. 'Riddled with gaol fever, this place, shouldn't wonder – should've been pulled down years ago. Turnkey! Where are you?'

The gaoler appeared with an alacrity that suggested he had been listening on the other side of the door. 'Yes, ladies?'

'We wish to take this prisoner to our own house to nurse him,' said Mistress Gooch. 'Otherwise, we fear he'll die in this cold. Look at it, sir, you ought to be ashamed of yourself – no fire to speak of, middle of February, snow on the ground outside and half of 'em are sick, and pillaged of most of their clothes into the bargain.'

The turnkey, withering, mumbled something about, 'Too soon, no chance to provide, no money to buy food or firewood, not my fault.' He added, more firmly, 'Is the prisoner prepared to give his parole not to escape?'

The prisoner was, and within ten minutes, Lucy in anxious attendance and supported by the 'stout fellow' the Widow had requested from the unfortunate turnkey, he was being taken back through the cold and snow to Pennyfarthing Street. The Widow and I handed over the basket and blanket to be shared amongst the remaining prisoners, and then followed them. I was quiet, my mind busy with the mystery of why Lucy's roving eye had fixed at last on Captain Daniel Ashley, cousin to Pym? He was not handsome, not particularly young, and she had met him but once before, very briefly and in most unpropitious circumstances. And of course, as an enemy Roundhead, he had very little chance of ever being acceptable to Simon.

And somehow, I could not bear that Lucy should have to go through the same torments and deceits of forbidden love as I had endured, and possibly with the same tragic end. Perhaps Simon, faced with another such situation, would prove adult enough to profit by his earlier errors. But I knew Simon's habit of forcing everyone else into the same rigidly moral armour in which he encased himself, and had my doubts.

The door was opened by Jamie, haggard of face and indignant of eye. His jaw dropped when he saw the ragged, half-conscious man carried past and transported up the stairs to the same second-storey room that had belonged to Francis. 'Who – what – Lucy, you can't bring him here! You can't! He's a Roundhead, a – he's one of the enemy!'

'Oh, yes, I can bring him here,' said Lucy, with some heat. 'It's not your house, is it? It's Thomazine's, or Dominic's, rather. If we'd left him there he would have died – can you look me in the face and tell me you'd *want* that to happen? I'll wager you can't!'

Jamie flushed, stared at his shoes, and mumbled something. Lucy, her battle won, swept regally past and up the stairs. The Widow winked at me and followed her.

'And what on earth is going on?' Grainne's sleek head appeared round the kitchen door. 'Lucy's brought her Roundhead here, that's what's happening,' said Jamie sulkily.

'Here?' Meraud demanded, stepping out from behind Grainne. 'But what will Dominic say? And Simon?'

We did not have the chance to find out the answer to either of those questions until much later, and meanwhile the house was thrown into busy confusion as the Widow flung herself with her customary gusto into the task of caring for yet another wounded man. Fires were lit, medicines fetched, fresh clothes and bandages and hot water and food; and at the end of it all, as dusk stole softly into the little gabled room that held so many happy and painful memories for me, Captain Ashley sat in the bed clean and well-clad in one of Dominic's nightshirts, the sword-thrust in his leg dressed and his arm in a sling, much restored by all this care, and thanked us.

'It was the least we could do,' Lucy said, smiling. The gentle half-light diffusing from the window emphasized the soft curves of her face and lent at once a shadow and a spark to her wide eyes. I glanced at Captain Ashley and saw him looking at her. Nothing showed on his face but a small smile at each corner of his mouth, but there was something about the quality of that smile that made me lean back, relaxed and relieved. At least Lucy was not wasting her charms on stony soil.

'Just a few minutes, I said,' the Widow told us, bustling in with candles and flint. 'Rest is what he needs, and he won't get it with you all gossiping round his bed, poor man. Now downstairs with the lot of you!'

Rather sheepishly, we filed out, leaving her in undisputed possession of the field and her prisoner. Halfway down the stairs came the rap of the door-knocker, and Lucy galloped down the last few steps to answer it.

It was Dominic, his cloak spangled with new-fallen snow, a look of something like hope in his cold-brightened face. And I stared in dismay, for with all the bustle and to-do of caring for Captain Ashley, I had quite forgotten that the Prince's army was expected hard on the heels of its prisoners. All thought of Dominic, of changing my attitude towards him, or trying to be a more loving and dutiful wife had flown from my head. And as he saw and interpreted my expression, the eagerness in his face froze and faded. He shut the door, removed his cloak with an ill-tempered flourish and hurled it at Heppy, who was making for the stairs with a small, evil-looking blue bottle containing one of the Widow's more noxious restorative potions. Faced with the choice of suffering the respective wraths of Dominic or the Widow, Heppy not surprisingly chose the Widow's. She caught the cloak and dropped the bottle. It smashed on the polished boards and a pungent, throat-catching aroma assaulted the air. 'Dear God,' said my husband, 'what's that?'

'Thass physick for Captain Ashley,' said poor Heppy, in between coughs, 'but I doubt that'll kill he, not cure.'

'And who, in the name of Mary Mother, is Captain Ashley?'

Heppy gave me an agonized, apologetic stare. I said hastily, 'He's wounded, and ill, and we've given him medicine, food and a bed in return for past kindness.'

'And what past kindness is that, pray?' Suspicion was plain in his voice and face; since it had become apparent that I cared nothing for him, he had scarcely been able to bear me even glancing at anyone else for whom I might feel any sort of affection. Thus had Drake been banished, literally on pain of death, to a cold lodging in the stable. I realized now, looking at him, that any answer would incur wrath, and decided on the truth as the safest course. 'We surrendered Ashcott to him, and he showed us every kindness and courtesy. When we saw him amongst the prisoners from Cirencester, it seemed only right to repay the debt and do what we could for him.'

'It's quite safe,' Lucy added. 'He's given his parole not to escape, and besides he couldn't very well, not in the state he's in. Heppy, please go and mop that mess up before it poisons us all.'

'Eh? Yes, Mistress Lucy, I'll dew that,' said Heppy with a cloak-encumbered curtsey, and fled to the kitchen.

Dominic looked around at our apprehensive faces, and shrugged. 'Well, as he's here I daresay he can stay. I'm not so inhuman as to pack a sick man back to the castle, or wherever he was before you rescued him. Now, Thomazine, I'd appreciate some food – it's been a long and cold day.'

Relieved at having got off so lightly, I gave him my best smile, and made for the kitchen. As I reached the door, my hand outstretched, it opened before me, to admit all in a rush a tangle of child, and dog, and kitten. They swirled shrieking and barking and miaowing around our feet until I grabbed Orange, and Grainne whisked Jasper out of the way with a shrewd underarm grip, and Drake was left panting hopefully in the middle of the floor.

'I understood,' said Dominic coldly, 'that that dog was to be kept outside. What's it doing in the house?'

Jasper, safe in his mother's grasp, squeaked, 'He was chasing Orange, sir, and the door wasn't shut properly.' He stood in some awe of Dominic, who was not the kind of man to indulge in easy camaraderie with small children. My husband said, with some anger, 'Well, take it outside, and tie it up where it belongs, and make sure it doesn't stray into the house again, young man, or I'll finally lose patience.' And, leaving Jasper silent and wide-eyed, he swept into the front parlour, with the four of us, the child and the animals in the hall staring miserably at each other. As I prepared a supper for Dominic while Grainne and Jasper took Drake outside to the stables, far removed from his former comfortable lodging on my bed, I had time to reflect unhappily about how, despite my good intentions, the relationship between my husband and myself was still of the sweetness of vinegar; and how his ill-temper was rapidly making enemies of the rest of the household, from Jasper upwards. I thought of Drake in his cold and lonely straw bed, and then my need and longing for Francis swept over me, overhelming all rational, sensible thought, so that a dozen fat tears dribbled on to the pigeon pie and diluted the steaming posset. Meraud, coming in as softly as Orange, found me there and put a friendly arm round my bowed shoulders. 'You can't go on grieving for Francis forever, you know.'

I nodded, and did all the sensible, rational things, blowing my nose and wiping my eyes and dashing cold water in my face, so that I would be able to return to my husband as my usual self. But beneath all this attempt at normality, I was realizing that even if I lived as long as Methuselah, I would mourn Francis for all that time. While I had been bravely pretending that nothing had happened, the death of Francis had torn away a fundamental part of me, and left a wound that would never truly heal. There was so much that my mind had shared with his, the same laughter, the same thoughts, the same interests and passions, and now there was no one to understand that part of me, and worst of all no one to comprehend fully what the loss meant to me. Deceived by my outward acceptance, they told each other, I knew, how well I was taking my bereavement, and the inevitable thought must follow, did she really love him as much as she professed?

But I had loved him more than I could ever say, and now there was a great empty aching void in my heart, to be filled inadequately by dutiful love of husband and, in the future, love of children.

I had told Lucy once, referring to Nan Blagge and Simon, 'I wouldn't want to be loved out of duty.' Nor, I suspected, would Dominic. I would do my best, but it was plain there could be no great love, not again, not after Francis.

And there was no laughter in Dominic; none at all.

Dutifully, I loaded a wooden tray with my husband's supper and bore it into the parlour. Somehow, the mistakes of the previous two months had to be put right, and I saw now what would do it. I knocked, and entered, and put down the tray on the hearth, and curtseyed decorously as any maidservant, and poured the wine and set out the food. Dominic stood and watched all this with a faintly surprised air. When I had finished, he said, 'To what do I owe this courtesy?'

'No courtesy, but what a wife should do for her husband,' I responded, with a humility which would have made Francis laugh aloud. I thrust his bright image to the back of my mind with an inward sob of grief, and gave Dominic what I trusted was a brilliant smile.

It worked. Still surprised, and a trifle suspicious, he smiled faintly in reply, and then drew me to the settle. Like true lovers we shared a wine cup, while he talked of Ciren-

467

cester, and the battle, and of the weather, so cold and raw for February; and at the end of it I said, 'Dominic, I have something to tell you.'

'Yes, little sparrow, what is it?'

I waited a moment, gathering courage, for to tell him this meant giving the concept shape and reality in my mind and in my future, and I was not at all sure I was fully prepared for it; but in the end I took a deep breath, and said, 'I am with child.'

The last clouds disappeared, the storm rolled back and the sun shone with delight in his face, so that for the first time I felt the stirrings of affection for him. 'Are you? Are you really? Are you sure?' I nodded as his eagerness over-flowed. 'How do you know? Are you truly certain? When will he be born?'

'How do all women know?' I said primly, as he gazed at me with happy, devouring eyes. 'In early September, I think. I'm not sure exactly when.'

'An heir at last,' said Dominic, still swept away on the tides of enthusiasm. 'A boy to carry on the name and our line! There have been Drakelons in Denby for nigh on six hundred years, and I swore to my father that I would not be the last of them. But I never imagined . . . so soon!' He stared earnestly into my face. 'It seems too soon to be certain. Are you truly sure?'

'I am,' I said, 'and Mistress Gooch agrees with me. She's not a midwife, true, but she's had wide experience of these things, and she's certain too.' I added, hesitantly, not wishing to dampen his delight, 'How can you be so sure it will be a boy?'

'It can't be anything else,' said Dominic. 'There's been no girls born Drakelon for two generations now; I had four brothers, who all died young, and my father had six. It's inconceivable you should carry a girl.'

I smiled at his unwitting pun, full of ridiculous delight at the success of my new leaf. Together we drank the child's health, and then Dominic needs must call in the other members of the household to share our news, and drink to the safe birth and long life and prosperity of the embryo Roger Drakelon, tenth of that name and twenty-fifth in direct line from the Fulk Drakelon who had been one of Norman William's henchmen and in return for the customary licensed rapine, murder and pillage on his lord's behalf, had received a fair proportion of Yorkshire. Perversely, the hope crept into my head that the infant might be a girl. Betty had to be sent out, grumbling, into the freezing snowy dark to the Blue Boar for a gallon jug of claret, and even Daniel Ashley was included in the celebrations, albeit at a distance, by being given a brimming cupful to accompany his supper.

That night I slept in Dominic's arms, the two of us at peace, as one; and dreamed a soft and gentle dream, full of snowy hills and vague comforting ideas of homecoming, and friendship, and rest after long and bitter hardship. We woke with a dawn made newly bright by the fresh snow shrouding the street, and looked into each other's faces with the first faint, hesitant smiles of mutual affection.

And I did not once think of Francis.

The snow melted, and spring followed hard in the slush, so that within a week of Dominic's return I was able to gather the first shy apologetic snowdrops from under the apple tree in the garden, and place them in a tiny glass jar, meant to hold simples, to fill the Captain's sickroom with their thin sweet scent. For after the first, rapid improvement effected by his removal from the castle, he had relapsed, and it had been several days before he again appeared to be recovering. Dominic was frequently out on army business, and the Widow had taken it into her head to visit daily the remainder of the castle prisoners with medicines, food and fuel; needing no permission from the harassed, overworked governor who appeared, from her indignant description, to be labouring almost entirely without assistance. So Lucy, Meraud, Grainne and I sat frequently with the Captain, exchanging, at first, information of mutual interest; thus, we learned that he was thirty years old, unwed, the eldest son and heir of a London clock and instrument-maker, and that he had a sister Keziah, and Harry, the brother-in-law in the castle, to whose farm at Cirencester he had fled after the surrender of Banbury, which had not long followed the siege of Ashcott. There he had once more been caught up in the fighting, and taken prisoner with the rest. Having given this information, he was then so rash as to inquire about this place Goldhayes that we mentioned so frequently, and was immediately favoured with an animated description from the four of us, but chiefly from Lucy, dwelling on its favoured situation, history, architecture, chief beauties and remarkable felicities, so that anyone not acquainted with the reality would have imagined a second Nonsuch. Following this, to set his head further in a whirl, there were digressions on family history, both recent, and in the more distant past, and culminating in the terrible events at Ashcott and after, many of which he had not of course heard. As she recited, hesitantly, the story of Francis's death, Lucy broke into tears, and I also felt my emotions overwhelming me once more. Captain Ashley listened with a face full of compassion and regret, and then gently reached forward to touch Lucy's hand. 'I am most deeply sorry, Mistress Lucy. I liked him very much – it's always the way, they say, to like your enemies as well as your friends in such a war as this, but he was a brave and enterprising commander, and I could have given the lie to anyone who asserted that he was not.'

'But too late,' said Grainne, her wide bleak eyes staring into the distance. 'And Lucy has lost a brother, and Thomazine her lover, whom she was to have married, and I a very dear friend, and all for some stupid matter of imagined honour.'

'But you are married to another now,' said Captain Ashley to me, and I flushed, and staring at my guilty, betraying hands, said defensively, 'I could think of nothing else to do.' And then, trying to joke in case I had put him at a disadvantage, added, 'I had Lucy importuning me, and that is the most difficult thing on earth to withstand!'

'Hah,' said Lucy, 'you didn't do much withstanding, as I

recall. But then Dominic and Simon were also very persuasive.' I realized with dismay that she evidently considered me flighty, eager to forget her dead brother in favour of the living cousin; rather an unfair attitude in view of the pressure she had put on me, I thought. And whichever way I leaned, my guilty conscience had me tied. When I remembered Francis, I was being unfair to Dominic, and vice versa. But Francis would always win in the end; I could begin to like Dominic, perhaps even grow fond of him, regard him with wifely affection, but I would never feel that leap of the heart when he entered the room, never be able to tell what he was thinking by the set of his mouth or the shadows in his eyes, never feel again that sense of oneness, of kinship, of *knowing* someone through to heart and soul as I had known and understood Francis.

All that, gone forever. But no good mourning, that would not work any miracles. I could only do what my wise grandmother had told me to do, when I stood a child of ten in the ruins of my childhood – 'Make the best of what you have.' And I had Dominic, and the coming child so triumphantly proclaimed, and my friends about me. It was not their fault that they were pale shadows beside Francis's ghost.

Spring came on rapidly now, the winds softening and the first spikes of daffodils sprouting green in a corner of the garden to dwarf the snowdrops, and on a fine sunny afternoon Captain Ashley took a stroll down the stone path, supported by Lucy on one side and Grainne at the other. Jasper rolled and shrieked with Orange on the damp grass, and because Dominic was out I slipped into the stable to release Drake from his irksome confinement. The dog was pathetically glad to be freed; he placed two hairy paws on my thighs and attempted to wash my face, and then went racing round the garden as if he were once again a carefree puppy, instead of eight or nine years old.

'You can see how he enjoys a run,' said the captain, pausing under the apple tree and smiling at the inextricable tangle of kitten, dog and small boy on the tiny patch of grass, 'it seems a shame to keep him tied up like that.'

'Oh, but Dominic doesn't like him,' said Lucy, with her usual thoughtlessness, 'he used to be Francis's dog, you see . . .' She saw my face, and her voice trailed away. Daniel coughed gently. 'For such a close-woven family, you do seem to harbour an inordinate quantity of disharmonies.'

I had to smile; the bare words might have come from Simon, but somehow Dan Ashley invested them with a dry gentle humour all his own, and which I was rapidly coming to appreciate. 'Oh, yes, worse than Montague and Capulet we are, worse even than that family in . . . what's that play, Lucy, where the brothers are jealous of their sister and murder her husband and her and one of them goes mad and thinks he's a wolf?'

'*The Duchess of Malfi.*'

'That's it, *The Duchess of Malfi*. Are you a lover of stage plays, Captain Ashley?'

'In the circles in which I move, Lady Drakelon, they are somewhat frowned upon. But I must confess to a sneaking, uh, liking at least for some of the works of Master Shakespeare and Master Jonson, although I must say I find Master Webster rather, how shall I put it, preposterous.'

'No, I never did like *The Duchess* much,' said Lucy, dismissing one of her erstwhile favourite plays without a backward glance. 'Nor *The White Devil*. But I do like *A Midsummer Night's Dream*, and *Romeo and Juliet*, and my favourite,' she added with a sideways glance at Captain Ashley to see his reaction, and a further glare at me for my silence, 'is *As You Like It.*'

I forbore to mention *A Woman Killed with Kindness*; indeed I could not, for Lucy and the captain were now deep in discussion of Touchstone and Melancholy Jacques, and a swift brilliant vision rose to my mind's eye of Francis, the level lines of his face dragged down in simulated melancholy, acting that latter part one rainy afternoon at

Goldhayes. Even if I wished to forget, my traitor's brain would not allow me.

Grainne stood by the stable door, her quiet smiling eyes on Jasper, now trying to dress the long-suffering Drake in an old hat of Jamie's. 'It's good he now has a sister, and your coming child too for company,' she said as I came up. 'He's not used to other children, and I can't feel that's best for him.'

I knew what she meant. Jasper even at his tender age had seen too much, and lived too long with adults. In the feeble sunshine his round babyish head shone with fire and every line of his thin, long-boned, graceful body spoke eloquently of his mother. 'I'm glad Henrietta has red hair,' she said reflectively, and then with one of her quick smiles, 'Do you know what Jasper calls her?'

'Hen,' I said, having heard him, unwilling to manage all four syllables, reduce his sister's name to that. Grainne grinned. 'No, not now. He calls her Fowl now. Chicken was the in-between stage, until he grew too pleased with his own cleverness.'

'I think Chicken would be more appropriate,' I told her, 'Fowl has connotations that aren't entirely suitable.'

'And of which he's very well aware,' said Grainne. 'He is too grown-up in many ways, isn't he? It's a shame there aren't more young children in the street, but all except that little Will are either too old or too young, and there is something about Will that is not right; he looks to me like a lack-wit.'

'Which Jasper is not, most emphatically. I may not have much knowledge of little children,' I said, 'but he seems to me to show exceptional promise of intelligence.'

'At the moment,' said Grainne, watching her son lying full-length on the grass apparently examining Drake's teeth, 'he seems to me to show exceptional lack of common sense. It's lucky Drake is even-tempered and long-suffering. A more uncertain dog would long ago have eaten him for dinner.'

'Poor Drake, the world conspires against him. I'm sorry,'

I said, making a sudden beeline for the mounting-block outside the stable door, 'but I must sit down. I hate this faint feeling I get now – it must be something to do with the child.'

'Most like,' said Grainne, sitting down beside me, and looking into my face. 'Yes, you look more than a little pale. And you're far more sick in the mornings than ever I was. Still, it passes off soon enough, and you'll feel much better.'

'It's as well it does, I'd run mad if I woke up every day for another seven months feeling as I did this morning. Still,' I said, lifting my head and smiling at her, 'it's made such a difference, hasn't it? Dominic is like a man made new.'

'And no regrets?'

'If Francis had never existed, no regrets. But you know, none better, how I loved him. I regret his death most bitterly, and will do for ever; but now that Dominic and I are in harmony, I have no regrets on that score. You could even say I was happy.'

'But,' said Grainne, 'I know too, how much greater happiness could be, if only . . .' She gripped my hand suddenly. 'It sounds terrible to say it, but you know I am almost glad that you share a similar grief to mine, for then at least we each know what the other feels and can have some measure of understanding. And now we each have children to assuage some of the loss.'

'But what I regret more than anything else,' I said, in a strangled whisper, 'is that my child is not Francis's.'

We sat in silence together, linked by sorrow and memories, until a piercing yell from Jasper brought us both to our feet. 'Orange! Orange, come down! Mother, Orange is up the tree!'

'It's all right, he can come down,' Grainne called, and then seeing his continued agitation gave me a wry grin and walked over. At that moment the gate in the wall opened and I turned to see Dominic's vivid blue smile. 'Hullo, I didn't expect you back so soon,' I said as, all feelings of faintness vanished, I went to greet him.

'I persuaded one of my lieutenants to sort out some

pother in one of the lodgings,' said Dominic. He pulled me into his arms and kissed me thoroughly. 'And how are you this afternoon, my little sparrow? Quite recovered?'

I had opened my mouth to say that I was, when a low, vicious growl interrupted. Startled, we turned, to see Drake, hackles raised, ears back, and his yellowing teeth bared in a ferocious snarl. The growl rumbled again in his throat; then he barked furiously.

'Sweet Jesu, I told you to keep him tied up!' Dominic said. 'Get back! Go on, back!' Still keeping an arm round me, he waved the other at Drake, and with a bloodcurdling noise halfway between a growl and a bark, Francis's dog leapt at his hand. The scream somewhere beyond us in the garden must, I thought blankly, be Lucy; then Dominic, cursing volubly, was shaking one hand, the other vainly lashing out at the dog, and Drake was on the end of it, teeth firmly fixed, his jaws locked on the object of his longtime hatred. Blood suddenly seemed to be everywhere. From past memory an idea came into my head; I ran into the stable, grabbed the bucket of water in Hobgoblin's stall, and from the doorway hurled it over man and dog. Drake's jaws opened, he dropped to all fours, with a yelp of surprise, and shook himself vigorously. And Dominic snatched up a heavy branch from the pile of firewood nearby and raised it to strike the dog's head.

I shouted something, tried to move, but someone forestalled me; like an arrow on his brief petticoat-hampered legs Jasper shot between them and locked his arms around Drake's neck. For a second I shut my eyes, so certain was I that in his uncontrollable fury Dominic would strike regardless. There was no sound of any blow, however, only Jasper's high desperate voice shrieking protest. 'No! No, you shan't! No!'

'In the name of God, man, put it down!' That, redolent with authority, was Captain Ashley. I reopened my eyes and saw him standing by Dominic's right arm as my husband stood rock-steady, his arm still held high to strike. 'Get that child away,' Daniel added to me. Since to do so was to sign

Drake's death-warrant, I hesitated, and Grainne, arriving at a run, grabbed her son by the shoulders and tried to prise him free. She might as well have attempted to disentangle the serpent from Laocöon; Jasper wound his fingers tighter round Drake's collar, and his voice climbed the scale into screeching hysteria. 'Dominic, please, put it down,' I begged. 'Your hand, look, it needs attention, put it down . . .'

'I'm going to knock that dog's brains out,' said Dominic in a voice as cold and deadly and distant as ice. 'And when that screaming brat is taken away, I'll do what should have been done years ago.'

Grainne was on her knees now on the soft muddy path, trying to separate dog and child by persuasion and main force, and Jasper, hand and face buried in Drake's neck, was shrieking like a banshee and warding her off with a beating fist. Abruptly, Daniel took the dog's collar and dragged the two of them, still entangled, the few steps to the gate. I ran to open it for him, and hissed in his ear, 'The Blue Boar, take them there, Mistress Mander will look after the dog and he won't dare gainsay her. I'll deal with Dominic.' And I dashed back into the garden, almost colliding with Grainne on her way out in pursuit of her son. Dominic still stood where I had left him, the wind taken utterly from his sails by the abrupt exit of his quarry. Sulkily, he hurled the branch back on to the pile, and as Jasper's yells diminished into the distance, he said, 'If I ever lay eyes on that animal again, before God I'll strangle it with my bare hands. And that brat should be horsewhipped.' He glanced round, at Lucy and Jamie and Meraud in a startled, shocked group on the lawn, and lowered his voice to hiss into my face, 'And what's more I'm tired, madam, mightily tired of sharing you and my house with a gaggle of your cousins and hangers-on and that upstart canting Puritan, and if I had my way they'd all be on the streets this night to make their way back to Suffolk where they belong.'

Sick with fury, and fear, I shouted back. 'And I'm tired of your stupid jealousy, sir! What's their crime, pray? That they're my friends, and talk and laugh with me? What was Drake's crime? Had he been the sweetest-tempered dog in the world – and save for you, he is – you'd still have found an excuse to be rid of him, for his fault is that he was Francis's dog, not yours!' And made bold by my anger I added spitefully, 'Can you see yourself and the spectacle you make? The great Sir Dominic Drakelon, scion of six hundred years of Norman landlords, Captain in the King's Lifeguard, jealous of his wife's affection for a *dog*?'

For a minute I really thought he would murder me where I stood. His hands came up to close on my neck, and Lucy screamed, and Jamie shouted something. But I was saved from an unexpected quarter; the gate banged open and the Widow's acid voice said, 'If you harm her, sir, then you also harm your son.'

Dominic's hands wavered, and dropped. A spot of his blood, still flowing from the ignored gashes in his right hand, stained my dress. The Widow Gooch stood, her laden basket over one arm, hands on hips, and surveyed us. 'Well, this is a pretty pass. Half St Aldate's is buzzing with the scandal already. Young Jasper being sick in the Blue Boar, Mistress Sewell half-distracted with fear, that harmless old dog chained up in their stable yard and Captain Ashley with a face like God's wrath, and to cap it all Sir Dominic Drakelon's lady yelling at him like a Billingsgate fishwife. Did she sink her teeth into your hand, sir?'

'No,' said Dominic. 'It was that dog you please to call old and harmless. And if my lady is behaving like a fishwife, then that is because her nature bears a strong resemblance to one – or to the ladies of a third-rate brothel.' And with that parting shot, he pushed past the Widow and through the open gate. She turned and called after him, 'Master Day is the surgeon, sir, opposite the Blue Boar, for sure as the Devil's in Hell I won't stitch you up!'

The only answer was the slamming of the gate, and the ill-tempered tramping of feet down the road.

I took a deep, shaky breath, unable to meet anyone's eyes. My three cousins exchanged embarrassed glances and the

Widow, summing them up, said, 'What d'you stand there gawping for? If you've naught else to do, then there's six onions need chopping for the rabbit pie, not to mention the syllabub to be whipped up . . .'

'I still think we shouldn't be eating meat in Lent,' said Meraud, and the Widow snorted. 'If the butchers are all allowed to sell flesh by special dispensation, I don't think you've room to quibble, lass – though of course if you *want* to eat that stinking mess those villains are pleased to call fresh fish, then you're quite welcome, but kindly don't bring it near my nose. As for you, young Jamie, I've a job for you; harness up the cob, and take the cart out to the farm for a load of fodder. He's expecting you, but it's not long till dark and you don't want to get caught by the curfew, do you? Or have the cart requisitioned. Now go on, lad, look lively about it.'

With a bad grace, Jamie dragged into the stable, and Meraud and Lucy, rather subdued, vanished into the house. The Widow took my arm. 'I don't know what that was all about, lass, but by Heaven he looked ripe for murder.'

'I think you saved me,' I said, shutting my eyes for a brief moment, and then told her what had happened. 'He seems to me to be almost insane,' I finished. 'Surely no man in his right mind would be so jealous of a dog? Or of a man three months dead?'

'It's not jealousy, lass,' said the Widow. She looked into my face. 'I want to talk with you, as private as can be managed. That was why I was at the Blue Boar, making sure there was an empty parlour set aside so we wouldn't be disturbed. Now, no questions till we get there. You look in need of a good restoring mug of Mistress Mander's best Lambswool, so that's what we'll do. The others can look to themselves.'

We walked up to the house, and I collected cloak and hood before going out again into Pennyfarthing Street. Still shaking and weak-kneed from the drama just enacted, I made no demur when the Widow took my arm and steered me briskly into Fish Street. As we threaded our way across to the Blue Boar, between carts and soldiers and the bustle and smell of the fish-stalls packing up for the day, I was consumed with curiosity about this mysterious 'private talk', but a glance at the Widow's small, wrinkled face revealed little but an unusual grimness. Apprehensively, I was guided into the warm dim ale-smelling fastnesses of John Mander's inn, down twisting corridors, up a flight of stairs and finally to a tiny dark panelled chamber looking on to the street. Through the greenish, distorting glass I could discern Grainne, accompanied by Captain Ashley with Jasper in his arms, crossing the street on their way back to the house. I could also see the premises of the surgeon, almost opposite, but there was no way of telling whether Dominic was within. Feeling sick, I sat down on one of the upright chairs by the table, and the Widow descended on to the other. A knock at the door heralded the arrival of Mistress Mander herself, red-faced and panting with a brimming aromatic mug in each hand. An ample, warm-hearted woman, she set the mugs down and said to me, 'Don't fret, Lady Drakelon. We'll look after your dog for as long as you wish, and John won't gainsay it, for we lost our watchdog last month, died of old age, and he'll not say no to another in these times. We'll see he's fed and looked after and the little lad can come over any time he wants and see he's well.' Her round face as she looked at us was bright with unsatisfied curiosity, but the Widow, said, 'Thank you, Dorothy, it's more than kind of you. Now, can you make sure we're not disturbed?'

'Quite sure,' said Mistress Mander, dropped a brief curtsey to me in acknowledgement of my own thanks, and retreated from the room. We listened in silence to her heavy diminishing footsteps, then the Widow turned to me. 'Are you ready, lass, for what I'm going to tell you? It may be something of a shock.'

I took a steadying sip of hot Lambswool, and stared into

her face, wondering whatever it might be. The Widow held my eyes with her own. 'You asked me why he was so jealous of a dead man. The answer, my dear, is that he is not dead. I know not where he is now, but your Francis is as alive as you or I, and that's for certain.'

'Francis? Alive?' I heard my voice coming from a great distance through the muzzy ringing in my head, then all of a sudden I found myself on the floor, with the hideous smell of burnt feathers making me cough and choke. 'That's better,' said the Widow Gooch, dropping the smouldering feather, doubtless purloined from the bed in the corner, on to the fire. 'Lass, I'm sorry. I forgot you'd been in the habit of fainting. Can you sit up?'

I did so, gingerly, and found to my relief that, although a trifle light-headed, I felt much restored. 'But, please, Mistress Gooch, tell me again, is it true? Is Francis really alive? How can he be?'

'It's true enough,' said the Widow. 'But it makes a sorry tale, and it grieves me it should have happened thus, and still more that you should have to hear it. He lives, and I have spoken to a woman who hid him in her house, until after you were wed.'

Only then did the implications of what should have been a joyous piece of news strike me. I had truly betrayed him: thinking him dead, however falsely informed, I had with indecent haste married another, to whom I was bound till death severed us. 'Oh my God,' I whispered, 'does he know I am married?'

The Widow nodded silently, and I broke into a heartfelt weeping that I could not stop. The cold numbness in my heart was being washed away by pain, and agonized regret, as the numbness of cramped, imprisoned limbs is dissolved by the hurts of returning life and freedom. My grief was for myself, and for him, betrayed by the woman he had thought loved him more than life; but not for his resurrection. Somewhere within me, I cried also for joy, that I was not after all alone.

'Come on, lass, he's alive, and that's no reason for weeping,' said the Widow. She took my hands away from my drowned face. 'Now get up, and sit yourself down and take a good long drought of your Lambswool before it gets cold. That'll calm you.'

My teeth chattered against the rim of the pewter mug, but I downed some of the appled ale and felt a deal better for it. 'Tell me what you've found out,' I said. 'Tell me everything.'

'It was partly as we'd been told,' said the Widow reflectively. 'He did try to escape that night, and was seen and shot by one of the guards, and fell into the river from the mill bridge. That far was true. What we didn't know, and your cousin Simon neither, was that he did not drown.'

'But I dreamed it,' I said, the horror of that night laid on me afresh. 'I dreamed I was drowning, somehow, I can't explain it, I shared his death. I knew he was dead, before ever Simon came to tell me.'

'So that was why you never doubted it,' said the Widow. 'I must say, I always did wonder why there was no body. And other things made me wonder, too. Your husband's great haste to marry you, for instance. If Francis was dead, there was no need for such hurry. Anyway, I decided in the end to make some inquiries of my own. I don't deny that I thought I was making a fool of myself, but you know how it is when an idea sticks in your head and nags to be proved. In the end, the chance I might be right spurred me on. And taking food to those poor lads in the castle gave me a good excuse. I managed to speak with the sentry who'd shot Francis. It was he told me that he'd fallen off the bridge into the water on the *downstream* side, and been swept away. So the fool who put it about that his body might have been trapped in the millwheel was wrong.'

I shuddered. 'I'm glad he was. It would be a horrible way to die . . . please, go on.'

'Well, the next time I came to the castle, I stayed only a little while, and then I set off to walk downstream, to see if there was anywhere he might have dragged himself out. He swims very well, doesn't he? I remember him being in trouble for it, as a student. So I thought if he hadn't been badly wounded, there was a good chance of him surviving where another might have drowned. Now, a little way downstream there's a house with a garden goes down to the river. I know Mistress Bailey, the woman who lives there; her husband and mine were friends long since, and since hers died she's been there alone. I called on her, and I asked her outright, had she taken in a wounded man, of his description, on that night? And she could not lie to me, and said that she had.'

I took in a deep quivering breath, my eyes locked on her face in the deepening light, too afraid of weeping again to speak. The Widow took both my hands in hers, and went on. 'She found him in her garden at daybreak when she went out. He'd somehow got himself up the bank and under some currant bushes, and her silly little dog found him. The cold had stopped the bleeding, but he was in the grip of a raging fever. Somehow he told her he was a fugitive from the castle, asked her to hide him, and she did.' A small grin appeared on the Widow's face. 'Even in that state he could charm the birds off of the trees, that one . . . She and her maid got him indoors and hidden upstairs in an unused chamber, and as she only has the one maid, and her loyal and trustworthy, thought it an easy matter to keep him hidden there till he recovered. The wound was a clean one, through the shoulder, and not beyond her competence to mend, but the fever was another matter, him being weak from the last time, and she nearly lost him. For a week or more, he was near to death, till he took a turn for the better.' She paused, and then said, 'Now comes the sorry part of the tale, lass, but I feel it's something you should know, whatever the consequences. Before he was on the mend, someone came to the house making inquiries. Now Ann Bailey she's a good woman, and honest as the day, and try as she might she could not lie convincingly. She said she had seen no one, had no one hidden, but he was not fooled. He searched the house, and found him.'

I drew a deep breath. 'Who was it? Simon?'

'No, not Simon.' Her hands gripped mine tightly. 'It was your high and mighty husband, Sir Dominic Drakelon.'

Tears began to spill over and dribble down my cheeks; I wiped them away and said in a whisper, 'Dominic? Are you sure?'

'Oh, yes, it was Dominic. She described him exactly, although he never mentioned his name. He told her to keep Francis hid, dropped hints that it would be very convenient if he didn't survive the fever; and he threatened her, saying that if word leaked out, or if she let him go or tried to spirit him away, he would have her taken up for harbouring a deserter, assisting escape, any number of crimes. He put the fear of God into her; and she was too cowed to do anything other than what he said. But she did refuse point-blank, thank God, to hasten his end; said she would denounce *him* if she suspected him of doing anything to harm Francis. They came to a rather uneasy understanding,' said the Widow caustically. 'From then on, as Francis recovered, your Dominic came to see him pretty near every day. And now comes the sorriest part of all; he came to gloat. He didn't tell him that you thought he was dead; didn't tell him that you were being pressured from all sides to marry himself. He deliberately let Francis think that you had allowed yourself to be seduced by his superior wealth, his lands and title. He said that you had willingly, gladly given over any feeling you had had for Francis, in favour of himself. And he stood over him on his sickbed, and told him with relish how joyfully you were preparing for your wedding.'

I began to feel very sick indeed, with guilty self-hatred and an even more overwhelming loathing of my husband, whose callous perfidy I had never dreamed existed. 'But . . . how do you know all this?'

'Ann Bailey listened at the door. Her honesty didn't stretch thus far, in those circumstances. She said that Francis refused to believe it at first . . . until Dominic produced the licence. Then he believed it.'

'Oh my God . . . so he thinks . . . he thinks that I . . .'

'Deliberately considered the choice between him and Dominic . . . and chose Dominic. If that husband of yours came into this room now,' said the Widow, 'I doubt I could keep my hands from his throat. There's only one thing to say in his favour – he refrained from returning after the marriage and telling him the details of bedding you. From what Ann told me, I should reckon he knew damn well that, sick or no, Francis would have laid hands on him, and half-killed him too, I shouldn't wonder. But that's it, lass – that's what you've wed, and God help and forgive us all, that we persuaded you into something best left well alone.'

'It's . . . it's all right,' I said. Something seemed to have happened to my voice; it was little more than a whisper. 'It doesn't matter. It's gone, and we can't alter it. The question is, what do we do now?' I spoke with the calm born of utter despair, for now I was trapped, imprisoned in marriage to a man who had deceived and cheated both me and my lover: and Francis believed that *I* had been deceitful. I added, my voice tottering on the edge of breakdown, 'I . . . I don't think I could bear to touch him, not now. I couldn't, I couldn't sleep in the same bed knowing what he's done . . . He sickens me, the thought that I have to spend a lifetime with him sickens me.'

'Well, you needn't spend a lifetime with him,' said the Widow, giving my hand another squeeze. 'How's your moral sense, lass? How strong's your belief in hellfire?'

I stared at her, a faint hope glowing at the back of my mind. 'Where Francis is concerned, very weak.'

'That's all to the good. Well, lass, in my book you've every right to leave him, and go to Francis. A marriage gained by trickery is no true marriage, I reckon. Your righteous cousin Simon won't agree with me, nor that prim-faced little madam, but the rest of 'em will, and they'd be glad for you, I know. So there's one good reason for steeling yourself to share that man's bed, and carrying on as usual – for if you don't, and he suspects you know Francis is still alive, you'll be kept closer than a miser's moneybags, in case you run off. No wonder the bastard's mad with jealousy, and sick with guilt and fear too, I shouldn't be surprised. So you must try and behave as if you were still his loving wife, lass, or you'll never get away.'

'But when? When can I go? He's always here, I'll never be free of him!'

'Your chance will come, lass, and if it doesn't we'll make a chance for you. But there's no need for haste; you can't go gallivanting off till the child's born.'

The child. I had forgotten it; yet one more link forged in the chain tying me to Dominic. 'If it's a boy,' I said, 'and I run off with it, he'll never rest till he brings us back.'

'So pray for a girl, lass, for I shouldn't imagine he'll care a toss for a girl. And there's another reason, too, for not running off straightway – where would you go? Where has Francis gone? All Ann could tell me was that he left two days after Christmas, with some of her husband's clothes, and a tidy sum of money she'd lent him, and said no word of where he was bound.'

'I know where he *might* have gone,' I said slowly. 'We have cousins in Scotland – he stayed two years there when he was a boy, and one of our cousins was his particular friend. And when he was in prison he sent a message by Jamie, to say 'Remember Catholm'. I think he meant that should he ever escape, that would be where he would go.'

'Yes, but you don't know, do you? If – I don't want to say this, lass, but you have to face the truth – if he thinks that all your love was lies and deceit, he's not likely to make for the place he'd set to meet you. He could have gone back to Suffolk, joined the King's army, or the Parliament's, gone to London, sailed for the New World – anything. There's one thing sure about that young man,' said the Widow, with a shadow of her old irreverent humour, 'and that is that he can be relied upon to do the unexpected.'

'I suppose I could write a letter,' I said, slowly and dubiously. 'But the only person at Catholm I've ever met was my great-aunt, and I haven't seen her since I was a child. She was sympathetic to Francis,' I went on, remembering her words long ago when Lucy and I had begged for her help in saving Drake from his father's wrath, and that letter she had later written about his exploits at Catholm, probably milder by far than any that might have been sent by the unknown Presbyterian, Grizel Graham. 'And if I wrote to her, she might help. It's the only chance I have of knowing whether he's there or not, so I shall have to take it – although she must be seventy or more, that is if she's still alive.'

'And is she truly the only one who could be relied on? At that age,' said the Widow, who was not much younger herself, 'her mind may not be all that it was.'

'Oh, I can't imagine Great-Aunt ever losing control of anything, let alone her own mind. She was bred at Goldhayes, but married a cousin at Catholm, and from all accounts entered into the true spirit of life on the Borders: cattle-stealing, raiding, feuds, she was involved in it all. And she's still a force to be reckoned with – *if* she hasn't changed. If I wrote and asked her to . . . to . . .'

'Put in a good word for you with Francis? That's not a task I should lay on anyone but yourself, lass.'

'Well, I could at the least ask her if he was there,' I said, trying to keep my feverish impatience in check. 'What chance, do you think, of a letter reaching Catholm safely?'

'Fairly high, if you send it by a carrier or some such, who has business in those parts, and if it isn't intercepted by either side. Not that you'd write anything of interest to a soldier, but you never know – wanton destruction seems to be the rule nowadays, and the wearing of a buff coat the excuse for any amount of it. And any letter to your great-aunt will have to remain a secret from your friends; in fact, I wouldn't entrust this news of Francis to any one of them, save possibly for Mistress Sewell – she at least has a head on her shoulders.'

'It will be difficult,' I said. 'And more difficult still keeping my loathing from Dominic, though I suppose that Drake could be used as an excuse for some coolness.'

'It could indeed. But bear that little scene in mind, lass.

It serves a useful lesson, to show you just how jealous and unreasonable your Dominic—'

'—He's not mine, no more is he mine—'

'—How he can be if crossed. Make it so that the first he knows that you've discovered his deception, is when you've upped and left him. Then you'll be too far away to be pursued, with luck, and with more he won't know where you've gone. And it's my bet that when he comes face to face with you again, and hears the truth from your own lips and sees how you've left your husband for him, then Francis will fall into your arms.'

'But it will be adultery,' I said in a small voice, remembering the wheelwright's wife at Adderbury, whom I had seen stoned for that very crime when I was eight.

'Until your unspeakable husband dies, you'll not get Francis without it. And besides,' said the Widow with her evil chuckle, 'since Francis is unquestionably destined for a hotter place than this, you'd be happier roasting along of him than sitting bored and lonely in the company of the saints.'

Which was, I supposed, one way of viewing the problem. And why quibble about adultery, when life apart from Francis, knowing him alive and free and yet being unable to reach him, was like being one half of a picture, or a book, or a song, never to be complete or whole or fulfilled until the two of us could be once more together? And I put aside my childhood, and the fierce teachings of my Puritan grandmother, and the fear of what Simon or Meraud or Jamie would think and say, and the uncertainty of Elizabeth Graham's being willing or able to help me, and then and there, in that dark room in the Blue Boar, I took my future in both hands and welcomed it gladly with a heart spilling over with hope.

'If we can have pen and ink and paper brought,' I said, meeting the Widow's compassionate wise eyes with a smile in my own, 'I will write that letter now.'

chapter ten

The valley of decision

Thus conscience does make cowards of us all;
And thus the native hue of resolution
Is sicklied o'er with the pale cast of thought.
(Shakespeare: *Hamlet*)

It did not take long to cover a sheet of the thick coarse paper that Mistress Mander brought, with a brief explanation of my affection for Francis, our thwarted plans, the circumstances of my marriage, Dominic's ruthless deception of us both, and my fears for Francis, who thought I had betrayed him. 'I desire only to know whether or not he is at Catholm, and how he does. I beg you, for the sake of the love and friendship between all of us, but most of all for Francis, to let me know if he be with you.' More I dared not say in case by some dire mischance Dominic or another friend should come to see it: and those few words seemed woefully inadequate to explain all the crowded, tangled relationships that had grown up amongst us since I had last seen my great aunt, and despite all my doubts I could do nothing else at all to assuage my anxieties and fears for my lost love, and so I signed my name firmly below with the spluttering, ragged quill: 'Your affectionate niece, Thomazine, Lady Drakelon.'

We presented the sealed packet, with its superscription, 'To Mistress Elizabeth Graham, at Catholm Tower, Liddesdale on the Borders near Carlisle', to Mistress Mander, who (so the Widow said) knew half of Oxford and their business, and she thought for a moment before saying, 'There's a man going to York, next week, an attorney who's a friend of my John's, to see about some estate. He'll take it and see it's put into the right hands to carry it on to Scotland; if it's an important letter it'll be safer with him than with some carrier or the Post.'

So the letter was entrusted to Mistress Mander, the first

step on the road that would bring me to Catholm and, at last, if the gods smiled, to Francis. And then there was nothing to do but wait.

At the best of times, I have ever been too impatient, too eager for action to bear sitting quiet and meek and womanlike for fate to befall me. It is, I suppose, a legacy of my wild and independent childhood, and my father's treatment of me, that I have always felt the unwomanly urge to be the shaper of my own life. But I had moulded it to the limit of my power now, and only time would show me whether the future was to be made whole, or broken in my hands.

Heaven knows there was enough in my life to distract me. There was the child to think about, the child that in a moment had changed from being the fulfilment of my existence to become the one obstacle to another and far more greatly desired fulfilment. For a little while I rebelled in my heart against this too easily conceived being who might well break my future for me. In some dark nights, lying open-eyed beside my slumbering, hated husband, I contemplated finding means to be rid of it. There were ways enough, but all my moral sense cried out against the slaughter, for my selfish convenience, of an innocent who after all was as much a part of me as of Dominic. I gave no clear thought to what I would do with the baby, once born; the idea of greeting Francis with the symbol of my betrayal mewling in my arms was not attractive. If it proved to be a boy, I resolved to leave it with Dominic; after all, wet-nurses would not be hard to find, and what fashionable young mother put her baby to her own breast? Certainly Mary Heron's contact with her children, nursed by a series of bountiful village women, had from all accounts been minimal. I hoped it would be a boy; the gift of the longed-for heir would do much, I felt, towards placating Dominic, if indeed he were still interested enough to pursue me. The brief uncertain flower of our affections had withered the day he had tried to kill Drake, and it was easy to allow him to think that that was the reason. He did not give up wooing me, and treated me with care; was I not the carrier of his child? But he meant nothing to me now, except as the man who had cheated me of all I held most dear.

I could never forgive him that.

There was also the war. Living as we did in Oxford, the King's headquarters, and not a hundred yards from His Majesty's lodgings, we had all the news fresh as it came in, and for spectacle the soldiers of the garrison, or those moving through the town on their way to some siege or raid or battle. Early in February some abortive attempts at peace negotiations had begun, and much ridicule had accompanied the arrival of the Parliament men in Oxford; believing the propaganda spread in London by their own side about the dire straits we were supposed to be in, they had come with plentiful stocks of food. No doubt their dinners at the 'Star' convinced them of the gravity of their mistake, even if they had not seen the abundance in the markets. But the negotiations came to nothing, despite the uneasy local truce which accompanied them. Meanwhile, the war went busily on. The Lifeguard, being bound to the King's person, was not involved in much fighting, although when a detachment from the regiment was sent with Prince Maurice to Gloucestershire, Dominic was one of those who volunteered to go. As before, Pennyfarthing Street was better and happier without him. Simon and Tom Sewell we hardly ever saw; as part of Rupert's Horse, our little band of Suffolkers were whisked hither and thither in that formidable and remarkable young man's shadow, this week to harry Bristol, the next at Aylesbury, then to Malmesbury and back again, only to be dragged out of their Abingdon quarters the next day to ride to Lichfield.

But Prince Rupert's vigour and dash was offset by the untimely loss of Reading, just as was the news of the death of Lord Brooke, one of Parliament's most able commanders in the Midlands and known to us from the days at Ashcott, lessened by the news that the Earl of Northampton was slain at Hopton two weeks later. There seemed never to be news brought of a victory that was not followed by word of some reverse elsewhere. The whole campaign was commented upon, scurrilously and with sharp wit, by *Mercurius Aulicus*, a weekly newspaper which had appeared in Oxford since January for the price of a penny, and was snapped up and read with delight as soon as it was issued. The embarrassing tendency of the rival Roundhead press in London to proclaim glorious victories and Cavalier generals slain without the slightest shred of corroboration was joyfully seized upon by the editor of *Mercurius Aulicus* and lampooned without mercy. Thus, the inhabitants of Oxford were supposed by one London newsheet to have been so terrified of the approach of Essex's army that they had totally deserted the place. 'The gentlemen and ladies bid me say,' commented *Mercurius*, laconically, 'that they have heard too much of His Excellency to be afraid of him.'

It was, I thought, greatly to Daniel Ashley's credit that he seemed to derive as much amusement from *Mercurius* as we did. He had endeared himself even to Jamie by his presence of mind in removing Jasper and Drake to safety that strange, terrible, joyful afternoon, and now during March became, especially in Dominic's absence, almost like a member of the family. He even joined in our music – for although only Grainne's Irish harp had survived the journey from Suffolk to Ashcott and thence to Oxford intact and unthieved, we had supplemented it by the purchase of a consort of viols, two lutes and two recorders from an impoverished Royalist family who needed the money. It was an extravagance for us; indeed, had Ashcott not been so close and comparatively unmolested, we would have been in like case, but from my tenants there and in Adderbury we now had a quarter's rents, almost complete, safely deposited with a goldsmith in the High Street, and that was enough to keep us in some comfort, though we lived simply enough. But music was our luxury and our delight, and when I took up the fragile trembling lute, or coaxed from the dark melancholy tenor viol the mournful, beautiful patterns of John Dowland, I no longer felt the emptiness at my heart as I played the music we had both loved; for although I lay in bed and sent my thoughts to seek his, and found no answer, I knew now that Francis lived, and music thus possessed another meaning than grief.

I had told Grainne of this, making sure that we were quite alone and not overheard. A stroll in Christchurch meadow one lovely spring morning, all birdsong and soft sunshine and promise, was sufficient for that. She took my hands and embraced me, not a usual act for Grainne, who was accustomed to show her affections in words rather than by gestures; and I was touched and delighted. 'Oh, I am glad for you – I am so glad,' she said, her eyes shining. 'And although there's still injustice, at least that greatest one has been set right – or, rather, proved to have been false. Will you go to him?'

'I can't,' I said, 'not till the baby comes. I'm not well enough, now, to embark on such a journey, and when all this stupid sickness and weakness goes – if it ever does – Mistress Gooch tells me it would be dangerous for me and the child to travel. No, I'm trapped here till the baby's born, but then, ah, *then* I shall go. If he is at Catholm.'

'Which he may not be, but it does seem probable; after all, he has friends there, does he not? But what will you do with the baby – take it with you? That might not be wise, in the circumstances.'

'If it is a girl, I may,' I said. 'But a boy would be better left with Dominic. You know how he longs for a son – it's the chief thing binds him to me. I tremble to think what he would do, to Francis, to me, or anyone else whom he suspected of complicity, were I to run off with his son and heir.'

'You speak of it lightly enough now,' said Grainne. 'You may well find, when you hold your new child in your arms, that it will not be possible to cast it so easily aside, however much you may hate its father – and God knows you have cause to hate him. And there are other things besides to be considered. If you leave Dominic, you leave also all your inheritance, your lands, your money. Everything you have is his, and you forfeit it all when you desert him. You may well feel Francis worth such a sacrifice, and I think I would feel the same, but you should remember that if things go

492

wrong you face destitution – and it may not be possible for any of us to rely on Goldhayes as our haven for much longer.'

I thought of that legacy from my ancestors, the manors in Yorkshire and in Norfolk, ships and yards and the house in Pennyfarthing Street and above all the beautiful Ashcott, and knew that she had made a very valid point. Should Dominic die in battle, a possibility I often found myself, guiltily, wishing for, not even in that event would my inheritance return to me – all, apart from Ashcott and Pennyfarthing Street which were my jointure for my maintenance in widowhood, would be the property of our child. Regret and anger at this injustice boiled within me. I said vehemently, 'Before God, I wish I had listened more closely to you, when you advised me not to plunge into marriage without thought. Had I done that, I'd not be in this coil – I could ride for Catholm tomorrow. Oh, God, I wish I hadn't married him!' I smacked my hand against a stout oak tree in my frustration, and then sucked my bleeding knuckles ruefully. 'And that, I suppose, proves how careless I am.'

'It's done, though, and cannot be untied, yet,' said Grainne. 'And I'm glad, and flattered too, that it was I you chose to tell.'

'Pure self-preservation – how long would it remain a secret if I told Lucy, or Jamie, or Meraud? I know with you that it will go no further. And besides, I know you grieved for him, and for me; and one less grief in these times is something of a blessing.'

'So many dead,' said Grainne, turning away from the tree, head down, and continuing along the path. 'In a little over six months of war, Ned and Henry both gone, and Hess, and those men at Ashcott. And all the others, killed or wounded or maimed or widowed or orphaned. Of all the evils on this earth, and there are many, the most evil is surely civil war. What could be worse than your own land divided and fought over, your own neighbours against you, your own kin, father, brother, son, cousin, facing you on the battlefield? At least that is one misfortune that has not befallen Sewells and Herons,' she added wryly. 'We are all alike, thank God, in our politics if in nothing else.'

'But think of Lucy. Have you seen her and Dan? He has fixed his affections on her as she has on him – and no wonder, for she's transfigured in his presence. I've never seen her like that before, though she's always been lively and vivacious enough. Now she . . . she glows. And he will be exchanged soon, and quite possibly the next time he meets a Heron or a Sewell, it'll be at the wrong end of a carbine. She should marry him now.'

'He wouldn't – he's too upright, too scrupulous, though in a better way than Simon; more tolerant of others' failings, more humane. And at least he has a sense of humour.'

'Which you need, to deal with Lucy. No, I suppose you're right – he would prefer to have her with Simon's consent, rather than split the family further asunder. And as matters stand at the moment, he won't have it; when Simon was here it was plain he could scarce bring himself even to speak to Dan, let alone be civil to him.'

'And yet, if Dan did anyone wrong at Ashcott, it was you and I. There is no accounting for human nature,' said Grainne thoughtfully, 'and never any accounting for anyone born with the name of Heron – save possibly for poor, dear Ned. You are all of you too stubborn, and wilful, and proud. An oak is broken by the storm, but the humble willow bends and survives.'

I hummed softly:

I leaned my back against an oak,
Thinking it a trusty tree,
But first it bended, then it broke,
And so my love proved false to me.

'And thus might Francis sing,' said Grainne. 'Will Lucy sing it also? Or Dan? One lovers' tragedy is enough in any family, and I should not find it in me to forgive Simon if he makes the same mistake with his sister as with you.'

I was glad, though also sorry for Lucy, when Simon was deprived of any opportunity to thwart another pair of sweethearts by the exchange of Captain Ashley, not ten days after my conversation with Grainne. After his departure, Lucy drooped like a flower without water, lay in her bed till mid-morning, and frequently burst into tears for scant reason. Even Meraud's patience wore thin, and the Widow was moved to say to Lucy brusquely, 'Now, lass, don't take on so. Thank God instead that he's living yet, and whole, and returns your feelings. Not many these days could say as much.'

As the beautiful spring, that should not have had to grace a country torn by war, slid softly into summer, my feverish impatience drained away into a calm placidness that was most unlike me. I grew bigger with the child, the sickness died away as I had been promised, and I felt the baby quicken within me; new life growing as the leaves burst forth on the trees. In my dreamlike state I was happy; too easy to pretend that all was well, that Dominic would suspect nothing, that the road lay clear ahead for me, leading to Catholm.

So June drew to a close, with one cracking thunderstorm to disperse the heat, and that bane of all good Royalists, John Hampden, was killed at Chalgrove Fight. A 'desperate man', *Mercurius* called him, and went on to describe a Cavalier raid on enemy forces to the east of Oxford around Wycombe, during which the Roundhead commander 'most valiantly hid himself'.

' "Whence you may learn",' read Jamie, grinning, ' "that the King's Army is sure to be besieged in Oxford for beating the Rebels most uncivilly out of Wycombe, and unkindly chasing them up and down Bucks." I do like *Mercurius*. Francis would have appreciated it, it's just his sort of wit.'

I tried to look suitably mournful, and not as though I had been memorizing that quotation to recount to Francis when we should meet. Lucy nudged Jamie disapprovingly and turned the conversation. 'Oh, do look at Hen! She's rolled herself into the beans.'

A loud scream from Grainne's daughter indicated that

she did not like the results of her activity. We were all in the garden, in the shade of the apple tree; Jamie reading from the news-sheet while I sewed baby-clothes, and Lucy and Meraud podded three pounds of beans from the heaps on their laps; and Grainne teaching Jasper, now nearly four and a half, his letters from a cheap hornbook purchased from a nearby bookshop. 'Go and roll her out again, Jasper, would you?' she said now to her son, and the little boy scampered down the path to the bean-patch and hauled Henrietta unceremoniously out by her petticoats.

'There's a letter for you all, from Suffolk by the look of it,' said the Widow, bustling down the path. 'Some ignorant yokel who didn't know our direction left it at the Blue Boar. Yes, Master Jasper,' as that young man came roaring up, his sister callously abandoned, to demand news of Drake, 'he's quite content, thank you, and happily occupied in consuming an ox's shinbone. Seal's not broke, and that's a marvel these days.'

'From mother!' said Lucy, seizing it. 'We've heard nothing from them for so long; the last came in March and that had been delayed while some Roundhead read his fill of it. Shall I read it?'

It was concerned entirely with affairs at Goldhayes, couched in ambiguous terms which would have meant little to anyone not intimately acquainted with our family. 'These late taxes and demands would have fallen hard upon us, but because of my son's foresight they can do nothing to harm us. Sir Thomas has used his influence to good purpose, and those who would wish us ill have been thwarted in their designs. They have taken four of poor Edward's best horses, and would also have had the grey colt bred from poor Francis's mare, but he being yet unbroken (there being no one left competent for the task, Master Sewell having lately been unwell), proved too difficult for them to handle, and when he had broke one rogue's arm they let him be. Master Sewell says now that he will not break him, but leave him accustomed to headcollar only, so that we may have one good horse left at the least, to get more. Sir Thomas has a lusty son by his new wife . . . Lady Pen. has gone beyond seas with Sir William and her children, so our life is quiet beyond our harassment by those on the Parliament's business.'

There was a lot of similar gossip, and perfunctory inquiries about our own welfare; plainly it mattered little to Mary whether or not we were at Goldhayes, provided her life was allowed to proceed on its usual tranquil, selfish course. The real news was contained in two lines at the bottom of the page, as if written as an afterthought: 'I must tell you that I am soon to be wed, to Master Trevelyan who has been of such great service to us all.' That was all; the next line held only, 'Your affectionate mother, Mary Heron.'

'Mother!' Lucy gasped. 'Married to . . . to . . .'

'My uncle,' Meraud said, in apparent astonishment. 'But why?'

'He must be all of five years younger,' I said, staring at her. It did not seem as much of a surprise to her as she wished us to think; there was a certain smugness about her mouth, like a self-satisfied cat. As to why, I could readily guess that. For Mary, not one to enjoy widowhood, the flattering attentions of a not ill-looking man several years her junior; while Richard Trevelyan, I was sure, planned to take advantage of the fact that there was no one but himself in a position to manage the estate, Sir Thomas Jermyn being of advancing years, despite his second summer and his young family, John Sewell in poor health, and Ambrose Blagge with no more than a polite and dutiful interest. And I wondered if he were looking ahead to some imagined future in which, the King's armies defeated and the male Herons dead or dispersed, his marriage to Mary and his previous connections would be the keys to possession of Goldhayes . . . I did not think that Mary was too old to have more children, and if all else failed, I could quite see Meraud tangling Jamie, or even, God forbid, Simon, in her sly selfish web.

It was an alarming vision which thus flashed into my mind, while the others, guardedly because they did not wish to offend Meraud, commented on the news. The general consensus was, despite their surprise, that they wished the couple well, although Grainne I could see was dubious. I did not like to speculate on what Simon would say, given the news. He had been remarkably friendly with Richard Trevelyan, but the thought that he would become his stepfather might well change things.

Simon, when he did find the time to visit us a few days later, seemed more relieved to learn that Goldhayes was safe from the sequestrations about which we had heard so many alarming rumours, and was filled with good-humoured self-satisfaction that his plan to vest his estates in trustees had worked so well, even if it had thus become much more difficult to receive any moneys from Goldhayes. For a long time now, he had existed largely upon his captain's pay and drawn as little as possible from his carefully hoarded store brought from Suffolk. Indeed, he even welcomed the news of Mary's marriage: 'I am very pleased that she has found a fitting husband; I had rather that than see her struggling alone at Goldhayes. And that reminds me; I dined last week with Tom Blagge at Wallingford – you know he's the governor there – and he told me that Nan is with the Queen in Yorkshire, and will come to Oxford with her. When she does arrive, I mean to make her my wife at last – she has waited for me long enough, and I for her.'

There was a flood of congratulations, in the midst of which I caught sight of Meraud's face, horrorstruck, her lips trembling, eyes spilling over with tears; then she turned and, unnoticed save by me, fled the room. I followed, more, I must admit, out of curiosity than compassion, and caught up with her in the garden. It was evening, cool and dim, the stars sparkling newly from the deep blue, incandescent sky. Meraud was crouched beneath the apple tree, her small fine hands cramped in the rough folds of its bark, her whole body shaking with sobs. Awkwardly, for it was now early July and the child was big within me, I knelt beside her. 'Meraud! What is it? What's wrong?'

No reply, only those agonized sobs that wrenched my own heart, despite my lack of real feeling for her. At last, however, she turned her head, fighting to control herself, and said bitterly, 'Isn't it obvious?'

It was, if my mind could accept it. I said gently, 'But you know Simon has always been betrothed to Nan. There is no surprise in this, save that nothing has been said for so long.'

'He may be betrothed to her, but that doesn't stop me loving him! It's him I love, I've loved him ever since he came to get me from Cornwall, I only came here to be nearer him!' Meraud wept, too overturned by emotion to be her usual secretive self. 'I thought if I could be near him I would have the chance, I couldn't bear not to be near him . . . and now he'll marry *her*!'

'But he is much older than you . . . you're but a child,' I said feebly, making the usual mistake of underestimating her maturity. Meraud's vivid white face blazed at me from the gloom. 'A child . . . Am I? Am I? I'm seventeen, I'm no more a child than you . . . and you loved Francis, didn't you, you loved him secretly for years; ever since I've known you you've loved him. So why am I so different? Why are you allowed a true love, and not I?'

There was no answer to that. Meraud went on, her voice shaking, as was her whole slight body, with the force of her emotions. 'I know he thinks well of me, I thought he would come to love me . . . and I'm beautiful! Admit it, I am, and *she* . . . she's plain and her teeth stick out, Lucy told me!'

But she is also quiet, and shy, and nice-natured, and altogether more suitable for Simon than a gilded, selfish butterfly child like you, I thought, and hastily put such uncharitable notions aside. I said, hesitantly, 'You mustn't let this go beyond me. You must put a brave face on it, never let him know how you care; that's the answer, unless you want him to see you as a humiliated little girl. It will pass, all things do, and one day you'll find someone else – heaven knows there should be no shortage; you draw all eyes in the street as it is. Even I,' I said, hating the sanctimonious tone of my voice, 'even I have come to accept my fate – and my love is dead.'

A snuffling snort from Meraud indicated that she thought a dead love preferable to one still living but in the arms of another. I suspected that more than anything else, her vanity and self-esteem had been struck a hopefully mortal blow. An idea then occurred to me with such enlightening force that I could not but speak it aloud. 'Is *that* why you took such pains to betray me and Francis to Simon? So that he would think well of you, as you put it?' And then, as her weeping began with fresh vigour, added quietly, with bitterness, 'So you see, in a way we are now avenged. Oh, I feel sorry for you, for no one knows better than I the pains of thwarted love – but I can't help but feel it's justice.'

'Go away!' Meraud hissed, her face hidden in the shadows of her hands. 'For God's sake go away, please, go!'

I stared at her rocking, convulsed figure for a moment, and then, already regretting what I had said, got with difficulty to my feet and walked heavily back to the house. Meraud, Lucy, myself, Grainne, all one way or another were suffering from the loss of the men we loved, and I prayed silently, from the affection I felt for both of them, that Simon and Nan Blagge would at last find the happiness together that had so far eluded the rest of us.

The Queen came in state to Oxford, on the fourteenth of July, and we stood in Fish Street with the cheering crowd, hemmed in on all sides and fronted by the soldiers of the garrison, to watch her pass. The carriage bearing her ladies came first, but though we strained our eyes between the rank of soldiers, we could not see Nan. The Servants' Troop came clattering past after, and then the heralds with their glorious coats and the Sergeant-at-Arms bearing the Mace, which sparkled in the warm July sun; then the Lord General, Lord Forth, notoriously deaf, and the Earl of Dorset, both gorgeously clad, on magnificent horses; and then the coach bearing the King and Queen and their sons, on one side riding the familiar figures of Prince Rupert and the Duke of Richmond. Last of all came the splendid gentlemen of His Majesty's Troop, on beautiful but restive horses that shied at the fluttering banners and waving kerchiefs in the crowd. Our ears rang with the cheering. Anyone seeing the people then would not have doubted their wholehearted loyalty, although I wondered whether it was Their Majesties or the show that was being so warmly applauded. Spirits were high, for the war was going very well in the North and in the west, while the presence of the Earl of Essex's plague-weakened army around Thame and Aylesbury did not exactly inspire terror; as *Mercurius* said, 'The Earl of Essex would have advanced towards Oxford, if much rain had not fallen and hindered him (and next time, the wind will blow).'

If Simon had hoped to see Nan to apprise her of his intentions, he hoped in vain, for the day after the Queen's arrival and her installation in lodgings at Merton, Rupert and all his army left Oxford: three brigades of foot, two of cavalry, nine troops of dragoons and an artillery train. They went to besiege Bristol, and we faced the very real possibility that Simon might be slain before he and Nan could ever be married.

It was not long before she came to see us, and I hardly recognized the shy plain girl of my memory in this gorgeously clad young woman, with her immaculate hair and the magnificent dress in the new style, featuring an elegantly lengthened waist which instantly made even Lucy's gown look dowdy. In astonishment, I saw that despite the slightly protruding teeth and mouse-brown hair and turned-up Blagge nose, she might easily be described as pretty. She came in on a waft of scent, attended by a supercilious maid who seemed to be assessing us and our humble surroundings with some scorn, and Lucy and I exchanged appalled glances. But the smile which greeted us was the old Nan, full of warmth, and we happily ordered wine and cakes from a goggling Heppy, for whom Nan had a smile and a greeting which made her goggle the more. Then we settled down to a good gossip, while the supercilious maid was hustled off to the kitchen and doubtless taken down a peg or two by the Widow. We heard from Nan of her experiences with the Queen in Holland, the dreadful voyage across the North Sea to Yorkshire, and the disgraceful behaviour of the Parliament ships in Bridlington Bay, which had fired on the house where they had gone on landing, so that they had all had to leave their beds and hide in a ditch. 'I confess I was shaking with fear,' said Nan, with a self-deprecating grin, 'but Her Majesty put us all to shame. We had forgotten to bring her lap-dog with us, and she actually went back and fetched it!' Then there was news of her half-brothers, Ambrose and Henry, now also fighting for the King, and of Tom in Wallingford – 'You can imagine how he delights in lording it over everybody,' said Nan. 'When a party from London came to negotiate with the King, they stayed at Wallingford Castle. The fools were rash enough to start talking politics with Tom over dinner, and according to John Snelling, they nearly came to blows.' I could well imagine the choleric Tom Blagge relishing an argument, and certainly he would not refuse a fight with anyone who contradicted his views.

The talk swung to our doings. Listening to the tale of the Herons over the past year or so, full of birth, marriage and above all death, Nan's face spoke astonishment and sorrow. 'Poor Ned, and Francis! And Henry Sewell and the little baby, too. Here have I been telling you my paltry woes, and you have had far more to grieve you.'

Lucy, who preferred not to think about such things, changed the subject. 'Have you heard from Simon?'

'Simon? No, should I have?'

'Ah,' said Lucy, with a coy wink. 'You would have heard from him, or even seen him, had the Prince not taken him off to Bristol.'

'Lucy,' I began, 'I really don't think . . .'

'Well, why shouldn't she know it?' Lucy demanded. 'Nan, he's spoken to Tom and it's all agreed. As soon as he's back from Bristol you'll be wed.'

Nan stared from me to Lucy, and then the poised, fashionable court lady bowed her shining pearl-graced head and burst into tears.

'Now look what you've done, can you never guard your tongue?' I hissed to Lucy, as we plied her with wine and kerchiefs and ascertained that it was relief and happiness that had caused this uncharacteristic lapse, and Lucy hissed back, 'It's just as well I did. Can you imagine Simon faced with this?'

I could see her point, and held my own tongue. Nan was speedily restored to her usual quiet, calm self, and with profuse apologies shortly left to resume her duties, accompanied by the now rather less supercilious maid.

We heard before the end of July that Bristol had been surrendered. The usual bonfires blazed dangerously in the streets, all the bells rang joyously, and the soldiers of the garrison got uproariously drunk and started not a few fights with some of those fiercer citizens not of their persuasion. On all sides, hopes were high for a speedy conclusion to the war; the Parliament's armies were defeated and demoralized, and Essex and Waller at loggerheads in London over the command, the latter's reputation having been shattered by his defeat at 'Runaway Down', and the former rather justifiably incensed at his rival's elevation to favour. Demands for peace in the capital grew deafening.

On the first day of August, Charles marched from Oxford, accompanied by his sons, and an army which included his Lifeguard of Foot. Before he left, Dominic urged me to have a care of myself, for the child's sake. 'Although it will not be born till well into September, I may not have returned by then. We go first to Bristol and thence, so rumour has it, to Gloucester, which is said to be ripe for the plucking. If that is so, we should not be long absent, but if it prove a harder nut to crack then it is quite possible that I shall not return until after you are delivered. You know, of course, that he must be named Roger. The eldest son is always given that name.'

'And if it prove a girl?' I asked. Dominic laughed. 'A girl? It will not be. If by some extraordinary chance it should fall thus, I leave it to you to find a name. Now I must leave. I shall pray for the child's safe delivery.' And he kissed my cold, unfeeling face and went away, without a backward glance.

It was undeniably infuriating to have dwindled into something on the same level as a brood-mare. Somehow, probably through my coldness towards him, his early passion for me had been transmuted into an obsessional concern for the child I bore. I was merely the clay vessel which contained such a precious burden, to be broken or heedlessly cast aside once my purpose had been fulfilled. I prayed, both for the child's sake and for my own desire to see Dominic thwarted, that my baby might be the despised girl.

A week after the army's departure, I sat in the garden, in a chair that Jamie had brought out for me and set beneath the apple tree. It had been a summer of variable weather, brief spells of sunshine interspersed with heavy rain, and the grass even in this morning's sun was too wet for me to sit upon it. I had been advised to stay within doors, for there were one or two cases of fever in the parish and the Widow was certain that there was infection in the air, but I could no longer bear to remain in the stuffy dim heat of the parlour, whatever the danger to the baby. So I sat and stitched at an embroidered coif for my child's head, enjoying the gentle breeze that cooled my face. Beside me lay Drake, panting softly, content to be in my company. Since there seemed little chance as yet of Dominic's return, we had taken him back from Mistress Mander and he now occupied his old place, ever at my side awake and asleep. Apart from the Widow and Heppy in the kitchen, there was no one else in the house; Grainne, Meraud, Lucy, Jamie and Jasper, with Betty, had gone for a stroll in Christchurch Meadow.

So engrossed was I in my stitching that I did not hear Heppy's excited approach until she was almost upon me, and Drake's inquiring head lifted to greet her. She stopped with a flurry of skirts and said, 'Oh, Mistress Thomazine, I mean my lady, there be a visitor for you, a-waiting in the front parlour.'

'A visitor?' I stared at her, running possibilities through my mind. 'Who is it, Heppy?'

My maid, aglow, said in tones of bewildered and delighted surprise, 'The Earl of Montrose, my lady!'

Montrose. I had heard of him, as a power in Scotland

whose services both the King and the Presbyterian party, led by Argyll, had at one time or another tried to procure. But what in God's name did a Scottish nobleman, from all accounts a man noble in every sense of the word, want with Thomazine, Lady Drakelon, who had never in her life been further north than Newmarket? And then I remembered that his surname was Graham, the same as my Catholm cousins, and rose so fast from my chair that Heppy grabbed my arm, counselling caution. 'I'm not ready to break yet,' I retorted, and picked up my skirts and ran, my maid bleating vainly behind.

He was in the same parlour that had seen Hess's body lying in her pathetic box of a coffin, and Charles Lawrence's disastrous birthday supper, and my subsequent interviews with Simon and Dominic. I paused for a moment in the little passageway outside to get my breath and smooth out the folds of my dress, and let Heppy announce me. 'Lady Drakelon, my lord.'

Awkwardly, I curtseyed to him, wondering how he would see me: a little woman, heavily pregnant, with untidy hair and an outmoded, high-waisted dress which nevertheless failed to conceal her swollen body. He took my hand and smiled: not a tall man, but neatly and strongly made, with brown hair and level, clear grey eyes and an imperious nose. There was something about him that I liked at once, a sense of honesty and resolution. 'A good morning to you, Lady Drakelon. I trust I find you well?'

'Very well, I thank you, my lord,' I said, hoping I did not appear too clumsy or rustic beside his quietly elegant tailoring. His voice too was attractive, low and calm with an intonation I took to be Scots. 'Would you care for some refreshment?' I asked. 'Wine, perhaps?'

Heppy was dispatched, and shortly returned with a bottle of claret and a plate of little sweet cakes, all dusted with precious sugar. I poured the wine with a hand scarcely kept from trembling, and we sat in twin chairs, one each side of the empty hearth.

'You must wonder why I am here,' said Montrose, accepting a cake (an act of great courage had he but known it, for they were of Lucy's baking), 'since we are strangers, and of two different nations who may yet be at war. The truth is, I have sought you out, Lady Drakelon, at the behest of a somewhat formidable lady who is, by marriage, distant kin to me, and whose grandson I am pleased to count my friend. This Mistress Graham, who is defied at the peril of one's life, instructed me to find you in Oxford and to deliver to you this letter which I have here, concealed in my doublet. Do I take it, Lady Drakelon, that you know this Mistress Graham?'

'Very well,' I said, hope lifting and sparkling in my heart and voice. 'If, that is, she is Mistress Elizabeth Graham of Catholm, in Liddesdale, then she is my great-aunt, my grandfather's half-sister.'

'That is the lady of whom I speak, and since you know her, you will be acquainted with her powers of persuasion. I am adjured,' said the Earl of Montrose, smiling, 'on pain of punishments too appalling to name, to give this letter into your hands and your hands only, preferably in the absence of any onlooker.'

The letter lay in my hands, addressed by the spidery hand that had struck terror at Goldstone, and years before dealt death to Border reivers; and in it lay my future, and all my hopes. I raised my eyes to meet the Earl's grey ones, and said, 'Thank you, my lord. I have waited a long time for this letter. It – it is very kind of you to have brought it to me yourself, you do me too much honour.'

'Not at all,' he said, finishing the cup of wine, 'it has been my great pleasure to meet you, Lady Drakelon, and besides, I could not have faced Mistress Graham without some report of you, so it is she you must thank. And should you ever come to Scotland to do it, then I hope we shall meet again.'

'I trust and hope we shall, my lord,' I said, trying to still my body's trembling as he bowed low over my hand.

'And now I regret I must take my leave, for I have an audience with the Queen which cannot wait, and so I will say goodbye, my lady, and leave you to read your letter.' He gave me a last smile which gave me a sudden feeling of having known him for years, instead of for ten minutes. 'I do not think that you will find it ill news, and if there should happen to be an answer, I will most willingly take it back. I shall doubtless be in Oxford some time. Goodbye, Lady Drakelon, and my thanks for your excellent wine and cakes.'

Heppy showed him out, quite overcome with the appearance of such an exalted personage, and when he was gone, came rushing back into the parlour, her mouth ready open to pour out questions. I forestalled her. 'I'm going back into the garden, Heppy, and I'd rather I wasn't disturbed for half-an-hour or so. I would like some peace.'

Grainne's maid Betty would have pouted and sulked; Heppy, with a cheerful shrug, picked up the wine bottle and cups and cakes and preceded me down the passage to the kitchen. I swept through and into the garden without a word to the Widow, although I gave her a hopefully revealing wink and grin, and hastened back to my chair under the tree. Patting Drake absently on the head, I withdrew the precious letter from my sleeve and broke the seal. 'My dear Thomazine,' it began.

He is indeed here, and safe in body if not in mind. Your story has explained much to me, for since his arrival here in February he has said nothing of his recent past, not even to Malise who was and is still his closest friend. I am sickened by your tale, and grieve most sorely both for you and for Francis. I confess that I was never easy in my mind about Dominic's character, nor absolutely content with that betrothal. I must say that I distrusted anything ever arranged by that overweeningly stupid mother of his (for it was she who promoted the match, once he had fixed his fancy upon you, for the sake of your inheritance, although she was doubtful of your fitness to be his wife). That woman was the ruination of the boy from the beginning.

That is as maybe, and past now. I have said nothing to Francis of what has happened, for he is bitter, and angry in his heart, and cares little for himself; his time is spent in furious activity, riding the dale with Malise, and drinking and wenching with Gib, going over the Border into England most often, since there is a shortage here of brothels and ale-houses, the Kirk being most concerned to stamp them out. I know that this news may tempt you to come to Catholm forthwith in order to prove that you were not after all knowingly false to him, but I beg of you, remember that you are a married woman, whatever your husband may have done to you, and that although I myself would not think less of you for so doing, there are very many, particularly here in Scotland, who look upon a breaking of the marriage vow as a most heinous crime, worthy of terrible punishment for those caught in the act, and you might be in some danger for openly committing the sin of adultery. Moreover, there is also the question of your inheritance – can you so lightly cast all your wealth aside? You can count on no other support but your husband's, and you may be reduced to penury should you desert him. However, the final decision must be yours; I merely give you the advice of my superior years, though that does not necessarily imply superior wisdom, and ask you to think on these matters most carefully before you decide what to do.

I have given this to a man to be trusted beyond the common run, a distant kinsman of my dear dead husband. Malise has spent much time in his household this last year or so, and has become in some sort his secretary, besides making music for him. He will bring me any reply you may care to make, should you find it impossible in the end to leave Oxford. If you do not, then I wish you a safe and pleasant journey, and remain your most affectionate aunt, Elizabeth Graham.

Below, where there was a space left at the bottom of the sheet, she had added,

I found these by chance, discarded, in his writing, and have copied them here for you. You may doubt, as I now do, whether Francis will welcome you, since his feelings towards you seem to have undergone a drastic change, but it rests with you whether or not you take heed of this warning. I merely point out that you risk losing everything you have, for the sake of a reunion that may be not at all as you would wish. E. G.

Underneath the postscript, she had written out a poem, and with my heart filled with a terrible sense of foreboding, I began to read.

As strong and steadfast as the ev'ning star
Thou seem'dst to be,
And though this war had sunder'd us so far,
I trusted thee.
But thy love prov'd as true
And constant as the tide,
And he that came to woo
Was not denied.

The honest, speaking eyes I thought so fine
Were but a ploy,
Thy virgin's body, innocently mine
He doth enjoy.
Thy faithfulness all lies,
Thy truth consum'd by lust,
My heart, defeated, dies,
Return'd to dust.

Thou had'st thy reasons, doubtless, to betray
A love so rare,
But should we chance to meet, some bitter day,
My heart, beware:
Remember what befell,
Repent not of thy choice,
For in this last farewell
I find my voice.

I stared at it, heedless of the flood of tears which poured over my face and made the spidery, unbearable words blur and dance in my sight. Their ambiguous bitterness pierced me to the bone; for the first time I saw truly what Dominic and I had done between us, and at the last, unable to face it,

I bowed my head upon Drake's warm black and white one, and wept.

Heppy found me, a long while later, still sitting there desolately with my arms around the dog. At her approach, I slipped the letter into my bodice and prayed that the long bout of weeping would not show in my face. As ever, I hoped in vain. Heppy stared at me in concern. 'Why, mis – my lady! What is it? Did he bring bad news, that Earl?'

'No, no,' I said hastily, 'no, it was just a visit to bring greetings from an – an old friend.'

'Oh,' said Heppy, obviously unconvinced. 'Now, why don't you come inside, my lady? Thass suffen too hot for you abroad now, and aside from that, there's infection about.'

In truth, I was beginning to feel uncomfortably warm, and consented. I placed one hand on the tree to pull myself up, and as I did so a great pain assaulted my body, so that I perforce sat down again, gasping. Heppy, suddenly alarmed, cried, 'What is it?'

'I don't know,' I said, and clenched my hands and face as another wave gripped me. 'Heppy, please, get Mistress Gooch.'

Within half a minute the Widow was beside me. 'What is it, lass? Pains? Dear Christ, don't say it's the babe come early.'

But it was, beyond a doubt. Between them they helped me inside and up the stairs to my chamber. Heppy was dispatched forthwith to the midwife who had attended Henrietta's birth, and as soon as she was gone I gave the Widow the letter. 'It's from my aunt, about Francis. Can you keep it safe for me?' Another pain sent my hands gripping the mattress. The Widow took the letter and pushed it crackling within the scrawny confines of her own bodice, and then finished unlacing mine. 'Now don't you fret, lass. For all your smallness, you've good broad hips, you're strong, and we'll keep you safe for him, never fear.'

'But the baby,' I said, staring up at her as she removed the hampering petticoats. 'What of the baby?'

'It's only a little over a month too soon,' said Mistress Gooch. 'My mother's fifth, God rest her soul, was two months early and a fine lusty boy, though the smallpox carried him off before he was eight. Now don't you worry, lass, you'll both be safe.'

It was a quick birth and, so the Widow said afterwards, a remarkably easy one. I remember only the pains, and trying not to cry out and biting through my lip with the effort; and somewhere in the middle of it all, Grainne, holding my hands and whispering encouragement. Before dark, the last and greatest agony convulsed me, and suddenly, with a rush, my child was born. In the fading light I leaned back, gasping, and saw the midwife sever the cord and slap the child heartily. A loud and angry scream was her reward. Above the sounds of my child's rage I said weakly, 'What is it? Boy or girl?'

'Boy,' said Mistress Gooch, with a meaningful look at me. 'A fine boy for you and Sir Dominic.'

They put the child in my arms, when I was ready. A small bundle he made, after Grainne's children, and to my eyes oddly shaped, his head a little too large and his body scrawny and covered with fine dark hair, of which there was also an abundance on his head. The midwife had performed all the customary rituals to bring good luck; she had wrapped him in a piece of old cloth, so that his first garment would not be new, and before he would be allowed to suckle, a cinder was dropped into a cup of water for his first drink. Mistress Gooch had also taken him in her arms and mounted briefly upon a stool, so that his first journey in the world might be upwards. In view of my plans for abandoning him at the earliest opportunity, I thought sadly, he would need all the good fortune he could get. His eyes opened briefly, newly and cloudily blue; too early to tell yet their true colour. And so small and perfect a scrap, with every detail of face and hands and feet and body the exact print of humanity, had been made by myself and Dominic, perhaps on that first terrible night of our marriage. Humble, wonderingly, I traced his features with my hand, that small as it was seemed so vast beside the baby's. His mouth made feeble, sucking sounds, his hands pawed like a kitten's, and with a smile, almost with reverence, I put him to my breast.

When the room had been cleaned and tidied, and the midwife out of it for a space, the Widow came to sit beside me. My son, replete, lay sleeping in the crook of my arm. She looked down at him, and said, 'No beauty, is he? Early babies seldom are – too red and scrawny, and enough hair for a beast, not man. But in a week or two you'd never tell he was born a month too soon.' She looked at me significantly, and weary and weak as I was, I took her meaning at once. 'You mean . . . when Dominic returns he might think . . .'

'That he was conceived before you married. It's quite possible, though of course he's only to ask me, or the midwife, or any of your fine friends who will doubtless be soon up here cooing over the lad, to know the truth. And of course, should he keep all that hair, and his eyes stay blue, he'll bear more than a passing resemblance to his father.' She looked at me. 'Still think you can do it, lass? Leave the babe here and go off to your Francis? Or are you too much the mother?'

'I don't know,' I said, feeling again the hopelessness that had overwhelmed me when I read that poem. 'Oh, God, I don't know . . . I want more than *anything* to go to him, and yet so much pulls the other way . . . the baby, and the lands, and the thought of committing adultery, and above all the fact that, according to my great-aunt, he may not want me even if I do go . . . and if I go, what happens to you all here? It's Dominic's house now and if I leave him he's quite capable of turning you all out from spite. He's threatened to do so once already.'

'He'll have a job to turn me out,' said Mistress Gooch stoutly, 'and besides, as soon as your cousin Simon returns I intend to make sure he knows the full sorry tale – which should properly cook Dominic's goose for him. Whatever Simon's faults, he at least knows where his responsibilities lie. But don't fret for us, lass. Think for yourself. *You* have to decide, *you* have to make the choice, and it won't be easy – and whatever you decide to do, you'll have to live with the consequences. So don't make your mind up in a rush. I'll tell you one thing, though – if you put the baby out to nurse, it'll make leaving him a good deal easier; you won't grieve for him overmuch, knowing he won't miss you, for one so young won't know the wet-nurse ain't his own mother. And if you decide not to go, then no harm's done. You can always say you were ill, that your milk dried up, and no one'll think aught of it – you'd be unusual if you did put him to your own breast. Such as Grainne are the exception, not the rule.' She looked at me and gave my hand a friendly squeeze. 'Well, lass? What are you going to do?'

I was so completely torn between the urgings of heart and head that I could make no immediate answer. My yearning for Francis was counterbalanced by my fear of what might happen to me, to my child, to my friends if I did succumb to temptation, and above all my terror that the longed-for reunion would turn to ashes and dust in my mouth, that I would gamble all the trappings of my life: husband, friends, child, wealth, on a love that might well no longer exist. But in any dilemma, choosing between the baby and Francis, my lover must ever come first, especially when my choice might mean the difference to him between life, knowing I had not after all betrayed him, and an early, longed-for death in ignorance of the truth. And the Widow was right; put the child out to nurse, as had been done to all my cousins, and to me when born, and he would with luck grow strong and whole without ever having known his mother, should I decide to go, or suffering any parting from her at such a tender age. And I would be safe from Dominic's pursuit.

But it was hard, looking down at my son, to reject him so deliberately, to cast such a helpless creature to the winds of fortune whilst I merrily set off for a life of adultery with my lover. It would forever damn me with Simon, and quite possibly with many of my other friends.

But I could not bear to desert Francis, not now. That poem had shaken me to the core, showing me the depths of bitterness and grief to which I had brought him. In the final account, casting the weights to one side or the other, Francis would ever hold far more in his balance than any other friend, or child.

The midwife was returning, I could hear her heavy tread on the stairs. I said quickly, 'Ask her to find a nurse for him.'

The Widow gripped my hand briefly, and rose from the bed. She said, cheerfully, 'And what will you name him? Dominic, for his father?'

'Dominic told me to name him Roger,' I said. 'But I won't. I think I shall have him baptized Christopher.'

'Well, he can't find much to object to in that,' said the Widow, 'apart of course from the fact he told you quite another name.'

'It's the name of the founder of the Heron family,' I said, 'and there have been many Christophers since. Christopher he shall be, and Kit for short.'

It was ensured the next day, the eighth of August, when my son was baptized in St Aldate's Church, and Jamie and the Widow stood godparents with Lucy and Grainne; not the customary arrangement, but any other possible masculine sponsors were absent at war, and it was felt advisable to baptize Christopher with all speed. He seemed strong enough, but was very small, between five and six pounds. The midwife had found a wet-nurse for us; a stout, good-hearted young woman in Butchers' Row not a hundred yards away, whose own first baby had recently died. She readily consented to join our household for the first few weeks of Christopher's life, and then when I was able to go abroad again, to take him back to her husband's shop. Christopher seemed quite content to be nourished by the buxom Eliza; for one with such tempestuous parents, he was a very good baby, spending most of his time fast asleep in his cradle, and only rarely did his cries shake the peaceful house. I made myself ignore him as much as possible, leaving everything to Eliza, who poured all her disappointed affection for her own dead daughter into her foster son. If I should be thought a cruel and unnatural mother, to thus tear myself from my own son, let me say that it was not without much agony and soul-searching on my own part, and in mitigation, that it was not for my own selfish whim, but for Francis's sake.

So the way now lay open for Catholm, should I decide to

take it, and still my bereft heart warred with my more practical, sensible head. I knew that it would be foolish to leave before my churching, a month after Christopher's birth; not only would I occasion much comment by so doing, but I would be unlikely to have recovered my full strength. And a pass would have to be obtained, and my route planned to take in the safest countryside. In my weakened condition, I shrank from the organization involved, from the dangers and efforts attendant on such a journey, and yet all the time my longing for Francis was like a permanent sickness, an ache in my heart that could not be stilled, would never be stilled until I was once more in his arms and at his side.

The dilemma in my mind was such that I could not long contain it within me, and when Grainne came one evening to sit with me, I once more made her my confidante, attempting thereby to justify to myself and her the impulses within my heart. We were alone; Eliza had gone down to the kitchen for a gossip with the Widow, and Kit lay quiescent in his cradle. We talked about babies for a while, comparing our offspring as mothers will, and then Grainne said, 'So you have decided to go to Catholm? Oh, yes, as soon as the wet-nurse was engaged I knew what must be in your mind. He is a lovely baby, do you not find the thought of parting hard?'

'I do,' I said, staring at my clasped hands, disfigured by Dominic's heavy gold ring, lying on the counterpane. 'Oh, Grainne, believe me, I do. But Francis has a greater need of me. It will make no difference to Kit now, if I go. He has Eliza, and he will have Dominic's devotion, and he will want for nothing. Francis is at Catholm, and if I do not reach him soon it will be too late; he will never believe I did not intentionally betray him. The day Kit was born I had a letter, brought by no less a person than the Earl of Montrose, from my great-aunt. She isn't given to exaggeration, and she told me that he was there, at Catholm, and that she feared for his safety.' I swallowed, having told no one else of this, not even the Widow, who had returned the letter to me as soon as was practicable, and had assured me that she had not read it, a statement I believed without reservation. 'She said he was drinking too much, and whoring with her grandson Gib, who from Francis's own description of him never sounded a very noble character, and she implied that he had no care for his life or safety. She said he was bitter and angry, and she sent me a poem which she had found and assumed he had written and then thrown away. It left his feelings in no doubt. Grainne, I can't leave him to go to an early death believing that I'm a light woman who betrayed his love and trust and married a worthless rival for the sake of his lands and title. Whatever the cost, I have to convince him that it isn't true, and the only way to do it is to leave Dominic and Kit and go to Catholm to be with him. And if necessary, go alone.'

'No,' said Grainne. Startled and upset, I looked up, and met her green, smiling eyes. 'Not alone,' said my dear friend. 'If you truly must go to Catholm, then I will come with you.' She paused for a moment, then reached her hand out to grip mine. 'But please, Thomazine, please, I beg of you, do nothing that you will later come to regret. Have you really thought it over completely? Have you realized what it will mean to go to Catholm: leaving your husband, even if you do loathe the sight of him, and your baby, and your friends, and all the things to make your life comfortable? You are going into the unknown, you may be throwing away everything for no return – you said yourself that his feelings had changed. Have you truly considered *everything*?'

'I have thought of nothing else,' I said wryly. 'And I have never in my life had a harder decision to make . . . and despite what I said to you just now, I still haven't made it. Even now, there is a little voice in my head that says, 'Fool, to throw it all away for love – and a love that may be as insubstantial as a dream.' And Kit is the biggest reason of all, not to go. I don't know if, when the moment comes, I shall be able to desert him.'

'And of course, you won't have forever to make up your mind – sooner or later Dominic will return, and whatever his feelings may be, I doubt very much if his pride will allow him to stand tamely by and watch his wife gallivanting off to another man. I'm not going to make up your mind for you, only you can do that – but I repeat my promise. If you do decide to go to Francis, I will come with you.'

'You can't,' I whispered. 'Not with the children, you wouldn't go without them, *you* wouldn't desert them, and Hen is too young . . .'

'I can,' said Grainne, 'and I will, if you desire it; the children will come too, they're strong and healthy, and with God's help the journey won't harm them. And as a widow, I'm my own mistress and can do what I like: even to the extent of suddenly packing my bags and moving to new pastures.' She smiled at me. 'Well? Have I made things any easier for you?'

In a sense she had, in that I would no longer have the dread thought of making the perilous journey alone; but it did not make the enormity of that striding into the unknown any the less. There were so many branches and turnings on the road of my future, and only one led to happiness. All the other chances were shadowed and marred by grief or betrayal or lonely tragedy. Mute, I shook my head. My friend said thoughtfully, 'It would be easy enough for me to obtain passes for us, for if it's the organizing of it worries you, I will gladly undertake to do that. As long as all this is kept secret, it commits you to nothing; but should you decide to go, all will be ready. Who else have you told, apart from me?'

'Only the Widow. She said much the same as you.' I laughed ruefully. 'What I really want at this moment is someone to make up my mind for me – me, Thomazine the strong-minded shrew, dithering like an old hen over a problem that Lucy wouldn't give a second's thought to – you know what *she'd* say. It's what my soul says, too, but there are so many problems and difficulties. We'll need the passes, and an extra horse, and baggage, and then there's the question of what to tell the others, and what will happen to them if I go, and whether or not Dominic will pursue me or try to stop me, and at the end of it all, will Francis even want me?'

'There is no other way to find out,' said Grainne. 'But I think Dominic might well be content now with his son – and pray God the child thrives, for if he does not, you will once more find yourself in demand as a brood-mare. The main thing, if you do decide to go, is to make sure that he and Simon are away with the army when we leave, for then they've no chance to stop us, and we'll be fairly safe from pursuit.'

'Well, at present they're sat before Gloucester,' I said. News of the start of the siege had reached Oxford the previous day. 'And how long they'll be there God alone knows; it could be a day, or a month. And I wouldn't be free to leave until the beginning of September. I haven't even left my bed yet, and Kit is five days old.'

'I think you must not expect to rise for another week at the least, and in the meantime, if you want, I'll make all the necessary arrangements. We'll need another horse if a groom is to go with us, and one for baggage too.'

'And where do we find a reliable groom?' I inquired.

That question was answered a few days later, when I heard a feeble knocking at the front door. I sat up abruptly in bed and then, disobeying orders, swung my legs cautiously out of bed and went over to the window. Of the visitor on the doorstep I could tell nothing, save that his arm was encased in a rough sling, and that his clothes were in tatters – and had once been blue. Then I heard below me the front door opening, Heppy's exclamation, and the figure abruptly vanished. Confused, joyful noises could be heard below. Intensely curious, I padded barefoot back to bed, cursing the convention that kept me there – apart from some weakness I felt perfectly well, and did not peasant women work again in the fields not a week after childbirth? – and waited to hear, as I doubtless would, who the visitor was.

Sure enough, I soon heard impetuous feet galloping up the stairs – Lucy, beyond a doubt – and my door was flung open. 'Guess who's arrived!' she demanded, breathlessly.

I did not like being put at a disadvantage. 'I can't think. Prince Rupert?'

'No, no, no!' Lucy cried, exasperated. 'Is that likely? No, it's Holly, Holly Greenwood!'

'But he should be with the Prince at Gloucester,' I said. 'Has there been a battle?'

'No – well, yes, the storming of Bristol, but we knew about that,' Lucy said. 'He's been discharged from the army. He was wounded in the storming, a bullet in his arm or something like that, and now he can't use a sword – which makes him useless as a soldier. So as soon as he was well, he came back here to see Heppy before going home to Suffolk.'

'Tell him I'm very sorry to hear about his wound,' I said, and added with a grin, 'you can remind him that it could have been much worse!'

As her steps clattered down the stairs again, I laid myself back on the pillows and gave my mind over to plans. It could be that in Holly we had found the stout male escort we were seeking. He had many advantages; he was big, muscular, sensible and reliable, he had had a soldier's training and could handle weapons, though obviously this wound had made some difference to that. And he had never forgotten that Francis had probably saved his life at Edgehill, and incurred disapproval for it. He would surely be willing to postpone a return to Suffolk, and go with us to Catholm, for Francis's sake.

But before I could speak to him, Dominic returned. He arrived with the King, Prince Rupert and a great company of other officers and lords on the 16th of August, having received special permission to leave his duties at the siege to reassure himself of my welfare. Either the reduction of Gloucester was proving so protracted and uneventful that his absence for a day or so would not be of consequence, or he had painted a very highly coloured picture of my health in pregnancy. But whatever he had expected on his entry into my chamber, it was not the loud wailing which erupted at the crash of the door. He stopped dead on the threshold and stared transfixed at the cradle which Eliza Parke was soothingly rocking. I said as calmly as I could, from my stultifyingly boring bed, 'You may go downstairs, Eliza,' and with a startled curtsey to me and to Dominic she left, shutting the door a good deal more quietly than was my husband's habit.

'I thought . . . I'd thought you were ill when your maid said you were abed,' Dominic said, staring dazedly at the cradle. 'Is . . . is that . . .?'

'Yes,' I told him. 'It's your son. Bring him here, perhaps I can stop that dreadful noise.'

Dominic went over to the cradle by the fire and gazed down at its occupant. In the ten days since his birth, he had, as the Widow had predicted, shed most of the signs of prematurity; his skin was no longer red and wrinkled but pale and well filled out with new-laid fat, and all the hair, including that on his head, had fallen out, leaving him as bald as a seal. Apart from his small size, and even that was no longer so obvious, he was just like any new-born baby who had spent the full nine months in the womb.

'When was he born?'

I detected the first signs of suspicion in his voice, and was perhaps too quick to provide an explanation. 'On the seventh of August. He's over a month early, by our calculations, and he was very small when he was born, and we were anxious about him; but look how fine and lusty he is now . . .'

My voice died foolishly away. Dominic had picked the infant up, rather gingerly. I said, 'You must support his head with your hand, he can't hold it himself yet.'

'He isn't small now,' said Dominic, not making any effort to hold my son properly. The baby screwed up his face and wailed louder, and with a sudden exclamation of impatience he crossed the room and dumped the unhappy child in my arms. It was what I had tried to avoid for days, such close contact with my baby, but I rocked him and spoke to him, and at last he slept again.

'Then he was only eight months in the womb, you say,' Dominic said abruptly, staring down at the small pink face, button nose and three folded creases to mark the position of eyes and mouth. 'He does not look like an early child, he's too big and fat.' His eyes shot suddenly to mine. 'Well? Is he truly my son, or another's? You should know, madam, or perhaps you do not.'

'Of course he's yours!' I said, keeping my voice under control for the baby's sake. 'Whose could he be but yours? I came virgin to your bed, as you well know. Moreover, if you'd been here when he was born, you'd have seen more than a passing resemblance to yourself, for he had black hair, before it all fell out, and I think his eyes will stay blue. Do you then think,' I added, indignant that my reputation should be held so light by my husband – though had he been able to read my thoughts, he would have found his suspicions about my faithlessness, if not Kit's parentage, amply confirmed – 'do you think, then, that you have been cuckolded, sir? And if so, by whom?'

Dominic gazed down at the child, the so dearly longed-for son, and said angrily, 'How should I know? That debauched rogue of a cousin of yours, most like.'

'Which cousin?' I cried, infuriated by his attitude beyond the bounds of sense. 'Which one? Simon, who's so pure and virtuous I doubt he's ever lain with a woman? Or Ned, who's been ten months in his grave? Or Jamie, who's still a child? Or,' I added, with a shaking voice full of bitterness and hate, 'Francis, whom you told me was dead?'

There was utter silence. Kit stirred and snuffled softly in my arms. The high colour slowly drained from Dominic's face, leaving only his eyes, blue and vivid and guilty, fixed on mine. 'I do not know what you are talking about.'

'You know too well. You let me think Francis was dead, when he was not, and trapped me into marriage by trickery and deceit – and not content with that, you foul-minded bastard,' I said, my voice sinking to a hissing whisper, 'you went to Francis as he lay sick and helpless and told him how I had betrayed him and agreed to marry you and you stood over him and gloated . . . Oh, God, to think that I once thought that I could love you. You! I'd sooner love a poisonous snake! Well, you've got your son now; yes, he is your son, your Christopher – I didn't name him Roger because I

couldn't bear to gratify any wish of yours, so I called him after
old Kit Heron instead. You've got your son, you've got what
you wanted – that *is* all you wanted, isn't it? You wanted me,
you wanted me and my possessions so badly you had to
wreck two lives for me and didn't care how either of us
suffered; all you wanted was your own way, and when even
after I'd married you you couldn't command my love, your
only need for me was as a brood-mare for your own stallion
lusts, to beget another Drakelon to trouble our family . . .
Well, you've got him now, and he's Kit, not Roger. Perhaps
that'll remind you that there was one thing you couldn't
possess by fair means or foul, and that was me, for I'm no
man's chattel to be governed so lightly. So look to your son,
sir, for I leave him to you as a parting gift, and you'll get no
more of me.' I laughed wildly, hearing the echo of some lost
quotation or memory. 'And perhaps there's enough of me
in him to ensure that he will not be your pawn either.'

'Leaving . . . what do you mean?' Dominic's voice was also
sunk to a whisper, as if we had a tacit agreement not to
disturb the slumbering child whose precipitate arrival into
the world had brought this matter to its last conclusion.

'Precisely what I said. I want no more of you, Dominic
Drakelon. The thought of you sickens me. I want you no
more in my bed, reminding me ever that you lied and
cheated to marry me. I am going, and do not think yourself
bereft, for you'll have Kit (and the wet-nurse has half-con-
vinced herself already that he's her own), and all my lands.
You'll have everything except me, and before God, Dominic, though you may for a time have owned my body, you
have never had my soul, nor my heart neither, and now you
will have nothing of me at all!'

'And let me tell you, you whoring bitch, that I want none
of you!' Dominic shouted, and with those last words, left
abruptly. The door slammed, with a crash that left Kit
screaming, and his footsteps pounded down the stairs and
crashed into the street. And then he was gone, to return to
Gloucester with the Prince that evening, and I prayed that I
would never see him again.

I drew several long, shaking breaths, utterly spent after

my tirade . . . and I had not said the half of what it had ever been in my mind to say to him, when the time came for the truth to be bared at last. Now it had come, I was glad of it. No more pretences now. I would leave him, and with never a backward glance, save for Kit.

Save for Kit . . .

Of course, after that final quarrel when I had vented all my long-withheld hatred and spite, there was no chance that the rest of the household would not know. Soon, they came silent and wide-eyed up to my chamber, and Eliza took Kit down to the kitchen on my orders, so that he would not disturb us, and the Widow told Meraud and Lucy and Jamie, and the Greenwoods, what she had told me that afternoon at the Blue Boar. When the last damning sentence was concluded, there was a long silence, and then Lucy, her face shiny with tears, got up and hugged me. 'Oh, Thomazine, I am so glad, so, so glad! That's the best news I have ever heard!'

'I'd like to kill Dominic,' said Jamie, between his teeth. 'I'd like to tell him just what I think of him, and then I'd like to torture him, slowly, just like he did to Francis, and only then would I kill him.'

'But he didn't torture Francis!' Meraud protested.

'Torturing the mind,' said Grainne softly, 'is as bad as torture of the body, and sometimes inflicts a different but greater pain.'

'But what are you going to do now?' Lucy demanded, disregarding these finer points of philosophy. 'You can't stay with Dominic, not now!'

'You must; for better or worse you're his wife,' Meraud countered. I said, 'In my heart I have never been that. Oh, I know it's wrong, I know I have vowed to live with him till death do us part, and all the rest of it – but if I'd known the truth I would never have wed him at all, as he well knew. No, I know where Francis is, he's gone to Catholm, and as soon as ever I can I want to go to him. To live in adultery, if you like, and to burn in Hell's everlasting flames if that is what you believe, but I cannot bear the thought that he is alive and thinks I was false to him.'

'And I am going with her,' said Grainne.

'Well said, Mistress Sewell,' the Widow remarked. The five other pairs of eyes stared at me, as astonished as if I had sprouted wings, or more appropriately horns and a tail, and I wondered unhappily what their reactions would be. Lucy's was typical enough. 'It's like something out of a play!' she said, emotionally. Meraud was more pointed. 'But if you go, what will happen to us? This is Dominic's house now, and he'd be within his rights to turn us all on the streets.'

'I'm trusting to Simon's sense of family duty to prevent that,' I said, with a great deal more confidence than I actually felt. For although my angry words to Dominic had in a sense made my decision for me, even now the doubts and uncertainties were crowding in on me, and at Meraud's words I felt my own sense of responsibility rising up; if a roof over their heads depended on my presence here, was I not doing them a great disservice by leaving them thus in the lurch? Meraud's sweet insistent voice went on, intruding on my guilty, unhappy thoughts. 'And if you both go, what will happen to the children?'

'Jasper and Hen will come with us,' I said. 'But I am going to leave Kit behind. If I took him with me, Dominic would pursue me to the ends of the earth, but if I leave him his son, I don't think he will bother.'

The horror which greeted this statement was further fuel to my guilt. Lucy and Jamie, of course, were ever accustomed to think with their hearts rather than their heads, and Meraud professed a prudish streak much at variance with her infatuation with Simon, but I nevertheless found this disapproval most disturbing, reinforcing still more my reluctance to desert my child. Through the chorus of it cut Holly's deep slow Suffolk voice. 'Thass right, Mistress Thomazine. You can't goo a-taking the little mite, and he won't miss you, he's too young. And thass another thing, mistress – you'll be a-needing a man if you're going a-journeying, thass not safe otherwise, for two ladies and two little mites to goo alone. I'm discharged now – if you want me, mistress, I'll come with you gladly. The farm, that can wait a few more months, my brother can manage it right enough.'

I was at once touched and embarrassed by his gruff diffident loyalty, another factor pushing me towards Catholm when, now that I had voiced my intention, I was rapidly coming to doubt the wisdom of my sudden decision. But I had not the heart, seeing that freckled, earnest face, to turn down his generous offer immediately, and smiled wanly at him. 'Oh, Holly, thank you. I was going to ask you if you would come with us, but I'm so glad you volunteered first.'

'Thass all right,' muttered Holly, going red. 'Thass only just and proper to help you and Master Francis. I reckon my mother would have words about wickedness and sin and suchlike, but to my way of thinking there's been grievous wrong done, and thass the best way to put it right. Now, when do we goo?'

And so, without my really intending it, my decision seemed to be made; and yet, while everyone discussed it, and poured encouragement or dissuasion into my ears over the next few days, still my secret thoughts chased each other in turmoil; all the old arguments, voiced by people whose advice I greatly respected, and ranged against them, only my love for Francis.

And his love for me – if it still existed. That sonnet of Master Shakespeare's, that he had quoted to me the day after we had discovered our true feelings for each other, returned now to haunt me. 'Love is not love, that alters when it alteration finds'. Would those words, that I could hear him saying within my head, as dark and clear and passionate as when he had first spoken them, still prove true? Would his love for me survive my betrayal? Up until a few weeks ago, I would never have doubted it, but now Great-Aunt's letter, and above all the poem, had changed everything. It was not the thought of the journey, not the prospect of penury without the money that had once been mine and now, so unfairly, was Dominic's; nor, God help me, my desertion of the child and the friends who depended on my presence for their security, that caused me to doubt so greatly the wisdom of what I had said I would do.

Beyond all these, the vision that terrified me most was that of myself riding up to Catholm, my boats and bridges burned behind me, and pouring out the whole fantastic, convoluted story to Francis and asking for his love and forgiveness – and being spurned with all the contempt and malice of which I knew him to be capable. Not only did this prospect haunt my waking hours, it also invaded my sleep; I dreamed it once, with horrifying vividness, and awoke weeping with grief and terror. Surely, I asked myself, it was better to cling to my memories of our love, and cherish that dear illusion, rather than have all destroyed by such a reality?

The humiliation of this, even when only as yet a product of my fertile imagination, was too great for me to confide it, even to Grainne, and like all such fears, it grew the greater for being kept hidden. While my dear friend busied herself with making ready – showing me in triumph the pass for herself and her children, Thomazine Lady Drakelon and a groom, to allow us safe passage through the King's forces wherever in the land we might be, telling me of the progress in packing our belongings, relating, with what in someone else might have been called glee, the machinations of the Widow Gooch in procuring an extra horse, and her generosity in allowing us the use of her old white cob, which like Grainne's own mare would be taken by a cavalry regiment only as a very last resort – while all this was going on around me, my inward terrors flourished. The acquisition of the horse, a great raw-boned brute with feathery heels betraying his plebeian ancestry, completed the arrangements. On the morrow, the last day of August, we would go, and yet still I was torn by doubts, still I did not want to leave my friends if it was for a mirage, a chimera, and possibly the bitterest and most terrible humiliation I had ever faced – a humiliation which I did not think I would be able to bear. By the morning of our departure, I had made up my mind. Even the thought of packing away my natural pride and going humbly to Grainne and the Widow with the news that at the last moment I had decided not to go after all, did not deter me; I could not face that greater abasement which surely awaited me when I arrived at Catholm. I had been walking around the house freely for a week or more, feeling fully restored to health, and yet when I woke that morning, with all set to go, I found my legs would not support me; I felt too weak to move from the bed. My body had provided the excuse that my mind desired, and the Widow, shrewd as usual, divined the situation at once. 'You don't feel well, eh? Sure you ain't having no second thoughts, lass?'

I could not deceive her, and gave her a wan smile. 'Yes, yes, I am, but it's nothing new – I've been having them for some time.'

Mistress Gooch sat down on the bed and laid a bony hand against my brow. 'Well, you ain't feverish, anyway. Look, lass, you've said you're going, all's ready, Jamie and Holly are saddling the horses, your breakfast's waiting down-stairs; why? Why don't you want to go? Don't you worry about them as is left behind, I'll look to them, never you mind them. You think of Francis and his face when he sees you were true to him after all.'

'But that's what I *have* been thinking of!' I cried desper-ately; and burst into tears. Fortunately there was only Mis-tress Gooch to listen to my sobbing explanation, to hand me her kerchief, and to say when at last I had control of myself, 'So it was because of that letter? And a poem he'd writ? Well, if he'd thrown it away as you say he had, perhaps he did that because he realized it didn't tell the way he truly felt about you. Perhaps he threw it away because he loves you, not because he doesn't. Have you thought of that, lass, eh?'

I had not. A faint renewal of hope stole surreptitiously into my mind, and would not be suppressed. The Widow saw my expression and patted my shoulder. 'Well, I'll be firm with you. I'll give you five minutes, no more, to make up your mind for good and all. No shilly-shallying, mark you, and no regrets neither. One way or the other, lass, and then do it. It's not like you to dither like this.' She gave me a final pat, as if I were a restive horse, and went out, leaving me alone with my milling thoughts.

Five minutes, in which to make the decision that would change my whole life – for better or for far, far worse. In five minutes, to go to Francis or to stay here, Dominic's wife forever. In five minutes, to decide whether or not to follow my heart or my head – to ignore or not to ignore the warning in that poem:

> But should we chance to meet, some bitter day,
> My heart, beware.

Great-Aunt's letter lay folded within the book of Dr Donne's poems, a gift from Francis, that lay always by my bed. Reluctantly, I removed it and unfolded the crackling paper, staring down at those last cramped lines of poetry as if somehow I could wring from them some hope, some talisman that could carry me through to Catholm and bring me at last to Francis's side.

'I have found these by chance, discarded, in his writing . . .' The words wavered in front of me, and I blinked away the tears; and then noticed for the first time the significance of 'these'. Yet there was only one poem on the page.

My mind made stupid, I stared at it for a few seconds longer; and then turned the letter over. On the other side, at which I had never bothered to glance before, was written another poem at the bottom below the seal, where it would be tucked inside; by its shape and structure a sonnet. Trembling at first with apprehension, and then with growing delight, I read:

> What is reality, and who's to tell
> The difference 'twixt that and thought's wild flight?
> The moon, that in the darken'd water dwells,
> Is't that which danceth in the sky by night?
> And does the Unicorn exist? And where
> On this wide earth are Dragons to be found?
> I know in truth they do not linger here,
> Yet still my heart can catch their distant sound.
> For what am I, if all the life I have
> Is made of cold reality, not dreams?
> I am worth nothing if I do not crave
> The glory of imagination's schemes.
>   And so, you sceptic stranger, do not dare
>   To prick illusion's bubble, for 'tis rare.

I knew it was truly his, a legacy of that far-off day when two children had built a bridge of Unicorns between them, a day which had lain ever since in my mind like a beloved jewel, a talisman, a precious stone for the memory to bring out and polish. I heard again the passionate childish voice of Francis, thirteen years old, 'In the deserts of Africa or the forests of Muscovy or the mountains of Hy Brazil – imagine your Unicorns!' And we had, building fantastic creatures in our minds, and made of 'water and light and ice and fire'; and thereby affirmed our shared love for the weavings of the imagination that bound us both with the same spell. And I knew then that, for the sake of my love for the strange, fascinating, enigmatic person that was Francis Heron, and more still for his own sake, so that the old flame within him could once more burn brightly, I must go to Catholm. Even if I was spurned, even if disaster struck, any sacrifice was worth the chance that our lives would be made whole again, and that we could be together, and complete.

There was a brisk knock and the Widow slid expectantly round the door. 'Well, lass, time's up. No one else knows of this, so don't you worry about saving face. What are you going to do?'

'What I should have decided to do some time ago,' I said, and my delight spilled over into my face and voice, my fears put at last to flight by a vision of Unicorns. 'To hell with the lot of you – I'm going to Catholm!'

It was a cold day, a grey and windy morning. The horses were ready, the cob slung with baggage. We would take it in turns to have Jasper ride before us, just as we would in turn carry Hen. And with us was Drake, ears inquiring, tail waving, as if he knew to whom he went.

Nothing to do now but say farewell to those whom we might never see again. I hugged Lucy and Jamie and Heppy, and all three of them wept and poured out their good wishes for a safe journey and a happy arrival at Catholm.

'We will stay here as long as the war lasts, even if Dominic does own the roof over our heads,' Lucy said tearfully, 'so please write to us, and give Francis my love – my best love – and tell him how happy I am for you after all you've been through, and keep yourself safe for us, please.'

'I will,' I said, 'and pray one day we may meet again and all be happy.' Vain hope – for only Dominic's death would accomplish that now.

'I'll look after your chickens for you, as well as I do my own,' the Widow chuckled, as I hugged and thanked her in her turn. 'And I hope for your sake, lass, that it'll be worth it in the end. If all goes well, it will. And I'll look to your little lad for you, too. Now you'd best be gone; dawn's up, and you've a long way to go.'

I had said farewell to Kit in my own fashion, holding his baby image in my mind forever as I stared down at his cradle; and then kissed him gently on his round hairless brow. 'Forgive me, little one,' I had whispered, and left before I could succumb to grief, or to the unbearable temptation to snatch him up and take him with me after all, in defiance of plans and decisions and common sense.

So now, I mounted Hobgoblin, praying that my hardly recovered strength would be equal to all this journeying. Holly took Jasper up before him, Grainne had Henrietta strapped in a basket to her saddle, and the baggage-laden cob was tied to Goblin's crupper. We rode out of the gate, and my friends and cousins waved and shouted farewells and called last tearful messages of good luck and good will, so that tears pricked in my own eyes because I was leaving my dear companions, perhaps forever, and the child I had tried not to allow myself to love.

But I had Grainne calm and smiling by my side, and Holly's reassuring presence, and Jasper's inconsequential chatter, and even Goblin and Drake were friends to me now; and as we rode through the empty, half-lit, golden streets of Oxford in the dim morning, my heart was light and hopeful, and my eyes strained towards the welcoming North; for at last I was going to Francis.

G. J. Scrimgeour
A Woman of Her Times £2.50

A woman's story that every woman will live as if it were her own. Through three continents, two world wars, through marriage and motherhood, love and pain and betrayal, Elizabeth Wingate is a woman of her times: a dutiful wife in Ceylon; a socialite in 1920s London; penniless and alone in 1930s Hollywood – journeying through decades in search of a destiny only time can reveal.

Annabel Carothers
Kilcaraig £1.95

A turbulent saga of three generations set against the grandeur of the Scottish isles. The Lamonts of Kilcaraig belonged to the Isle of Mull as surely as the proud birds of prey belonged to the mountains of Glen More – Catriona, the grandmother whose dark secret shadowed the family's future; Grania, the daughter who finds love only after she has chosen a husband; Niall and Rorie, twin grandsons of contrasting destinies; and Catriona the granddaughter, as beautiful as her namesake.

Gail Godwin
A Mother and Two Daughters £1.95

'A novel about that richest of all subjects, families . . . funny, sad, provocative, ironic, compassionate, knowing, *true* . . . everything that a novel should be' WASHINGTON POST

'A major novel from a talented writer really hitting her stride' KIRKUS REVIEWS

'A novel to live with and live in' NEWSDAY

Laura Black
Strathgallant £1.75

The indomitable old Lady Strathgallant had decided. Her ward Perdita was to be married and to inherit the Strathgallant estate. Rupert would have been the perfect match, but Rupert had fallen in the damned Indian Mutiny. The four Ramsay boys, the great-nephews Harry, Colin, James and John, would be summoned to attend Perdita's eighteenth birthday ball. As each arrived, Perdita fell in love with each in turn. Then came Jules Delibes, connected to the family by a French marriage and keen to be the fifth suitor.

E. V. Thompson
Chase the Wind £1.95

For the men who dug the Cornish earth of Bodmin Moor, the flourishing copper trade brought little but poverty and exploitation. Josh Retallick, son of a respected local family, and the wild Miriam, daughter of a drink-sodden miner, explored together the wild moorland until fate swept them apart . . .

'A keen eye for detail . . . astonishing energy' SUNDAY TIMES

The Dream Traders £1.95

The China opium trade of the 1830s was a maelstrom of greed, intrigue and misery – the way to power and wealth for the men who traded in drug-steeped dreams – and it spawned a conflict that would change the course of Asia's history. Luke Trewarne was a young Cornishman who came to China to make his fortune, but he fell in love with a country, an ideal, and a beautiful Chinese water gipsy . . .

Susan Howatch
Penmarric £2.95

'I was ten years old when I first saw the inheritance and twenty years older when I saw Janna Roslyn, but my reaction to both was identical. I wanted them.' The inheritance is Penmarric, a huge, gaunt house in Cornwall belonging to the tempestuous, hot-blooded Castallacks; Janna Roslyn is a beautiful village girl who becomes mistress of Laurence Castallack, wife to his son.

'A fascinating saga . . . has all the right dramatic and romantic ingredients' WOMAN'S JOURNAL

Cashelmara £2.95

A glorious, full-blooded novel which centres on Cashelmara, a coldly beautiful Georgian house in Galway, ancestral home of Edward de Salis. The fast-moving plot follows the turbulent fortunes of an aristocratic Victorian family through half a century of furious encounters, ill-advised liaisons and bitter-sweet interludes of love.

'Another blockbuster from Susan Howatch' SUNDAY TIMES

Fiction

☐ **Options**	Freda Bright	£1.50p
☐ **The Thirty-nine Steps**	John Buchan	£1.50p
☐ **Secret of Blackoaks**	Ashley Carter	£1.50p
☐ **The Sittaford Mystery**	Agatha Christie	£1.00p
☐ **Dupe**	Liza Cody	£1.25p
☐ **Lovers and Gamblers**	Jackie Collins	£2.50p
☐ **Sphinx**	Robin Cook	£1.25p
☐ **Ragtime**	E. L. Doctorow	£1.50p
☐ **The Rendezvous**	Daphne du Maurier	£1.50p
☐ **Flashman**	George Macdonald Fraser	£1.50p
☐ **The Moneychangers**	Arthur Hailey	£2.25p
☐ **Secrets**	Unity Hall	£1.50p
☐ **Simon the Coldheart**	Georgette Heyer	95p
☐ **The Eagle Has Landed**	Jack Higgins	£1.95p
☐ **Sins of the Fathers**	Susan Howatch	£2.50p
☐ **The Master Sniper**	Stephen Hunter	£1.50p
☐ **Smiley's People**	John le Carré	£1.95p
☐ **To Kill a Mockingbird**	Harper Lee	£1.75p
☐ **Ghosts**	Ed McBain	£1.25p
☐ **Gone with the Wind**	Margaret Mitchell	£2.95p
☐ **The Totem**	David Morrell	£1.25p
☐ **Platinum Logic**	Tony Parsons	£1.75p
☐ **Wilt**	Tom Sharpe	£1.50p
☐ **Rage of Angels**	Sidney Sheldon	£1.75p
☐ **The Unborn**	David Shobin	£1.50p
☐ **A Town Like Alice**	Nevile Shute	£1.75p
☐ **A Falcon Flies**	Wilbur Smith	£1.95p
☐ **The Deep Well at Noon**	Jessica Stirling	£1.95p
☐ **The Ironmaster**	Jean Stubbs	£1.75p
☐ **The Music Makers**	E. V. Thompson	£1.75p

Non-fiction

☐ **Extraterrestrial Civilizations**	Isaac Asimov	£1.50p
☐ **Pregnancy**	Gordon Bourne	£2.95p
☐ **Jogging from Memory**	Rob Buckman	£1.25p
☐ **The 35mm Photographer's Handbook**	Julian Calder and John Garrett	£5.95p
☐ **Travellers' Britain**	} Arthur Eperon	£2.95p
☐ **Travellers' Italy**		£2.50p
☐ **The Complete Calorie Counter**	Eileen Fowler	75p

☐	**The Diary of Anne Frank**	Anne Frank	£1.50p
☐	**Linda Goodman's Sun Signs**	Linda Goodman	£2.50p
☐	**Mountbatten**	Richard Hough	£2.50p
☐	**How to be a Gifted Parent**	David Lewis	£1.95p
☐	**Symptoms**	Sigmund Stephen Miller	£2.50p
☐	**Book of Worries**	Robert Morley	£1.50p
☐	**The Hangover Handbook**	David Outerbridge	£1.25p
☐	**The Alternative Holiday Catalogue**	edited by Harriet Peacock	£1.95p
☐	**The Pan Book of Card Games**	Hubert Phillips	£1.75p
☐	**Food for All the Family**	Magnus Pyke	£1.50p
☐	**Everything Your Doctor Would Tell You If He Had the Time**	Claire Rayner	£4.95p
☐	**Just Off for the Weekend**	John Slater	£2.50p
☐	**An Unfinished History of the World**	Hugh Thomas	£3.95p
☐	**The Third Wave**	Alvin Toffler	£1.95p
☐	**The Flier's Handbook**		£5.95p

All these books are available at your local bookshop or newsagent, or
can be ordered direct from the publisher. Indicate the number of copies
required and fill in the form below   7

Name_____
(Block letters please)

Address_____

_____

Send to Pan Books (CS Department), Cavaye Place, London SW10 9PG
Please enclose remittance to the value of the cover price plus:
35p for the first book plus 15p per copy for each additional book ordered
to a maximum charge of £1.25 to cover postage and packing
Applicable only in the UK

While every effort is made to keep prices low, it is sometimes
necessary to increase prices at short notice. Pan Books reserve
the right to show on covers and charge new retail prices which
may differ from those advertised in the text or elsewhere